On Behalf Of:

THE PRESENTER

BY REQUEST, THE AUTHOR HAS PRODUCED
THIS SELF-PUBLISHED, SIGNED, AND DATED
LIMITED-EDITION VOLUME
ESPECIALLY FOR THE PLEASURE AND BENEFIT OF:

THE PRESENTEE

SET_____ VOLUME_____ EDITION_____

THE M HART EDITION

In honor of the

MILLENNIUM
CHRISTMAS

2000

Book Designed & Printed By:

C. John Coombes

EBOOK ISBN 9780982221310   0982221312
PRINT ISBN 9780982221327   0982221320

All Rights Reserved By C. John Coombes
Copyright 2000 2008 2010 2013

CLAUS

A CHRISTMAS INCARNATION

A novel by
C. J COOMBES

Escape to a time
When life was an adventure.

Our nation was young,
And so were her people.
A time of struggle and setback,
Of pain and perseverance.

A time also of freedom, joy,
And the birth of new traditions.
The future was fearful and uncertain,
But no more so than for the children.

For them, let us say,
Fate brought forth a man.
He was wealthy and influential,
He was good-hearted and generous.
A man of conjecture and mystery.
He was there for them, a savior,
A second chance, a hope.

Only one person may have known him.
A person who struggled to understand him
Through the eyes of a child,
Through the heart of a woman.

A disciple named Elizabeth.

ILLUSTRATIONS BY:
C. JOHN COOMBES

THE M HART EDITION

THIS EDITION REPRESENTS THE FOURTH EDIT
OF VOLUME ONE UNDERTAKEN SPECIFICALLY FOR A
6X9 PAPERBACK PRINTING

**It would be preposterous
To assert that
Fact is born of myth.**

*Conversely...
It has been proven
Myth is a child of truth.*

BOOK ONE

The child

THE M HART EDITION

ONE

During my years of study, I read many a fine book. Some could enrage gentle men into battle; others could drive the heartless to cry for peace. They spoke of our humanity, our cruelty; they recorded the birth of our civilizations, the splendors of Rome, the death of Christ. All were fulfilling accounts of who and what we are.

I am compelled to write of something that may prove no less trivial by comparison: the remarkable yet disquieting occurrences behind the advent of the Rebecca Foundation. Suffice it to say, as of late, during those months when the Mistress of Winter embraces our land, I find myself investing more time beneath my old ship's blanket and curling up close to the fire and heat of hearth. Increasingly, I wait out those blustery winter nights gazing upon the coals, while turning my ear away from the howling wind so I might hear the crackling embers speak to me of life.

I struggle to retain my memories, finding solace and inspiration in my diaries, so too, in the personal memoirs of Christopher Claussen, the logs of his good ship REBECCA, roundtable tales, and countless missives penned by the orphans. These journals have filled me with every emotion, especially during those days that border Christmas, for my memories are forever sewn into the fabric of that season. Feelings are forced back upon me by these pages from my past, sentiments forever fastened into the spines or preserved within the folds of this intimate collection of papers.

The Christmas seasons have always brought change to my life; and as I look back, my belief in good will has only been strengthened, and this not just for me, but for many others across this newfound land. I suppose I came to feel that being the only soul in existence bound by history to know this story complete, and the unsettling notions and questions left to be answered in its wake, was for me a burden unbearable. But for you—*call it gossip.*

Elizabeth Dennison Claussen

AN 1850'S HANDBILL PROMOTING THE RMR TO SETTLERS
AND MERCHANTS EAST OF THE ROCKIES

TWO

1854. The heat of the sun dropped mercilessly downward through the cloudless blue Colorado sky and baked the desert dry. Twin rails of scorching hot iron, staked to their timbers, split this unorganized territory in half from the tips of one's boots to the wavering eastern horizon. Standing here and looking westward, the land appeared parched and starved for life. So it seemed in every respect, save for a nightmarish collection of snakes perplexed by those iron rails, and the black biting flies, which served no purpose other than to claim top rung on life's ladder of miseries—even surpassing the heat.

Elizabeth Dennison waited patiently in the cooler shadows of the station. Deep in thought, she stared down the tracks while waiting for the westbound RMR to arrive. The years struggled to show themselves on her face, and even at her present age of fifty-six, having confronted desert, mountain, river, and sea, she remained most comely.

Entering the autumn of her life, she found peace and tranquility outside the raging currents of "daily goings on" that all too often swept away the young. Avoiding those anxieties, and on this day any other unnecessary labor in order to remain fresh, Elizabeth positioned herself comfortably on the silvery unpainted and well-worn slab of pine that served as the station bench. It stood firm on the raised platform, being wedged back against the slatted building wall, and provided an ample view of the tracks below.

In contrast to the vertical lines of the siding, the bench seat rested with a slight slope to the east, not unlike the lay of the land as it flowed toward the rising sun and away from the also vertical walls of the Rocky Mountains. Through a collection of carvings created by idle minds and fidgety fingers, the pine plank revealed the degree of monotony one might face while left sitting in the heat with nothing to do but wait. Still, it offered sufficient surface to support the various sized butts, which counterbalanced heads leaning carelessly forward. Faces young, fresh, beautiful, or old and worn, twisted around on their out-stretched necks to look eastward along the rails for the first sign of an approaching train.

Elizabeth wouldn't lean back against the wall, nor would she lean dangerously forward. She did look down the track in earnest, but sat upright as would be expected from a lady of good grooming. Impatiently, she tried to make the best of each passing breeze, light as it might be. She repressed her nervousness by chatting away time with Ernie, who was her dear friend, confidant, and driver.

"Been a spell since we come down to the Junction, Ernie. Can't say I really miss it—too hot. I don't ever remember it being so hot. Is it the weather or is it my age?"

"Got t' be the weather, Mrs. Claussen. You don't look a day o'er twenty t' me."

"Ha! Oh, lord! You need to get out of the sun, Ernie. *Day over twenty*, my word…you *are* a pistol."

"Gosh darn, Mrs. Claussen, I'm tellin' the truth, believe you me. My eye hain't that bad yet, no ma'm. I still know a pretty face when I see one." Ernie squinted as he looked at her.

"Ahh! Listen to you, what fiddle-faddle! Either you are blind as a bat, or your brain must be baking and shrinking same as everything else out here. I bet it's rolling around in your head like dried-up tumbleweed."

Ernie laughed. Elizabeth and he went on to ponder the distance tumbleweeds might roll, the centuries cacti might live, the sweet scent of sagebrush, or whatever small talk took their fancy. They discussed the rugged beauty of this still untamed country, and together they recalled their memories of first times setting eyes upon it. They talked of their early years in this land, and they laughed about the characters that arrived as strangers, many stopping momentarily before moving on, many stopping for good, many stepping in and out of their homes and hearts. They spoke freely of Emma and Raven.

Predictably, the discussion would center on their amazement at the number of folks turning up in these parts, especially at the watering stops, the poles, and the junction of the tracks. These were the travel routes favored by the settlers migrating west. It was a testimony to all those who were putting down roots, and there was a certain confidence gained from that realization, for security came with the influx.

"I swear, there's so much changing around here, I am constantly lost. One scarcely learns a place-name before it is made over into something new. Seems like ever since forty-five, when the Union lay claim to Texas, nothing's been the same. The place has gone crazy—nuts."

"Yes, ma'am. Them Mex'cans were fit t' be tied, weren't they though? Claimin' Texas only went so far as the Nueces River. Ha! That was a spit. Kinda funny how big Texas is when we're a takin' it an' how small it is when they're a givin' it up. Gosh darn, they wanted a war; they got one. It cost 'em plenty an' I'll bet they'll be thinkin' twice next time 'round."

"I never heard anybody say we got it for free. Seems by all I heard it cost us plenty as well. I should hope a lesson was learned and there will be no *next time around.*" Elizabeth implied a moral lesson.

"Yeah, I reckon so, I reckon so."

Ernie looked down at his boots. It was a sensitive issue, for half the folks in these parts were Mexican or part Mexican or married to a Mexican. When the war was over, Mexico had ceded a fair amount of land to the United States, but not without compensation.

"So what's it been since the war, Ernie? Oregon in forty-eight, then all that insanity in forty-nine with the rumors of gold."

21

"Oh, yeah. Girls n' glory in California!" He shook his head as he fantasized.

"Down boy, it didn't say much for your gender then, and it still doesn't. I never saw anything like it, and I don't believe I care to again. What a disgrace you men can be."

"Amen!"

"My word, when I think of the way those hooligans ran around. They were crazy, pure and simple—out of their minds. I can't imagine anybody leaving family and friends behind to dig in the mud. That gold fever was worse than cholera, I swear. There sure were a lot of them, must have been every degenerate kicked off the East Coast. I'm surprised there is any room left to breathe in California."

"Yeah, but then look at all the good that come of it. Folks here in the Junction made out all right, ya gotta admit."

"I must admit, I never saw so much heartbreak in my life."

"Aw, now Mrs. Claussen, I hain't denyin' the girls and boozin' a bit. But then California might not ever been settled if'n it hadn't been for all them miners an' fortune seekers millin' 'bout out there. 'Member how they went right on an' voted 'emselves inta the Union without Congress? Wasn't that sumpin', now? Them Washington fellers had t' do some real horse whippin' t' catch up with us out here, an' you know it well as I do. Ya gotta 'gree that was pretty darn funny. 'Sides, if'n it hadn't o' been fer them crazy panners, California would o' never been made no territory in fifty. It might not o' happened in sixty or seventy, far as I can tell. Who'd go plum out to the West Coast for any other reason?"

"Don't you even bet on it, Ernie. Utah and New Mexico weren't overrun by lunatics and they both made territory in fifty. And Oregon is also on the coast and it made territory last year. And look at this year; the unorganized territory isn't so unorganized after all. Now, we have Nebraska and Kansas, and they didn't come about for reasons of gold fever. Good people don't lose sight of their morals and go leaving their family and friends to suffer, while they're off searching for a better life in order to settle a land. Face it, Ernie, greed is greed, plain and simple. Matter of fact, any fool can see that it's families that do the settling. It's families that build communities. It's God-fearing people, not drunkards in taverns drinking whiskey and fondling whores." Elizabeth was now glaring at Ernie.

"Gosh darn, Mrs. Claussen, have I gone an' said a thing or two t' get ya upset? I mean if I have, I din't mean it for certain." Ernie's eyes reflected his concern. Elizabeth sat back a moment, then started to laugh. She looked puzzled.

"Forgive me, Ernie, I have no idea what just got into me. I sure got my backside up, didn't I?" She shook her head in amazement. "Oh, well, I reckon I'm a little edgy, a little nervous, I guess. There's no point in denying it."

"Mrs. Claussen, it ain't my nature to meddle an' I don't suppose to know yer business with Miss Rings, but I am a might surprised to hear ya talkin' 'bout being nervous. I never known ya to be that-a-way, an' t' me ya look as cool as a cucumber. Don't ya be worryin' 'bout nothin', everything'll be jus' fine."

"You're a good man, Ernie. Where would I be without you?"

Elizabeth took a deep breath and settled her nerves. She looked out across the flat lands that rolled away like carpet up to a distant range of mountains to the south. There were no people to be seen out on that torturous land, but it was true that in any direction you chose to travel, signs of settlement were to be found. The Unorganized Territory of the Louisiana Purchase was being settled by the wagonloads. People from the East and South were pouring into the Territories of Kansas and Nebraska, and it was said that many of the settlers were Swedes. Those rumors warmed her heart.

Elizabeth was as familiar with the Rocky Mountain Railroad as any person alive. She had been there almost from the start and had personally witnessed endless miles of rail bed being surveyed by Christopher in the early forties. It was laid out to form a wide-reaching cross. It was made up of two nearly straight lines, one laid out north and south, the other east and west. They intersected each other about midpoint.

She recalled standing beside Christopher while he was tending to business; the men hammering rails to their timbers had drawn her attention.

"Claus?"

"Yes."

"Why are these rails spread this exact distance? Do you know what I am saying? How far apart are they? I mean, who decided they should be that distance?"

"How far apart? About a meter. Why that distance? Because that's the distance between the wheels on the cars," he teased. *"Who decided? The Romans."*

"The Romans? Oh, I see. The Romans were in the business of building trains. That makes perfectly good sense to me," she quipped.

"Well, no, they didn't build trains. However, they did build roads, and they built them all across Europe, and they built them to last. They also built ruts into their roads that trapped chariot wheels or cart wheels to keep them in place. The wagon makers of their day began building wagons to fit in those ruts. Eventually there became a standard distance between the wheels. As those wainwrights and wagon-makers moved out across Europe, they brought those standards with them. And so, all wagons and carts, carriages and buggies, were built more and more to that standard. When the first rail cars were built, they were naturally based on the standard. So, incredible as it may seem, these modern-day rails are a duplicate of the ancient ruts in the Roman streets."

"Maybe, I should have never asked."

"You didn't like the story?"

"Is it true?"

"Very much so."

"I loved it."

* * *

Elizabeth knew well the layout of the tracks set down by Christopher's plan. She had traveled to the end of each run many a time and saw the *Poles*—four large timbers driven into the ground. They stood straight up, one marking the end of each run and visible for miles beforehand on approach. Each pole became a flagstaff to the railway station and the centerpiece of a growing town, Northpole town, Southpole town, Westpole, and Eastpole or Forktown as it was also known.

The north pole was driven into the ground at the top of the north-south leg. Its flag flew east of the Big Horn Mountain range near the southern bank of the Powder River. It was from this point that travelers could descend southward 150 miles from the Upper Missouri region in a timely fashion toward the South Pass Junction where the two legs crossed. South Pass Junction was the hub of the four smaller 'Pole' towns, and was the focus of the greatest activity since it was centrally located. It was also strategically situated in a mountain pass that provided the best natural gateway to the west.

The South Pass Junction marked the center of the east-west leg that began its run westward from Eastpole, or Forktown, near the forks of the Platte River. From this point the tracks headed two hundred and fifty miles west to the South Pass Junction, and then continued onward another two hundred and fifty miles beyond the pass. There it traveled along the Sweetwater toward the Green River, and finally a hundred miles in a northwesterly direction toward the Snake River.

The southern leg of rail bed dropped from South Junction Pass, somewhat following the southward turn of the northern branch of the Platte River. It skirted the eastern slope of the Southern Rockies for about one hundred and fifty miles until meeting up with the South Platte River. It then continued another one hundred and fifty miles farther south until it reached its last timber at the station platform in South Poletown near the banks of the Arkansas River.

The RMR represented a thousand miles of relief from the bone-breaking, wheel-busting trails that killed many of the teams and travelers who were westward bound. The railway was a natural channel for the increasing numbers of trappers, speculators, gold hunters, and sightseers who had worked their way north by way of the Missouri or west along the Platte River. It was there for those who now wished to continue west by a method other than facing the daunting heights and snows of the Rocky Mountains, the sand blasting desert, the alkali waters of the plains, or the Indians who had been driven into hating white men. It made for quick travel and offered a reprieve from the brutal and unforgiving harshness of the land. Undoubtedly, it saved many lives.

The railroad was never used profitably in the early years, but Christopher was unmatched in his insight and ability to understand the future. He always bought cheap and looked far down the road. Only he would have given thought to the ore in the mountains that would provide the iron to make the thousands of miles of rails. It came to be that an ambition originally thought by investors nationwide to be a supreme folly was now the envy of financiers globally and the pride of wayward travelers who hop-scotched the latitudes for distant parts. In New York or Boston, if the topic of discussion fell upon western travel, it was impossible to conclude the conversation without mention of the ROCKY MOUNTAIN RAILROAD.

This knowledge and other memories filled Elizabeth's head and fashioned the innumerable details that built her character.

She mused over these facets of her life with Ernie until the telltale sign of smoke, off in the distance toward Eastpole, signaled the approach of a train.

It bore its lofty cloud right on schedule, and Elizabeth felt a rise of anxiety in the pit of her stomach. This time the train ferried a passenger who had long resided in the shadow of her past. Always in the background, out of reach, on the fringe of her awareness, a person for whom she felt some envy, some jealousy, maybe even despised for no sound reason; but now more than ever before, a person who stirred within her a burning curiosity.

This was a person who possibly possessed information that might shed a little more light on the many questions that now haunted Elizabeth, questions she had wrestled with over the past couple of years. It might be the smallest detail, the infamous needle in a haystack, a detail undoubtedly camouflaged, hidden by the colors of everyday life, or better yet, a bright 'look up and take notice' missing piece of the unfinished puzzle spread out in Elizabeth's head.

Her understanding of this woman barely extended past the pronunciation of her name: Britany Allison Coombes. She had been a lost figure, a fragment of memory reaching back to the earliest years, back to the ship—so long ago. Elizabeth could no longer put a face to this person. In any event, she would have one soon enough. Many years had fallen to the side, and with them, so too had many petty differences and misunderstandings of the heart. Elizabeth now only wished to extend a warm and genuinely sincere welcome.

The steam billowed across the platform as the train slowed, offering nothing in the way of relief from the oppressive temperatures. Here and there, an iron wheel screeched a drawn-out complaint, skidding itself thin in order to halt the mass upon the hot rails. The locomotive, baking from its own internal fire, sucked down the cool stagnant tower water like a spent dog as it quenched the dried out innards of its dusty black and overheated hulk.

To this day, Elizabeth remained somewhat wary of the awesome and frightening machine, but this massive steel bull was Christopher's pride and joy. It represented everything about the man and might have been Christopher in spirit, escorting this special guest, this dear friend of his from so far away to meet Elizabeth.

A door at the rear of a private coach opened to the platform. From there, stepped down a woman, who by the very nature of her moves commanded respect. She was dressed in the latest fashion from back East, which made her appearance somewhat masculine. Bloomers were all the rage, so it was said. They were a departure from the large sweeping hoop skirts and crinoline that had adorned women during the past decade.

Bloomers gave this woman a more authoritative posture. Her dress consisted of an embroidered frock of crisp organdie with raised collar and an unpretentious lace lacking the usual frill. It cascaded down a line from either side of her neck to her waist forming a vee. Her sleeves flared out, being fitted with ruche at the wrists. The light muslin ruche contrasted with the black velveteen sleeves of her bodice. A crinoline petticoat supported a very short skirt, about knee-length, dyed pale blue and trimmed with a conservative pattern embroidered along its hem. From there was visible white full-bodied Turkish pantaloons. At her feet were polished black dress boots.

Upon her head she wore a wide-brimmed hat, flat in shape, almost saucer-like and noticeably free of any ribbon or decoration. Her hair was blonde with white coursing through and pulled up tight at the back of her head. She wasn't bashful about jewelry and sported many rings. The overall impression was one of a cross between a woman and a man in a business suit. She was a woman of large frame, not overweight, but certainly not frail. A male escort accompanied her, adding to the impression of her importance. There was no doubt that she was a person to be reckoned with—and inside, Elizabeth fought her increasing nervousness.

Elizabeth watched the woman's blue eyes sweep the station and lock onto her. At once the face broke into a broad and gracious smile that instantly relieved Elizabeth of her anxiety. She understood at that moment how Christopher had been attracted to this person.

"Elizabeth!" The passenger roared as she turned in Elizabeth's direction.

"Yes! You must be Britany," Elizabeth responded.

"Oh, God! Nobody calls me that. That's a name befitting someone such as yourself. You are as beautiful as I imagined— I'm sorry to say." The woman feigned disapproval. "Call me, Brig. Brig Rings." She extended a hand, her rings sparkling in the sunlight. "The rest of the world does, and I've always stood up to it." Elizabeth offered a hand in return, and it was immediately taken by Brig Ring's firm grip.

Again, the gracious smile. The two women studied each other's faces, trying to connect them to bodies of young girls long since grown; faces now changed by the passing of time, by oceans, deserts, and thousands of traveled miles. They sifted through years of memories that reached back to the REBECCA. Releasing her grip, Elizabeth couldn't help but laugh.

"As you wish—Brig Rings it is. I am struggling to remember your face, but I am afraid it has been too many years. Nevertheless, I'm pleased you're here, Brig. Welcome to South Pass. I've waited and wondered about this moment for days—for a lifetime. It's more nearly a relief, but speaking of relief, let us get your belongings and refresh you."

"Oh, that sounds wonderful. Don't fret about the face, child, it hasn't looked that pretty in thirty years. Salt and sun...hard on

29

the skin, but I see you have been spared most of that. You're a handsome woman yet, Elizabeth."

"Enough, enough, you embarrass me."

The two women directed their men to collect the baggage, and then proceeded to the station grounds where the carriage was waiting. They chatted amiably, feeling each other out and beginning to build the framework of friendship.

"So was your trip agreeable?" Elizabeth asked.

"Aye, as much as any other, I suppose. The last time I saw this much flat space I was in the middle of the Pacific Ocean."

They both laughed again and rounded the corner of the train station. Brig stopped short, her eyes lifted in surprise at seeing a common carriage.

"Brace me, darling! No *vermilion* coach? I'm truly disappointed."

Elizabeth was completely taken aback. The shock wiped all expression from her face and Brig took immediate notice.

"Oh! Brace me, child! Have I said something to offend you? Aye, I've upset you; it's true. Please! Forgive me if I've been insensitive; but pray tell, what is it I have said? What have I said?" Brig fell over herself with apology and concern.

"No, no! You've done nothing." Elizabeth stammered. "I—I am sorry. I can't even explain why the question stunned me so. I suppose I wasn't sufficiently prepared for the fact you *should* know about these private and personal aspects of my life. And of course, you *should* know things about my life, as I yours. For whatever reason it felt quite unsettling, I must admit. I suppose I was caught off guard. The apology must be mine." Elizabeth gathered her wits. "As for your inquiry, Lady Rebecca's coach is presently at the ranch in Northpole, a final resting place of sorts. Christopher kept it stored in warehouses for years. Apparently, you've seen it before, but it isn't the same. You wouldn't recognize it as it once was. This carriage belongs to close friends of mine here in South Pass. They were good enough to allow me the use of it while they were away."

Brig took Elizabeth's arm with care and led her toward the black, dust-covered carriage. Her man opened the door as Ernie seated himself and took up the reins. Brig encouraged Elizabeth to climb in. She spoke to her from behind.

"Give me a chance, Elizabeth. You shouldn't feel it necessary to be on such guard. I think we'll be great friends. I can feel it, and I pride myself on being a superb judge of character. I could feel it the moment my eyes met yours at the platform. Our ties run deep like the blue sea. You and I go back a long way and we have much to share. We already know secrets about each other that only intimacy affords. Time is all we need—a little time to learn we're already intimate, that's all." Brig settled into her seat and glanced around the desert.

"How ever do you put up with this heat?" She pulled at her frock, sensing the discomfort of the material sticking to her body.

"Enjoy. It will soon change and within hours you will find yourself chilled to the bone." Elizabeth smiled.

Ernie coaxed the horses to follow the sandy ruts embedded into the main street of town. He passed the trading post, the feed store, the livery and boarding house, the local tavern and the post office. Brig noted that even beyond these prominent structures was to be seen a great deal of activity. The buildings stood completed and doing business, but their walls were crisscrossed by the shadows of new framework construction that crowded the main street from alleys and back ways. One for a barber, another a lumberyard, a tinsmith, a wheelwright; a general feeling of vigor and growth was everywhere.

Anticipation was the blood and gut of these western folk. Brig could feel it in the air, see it in the passing faces, and hear it in their salutations. Impatience was the plague that suffered

31

all. It ran rampant, fed by boastful tales that exaggerated the glories of open land, wild women, gold and fortunes yet unfound. Betting and gambling permeated the spirit of these people. Everybody wagered and speculated on everything, from the next rainfall to the number of buffalo in a herd. The mania infected nearly all it touched, spreading back to the eastern shores, where business circles hummed about the money to be made out west.

One of the largest speculations to date in this young exploding country was guessing where the railways would be constructed that would one day link the continent together from ocean to ocean. Untold fortunes rested on the final outcome. Politicians, socialites, military leaders, scientists, and financial barons all squabbled relentlessly over the best routes to establish. Many had staked their personal fortunes on the outcome. Even Brig herself had played some of her investments west of the Mississippi.

She could boast the proper connections, for she had been given advice from one of the best. Christopher Claussen was the one-in-a-million man, who possessed an uncanny foresight and the unlimited resources needed to take it upon himself and build stretches of track such as the Rocky Mountain Railway. He and a very select group of others held the best odds of linking up to the main continental routes, or at the very least, securing a foothold in an area that revealed good promise of great fortunes to be had.

It surprised no one who knew him that Christopher was able to develop one of the most significant stretches of railroad on the continent while defying every obstacle put to him by Mother Nature and the competition. Those few having the benefit of knowing him personally agreed it was solidly within his character, and for someone like Brig, it was a very profitable relationship. The rest were left to fume at being beaten out by this successful but secretive man.

RMR tracks traversed the now well-known South Pass, but its bed was laid in a vision that occurred in a time when a white man was as scarce as comfort in these parts. The tracks seemed hidden from awareness until their need was realized. Then overnight they spawned the birth of settlements turned towns, and investors came in droves to reap the profits of growth and traffic. There was much money to be had, and with the potential profits came all the intrigue and corruption one would expect.

So too came the losers, the lost, the left behind, and the lonely. So too came the widows and the weak, the sick and injured, and of course the orphans abandoned to the mercy of others. The downtrodden were plentiful, far outnumbering the hopeful and successful, but never acknowledged, shunned, because they represented the vast array of misfortunes that lurked at every turn. It was they who provided the darkness and fear within the shadow of every new structure. Elizabeth knew this well and spent much of her time trying to bring relief to their kind.

"Where do we go?" asked Brig.

"Not far—a mile or two at the most. The owners of this carriage were also kind enough to allow me use of their home. They have headed east and aren't expected back for three or four weeks at the earliest. I am most appreciative of this favor, for the ranch is conveniently located close by the station, and I pray the least burden for you. We'll have it to ourselves, as the men have rooms reserved at the boarding house. If all is well at the cabin and you have no objections, they will then arrive back in the morning at eleven to see to our well-being and return you to the station."

"That sounds perfect to me—a good chance to talk without interruption and no lack of privacy. Richard!"

"Yes, ma'am," answered her escort.

"Go to town and procure whatever stores you feel necessary for our return trip, and for God's sake be back before the train leaves."

"Yes, ma'am."

"Brace me, darling, but Richard is the best damned cook I ever had the pleasure to enjoy. You probably thought he escorted me all the way out here. No ma'am, I escorted him. I'll sooner die than be left wanting for his culinary expertise."

The cabin was found to be comfortable and accommodating, having two separate bedrooms and a kitchen removed from the main dining and living areas. It was square by design with a spacious front porch. The walls were constructed of adobe, in good repair, and a full two feet thick providing ample insulation against the heat of day and cold of night. They were well windowed for ventilation. The floors were planked in wood, raised, and carpeted. The ceilings were beamed with large timbers brought down from the mountains. The rooms were nicely appointed and swept for spiders and bugs, the beds freshened, and the kitchen overstocked as bespoken by Elizabeth a few days before. Best yet, the well water was sweet, cool, and clear to the eye.

Ernie and Richard deposited the baggage into the ladies' respective rooms, and after Elizabeth assured Ernie that all was well, the men excused themselves and rode back to town. Elizabeth and Brig took some time apart to sort their belongings and freshen up. Soon thereafter, they drew up the cool water of the well and mixed it with the extract of lemon. They moved to the porch in hopes of enjoying a breeze and taking in the splendid view of the mountains to the north.

They sat down at a table and began with light conversation. Getting to know one another, they touched on their past, their travels, their experiences, and surmised almost at once they were kindred spirits. They felt more like sisters than strangers. Now fully relaxed and enjoying new energy, Brig spoke on a much more personal note.

"So tell me of your life, Elizabeth, please. I am so curious and impatient to know, you wouldn't believe. Tell me everything, child! All I know is spotty, half-truths—so much left to guessing and wondering. It's terrible. I want to know all there is about you, if you so choose to speak it."

Elizabeth grimaced outwardly. Inwardly, she thought how she wished to know everything about Brig and also her past association with Christopher.

"You embarrass me! You are so kind to ask about my life, but enough! You, a woman who has captained her own ship! Who would believe such a thing, no man for certain, for it is unthinkable by their gender. It is remarkable. I am in awe of you. You who traveled to distant shores I can only imagine! The West Indies, the Sandwich Islands, Cape Horn, China! Imagine—*China* of all places! More intrigue than one can stand in a lifetime! Christopher spoke of it often with great fondness. To follow your dreams and the trade winds, the excitement and all, it must certainly be you who has the life to tell, not I!"

"Oh, no! Elizabeth, please!" Brig pleaded earnestly. "It is true my life has been both adventurous and full, but let's be honest. We have but precious little time for conversation. Allow me to open my heart to you in this privacy, without further ado. I have traveled a great distance for the pleasure of your acquaintance." Brig studied Elizabeth seriously and then spoke from her heart. "Surely, you must know that I loved Christopher, possibly even imagined how I longed for him over the years. The difficulty I endured leaving his side to sail off for months or years before I should see him again. It tore the very heart out of me! The tears I shed in the darkness of my nights, in the loneliness of my cabin, were enough to float any vessel I ever mastered.

35

"Aye, he knew how I cared for him, although I wasn't nearly ladylike enough to show my feelings proper. Don't misunderstand me; our bed manner was all I had ever imagined it should be. What I mean to say is, try and picture me attempting a convincing proposal to scrub his trousers and blouses, to darn his socks and scrape his dishes forever in wedded bliss while I covered my tattoos with leather boots, strapped a furring knife to my side, and pinned my hair up with a marlinespike—not exactly a picture of sweet virgin innocence. A sturdy companion on the high sea maybe, but not the landlubber type, not the accepted picture of mother with child. Not what one would deem the embodiment of moral, spiritual, or maternal instincts."

The two women looked at each other for a moment.

"You really loved Christopher, then?" Elizabeth asked as she studied another who had held strong emotions for this man.

"Oh, brace me, child, did I! Aye, yes, yes, I did dearly. Was he not every woman's dream? Was he not the most handsome man a girl might lay eyes upon? Or better yet, lay next to? That thick blonde hair and those deep, deep blue eyes, deep as the sea. They set my heart to fluttering something terrible. He was tall, strong, commanding. He was rich. I never knew how rich, 'tis certain. But there were stories, and I believed he was as well heeled as a man might be. In later years, I began to get a pretty good notion of just how rich, but back then, if not for rumor, one might never have known. There wasn't an arrogant bone in the man, at least not as I knew him. He was kind in every way. Aye aye, that he was, kind to a fault, especially with the children. Do you know of the children of the sea, Elizabeth?"

"Rebecca often made mention of them, but only through her."

"They are real. A pitiful lot they are, poor and wretched. Christopher took to them like a puppy to a teat. Whenever the REBECCA came to port the children were all about the docks, waiting, watching, wondering, and talking amongst themselves, looking for the first sight of him. He always had a few gifts on board for the children. Aye, the children loved him. They mobbed him at every port. He never forgot them. I would see this and dream of the father he would be to my children."

"What happened between you—?" Elizabeth stopped short. "Oh! I beg your pardon, Brig. It is none of my concern and I apologize for my rudeness, uh—."

"No, no, it is nothing. I would ask myself the same questions. Besides, it would be just as rude of me to leave you with only half of a story." She took a breath. "Looking back and having plenty of years to see it plain and clear, I would say it was a simple matter of him not loving me. I mean, he cared for me. He cared for me a great deal. I never doubted it. He fussed over me and spoiled me rotten. We slept together and he was a gentleman in every respect. But he never loved me. That part of him was devoted to someone else—Rebecca. I can see that now. That part of him was beyond my reach. That part of him was sad and lost. There was no chance of taking him away from her, at least not for me. So I cried and I sailed away. I wept for him more than I care to recall. I had to accept that fate wouldn't allow me this love."

"You were wiser than you know. Lady Rebecca was his life."

Elizabeth studied Brig with much empathy. How well she understood this kind of despair. But something else was playfully annoying her, muddling her thoughts. It had to come out.

"You really have a tattoo?"

"Huh? Oh, God forbid, child! Don't ask!" Brig hammered.

"No, I must. I have never imagined a woman who might dare such a thing. I envy your courage. I must see it. Please, show me, I beg." Elizabeth pleaded.

"Brace me through hell, darling! I am afraid that is impossible. It was one of my more serious mistakes in youth—an act of sheer stupidity, while under the influence of the damned devil—and rum. Not a soul has laid eyes on it in more years than I care to count. I might add…that in itself is depressing enough."

The two women sat looking at each other again in silence. Brig realized this small slip of the tongue had turned into a secret, the first obstacle in a relationship that had the potential to become a long and lasting friendship. It was she who was holding back, she who was first to imply that boundaries existed between them. It was a moment of truth. She relented, exhaling with a low moan.

"Oh, Elizabeth! *They are not at all* in a proper place. Trivial things, really—nothing to brag about, nothing worth seeing, really—an embarrassment," she stalled.

They sat in awkward silence until Elizabeth backed off for the sake of politeness.

"Forgive me. It was rude to press the issue. I might have exercised better manners." She smiled at Brig, who was now visibly in despair.

"No, no, it's too late. I can see that plain as land. You *truly* desire to see this tattoo, is that it?"

It was an opportunity that was hard for Elizabeth to pass up. "I am honestly ashamed to admit it, but my curiosity burns like a child's." Elizabeth grinned sheepishly.

"Trust me, darling. Only one of us will come out of this feeling ashamed. I have the gravest reservations about this." She spoke mostly to herself.

"Go on then, Brig! At our age, who do we answer to?" Elizabeth prodded.

Brig returned a most cynical expression and then stated, "To ourselves as we lay in bed at night thinking aloud, *I can't believe I actually did that! What an ass!*"

That being said, they both started to laugh. Brig glanced briefly around the yard for onlookers.

"Aye, then. This is it—only for you—for the sake of your curiosity. However, I must warn you in desperation for decency that my boots can't really cover it because it's too high. Must I go through with this?" she whined.

They stared at each other.

"How high?" Elizabeth asked with a dare in her voice.

Brig thought a moment. "If I were a man I would say, aye, it nearly touches heaven."

Elizabeth squealed. "Let me see. Let me see it at once! This is too much, indeed!"

Biting her lip and squinting her eyes, Brig looked directly at Elizabeth. "So be it. Mark my words, darling. It's a good thing for you I haven't a bashful bone in my body. For heaven's sake, I don't even know you." With that she stood up from her chair and reached under her skirt. She let out another breath. "Aye, here goes." She fumbled a moment beneath the fabric, raised her skirt, and lowered her pantaloons just enough to expose one inner thigh—still a very shapely leg.

There within the folds of her garments, done by an artistic hand in admirable detail, in deep blue and red, was a curvaceous nude angel, wings and all, blowing her trumpet and pointing a delicate finger directly toward Brig's graces. Inscribed along a banner about the angel's feet were the words 'THE GATE'.

Elizabeth's hand rose to cover her mouth. Speechless, her eyes stuck wide open with amazement until finally she gasped for a breath and blinked. All the while, Brig hurriedly corrected her clothes.

"The gate?" Elizabeth inquired in a voice of disbelief.

Brig frowned as she reseated herself at the table then stated sarcastically, almost contemptuously, "An angel on the other leg says '*to heaven*'!"

Elizabeth was lost to fits of laughter.

"Brace me, child, what did you expect from a young girl who mastered a ship of fools! They never made undergarments that colorful," Brig exclaimed.

Just imagining Brig lying prone with a banner of sorts across her bottom to direct an approaching lover was more than Elizabeth could bear.

"I suppose you thought I led a sheltered life at sea. Is that it?" Brig admonished her.

Elizabeth moved to wave her hand, a plea for Brig to stop before she succumbed to death by laughter, but in doing so, her gesture inadvertently clipped the pitcher of lemonade. She fumbled in a mad attempt to steady the drink, but instead of grasping it, she knocked it flying. Elizabeth shrieked as the liquid soared directly toward Brig, who instinctively pushed herself away from the table and the imminent shower.

The rearward slide drove Brig's chair leg into the crack between the boards of the porch, and being held there fast, Brig toppled over backward in an almost slow-motion dance with flailing arms and outspread legs, soon disappearing from view. The scene was enough to drive Elizabeth into a near state of hysteria, and at once both women were convulsing, rolling in laughter with tears streaming from their eyes. They remained out of their wits for the better part of five minutes before they were finally able to catch their breath and composure. The friendship was being well cast to last.

Brig brought her large frame back to its feet, and impulsively flipped her dripping hands to fling a spray of lemonade at Elizabeth, who spun about in fast retreat. Brig shook the drink out of her clothes, and began spanking herself to drive out the dust her bottom had collected from the porch.

"Oh, darling!" Brig exclaimed, while drying her eyes and face with a handkerchief. "Understand this! I so wish to enjoy your friendship, but I fear I've lost my reasoning and respect as an old lady. Aye, it is I who has paid the steeper price, my love. Look at me! What a mess!" Brig then drove her forefinger into the table in a gesture of demand. "And I expect answers and information in return to fill this void within my chest, not to mention the loss of whatever shred of pride and decency I may have once laid claim to." She then snapped that forefinger, sending one last drop of lemonade in Elizabeth's direction.

"Whatever I might do, just ask." Elizabeth barely managed to spit out the offer as she collapsed onto her chair, her head falling across arms now folded upon the table. She was fighting the compulsion to laugh again and refused to look at Brig lest she lose all control and relapse. Then with a fresh thought, she quickly raised her head.

"But first!"

She held up her finger as if to stop the world and stood up. She stepped into the cabin. A moment later she reappeared on the porch with a package, carefully wrapped and tied off. The label was addressed to Brig Rings.

"In my letter, I mentioned that Christopher included you in his will. My instructions as executor of his estate were very specific in that I locate you and notify you of this package. He was most adamant. This was very important to him." Elizabeth handed Brig the package. She retreated toward the cabin door.

"I will leave you your privacy, so you—"

"Nonsense, child!" Brig interrupted her. "Sit down, please. I possess no secrets. Do you know what it might be?"

41

Elizabeth shook her head. "Not the faintest, but he certainly was most decided in his instructions about it. I was to place this in your possession at whatever cost."

Elizabeth sat back down, hands folded in her lap. The truth, as much as she hated to admit it to herself, was her desperate desire to know what sort of gift Christopher would have taken such great pains to see presented. What sort of gift would be offered to this person, this other woman so special to his heart?

"Go ahead and open it."

Brig looked at her. "Isn't it strange how I should find myself so full of apprehension and restraint? It's so unlike me. I *hate* that feeling."

Elizabeth shrugged her shoulders. "Go ahead and open it. He cared for you. I am sure it will bring you pleasure."

With that bit of encouragement, Brig slowly parted the wrappings to reveal a fine wooden box. The quality could not be hidden by its notable disrepair, the worse for weather. But for her own curiosity, Elizabeth being so intent to observe the contents of Christopher's package, she failed to realize the shock on Brig's face at seeing the case now brought to light. It was the flash of a tear fallen, splashing across the inlaid wood top, deepening its color that prompted Elizabeth to look up. Brig was staring directly at her, unashamed of her emotion.

"This is impossible!" she stated with a broken voice. She shook her head in disbelief.

"Do you have any idea what this is, Elizabeth?"

"No." Elizabeth shrugged.

"Have you never seen it?"

"No, I can't say I ever have."

Brig cleared her throat. "This is my name. This is impossible, this is impossible." Brig rocked her head back and forth, wiped

42

her eyes, and then carefully raised the top. Her eyes continued to weep. She placed her hand upon her chest and spoke.

"How is it with memories? On one hand the years pass in such number it would seem impossible to measure their time. Yet, from somewhere within that distance, there arrives a forgotten feeling that can turn a tear between the blink of an eye as though this emotion was born only a moment before. This is so unsettling. The sight of this gift grips my heart."

Without removing the contents, she handed the box to Elizabeth and encouraged her to open it. The box measured about eight by twelve inches in size. It was only about two or two and a half inches high, but very heavy. Elizabeth raised the lid and her eyes opened wide; she gasped.

"Oh...my...lord. It is absolutely divine."

Before her eyes, there flourished the intricacies and splendor of Florentine engravers from Italy, famous for their unsurpassed mastery of silver and gold. Set into a burled wooden plaque, a combination of both precious metals had been worked to produce two exquisitely detailed sailing ships upon the high seas. Two suns fashioned out of a whitish yellow gold bordered each side of the work. Their rays, a deeper yellow, ascended upward from the horizon to streak above the ship masts and hulls which were planked in the darkest of coppery gold, then higher through the silver sails that merged to disappear into clouds of a similar silvery hue. It was nothing, if not the finest in craftsmanship. It was priceless.

"What a day this is!" Brig exclaimed, shaking her head. "I haven't shed a tear of emotion in thirty years, and now I cry from laughter and sadness in the space of a minute. This will be the death of me unless I take care." She let out a deep breath and patted her chest with the damp, fluttering handkerchief in hand. "I am emotionally out of control." She paused. Then, in a voice filled with fondness, she said, "Turn it over and read the back, child." She smiled, knowing this piece well. Elizabeth removed the plaque and carefully turned it over in her hands. Engraved in a wonderful calligraphy it read:

Elizabeth looked back to Brig to listen to her words.

"Aye, this was my christening of sorts. I had this young girl passion for rings, and I would purchase them at every opportunity from ports up and down every coast in the world. When I was first aboard the REBECCA, her maiden voyage in fact, I was then a very young girl, as were we all, but I had the great misfortune of losing a ring that had belonged to my mother. I was crushed."

"I seem to remember something of that day."

"Aye, it's possible, for I searched high and low days on end aboard that ship, all to no avail. Don't ask me how it was possible, child, but Christopher found that ring and returned it to me freshly polished, then proceeded to scold me for wearing something so precious while I worked. It was careless, he said.

"When we arrived in America, he sent for a man to escort me into town, to the jewelers no less, and gave him instructions to buy a ring for each of my fingers. With each one now adorned, he said I could wear my mother's ring around my neck or place it in safekeeping. He called me Miss Rings from that day on."

"Yes, yes, I am certain I remember this. It is so vague to me at first, but I am remembering now that I hear you speak of it." Elizabeth strained to recall the incident.

Brig raised both her hands and spread her fingers.

"You know, I would wear those rings on every finger, not so unlike now, and I went right on losing them all about the ship,

44

but my mother's remained safe. Years later, when I became master of my own ship, a brigantine, my nickname *'Brit'* was quickly trans- formed to *'Brig'*, and my size went a long ways toward reinforcing it. The nice thing about Christopher, his size always made me feel petite, can you imagine? Anyway, he never stopped teasing me about my rings, and gave me the name 'Brig Rings' on this plaque when he presented me with my first ship. I loved the ship, the gift, and the name; I used it as my signature from that day on."

She shook her head in amazement. "But, Elizabeth! What overshadows all of this is the fact that this box was lost at sea, three or four leagues off the coast of Boston in eighteen-fifteen. How can I accept this? No, wait. May I see it?" A doubt had arisen.

Elizabeth handed the piece back. Brig scrutinized the piece and quickly confirmed its authenticity.

"Aye! Aye! Look here, Elizabeth!" She placed her finger on the piece. "Do you see the slight indentation in the engraving? When I first received it, I was so thrilled, so proud of it, I ignored my own good sense, and I kept it on my side table to be displayed in my cabin. It was only about three, maybe four days before a wave heeled the ship hard to starboard and sent it flying across the cabin. It was marred only slightly, but I, being utterly distressed, determined from thence on to always keep it boxed and out of harm's way.

"And so it remained safely stowed for many a voyage out and back until one most unfortunate night, the 15th of March, a Wednesday to be precise—aye, it will not be easily forgotten. I was homebound from Caracas atop South America, concluding a very profitable journey, and standing for the port of Boston to drop anchor. With scant warning we were overtaken by a storm of short duration, but preceded by a gust of wind of such force that it drove our ship upon her beam-ends.

45

"The sea staved in the deadlights, and my cabin flooded. Everything was strewn about and floating. After the ship righted and the damage could be assessed, I was horrified, horrified to a degree beyond any ability of mine to express even now as we speak. I discovered among my belongings carried away to sea was his gift, my most treasured possession. We had been sounding just prior and I knew us to be in over thirty fathoms. The piece was lost for all eternity." Brig took a deep breath.

"I pined for years over my loss. But here, now…this? I ask you, Elizabeth, in God's name, how can this be? I say in all my years upon the sea, years of having seen many strange things, this is a mystery of no small measure. This, I dare say, is impossible."

"Do you suppose it was taken in by a fisherman's net?" Elizabeth suggested.

Brig nodded her head. "Aye, indeed, I would say so. Whatever else could give such an explanation? Even that as it may be, I swear, would be no less a miracle in its own right."

The two women sat pensively as they considered this seemingly mystical event.

Brig commented. "Isn't it just his nature to return this, my most precious belonging from the unyielding grip of the sea? And doing so without the least explanation, knowing full well I shall be beside myself until my dying day wondering how this might be. It was the same with my mother's ring. I was so disappointed, and then he raises my chin upward, smiles knowingly, and places the keepsake in my hand. How could he have possibly come by it? Surely, it had been lost forever.

"He was like that. Do you know what I mean? Always secretive, Elizabeth—he was always so secretive. I could have him all night, sleep in his arms, but only to awake to the feeling he was being taken from me, drawn to some other place far, far away. To a place I was never allowed to go, a place that fought me for his heart and soul." Brig mused momentarily.

46

"But then, isn't that the reason I'm here, to unlock some of those secrets? Aye, so take me back, Elizabeth, take me back to the beginning. Tell me about Christopher and his life as you knew him. He was so elusive most of the time. Tell me about Rebecca. I was so jealous of you both. Sometimes I would cry at night, longing for a place in his heart. I was filled with resentment, knowing you both were so special in his eyes. Forgive me for confessing how I cursed your existence.

"Aye, I always thought of you as the power, the world that drew him away. Right or wrong, it makes little difference now, and I am not now about to deny I had feelings for the man. So, take me back to the beginning, darling, take me back and tell me all. A good deal of my life now is spent pondering my past and wondering about many such things as this, especially those things associated with Christopher."

"Very well, Brig," Elizabeth said softly. "I must admit you certainly have earned it." Elizabeth placed her hand affectionately on the back of Brig's wrist. "We have much to share. Similar thoughts, similar questions—I hope you may ease the burden of my own heart, for the story I shall tell is not only bizarre, but also unnerving and yet, full of inspiration. I have questions I pray you may answer for me as well."

Elizabeth settled back and fondled her empty glass. She hadn't anticipated Brig being as curious about Christopher as was she herself. It came as an interesting twist of events. She took a breath and began.

"We must go back, far back into my earliest years as a child. Back to the year my mother became deathly ill. This was about eighteen-o-six, a year or two before we first sailed upon the REBECCA. I was too young then to understand the events of the day, but I knew my father loved my mother dearly, and I remembered overhearing his attempts to ease her fears about the six of us children. I remember him consoling her at her deathbed, urging her not to worry for us. We were all spoken for and would see good care.

47

"Father told me I was to take a short stay at a very fine house in the country, a day's ride distant. I believed myself to be going on an outing of sorts so as not to bother my mother in her illness. I would be allowed to play and make all the noise I wished, and this would make my mother happy. I was agreeable. It sounded like great fun, a change from the gloom about our home." Elizabeth paused. She drew a shawl up over her shoulders to ward off the approaching chill of the evening air, and then looked at Brig soulfully.

"Never again did I enjoy the comfort of my mother's caress, nor the love in my father's eyes."

THREE

1806. Off in the distance, a most magnificent red coach fitted with winter skis glided along silently, briskly, through thick clouds of breath left in the wake of trotting horses. In the stillness of night, it drew past sparkling moonlit fields of undisturbed snow, leaving unseen creatures to fall by the wayside, mesmerized by the enchanting lullaby of a thousand bells singing in chorus.

Row after row, bells chimed upon gilded holiday dress blankets draped carefully over the well-groomed backs of the stable's pride. The prancing hooves jostled them to life and they rang out in perfect time with every step. The wonder of their harmonies carried across the meadows, deep into the dark solitude of a country night. As they heralded a forthcoming, the coach made its way up the winding snow-covered drive to the gates of the renowned estate of Claussen.

Drawn under a canopy of winged angels celebrating the wrought iron passageway, the vehicle moved through the expansive gardens, now asleep, but still the signature of a formal

CLAUSSEN ESTATE, SWEDEN

courtyard. Approaching the threshold of the main entrance, the coach was dwarfed by towering granite columns, each soaring up to a crown of flickering nightlights. They bordered a porch paved with reflections of firelight upon stunning patterns of inlaid Italian marble. It humbled all that trespassed.

The coach was a masterpiece of craftsmanship. It was unusual because of color. It gleamed vermilion. A dazzling hue of red, adorned with ornate cast bronze embellishments. Metalwork, engraved by hand to depict the most exquisite flowers and birds, brought up to a flawless mirror-like finish through hours of buffing with polish. To show respect for the workmanship, the coach was never drawn with less than four, and nearly always showed with six white and impeccable, imported Lipizzaner horses of the best breeding.

This evening the coach moved quietly past the beckoning lights of the front entrance, and came to rest in the privacy of a rear corridor used primarily for service to the kitchen. The chauffeur stepped down then assisted the lady and her maiden servant to the pavement with great care, for it was covered with trampled snow and slippery. He escorted them both inside, bade them good night and locked the door as he disappeared into the darkness.

From within the kitchen, through frosted windowpanes, a desperate herd of deer could be seen pressed together tightly. They struggled to keep the pervasive cold of northern arctic air from stealing away what little warmth they could muster. They stood between massive pillows of white snow, propped up by the straining limbs of dark green spruce. Many would die this night. Their breath rose in a giant cloud of mist. It floated upward through the stilled pristine air, until consumed by the blackness, which seemed to be waging its own battle against the stars for dominance in a crowded night sky.

Everything on the grounds of the Claussen estate seemed to crack from the merciless cold. A cold that one knew by instinct meant death to the careless, a cold that sucked the heat of life from all living things—cold that split the very rock beneath the lifeless grounds of the estate. It was the kiss of winter. A mistress returned every year to test the will of men in a land that was as harsh as it was beautiful. It was said that all women were accursed with cold hands by the Sun God, after the warmth of his affection was rebuked by this Mistress of Winter.

The fear of this brutal cold was soon forgotten once inside the spacious kitchen of the Claussen home. Its thick walls returned heat from the fireplace, which in recent days had been the focal point of many Christmas holiday feasts. The kitchen candles were extinguished and the maids all departed, for in light of the holidays, they had been excused early in the evening to go to their families. It was late and the dinner guests as well had retired to their rooms. Only the orange light of embers with the occasional lick of flame moved about the room.

The hearth continued to push aromas of the evening's repast out into the great hall. Now lingering were smells of roasted chicken, venison, baked ham and honey, breads, and the delicacies of apple and cinnamon. Fragrances that flowed like incense in unseen currents of air, moving across the endless oak dining table, around the porcelain and goldware, brushing gently against the half-emptied hand-blown Venetian goblets. Rising to swirl past the filigreed candelabras, they moved upward, attracted by the majestic tasseled tapestries that hung on the walls. They clung to the delicate and colorful embroidery, reaching even higher to lofty beamed ceilings. No space escaped the tantalizing taste of the air.

Behind the heavy door that closed off the kitchen from the great hall, shrouded in shadow there stood a weeping bride. Silently, each tear that fell from her face reflected not only the firelight, but also the beauty that marked her presence like the halo about an angel. She was, in the eyes of many, unsurpassed in loveliness and grace. This beauty might only be matched, and most certainly enhanced by her inescapable charm, her intoxicating demeanor that was more than merely captivating.

It was supremely seductive. Friend, family, and stranger alike longed to be near her, but none more so than one equally remarkable man—her husband, Christopher N. Claussen.

He was far removed from the fools of everyday life. He saw clearly that this woman, who was bred from common stock, had about her a silent wit and determination that raised her above her own. He was captivated by her childlike innocence. It mystified him in every way. He attributed this appearance of naiveté to an honest sincerity in her manner and an acceptance of everyone she met as persons of good intent. This assumed naiveté instilled within him an uncontrollable need to protect her from all those he felt were filled with potential to do her harm.

He desired to give her the things in life of which she never dared to dream. To shield her from pains, which he understood resurfaced not only from her past, but his as well. He was driven to drown himself in her ambiance—to gorge himself wantonly of her presence—to smother his self with her essence. Her merest wish was his crusade. His desire to please her knew no bounds. It gave him purpose. She was his life.

She was Lady Rebecca. She wept because of his devotion. She wept because she was powerless to stand in the way of a man who made her the focus of his being. With all her heart, she thanked the Lord for this man; she begged that his dreams might be fulfilled, his ambitions realized. She asked the Almighty to quell her fears, to give her the strength needed to support her husband, to stand by him. It was difficult. She was afraid. She prayed to God that this night's conversation between her husband and his father would go in her favor. In her heart, she knew the outcome. She knew Christopher.

The two men were close. They sat together before a purposeful fire in the great room. They conversed over snifters of brandy, pausing only long enough to note the sound of the bells and Rebecca's return home.

A proud father and a respectful son full of admiration, the blood was obvious to all. Christopher was the youthful image of his father in wit, temperament, and good looks. Blonde hair crowned his strapping six-foot-three, two hundred and forty-pound frame that belied the steady temper and considerate character inside. The senior Claussen reveled in living vicariously through his son during his boyhood years, his apprenticeship into the business, and above all, his wedding to Rebecca.

Christopher's mother, Angelica Claussen, passed on from his life at age nine. The Mistress of Winter reached for her, never to relinquish the grip. Devastated, he stood in silence alongside his father only to watch in helpless torture as the warmth of this woman slowly slipped away. One last kiss, one last farewell; one final realization; he was the only child, a boy crushed by his loss.

Tears of his despair decimated Christmas. Christopher never understood why someone so perfect would be taken from him during the season when all rejoiced in the spirit of generosity. Why, in this season when all men praised the Lord, when all men opened their hearts and purses, when all men gave what they could spare to ease misery and want, why now did God choose to take?

He turned to his father, but was old enough to realize his loss was reflected in the broken man's sorrowful eyes. The senior Claussen changed that day as did he. They sought out one another for love and affection, and they built a relationship between them that was the envy of many a father and son. They grew to understand and respect one another, to shore up their lives, to share their love, and to appreciate their coveted bond.

When the charm of Rebecca breezed into Mr. Claussen's life by way of his son, he threw open his heart. He welcomed the sunlight she brought to the dark, dusty corners of his home. She filled the place with warmth, as only a woman is able. She became an object of worship, the love of a son, the adoration of his father. If ever by chance Christopher should overlook some minute detail in Rebecca's needs or desires, his father stood by

LADY REBECCA GREYSTONE CLAUSSEN

ever ready to step into his place, for she could do no wrong in his eyes, and he planned on spoiling her rotten in his son's name.

It is true that Christopher gave Rebecca her coach on their first Christmas, but she knew it was too expensive a gift without certain consultation and consent from Mr. Claussen. She often commented aloud to her father-in-law that she believed the coach was probably more his gift than Christopher's. Christopher never argued the point, instead choosing to nod with a knowing grin. The senior Claussen would never admit to it under any circumstance, but he would glow like a summer sun at the suggestion.

FOUR

Although the senior Claussen was not one to be often seen in distress, there could be no mistaking the torment he was going through this night. Christopher was pleading his heartfelt case with sound judgment and enthusiasm, while his elder reached for every straw to support a passionate argument against his son's intentions.

"I beg of you, Christopher, reconsider. I will see to it that your inheritance will be at your disposal whenever you wish. The business in its entirety is yours to administer. I'm not blind and—thank the Lord, not dim-witted at this time. I can see clearly that you are restless. And I say go, travel! See the world for all it is! Go with Rebecca! But remember, forever this is your home, Christopher, not some deep woods or desert canyon, or some godforsaken Indian plain.

"This is home. This has always been home, and this is where you belong. This estate has been in our family since the beginning of time. It belongs to you, son. Heavens above! There is plenty of wealth to be earned and activity to be had in Copenhagen or Oslo. Take up residence in London if you must, but spare me the distance of the New World, Christopher." He let out a deep, discouraged breath.

"Father," said Christopher, with compassion. "...I know how hard this is for you. I too wonder how I will go on without our evening conversations over brandy without you to share my interests and accomplishments. These things will be difficult for me, and I too will find no one to fill these empty spaces. These will always be sacred longings of mine that even Rebecca, with all she brings, will never satisfy."

He continued. "Father, please understand how the world appears to me. I possess more wealth than any man has a right to claim. I own forest and field beyond measure. A week's carriage will not bring my eyes to see all that I am to inherit. Is the sole purpose of my life to discover what is to be my bequeathment? Am I to reflect upon my deathbed, and see the sum of my years as nothing more than a balanced book, a tally of the fruits of my ancestors' labor?

"Father, please, I beg, support me in my dream. The New World is fraught with peril, it is true, but it is also blessed with incalculable wealth and riches. Its borders are unknown and certain to be filled with splendor and adventures worth more than gold in a man's life. Father, gold weighs a man's soul down—*adventure* gives him wings! If the Lord gave me but half a brain, I should at least triple the family holdings with investments abroad. Not one of my ancestors has seen the likes of these opportunities that are here and now presented to me.

"Hear me, Father. Recently I had occasion to visit with the administrator of Capelo's, a trading firm in Portugal. Whilst en route, I took notice of a sizable crowd upon the dock at a ship called the SPANISH MAIDEN FAIR. There was on this dock, being promoted with great pomp, a section of a timber. With God as my witness, I swear before heaven above that this slice of wood was all of thirty-six feet in girth. It had been quartered in order to ship but for its enormity.

"This master, I say was all about the wharf trying to raise interest and thereby fund a fleet for the purpose of moving an unlimited supply of this tree to the timber-starved shipyards of England. He claimed to have seen the forest itself, and stated with all assuredness that a brig could be built complete by felling a single tree! I will speak freely and state there was no lack of interest—and for good reason! Father, mark my words. This speaks of a wealth greater than gold or silver. This is a commodity that is attractive to the poor as well as rich. Imagine an unlimited supply of virgin stands, three hundred feet tall! What tree do we forest that might compare?

"And who better to mount this venture than I? Foresting is the heart of our fortunes. I was bred on bark. Or, do you prefer that I leave it to others and fight a losing battle from this side of the ocean as we are undersold and ousted from the business?

"The Land Act in the states is offering quarter sections; one hundred and sixty acre parcels at just over a dollar and a half an acre. Think of it, Father!" Christopher warned, "With respect, I beg to remind you that we already own the shipyards and the fleet. We already possess the knowledge to process these vast forests. This matter must be investigated. I see no other way." He studied his father, awaiting a reply.

"I understand your enthusiasm, son, but I disagree with the notion that shipping these goods is going to be easy, 'treasures for the taking,' as you seem to imply by your convictions. The situation between England and France is unbearable. Napoleon is doing his best to strangle Britain with his Berlin Decree and his proposed Milan Decree. Those blockades not only suffocate England, but the Continent as a whole. It makes shipping a very dangerous proposition. The man is running amuck. He subjugates all the countries within reach of his armies, and I say he may very well succeed with his blockades. He must be reckoned with, Christopher.

"But let us suppose you clear the English Channel and that you make way past all the possible fears of the French coast and Napoleon. You still have to face England's blockades up and down the American coast. Remember the relationship between England and the States may be better than that with France, but it is far from cordial. It is no secret that England has been commandeering American ships and impressing their crews into service for the king. The American Minister Monroe practically lives in England trying to put an end to this business, and what has he got to show for his time? Worthless treaties and empty promises. The English care little about impressed Americans and it will soon boil over. And if what I say isn't compelling enough, consider then that the Americans have recently implemented their own Nonimportation Act and have banned a good many general stores from Europe. This is a time of war and tensions run high. I assure you, business upon the seas will be stormy, son!"

Christopher would not be daunted. "True! True, Father! True enough! Yet, I see it entirely different. Napoleon cannot possibly enforce his decrees. Blockades of the channel require far more resources than even he can muster. Remember our amazement at hearing how he sold Louisiana to the United States? I tell you, sir, either he is stretched to his limits or he has gone insane.

"Louisiana is so vast, it's said to be virtually immeasurable. I hear tell the latest estimates exceed eight hundred thousand square miles of virgin country. The fool gave it up to possess lands that are overpopulated and stripped of their wealth. I have also heard that the American President Jefferson is reported to have dispatched a scouting party to map this new frontier, and they have made claim it exceeds two million acres. Two million acres, Father! I cannot even comprehend the vastness of such space! And most of it has never been trodden by a white man's boot. This frontier is enormous, Father, and open to all. The activity within the markets will explode!

"I say the day of Spanish influence is over, and they no longer are contentious. The U.S. Congress has legislated plans for a national military force and also a national road to stretch from the East Coast well into the western frontier. I can't imagine that England and France can be so blind they cannot see how they must put aside their differences and become a part of this new wave of exploration or their citizens will bring the governments to bear.

"It is beyond me, Father. However, I must admit the more they squabble, the better for the Scandinavians. The ports are overflowing with new trade, and our yards can't keep up with the demand for new ships. English and French ports are becoming too dangerous. Even the English merchants are now in fear of ports that were always considered safe, such as those in Holland and Germany.

"As it stands for now, we are perfectly situated at England's backside. We are protected by her fleets and comfortably out of the reach of Napoleon's armies. Now that our king is sympathetic to the British cause, and after that devastating defeat of the French navy at Trafalgar this year past, the fate of the French upon the open seas is sealed. The business of shipping for us Northerners can only flourish. It is not as dire as you might at first believe, father.

"I know I am rambling on, but it is all that I think about. It is all that I dream about, and I speak of only limited issue. There are many wonders to be discovered, opportunities beyond all our expectations. Father, I see what is to be my life. I never will know contentment so long as I remain strapped to this shore. I am sorry, Father. Please, I beg you, try to understand." Christopher looked deeply into his glass of brandy. Then he spoke in a lower tone of voice, so as not to be overheard.

"Let us also not forget that as long as I remain here, I may very well be called upon to serve. I will be handed a commission and a gun. I am not a coward father, but I care not for either." His father rolled his eyes in despair and nodded with comprehension.

He fully understood his son's concerns. They were real enough. Christopher continued to speak.

"Napoleon is a solider of great merit. Unfortunately, he's not on our side and he seems bent on overrunning much of what we call ours. Now, with all due respect to King Adolf, we are party to the Third Coalition and find ourselves embroiled even deeper into these hostilities. I support him in many of his views, but Russia and France are in accordance and signing treaties to our demise. Not to mention that our own throne leaves much to be desired.

"There is no successor to Gustav, but there is plenty of bickering among the forces that surround him. Where are we going here, father? I am convinced of one thing, and that is to say, I have no need for any of this. In America, people of every nationality sit together at the same table. I am sure there is plenty of distrust and even hatred, baggage they carry with them from Europe. That's our legacy. However, I don't believe they go on Napoleonic crusades slaughtering each other into submission."

Christopher knew he would leave, but he had to rinse his conscience clean. He also knew that his father realized the awkward position he was in, being a member of one of the wealthiest families in Sweden. If Sweden was now at war, he would be expected to partake heavily in the king's service. His father looked upon him with great love and resignation.

"I understand, my son. That is my problem in its entirety. I understand all too well. I worry. I fear for you and your wellbeing, and for that of Rebecca. Someday, you will have a son, and a different perspective will slant whatever decisions you make. My world will never recover from the absence of you and Rebecca, bless her heart, but what can I say—stay? No. Your assessment is well thought out and accurate. I have no choice, but to say with heavy heart, go. Go, Christopher, go with my blessing, son. Seek out your life and fortune. I have lived my life. The turn is now yours. Go with God."

Rebecca sobbed.

FIVE

Timothy Anderson sat quietly with his mess, immersed in the sounds of the sea and the bone-chilling damp. The table, lowered from the deck beams overhead to a position in-between the cannon, swung gently to the ocean's roll. Resting upon it, in addition to the elbows of his friends, were pans filled with dandyfunk, a cracker hash concoction made up of water-soaked biscuits, baked on this rare occasion with unsalted beef, fat, and molasses. There were also potatoes and green peas. Lemons, fenced in by the fiddles, rolled about recklessly dodging hungry fingers. Eyed with relish, they were snatched up within the grip of the men's fists, stripped of their skin and readily downed. Fresh fruit was a rare commodity to be found onboard. Now it was plentiful, following welcomed rations of maggot-free bread and unsalted meat. The repast of late was better than usual—supreme in fact. A sure sign the ship was sailing in waters near home ports.

Over the past couple years, Timothy's mess had become entirely American. They would never have been allowed to congregate openly in the beginning for fear of scheming. But years had gone by and their nationalities had blended into the framework of the ship. Except for the darker-skinned islanders and slaves, it was difficult to tell the Americans or Englishmen from any other onboard. Ironically, the one freedom upheld for all sailors in the English navy was the choice to mess with whomever one pleased. And so the Americans ate together as a group sharing three or four tables. Tonight they ate silently and out of character. An attentive guard might have noticed how they concealed the inner nervousness they shared. Meanwhile, from out of the corner of their eyes, they stole furtive glances about the ship and worked hard to keep up an appetite.

This was not an ordinary night. The ELIZABETH ANNE man-of-war, 104 guns, was anchored with her escort of frigates in the port of Copenhagen. Here, the mammoth ship would find very little, save a frosty welcome and deep suspicion from the city dwellers upon news of their arrival. Years before, a similar British warship devastated the harbor front by broadsiding it with cannon from this same anchorage. It caused enormous destruction, including fire, much mayhem and loss of life. The wounds were deep and slow to heal; the scars, both visible and invisible, were numerous.

What this port did have to offer, much to the chagrin of the ship's officers, was safe haven for those unfortunate souls who were impressed into service for the Crown. For them it was just a matter of getting to shore. For certain, the captain was no dimwit and the ship stayed far out from dock to thwart any misguided attempts by the foolhardy.

Timothy's table and the three just aft were seated with impressed sailors. That was not so unusual. What was unusual, again, was the fact that these tables were made up entirely of Americans who had come to form a tightly knit group. Their attitude was markedly different than sailors impressed from other countries. Many of the others faced oppression either on board ship or on land in their home countries. They could often be indifferent between a choice of two different forms of misery. Americans on the other hand could be defiant unto death. They were free men, a fact never forgotten and never to be forgotten. Not unlike cats pacing the bars of a cage, they seldom slept peacefully whilst in captivity.

They had spent most of their years of forced service on board vessels of war sailing the seas about the Mediterranean, the Barbary Coast, the sea of Trafalgar, or the Spice Islands and Trades. Their captain kept a sharp lookout for French and Spanish merchants' ships, or better yet, warships. Nothing brought a smile to the officers of the ELIZABETH ANNE like the possibility of engagement. There was booty to be had and rank to be gained, and this being the only viable means to support their preferred lifestyles, engagement was a most welcome event.

Not so for the men on the lower decks as they stood flanking the massive castings of iron, inhaling the acrid smoke of black powder so thick one could choke to death on it or his fear. Through eyes stinging with the sweat of impending death, it was they who stared down the barrels of enemy cannon often little more than a hundred feet away. It was they who saw their own fear reflected in the faces of the enemy so near.

In union, as though dancers before a mirror, opposing forces clapped torch to wick—as if partners moving to perfect step—soul mates staring into each other's eyes but never to embrace. The cannon roared, and the ships disappeared into a cloud of smoke perforated by shot, ball, and chain. This followed by morbid confusion as the resonance of horror reverberated across the water between the lumbering hulls—the piercing screams of friends and foe. Like dying porcupines, men stumbled blindly along the bulkheads with shards of splintered oak protruding from their bellies in a pointless attempt to escape the harbinger of death.

The rain of blood and flesh abated, and the gunners retreated from the flood of crimson creeks that cut back and forth across the rolling deck. The liquid of life, driven by the motion of the sea to seek out the arms and legs blown hither and thither, to be found flung into corners or strewn under the carriages and blocking the guns from moving forward once again into position.

Timothy knew the look of terror in an armless man's eyes as he was thrown overboard to the sharks. Whether he was eaten, drowned, or bled to death, this life was over for him in a moment's time. The distance from heaven to hell on a man-of-war was six feet below the upper deck, or the length of a prayer.

Except for when taking on water, the ship only neared land in England, and then only where shore crews maintained the strictest surveillance looking out for deserters. In the most stringent terms a man-of-war could easily be called a floating prison.

This night was different. This was the night the Americans had waited for years to arrive. It was bound to happen, a foreign port where press gangs couldn't walk the streets in defiance of the community, a port without informants at every inn, a port steeped in resentment and having little desire to appease the British who burned them out. Unlike any other night, tonight Timothy and the others would risk their lives to gain freedom. They had all worked feverishly to form a plan of escape for this night since way back when word first made it down 'tweendecks' that the ELIZABETH ANNE was standing for Denmark.

It was Currie Larson's turn to be the mess chief. He would, according to plan, return to the cook twice for slush, a hot greasy slop that was often thrown on bread to kill the maggots and the taste. Each man had obtained and hidden a length of line and a round piece of sailcloth, eighteen inches in diameter. Over the past couple of weeks, the man whose turn it was to be mess chief would request the slosh, and one by one each man would saturate his sailcloth with the grease, working it in while hot and burnishing it smooth. This made it quite waterproof. The pieces were stored flat in bedrolls for safekeeping.

The main concern was the sentry who patrolled the forward gun deck. The man would be a marine and even if nice enough off duty—a regular guy, while on watch he would have to be subdued in no uncertain terms or he might get hanged as an accomplice. He didn't patrol the deck for invaders; nobody stole aboard a ship with five thousand men on board. He patrolled to stop deserters. The Americans had already checked the roster and knew well in advance that the man was Charles Cooper. He was a man slight of frame, and of no concern to the Americans who planned on overpowering him.

After the evening mess was over, the mess chief removed the pans and went off to wash. The others raised the table and tied it off overhead as required. Shortly thereafter, the men of the forward starboard gun deck were ordered above to retrieve their bedrolls. These were stored in nets affixed above or alongside the bulwarks to protect the men on the upper deck from wood splinters and musket shot.

As Timothy and the others walked the waterways to retrieve their sleeping rolls, they studied the lay of the bay and the mooring of the frigates as best they could with short glances through the passing gun ports. They were anchored a quarter of a mile off shore. It would be a trying swim in the current of these cold waters.

The call to bed down was made, and the men who had already strung their hammocks to the beams overhead climbed in and extinguished the oil lamps. Slowly, the ship darkened and the noise dropped off to the ever-present drone of activity on other decks, this broken only by the rhythmic steps of the passing sentry, Charles Cooper. The men tried to rest, for their bodies would need every ounce of energy that could be mustered when fighting the cold water. It was an effort in vain; their nerves were altogether too agitated by anticipation.

By plan, Kenneth Steward would feign illness and draw Charles deep into the mire of hanging hammocks. Timothy was berthed next to Kenneth and would be counted on heavily to be the first to reach for Charles. It would have to be quick and silent. He felt for his knife.

"Oyeee, Charlie!" Kenneth whispered. "Step o'er here wi' ye light, I feel I gotta rash a coverin' me. Bring yer lant-ern, Charlie, an' give us a look." Charlie sighed, not wishing to work his way into the tightly packed hammocks.

"You'll be fine. Go to sleep."

"No, I can feel it, man. Bring us yer light."

"Go to sleep."

"Damn it, man! I be needin' a light!" Kenneth started to raise a ruckus. The sentry, standing among so many mates expecting to sleep undisturbed, wanted no trouble and so relented.

"Oh, all right. Hang on then."

Suspecting nothing, he dropped down on all four, crawled beneath the layer of suspended bedding, and arose at Kenneth's side. He leaned over with the light as Kenneth pulled up his shirt to expose his belly.

"Naught! Don't see a thing."

"'Ere must be. I kin feel it. Feels bumpy. 'Old the lant-ern closer, somethin's 'ere, I kin feel it." Kenneth protested as he rubbed his belly, feigning discomfort. Charlie held the light up, nose nearly buried within Kenneth's navel. At that point, Kenneth exposed his penis, which utterly disgusted the sentry, but fully distracted him from other goings on.

"There ain't nothin', ugh, you bastar—mmmph!

In a split second, near twenty men dropped quietly to the deck. Timothy held Charlie hard by the mouth and kept a knife firm to his throat. He prayed he would not have to hurt him. Timothy wasn't a killer, but he had passed the point of no return, and was now desperate. Kenneth relieved the sentry of his lantern.

"Keep quiet, Charlie. You're a good man an' a good marine. I hold nothin' against ya, but I'll kill ya this instant if ya so much as breathe contrary." He could feel Charlie start to quiver. "Calm yourself, ya been overpowered and ya won't be hanged."

The sentry understood the importance of that fact. He would still have a lot of explaining to do, but he could now see how many men were involved in the plot, and he would surely be forgiven. Timothy continued to whisper in Charlie's ear.

"I've had four years too many on this prison barge, Charlie. I never asked t' be put on 'er. I was married four weeks, taken without compassion to live in this miserable bloodletting dungeon afloat. No more, Charlie...now ya just keep quiet an' stay put an' I'll buy ya a drink the next time we meet."

The others quickly lowered their mess tables and used the attached lines to fasten their belongings securely to the tabletops. The remaining lines were used to immobilize Charlie and for lowering the tables into the water quietly. A number of others watched in silence, but had the wit to know nothing and feigned sleep.

Time was not on their side. With haste, they moved throught the ship retrieving the fire buckets, which hung slowly swaying from the cross-timbers overhead. The produced their pieces of greased sailcloth and stretched them over the buckets. Folding the cloth down over the rim of the bucket, each man wrapped his line trightly around it a time or two and then tied the rope off. The result was a watertight float. These were all strung together and lowered through the gun port on a line. At the same time, the hammocks were tied together to form a rope, which was secured to a deck beam and lowered out a port in a likewise manner. Sound traveled far on the water, and the men would have to lower themselves quietly into the sea lest they be found out by marines stationed topside. The tables were set out to float, and immediately followed by a line of men who quickly but quietly slid down the hammocks, one after another, into the sufferable cold of the water.

Within minutes they were moving toward the ship's bow to avoid the light of her stern lanterns. The night was in their favor, there being little moonlight and heavy fog lying upon the water to hide them and muffle sounds. They cast off quietly in the same single file until out of sight of the anchor watch at which point they joined up.

The buckets were passed out among the men and eased their struggle to stay afloat. One hand on the bucket rope kept them floating above water easily while at the same time keeping the bucket upside down to hold trapped air. They kept whatever belongings they could manage on top of the floating tables. The belongings didn't stay dry, but they remained secured and were not carried away to sea.

It was just shy of fifteen minutes before they were discovered missing, and at which time the alarm was sounded onboard the ELIZABETH ANNE. She sent up her flares, and shortly thereafter a couple of nearby brigs did likewise. The other ship officers assumed correctly the cause for alarm. Orders were given to lower a longboat because the captain was ashore and no skiff was readily available. It was also determined, due to the number of deserters gone over the board, a larger longboat was needed to bring them back. It was no small matter getting the boat into the water, and for that reason precious time was afforded the Americans to swim well away. Once in the water, however, the longboat rowers made way with speed.

"She'll be upon us in a matter of minutes, losing time only to seek us out," Kenneth noted to the others.

The men were concerned, and for good reason. There would be some serious flogging and possibly a hanging from the yardarm should they end up back on the ship.

"We're going to turn this into our favor," Timothy stated with an air of confidence.

"How's that!" The men asked in desperation, for now the longboat's silhouette could be made out on occasion when sufficiently backlit by the ELIZABETH ANNE's lanterns.

"You see, the crew hasn't lit their bow lantern." The men took note and agreed. Timothy continued. "They don't want us to see them coming any sooner than necessary, so they might get the upper hand on us by surprise in this fog. These tables will make a fine target to sight on as they come across. I say, half of our number should remain with the tables. The rest swim with your buckets out to each side and wait for them to come. Let them pass through our flanks, and then we will close in, quietly swimming up from behind. The fog is very much in our favor.

"Those at the tables must make enough noise to draw them into our trap. Appear to be surprised at having been found out, but once they have spotted you, raise a tremendous ruckus as they approach so they will remain intent on the situation at hand. Be especially belligerent and rude. Curse them to hell. This will make them fighting mad and they will pay little mind to anything other than punishment and wringing your necks. As long as their eyes don't waver we will upset their boat. Remember this above all else, they are not coming for us; we are going for them. We want the boat, and I assure you that when you have your mits on the gunwales, you will have no problem taking command of it." The men started laughing quietly among themselves, their confidence renewed even as they shivered. It was just a matter of perspective. The prey was now the bait.

The Americans had one distinct advantage over those in the longboat. They had floats and knew they were unlikely to drown from exhaustion. If they could conserve their body heat and keep from cramping up, they could float forever. Not so for the longboat crew. To have their boat rocked violently without warning would plunge them into a certain state of panic. They had only their frightened wit to ward off drowning once spilled into the black night waters of the bay midway between ship and shore. It would be total chaos for the crew, every man for himself. For this reason, the more confusion the better because unlike the unsuspecting longboat crew, the Americans were

70

suddenly working together according to a plan—to get out of the freezing water and into the boat.

It was as though the English in their longboat wished to help the Americans. The moment they took notice of the floundering swimmers, they bore down as quickly as possible upon the tables and deserters, in order to effect the greatest surprise and terror. Their attention was fixed rigidly upon their prey with the arrogant expectation of inevitable success.

Having emerged from the fog within a couple of rods of the men, the pressmen ordered the deserters to remain still and prepare to be removed to the boat. A man stood at the bows pointing a pistol in their direction. At this, the swimmers let loose such a flurry of obscenities and insults toward the boat crew, and with such exuberance that even the Lord in all His understanding must surely have winced. The crew was belittled with insult. So enraged were they from this unexpected boldness, they allowed themselves to be provoked into the trap of men they intended to snare.

While the Americans moved under the cover of fog, floating silently toward the stern of the boat, the pressmen were foolishly looking forward without caution, their backs exposed to attack. The insults had brought them to their feet, eager to announce in grizzly detail the punishment awaiting those whom they didn't first shoot or drown. So thoroughly were they distracted by the insults and blinded by revenge, the remaining Americans were handed an easy approach.

In an instant, after one forceful pull of the American's combined weight upon the gunwale, much of the crew was knocked completely off balance as anticipated. Each fell into the other causing all to trip and tumble into a great tangle of flailing arms and legs, pushing and pulling to save themselves, but to no avail. They spilled over the heads of the Americans, subject to the full shock of surprise and bone chilling water as they plunged beneath the surface of the darkened sea.

Those who were more agile were pulled overboard before gaining time to resist. All the while, having kept their hands firmly gripped upon the gunwales, the Americans immediately pulled themselves aboard, assisted their own into the boat, and made quick claim to it.

With an obvious victory at hand, the Americans were propelled into action with renewed vigor and took up oars in a threatening manner to crush the skulls of any pressmen within range. This quieted them quickly and turned them to thinking of their own demise in the frigid sea. The two remaining pressmen seeing that they were badly outnumbered stood immobile and bewildered before accepting sound advice to jump over the board. Indeed, they were quick to make room for the remaining deserters still swimming into view from the shadows.

There were a good number of Americans, near twenty in all, many still in the water awaiting their turn to be hauled aboard. They kept a wary eye on their adversaries who now had turned toward sea, disappearing in the night amid a stream of curses hurled by both sides as they swam for the ELIZABETH ANNE.

The longboat was large enough for all in spite of the fact her crew had numbered only nine—eight pressmen at the oars and one officer, this by plan so there might be ample room to lay in their failed catch. Timothy helped the others remove their belongings from the tabletops and everything was placed into the boat. They left the floating tables along with the buckets to the losers and dumbfounded for whatever advantage they might offer.

As Timothy and the others began to make way for shore, they hurled one last barrage of insults at the pressmen. There was no love lost for the spilled crew of the longboat. They were not the same sort as Charlie Cooper. He was a mate much like themselves, a regular—a good man. There was nothing in common between Charlie Cooper and the boat crew that held little pity for the likes of Timothy, newlywed or not.

Strong-armed, most of these men were kidnapped and forced to the farthest reaches of the world with scant hope of returning home to friends and family. Equally dismal was their chances of living through the ordeal, all the while their captors laid about on land roaring with laughter over ale as they sat in the taverns describing in detail and delight the looks of panic upon the unfortunate whom they managed to collar and carry off.

One particular memory was carved eternally into Timothy's mind. That of a young girl sentenced for some crime, probably very petty, no one ever knew. Her punishment was to service the men onboard the man-of-war. This was a daunting task for the experienced woman of the night, let alone a young girl who obviously was not so inclined by reason of faith or upbringing.

At no time in the three weeks she was aboard the ELIZABETH ANNE did she relent from her crying. So pitiful was she to see that the men respected her good nature and tried in vain to comfort her, to ease her fears, but to no avail. She never raised her eyes, spoke a word, or took of nourishment save for a little drink.

As she wasted away before the men's eyes and their pleas for her release, she accepted only a Bible upon which she cried without stopping until she was discovered one morning clasping it in the grip of death. Silent at last and set free, she died from nothing other than fright and distress. She was young in years and surely innocent of any malicious wrongdoing. It saddened the men greatly and they resented the officers bitterly for their lack of compassion, leaving her to despair unto her death.

For two weeks following her passing, the men stalked the ship's decks in a state of great anger and belligerence. The marines were on full alert. The officers did well to leave it alone and watch their backs, keeping safe distance from the men who boiled with a vengeance and would have taken many an officer down under the guise of an accident.

Timothy and the Americans put these thoughts and many others behind them as they pulled upon their oars and made way to shore. They landed in great style and good humor. Making every attempt to avoid the English officers, they split up into smaller groups to be less conspicuous while they searched out ships bound for the States. They offered quick farewells and made hasty plans to meet up and swap information on departures. Like the others, Timothy went with a group of six, searching for an American captain to employ them in their return voyage to the port of Boston.

SIX

The month of December was one of rest and relaxation for many, but not Christopher Claussen. He kissed Rebecca good-bye long before the first light of day. He was not expected home again until the week before Christmas. This may have been for the best in Rebecca's mind because she found herself depressed and unable to sleep at night. She feared herself to be dismal company and a burden to her husband. These feelings had ensued for many weeks. Christopher was off to the wharves of Malmo and Copenhagen with much business to accomplish before returning. Maybe by then she would feel revived.

Christopher journeyed two days by coach from the Claussen estate to Malmo on the coast. After completing a few days of business there, he boarded a ferry to Copenhagen. He was in need of an experienced American master to captain the ship he was currently having fitted out. The American shipmasters were hesitant to call on ports of England for fear of having their crews or vessels, if not themselves, impressed into the naval fleet of the Crown. Instead, they would be found wandering all about the Scandinavian ports doing business by transferring cargo destined to and from English ports.

Christopher needed a man with experience and knowledge of the American seaboard as well as the customs of the harbormasters and locals. He interviewed many a competent master, but in the end he found himself desiring one master in particular—one who had a serious drawback. The man was Captain James Ward of Baltimore, Maryland. His knowledge and experience of not only the American seaboard, but also the trade routes, surpassed thirty years and was notably impressive. Unfortunately, he wished only one last return voyage home, it being his desire to retire from the sea in style to be forever 'spliced' to his spouse. To 'swallow the anchor', as old seamen would say.

74

Christopher admired this man from the start, if for nothing other than the confident, steady demeanor that reveals itself only after a lifetime of experience. They spent a great deal of time discussing matters of shipping and ships. They conversed openly of their likes and dislikes and places of interest. They had bonded as friends almost at once. Christopher honestly enjoyed this man, but no matter how he might try to convince Mr. Ward of his need, there was no changing the man's mind about his return to land.

In the end, Christopher decided even a short trip abroad within the captain's company would serve him well in ways he might not presently foresee. His decision was free of concern. Therefore, from the start, after signing the papers and setting contracts aside, conversations focused on the hazards of the voyage before them, especially the state of near war between Britain and France. It was here that Christopher made mention of a special armament he had designed. The announcement brought an interesting response from the captain.

They were seated at the table in the captain's quarters of the ship MARYLAND III moored in port. Over a glass of fine porter wine, Christopher was speaking.

"So being burdened with the distasteful situation between Britain and France, not to mention the many other thieving pirates off the African coast, I was forced to consider some type of defensive weapon. As you know, this would normally be cannon. The trouble is, cannon take up a great deal of space and are of substantial weight. Even the smallest 'three pounder' is a cumbersome piece with its four to six foot chace, plus carriage, training tackle and all. Even worse, anything larger, such as a 'six pounder' or more, brings with it a need for gunners who must be reasonably well trained to man them. They also must be fed like any other sailor, but often contribute little to manning the lines or moving stowage, that being work they often shun.

"It came to be, after a great deal of thought and study of arms that I did employ the Carron Cannon Works in Scotland to build for me a long-barreled weapon of light weight—a cross between cannon and musket. The idea being, it projects a ball about an inch in diameter or small grape shot. Underneath the front of the barrel is fitted a ball-like protrusion that settles into a socket mounted upon the bulwarks, most generally at the timberheads.

"One man can easily mount, or remove and remount the piece quickly—say from larboard to starboard. He will find no hindrance in maneuvering for target. There is also the ability to load the shot with a charge at the breech, which makes this a fast weapon. I admit to being a braggart when I say with much pride and satisfaction that the gun possesses superb accuracy and range, surely the best elements of a well-designed piece. I now am only concerned with the manning of possibly five or six cannon at most. I am thinking possibly two 'twelve pound' long guns at the bows, possibly four 'sixteen pounders' abeam, and I am not sure maybe a 'three pounder' or two astern for good measure. All in all, a much more manageable situation."

Mr. Ward studied Christopher at length before proceeding with an air of cautious reserve.

"Sir, I have desire to present you with a plan which might be of great assistance. However, it comes with risk, and its nature may be of distaste to you. I emphasize, I mean no offense, and offer it only as a plan for consideration." He stopped as if to put order to his proposal.

"Go on then, Captain, let's hear it."

"Very well. It is common knowledge your ship sets sail for America on her maiden voyage. Obviously, there is little hope for secrecy on the docks. Even here in Copenhagen we have heard. She builds as a magnificent vessel that has caught many an eye in London and stole as many a conversation. To speak the truth, her beauty contributed greatly in my decision to hear you out. I was swayed no less by your reputation as a gentleman, and I trust you will take my words into the strictest of confidence. Many lives depend upon it."

"You have my word, Captain Ward. And I promise it untarnished as is the gold that backs my name."

"Much appreciated, sir. Let me say, when the construction of your vessel commenced two years ago, all upon England's docks strove to discover the rightful owner. It wasn't long before the clerks of the warehouses put two and two together and compiled sufficient evidence to point a finger in your direction, sir. At that point, scraps of information about your person came in with every arrival in port.

"Time and time again, it was said that the owner was a man of great wealth, compassion, and generosity. It was said, whenever he appeared, children who held him in great favor swarmed about him like bees about a hive. I learned later, you were the administrator of a large fleet of ships in Sweden, and your masters swore to your honesty and fairness. Stories of your charity abound, sir. I am particularly drawn to you by reputation, and pleased to have made your acquaintance for you have certainly earned my respect.

"As you know, I claim allegiance to the flag of the United States. This has made me the target of many seamen, mostly American by decree, who are deep in hiding for being deserters of the English man-of-wars, frigates, and what not. They have all been impressed upon for service to the Crown. Most, I will vouch have been taken from the harbors of their own homes. It is a sad situation and one in which my God-fearing country, proud as it might be, is unable to prevent. We are too young as of yet for a navy of consequence, however, as God is my witness, it will surely come. In the meantime, I offer my assistance in whatever manner I am able to help these unfortunate lads back across the sea that separates them from their roots. Many have been away from wives and children for years and are desperate to return.

"At first, I felt compelled to call upon your good conscience and compassionate heart to relieve these men of their suffering. Now, however, I would much rather suggest that I offer you their service as experienced gunners to man your cannon. These are men who can sort out gun and training tackle in their sleep. These are men trained on the man-o'-wars, yet, men who were formerly merchant seamen.

"As a rule you will find them most capable of going aloft to give hand with the sails or a-low to manage the lines, ground tackle and anchor. They make a fine lot of waisters, and there's certain to be an idler or two in the lot, maybe a barber or surgeon's mate, maybe a carpenter. Even if not, they'll earn their keep. They have plenty of work cut out for them keeping ordnance and gun in proper order, and training fresh crews to man them. Finally, there would be no cost to you other than sustenance during their journey home. I hope you find it not only an attractive proposition, but one with a noble cause."

"Hmmm." Christopher remained pensive while digesting all that Captain Ward had presented. "I am flattered by your assessment of my good nature; I feel I hardly deserve it. Yet, I can't help but to make mention of the fact that my ship is berthed in London's most visible dock. To say the least, it draws a great deal of attention. To me, this seems no small matter. Eyes are upon her sun-up to sunset, day and night. Surely, suspicious sorts would be arrested on site and I would find myself in rather embarrassing states of affair.

"Regardless of where my heart might be in this tragedy, anchoring at any other port would be a great inconvenience and of no assurance conditions would be safer for my ship. On the other hand, I should have little trouble finding sufficient numbers of jacks with at least some experience behind a cannon."

"You speak truth to the last word. Yet, I ask you to consider at length this fact. God forbid the need would arise, but should things go for worse, these men are battle-hardened. I guarantee they will remain steadfast at your side with their wits intact. They will be especially driven to see you through hard times, as they stand to lose the most. Should they cower or flounder before the enemy, they may well never again find their way home, never again see their families. These men truly understand what it means to be impressed into service against their will, to be hung from a yardarm if boarded, or sent to a slower death on the plantations.

"Believe me, Mr. Claussen, these are not forgotten souls. They are remembered by the Americans who await their return, and this may open many now unforeseen doors. Allow me to add that you should enjoy much praise from the citizens, who are fond of these luckless lads. I should expect for your efforts you will be repaid handsomely in status and favor."

It was not a matter to be taken lightly by either man. It was not a question that expected an answer. The affair was dangerous to all involved. These risks went unchallenged except where lived the moral resolve of men like Captain Ward and Mr. Claussen.

"I will give your proposal my sincerest consideration, this I promise. I find it as much heartfelt as interesting, certainly worth merit. Still, as I mentioned earlier, they are not onboard, Captain Ward."

"I understand. Yet, I would rather not bother you with details, for the less you know of that matter the less you suffer consequence in the event of mishap. Suffice it to say, we will be loading a hold with crates of Danish glass buried in flour for protection. Two commodities shipped for the price of one. The guise has worked well in the past, for the white dust keeps snoopers at bay. I will supply you with the proper articles for shipping the glass to America. We will transfer the cargo to your vessel from another berthed at London Dock imports."

And so the conversation went until that time when the men parted. In the end, Christopher found himself amused at the depth to which he had been drawn into this covert affair. It started out as harmless conversation, a natural progression of thought that belied his conveyance farther into the matter with each passing word, with each sip of wine. It was only afterward, in thinking back over the night's events that the full scope of his involvement settled in. This captain was no fool, he was interesting, his path somewhat dark, somewhat unknown, most certainly a man to be regarded. But for now, he was of clear conscience, and so with a grin he prepared himself to return home.

SEVEN

Christopher arrived back from Copenhagen in time to be with Rebecca and his father during the holiday festivities. They were often gathered together with friends, and Rebecca was generally the focus of attention. Unfortunately, as of late, she found it increasingly difficult to maintain an entertaining and sociable spirit. This didn't go without notice in the Claussen home, for when Rebecca was happy the world was vibrant, filled with life and the music of laughter. When she was depressed or away on travel, the estate seemed to be in a sluggish, dreary sleep. Her condition did not give reason for alarm. It didn't stop the world from going about its business, and anyone who didn't know Rebecca would have missed this small change of character.

Christopher, on the other hand, was very sensitive to her subtle ways and had no trouble picking up this mood. He questioned her repeatedly about her feelings over the past months, but she remained vague. Christopher, decidedly confident of the house servants and the presence of his father's watchful eye, knew Rebecca would be well cared for while he was away making preparations for their trip abroad. And so, he left again on the fourth of January. It would be two weeks certain before his return.

Have you seen the brigantine, Saralinda, on the sea?
Homeward bound from China, her holds chocked full of tea

She being fitted well to voyage, one-eighty out then back
Give or take a month or two, should winds be fresh or slack

Her sails let loose in August past, filled and billowed bright
We watched her go hull down at last, in remnants of day's light.

We cried ourselves to sleep that night for those before her wake
In the brigantine, Saralinda, a vessel of heartache

Oh, how we did our business to forget the length of time
Watched winter go to summer while awaiting bells to chime

Ding-a-ling the brigantine, Saralinda,'s on the sea!
Returning after leaving us in eighteen hundred three

Alas, neither ring nor swing, the steeple bell stays still
No such salutation from its tower atop the hill

We turn our backs on family, our labors, and much more
Going down in desperation to pray upon the shore

Dear God, we beg you sound her, pray tell them how we fear
To face the sea, the reality, of misfortune drawing near

Oh, God, we beg you bound them across the beating wave
To berth back home belated, but free the watery grave.

Rebecca closed the book and laid it upon the blanket. She looked up at the ceiling and stared blankly at the patterns of shadow in the woodwork that shifted with each flicker of her night candle. She took a deep breath.

"Why do I torment myself so?" She spoke aloud.

She placed the book upon her bed table, leaned across to blow out the candle, and fell back into the warmth of her bed. She lay in the silent darkness wishing to go to sleep, wishing to be freed of the inner anxiety and depression that plagued her with unending torment.

Slowly, throughout the long hours of these sleepless nights, Rebecca began to untangle the knots of frustration and distress within her troubled soul. Rebecca was an orphan. That fact was as much a part of her makeup as were her brilliant blue eyes, a part of her that could not be seen, but was always felt—a phantom of sorts. It stayed with her during every living breath of her existence.

Christopher had a profound effect on this matter. On the one hand, he was able to nearly erase this past injustice with his affection, which he used to smother her at every opportunity. On the other hand, he was always off addressing affairs of business, affairs of which she never fully understood. It kept him from her often, heightened her sensation of being alone, and often revived the dark misgivings and apprehensions of an orphan child. It would dampen her spirit and cause her to brood although she despised herself for being so shallow. She would escape these terrible feelings by going out for a ride in her coach—the vermilion coach that was his gift to her. It surrounded her in peace and comfort, not unlike his arms.

Rebecca never doubted Christopher's love for her, and that above all else was her life's joy. Love was something she had never known. Lust was something she grew up with in the tavern as a table maid. She had seen that craving in many a man's eyes. It had often put the fear of God into her; and when cornered, she was all hell to behold, teeth, nails, and spit. It was no time at all before her reputation for being an angel with a devil's swing drew as much business to the West Indies tavern as the brew itself.

She had always been cared for, even as an infant. She had never faced neglect or physical abuse. Her life was better than most without families. Still, it was an experience empty of compassion or affection. As for love, it was never more than a dream during her nights spent alone when only a pillow offered her comfort from bad dreams and demons prowling in the dark.

She saw her childhood as that of another little girl. A little girl for whom she grieved, a little girl for whom she cried until sleep relieved her of her torments, her worrisome thoughts each night. She now was able to recognize and understand the meaning of emptiness because she now knew about love and fulfilling relationships. The little girl of her childhood never knew enough about the injustice of life to cry, but this older and wiser Rebecca, although still dry-eyed, had learned a great deal about things to fear.

It was about change in her life from this newfound comfort called peace, called stability; this new thing that felt solid unlike the threats of change that were now coming toward her.

The closer the day of departure became, the more she suffered from panic and anxiety. It was the voyage into that unknown— heading back into the void that had been her whole life. Against her every instinct, she was being led away from the comfort and protection of the Claussen home, which seemed her only tangible security. It stood before her as a monument to tranquility; a centuries-old estate bound as firm and solid to the land as the nation that surrounded it.

Yes, she could see it now. She could feel the nervousness returning, the once all-encompassing loneliness that had been buried so carefully as of late. The emptiness that had been her mother, her constant companion as a child, was now drawing near to embrace her again. Now, she understood what it meant to be an orphan. She understood now what were these fears faced. It was about learning to make roots and being uprooted. It was about building foundations and feeling them shake. It was about having given all heart, leaping with blind faith into a love that could only be a dream. It was about standing in the light and looking back into that terrifying dark emptiness and turning to run for all your worth.

She tossed and turned and worried. Then from somewhere within these troubled thoughts came a wave of warmth. She was suddenly washed in a nocturnal bath of serenity. It was an awareness, a realization that home was not the estate or the land, but very clearly the man whom she married; the man who gave her love. This is why she was so depressed. When Christopher left on business, it was as though he took away her foundation. She only felt at home, at peace, when she stood by his side or within his embrace. Of course, it was clear now. Christopher was her tabernacle.

Rebecca sat up in her bed. She looked into the darkness of the room, and spoke aloud to her heart. She vowed with illimitable determination to face her fears and keep her home intact at whatever cost. If it meant she should live in a tent pitched among a godforsaken plain of Indian heathens, so be it. Should Christopher make his bed there so too would she, for that place was home. Only in that place would she belong, and only in that place would she find happiness. It took a long time to get there; but with that determination, at last, she slept in peace.

EIGHT

1807. On Saturday afternoon, the 17th of January, Christopher returned from England as promised. To see the look in his eyes, after he'd been away from her side, thrilled Rebecca to the heart. He wanted her. His eyes would never lie. When he gazed upon her, every worry in her world was drawn out, all the exaggerated fears and concerns, all the scars from thinking too much alone, all burdens of the heart dissolved into a sea of joyous reunion.

She had bathed and misted her chocolate-colored hair with the fragrance of lavender. Her maidens fitted her with great exuberance and saw to it that her dress was exceptional. She stepped through the gigantic front doors and braved the arctic winds. Wrapped tightly in Christopher's favorite mink coat, she stood centered in the great circle of inlaid marble. She shivered among the shadows of the great granite columns and waited impatiently as he approached.

All the gray granite in existence couldn't subdue the radiance of Rebecca. Christopher's pulse quickened at first sight of her. Her thick locks of hair lifting to catch the winter gusts, concealing the color of her face, the blue of her eyes, then parting before mists of breath and the flash of her smile, settling back down lost in the luxurious fur that protected her graceful shoulders. He could feel her effect course through him like bloodfire. There was no time to wait for his coachmen, and the cabin door was flung open before the horses stood still. He raced up the steps to meet her open arms, and lifting up her delicate frame ever so carefully, he twirled her within his embrace—she held fast by a kiss filled with his longing.

Their lips parted and he gently scolded her for waiting out of doors in the bitter cold air. He reminded her of how he lost the only other woman he ever loved to the Mistress of Winter, but Rebecca scarcely heard him as she chattered on about things of no consequence just to have his attention, just to hear his voice and bask in the warmth of his love.

They floated and fussed over one another until Rebecca escorted Christopher down to a spectacular dinner spread out across the massive oak table prepared especially for his return. There were seated a number of guests who had arrived beforehand to join the household in welcoming Christopher home, for the holy day season was still being celebrated. They ate and drank. They joked with one another. They teased and they laughed. They listened to Christopher's stories and of news from abroad. Rebecca never stopped smiling in his presence, but she longed for the evening to end. She wished only to leave the bright lights and fanfare, and retire to the privacy of their chamber where she might have all of him to herself, heart and soul.

Throughout the evening, Rebecca conversed with Christopher in a language free of the constraint of words. A language of glances, touches, and subtle expressions, those only lovers might know. She was offering herself to him both consciously and unconsciously. She was expressing her desire to be with her man and she was driving him mad. For the one man in the room to whom she called, her message was loud and clear, and he was forced to contain himself, as was she. The agonizing wait only served to make their desire all the more intense.

At last, for the two of them, a respectable amount of time had been given to their guests, and Rebecca announced that certain affairs important to the cohesion and tranquility of their marriage had to be addressed without further delay. Inside, her heart was racing with anticipation as she moved away from the table and stood behind Christopher's chair amid a round of applause and encouragement from the guests. The senior Claussen arose to his feet, offered a toast in honor of their love, and then bid them a glorious good night.

Rebecca and Christopher played, and kissed, and loved late into the night. They slept soundly until well after the sun made its appearance the following morn. It was the aroma of breakfast from the kitchen hearth wafting through the dining hall, up the great staircase, past the tapestries, and along the corridor to their room that finally brought them back to life. They were famished and entirely ready to enjoy a hot breakfast in bed. With their bellies full and hearts content, they pushed away the trays and once again gave in to their sexual desires.

Afterward, feeling satiated, they lay about lazily in each other's arms until mid-afternoon, at which time they felt compelled to visit with Christopher's father. The visit extended into the dinner hour, and this time it was a private affair for only the three members of the family. Satisfied with his supper, the senior Claussen removed himself to the study. Christopher and Rebecca joined him for a brandy and conversation before the fire; and when finished, they left the elder gentleman with his blanket and book, as they retired to their chamber.

By fashion of an ages old habit, Christopher took up his chair at the study and became at once absorbed by the endless assortment of paperwork and details spread out before him. The litter of documents represented every manner of issue pertinent to his business ventures and other involvements either unknown or barely comprehensible to Rebecca. These lifeless scraps of parchment conspired in a common distraction to turn his eyes from hers. They were chains from which he never seemed to break free or find himself even a moment's reprieve.

Rebecca likened his business affairs to a reckless and overbearing ogre that she was determined to subdue. It was her mission to thwart the beast's unchecked advance, its insatiable appetite for Christopher's time—time that belonged to her. She used every weapon, every shield, every charm in her arsenal, and due to those charms and persistence she seldom saw defeat.

Rebecca seated herself at the lover's couch adjacent to Christopher's desk. She studied him and her attention didn't escape him unnoticed.

"Rebecca, you are staring, my love." He sat back from his work, crossed his arms, and met her eyes.

"I know. I was using my mental powers to distract you."

"You succeeded, you wanton witch. Now, tell me, is there something on your mind, my dear?"

She looked around the room, and then faced him with apprehension.

"I very much wish to ask something of you. However, it is difficult because you know no restraint in trying to please me."

"Rebecca, I live to please you."

"And you do please me as no other." She spoke sincerely.

"Hearing you say it makes it all worth the while. I hope at last you will tell me what troubles you. I have been distracted but for my concerns about you these last few weeks. You haven't been yourself, a little down—a little sad, it seems to me. I know this upcoming move abroad has had an effect on you. One, I fear, that has been unpleasant. Is this it? You must speak frankly, Rebecca."

"Yes, I am afraid so."

Christopher winced with pain. "You wish to remain here at Claussen. I am correct, am I not?"

"I love it here. This is my first home. I feel so safe here and I am nervous to leave, I admit it. But I couldn't bear to be left behind, Christopher. Not alone without you."

"Yet, on the same hand you can't bear to leave either. Is that it?"

Rebecca smiled. "Well, it was that way, true enough, for it has been difficult. I spend many a night lying in bed worrying about what will become of us once we leave the security of Claussen and your father. But I am done with all of that now, and I want you to know that I have found the courage to stand by your side and support you in whatever dreams you have. I love you, Christopher, and your happiness is my happiness."

"Oh! Thank you, dear God! Rebecca, you cannot possibly imagine the burden you have removed from my mind." He closed his eyes and the anxiety left his brow.

"Ask anything of me, love, anything at all. If you do so choose to stand by my side, I swear to you before God there isn't anything I won't attempt for the sake of your own happiness and peace of mind. Just say the word, Rebecca. Please, I beg, just tell me what it is you wish." He was euphoric.

She watched him closely. "You have asked me repeatedly what troubles my heart. I was never able to satisfy you with a sound answer because I never understood these feelings myself. I tossed and turned all the nights of your absence, and I prayed to God for my peace of mind. I believe He has shown me. I have given this a great deal of thought and…." She steadied herself. "I would like to bring some children with us. There, I've said it." She looked away from him. At times it was difficult for her to meet his gaze. However, there was no turning back once she made a request.

Christopher's face folded up. "Children?" He was dumbfounded.

"Yes."

"You mean more maiden servants besides Mary and Elizabeth?"

"Not exactly."

His eyes suddenly grew wide. "You're not saying…." Christopher looked at her belly with some concern.

"Oh, no! Not that, my Lord, no. We don't need that right now. Oh, Christopher, I knew this would be difficult. I shouldn't bother you with this so soon after your arrival home." She regretted taking this initiative.

"No! No! My darling, I insist! I was so afraid you would ask me to leave you behind. Anything, anything now is easy. Go on, tell me what you mean."

"Orphans," she said sheepishly.

"Orphans?" He returned slowly, further confused.

"I have listened very carefully to everything you have said about the New World over this past year. Everything! Maybe that is because I worry so much. I have even taken it upon myself to seek out books to study; and I know from this and what you have said that there is plenty of room and opportunity for orphans who might go to families abroad.

"Christopher, you know what my life was. I had no life. Even worse, I had no future. Nothing! You saved me from a life of prostitution or at best the drudgery of a seamstress's toil, working my fingers to the bone trying to eke out enough money to buy food and clothes. I never deny it. I know this all too well and so do you. You are too much of a gentleman to remind me of it, but I never forget. It makes me feel guilty that I should be so blessed. I ask God every night, why did He send you to me? I wake up every morning, and I am afraid to open my eyes because I know this has to be a dream. But…if it isn't a dream, then I want to give some of that blessing to others. Can you understand? Please understand, Christopher." Rebecca bit her lip and waited.

Christopher waited. Then cautiously he spoke.

"How many others do you want to bless?" He braced himself.

"Forty–nine," she whispered.

Christopher's mouth moved to the words, but no sound came out. In the three years she had known her husband, she had never seen this expression he wore. They both sat staring at each other—he afraid to ask, she afraid to offer.

Christopher made a mental note to post Captain Ward—*bring as much flour as you wish, there will be many mouths to feed… multitudes. PS, bring Jesus.* Next, it occurred to him the irony in knowing he might be showered with great pomp and ceremony for transporting these orphans to America, whilst under their very feet amid all the ado would be crateloads of smuggled Americans. He was first to break the silence.

"Did you eat well tonight, my love?"

"Yes."

"Have you been eating well as of late?"

"Yes. Why do you ask?" Her puzzled look quickly changed to contempt. "You think I've gone daft, don't you!"

Christopher ducked from her look of disdain. The taunt brought her closer to him, and without another word spoken, he rose from his chair and took her hand. He escorted her to their bed. He felt he had been gone forever. They fell with the shadows of night as he inhaled her fragrance, as he immersed himself in the softness of her hair, in the bliss of her love

NINE

The following morning, during an invigorating breakfast, no mention was made of Rebecca's request. She did not attempt to rekindle the conversation, for she knew the request would, as always, become Christopher's preoccupation. This request in particular would be taken straight to task, for not only was it her wish, but it was a wish for the sake of charity, an issue held close to Christopher's heart. He went to great lengths to offer assistance to others, especially children, for he was supremely fond of children, and could never turn his back when it was within his power to do them good. It was only a matter of time—and whatever she might do to expedite the process.

I was new to the household, and because of his numerous trips, this was the first Mr. Claussen had seen of me. The breakfast table was being cleared when he motioned for me to step forward. I was the youngest of the maiden servants.

"Elizabeth! That is your name, is it not, child?"

His sudden attention frightened me.

"Yes, Milord," I answered. I offered a stilted curtsy on very shaky legs.

"Welcome to our house. I hope you enjoy your stay in service. Could I trouble you to bring Rebecca and me fresh coffee?"

"Yes, Milord," I answered. I was so nervous I could feel the onset of hives, so I turned and ran for the kitchen.

"She is a darling one. You said eight, didn't you?" He looked over to Rebecca.

"Yes. However, I must point out I was admonished for saying so. Her birthday was the 16th of December last, and I was informed she is fully nine, two weeks, and some three or four days to boot. She was most precise about it."

"Sounds like a child with a good head for details. Do you believe she'll earn her keep?" he asked. Rebecca began to speak in a lower tone.

"I have little doubt—special she is—such a character, so funny to watch. Almost peculiar in the manner with which she studies everything that is new to her. She is very observant. She loves to draw, and I am constantly searching for scraps of parchment to delight her. I must tell you, I follow her all about the house when she is unaware, and I just watch her. I can't help myself. Sometimes, I hide behind walls or doors. Usually, I just watch her out of the corner of my eye or from behind the furniture. And the things she says. There is innocence about her I cannot resist. She is so adorable, she simply runs off with my heart. I am fully taken in by her, I'm afraid."

"My darling, it sounds like someone here needs a baby to cradle."

"No! Oh, no, no, no!" Rebecca slapped his shoulder, shaking her head emphatically. "With all that is about to happen in our lives, I don't believe this is the time for babies. I would only worry myself sick for their well-being. No thank-you, kind sir."

"Excuse me for the thought," he toyed. "I suppose then I am to keep reminding you that young Elizabeth is your maiden servant and not your daughter, or will you manage to keep it sorted out on your own?"

"Oh! Don't concern yourself. I just enjoy her and I worry for her—with her mother and all. She was raised proper, with good sense and manners. Although I can't speak from experience, I imagine it to be the work of a good, loving mother."

ELIZABETH

Specifically nine years, two weeks and four days.

"And *how is* Mistress Dennison doing these days?"

"Very poorly, I am afraid. I spoke with Mr. Dennison, and he has informed me that she will unlikely last the month."

"A shame indeed."

"I feel for the child. She deserves better, *much better.* I asked her to join me last night in the coach as I accompanied Jannette back to her home. We were both thoroughly entertained by her wit. I could see she was deep in thought, so I asked her.

"Elizabeth, what is on your mind, child?"

"Nothing, Milady."

"That is not true. For Jannette and I both can see your little mind is just working away on something. It must be important and worth discussing."

"She gave us that wonderful expression of hers, as if to say, you two are playing with me. I see it often.

"Go on, child," I said. *"Tell us what it is you are thinking on."*

"Well, Milady, I have this problem with numbers. It isn't anything, just a problem that I have. That's all."

"Really?"

"I responded, quite surprised. *"This sounds serious. Go on then. Tell us about this problem, we wish to know. Maybe we can offer some assistance."*

"We weren't kidding either. We really were surprised. Who would imagine a nine-year-old child has problems with numbers?

"Well, you know how the day is split in two, morning and night?" she started.

"Yes."

"Well, that is one and one. And one and one is two, and two is an even number."

"That would be true."

"You know how one half of morning is before breakfast and the other half is after, and how one half of afternoon is before supper and one half after?"

"Yes."

"That is two and two again. And two and two is four and that is an even number as well. And there are twelve hours in the morning, and that is an even number, and there are twelve hours in the evening as well, and if you add them up you get twenty-four hours, and that is an even number. And there are twelve months in a year and fifty-two weeks as well. There are four weeks to a month. I wonder if everything is supposed to be even. We have two hands, two feet, two arms, two eyes, two ears.... Bugs have six legs or eight legs or a hundred legs. How come nothing has one eye or three legs?"

"Well, you only have one nose," I commented. She looked at me for a moment, and then continued on.

"But it has two holes. See what I mean? Sometimes, when I wash my hands, I think I have to wash each hand the same number, so the scrubs are even and each hand would be equally clean. You know...four times this hand and four times this hand. That makes eight. When I eat, I think maybe I should chew my food ten times or twenty times, but not seventeen. It just doesn't seem right. That is why I think I have a problem with numbers."

"Well, I looked at Jannette and she at me. We just stared at each other like dimwits. Finally, I looked back to her, trying to appreciate the gravity of her situation, and said,

"What is the worst-tasting food in the world?"

"Onions, Milady. They are awful."

"How do you know?"

96

"Because my father always makes me eat them, and he knows I hate them."

"Do you eat them often?"

"Too often. He eats them like apples. I fear he puts them into everything we eat, so I have to eat them."

"How many times do you chew onions?" The question caught her up, and she looked at me cautiously.

"I don't know, Milady. I try not to chew it. I try to swallow it whole and drink something quick. Ugh."

"There. It's settled then. You can't have a problem with numbers or you would know right off that you chew onions an even number. So this means you only think about even numbers when you are playing games with your mind. You don't count evens when you don't like something. You wouldn't strive to chew onions ten times for the sake of an even number, so it can only be a game. Your mind wants to see everything in order, and you see order in even numbers so you try to make everything even. It's a natural thing. You're cured, my child."

"She seemed to feel better hearing that, but Jannette and I were raising brows and shaking our heads with wonder. We couldn't help but laugh. It was so nonsensical, yet too mature a thought to come out of a nine-year-old. I don't believe we stopped laughing from the moment we left the estate. It was all we could do to keep the poor child from thinking we were mocking her. Whenever we got out of hand, she would give that look again and make it all the worse. You could see there is a temper behind those big, brown, teddy bear eyes.

"Oh, I do worry for her, Christopher. I had a most touching conversation with her during our return, after I dropped Jannette off. She possesses sincerity that I find hypnotic. My heart goes out to her, for she is afraid, having always been with her family, and coming to realize her departure from home may not have been the holiday stay she had first thought. She doesn't fully understand. I fear she spends time crying. She doesn't know her mother is soon to pass on, and it troubles me to think about how she will accept the news. She feels as though this home is paradise, but she is becoming both wary and suspicious of not seeing her family. Lord knows I understand those feelings of insecurity. It is strange to me how she pulls at my heart. I sense we'll become very close if she'll allow it. I can feel it." Rebecca smiled.

"Wonderful! You're developing maternal instincts. I plan to take full advantage of these newfound talents," Christopher jested.

TEN

I ran to Maid Anne and told her that *he* wanted coffee for both of them. Maid Anne's eyebrows shot right up.

"Stay put, child, and you can bring *he* his coffee."

I walked over to the door and waited. He made me nervous. I peeked through the kitchen door into the dining room and listened. I could hear his voice echoing along the walls. They were talking about last night.

I thought a lot about last night. The carriage ride was the best I felt in some time. Lady Claussen told me I could call her Lady Rebecca when we were alone if I liked, but I don't think I will. She asked me if I missed my mother, and I told her I did. Sometimes I would cry. I told her I knew my mother didn't feel good, and that Daddy told me us kids had to go away for a while until she was better because we made too much noise and she needed to sleep. I told Lady Claussen I missed my mother because I have been gone for five or four weeks. I worried my head off for my mother, and I talked to God about it at night in my bed.

Lady Claussen told me she never had a mother or a father. I couldn't believe it. I thought that maybe God could be mean.

"No," she said. "God was wise." She might never have met Christopher if she had a family. I told her I was lucky. I did have a mother, but I was afraid she might forget how to find me. She told me not to worry, and put her arm around me. She gave me a big hug. I think she is wonderfully kind.

She brought me to my room after the coach ride and undressed me. She washed me, and afterward we sat in the big cushioned chair at the fire. She read stories of Christmas to me from a large book that she had brought to my bedroom until I fell asleep. I remember her tucking me into bed and kissing me on my head. She never did any of these things before. I think she must have been sad last night. I think she needed someone with whom to talk. She learned me this prayer. She prayed it when she lived at the orphanage.

> *Angel eyes and Angel ears*
> *Guard all children sleeping here*
> *They have no one to call their own*
> *So, sleep with God, and not alone.*

> *His sentinels stand at every bed*
> *For, so it goes, without being said*
> *Above, in Heaven, God doth keep*
> *Sacred, children of the street.*

"Child!"

I was daydreaming.

"Get on with it! *He* is waiting!"

"Yes, Maid Anne!" I reached for the tray of coffee and entered the dining room. I walked one step at a time, and I never took my eyes off those cups. Nothing spilled. I couldn't believe it.

"Thank-you, my darling Elizabeth."

"Yes, Milord."

I placed the tray upon the table and stepped back. I looked up at the two of them. They always looked like they were going to laugh at me. I don't know why. They might have wanted to laugh at me, but I know I didn't spill. I went back to the kitchen.

Christopher studied Rebecca for a moment. "Now, about last night.... Were you serious about this desire to send orphans abroad?"

"Very."

"This presents me with...challenges. I must admit—."

"Please forgive me my foolishness," Rebecca interrupted. "I was so insensitive, having not given you proper time to consider." She frowned with embarrassment.

"Rebecca, you know nothing of insensitivity. Furthermore, for me, it has always been more than just a game of the idle rich to fulfill your wishes. Please...hear me out.

"It isn't a question of expense. It is a matter of contracts drawn and obligations to be honored. I was in the business of contracting stowage even before the ships went in for fitting. Have no fear; I will find a way to accommodate your orphans. However, it is a serious matter you have chosen to undertake, and I need from you not a wish, my love, but a commitment by your word."

Christopher spoke with businesslike authority. "I will need a list of stores required, an estimation of space for belongings and berthing. I will help you in whatever manner I might. But, trust me; we have precious little time at this stage."

Rebecca asked to be excused briefly from the table, this somewhat to Christopher's surprise. Within moments she returned with a folder in hand. Leaning over his shoulder, she opened it and presented him with a sheaf of papers, lists to satisfy his concerns. He was lost for words.

"I keep telling myself I married you for your silent wit and determination, but the more time goes on, the more I believe *you* married *me*."

Rebecca smiled with satisfaction.

"What is this list of names I see here?"

"Oh. Those are couples who are taking passage to the New World and have arranged to take children into their homes."

"Thirty orphans are already spoken for?" His eyes opened wide with surprise.

"Or more."

"I give up! How did you manage that?"

"It was quite easy actually. The major obstacle is the cost of transportation, so I offered to cover the expense, with your approval of course. That delighted both the menfolk and their wives. What worked much to my benefit was mentioning that a child kept womenfolk entertained and busy at home while their men were farrrrrr away for a loooonng time." She grinned coyly.

Christopher shook his head in disbelief. He closed the folder, then looked upon her with great affection.

"Come. Join me in the sun room."

He rose from his chair and held out his hand. She took it and he led her down the hall. They settled into a loveseat, sitting in close embrace. Christopher covered Rebecca with a blanket, and they situated themselves to take best advantage of the midday sun while its warmth poured in through the large window. There could never be enough heat in the chilling winter months. They sat in silence for short time, both lost in their thoughts, but supremely content just to be together basking lazily in the sun's rays. Rebecca was first to break the stillness.

"If you could have your way, you would do this, would you not?"

"Do what, my darling, sit here in bliss with you?"

"No." She frowned. "Bring the orphans to the New World!"

"Oh, that. In all honesty, the idea never would have crossed my mind, I'm afraid."

"Be that as it may, I'm certain it would have soon enough. I believe you would do such a thing. I am right, am I not?"

Christopher chuckled lightly.

"What is it you are saying, Rebecca?"

"Nothing, really. Only that I have come to know you well, and I have seen the many deeds of kindness done in your name or by your hand. You are a very generous man, Christopher. You do a great deal for children."

"You embarrass me, love, for not only is it not my wish to draw attention, but believe me whilst I confess it is no great feat for a rich man to reach into his purse. You see, when a common man gives from his pocket, he feels the pinch. He might go without bread or miss a meal for his act of good will. I, on the other hand, could go on building orphanages from the ground up, which I have done on many occasions, and never miss so much as a spoonful of soup. It is hardly a test of generosity, hardly a sacrifice when one's purse remains overflowing, when one's stomach remains full, when one feels no pain."

"If that is the truth of it, then why do you continue? Remember that I am an orphan and I know these people. I have seen the many bronze plaques with your name affixed to the entranceways. Does it not bring you some joy, some sense of accomplishment?"

"Not the plaques, they are engraved by the dozens, a repetitious assortment of testimonials that are uncomfortably close in appearance to headmarkers. When I see them I feel as though I am but one step ahead of the grim reaper. I won't say there is no reward to be had, for when I see the eyes of a forgotten child light up with surprise, I am able to carry that joy in my heart forever it seems. Certainly, I remember it longer than the plaque.

"I must tell you, Rebecca, you will discover as time goes on that all too often the burden of wealth is guilt. You will ask yourself over and over, why should you enjoy such fortunes, and be witness to so much misery? Why should there be a child who revels to feel the warmth of a single blanket? The only thing he can claim to be his own. It is as though these things are presented as a reminder of what is expected of me. So the question you must ask is this. Is my generosity due to an act of goodness on my part, or is it an act of retreat, an act of repentance for the injustice I fear I perpetrate?"

"You are good with words, Christopher, but actions speak louder, and I have seen much of the work for which you take no credit. I am convinced you are a truly good man—and who might know you better than I?"

"Possibly no one, yet I fear you'll find me utterly ordinary." He paused. "On this subject of knowing...do forgive me, Rebecca, for I understand I am out of line, but as our discussions have been centered about orphans and the like a great deal as of late, I confess my curiosity is forever unsatisfied when it comes to your youth. I would never wish you to expose or endure explaining your past if it brings you discomfort. However, at times like this, I find my curiosity knows no limit. I desperately yearn to hear more of your own life at the orphanage. Tell me more about it, for I am embarrassed to admit how far removed I am from those hardships, how nearly impossible it is for me to imagine such deprivation."

"Christopher, it is I who should be the one to apologize for keeping so much from you. You are too kind so not to ask. I have always been afraid to reflect upon those times, lest they return to steal me back. As time passes, it becomes easier to look back, to see things with a sense of understanding. There are times when I am here in your arms that it seems an impossible past, some foolish daydream.

"Let me say in many ways I was fortunate. My home was virtuous. The Elders of St. Katherine watched over us. We were always fed and never given the strap without due cause. It is true, we never enjoyed the love of a mother, but then we never feared the abuse of a drunken father either. It was a strict environment, terribly strict, but always fair. And as I have mentioned previously, even as a girl, I was allowed to study the Bible.

"To allow me to read was very forward thinking, not at all common knowledge. It was mostly meant for the boys, but if a girl such as myself was so inclined, a head was turned so as not to notice. A few of the elders were more open-minded and understood the importance of knowledge. They kept it in balance with the Scriptures. The Bible was my reader. Yet, there were other books that gave substance to my dreams. I lived the lives of all the characters that crossed the page. Every experience in the world that wasn't my life was buried within the books that fed my imagination.

"The books were very expensive and we were rarely let out of sight while in possession of any printed page. I was cautious as well, for if I showed too much interest in reading, it tended to raise both eyebrows and suspicion. Still, the church was good to us in that respect, providing us with an opportunity to learn, teaching us to read if we so desired, or overlooking a book purposely left behind.

"There were also plenty of papers and daily journals, flyers and placards, and calls to travel. Everywhere one turned, in the city, they could be found plastered to the walls and storefronts of the streets we worked. They were all full of sensational stories or bits of information. I was beginning to read them as naturally as I might walk. They filled me with wonder and encouraged me as a young girl to explore, to seek out the truth of what I read.

"You must understand, Christopher, it is very difficult for a female orphan to marry. Most men believe she has no under-standing of love or affection, and may fail to give satisfaction in bed or with raising children. They often believe orphan girls must be so starved for attention that they are most likely to be untrustworthy or unfaithful by nature, and doomed to become uncontrollable whores to fulfill their cravings.

"Then, there is the matter of parents and family to help with the new home and the expenses. What dowry does she possess? What value does she bring into the marriage? She has nothing. What if she is the child of parents who have gone mad? Will she breed that trait into her husband's offspring? Of what value is she? It is only learning a skill that offers her salvation from working the streets or worse.

"Of course, there was never a lack of work. We all worked. We didn't have to face the life of the young boys in the mines or laborers. As an orphan my life was a great deal better than that, I am certain. We would hear of many children dying at fifteen or twenty years of age, wore out, through and through. No, I believe it was more like a child doing chores. Except for the constant worry always lurking in the back of our minds, or in our dreams, of no money or maybe no food, or worst of all, maybe we would be forced to leave, forced to go onto the streets.

"I remember poor Jennifer Bollins. They turned her out when she reached the age of thirteen. She knew it was coming, and for months she would lie at night and cry. She slept in the cold upon the steps at our front door for four nights and cried until hunger drove her to the church or somewhere. To think of it burdens my heart and surely will bring me to tears should I dwell upon it. She was fond of me, and I remember her as most kind and gentle with us younger children. She was what a mother might be. I am certain her life was reduced to walking nights through St. James Park performing favors for food. That was the way it usually happened. No one discussed it because it was objectionable before the elders of the church. It was left unmentioned, but we accepted walking the streets as our fate. We didn't dare dream of marriage.

"Actually, it wasn't the prostitution that we feared as much as the loneliness. There were plenty of people with good hearts who tried in earnest to help those of us who were forced out one way or another. What frightened us most was giving up the only roots we ever had. Even if it was only an orphanage, severing those ties and being left with absolutely no connections, no one to turn to for support, no one to quell your fears was cause for terrible nightmares. It became only you and whatever courage you might muster to face a world that 'shan't slow a step' to take note of you.

"In fairness, you can't blame the orphanage. They had little choice but to force open bedspace for the young who could not fend for themselves. Lord knows there were many turned away for the sake of the very young, those who were often just babes. That's how it was with me when I arrived. I came in a basket, so I was told."

"I can't imagine such a thing. I simply cannot imagine it. Tell me, Rebecca, when did you notice your life was different than most? When did you realize that you had no family? I mean at what point did you look out a window or a door and ask yourself, how is it that they don't live the same way as us? Surely, it must have come sudden and with a shock."

"It wasn't quite what you might think. It wasn't as if I woke up one day and felt cheated. I lived much the same as everyone else in my life, so to me having no family was normal, or you might say all those about me were my family. What was different was that we were always told wonderful stories from the older children about *families*. Stories that I suppose were passed down for years, one child to another. We were keenly aware of being turned out of the orphanage, and it was said that families never turned out their own. We all knew that was a big difference.

"I suppose as a small child, the closest I ever came to wondering about mothers and such happened one bitterly damp night in London during the Christmas season. I was about six years old, I believe, and I was left to stand in front of a tobacco shop in Charing Cross, near where the stables used to be. I couldn't go anywhere and didn't know where I might go, so I stood there for hours with a tin of fusees to sell.

"I remember shaking so hard, being so cold that my fingers refused to uncurl, my hands and feet ached, and my teeth chattered so, I was unable to speak. I desperately wanted someone to come and ease my suffering, but of course there was no such person.

"Then out of nowhere came this lady of some standing with a young boy of about three. She stooped down beside him as he placed a coin in my cup. She must have noticed how I shivered, for she reached out her hand and placed it upon my cheek. At that instant the whole world seemed to stand still. I could see she was upset.

"She became the sole focus of my awareness for that one moment. I could see every lash upon her soft brown eyes—the shape of her lips. I could feel the warmth of her breath when she embraced me. She glowed. She spoke to me all the while, but instead of hearing words, I was captivated by gentle sounds. I remember my whole self being filled with a sensation of warmth and comfort. She removed her scarf and wrapped it around me with such care. She looked at me with great sadness and then brushed my cheek once again, leaving me with a kiss.

"I remember thinking for the first time that this was a mother. I suppose what I find most amusing is that she never had any idea what a profound effect she had upon my life. It was nothing more than an encounter of two minutes at the most; yet, I slept with that scarf for many years, and it never lost the scent of her. It's the reason I so enjoy the fragrance of lavender."

Rebecca's voice trailed off. She thought a moment in silence while staring out the window, lost in the shadow of another world, another time.

"The greatest pain of an orphan is the pain I feel now as we sit, Christopher. It is not the cold, not the hunger, often not even the loss of affection. It's the inability to share these memories—having no one to remember your triumphs or your wounds. All those years of life and living that exist only in your own mind. All the past experiences which you can only attempt to explain to another with empty words. It is nothing like having them there to laugh hysterically over the recollection of childish pranks done together.

"It is like telling one of a good book, instead of him reading it for himself. Do you understand what it is I am trying to say, Christopher? When you can't share your life, you don't really have a life, you never existed before anyone," she paused. "You gave me my life." She looked at him and blushed. "I know, I am being overly dramatic, aren't I? Forgive me."

The sun formed a halo in her hair. Christopher was moved to emotion.

"I love you with all my heart, Rebecca."

She felt herself relax at the sound of his words. Certain fearful tensions dissipated as she melted into his embrace, and she whispered.

"I know."

ELEVEN

"Damn ya! Damn all o' ya! Damn dis place an' me fer bein' in it!" He swore at both his family and the ghosts in his head as he brought the blade of his knife down with all his might onto the old wood of the tabletop. It wasn't the first time, and the table wore the many scars of his tantrums and hallucinations. The knife stood erect and this sight pleased him.

Gustaff Borislav was again seething with anger. He was brutish, ugly, his irritation amplified by a rum-induced state of mind. He supported himself at the old wobbly table with a bottle in his clenched fist and stared at the standing knife. The crowded one-room cabin reeked with his odor, reeked of his presence. Over the years, his disposition had grown more disagreeable with each passing season. He no longer realized any reason for his living except to face the misery of his poverty and the hopelessness of his future. Work was difficult to find, and when he did chance upon it, his health more often than not stood in the way. The drinking had taken its toll.

The last of his pleasures, the heat of a woman, also came at a price—three children under the age of five. Three children entwined like strands of a rope around his neck, choking out the last trace of freedom in his pathetic, miserable existence. Their incessant whining and squeaking, their shrill little noises piercing through the solace of his intoxication—the predictable manner in which they hovered about their mother, keeping her distracted from his needs. He would willingly wring each one of their scrawny little necks with his bare hands, given just half a chance. He could see little difference between the neck of a brat and that of a chicken.

Understanding this truth, as often as not, the children stood corralled in their mother's arms cowering in a darkened corner beyond the bed, not daring to utter a sound lest they get beaten senseless. Only after Gustaff vented his rage would he sleep. It was a nightmarish game of cat and mouse with unpredictable outcomes. A scene first played years ago and now repeated almost daily, each time further refining a strategy of avoidance by mother and child. Their best weapon was their greatest enemy. They prayed the rum would drop him.

As of late he had been both drinking and thinking hard. With glazed eyes half open to the world about him, he chewed a leftover piece of tough dried fish. Slowly, methodically, his head rose and fell upon his jaw, up and down, up and down. It teetered back and forth, precariously balanced upon the neck of his bottle. With what little functioning mental capacity he still possessed, he concluded once again that his only hope for a decent life would be in the New World. The stories on the docks about the Americas had prickled him like thorns for years, stories that were at the very least amazing, stories that covered every possible dream of man. Be he rich or poor, there was something for everybody in the New World.

The main obstacle for Gustaff was the inevitable passage by ship. He was deathly afraid of the sea, of the monsters that lurked in the deep. He would break out into a sweat at night, imagining some dark, stony-eyed creature coming up for him out of the blue-black depths below, taking him into its cavernous jaws. Instead of dying instantly, he would be held immobile, then slowly drawn down into the deep, impenetrable murkiness. He would lie there upon his bed in a drunken stupor holding his breath until he exploded.

He was afraid of the fury of the storms that took so many lives. He would envision angry black clouds rolling across the sky, boiling and seething, prodding mountainous waves to batter ships and stave in planks. He shuddered as imaginary lightning seared its way through his mind, through the masts and rigging, setting sails afire, bringing yards and spars crashing down about him. He struggled, fought to free himself from the rigging that entangled him like a frantic fish desperate to escape the net. Coils of raveled line crossed his chest, pinning his back to the flooding deck while the sea rose higher, inch by inch to claim his unlucky soul.

The debris and entanglements were endless, a thick field of seaweed reaching for him, tripping him, trapping him, dragging him down. He could see himself being swept off the deck by a rogue wave. Terrified and alone, he clung to a single shredded line, holding on to the twisting strand of thread for all he was worth—it being his only connection with the now distant ship. Straining against the pull of the sea, he suffered. His arms and hands went numb from exertion and exhaustion. He prayed for relief from this nightmare. Then, as if to answer his pleas, up from the depths came the dark, stony-eyed creature.

Gustaff was even afraid of shipmasters. This seemed almost comical knowing what a brute he was, but at least this fear was not so far-fetched. He knew enough to realize that with his temper and belligerence, his chance of ending up in leg irons or whipped with the cat o' nines for insubordination was too good for comfort. A sailor's life was worse than that of a slave. Slaves were protected, for they had worth. A sailor, on the other hand, was not the master's property. He was not owned and therefore was viewed as something to be used up and expended. Unlike slaves, sailors volunteered to board ships and took what abuse was dealt them for they had no one to blame but themselves for signing on. Gustaff spent many years taking wage for work on the docks, but inside he was and always would prefer to be a woodsman and hunter with feet planted firmly on solid ground.

What had him thinking hard of late was a chance occurrence, a devilish opportunity to make a tidy sum of money with very little effort. The makings of this plan rolled over and over repeatedly in his loathsome mind. What little conscience remained in his unsalvageable character forced him to think, often aloud, until he managed to twist the nature of his scheme from a purely despicable act into something reasonably justifiable. The rum removed the weight and distraction of his surrounding misery and left him to concentrate on his recollection of events.

He had been on one of his routine pilgrimages to wander the wharves of Malmo or ferry across to Copenhagen. The moorings were plentiful and work was generally available to those in need, those who wished to travel to the shore. He had been milling about the wharf looking for an unsuspecting sailor of foreign birth to rob, when he took notice of the ELIZABETH ANNE man-of-war, 104 guns.

It was an impressive sight and rarely seen up close in the harbors of Denmark. Unfortunately, it was also a bad omen. He wondered if he was safe where he stood or if they were about to blow him to smithereens. The thought made him uneasy and he looked back over his shoulder for a fast escape route, should he be in need of one.

The last time English warships were in this harbor, they had been bent on leveling the place. The man-of-war did little to raise his spirits or those of anyone else on this shore. This was a vessel normally committed to the coasts of England, sinking French and Spanish vessels, or deployed to the colonies of the New World to enforce embargoes. Then, with a shudder, he realized it most likely was a harbinger of the war with Napoleon. Gustaff knew he was just the kind of peasant to be shackled and sent off to die for some king who was working him to death anyhow.

It was while crossing the road for purpose of closer observation that he was obliged to step back and give way to a fabulous vermilion coach. Among a collection of curious onlookers, he stood by to watch the footman step down and aid the passenger in her exit. She was a lady of upper standing, and Gustaff was quick to notice that she traveled without the service of an escort on the wharf. The thought of a robbery brought a rush of anticipation to his heart.

Instinctively, Gustaff headed for the coach. Stepping quickly, he moved in close to make note of any detail, any sign that might signal a chance to better himself financially. The lady made a few inquiries and was directed toward a gentleman who was already crossing the yard and headed in their direction. By the respect he was given, he was either the administrator or the owner of Bergen's Trading and Stowage. It was obvious the two knew each other, for he had broken into a broad grin at first sight of her, and she had taken his arm.

Gustaff kept his ears open. He approached one of the yardmen.

"Oyeee! Mate! Ooo'd be dat princess?" He nodded toward the woman being escorted by the administrator as they walked away. The yardman looked up.

"That's Lady Rebecca Claussen. Seen 'er 'ere a time or two before. You're not from this port then, are ya?"

"Do I sound like I'm from dis port?"

"No offense, man. There's no need t' be getting' gruff. Most folks in these yards are from elsewheres, but if ya been 'round 'ere any time a' tall ya'd 'ear stories 'bout the Lady. She's a fair one, they say."

"Va' vould bring da likes o 'er down t' da yards anyvays?"

"Word 'as it, she's a fixin' on takin' a lot of orphans to the States. I got t' run now. Good day to ya, sir."

Gustaff's face twisted about. Very curious, he thought to himself. Why would anyone wish to waste time shipping a fool lot of sniveling brats across an ocean? The sheer stupidity of it amazed him. It mattered little to him at first, for nothing that amused the idle rich would surprise him. They were all extravagant in their debauchery as well as their demands.

He continued to listen and nose about the coach. He paid little mind to the Lady as she returned on the arm of the administrator. When he looked up to see them both studying him, he could hardly be bothered, but he was mildly annoyed by the manner in which the Lady met his eyes. There was no sign of fear or concern in her look. In fact, her eyes appeared bold, almost aggressive. It was as if they spoke aloud to say *'I know your kind, and I will confront you without pause.'* She looked straight through him. He stepped away irritated.

113

Gustaff knew the Passenger Act had been made into law a year or so past in England to restrict the number of passengers aboard ships heading for the New World. "It was about blessed time!" he said to himself. His aversions to sailing to the New World were not totally founded in an overactive imagination. He had worked the docks on and off for years. He knew that the banners all about town made the voyage appear a holiday. He also knew, in fact, it was usually a horrific experience, one of utter misery in over cramped steerage sealed off from fresh air much of the time with little or nothing to eat and an impossible amount of retching and vomiting from a starving lot of souls.

The proclamation of the act was no small matter. It raised plenty of stink in England, and it would be no different here. It wasn't all that much of a hindrance or particularly bothersome if you were a ship's master or owned a trading company. There were hordes of people leaving the country like rats on a sinking ship, all paying customers, especially in the Scandinavian countries. He watched crowds of them departing the docks daily in Malmo and Copenhagen and heading for the ports of England en route.

The people who cursed the new regulations were in the business of placing indentured servants or general labor. This declaration severely diminished their profits in business, for New World establishments immediately curtailed their requests for labor due to the elevated prices for passage.

Gustaff stepped back into the crowd and away from the unsettling glare of the Lady's eyes. For a passing moment he was taken up by the splendor and craftsmanship of her coach. He was amazed at the quality of the worked brass that shone brightly against the fine woods and rich red paint of the cabin. He marveled at the delicacy of the gold paint striping. It resembled lace embroidery as it caressed the name Rebecca Claussen, a name that he could not read. The idea that one person could lay claim to something of such extravagance made it only a very short spell before he slid deep into a grumbling state of contempt for the snooty bitch and her lifestyle.

114

"May ye rot'n hell vit' da rest o' da rich'n royal!" And with
that he spat toward the coach, catching the back corner. A
string of his mucus and saliva hung suspended in the air while
he sneered before the crowd of stunned admirers surrounding
him. He viewed them all as mindless gawkers, sheep to be
led to slaughter, puppets pulled from the pockets of the rich to
bow and grovel in adoration at their slightest appearance. He
took leave of the worthless lot in order to find a more appealing
environment, a favorite haunt nearby where he could fill his
mitt with a mug of rum and a woman's breast.

Boom! The table utensils rattled out their disruption. It
wasn't a deafening explosion of a man-of-war cannon letting
loose that rocked Gustaff. No, he had finally lost his senses,
dropped off his bottle, and hammered his head upon the table.
In clouded confusion he raised himself, befuddled, and then
collapsed alongside his knife; it still standing erect like a head
marker.

Moments passed—and then the cautious scrutiny, the need
for assuredness. The family, feeling confident Gustaff was
finished for the time being, stepped forth quietly from the
shadows of the corner. Much like creatures of the night, they
tiptoed about their surroundings. The whispering chatter of
children began to fill the air.

TWELVE

Winter was now but a memory, and even that was being
blown out of mind by the warming winds of March. The air
was thick with damp and chill, but free of the frigid grip of
death that had hovered about us during the months prior. Still,
I was to be one of the last to escape winter's wake, and it was
Lady Rebecca who eased me out of the brutal reality of its
lingering vestige.

Mary entered the kitchen where I stood working before open drawers of silverware, bored to tears and lamenting over the possibility of never completing the chore at hand.

"Liz, Lady Rebecca is asking for you. She asked that I send you over to the sun room."

"Oh! Gracious! Thank-you!" Then came a second thought. "Am I in trouble?"

"She didn't make mention of it, but I sensed she was concerned about something." Mary shrugged her shoulders.

I frowned. I put down the tableware, attempted to wash most of the black tarnish off my hands, and made my way to the sun-room. Lady Rebecca was sitting at a small settee that had been moved into the light of the sun. It now rested at a place where the rays passed through a large window, illuminating and warming the room. She was facing the window when I entered, and appeared lost in thought as she gazed out onto the grounds.

"Yes, Milady."

She turned about slowly. Her gaze was still distant as it crossed the room to meet me. At first, she said nothing and only looked at me as I stood there. She studied me briefly in silence.

"Come to me, Elizabeth."

Her request was gentle, yet commanding. I walked over to her side sensing something amiss. She drew me in close and wrapped her arms around me. Lady Rebecca was always showing me her affection, but this was something more.

"Have I done something wrong, Milady?"

She leaned back from me and looked into my eyes. She ran her fingers through my hair, pulling at my curls and snarls. She took a deep breath.

116

"Elizabeth, my dearest child." She shook her head and looked at me with such sorrow, I could see she was troubled deeply.

"What is it, Milady?" I asked.

"This is about your mother, Elizabeth."

The words slammed into me with a crushing blow. The breath sucked from my being. Instantly, I knew it was to be dreadful news. I froze.

"The Lord came for your mother last night, Elizabeth. She is fine, but she has passed from this world, and is now living with God in heaven. She is worried about you. She loves you so very much, Elizabeth. You must pray to her, child, let her know that I will take good care of you; and I have promised you will want for naught. She needs to know you'll be safe here on earth. She wants you to know that she loves you with all her heart and misses you, and that she will always be looking down from heaven to watch over you. Do you think you can pray to her? Do you think you can ease her mind? Do you understand what it is I am saying? Elizabeth?"

I heard her question from far, far away. My head swam, the room began to spin, and I felt myself sinking, sinking into nothingness. I was lost, confused, terrified. I couldn't accept what Milady was saying. It couldn't be. But Lady Rebecca would never lie. Lady Rebecca was kind, very kind. Lady Rebecca tucked me into bed at night, she read me stories, she sang to me. Could it be true? What if it was true? I was so worried that my mother might not find me. I hadn't seen her for such a long time.

"Elizabeth?"

I knew she was tired. I knew I had to go away. I knew she had to sleep. Papa said, *"Go to the country and have fun."* He said he would come for me soon. But it hadn't been soon. It had

117

been a long time—*too* long. I wasn't there. I wasn't home when I was supposed to be. I was having fun…and my mother died. She didn't say good-bye.

"Elizabeth!"

My mother was dead. My mother was dead. No, this couldn't be. I wouldn't let it be. My mother was home. She was waiting for me. She loved me. I knew she loved me. Was she calling me? Had she been calling for me? It is possible I didn't hear? Did she think I left her? Did she know I was waiting?

"Elizabeth."

"I was waiting!" I cried out in disbelief.

"It will be all right, Elizabeth. Your mother loves you very much. You must believe—."

"I didn't forget. I was waiting," I sobbed, horrified to think my mother may not have known how I waited to return to her.

Milady held me firm, my head buried deep into her shoulder, in the warmth of her neck moistened by my tears. I was alone. No, I had Lady Rebecca. What did she think? Was it my fault? I should have been home. I didn't know where home was. I didn't know where I was. I stood up and looked at Lady Rebecca. Her eyes were moist. Was she sad for my mother? I hoped she understood that I had waited.

"I waited to go home, but Papa never came," I cried. "I didn't forget her. I promise; I didn't forget my mother."

I could hardly get the words out. I fell back into Lady Rebecca's arms and wept. She said nothing. She rocked me gently. Together, we passed the remainder of the afternoon bathed in the melancholy rays of the late-day sun. I cried until I was utterly exhausted and finally succumbed to the mercy of sleep.

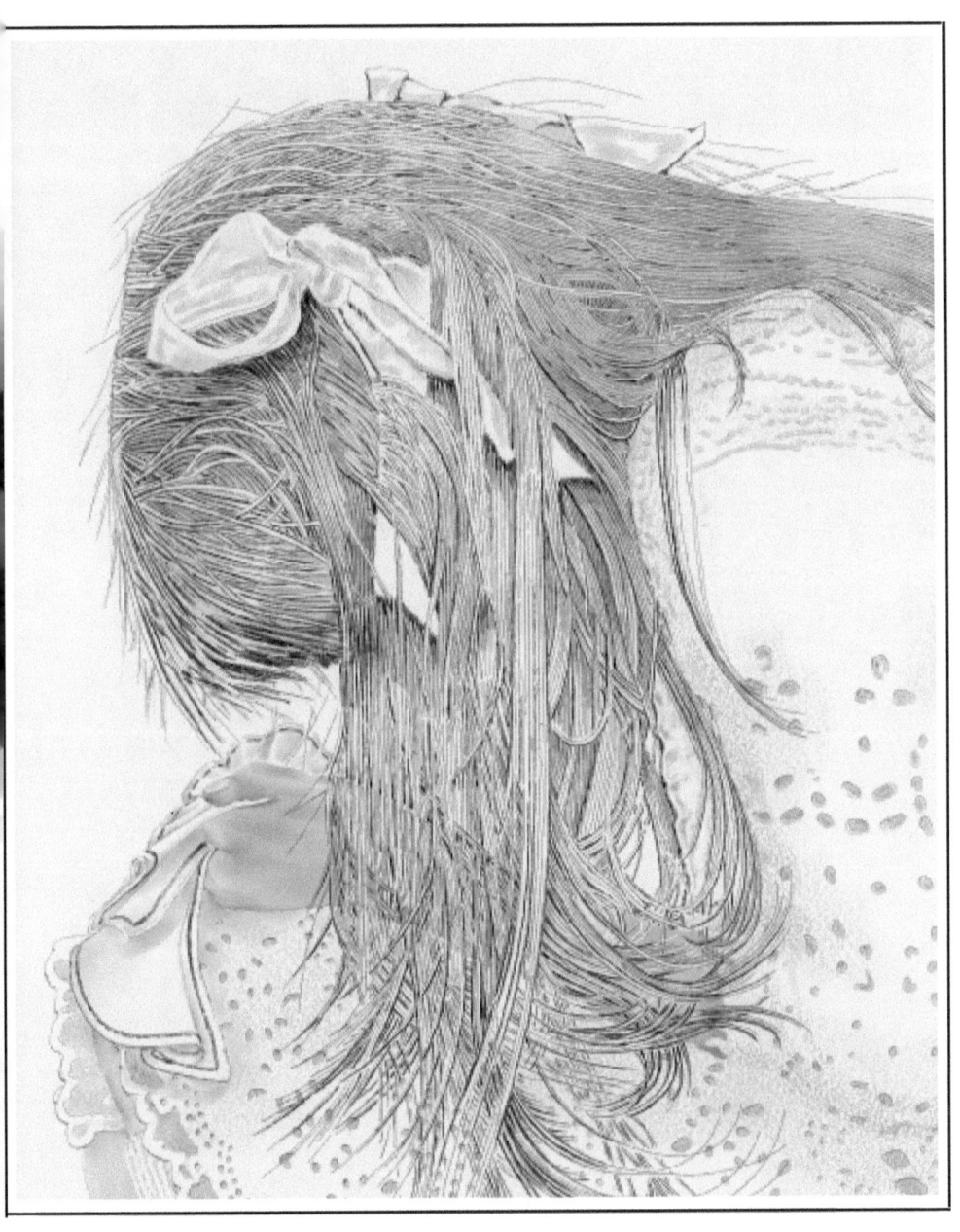

ELIZABETH

I had waited

THIRTEEN

My tears eventually disappeared, as did the ice formerly upon the small bays of the northern lands, all having evaporated into the air of the distant horizon. The hustle of carpenters and shipwrights was again the movement and sound of the docks and yards. The rapping of swinging hammers and the laugh of a drawing saw. Seaside villages and towns dotted thousands of miles of coastline from the eastern shores of England and Scotland, across to the western shores of Norway, then south into the harbors of Denmark and Sweden, and finally northeast through the Baltic Sea toward Finland and Russia. All places rejuvenated by the spring of eighteen hundred and seven and the hint of fair season.

The influx of trade to and from the New World made an enormous impact everywhere on the globe. No place was more affected than the seafaring countries of Europe. Merchants of all nations scrambled in a perilous manner before a backdrop of war and greed to fill their coffers. This rush to reap the treasures of the Far East and New World pressed hard upon the ships and masters to bear on past the safe season of the year and to hold firm through the winter months. For this reason, untold lives were lost to winter storms and tempestuous seas. Calamity and misery was the reward for the seaman who endeavored to satisfy the greed of the insatiable and unscrupulous trading companies that buckled under the pressure from their investors and political leaders.

Scandinavian sea trade with England had been growing steadily, but surged in eighteen and three after Napoleon declared his intention to bring down England and its horde of shopkeepers. English trading firms were booking record stowage with Scandinavian ports.

The Revolution in the colonies had placed a severe strain upon business and trade concerns between England and the

United States for some years. Many Americans resented the English for their arrogance and desire to dominate. This was especially noticeable the farther into the interior one traveled. The war had been many years past, but tensions were escalating and another conflict seemed in the making. Boiling tempers rose to the brim of a cauldron filled with lies, jealousies, and hatred fed by the sniping of English, French, Indian, and American design.

Along the eastern seaboard the relationship was tumultuous at best. If you were a merchant, you had to be forgiving of English sympathies and abuses in order to remain part of the profitable business community. English merchant ships were the key to financial success. England was fast becoming the workhorse of the world. An industrial revolution was in its infancy and growing explosively. Britain's fleet of ships dominated the oceans. They scoured the world for resources, returning with the nourishment required to feed the voracious appetite of England's fledgling industrial enterprises.

Clever English merchants often sought the safety of a lower profile by contracting stowage with foreign fleets as fronts to avoid French warships and piracy, as well as the distaste of hostile Americans. The harbors and wharves in Denmark, Sweden, Holland, Ireland, and Scotland, to name a few in Northern Europe, benefited enormously from the heightened activity and distrust.

If one thing surpassed trading of goods from the New World it was trading of rumor. The stories spanned the entire gamut, from the absolute absurd to the bloodcurdling horrible. The journals thrived on this frenzy of interest and supported much of their circulation by whipping up emotions with questionable articles on the New World. Cover to cover, the stories revealed accounts of discoveries, including diamonds the size of boulders, trees 100 meters tall, plains of prehistoric animals, Indians burying settlers alive up to their necks and then roasting their heads with small campfires. Much of it was silly, based on ignorance and wild imaginations, much of it unbelievable, but some of it, such as the story about the Indians was true. That was called Head Pudding.

True or false, silly or not, all of it fanned the passions of the common folk who were suffering from life in conditions close to, if not completely unbearable. Unemployment was high; the land overpopulated and underproductive. Fear and insecurity hung heavy upon the shoulders of ordinary people—fear in knowing they lived in the most modern of times, yet their futures appeared ever the more bleak.

It seemed every page of town papers carried stories about new inventions or new machines, or the latest wonders of science revealed. There were always stories to be found describing new and mysterious lands explored. The New World left no reason for a page to be blank. Everything was changing except for the plight of struggling families. If they could perceive change at all, it was for the worse. The structure supporting class and income had been embedded in the culture of these Northern European countries for hundreds of years. Since the time of feudal lords, a specific manner of passing down land and wealth was adhered to—a manner that propagated a burgeoning underclass of desperation.

The talk at taverns was always the same, tales of the New World, tales wild with wonder and rapture punctuated with gossip about friends who had courage enough to make the trip, stories about hims and hers who struck it rich, and 'what's their names', who drowned at sea.

When spring showed sign, people were drawn to the sea, and left wondering how they might fare, imagining what life would be like on the bountiful coasts or in the forested heart of the Americas. Warm winds stirred men's souls with wanderlust. An exodus like nothing ever seen in the western world was building within the womb of misery.

FOURTEEN

The morrow would usher in the fifteenth day of June, and with anchor aweigh at the ebb, sail would be set. From those early days of March in eighteen and seven following my mother's death—especially after we set out upon the open sea, I remained fearfully close to Lady Rebecca's side and very much under her protective care.

She had tried her heartfelt best to save me as much pain over my mother's passing as was in her power. I was her servant, but she doted on me as if I was her only child. She quickly became the central figure in my life for nurturing, filling the enormous void left by the loss of not only my mother, but also my family, which had been split up and taken in by others.

Our relationship washed back and forth, flowing across boundaries and all acceptable lines of behavior between servant and employer. It was indistinct and confusing for me, but I made it a point to remember above all else, no matter how I felt for her emotionally, I was enlisted to serve her needs as a maiden. I welcomed this aspect, for it was something I could control and it was my only means of showing her my gratitude. I wanted to make Lady Rebecca happy, and I strove to win her praise. Unfortunately, it seemed the harder I tried to perfect my service to her, the more distressed she became. She was searching for something. She wanted something from me that was beyond my ability to comprehend.

Often I would see Mr. Claussen looking at me with a slight frown; he would then conclude his thoughts with the shake of his head and a gasp or a groan. He never reprimanded Lady Rebecca for treating me special. I believe he came to understand these were her natural mothering instincts—instincts she was driven to pursue, questions he felt she needed to answer about her own ability as an orphan, to mother—to raise children. I was her pretend child, her opportunity. We were bound to each other out of need, and she would have spoiled me rotten, if not for the rumor and gossip; for ours was a relationship that raised many a brow.

Mary Fallgren was Lady Rebecca's most trusted maiden servant. I thought her to be five or six years older than myself, some fifteen years of age. She was most fair, and I was attracted to her from the moment we were introduced. The color of her hair was extraordinary. She called it strawberry blonde. It looked like polished copper to me. It changed its hue from reds, to golds or ambers every time she moved her head in the sunlight. It glowed. I loved it best when she was done working and unfastened her bun, so her hair might hang free across her shoulders. I was forever asking if I could brush or braid it. Her eyes were amber, speckled and spellbinding. Looking into them was like looking through clear water to the bottom of a streambed covered with polished pebbles. A face full of freckles complimented her eyes and softened her features. All of this was enhanced by a gracious smile, giving her a warm and comforting presence that brought me peace.

Mary taught me most everything I was required to know in order to perform properly in an environment that was demanding and designed by the social expectations of the elite. These people permeated the lives of the Claussens. It was by this working relationship that birth was given to a personal bond, a natural attachment that drew me to idolize her, to trust her, to look up to her as an older sister. I adored her.

FIFTEEN

Lady Rebecca, Mary, and I remained seated within the privacy of her coach. Lady Rebecca had honey-sweetened tea brought for our pleasure. It seemed as though her life over the past four months was plagued with nervousness and nausea. She mentioned a desire to ask Mr. Claussen for a small glass of port, or better yet Chambord to settle her nerves, but believed it would appear arrogant to imbibe such a luxury in public, especially as a woman. To be sure, her decision was prudent, and her request was for green tea and honey.

We three, being parked upon an elevated lot, enjoyed a splendid view of the port and watched with the utmost interest the goings on about the wharf and docks. The docks were buried deep under the usual stores plus swaying towers of rummage and stacked crates of unclaimed freight.

This brought the bustle of businessmen and bargain hunters from every walk of life. They responded politely or not so politely to the various hawkers peddling goods amidst the ships. They streamed through the ever-shifting maze of unloaded cargo. They swarmed over the decks with impatience, peering into darkened holds filled months before in faraway ports and watched the emerging goods being hoisted up into the sunlight above raised faces waiting with anticipation. They could be seen and heard haggling price, arguing quality, poking away, pushing and pulling at everything they could reach, searching out those special treasures that found their way to these Swedish shores.

I believe Mr. Claussen had scarce time to breathe as he walked endlessly from dock to dock with his captains in service, their mates, the harbormaster, and a large troupe of agents, who were all engaged in reviewing the ship articles and stores. Meshed within this party of businessmen was a ragtag lot of urchins—street kids who followed and pestered Mr. Claussen, not because they disliked him, quite the contrary in fact; it was because he paid them mind. He was their hero, and they hoped to be called upon to serve him in one manner or another to earn a coin.

They were homeless as a rule, and Mr. Claussen always found an excuse to put a coin or two into their pocket by way of an errand here or a favor there. They loved him for it. Periodically, he would return to our coach to gage Lady Rebecca's state of mind and also to keep her informed of all that was taking place. He fussed over her a great deal. I would get a good look at the boys and girls as they approached the coach in his wake, often breaking through the restraining arms of Mr. Claussen's aides in order to ask if they might run an errand in his behalf. They were a desperate-looking lot, and the thought of living in such manner made me nervous and uneasy. It seemed all too possible a life for me.

It was unusual to have Mr. Claussen about to such extent. He was so often employed elsewhere in dealings of a nature unknown to us. We were quite accustomed to making do without his presence. Now, though he was involved in his affairs of business at hand, we were a part of that business and in his company more than ever before. The experience was much like watching a new neighbor on the street rushing in and out, moving his belongings to and fro.

I don't know that anyone understood exactly what business Mr. Claussen attended to on his trips and so this experience was somewhat of a lesson. It allowed us to view up close the unknown side of the remarkable Christopher Claussen. He was a figure who commanded everybody's attention. He was central, and Lady Rebecca could hardly turn away her eyes of adoration, lest he vanish on the spot.

"I am so lucky to have such a man. Look at him, isn't he special? Look at the way the children take to him. They're all street brats, but he doesn't turn them away. He has such a good heart. See, even they know it. Won't he make a wonderful father?" She simply beamed.

Lady Rebecca influenced me in every way, and I too saw Mr. Claussen as more than just an ordinary man. To a young girl, a man is a creature apart. Like a great bear, something terribly attractive, but often fearsome and frightening. A man's actions are rough and less consoling than the embrace of a mother, but when a father embraces you there is nothing in the world to fear.

Mr. Claussen carefully inspected his ships with his masters, and then returned once again to share with Lady Rebecca all that was taking place.

"These are magnificent vessels, Rebecca. They are of Norwegian design. Father commissioned them some six or seven years ago to be built in our yards at Goteborg. Can you see how they are round and full by stem and stern?" He moved his arms, shaping the hulls out of air. "They look heavy; they are heavy. They are slow to make way, but they are strong, worthy of their masts and sail confident against the North Sea. I have had them lightly refurbished for our voyage, for in these chilly northern waters the hulls hold long and fast and little more needs be done. You will find them comfortable to board, my love, of this I am certain."

I listened as Mr. Claussen and Lady Rebecca discussed a number of issues. Even Mary's concerns were acknowledged. I paid little mind to most of what was being said until they began to make mention of pirates. The discussion took on a different tone as it moved into this new direction, taking with it my full attention. I was to learn that piracy was a grave concern for the masters of all ships, and not to be taken in jest. One of Mr. Claussen's masters had approached and now joined in the conversation.

"There be little need t' wait for Africa, t' spy pirates abreast, Milady. One need only sail the Channel. France n' England support piracy by turnin' a blind eye. Aye, the seas can barely contain their numbers with the way they go 'bout raiding each other's ships. They're at war, Milady. An' if they ain't up t' mischief 'nough, then every rascal in them parts is stealin' ya blind an' claimin' t' be sailing for the flag or the Crown so they might fill their own coffers. They're thieving pirates plain an' simple, 'specially them Irish." The man shook his head in disgust at the thought of the mess. Christopher took up the conversation at that point.

"Have no fear, Rebecca. I shan't be caught off guard. Look over there, beyond these ships. Do you see the two vessels farthest out?"

"Yes." Lady Rebecca answered as we strained at the window to see of which vessels Mr. Claussen spoke.

"Those are both East Indiamen. They are able-bodied vessels, and not only come with spacious holds for cargo, but also readily suitable for mounting cannon. It is not my intention to go to war, Rebecca. I have only lightly outfitted these vessels with defensive armaments. I would hope I am in the business of shipping goods, for I see no profit to be had in hauling cannon from shore to shore. Nonetheless, I have employed eight additional men, for the purpose of manning the guns and assuring your safety. Both ships have been outfitted with four cannon apiece, along with four experienced gunners to instruct a crew of men in their use if need be.

"I was fortunate to discover a unique style of cannon being fabricated in Scotland by the Carron Iron Works. They call them Carronade. They are a reasonably lightweight piece requiring no deck space for training tackle, as they are pinned to the hull. A very interesting approach, much the way my own weapon is designed. They even swing about the pin, as does my own. The beauty of this feature is in the fact they can be secured sideways up against the bulwarks and completely out from under foot whilst underway. They seem to be a perfect choice for a merchant vessel. I chose to go with twelve pounders and am entirely confident they shall be capable enough as a deterrent for any rascal thinking of coming in too close." Mr. Claussen turned away from us and spoke to the master of the East Indiaman.

"Mr. Olsten, did you see to it that any cargo made up of small hardware was stowed close in to the cannon for use as fodder, should the need arise? I was very specific in my request."

"Aye, Mr. Claussen—that we did, sir. All is as you asked."

"Very well then. My dear, I must be off for a time. Sit tight and I shall return shortly." He leaned in the doorway, kissed Lady Rebecca upon her cheek, and then headed back down toward the docks with a lollygag lot of children in his footsteps.

I kept my thoughts to myself, but the conversation I was just privy to hear scared the daylights out of me. Lady Rebecca must have noticed the fear upon my face because she turned her attention to me at once and grasped my hand.

"Oh, dear me, child. Have we frightened you? What were those men thinking, giving rise to such concerns before young ears? Pay them no mind, Elizabeth. If I thought, even for a moment we were in peril of pirates or anything else for that matter, I would simply refuse to be part of such folly. Put aside your fears, Elizabeth. I promise to keep close watch over you."

SIXTEEN

Our time of departure was now close at hand, for the tide was beginning to ebb. A specially constructed wagon fitted with a large boom and tackle was en route to lift Lady Rebecca's coach onto the deck of one of the ships. Mr. Claussen came by to explain how the coach would be chocked athwartship, that is to say, crossways on deck, between the fore and main masts above the grating. It would not only go to London with us, but all the way to the New World.

Milady was greatly relieved to know that efforts to transport he coach were moving along without setback. She was supremely fond of the coach, as it was her favorite possession by far—this Christmas gift given by Mr. Claussen. It brought her cherished memories of their first Christmas together after

130

being married. Lady Rebecca was very good about not showing off her wealth, but she couldn't help herself when it came to the coach. It was her pride and joy.

We three remained seated inside, surrounded in its luxury and kept well out of harm's way upon the high ground, but I was on pins and needles. I was filled with butterflies and barely able to remain upon the seat. I was fidgeting terribly, for all the anticipation had me so wound up that I really needed to be set free to run and work off my energy. Lady Rebecca sensed this, and having finished her tea and wishing to be distracted, she sought to have us all entertained. She summoned our driver and instructed him to inquire of a nearby seer, a reading of her leaves.

Escorted back by the footman and visibly wary, the elderly woman stepped up to the coach as requested. She appeared clean. Her scent was of cinnamon. She spoke with respect and in a gentle manner. The old woman was most surprised and somewhat suspicious when Lady Rebecca invited her inside to take up a seat. Nobility kept a steady distance from the common folk in order to avoid the torments of lice, fleas, and the like. It was apparent that the sight of us children eased her mind a good deal, and after having hesitated, she set aside her fears, entered the coach, and made herself comfortable.

In the oddest fashion and quite out of character, the woman suddenly looked up confused and studied the cabin. She looked back over both her shoulders, then seemed to dismiss her thought and received Lady Rebecca's cup to peer inside with all seriousness. She uttered sounds of understanding and acknowledgment as though she were being told many things. I watched as she repeatedly interrupted herself to again gaze warily about the inside of the cabin. I was completely caught up in this mysterious affair, as Milady assumed I would be. The anxieties of our departure and my fears of pirates upon the open sea gave way the instant the old woman looked up at Lady Rebecca with surprise.

"You are with child, Milady?"

My mouth dropped open. Lady Rebecca went pale.

"No! My god, I leave on the ebb for the Americas. You are surely mistaken." She admonished the old woman firmly but gently.

"I beg your pardon, Milady. My feeble eyes do the leaves no justice. I see children. I see you upon a distant shore. You will travel far. I see your heart bursts with kindness."

"You are too kind, old woman. You make me blush. The children are orphans soon to be under my care. It must be this of which you see, *or possibly heard,* for it is becoming common knowledge about these parts, and is it not also plausible that I wait at the pier in order to depart."

"It may be so, just as you say."

The old woman continued to study the patterns. Slowly her face turned dark. Her eyes darted about the inside of the coach more frequently, more nervously. She frowned as she re-read the leaves in the bottom of the cup, looking at them from every angle. She stared at me for the longest moment and then again looked about the coach. She shook her head warily. She was increasingly suspicious and uncomfortable. Then her eyes snapped back to lock onto mine.

"Who are *you*, child?"

She nearly glared at me, and I was shocked speechless to be so suddenly singled out. Milady spoke in my behalf.

"She is Elizabeth, my maiden servant—a good girl and nothing more."

The old woman continued to stare at me and spoke. "The leaves say this coach will bring *you* great sorrow and everlasting joy." She looked back to Milady. "This coach is touched by His hand. I must be off now." The old woman moved toward the door visibly distressed.

ELIZABETH

The chosen one

"Old one, you leave so soon? Pray tell, why the rush? We wish to hear more. How might the coach bring such great sorrow and joy? That seems such gibberish. What is it you see? I know your kind. There is always more."

The fortune-teller began mumbling under her breath, but would not be restrained. She arose without further ado and fumbled with the cabin door handle, which the footman heard and opened at once. She took his arm and stepped out before anyone could forward an objection. Then, once free of the confines of the coach and obviously much less worried about retribution, she turned back to Lady Rebecca and addressed her sternly.

"Understand, I cannot say of things I see, for to speak it surely makes it ring true, Milady. But believe the leaves. You are kind. God is with you. He will be with you always. You have purpose in His eyes." She looked across the cabin to me. "The spirits protect you, child. You are a chosen one. I must go now." The old woman ran off.

"But your fee! Wait!" Milady called out to her.

"No, no, 'tis nothing. There should be no talk of money." The old woman's voice trailed off as she moved into the crowd.

"Daniel." Lady Rebecca addressed the footman who still held open the cabin door.

"Yes, Milady." He snapped to attention.

"Seek the old woman out and see to it she is paid for her service. I fear we have frightened her off." She handed him some coins.

"Yes, Milady." With that, the footman was off at a run.

Lady Rebecca's eyes followed the old woman until she disappeared into the bustling crowd, and then turned her attention toward us.

I had never experienced anything the likes of this before. It all happened so fast, a matter of moments, and yet it was as though we had stepped into another world for an unknown length of time. The old woman's presence lingered within the cabin, and it was more than just the fragrance of cinnamon. The entire affair left my hair standing straight on end.

I took everything she had said right to heart. Why would she lie? It all seemed so foreboding to me. It gave me concern enough, that now I didn't know which was my worst fear, boarding ships and pirates, or great sorrow and being the chosen one. Indeed, from what *did* the spirits protect me; I wondered.

I was amazed at what little stock Lady Rebecca put into the reading. She brushed it off with laughter and went about chatting in a festive mood. I was more than happy to fall back on faith, as it encouraged me to dismiss my concerns, and accept Lady Rebecca's understanding of the event.

"I feel somewhat left out," complained Mary. "Am I unnoticed by the spirits then?"

"Girls, you must know the readers are unchanging. It is their art to leave you feeling good about yourself and worried about everything else. You will never make sense of their ramblings no matter how long you ponder them so you keep going back for more incomprehensible advice. It is how they earn their keep. If you are of their kind they will give you much information. If you are of the upper crust they keep mum for fear of your anger. I know of these things all too well."

"But why would she refuse her fee?" I asked. Lady Rebecca shrugged her shoulders.

"I fear we frightened her."

"What did she mean when saying I was the chosen one?"

"She meant you were special, Elizabeth, but I have known that since the day I met you…and, I am no spirit."

"Yes, but—."

The issue was brought to a quick close by Christopher's return, which overshadowed all. We were removed from the coach by his own hand and escorted to the ship FAIR WIND. I looked back to see the dockmen scurrying about the coach, and in a matter of minutes, she was a cabin without wheels, resting atop a pallet and suspended by straps to the wagon boom.

As we walked across the boarding plank my stomach was in my throat. I felt as though I were surrendering myself to a watery grave. It was unsettling to walk a plank bridging so far above the water and know, to fall would mean to disappear into the murky bay, to what depth, I couldn't bear to imagine.

Lady Rebecca took notice of me. "Elizabeth! You grasp my hand with such firmness, child. Are you frightened?"

"Yes, Milady." I moved in close to her, for my heart was racing as I crossed over the water. I felt light-headed and unbalanced.

Mr. Claussen stepped across the gunwale, then turned about to assist Mary and Lady Rebecca with me in tow. When he felt we were all safely aboard ship, he spoke to Milady.

"Rebecca, I hope you will forgive me any inconvenience these next few days. I have made every effort to see you endure as little hardship as possible. Nature, you must know, is her own mistress and pays no mind to my wants. However, the ship is fitted well for a short stay, and I feel you will long for nothing. We will soon set sail for England, and God willing, shortly there-after drop anchor at Londontown, the place of your birth and my good fortune."

"Only you can surpass yourself with worry over me. I can fend for myself, Christopher. Take care to attend to your business of shipping. I have my Mary and Elizabeth to keep me company, and we are all of high spirits. Now, take me below so I might see my cabin and we shall settle in."

"As you wish, my love."

SEVENTEEN

The vessels weighed anchor on schedule at four past Meridian, Monday, the fifteenth day of June, eighteen-hundred and seven. The weather was fair, winds light with agreeable seas, temperatures in the mid-seventies.

We departed Malmo and made way along the shipping lanes past Copenhagen and on to Helsinger. We moored briefly in Helsinger, where we loaded a cargo of glassworks and silver. We again set sail and followed the Swedish coast north to Goteborg. Here we dropped anchor; and after Mr. Claussen concluded business with his shipyards, we supped. We enjoyed a peaceful evening after persuading Lady Rebecca to give Mr. Claussen, Mary, and me a reading. After a good night's sleep and an early breakfast, we prepared ourselves for the North Sea.

We left Goteborg and stood west until we doubled the cape at Skagen. Here the Westerlies were upon us with head winds and high sea. We stood south and west, and bore along the Danish coast. Following the coast we bore to starboard and again into the Westerlies. Mr. Claussen called on a number of ports in both Germany and Holland, and thankfully, we encountered no foul attempts to encumber our voyage. After three days of business at various anchorages, we made for Londontown. I had always heard great stories of London and England—some good and some horrible, but all fascinating and able to light the imagination of a child.

Lady Rebecca was jubilant to be back. She had been removed from the poverty and place of her youth to enjoy the luxury of mansions and servants, but this would always be her home. I could see a fresh exuberance take hold of her, and she promised Mary and me a wonderful time ashore. There were obviously many old friends and good memories to be introduced.

Our approach to London was unlike that of Copenhagen, Malmo, or Goteborg. London seemed to be far inland from the sea. We were now sailing on the lee side of England and the sea

138

was more agreeable, being protected from the prevailing winds. The night air was fair and many lingered on deck anxious to observe landfall.

Removing ourselves from the stuffiness of the cabin, I took Lady Rebecca's outstretched hand and followed her above deck to enjoy the fresh air outside, which was light with little breeze. The water was nearly still about us, glasslike with low gentle swells and giving off reflections of firelight now visible at this darkened hour.

"Are we there, Milady?" I asked.

"Not yet, Elizabeth." Mr. Claussen answered in her place, and then went on to explain further for our benefit. "We are nearing the mouth of the Thames. She is eighteen miles across at this point. We are now making way toward the Nore, which is a large island of sand that marks the estuary from the River Thames. Do you see the bright light...there just off the bow?" He pointed and we all agreed to seeing it. "That is an enormous oil lamp, perfectly situated to guide ships home safely from the tempestuous North Sea."

Its swath of light streaking across the water brought the silhouette of many a ship's mast into view, most slumbering peacefully upon the dark placid sea.

As was luminous the light of the Nore, so too my curiosity was aflame, and I listened with great interest as Mr. Claussen gave Lady Rebecca an account of our course.

"When might we go ashore, Mr. Claussen?" I asked.

He laughed knowingly.

"Might be as soon as noon on the morrow...or as long as two or three days...but, I would suspect the morning after next." He turned to his master. "How distant be the West India docks, Mr. Olsen, forty is it?"

"A good forty t' fifty miles, Mr. Claussen. Ten t' the Nore an' another forty up river t' follow."

139

"Unfortunately, Elizabeth, the Thames and the wind are good friends and travel together in the same direction for the most part. This is a well-known fact in these parts, and a most frustrating obstacle for the masters who wish to make way to London. They have little choice but to wait for an easterly or pay the rowers. When those Easterlies come, it's all too often fast and furious with little warning, leaving those masters to scramble and sort themselves out as they rush in to enter the river. A good many have been known to end up on shore far sooner than they expected. As for us, we will not be subject to the dangers nor the whims of an easterly, for I have enlisted the service of a tow." Lady Rebecca spoke up as well.

"The Thames doesn't change much. Since the beginning of time, it keeps getting narrower the farther upstream one goes. On the other hand, every year the ships are built larger, the congestion gets worse, and the passage upriver to London becomes all the more difficult. Ships that have been out for a year or two think nothing of mooring another week or so to await a favorable wind. Now the newer packets are just the opposite. They are crowded with impatient passengers, and don't enjoy the luxury of waiting about to watch sunsets. They unload their passengers into longboats as quickly as possible to be taken up to London by oar. They keep to a tight schedule and stay out of the river. It's just too much trouble."

It was as they explained, word for word. I watched in the distance dim lights of bow lanterns that seemed to break away like sparks from the bright light of the Nore. They were affixed to the longboats that surged upriver beyond the Nore and glided back to the various packets that surrounded us in the bay. Their tiny lights moved slowly past the brighter anchor lights of the ships, but all lamps, large and small, were reduced to reflections of narrow lines of light that floated across the black water to meet us. Throughout the night, I listened to the muffled voices of passengers, or the squeak of an oarlock in need of grease. The sounds seemed to travel miles across the tranquil water.

EIGHTEEN

It was late the next afternoon, and I had been in and out of the cabin a number of times before I looked toward shore and took notice of an enormous cloud of whitish smoke rising upward into the onset of an evening sky. Curious, I followed it down to its source. Filled with alarm, I broke into a run.

"A ship's on fire, a ship's on fire!" I dropped below deck still screaming at the top of my lungs. Mr. Claussen, who had gone below only moments earlier, flew back up through the companionway. I turned to follow him, because he knew how to right every wrong, and would surely have something to say.

"Where, Elizabeth?" I was surprised by the question, as he and Master Olsen spun about looking in all directions.

"Right there!" I pointed, somewhat confused. Lady Rebecca, Mary, and a few of the deck hands had now crowded in amongst us as well. There was a brief moment of silence…and then a rash of snickers, and finally an eruption of laughter by everyone at my expense. I knew I had made a mistake. I felt like a complete fool, but I didn't have a clue. The boat was clearly going up in smoke, and lots of it to say the least.

And so it went with my introduction to the mighty steam engine. I let out an alarm all for naught, and now I wished only to hide, feeling dismally stupid before all hands on deck. Even Mary was laughing. I was red as a beet and much put out by the time Lady Rebecca came to ease my embarrassment. Unfortunately, aboard ship there was little comfort in having no place to run or hide.

"Don't let this bunch bother you, angel. I myself have never seen a steam engine, and as far as I can tell the boat is surely charred to the waterline. You were very grown up to take it upon yourself and beckon us instead of lulling about on your laurels

141

the way most of this lot might." She gave the rest a glaring look of disapproval.

"You did the proper thing, Elizabeth," remarked Mr. Claussen.

Lady Rebecca embraced me tightly from behind. She nuzzled me and kissed me repeatedly on both sides of my head as I stood watching the clouds of white steam rise above the small boat during its approach. It was heading straight for us, but I could have hardly cared by that point.

"Elizabeth."

"Yes, sir." No matter what my frame of mind, I had to remember my place as a maiden servant.

"You ever see a log explode in the hearth? You know, one that blasts hot embers and ash across the kitchen?"

"Yes, Milord."

"Let us assume that you were holding onto that log when it exploded. Do you know what it would do to your hands?"

"It would burn them, Milord."

"Umm hmm. It would do that for certain, but it would also push them apart like this—boom!" He moved his hands apart in the air over my head. "Because of the force of the explosion, they would fly away just like the embers. You see, there is a small chamber in the log, a small space that has water in it, like a tiny tea kettle, and when the water gets hot it turns into steam and that steam gets bigger and bigger, all the while pushing on the inside of that log until it can't hold the expanding steam back any longer. The log blows apart from all the pushing and the embers fly across the kitchen.

"Something similar happens on that boat. Only, the water is in a giant tea kettle sitting over a giant fire and it gets very hot. It too expands, but instead of pushing on the inside of a log, it pushes on pistons, things that go up and down, and they are connected to things that go 'round and 'round such as the paddles that makes that boat go forward.

"Boats like that no longer care which way the river flows or which way blows the wind. It will chug upriver and down, whenever it likes because using steam to push paddles 'round n' 'round mean...no need for sails. That is why it can tow a ship like the FAIR WIND upriver against the forces of current and wind as well. All that smoke.... That's nothing more than wood burning to make the steam.

"This may be the first time you have seen it, but you have seen it before most. In years to come, when you are as old as I, you will see steamboats everywhere. You will travel on ships powered by steam. Mark my words, child, for it won't be long." He placed the weight of his hand upon my shoulder and then left our company to return to the cabin.

That little smoking boat came alongside and after an exchange of commands the FAIR WIND was in tow, leaving the remaining vessels behind in the estuary as we headed for the Nore. I had wanted a closer look at the boat, but Lady Elizabeth wouldn't hear of it. She kept me at her side in the cabin or at the stern. Apparently she had never seen such a vessel either, for she seemed somewhat fearful of it.

Our ship entered the Thames proper as the little steam-powered boat towed us upriver past many parishes and most of the night. The towboat relieved the mates of most of their work and so a mood of relaxation and joviality was building in the air. There was little to do other sing, laugh, and keep a sharp eye out for flaming embers that were often seen to land on deck. Even that was a game as the men raced each other to stomp out the glowing ash.

As for me, I was soon fast asleep, and remained so for some time before being awakened by Lady Rebecca. My senses were greeted by a great deal of commotion that also awoke my curiosity. I began pushing back my heavy woolen blanket, my protection from the damp night air about the water. Lady Rebecca had made it for me during the long winter evenings whilst Mr. Claussen was away on business. She and Mary would sit for hours talking, while keeping warm under the blankets they were in the process of knitting in front of the fire.

Mary made one for herself, and Lady Rebecca made mine, as I watched and learned something of the art. To please my childish desires, she knitted into the pattern a large sailing ship with a red hull. I thought it very lucky, and gained a great sense of security and comfort when wrapped by it. Now, I sat up within its folds somewhat groggy. I tried to make sense of what was taking place about the ship.

We had just been secured at the West India docks as planned, and my eyes opened to a show of flickering lights all aglow like countless giant fireflies. Their numbers were multiplied many fold by the reflections dancing off the droplets of dew that covered the surfaces of the ship still deep in shadow. I could see these reflections through the arms of Lady Rebecca, who brought me to my feet and pulled the blanket tightly about me. I stood there leaning into her as my attention was momentarily taken in by the new and strange collection of sights.

All about us were ships, seamen, and stevedores. There was much going on. I believed it to be only an hour before sunrise, but it mattered little for this seemed to be a place that didn't sleep. There were languages in the air that were strange to me. Many people of dark hair and skin, strange-looking folks they were. They, along with others, moved in and out and all about stacks of crates, piles of rummage, and wagonloads of goods that seemed to block all of one's attempts to course along the wooden docks. There was an undercurrent of noise that surrounded us, much of it from cages of chickens and ducks, and animals in pens.

Our ship was made fast to the docks, and all on deck, save the anchor watch, were relieved of their duties and allowed to repair to their sleeping quarters for the remainder of the night.

"Come along, Elizabeth. Come on, honey, we're going below." Gently, Lady Rebecca took hold of me and walked me back to the cabin. Once below, she tucked me in alongside Mary.

At daybreak, a time not so easily realized below deck, I was awakened again by the hustle-bustle about ship, much the same as the night before. This time, hull-shaking vibrations and loud drum-like poundings sounded everywhere. It was the slamming of cargo being ferried out the holds. Inside the cabins, it made enough noise to wake the dead.

I lay in my berth for a spell watching Mary as she poured the water she had fetched for our basin. After we washed up and brushed out our hair, we breakfasted. It was a dandy meal of oysters, eggs, bread with butter and jam, punch, and best of all, a large piece of chocolate. The ship's cook was kind to us, and our portion of chocolate was fit for a king.

Lady Rebecca was never one to be found in her bed, and by the time I arose from breakfasting, she was already dressed and singing cheerfully. Today, she was to go to the orphanage for conversation with the head mistress on details pertinent to the passage of the orphans abroad.

Mary and I were left with no instruction other than to enjoy ourselves and to keep out from underfoot the deckhands. I spent the early morning blissfully purring, while Mary groomed me affectionately. We took turns fussing over each other, seeking out nits and brushing out snarls. I so loved her coppery hair. After some time, Mary found herself a warm place to laze in the morning sun and curled up with a book, for Lady Rebecca was teaching us both how to read English.

I, on the other hand, cared little for book learning and much preferred to satisfy my curiosity by investigating all the activity on deck. Still clutching my woolen sailing ship blanket, I climbed atop the cabin and seated myself just ahead of the companionway going below. It was a great vantage point. I watched hour after hour in endless fascination all that took place and learned something of the work of riggers, deckhands, and dockmen. The other ships of Mr. Claussen's fleet came gliding into the docks amidst a round of cheers by all hands, and were promptly secured nearby.

Lady Rebecca's coach was the first item to be set ashore. The beauty of it compelled the men to handle it with great care. They went about checking and double-checking the hoist and lines. They packed layers of rags between the straps and the finish so as not to mar it. Once done, the coach being safely removed from the FAIR WIND and out of harm's way, the hatches were all slid back or removed, opening the ship's holds and exposing our cargo of lumber. The men set out at once to remove all that burdened us. Toward late afternoon the emptied holds were beginning to fill with crates of tea, spices, wines, hardware, tools, machinery, and numerous other items incomprehensible to me.

This was my entertainment for the next two days. The routine altered only when one of the jacks might take it upon himself to set me off screaming as he chased me about the deck, whilst swinging a tar bucket and threatening to glue me to a mast—all to the amusement of his mates.

In conversations overheard about the docks, I realized that it was strange Lady Rebecca had not removed us to one of the fine hotels in the city. I was curious about the city and would very much have enjoyed seeing it firsthand. As I heard it, Milady chose to remain on board for my sake. The men had said they were asked to keep an eye out for me, and I would be happier to run the docks in fresh air than stand about in smoke-filled hallways of a hotel. Of course, I also noticed that Mr. Claussen spent all of his day on these docks, and I was certain I was not the only reason she stayed on board.

NINETEEN

The morning of the third day in port, I awoke to hear Lady Rebecca receiving a stern lecture from Mr. Claussen. Never before had I heard Mr. Claussen raise his voice. I determined he wasn't angry, but he certainly wasn't happy either. It was in Lady Rebecca's mind to visit the haunts of her unmarried life, those places in which she grew up. In spite of Mr. Claussen's cool reception to the idea, she continued planning and talking about her intentions to do this and do that. She wished to call on many, especially friends at her old workplace, the West Indies Tavern.

At first, Milady sat alongside Mr. Claussen listening respectfully to everything he had to say. She appeared unwilling to discuss the matter, for she knew all parties were obliged to wait until the ship's holds were filled, chocked, and secured. There was ample time, to be sure, before any thought might be given to our departure. Second to that, she could think of no pressing matters at hand (the issue of the orphans having been concluded), nor any basis for Mr. Claussen to object to her going visiting other than his nervous concerns and protective nature. Mr. Claussen, I must say, was of an *entirely* different mind.

Consideration for Milady's well being was foremost on his mind. And the prospect of Lady Rebecca heading into Stepney made him feel profoundly uncomfortable—feelings which he expressed in no uncertain terms.

Milady asked on more than one occasion if he might lower his voice and save the others on board the embarrassment of enduring their difference of opinion. He was neither indiscreet nor offensive, but it mattered little within the cramped quarters of the cabins, for privacy existed only in one's dreams. Mr. Claussen was never one to deny Lady Rebecca her wishes, but he was fit to be tied over this matter and biting his lip to contain himself from speaking coarsely.

The passion of the discussion was enough to cause me to rise from my bunk and wander down the passageway toward Milady's cabin door. It had swung partially open with the rocking of the ship, and I was shocked indeed to see Lady Rebecca standing before Mr. Claussen dressed in the rags of a commoner. She was also wearing an expression of defiance.

My movement must have distracted her, for she glanced in my direction a number of times while Mr. Claussen proceeded in his attempt to dissuade her from "a most unconscionable and ill thought notion," as he put it. Convinced of the risk before her, he was insisting that she be accompanied by no less than two escorts, preferably four, which she steadfastly refused. He was beside himself with disconcertment.

At first, Lady Rebecca pleaded with Mr. Claussen to understand the inappropriateness of visiting old friends, all commoners, while flanked by the vestiges of wealth.

"I find it rude, thoughtless, and degrading to those people who mean a great deal to me, Christopher. I might as well say to their face that I fear one of *them* may strike me from behind."

"You *have no fear*, Rebecca. It is I who fear someone may strike you from behind. You must not turn a careless cheek to your position. You are no longer their table maiden, but a Lady of substantial means. That fact is not secret in these parts, nor is your presence, and wealth, my dear, is a perilous crown to wear in the back alleys of London, especially in Stepney and about the waterfront—no, not just the waterfront, I wish it could be *just* the waterfront. It is any place one steps in London. My word, a *man* must proceed with all due caution, let alone a woman, particularly one without the good sense to employ an escort. I say emphatically, this place didn't earn its foul reputation by breeding a city of good Samaritans.

"It is obvious you don't believe I have sufficient cause for concern, but I am well traveled, Rebecca. It is no secret that London is a notoriously dangerous place. In all of Europe, no city equal to her size harbors the dismal collection of highwaymen, robbers, thieves, rapists, or drunks one finds at this port. To be sure, no place else in Europe tolerates anything like the state of debauchery that makes up the common character of this city. To me, it seems incredulous that a city of such breadth, a city of such magnificent parks and palaces, a place of structures built so high—might rise up by the hands of people with morals so low." Mr. Claussen shook his head in exasperation. Milady was immune to the condemnation.

"I must say, that is especially harsh criticism from someone who knows the port and her people best through a small window in the side of a ship."

"I hardly believe that is the case, my love."

"I beg to differ, Christopher. You choose to argue the issue with me, yet it is I who has lived all but two years of my life in this city, not you. I don't dispute there is plenty more to be desired. From where you stand, distant and apart, you only seem to spy the criminals and the horrors of living in cramped squalor. Pay me mind, sir, if you are hungry and you steal food to eat, and your brother steals food to eat, and your neighbor steals food to eat; you don't see stealing food as a crime. You see it as a way of life, a necessary act to survive. When people don't steal food to eat, they die of starvation or disease. Ironically, that is a crime of the crown that goes on forever unpunished. Isn't it odd to realize that ten thousand people can drop dead of starvation, and no one will be brought to bear? Yet, if one person gets caught stealing a loaf of bread, he could be hanged. When those people look afar, they see you, Christopher, and you are the criminal."

"Rebecca, please, I must insist you…."

"The city employs a force of police where it is necessary. The Thames River Police have been around for a good number of years now. That is certainly a testimony to the will of somebody to curb lawlessness. I am told there is even talk of expanding their authority into the city itself. Maybe, the city as a whole has changed for the better since you last looked." Lady Rebecca added this additional thought with some cynicism, but Mr. Claussen wasted no time with his rebuttal.

"Oh! That is rare indeed! Imagine a force that is named with a *French* word during a war with France. It must garner wonderful support from the general public—a public that puts absolutely no stock in the concept, whatsoever. The docks are filled with—."

"Are you belittling these people, Christopher?" Lady Rebecca stared down her nose at Mr. Claussen. "It has nothing to do with a French word. It has to do with getting strung up by the neck for being poor, no matter how right you might be in the eyes of the Good Lord. Now, we have a cadre of men working in the king's name who are supposedly above dishonesty and abuse, they being dispatched for the betterment of all. You can't blame the people for thinking that sounds a bit far-fetched. How well do you know King George the Third? After all, if the common man is lacking in virtue, it is only because he has picked up his traits by example. What better for the elite than an official body to enforce their bidding?

"In your position, Christopher, how can you possibly understand these things, how can you judge so freely? You know little of the life of a common man. What fears do you know? We grow up worrying day to day that someone will spread a lie about us for the sake of a reward, and if we cannot pay the authorities more than they have paid the informant, we are doomed. Only poor men face the gallows, Christopher. The wealthy have no respect for laws; they are unaffected by them, but they do have a need for laws. It is how they keep the poor and wretched poor and wretched."

Mr. Claussen must have wondered if it was he or the soil of England that suddenly gave rise to a side of Lady Rebecca that was generally kept at bay. It was a strange experience to see her emotions surface with such conviction, emotions he could see were rather explosive. He had disrespectfully crossed a line marking sacred territory, not the limits of Londontown, but the boundary of her heart. The lay of this land was defiant inner strength, a strength acquired through a lifetime of hardship and struggle in order to survive—concepts unfortunately, he really could not comprehend.

"I would spend less time peering through the small hole of a ship, as you put it, if I didn't share the same fate every other foreigner faces on this shore. To make matters worse, a stranger who elects to venture inland is simply asking for trouble. Londoners prey upon their own without mercy, and the vision of a foreigner within their midst is enough to set off the unscrupulous to drooling like famished wolves." Mr. Claussen chose to persist, but Milady would have none of it.

"I believe you may have forgotten that I earned my keep tending to the people of these parts. Who do you suppose they were, English? I think not. I've seen them all, the Germans, the Danes, the Irish and Scots, the Negroes, the beloved French, and this may startle you, Christopher, but there are a good many Swedes about as well. I can only assume when you say the foreigners are appalled by the affairs of London you must mean we are taking stock of our own lot and moving to improve ourselves. Is that what you were saying?"

"Apparently, it was." Mr. Claussen relented. "Please, Rebecca, I implore you take an escort, if not for yourself, then for me. Please."

"Fine! Fine!" Lady Rebecca nodded her head. "I'll take young Elizabeth at my side. That should be more than sufficient. She shall watch my back. I shall appear a woman with child and spoken for. Does that make you happy?" Lady Rebecca spoke through clenched teeth, and looked straight at Mr. Claussen, who went abruptly silent.

She remained adamant, and on one of the rare occasions where she spoke out against Mr. Claussen's will, it was he who relented, albeit with a worrisome wind and a fearful heart. He stood a moment looking at her, then turned, following her gaze to see me just outside the doorway. Dumbfounded, and understanding there would be no reasoning with Milady, he started to say something, stuttered, and then overcome by frustration and a loss for words, he left the cabin. He brushed past me and went topside. He was in a mood, but Lady Rebecca broke into a grin and held her hand out to me.

"He means well, child; he loves me very much. This is how I know. And he isn't altogether wrong in his opinions, for he is no fool. But London always seems much worse to the outsiders. Come, darling, I shall dress you in all the rage of Stepney."

As for Lady Rebecca, she was born of London stock, loved her city and remained unmoved by any outsider's view of a place she knew as home. She had heard all their opinions and complaints a thousand times over during the years she tended tables at the West Indies. It was a state of bedlam that she dismissed with a flip of her wrist. She handed me some rags to wear.

TWENTY

Within the hour, we were off into the parish of Stepney. I was thunderstruck by Lady Rebecca's revelation that this was the place of her rearing. It was a rough-looking parish and set me to worrying about all Mr. Claussen had aired.

"So, you too are frightened. Would you rather have stayed with Christopher on board the FAIR WIND?"

"No, Milady. This is where you were born?" My question seemed to catch her off guard. She hesitated.

"Now, I never said that. Truth be known—I don't know, Elizabeth. I *have* no way of knowing. In my heart, I like to think not. In my heart, I was born far away on the open sea.

You know… Stepney is a famous place. You might not realize this by the look of it, but it's true. All around the world it is said that *children born about at sea—find sanctuary in Stepney*. That is why there are so many orphans in this area. The children come from all over the world."

"Are there a lot of children in Stepney, Milady?"

"Lots. Lots and lots. They're everywhere."

"But, are they all orphans?"

"Not all, a good many."

"Did your mother and father leave you in Stepney then?"

Lady Rebecca didn't answer me. She looked down at me with a half smile and shrugged her shoulders as if to accept this mystery in her life. Still, I sensed this bothered her, and that saddened me.

"I promise I will never leave you, Milady. Wherever you go, I shall stay by your side and care for you. I give you my word." My sincerity brought a smile to her face. She looked at me with much affection and pulled me in close to her.

"Take care to stay by my side, now. It is too easy getting lost in this crowd."

"Yes, Milady."

It wasn't possible for a nine-year-old country girl such as me to be prepared for the onslaught of commotion I encountered upon these narrow, dim, smoke-filled streets. My eyes burned and my mouth tasted terrible. If the air didn't prove suffocating enough within the haze of blue smoke from wood fires, or the gagging stench of garbage piled in heaps, then the crowds took up the slack as they pressed tighter and tighter until they seemed to squeeze the very breath out of me.

"Stay to the wall! Stay to the wall. Elizabeth!"

Every passing moment presented another near-escape from death as reckless and indifferent drivers, one after another, raced their carriages and coaches down the cobblestone lanes in threatening fashion. Between them, the hordes of chairmen screamed obscenities and verbally threatened us with death itself if we were too slow to move 'against the wall'.

The din was beyond description. These fleets of wheeled vehicles rolled in quick succession, their iron-rimmed wheels clamoring noisily upon the puzzlework of pavers. It was impossible to hear anything Lady Rebecca instructed, but for the noise. It seemed everybody was compelled to yell. It was all out competition between the stalls of costermongers, the sandmen and cherry girls, the tinkers with their swinging pots and pans, and milkmaids all a-calling. Not to mention the yelps of barrow boys, bread sellers, and a thousand others.

"Ring! Ring! Ring!" I spun about in response to this call, this demand for space, as the curious moved back to form an area in which two angry men were squaring off to fight. They were soon blocked from my view by a jeering mob of on-rushers pushing rudely inward to place bets. Men, women, and children alike were yelling at the top of their lungs, screaming out their wagers or taking sides and arguing out differences of opinion. Attracted by the commotion and chances for profit, there came the pickpockets and a troupe of musicians including a fiddle player, a drummer, and a guitarist in the company of a young couple that sang songs for coins. Ears, eyes, nose, mouth, every element of the street was an assault to the senses.

"Elizabeth!"

"Yes, Milady." I looked ahead to see Lady Rebecca glaring my way from her place a number of paces ahead.

"Come along, Elizabeth, before I lose you! You must pay attention, child. Stay at my side for your own good, and stay to the wall for heaven's sake, *stay to the wall*."

"Yes, Milady."

TWENTY-ONE

I was offered a chair alongside Milady at a table in the family room of the West Indies Tavern, the establishment of which she was so fond. There was quite a stir when we arrived. I didn't know anybody, but they all knew Lady Rebecca. There was a lot of hugging and kissing, a lot of laughing and carrying on. Everybody wished to get close to her. We were nearly carried to our seats by the crowd, and remained a disruption to business and the center of attraction for some time until the mistress of the inn arrived with a squeal of delight and joined us at our table. At that point things quickly settled down and went back to normal.

"Elizabeth, I want you to meet Mrs. Hattie Parker. She and her husband, Holland, own the inn. She watched over me for almost five years, while I worked in her employ. I was a table maiden much like yourself. This is where *I* worked." Lady Rebecca stressed the fact she had also worked to earn her keep.

"Hello, Mrs. Parker."

"Hello, Elizabeth. You are such a fine-looking young girl. I would take you in a second. What might I bring you, child? Would you like some punch? Are you thirsty then?"

"Yes, ma'am. Thank-you."

Lady Rebecca had ordered sweet tea for herself, and biscuits to go with my punch. Mrs. Parker brought me pieces of lump sugar, or 'candy' as she called it, for my pleasure. I passed my time enjoying the treats and watching the patrons, faces of strangers who approached one after another to greet Lady Rebecca. I believe she knew every regular in the inn, and until they all paid their respects, Milady was unable to converse freely with Mrs. Parker. Eventually the conversation gained momentum, and I sat quietly half-listening. I gathered there were would be no end in sight to the amount of catching up that had to take place.

"In what hotel have you put up?"

"I haven't. Originally, Christopher and I had intended to take a room during our stay in London, but after we arrived, I found I had no desire to deal with the headaches of moving all my belongings plus that of Mary and Elizabeth. What was the point, I ask you, only to repeat the ordeal four days later? It seemed more sensible to me, to simply leave it all be—aboard ship—and then move it only the once from the West India Docks to the London Docks where lies the REBECCA. Why encourage an episode of stolen or lost baggage at this time, and besides, the girls are nicely settled in and calm. I figure I might as well get accustomed to living on board while I can still go ashore for a break. And quite frankly, the attention paid us on board far surpasses anything one finds ashore. The service may be crude, but it is heartfelt and most personal."

After what seemed to be hours of gnawing on biscuits, sipping punch, and listening to discussions on the latest news about everyone in London, I finally became too fidgety to remain seated in their presence and was given my leave to wander about the tables as I wished. I was most attracted by the men's room. The gentlemen therein found me amusing as I peeked in and beckoned me to enter. I was eager to do so, for my attention was drawn to the walls, which were covered with charcoal portraits of the many patrons. I liked drawings. Beneath each likeness was a peg upon which hung that man's mug.

I was quickly put into a game of searching out drawings of the men seated in the room. To their surprise I did it very quickly. They were truly amazed at how fast I accomplished the feat and were quick to fill the air with applause and compliments. I was certain they had tipped a few too many, for they never seemed to realize that by removing their mugs from the wall in order to drink ale, they had given me the key to finding their portraits.

By the time I had returned to the table where Lady Rebecca and Mrs. Hattie sat, their conversation had taken on an entirely different nature. A serious and sorrowful air had replaced the laughter and lightheartedness of before.

"You're certain she'll be there?"

"It's her routine. It would be strange if she wasn't."

"I fear I am putting you out so."

"Nonsense—I am thrilled to accompany you. We'll see it through."

"Hattie, I am indebted. Have you someone to run an errand for me?"

"For certain. There's young Oscar. He is both quick and smart to boot. He knows the area."

"Excellent. If I might trouble you for a quill and sheet, I will send word to Christopher to bring around a coach, and to expect me in late this evening."

Lady Rebecca penned her note to Christopher as Hattie looked on. Upon completion, Oscar was dispatched in all haste to the West India Docks with message in hand. I found myself becoming very interested in what was taking place, for I sensed an air of mystery about us.

The coach came as Lady Rebecca had requested, and it didn't go without notice that it had arrived accompanied by two additional footmen. Between the driver and the three footmen, Christopher had managed to get his way. *Four escorts in Stepney.*

When we departed the comfort of the inn, a thick fog confronted us, the kind of fog I soon learned that contributed to much of London's infamy. It pressed in close upon the street and was as much a mix of smoke and soot as anything else. Everything was dripping wet and the air was cool. It was a notable change from the sunny weather we had enjoyed during the morning walk to the inn. It was cozy inside the coach, but it was impossible for me to make out anything of the city that passed by the window. I could do little more than sit quietly as I had been expected to do most of the day. The conversation between Lady Rebecca and Mrs. Parker continued on in hushed tones and half-sentences. I desperately wanted to ask what all the secrecy was about, but I had been trained to hold my tongue and never ask or intrude into the business of the Master and Mistress of the house. It was a cardinal rule, so I sat mum and attentive.

The coach came to a halt at a large set of gates. Surprisingly enough, Lady Rebecca held out her hand to me so I might step down and join them instead of insisting that I stay in the company of the driver. Once removed from the cabin, I looked up to see a wrought iron mantle straddling the entrance; it read, 'St. James Park'. We passed through the gates and entered the grounds on foot. The night was dreary and darkness came early due to the heavy fog. It was an eerie atmosphere, and it spooked me to walk through the murkiness even though there were a good many people about. I was relieved to see two of our footmen following close and watching over us.

"Hattie?" A stranger called out from amidst a group of men.

"Why, Mr. Berkely, what might you be doing out so late this night?"

"I was of a mind to ask the same of you." He smiled teasingly.

"I am out looking for a friend."

"Aren't we all."

"Yours must be a friend of Mrs. Berkely, I assume?" said Mrs. Parker, and with that the men behind Mr. Berkely roared in laughter.

"Nothing other, I assure you," he responded.

"Then my faith in you has been restored. Give your wife my regards, I beg."

"You have my word, Hattie. Good evening ladies." Mr. Berkeley removed his hat and bowed graciously. The others were still laughing. We continued on into the park while Mrs. Parker went on to express her disapproval.

"The scoundrel! The man has four children at home as it is. A fine thing, he should be gallivanting about here of a night."

It turned out Mr. Berkeley was only one of a number of men who recognized Hattie as she escorted us through the park. Voices of both acquaintance and stranger called out to us from within the darkened underbrush and wood.

"Are you certain you haven't visited these grounds before this night? You certainly are well received," Lady Rebecca teased.

"I beg your pardon! I don't believe my ears. Talk like that will get you left with these admirers who seem to have caught your eye."

"Caught my eye?" Milady answered feigning shock.

"Indeed! Isn't it like you to have it all and still look for something better."

Lady Rebecca laughed. "There couldn't possibly be anything better."

"One never knows."

"This one does know. I have the best. You may have the rest." She laughed as she brushed imaginary crowds of men aside. They went on teasing each other and acting much more like children than ladies.

A number of times as we walked, Mrs. Parker stepped to the side and spoke with strangers we came upon. Some seemed to understand whatever it was she asked, while others shook their heads in obvious ignorance. Those who knew were directing us to a specific place. I now understood that Lady Rebecca was looking for someone—a woman named Jennifer. The fog blanketed the bushes and trees, and they were forced to keep a sharp lookout. My instructions were to walk a few steps ahead and keep an eye to the ground. This was to save us from stumbling upon rock or crevice, but also to keep me from paying witness to certain activities that should remain unseen by a young and curious girl.

"There!" Hattie whispered. We stopped to look in the direction in which she pointed. I could see the glimmer of a lantern off in the distance. We headed for it. As we approached, a woman with a shawl wrapped about her shoulders, and dressed in a frilly outfit that was probably quite splendid in days prior, stood waiting in place alongside a statue. At hearing our approach, she turned toward us. As we neared her, I could see the strain on her face as she tried to determine who we were. Hattie began to fall behind and reached for me, but I resisted. It was a bit too dark and scary for my comfort, and I sped immediately to Milady's side.

"Jennifer?" Lady Rebecca called out cautiously.

"Who are you?" the woman responded nervously.

"I am someone who thinks of you often."

"Look, Milady, I dunno why ya'd be wastin' time thinkin' o' me, but if it's t' do wit' your man, I don' go chasin' men. They come here." She sounded hard.

"Have no fear, I mean you no harm. I have come to say thank-you. I am not Milady. I am Rebecca Greystone. Do you remember?"

The woman stood silent for a moment, staring, running back through her memories to find this face or name. A remembrance came to her at last, and it did much to soften the look upon her face.

"Rebecca? Little Reb from St. Kath'rine's?"

"Yes, yes, little Rebecca from St. Katherine's. You remember. I didn't know if you would." The other woman laughed and shook her head in amazement.

160

"For me, there be precious few recollections worth keepin', but I still 'member you. Them were good days. What brings ya t' call on me?" she asked, the sound of suspicion much diminished in her voice.

"Well, I am embarrassed to think how silly you might find me for what I am about to say; yet, for my own peace of mind it must be said. I wanted to tell you—this is awkward, I know I must appear mindless, you hardly know who I am. I—I wanted to say thank-you. I wanted to tell you how much I appreciated the kindness and the care you showed me at St. Katherine's. I wanted you to know that I never forgot how you took me under your wing and protected me. I wanted you to know how hard I cried when you were put out. I still remember watching you on the front steps, listening to you pounding on the door and crying to come back in. I cried as well. I begged them to let you back in. Of course, I didn't understand. I don't know quite how to put this into words, but I never forgot you, Jennifer. I never forgot all that you did for me. I have always hoped to see you again—if only to say thank-you."

Jennifer studied Milady, and I could see by the light of the lantern that she was moved by Milady's sincerity. She almost looked embarrassed at having been a person of kindness at some point in her past. She reached out for Lady Rebecca, who stepped forward to receive her. They embraced and remained so for a long time. With a softer voice, in a matronly manner, Jennifer spoke.

"Ya look t'ave done good for yer self. I ain't surprised. You were diff'ernt, child—headstrong. I s'pose that is why I fussed over ya so much. You could always make me laugh. You were so full o' spit an' sass. The elders couldn' break ya. Ya took me from my worries—my fears 'bout things t'come. What ya done with yerself, Rebecca? I too, of'n wondered 'bout how ya got on, 'bout the li'l girl I used to cuddle in my arms. Ya married in t' money, din' ya. Tell me that ya did. Tell me that ya did. 'At's what I wana 'ear. Make me happy."

161

"I have been fortunate. I feel guilty. I have been given more than my fair share. I fear every morning that I should open my eyes and find it all a dream. I fear I will wake up to find myself a little girl back at St. Katherine's. I can't escape those nightmares. Still, the Lord has been very kind to me."

"Then, I'm happy to 'ear it. I'm happy t' know that at least one o' us done well. I'm thinkin' that maybe yer the only one. Most o' the others are here. You'll see 'em all in the park. All but you. Fate smiled upon ya hon, jus' as ya said.

"What a life we've had, Rebecca. All them years at St. Katherine's list'nun t' the teachings o' the church. Look at you, an' look at me. I been part o' every sin imaginable a thousand times over, lost every virtue. At least I ain' alone. If I am going t' hell, I'm goin' with plenty o' company. Last I heard, there were five or six thousan' of us here a night. It's the most pop'lar place in the country once the sun hits bottom. We're all the same ere, Rebecca. We tell all the same lies. We lie 'bout where we come from. We lie 'bout what we do. We lie 'bout where we're goin'. Then we rob people blind so we might keep up with our lies. Ain't it a life, hon? You're blessed t'been spared, baby."

"Is this here yer daughter?" The woman smiled down at me. Milady was slow in offering her answer. She put her arm around me.

"No. I would dearly love to have a child the likes of this one. She's a good head and I am most fond of her—too fond of her I fear. She's in my care for the time being. She earns her keep as my maiden servant." Lady Rebecca hugged me tightly and suddenly there was silence.

Nothing else in common was left between these two women, and for lack of knowing what else to do, they were soon to part; but not before a reluctant Jennifer was convinced to accept a gift from Milady. She was asked only to refrain from viewing it until after we had departed.

162

We headed back across the grounds with the footmen still at our heels, and found our way back to the gates and the waiting coach at the place we parked it. Little was said between Lady Rebecca and Mrs. Parker as we headed back to the inn returning her as requested. It appeared that both women were lost in the fog of thought, deep and dark as the night that surrounded us. After a difficult farewell, Lady Rebecca and I continued on down the now empty cobblestone streets that led toward the docks. In contrast to the morning, the only sound now was the sniffles of Lady Rebecca, the echoes of coach wheels crossing the pavers, and the clippity-clop of horseshoes bouncing back and forth between the walls.

Mr. Claussen was also moving back and forth, pacing aboard his ship, and threw up his arms expressing a great sigh of relief at the sight of our approach. He came across the plank to meet us, and then escorted us back to the warmth and security of our cabins. He looked at Milady and at me. I said nothing, but shrugged. Lady Rebecca was visibly upset. His words were kind and soothing, and one might never have known of the objections he had raised so strenuously during the morning.

TWENTY-TWO

On the fourth and final day aboard the FAIR WIND, our personal belongings were removed to shore and transported by cart from the West India Dock to the London Dock where lay the ship that would take us to America. Before disembarking, Mary and I dressed in our finest attire as instructed by Lady Rebecca so that we might accompany her and Mr. Claussen on a trip into London proper.

We boarded a riverboat manned by three oarsmen that had been summoned for our service. Mr. Claussen pointed out the

163

fact that a coach would have been expeditious, but not nearly as romantic, and we all happily agreed. We were docked in the import basin of West India Docks, which was farthest inland. As we departed we passed by the export basin, it being closer to the river, and the place where the FAIR WIND would soon be secured to take on cargo for the Americas.

The oarsmen made good time against the current, not that we were in a rush, and having gone upstream a short distance, we reached the Lower Pond. Right from the start, I could see that London was to be everything Milady had claimed. My imagination would be left wanting not. To our right, Lady Rebecca pointed out Stepney for Mary's benefit, who unlike me would only know it from afar. She then began to tell us of London.

"For ages London was a Roman port. They called it Londinium. They also called it Augusta because it was one of the most prosperous cities in the world. It was the greatest city in the Roman Empire north of the Alps. When Rome fell to ruin, so too did London. It was next invaded and conquered by the Saxons and no one knows what happened to the city for at least the next one hundred and fifty years. The Danes also invaded it. It was also called Lunduntown. We still call it that with affection. Eventually the city was revived and it went through a number of transitions, usually for the better, all of which has brought us to the London of today. It is a very old city, as you might imagine."

In contrast to the age of Milady's city, a mile farther brought us to a very modern feature of London, a feature of the city that was squarely within Mr. Claussen's area of expertise.

"Look here, girls! London Docks! These are recently built, constructed within the last two years. These are the finest docks to be found anywhere in Europe—in the world for that matter. See the size of those warehouses? They are enormous, are they not? Those large ones just there are rented by the Crown to store mountains of tobacco. Those over there are filled with sugar, tea, spices, wool, drugs and all assortments of goods, too many to mention. These here contain huge mixing vats for making wine. Look beyond. See the wagons loaded with grapes and fruit."

Enormous structures indeed, and the amount of river traffic going to and from these warehouses was unbelievable. Mr. Claussen instructed the oarsmen to head into the basin for a ways, while he continued to speak in an excited manner that was most unlike him. He was certainly cheerful.

"During the past four or five years, a total of four large docks have been constructed here on the river. There is the London Dock, which as you have seen is very nice, and of course the Surrey Dock. More importantly though, there is the East India Dock, which encompasses some eighty acres and adjoins the West India Dock, the place of our arrival and most certainly the largest dock of all, covering some three hundred acres all told. Together, they have assured England her command of the seas and have made her the most powerful and profitable shipping port in the world. Now, if you look carefully...right...over... *there!* See the vermilion ship? See it? That is the REBECCA, and that is the vessel we shall soon board. Do you see it girls?"

"Where? Where, Milord?" I struggled to make out this ship among the thousand masts before me. "I can't find it, Milady. Where is it, Mr. Claussen? Where is it?" I was young and momentarily forgotten as Mary, Lady Rebecca, and Mr. Claussen busily engaged themselves in sighting the ship.

"It is there, Elizabeth. Do you not see it?" He and Lady Rebecca pointed into the thicket of masts, yards, and rigging. "There, there, it's right over there!"

"Where?" I stood up in the boat and put a fright into Milady.

"Sit down, Elizabeth! I shan't have you falling overboard."

"But, I couldn't see it."

"I guarantee you will see nothing from the bottom of the basin."

"Don't fret child. You'll have all the sight of it you wish in a few more hours." Mr. Claussen consoled me.

I saw nothing. Our passing of the channel that entered into London Docks offered only a brief view, and within moments all hopes of my seeing the REBECCA vanished in our wake. I was truly disappointed, but it didn't last long. It was forgotten as soon as the next sight was offered up to us. And what a sight it was.

"The Tower of London!" I gasped, somewhat fearful. *Everyone* knew about the Tower of London. "It's huge! It's scary."

"You have nothing to fear as long as you are on the outside, child. So behave yourself, you hear."

"Yes, Milady." I kept mum all the while we were ferried past the walled structure with its enormous white tower. Just being near it was enough to keep me in line.

We were soon upon a large waterside structure called the Customs House, but I was infinitely more interested in the bridge of London as we approached it. My eyes were glued to its arches until the distractions of a chorus of screaming voices reached out across the water to overwhelm me.

"This is the Billingsgate *fist* market," Milady announced with a grin and a sense of demented pride. Her play on words rang truer than the fish market it actually was. It appeared to me more like the Billingsgate brawl, a free-for-all between the lot of England's old ladies and fetid fishmongers. What a raucous! In the middle of the fray were barrels and crates chocked full of every seafood that could come to mind. There were mountains of cod, sole, flatfish, whiting, and oysters, to name just a few. There were rows upon rows of smoked, dried, and cured fish of every description hanging above the maze of old wooden stalls. Like flipping through pages of a book, I could only briefly glimpse the whole of it, for I was compelled to pay attention to Milady as well, who continued to speak on the most interesting aspects of her town and its sights.

"Girls, before you is the most famous bridge in the world. Surely you have heard its name—*London Bridge*. This bridge of stone was built almost six hundred years ago. Twelve hundred and something—I think ten. Isn't it remarkable that something that impressive was built so long ago and still stands today? Before it was stone, there was a wooden bridge that stood in its place even longer, for almost a thousand years. Can you imagine—*a thousand years?* It is difficult to believe anything could exist for such a long period of time." Lady Rebecca was pointing out features of the structure and beaming with pride.

The whole of it was a climactic scene, and it held Mary and my attention steadfast as the oarsmen rowed our boat into the shadow of the great structure. It was magnificent. Mr. Claussen added to the conversation.

"Remarkable she is. You might also find it interesting to know that the bridge marks the indisputable end of passage for seafaring vessels going upriver along the Thames. For as grand as she may be, her arches are too low for those lofty masts upon seagoing ships."

In our riverboat we easily slipped underneath its arches, and made for the steps leading up to the Old Swan Inn just the other side. Here we would climb the embankment. My eyes were wandering every which way, and Lady Rebecca and Mary both were warning me to keep my attention focused on my feet, lest I fall into the river and drown. It wasn't easy for me to comply, for everywhere I turned there was activity. There were people and buildings, tall buildings, rows of buildings, buildings that stretched out as far as the eye could see. *This was London!* This was London! If only my brothers and sisters could have seen it!

Without forewarning, Mr. Claussen turned about as if he had specifically heard Lady Rebecca's warning to me, and before I knew it, he took hold of me under my arms and lifted me free of the boat. I wrapped my arms tightly around his neck and found myself at once tense in this close encounter. He didn't set me

167

down directly, as I had expected, but held me to his chest for some time, longer than I thought necessary. At first my breathing was short and rapid, for his embrace thoroughly unnerved me. Then as I calmed down, I was filled with a feeling of wondrous contentment. To my dismay, he lowered me to the ground. I looked up at him, and he met my eyes. Something subtle passed between us. I had never experienced a sensation quite the same, but the feeling stayed with me for a very long time.

When I was forced to return my attention to those things about me, I focused upon the goings on a few steps down the bank. For there, milling about in the shadow of the bridge and darting into the light long enough to be chased away by passersby, or those employed by either the inn or the fish market, was a motley gang of young children. It was made up of boys for the most part with a girl here and there. They were of all ages, some younger than I, others as old as Mary. I am not sure if it was the activity or the distasteful appearance of their dress that so transfixed both Mary and me. Plainly, we stood staring at them. They were running about the banks picking their way through the mud, the trash, and the crowds, then disappearing within the sanctuary of the sewer whenever angry merchants bolted for them.

Lady Rebecca took notice of our fixation and came to us.

"What is it you find so interesting, girls?"

Mary raised her arm and unabashedly pointed at the boys. "Those boys are a dreadful-looking lot. Look how filthy they are, it's a disgrace. And what is that they carry on the sticks? Huh! Oh…my…word!" Mary gasped, "Are those rats?"

"They are mudlarks," Lady Rebecca stated.

"No, Milady, those are rats, I am certain!" I exclaimed. My eyes were as wide as saucers, not unlike Mary's. The dead rodents were impaled upon the pointed ends of the sticks, and the sight of it was utterly revolting. It was highly improper for me

168

to correct Lady Rebecca, but due to my profound distraction and lack of experience, Milady let it pass.

"What you say is true, Elizabeth. Those are rats skewered on the sticks. It is the boys who are called mudlarks. They spear the rats for food."

"Food for what?" I asked innocently enough.

"Food so they might eat," Lady Rebecca answered. Mary's jaw dropped instantly.

"You mean eat *those!*" She pointed again. "You mean eat *those!* They're going to eat them? I'd rather be caught dead than eat rats. Ugh!" Mary was horrified. She shuddered, her face a twisted contortion, not unlike my own.

I was listening to Mary as she blurted out her revulsion, but my focus moved past her and toward Lady Rebecca. While Mary was gawking at the boys who were standing in the shadows of the bridge, I saw the unmistakable look of disdain move across Milady's face as she considered Mary from the side. It was a look all children learn early in life. Her eyes raised above Mary's head to look at me. She said nothing. Instead, she turned and called out to the boys. They were quick to congregate, for she appeared a lady of obvious standing, a person bound to have something to spare.

"Good morning, boys," she called out.

"Good morning, Milady." They all responded in kind.

"Have you boys been working hard today?"

"Yes, Milady." Again they answered as a group.

"And what have you to show for it? Have you found anything of value? Have you anything to sell? Anything that might fetch a price?"

The boys quieted down. One stepped forward. "I got this here." He held up a small piece of cloth about the size of half one's palm.

"I got this." Another held up a short length of twine, about eight inches long. Another held up his arm and dangled a fragment of a fish net impaled by his fingers.

I looked down at their bare legs, and was mystified by the scars they sported below their knees, especially about their ankles and just above. I thought them to be diseased or possibly they were the marks of their gang. I tugged at Lady Rebecca.

"Milady, did you see the marks on their ankles?"

"Yes. I saw them."

"Why do they look like that?"

"Rat bites."

"Rat bites?" I repeated. I was uncertain of what she meant. I kept looking at the rats on the sticks, and then the connection was made. The scars were from rat bites. *Rat bites!* My blood ran cold and it wasn't warmed any by the ensuing conversation.

"Have you all eaten today?" Lady Rebecca inquired of the boys There were some nays among the bunch, but the majority claimed to have eaten.

"And what was on the table?" With this the boys laughed.

"Fish guts! Rats!" They all chimed in.

"Jokers you are. All of you."

"Fish guts and rats!" They howled.

"Why would you eat such stuff?" The boys simmered down. They looked at each other, then back at Lady Rebecca.

"What else is there—*leg of lamb?*" one asked. The others roared.

"My Mary here says she would rather die than eat a rat. What do you say to that?" The children's faces went emotionless and they stood quieted, when an older boy, not nearly as amused as his younger counterparts, stepped forward from the group. Looking squarely at Mary with a searing intensity in his eyes, he addressed her.

"I'd say dyin' ain't never been that easy, Mary. You never been hungry or ya'd know well the taste o' rat shit an' worse long 'fore ya'd know the blessin' o' the grave. That's whu'd I'd say. Whu'd *you* have for breakfast, dearie?"

His eyes never backed down and Mary was forced to step back. She turned away and the boy moved back through the crowd of boys. Mr. Claussen had moved in closer upon sight of the older boy, fearing mischief. He wasn't as nearly at ease as was Lady Rebecca. She could relate to these impoverished souls; it was something understood.

She turned to Mary, but said nothing. Mary's eyes were downcast and misted over, for she was very good in heart, and knew at once the arrogance she had conveyed. She was deeply embarrassed by these truths presented to her, embarrassed to have it pointed out so harshly by the boy. I understood well, this was to be a lesson directed toward both of us. Lady Rebecca raised Mary's chin toward her. Mary's face was glowing red.

"I trust by the look in your eyes, you see the error of your judgment and the stupidity of your words."

"Yes, Milady."

"I know of nothing you have done, no task, no marvelous deed, no payment out of hand that should warrant the place you hold in life. If I should so choose to exchange the two of you for two of them, I am certain they would never quip that they were above eating the rats of the sewer."

In shame, Mary bowed her head even lower if that could have been possible. Lady Rebecca's words cut deep into a gentle heart, and Mary began to shake as she fought to restrain sobs that gushed forth. I watched the tears slip off her cheek, falling to her feet. I felt terrible, but I couldn't cry for her, because I was horrified to think Lady Rebecca might have considered exchanging me for a mudlark. I kept looking at the speared rats and scarred legs, and wished only to leave both the bridge and the lesson. I wasn't so sure about London.

Lady Rebecca called out to the older boy, who came as beckoned, and she handed him a stack of coins. She made him promise to spend it fairly among the thirteen, and assured him we would return to this very spot and ask if he had done as she ordered. The boy knew better than to cross the powerful, and there was but little fear in Lady Rebecca's mind about what course he would take. I, on the other hand, endured even more fear at the dismal news we would return this way and again face the risk of being exchanged a second time.

The incident was nearly over, hastened to finality by Mr. Claussen when he called out to an unsuspecting father of a nearby family that was also foraging along the embankment. He opened his purse and quietly gave the wide-eyed man a few pieces of gold, then asked, "What will you do with it, my friend?" The man stared at him in utter disbelief.

"I believe I'll purchase a boat an' net. My family should never go without food again."

"A wise decision. See to it that before you sell your catch, you give something of it to the needy."

"Aye, that I will, Milord, ya 'ave my word on it. I promise. Are ya with the church then, a man o' God or the likes, Milord?"

"No sir, nothing of the kind I assure you."

"Is there—." The stranger was about to ask if there was something Mr. Claussen needed in return, but Lady Rebecca interrupted him.

"Don't you believe it, sir. Is there anything that is not controlled by the hand of God?"

"No, Milady, I don' b'lieve so. At least not this day, I'm certin' o' that."

"Then it is possible Christopher's hand is the hand of God, doing God's will. Do you not agree?"

"It surely would seem to be, Milady."

"I agree. Now go to your family and give thanks to the Lord."

"Yes, Milady. Thank-you, thank-you. I must tell my wife. If she weren't here t' see me talkin' t' ya, she'd say I stoled it, pure an' simple. She ain't gonna know what t' make of this. Hah! Ha hah! Who'd believe it? Ha hah!"

The stranger trotted back to his wife and children, who were standing motionless, concerned about the encounter between their man and the highborn. Christopher turned to Lady Rebecca.

"I am uncertain as to whether you were given to me in order that I might find happiness or that I might find further guilt about my station in life."

"What difference does it matter as long as it serves God's needs, the poor, and your conscience? Would you take it upon yourself to help these unfortunates without the Lord's prompting?"

"I would hope it be my way. However, I confess that the business of the day generally blinds me to such matters."

"Imagine how much clarity one gains viewing the world through the clutches of poverty as opposed to purse, my love."

"You are making me feel shameful, Rebecca."

"Then I beg you forgive me, Christopher, for I know you are generous and of good heart. That is why I married you. Besides, many men have the ability to go among the poor and distribute what they might, but only a rare breed have the ability to produce

173

enough, that something extra of it might be given away. Do what you do best, Christopher. You make your fortune and I will give it away."

"Oh, now that is priceless. I work myself to the bone, and you give it away. That strikes me as somewhat unfair. I rather think you should do the work and I will give it away. I might like that part better," he teased.

Lady Rebecca took the hand she held and turned it over. She kneaded the soft skin of his palm.

"How hard have you worked for it, my dear?" Christopher retracted his hand at once. He was visibly caught off guard. The act reminded him of time he had been caught red-handed partaking in a farce at the West Indies. She had inspected his hands then. He looked at us with an expression of embarrassment.

"Well, girls, I feel we all three are in the doghouse." He put his arm around Mary to cheer her up; and we walked up toward the inn, a troupe in despair, but still able to laugh at our short-comings. Lady Rebecca followed, laughing as well.

TWENTY-THREE

We put the lessons of the morning behind us. In no manner did I feel Lady Rebecca was harsh or cruel. In matters of benevolence, she was a driving force. She was a person of action, a person who performed the deeds that others only talked about. She was of a heart that knew no boundaries when it came to helping others. Nothing would upset her more than to see a person look down upon the unfortunate.

Milady had made her point, and she had no desire to revisit the issues surrounding the incident; however, the episode ranked as one of my first great lessons about life—a lesson I knew would be with me as long as I lived. I was beginning to understand what it meant to be fortunate and to appreciate the blessings in life I possessed. I couldn't possibly know of all that surrounded me in the way of wealth, but I could plainly see the misery that filled the lives of others. I was developing a sense of life's injustices. It was the first time I wished with all my heart to help another.

I doted and fussed over Mary. She would have preferred that I did nothing to remind her of the event, but she knew it had caused me pain to see her hurt, and she didn't rebuke me for my actions. Her spirit was soon to return, for Lady Rebecca was most fond of Mary as well, and would never have allowed her day to be ruined by the lesson given.

So, having enjoyed a good breakfast, feeling fully refreshed and in high spirits, we bid farewell to the patrons of the Old Swan Inn and then removed ourselves to a coach called to our service. We hoped to crisscross the city and listen to the wealth of knowledge that Lady Rebecca had amassed during her years as a youth on these streets. It was impossible not to be interested, for Milady was so exuberant in her manner and so impatient to share these highlights of her life that we hung on her every word. Unlike the night before, the morning was clear and enabled me to see far and wide, taking in all that Milady pointed out for our benefit.

Our journey was surely going to take us through the times past, both of London and Lady Rebecca; and I prepared myself to absorb all to be said about the many monuments, parks and palaces, and places of legend and lore. Brimming with antici-pation, I tried to sit still upon the comfortable seat of the coach as we headed up toward the top of Fish Street Hill at what seemed to me to be an agonizingly slow pace. At last we came to our first stop; a place called the Pudding Lane Monument, or the 'Monument'.

"What's it for?" I asked.

"In memory of the great fire of sixteen-sixty-six. It burned out the heart of London. Over eighty churches and thirteen thousand homes burned to the ground. See, up there? See the bronze flame?"

"Did all the people die that lived in those homes?"

"No, it seems nearly miraculous, but only six or seven were known to have perished. I have no doubt there were probably more, but not according to record. The first one to die was a maid servant not unlike yourself."

"Ohhh." It was a terrible thought.

"How did it start?" asked Mary.

"The king's own baker. He lived on the next street over, Pudding Lane. If the monument were to be laid on its side, the tip of it would touch the place where the baker's house once stood. It was his maiden servant that died. She didn't dare climb out onto the roof, but for her fear of height, and so she perished in the blaze. See those Latin inscriptions on the base? They tell the whole story. Would you girls like to go to the top and see the city? The view is beyond description."

"Oh, yes! Let's go at once. I wish to see the city. Let's go up!" I said.

"What!" said Mr. Claussen, horrified.

"Oh, come along, Christopher. It's a great view from up there. You will love it. Girls, tell Christopher how you wish to see the city from high above."

"Oh, please, sir! Please, let's do so. 'Tis certain to be fun," Mary exclaimed.

"What could possibly be fun about that? Sounds like a tremendous lot of work to me. Three or four hundred steps on a full stomach, going 'round 'n 'round, getting dizzy and all. I don't know. I think maybe you should all go and enjoy yourselves while I stay and watch over the coach to preserve our ride. I insist you take your time and enjoy yourselves. I will be fine right here where I am. I will wait, thank-you."

Lady Rebecca looked at Mr. Claussen, positively dumbfounded. "How is it, my love, you can climb to the clouds on the spindly strands of a shroud in the face of a hard blow—a full gale no less, a hundred feet above the decks before a storm that would sweep me off my feet!"

"That's different—."

"No, no, listen girls. All the while his ship is pitching back and forth, side to side unto its beam ends, and flinging all that is unsecured over the board—this, mind you, at any time day or night, hungry or full, sun or snow, while freezing or sweating. Yet—he can't fathom scaling these few steps with his wife and two young girls? *Lazy, is he not?*"

"Lazy!" Christopher repeated with indignation.

"If ever I saw such a thing."

"I hardly accept *that* as one of my traits."

"I see no *ladies* shilly-shallying here."

"Shilly-shallying! We shall see who shilly-shallies when we are half way up, my darling."

Mr. Claussen immediately stepped from the coach in haste. He offered Lady Rebecca his hand to help her down, and just before she stepped out, she turned to us and winked with a smile.

It goes without saying that within the first ten steps of our climb, Mr. Claussen transformed himself into a dastardly ol' captain of the seas, a man with so much salt in his veins (as he put it) that by merely touching food, he preserved it for all time. He drove us before him, and at the slightest sign of weariness, hounded us to step lively and be cheerly about it, he wished not, 'to see an old sailor among the lot'. It was all a great deal of fun, and I was worn out more for the laughter than the exertion of the climb. At the top, Mary and I were utterly thrilled, so too was Mr. Claussen who eventually agreed the climb was worth it. We could see clear back to the London Dock and Mr. Claussen was convinced he could see the vermilion hull of the REBECCA. The view was indeed everything Lady Rebecca had promised.

We returned to our coach, and Mr. Claussen instructed the driver to head straight up Gracechurch where we stopped briefly at the large market of Leadenhall. From here we headed west along Cornhill and headed past the Bank of England and the Exchange. It was obvious that Mr. Claussen was very familiar with this area.

"He knows his way about the inside of the bank, better than I know the streets of London, and I have lived here the whole of my life," Milady teased.

We continued on westward, traveling along Cheapside until we reached the north side of the grounds that surrounded the wondrous St. Paul's Cathedral. Lady Rebecca insisted on being driven around the church a number of times before she was fully satisfied with seeing it. Sadly, I lacked the wit to appreciate the architectural beauty and the immeasurable amount of work that went into its creation. I was merely astounded by the size of it, and the way its spires reached to the sky. I listened to Mr. Claussen and Lady Rebecca speak of Mr. Wren, a famous man who drew up the plans for the church and many of London's other famous buildings, and about how he was buried beneath the church floor near its center. It made me wonder how much the church weighed.

From St. Paul's, we continued west along Ludgate Hill and on to Fleet Street where we passed by the steeple of St. Brides. Fleet changed into the Strand where we passed the church of St. Clements Danes and soon thereafter, St. Mary Le Strand, each and every one a wonder to see. I had never seen so many churches in one place in my life. Across from St. Mary Le

Strand was a magnificent Italian house called Sommerset. We continued on along the Strand and turned northerly onto Cockspur; then we traveled a large square, heading north on Regent's, then west past the fine shops of Piccadilly, south on St. James passing the King's palace, and finally east on Pall Mall.

It was pointless for me to keep up with all we saw. I was unable to either digest or sort out the myriad of shops and structures that flooded my view. London was big, it was great, it was magnificent—it was too much. It was fast becoming a blur, and I began to daydream about what America would be like. At first, I thought that Lady Rebecca was thrilled to see all we passed. Then I came to understand she was actually sad, for she knew it might be the last time ever her eyes would fall upon the city of her youth, the place she called home. I felt sorry for her.

Pall Mall caught my attention only because it led us to St. James Park. I took in a completely different view of St. James Park during daylight as opposed to the eerie, foggy night before, and it brought to mind the gift Lady Rebecca had left for Jennifer. I imagined it was generous and that Jennifer was very happy this morning.

"Do you believe Jennifer is happy this morning, Milady?" Her eyes darted in my direction. She said nothing, maybe not wishing for Mr. Claussen to know what she had been up to last night, but her eyes expressed her thoughts and she smiled at me.

Our ride through the park was relaxing and a welcome relief from the traffic upon the city streets. About the time I was convinced I had seen it all and there was simply no room left in my brain to accept another wonder, we happened upon the Abbey of Westminster and the hall. We stopped a moment to watch the masons working on the hall. By the look on her face, I could see Lady Rebecca was amazed at the amount of change that had taken place in just the past couple of years while she had lived in Sweden. There were many things new to her as well.

179

We followed the flow of the river back to where we started, riding a good stretch along the embankment until we reached the Tower of London. On one hand, Milady delighted in telling some of the grizzly stories behind the tower, but on the other she was disheartened by the many innocent people that fell prey to a corrupt system.

Our tour of London lasted for the better part of six hours, at which point it was deemed necessary by Mr. Claussen to proceed to the London Docks and await the arrival of the orphans. Time was drawing near. The driver was instructed to return, and on the way back to the docks we drove though Stepney. Mary was given her own opportunity to see and hear the activity of the street. This time it was up to everyone else to 'stay to the wall' as we raced by. This time, at Lady Rebecca's request, the coach traveled down one street in particular, the street where Lady Rebecca lived as a child. We passed by the orphanage. It appeared bleak to my eyes and left me with an uncomfortable sensation of loneliness.

The day was memorable in many ways, but for two reasons especially. One was for the lesson of life learned, which I believed would remain with me always. The other reason was most unusual, and far more difficult to explain. It marked the first time I had ever spent my day in the company of Mr. Claussen as something of a guest. I was allowed to be more than a servant girl.

I found him to be very attractive in character. I found him irresistible, and I felt myself very much drawn to the man. I tried to stay close by his side because I wanted to know first-hand what it was about him that brought me so much pleasure. I wanted to know why Lady Rebecca was so taken by him. I wanted him to notice me. I wanted to be the center of his attention. Did I wish him to be my father? Did I possess a subconscious need to have the security and love that only a father could give? I didn't know. I didn't understand my feelings for him other than to say they were overwhelming, too powerful for a man I didn't know and mostly feared. I knew he was a man that controlled my life.

TWENTY-FOUR

The city, now falling behind us, was disappearing into the realm of memories. The coach found its way to the massive expanse of London Dock, and hoped to work its way safely through the throngs of people crowding the way to the export piers. We inched forward past the import docks and made our way to the south side, where departing ships were burdened with cargoes heading out to the rest of the world.

It was then that we came into full view of our ship. This time I had no trouble spotting it, for it was two times the size of anything else on the water. Even I could appreciate the significance of the ship before us. It was unlike anything else at the dock; for one thing, it was *red!* I thought it to be enormous and by far prettier than anything else in sight. I dropped the cabin window to better see the whole of it, and the conversation of the crowd outside flooded into the cabin. Everywhere talk was in tones of awe and disbelief, and the raves proved to me that I knew a special ship when I saw one.

"She is of nineteen hundred burthern," one man claimed, while others shook their heads in amazement.

"Three-masted, d' likes of which ya don' see lessin' it'd be a ship o' d' Crown, a bloomin' man-o'-war."

"Isn't she fine? Ain't a coil o' hemp on 'er. All manila stem t' stern, first-class vessel that one is," cried another.

"Aye an' spy 'er sticks. Ya know she'll be carryin' full courses o' gallant, royal, an'...an'...what's that I see there 'bove the royals? Bloomin' eh! She's rigged with another set of yards! N'er seen such a thing before. Can ya imagine 'er looks under sail! A true three-masted sky sailor, she'd be."

"What a lady to behold!" said another.

"Aye aye! I dare say, an' I'll wager she'll better a half cable in length!" challenged a seasoned jack.

The sailors gawked and pointed in every direction.

"Look at all these people! Could they be here to see the ship? Is that possible?" Milady asked Mr. Claussen.

"Oh, indeed it is possible. Have you not always said that this is the land of sailors, my love? Believe these men know a fine ship when they see one, and they will stop everything to stare at her for hours as though she were a young maiden."

All about our coach, everywhere I looked, townspeople mingled, crowding each other for open space on the docks whereby they might better see clearly and feast their eyes upon the ship's resplendency. Mr. Claussen was gushing with pride.

"Have no doubts, these wives conceal faces of jealousy and nervous hearts behind those masks of admiration. They come with their fear arm in arm at their husbands' sides knowing full well, given the slightest opportunity, they would lose their men to such a fair lady of the sea. A sailor seldom gets the opportunity to work this fine a vessel. He wonders in his heart what she is like. Is she full of life? Will she sail like the wind when he caresses her? I assure you these women have good reason to fear."

To my young eyes, the ship sported all the activity and makings of a country fair. It was so large I could barely comprehend it was afloat. Looking fore and aft and sighting with my finger, I traced the bright manila lines that streaked about the masts to angle upward high above me, drawing my eyes skyward to follow them to their ends at the trucks.

There, in sharp contrast, blackened lines of standing rigging sprayed downward, spreading out like tufts of hair from the dizzying heights of the masts, topmasts, and topgallant masts. Above all of this flew the Blue Peter, unfurled in a breeze that we were unable to enjoy on the dock.

"Look! At the very top a blue flag, Milord. I like that." I thought it was perfect as it wagged about in the light gusts of wind.

"Do you? It has meaning, Elizabeth. It waves a message to the sailors moving about us and those few off having their last pint of ale that we shall soon set sail. They can see her calling them back to ship from way down the docks, and they know they better get a move on."

The shrouds were hauled taut from their masts and bolsters by purchase and deadeyes and then secured and set up fast to the chainplates mounted to the brilliant vermilion hull, a color not unlike Lady Rebecca's coach. The hull was designed to show a line of gun ports, which stretched the full length of the ship. Their hatches were painted in stark black to be highly visible and thus ward off pirates. They were now open, their hatches raised, but no cannon were visible. Instead, they were being put to good use as light portals and points of entry for numerous small stores.

Running parallel above their line, the ship's bulwarks were painted white inboard, as was her taffrail, all her stanchions, and much of her trim about the quarterdeck and forecastle. A variety of other details about her were highlighted in black or matching vermilion. The pilothouse, forecastle, quarterdeck beams, companionways, and planking, as well as the towering masts were done up in a varnish, rich as the color of honey. They were much more attractive than the surrounding masts on our neighboring vessels, which were scraped and oiled in the traditional way.

Finally, holding me spellbound for the longest time, there was at the base of her bowsprit, carved gloriously into a tree of teak, a maiden of the seas with hair thrown to the wind and flowing freely across the folds of her gown. It draped heavily over the bows, and enshrined the trailboards upon which there stood, chiseled and emblazoned in gold, the name REBECCA. It gave me gooseflesh just to look at it. I was impressed beyond words, but have no doubt; I was not alone. While I sat there with my mouth silently agape, Milady provided the sound.

"My word!" Milady held her gloved hand up to her mouth. "Is that not the most spectacular vessel you have ever seen?"

"Yes, Milady." We agreed wholeheartedly. I for one had seen little of ships, let alone red ones.

"Ahh. Bless my soul. At last you can see her worth." Mr. Claussen beamed.

"I cannot believe this is the same ship!" Lady Rebecca was astonished. "I recall accompanying you twice to the shipyards, while you attended to your business with the chandler and reviewed progress on its construction. Once, I remember it was in the shipway, and the last time it was in the fitting-out berth. It didn't show like this, Christopher. It never took my breath away."

"My love, first we must build muscle into a ship, then we dress her in finery."

"Maybe it was the weather—the winter season. You know how dismal it can be. I mean it looked so bleak and gray on the water. As I recall, the ship had no warmth to it. To me it appeared cold and massive, and barren at best. It was impressive, but in a repulsive sort of manner, I'm afraid. I apologize, Christopher. It meant so much to you, but it held absolutely no attraction for me whatsoever. Was I cruel? I didn't mean to be. I know how proud of it you are. I should have said something good about it, I know, but it certainly didn't appear as thus."

"Oh, I might have had a painful moment or two." Mr. Claussen inserted his knuckle between his teeth and bit down upon it humorously to signify his pain. "You had a way of disappointing me at times. I won't deny it." He bit down again. "But I did my best to see it from your point of view." Now, he grew serious. "I tried to understand that in your eyes this was the vessel that would whisk you away to strange lands; the ship that would remove you from London, from Sweden and the security of the Claussen estate. I understand for you it represents new and strange things, most of which bring fear and nervousness. I accept your apology."

"I could see the thought of these travels were not nearly as frightful to you as for me. Just speaking of it still fills me with worry. I keep thinking, I am leaving all this, and for what, to be pitched about upon the open sea?" She turned to us. "I confess, girls; it did nothing other than depress my spirit. I simply couldn't see all the fascination it held for him. I often wondered if ships could drive a man mad. It seemed his only obsession, truly it did. I am positive he forgot he was married."

"Dear, dear, Rebecca! *You* are my only obsession. Why would you ever think differently? Is it because of times such as this moment when I must leave you, this moment when there is so many issues that require my attention, this very moment when I must beg to be excused so I might return shortly and give you word on when we shall board." Christopher was grinning broadly as he teased Lady Rebecca.

"Yes, yes, all those things, and many more, I am certain. Now, go, go." Milady waived him off. "Do what you must then come when you wish. I shall be waiting—*patiently.*"

Mr. Claussen exited our company laughing heartily. As soon as he stepped away from the coach, he was met by a group of men dressed in business attire. They all seemed to converse simultaneously as they drifted toward the ship leaving a whirlwind of discussion in their wake. Lady Rebecca watched the men walk away. She resigned herself to accepting the wait at hand and so settled back to study the ship.

"Ladies, have you ever noticed that a sailor's concept of a bosom is most decidedly different than that of a woman's? Do you see what I mean?"

185

"Yes, Milady," Mary answered. I looked back at the ship and noted the gleaming vermilion coach chocked and strapped into place within REBECCA's waist.

"He certainly likes red!" I offered.

"Yes, well, there's a story behind that. Someday I will tell you. In any event, I would have never imagined red or anything like it. I only see these things as plain Janes, gray and dismal. He sees them in full regalia, jeweled and crowned and glorious. When he looks at the unfinished hull he sees a lady of the seas. And isn't that exactly what she has become? Look at her all done up the way she is. Look at how the men stare. She draws them 'a callin' from miles around. I swear there isn't a place left for feet without fear of being run over. A woman should be so lucky." Lady Rebecca shook her head in amazement.

I looked across this scene vibrant with life and motion. Men were hollering and boys running to order, jacks and stevedores moved up and down the gangplanks, and 'round and 'round the docks like ants circling a cake. In a shipyard adjacent to the docks, riggers were tethered to lines suspended from ahigh, mimicking little spiders as they rose and fell. Their feet searched out the web-like rattlins of shrouds, while they tarred everything they could reach with their buckets of tallow or hot pine resin and oakum.

At our own dock, ropes were tossed, blocks rove, tackles shifted, and cargo lifted, lowered, lashed and chocked, heaved to the left and hauled to the right. Casks of wine and liqueur, water, salt beef, and more were being rolled about and put in place for hoisting. A stream of wagons rolled down the dock, each waiting their turn to unload barrels of whale oil upon the dock. I counted at least a hundred. Hoist horses strained at harness and tackle as the collections of barrels and other goods were raised from the dock and moved slowly up the skids, or swung overhead by the booms that brought them to their final resting place in the hold.

The ship absorbed it all like a parched sponge. It was most entertaining, this flurry of congestion and commotion, and I was both hypnotized and invigorated by the excitement of it all. Over a course of days, the ship's holds commenced to be filled and readied for the business to be done in the Americas. It was also Mr. Claussen's concern to see to it that his stateroom was put into order down to the smallest detail; it being outfitted in replete accommodation for Lady Rebecca's every comfort. Now he was standing on the dock frequently looking back over his shoulder toward town.

"I'll wager Christopher is discussing the issue of the orphans as we speak. He is watching for them. It won't be long now, girls." Milady raised her chin and released a breath of confidence. She folded her hands in her lap.

It was as if Mr. Claussen could read her very thoughts, for no sooner had her words been said, when he parted company with the master and made his way back along the crowded dock toward the coach. Looking up toward us, he motioned to Lady Rebecca, whose attention never seemed to leave him, so she might turn toward the street behind us that serviced these docks. In response, she slid across the coach, and leaning over me in a cloud of fragrance and frills, she stretched out to better observe from the coach window a disturbance some distance off.

It was an exceptional and entirely unexpected sight. Flowing onto the docks, there came a procession of six horse-drawn wagons loaded with children and what few worldly belongings to which they might lay claim. Yet, to see them was no easy task for although at last count there were only forty-nine children total, there were at least five hundred city folk walking alongside the wagons as they rolled toward the mooring. Mr. Claussen made his way back to the coach.

"Well then, my love, it appears as though the news of your intention to find good homes for these unfortunates abroad has raised a swell of compassion that crosses the whole of the city. Now, there is a collection of faces, rich, poor, mothers and fathers, ministers and maidens, the famous and the not so famous. Do you suppose they are all sharing in a common guilt?"

"Be nice, Christopher. These citizens appear to be filled with sympathy and remorse, and a desire to offer the children their hearts so they might remember the world they were leaving as a world that cared. I certainly prefer this over the hypocrisy of protesting their departure when nothing else is offered these luckless orphans, save for empty promises of a meaningful life in the already overcrowded, poverty-stricken back-alleys of this city, no matter how much I love it."

The people wanted to believe the children would find a brighter future, and so they wished them luck and showered them with small gifts, foods, and sweets to take with them on their voyage. The display of generosity moved Lady Rebecca to tears, for she understood these people. She was raised among them. She had spent much of her life at the West Indies Tavern listening to their tales of hope and despair.

For whatever other reason, they were all here showing their feelings, and the children were beside themselves with glee. The orphans could see no farther than the present, for they had never been given reason to look beyond. The excitement was here and now, and being so starved for attention, it was altogether too much for their young minds to handle and so they became riotous and disorderly.

The procession slowed to a stop a couple of rods behind the coach. The city folk surged past the children and moved to form a great circle that surrounded the wagons and our coach as well. They stood many deep and bobbed back and forth as they looked over shoulders to see in our direction, while displaying their delight by expressions of laughter and joviality.

Lady Rebecca was astonished. She reached for her door to greet them and Mr. Claussen moved quickly to offer her assistance. In that manner of hers, which was so unpredictable, she asked him to help her upon the coachman's bench.

"What is it you wish to do, Rebecca?"

"I wish to be put upon the driver's seat as I have asked. Now be quick about it, Christopher, for there are many people here in our behalf."

The request was certain to have made him nervous, but with careful grip and a welcome hand from the driver, he lifted her atop the driver's bench, high above a rousing cheer from the crowd.

Milady was a breathtaking figure of beauty, a queen in her own right. She was in a class by herself, and stood tall to greet the rabble of raised faces. They grew silent. They were as surprised to see her take her position above them, as she was to see them arrive. She spoke with the song of a woman, but the strength of a man.

"Hello! Hello! Good day to all of you! I am overwhelmed! I am lost for words." The crowd applauded. "I must tell you that I am moved to tears by your display of affection for these children. For those of you who may not know, I too am an orphan. I can say from my heart with conviction that this moment of kindness and generosity shall be forever remembered in the hearts of these children, as well as my own. Go in peace knowing over half of these children have been spoken for. Thank you and God bless." She did well to maintain her composure, but the charged emotions of the moment misted her blue eyes even as a winning smile lit her face.

The crowd was bent on having a good time. They were in a generous frame of mind and appeared nearly as excited at the children. A rousing cheer went up. These were common folk and there was certain to be many among them who knew some version of the rags-to-riches story of the Lady Claussen. The stories endeared her to them. She was well known in these parts, having worked at the West Indies Inn as a table maiden from the time that she was twelve or so, until her engagement to Mr. Claussen.

A man approached, a stranger to me but apparently an acquaintance in good standing with Mr. Claussen, for he spoke freely outside my window in a personal manner.

"She is truly an angel, Christopher. She is decent and virtuous, and in spite of her good fortune, she never holds her head above her former friends. You can see how she gives these people hope and fills them with happiness and pride. They love to mention over tea how they recently rubbed elbows with the Lady Claussen. Poor as they might be, they believe she respects them, sir. They know she is born and bred of their blood and they understand; orphan or no orphan, she belongs to them. You are a very lucky man, sir. God has been much too good to you. Make sure the king doesn't find out about her." The men laughed.

Lady Rebecca looked down to see Mr. Claussen, who was now standing at her feet, looking up and studying her with that mixture of disbelief and pride that made her feel like his idol. He reached up for her.

"Rebecca! Take my hand, love. I will escort you aboard our ship and show you the cabin I have prepared for your journey. I spared no expense, and I pray you will be pleased, although…," he sighed, "compared to all of this, I fear it will prove an experience rather mundane." He made an effort to keep up appearances.

Lady Rebecca seemed to understand that behind her man's unshakable character there might be a little hurt, a burst bubble behind his bold blue eyes and stiff upper lip. Mr. Claussen had waited anxiously all morning for this special moment to arrive. He had mentioned it a number of times during breakfast and as we rode through the city afterward. I knew he was impatient to show her the ship. I was certain he never imagined anything could compete with this long-awaited day to present the ship built to honor the woman he loved. Yet, he found this moment overshadowed, pushed into the background by cheering crowds and well-wishers forcing another agenda.

Mary and I could see it in his eyes. His excitement was subdued. Lady Rebecca could read not only his eyes, but his thoughts and wishes, and she knew how to soothe him. She whispered in his ear as he lifted her down off the coach. The remark caught him by surprise and his smile was invigorated. She kissed him lightly in front of the crowd, a show of affection that left no mistake as to his position in her heart—an act no self-respecting person of upper class would display in public. But here and now, and in the midst of these people, she was cheered with approval. Mary started giggling.

"What's so funny?" I asked.

"Do you want to know what she said to him?"

"Yes! What was it?" I leaned forward, so as not to miss anything.

"She asked him if their bed was cozy." Mary started giggling again. Outwardly, I laughed along with Mary. Inwardly, I couldn't figure out what was so funny. Beds were always cozy.

Lady Rebecca turned to face us, and motioned for Mary and me to leave the coach and follow. She took Mr. Claussen's arm and led him to his ship of pride with Mary at her side and me in tow. His enthusiasm was infectious.

"Look at you!" Lady Rebecca laughed.

"What?"

"You are just like a little boy. A woman can tell just what a man was like as a boy by making him really happy or really angry. You men can never hide it."

"It may be true. It is true. I have all I can do to walk to the ship instead of run. All I know for certain is this: I want you to be thrilled."

191

TWENTY-FIVE

Mr. Claussen led us across the boarding plank toward Captain Ward, who introduced himself properly by welcoming us aboard and graciously committing himself to our service. He extended a supporting hand to Lady Rebecca, Mary, and myself. I looked to my right and saw the men covering up the Claussen coach. We turned to our left and I followed obediently as Mr. Claussen and Lady Rebecca strode leisurely down the waterway toward the quarterdeck.

We were obliged to stop every few feet in order that Mr. Claussen might point out with great satisfaction the numerous items wedged tightly within the holds. The hatches were both large and open. At the expense of Lady Rebecca's fright, by leaning over to peer inside, I was able to see the sailors moving about below along the gangways of the lower deck. Everything was chocked securely, and explanations were given on the dangers of loose stores in a high sea.

"I trust you recall I have said on many occasions, the REBECCA is a cargo ship by design. She was not meant to be a vessel of luxury and comfort. Yet, I am confident you will learn soon enough that when cargo ships are to be compared, she proves to surpass them all in beauty and accommodation. The crafts-manship in our cabin and the staterooms is superb. You will find it varied and generous in carving and relief. The cabins are fitted out in a fine selection of woods, oiled panels of oak, cherry, and satinwood. All of this has been added for your benefit, Rebecca, in order to make your journey more bearable. However, if I fail to meet with your satisfaction, I assure you that Captain Ward has thanked me profusely, as he has reaped many of the benefits for himself by way of my attempts to please you." The men laughed heartily.

"Aye aye, sir! I won't be denying it." In spite of his impeccable manner, he stood utterly glowing with pride to command so elegant a vessel. It would be safe to say that nearly every captain on the coast of England, and then some, had set foot aboard the REBECCA on the quiet by his invitation. The captain was sailing back home to America in style. Lady Rebecca understood his pleasure.

"As you can see for yourself, Captain Ward, Mr. Claussen spoils me rotten. I fear my character shall be ruined for good unless he pays a little less mind to my happiness. I can imagine that everything in my cabin will be nothing short of the finest that money can buy. It's Christopher's way." The captain smiled knowingly.

"I suppose I do go overboard, but I have learned this for certain; there are things money cannot buy. I cannot buy your love, my dear, and I cannot buy happiness, but you give me both freely."

"You sure know how to talk to a girl." Lady Rebecca pulled him in tight. She was looking about, maybe considering another kiss. She looked first at us, then beyond to see who might be watching at which point she happened to glance skyward.

"Oh! Look, there's Darrin!" Lady Rebecca pointed high into the yards.

I looked up and at once shuddered at the mere thought of someone perched so precariously at that height. It made me both dizzy and queasy just to look at him. However, I immediately understood Lady Rebecca's excitement in seeing this person, for he began to sing with such a robust voice that all those about stopped whatever occupied them and gave the man their ear. His song carried out across the docks.

I'm atoop th' toop gallant mast
T' see that th' gaskets be fast
Should th' sails come unfurled
Aboove th' whoole world.
Me time wit' th' Capt'n woon't last

"Ahoyeee, me Lady Rebecca!" High above her, he bowed, swinging his arm out in a great dramatic sweep. The captain saluted the man and laughed, then turned to Mr. Claussen.

"You were right. He is a character indeed."

"Isn't he though? I am pleased he is with us."

Lady Rebecca responded playfully in a male-like voice.

"Ahoy! Mr. O'Kurk!" She returned a vigorous wave and followed that with an exaggerated curtsy. Her gestures given to a common sailor instantly pleased all the jacks about the deck, and they demonstrated their approval by applauding her vigorously. That caught her by surprise and brought both a flush and a flash of her smile. Her beauty and charm was readily apparent to the men on the deck and the sense of a warm welcome was all about. It was her first encounter with the crew and it went well, dispelling any misgivings or talk of bad luck brought on by the presence of women aboard ship.

The ship had been substantially redesigned from the original plans in order to accommodate Lady Rebecca and the orphans. The newer design offered larger cabins, better access, and more privacy from the mates. As we approached the cabins, I took notice of the steps fitted flush with the bulwarks at each side of the quarterdeck. They offered one an approach to the higher elevation of the quarterdeck, which was an attractive place for a small person such as me to enjoy a view of the activity on deck. Just inboard of each set of steps was a door that offered entrance to the pilothouse and main cabins beneath the quarterdeck.

Next to each door, farther inboard was a glassed window facing forward. The beams and planks about the hatches and windows were done proper in a rich varnish.

Lady Rebecca and Mr. Claussen led the way as they stepped through the starboard doorway and entered the pilothouse. The captain stood aside courteously and encouraged Mary and me to enter before him. Moving aft, we followed Milady inside and entered a protected place in which to observe the workings of the ship. It provided ample view of the helm, the masts, sails, rigging, and deck. As I faced the stern, to my immediate left and leading below, was the starboard galleyway that descended forward into the galley situated below the main deck. This was also a way to access the ship's innards.

At my right shoulder, or larboard, there were two small windows. They faced inboard toward the center of the ship, giving view to the helmsman. The helm was situated amidships as one would expect, but it was surrounded by the quarterdeck, which was horseshoe-shaped and wrapped around the helmsman, offering him better protection from the elements.

Stepping farther aft, we turned a corner to our right, toward the center of the ship where four additional glassed windows were fitted to face forward, they being situated directly behind the helm. At the center of these windows was the bulk of the mizzenmast. Mr. Claussen informed Lady Rebecca that it was very unusual to have the mizzenmast behind the helmsman. It was a peculiar design found only recently in England. He chose the design because it offered a more spacious layout for the cabins and her comfort. Now, I stood at the center of the ship alongside the mizzenmast and faced forward. Beneath the windows, to the right of the mast, to starboard, stood a desk with a large opened book upon its surface. It was the log and above it was a framed piece of black slate with writing in chalk upon its surface.

The four windows also provided light, which streamed past my shoulders and illuminated the corridor that led aft from the mizzenmast toward the stern and ended at the double doors of the Claussens' cabin. Four additional cabins flanked the corridor, two to starboard, two to larboard. One belonged to Captain Ward. One belonged to his officers. One belonged to the surgeon and the last was reserved for needs specific to the orphans.

Also flanking this corridor at its forward end were two additional staircases, again one fitted starboard and one larboard of the corridor, both leading down from the pilothouse. The steps descended aft, parallel to one another and entered the children's quarters, which were situated in steerage directly below the quarterdeck aftcabin and staterooms. The double staircase was another revision designed to facilitate the movement of children. As one group went topside on one staircase, another group would be free and unencumbered to go below decks on the opposing staircase. Considering the number of children on board, this would come as a welcome feature.

We moved aft along the dim corridor, at which time Mr. Claussen swung open the double doors to the Claussen cabin and immersed us in a flood of light. It poured in through numerous windows and washed over the polished wooden surfaces, striking fire to the gilded carvings found all about a most luxurious aftcabin. The number of windows, some with colored panes of glazing would certainly raise the spirits and provide a splendid view of any port o' call on the open sea.

Milady stood in the cabin doorway and there before her, like a mural, was a large painting of merchant ships moored in harbor at Bristol. It was secured to a blind that concealed their bed from view. The blind faced the double door entrance and stood before us some ten feet wide. Mr. Claussen didn't have to wait for Lady Rebecca's approval. Her face was aglow. She needn't have said anything as she marveled at her surroundings.

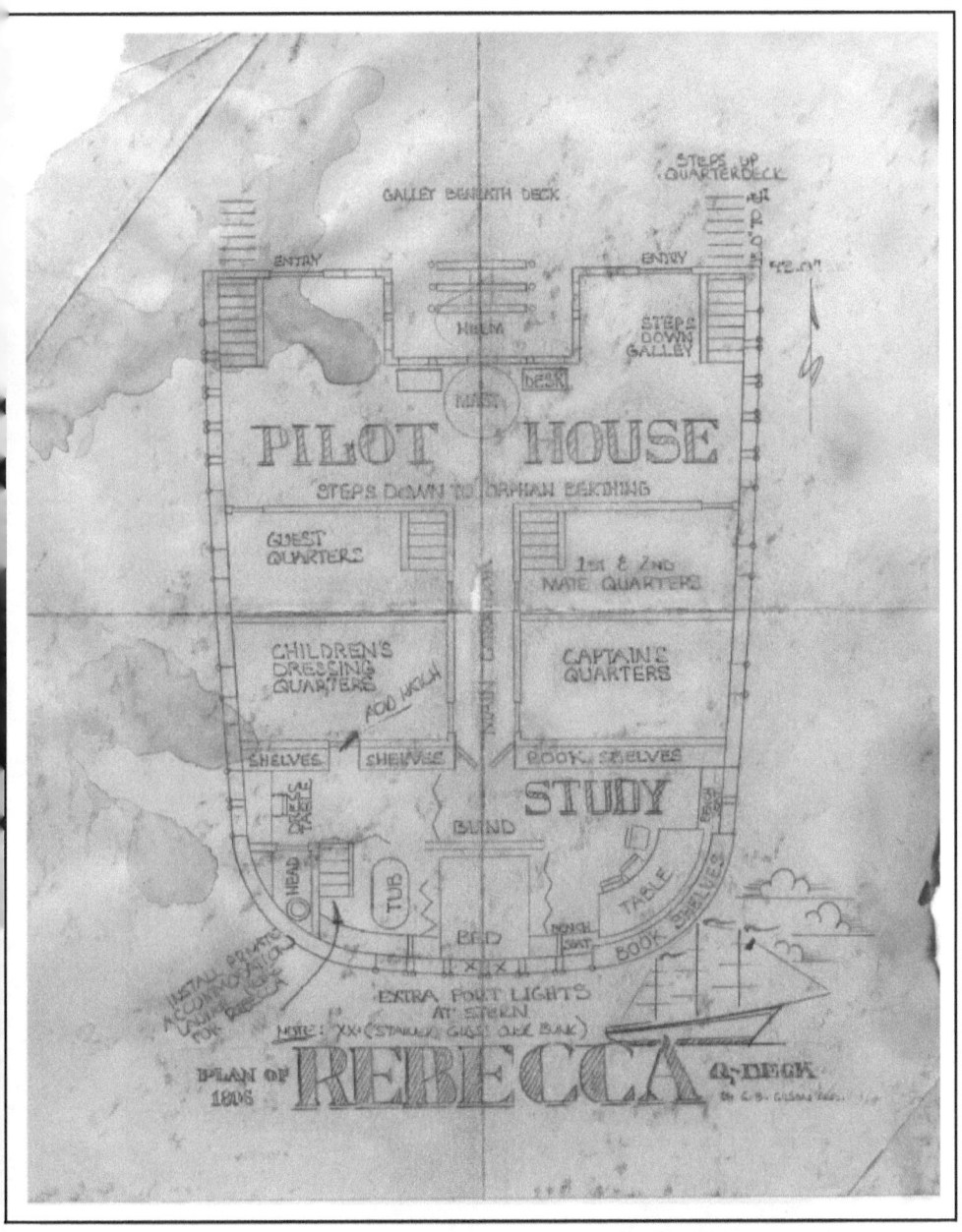

CHRISTOPHER'S NOTES ON REVISIONS FOR LADY REBECCAS'S
QUARTERDECK ACCOMMODATIONS

To our right, to larboard, was a dressing area against the ship-side with a private water closet just aft, it being situated in the corner of the cabin. Inboard of the water closet, along the stern was a large wood and brass tub. Between the tub, which was visible from where we stood, and the bed, which was hidden behind the painting, was a small hatch in the floor. It was lifted and secured open to reveal a private staircase, an accommodation ladder, which led below to the children's berthing in steerage. Just forward of the water closet in the corner, along the larboard shipside, was a nicely crafted dressing table with a comfortable chair and two large windows. They offered a splendid view to the outside and an abundance of light to the inside by which to prepare oneself.

Forward of the Claussen stateroom to larboard was the adjoining cabin that opened to provide an area for the children to collect themselves. Here, they could dress and undress for a bath; or it could be used for classroom study, for indoor play in foul weather, or at the very worse, for purposes of quarantine. Overall, the ship had been designed to afford Milady enough space to handle the children in a reasonable manner.

To our left as we faced the stern windows, all along the starboard bulkhead from the doorway to the shipside, and equal to impress, was a superb collection of books. It continued aft along the shipside covering every square inch of the hull as though it might have been a large tapestry. The books were grouped in classifications such as geography and trade, or shipping and seamanship. There were maps of the world and a bountiful assortment of novels for Lady Rebecca's pleasure and for the mates on board that could read.

Not to be overlooked were the shelves of books for children. Lady Rebecca aimed to see that books would accompany the children all the way to their newfound homes if need be. She was determined the children would be encouraged to keep up their studies and become persons of knowledge and information. Mr. Claussen saw to it that the books were made available. This gesture came at substantial cost, for books and fineries covered the bulkheads on either side of the double door entrance. Who could ever imagine such elegance aboard a ship? It was the largest private collection of books I had ever seen aside from the library at the Claussen estate.

Lady Rebecca appeared as if her fears over the past year were unfounded. All before her now seemed positively exciting and quite secure. She slid her fingers over the gilded mahogany carvings that were often complemented by adornments of delicate ivory scrimshaw spread copiously throughout the cabin.

Mary and the captain turned about, seemingly in the know, while I stood by and watched Mr. Claussen take Lady Rebecca's hand and lead her around the blind to their bed. I followed to see how cozy it might be. It was full and inviting. It would be warm. She spread her hands on it then seated herself, and finally lay back on the pillows. She pulled Mr. Claussen toward her. He looked positively flushed.

"My lord, Rebecca, there are people all about!" he protested.

"I can see that. Kiss me," she whispered. Mr. Claussen bowed only to one, and kiss her he did—right in front of my wide-open eyes.

"It's beautiful. And I love it, truly," she whispered into his ear.

I believe he was about to fall into the rapture of a second tantalizing kiss when the clopping sound of little feet supporting a herd of half-crazed children, recently spoiled beyond all salvation, stampeded along the waterway, through the pilothouse, and flooded into the main corridor. They came to an abrupt halt, stopping short to gawk at us from the double door entrance. Mr. Claussen stood up smartly and stared at them in an obvious state of embarrassment.

"Move along, children," Lady Rebecca warned gently.

Two of the older children took stock of the situation, quickly formed an opinion, and rolled their eyes with a giggle. Mary shooed them back along the corridor and followed them down below. Lady Rebecca still gripped Christopher as he held himself over her frame, motionless and silent. They listened to the clamor of children congregating at the forward end of the corridor, crowding each other at the steps and descending either farther forward into the mess, or else aft, where they filled the steerage berths underneath the Claussens' quarters. At that point Lady Rebecca and Mr. Claussen turned to look at me.

"Have you no wish to see the remainder of the ship, darling?" Lady Rebecca asked.

Almost instantly, before I could give it a thought, the captain, who had remained on the forward side of the blind respectfully out of view, reached for my hand and offered to escort me away, thereby conveniently excusing himself from the situation at hand.

"Miss Elizabeth, might you join me in a tour of this fine ship?"

"Do you live on this ship?" I asked, placing my hand in his.

"I do now."

"Is it fun?"

"It is if you're the captain."

"Do you tell everyone what to do?"

"Not if I want any peace. I tell them what I need. The first mate tells them what to do, and I stay out of his way if he's good at his job."

"Do you tell Mr. Claussen what to do?"

"Oh, no, Miss Elizabeth. I have it in my power to do so, but no need—unless the safety of the ship becomes an issue. I must tell you, Mr. Claussen is a sensible man of good character, whom I have come to hold in a most high regard. I fear no problems with Mr. Claussen."

After exiting the Claussen cabin, we walked forward along the corridor and upon reaching its end, turned about at the staircase to head below. From the point of our exit in the main cabin, and along the length of the corridor, the intensity of the clamor from below increased dreadfully. The racket reverberated off the bulkheads, became amplified and pierced every nook and cranny beneath the quarterdeck. The ship literally shook with noise and pounding feet. We descended warily into an inner sea of bedlam. Mary stood before us immersed in the confusion, screaming to bring order to the current state of pandemonium and succeeding about as well as one trying to herd kittens.

"This is where you young ones shall retire, if that will ever be possible," the captain stated, but was mostly drowned out by the din of forty-nine children fighting over whom would sleep where.

To fulfill Lady Rebecca's wishes, the children's quarters were isolated from the rest of the ship. A private accommodation ladder was fitted between her cabin and steerage below where the children were to sleep. She fully anticipated being on call during the many nights ahead to attend to the sick and frightened, and she had no desire to dress each time she arose from her bed for the sake of modesty. Her mind was put to ease at the sight of a private and unencumbered route below to berthing. And what berthing it was.

I could only stare wide-eyed at the scene before me. Space aboard the ship was a very valuable commodity, and the berths were built with no room to be wasted, two children to a bunk. Each bunk was made up of a sturdy frame crisscrossed with rope and fastened to temporary bulkheads and stanchions fitted between the overhead deck beams and the deck itself. The assemblies stood four bunks high, with belongings to be stowed away underneath the bottom berth upon the wooden deck. It was being advised that those with the weak bladders sleep to the outside and bottom.

I was born and raised in a small cottage with my siblings, and entirely accustomed to tight quarters and noise. In fact, it was almost unsettling to experience the absence of commotion when living my life in the Claussen mansion. My bedroom there was nearly as spacious as the entire quarterdeck of this ship. This place looked more like a cellar stacked to the ceiling with rat traps. It reminded me of the rows of crawling caged vermin stampeding each other in the back of a wagon ready to be hauled off for a drowning.

Tight as these quarters were, good ventilation was obtained by use of the gun hatches that reached back to the stern and opened wide for fresh air and light. Needless to say, there were no cannon, and the openings had been fitted with iron grates hinged to close securely and prevent children from falling out. Another blessing was fresh bedding in a fresh ship, new enough to be free of annoying bed bugs.

The captain appeared horrified by the onslaught of din and disarray. He assumed I was pleased with my new surroundings, and finding me to be of little trouble, he drew me back from Mary and the mob of children. We retraced our steps up the starboard companionway and passed Lady Rebecca descending the opposite staircase, on her way down to rescue Mary. She flashed us a knowing glance of what she was about to face as we reached the top step and retreated to the less riotous pace of the pilothouse. We moved across to the staircase going forward and below into the galley.

Captain Ward pulled the galleyway door closed behind him and exhaled a cloud of invisible relief. He found limited refuge. Indeed, the noise was reduced considerably, but it was impossible to escape entirely, for the children's berthing in steerage and the galley in which we now stood shared the same bulkhead. If built two feet thick it would still be hard pressed to fully contain the level of noise on the opposite side. The captain spoke to me in a more normal tone of voice.

"Miss Elizabeth, I believe I must leave the matter of children's care to you, Miss Mary, and Lady Rebecca. I am afraid I much prefer a full gale or the peace of war." He shook his head. He then looked about in some surprise.

"An empty galley. This is a surprise. I must have a shiply crew or a dandy first mate."

Before us, laid out athwartships, was a long common table with equally long benches running its full length on both the forward and aft sides.

"Now, see here, Miss Elizabeth, how large is this table? Don't be caught thinking this is standard fare on an average ship of any sort. It's been put in place only for the benefit of the lot of you. The jacks, as a rule don't eat at a table. They'll use tinware now and then, but you won't see any stoneware on a ship. I'll bet you a piece of chocolate you weren't aware of such a thing. Am I right?"

"Do they eat out of their hands?" I asked.

"They eat KIDS!" He made a lunge for me in a teasing manner. "Well not exactly *eat kids*, rather eat out of kids."

I was stumped, my mind racing as to what he could possibly mean by eating out of kids. I could sense he was amused by my lack of understanding. He turned about and removed a large wooden tray, which was somewhat hollowed out, troughlike. He placed it on the table.

"This, Miss Elizabeth, is a kid. The men eat out of these because it is much easier than having twenty sailors reeling about in a heavy sea with fifty plates in hand. The cook places the meat, potatoes, and dessert, if there is any, all together on this slab of wood. Only one person has to manage it from the galley to the fo'c's'le. You see Miss Elizabeth, as a rule the men don't eat in the galley, as your lot shall. The men eat forward, where they sleep in the fo'c's'le, and it can be an effort indeed getting their fare from the one place to the other in a heavy sea. Afterward, when they're finished with their mess there is only one item to return to the galley, wash, and put away—saves water. That, my child, is called efficient."

"What about knives and forks?"

"Each man has his own."

"Will we eat off a kid?"

"Not likely. At least not as a rule, of that I am certain. Lady Rebecca wishes you to have manners. See here, a number of tin plates on board. We wouldn't have them for the men. A waste of space." He pulled one off a stack and set it alongside the kid.

"You like salt beef, Elizabeth?"

"Yes."

"Good, then you'll like ship food, child." He handed me a piece of chocolate.

I looked about the space and noticed another set of steps that entered into the galley from the larboard side of the ship. The galley was laid out symmetrically. Between the two staircases, centered against the aft bulkhead rested a great stove attached to a chimney that rose upward and passed through the top deck planks to exit near the helm. According to the captain, its heat was much appreciated by cold hands of the watch, as he stood confined to the wheel hour after hour in the cold of night.

At this point another man entered.

"Good day, sir." The captain turned about.

"Good day, William. Allow me to introduce you to Miss Elizabeth, maiden servant to Lady Claussen. Miss Elizabeth, Steward William."

"Miss 'Liz'beth." The man nodded his head respectfully.

"Steward William," I acknowledged.

"I was just showing Miss Elizabeth about ship. We were forced to flee steerage for the sake of our wits and sought refuge here in the galley."

"Aye, sir. Isn't it a reg'lar hen house in there?" he snickered.

"I was explaining to Miss Elizabeth here, that as a rule we don't have much use for such luxuries on board, the likes of this table and tin plates to boot."

"'Tis a fact true, Miss Elizabeth. This here'd be no reg'lar ship She's fitted out fer a queen if ever I did witness such a thing. There'd be many a thing diff'ernt that someone such as yerself mightn' not notice right off, but ya can bet yer pretty curls the men see it firsthand. Take that there tin plate fer 'xample, an' looky here at all these forks an' stuff. Takes too much water t' keep the likes of that clean after 'ery meal. But here they be a whole stack of em' an' a draw full of utensils." He pointed to the stack of tin plates secured alongside the stove. "There be a row or two o' water casks on board an' they ain't here fer scuttlebutt, I'll promise ya. Fer that matter look at me. My employ wit' the captain is to assist the cook an' assist with caring fer the likes of you. Ya like salt beef?"

"Yes."

"Hey, there's a regular now, ain't she?" He looked up to the captain, then continued.

"I'll tell ya, Miss Elizabeth, if the blessit Lord put three hundred an' sixty-five days into a year we would normally be eatin' salt beef, pork, an' hard tack 'bout five hundred o' them three hundred an' sixty five days. But not on this ship, no, Miss. You'll be sittin' up to a plate o' mutton stew or beef soup wit' biscuits. Lots o' fish an' soft bread wit' everything but the worms. Not that the worms are all that bad. They's the only things that can put enough holes into the stuff we norm'ly call bread t' keep it from breakin' yer teeth. You'll be lickin' up sugar on the end of yer fingers instead o' molasses, an' your tea will taste like tea. Not like hot water wit' a leaf in it. This ship is special, Miss Elizabeth. The men are callin' it the Christmas ship cuz, it's bright red an' brimmin' with goodies." The steward laughed and handed me another piece of chocolate. I looked at the captain for approval and he turned his head so as not to observe my overindulgence.

"You best keep a keen eye on those stores, Steward William, or I'll be serving you up on that kid instead of salt beef." The captain winked at me.

"Aye aye, sir. On that ya can rest easy."

We rose from the bench seat and walked over to the forward galley hatch, which led directly into the holds of the ship where stores were packed in tightly everywhere except at the hullside waterways. This allowed for movement below decks, which was safer for the children if need be, and to allow the opening of the gun ports for fresh air and light to ward of damp and disease. We returned to the pilothouse, where the captain thanked me for keeping him company and asked if he might be excused to attend to his duties. The level of noise was now notably diminished and judging all to be well, he made his way on deck leaving me to my own care.

Looking through the pilothouse window onto the upper deck and deeming it safe, I stepped though the hatch myself and watched the captain as he walked away. He began at once to inspect his vessel and question his men. Turning about, I scaled the steps I had spied earlier leading up to the quarterdeck from outside and had a good look about myself.

Mr. Claussen took it upon himself to see that the ship's carpenter, while moored here in London, constructed a corral atop this upper deck. This done for the purpose of confining the youngest children to a safe place where they were most removed from the elements of weather and traffic along the waterways and in the waist of the ship while under way.

The children could be led from steerage below, up the companionways, through the pilothouse, and up onto the quarterdeck to benefit from fresh air and sunlight without crossing over the ship's deck or underfoot of the crew. The corral was centrally located on the quarterdeck above the main corridor amidships and underneath the boom of the spanker. It would be here that the children would spend most of their time. A canopy was provided for protection against the sun. As the day drew to a close, the children would be called down from the corral for an inspection of cleanliness and health. They could then proceed to the galley and eat or go back to berthing and retire for the night.

I spent the remainder of the afternoon close to the starboard steps of the quarterdeck, which seemed to provide the best view of the docks from the ship. I wasn't tall enough to see over the bulwarks, but I was able to see through the stanchions of the quarterdeck rail with little problem.

TWENTY-SIX

It was early in the morning of Wednesday, June twenty-fourth, year of our Lord eighteen and seven. The sun was not yet in the morning sky. This I knew, for the gun port hatch had been left ajar so we might benefit from the fresh air. At this hour, as I looked through the port, only the peaceful flicker of oil lamps was to be seen scattered randomly along the docks and upon the vessels, keeping their silent vigil. They hung motionless, attracting a myriad of tiny flying things, while at the same time warding off suspicious souls and the heavy morning dew. Their gentle beams entered our berthing and painted the planks softly with a slow-motion brushstroke of pale yellow light that pushed the shadows up and down as the ship rocked with each passing breeze.

Knowing that we would weigh anchor this day, if the weather was agreeable and all went well aboard ship, made me anxious and dispelled any notion I might have had about sleeping further. I wasn't suffering alone, for most of the children were unfamiliar or uncomfortable with these strange surroundings and tossed and turned in their bunks the whole of the night.

Tomorrow would be the last possible day to sail this week. No sailor, so it was said, would begin a journey to sea on a Friday. It was believed that to do such a thing would summon the worst of luck, if not a mutiny. Captain Ward made it public knowledge that he intended to leave this Wednesday; and for that reason, we all suffered from a mix of the butterflies of anticipation and secret fears, which surfaced in our dreams.

Due to my being the younger and unable to sleep as sound as Mary on an ordinary night, let alone this night, I was allowed to lie on the outside edge of our bunk providing I didn't run off excessively. I lay as still as possible, as long as possible, until I felt I would go crazy. I was too nervous to sleep, and had laid awake for some time listening to the others stirring about. I had listened to Mary's soft breathing, and would have been lulled back to sleep, but for sounds passing through the bulkhead that came from a cook working his stove in the galley. The subdued raps and taps, and clinks of cookware finally got the best of me. If the cook was up, I might as well be up also. My mind was racing before the dawn, and being aware of the small freedom handed to me, I slipped off the bunk and set out to entertain myself.

Carefully, so as not to disturb Mary, I removed my sailing ship blanket from the foot of our bunk and wrapped it about me. I tiptoed away quietly with intentions to go outside onto the quarterdeck. I climbed the stairs to the pilothouse and found myself suddenly engulfed by the sweet aroma of freshly brewed tea. Everything else would have to wait until I determined if it was at all possible to fetch a hot cup for my own. It would be perfect to ward off the chill awaiting me up on deck in the cool of the morning. As I stepped across the pilothouse, I stopped a moment to glimpse through the starboard window and beyond into the darkness where the view of twinkling ship lanterns and dock lamps reminded me of fairies in the night. The darkness looked cold and uncaring, and I pulled my blanket tighter about me before descending the staircase and slipping cautiously into the ship's mess.

The galley was lit by the glow of an oil lamp and pleasantly warmed by the stove. The smell of chocolate, coffee, and tea was thick in the air. My mouth watered and my stomach kept me from being bashful so I approached the cook with the need of a handout written all over my face.

"Lordy me, und phat 'ave ve got 'ere, an angel flittin' ah-bout or zit joos me dreamin'. Ya-ah?" He stepped back from the stove with a clunk where a foot should have been. My jaw dropped in one direction; my eyebrows shot up in the other. I completely missed his question to me.

"Pfat name jou go by, child?"

"Elizabeth," I uttered, not wishing to be distracted from the sight before me.

I was finally able to look up at him long enough to meet his gaze. He was broad through the belly and wore a wonderfully inviting smile of good teeth set deep into a black stubby set of round cheeks. His bushy eyebrows bobbed up and down, while his eyes snapped back and forth. He laughed easily, and it was obvious he enjoyed children.

"By George, de pleasure be mine, all mine." He extended his hand. "My name tis Hans Swarensen, boot I hain't been called it in 'jears. Not shince I schtarted shipping as de cook. Since den I been called 'Doc,' 'Peg leg,' 'Leg o' lam,' 'Club foot,' 'Schplinter butt,' 'Voody,' 'Rap n' tap,' 'Schtick man,' 'Oakey'…. By George, I t'ink I can arly 'member alf de names I go by, ya-ah. On dis ship it's Cookie Jar und I likes fer t' be called dat.

Cheptin' for 'Doc' vich I gets called a lot, everyt'ing else as fer t' do vit me vooden peg."

"It's a pleasure to meet you, Cookie Jar." I looked back down at his…well, whatever. He must have seen my wide-eyed expression, for he began to stomp out a little dance step with his peculiar appendage. Clunk, tap tap, clunk tap clunk, clunk.

"Dis a true life vooden peg, ya-ah. I can't beliefs it myshelf, und I own it, ya-ah." He laughed.

He stopped his hopping and I moved in toward him, bent down, and took a close look at all the carvings and decoration that covered its surface, they being mixed with countless names of friends and past acquaintances.

"Vould jou likes me fer t' tell jou 'ows I coom fer t' own oon peg fer oon leg, ya-ah?"

"It must be a pretty good story, I'm certain."

"De best damn yarn jou'll ever 'ere, me schveets. Let me get jou a copper o' tea und I tell it fer t' jou, ya-ah. Howsh zat, ya-ah?"

"I'd like that very much thank-you." A cup of tea and a story to boot, I was all ears—this cook was a one-man sideshow.

He dipped the cup into a large pot of boiling tea. He scooped some sugar into it then set it on the table while motioning me to sit down. I sat down and he began to give me the account of his misfortune accompanied with great facial animation and large sweeps of his arms. He was a show indeed.

"Veez out in de middle oon de Atlantic. Aadn't sheen oon schpeck o' land fer t' better 'n of oon mont', ya-ah. Been 'gree-able sea vit oon fresh vind fer oon full veek before. Den ve coom fer t' fine ourshelves becalmed. Ve juce sit there, floatin' like oon dried leaf on de pond. Jou know phat I'm shayin' ya-ah? I had juce coom off de first vatch, dad be 'bout four in de mornin' fer t' jou, shveethart. Und I vent below fer t' get soom rest und I vas half dead shleepin' ard, vhen de mate cooms a yelling, 'First vatch oon de deck und be lively bout it boys.' Vell, I joomped up fer t' threw on m' clotes und tumbled out oonto de deck. I noticed de ship vas actin' lively alst de vhile I vas dressin' und vhen I schtep oon de deck de vind vas oon ard blow, ya-ah.

"Da Mate he 'ollers 'First vatch aloft und' send down de studn'sls. Second vatch aloft und dooble reef de fore top'sls. Schtep lively boys, oon gale's upoon us.' It vas as black out as tar und impossible fer t' see oon's nose scheptin' fer de flashin' o' lightnin' dat ve knew vas goin' fer t' be da det' of us all in da riggin'.

"Da vind vas fierce soon und brought un blast o' snow und sleet vit it. Balls of ice de size o' eggs. Dey vere 'alf knockin' us senseless und ve vere caught betveen trying fer t' 'ang on fer t' de jards, vork de sails und cover our 'eads. Vell dat's t'ree t'ings fer t' do und man's only got two 'ands. So de only t'ing ve could do vas do phatever ve vere doin' fast. De faster de better. Ve best get down lively or ve vere all 'bout to be knocked off de jards.

"De vind vas puttin' too much pressure on de ship und she vas 'eeled over fer t' port vit' 'er scuppers avash. Ve 'ad no choice, boot fer t' get de studn'sls sent down or de mast und riggin vould all be carried avay. It vas a terrible blow. Me und two mates vere trying fer t' send down de stun'sl boom from de jard arm vhen all at once de ship pitched fer t' veather und de boom freed herself. De next instant ve vere 'eeled over fer t' lee und de boom came svingin' back und caught me right 'ere." He pointed to the place where his leg ended and the peg began. "I vas so busy trying fer t' keep from gettin' knocked silly by de hailstones dat I blinked for oon secont und dat's all it took." He snapped his fingers. "Just like dat de boom vas forced back by de roll oon de ship und de force oon de blow. Schmack! Right into me leg it vent. Never saw it comin'." He took a breath and looked at me.

"It must have really hurt?"

"Oh, forgive me me sins, sveets, it 'urt sometin' terrible. Un foot 'igher and de boom vould o' knocked me onto de deck or into de sea. Boot I 'ung on de yard. It vould o'been oon might easier if I 'ad gone down. I prayed fer t' die. Let me die, dear Lord, joost let me die. Boot as jou can now see, I din't. Only de leg did. So dat's 'ow I ended up vit' oon peg fer oon leg, ya-ah. I don't go aloft no more. No, Miss. I schtay below in de galley. Boot it ain't all dat bad. It gets 'ot, bless me lord, it gets 'ot indeed. Boot dis is better dan tryin' fer t' 'ang on de riggin vhen it be covered vit ice und jour 'ands dey freeze up 'ard und don't move none, ya-ah."

"That's quite a story, indeed."

"Und' didn't I say it vould be, ya-ah?"

"Yes."

"Und' vhere jou be headin' off fer t' at dis 'our, sveets, it ain't 'ardly light as o' jet."

"Atop the quarterdeck to watch the sun come up."

"Vell go oon den und take care not fer t' fall in."

"I won't, I promise." I rose from the table.

"Take dis vith jou, Miss Elizabeth." He handed me a piece of lump sugar.

I thanked him and took leave of the galley.

I believe most of the sailors enjoyed us as a rule, even when we were in the way because their lives were often lonely without wife, family, or kin. It needn't be said, there would always be a few that disliked children and they made no secret of it. William Morrison, a man named Torrie Harper, and another called Gustaff Borislav, who always wore a striped bandana about his neck that had bear claws sewn along the edge. We were warned to keep clear of them by the others, but even without warning, their eyes spoke for themselves and nothing further need be said. Aside from the few unfriendly blokes, the children would accept the men as they were without question, without judgment, and looked up to them as heroes of all sorts. In turn, the crew's consumption of rum was already notably below their allotment. Often, with what little free time they had, instead of pacing the decks, as was their custom, the men might be found near, if not inside the corral upon the quarterdeck, singing and playing with the children. They brought sail needles and balls of twine for entertainment and the teaching of tricks and fancy knots.

Cookie Jar, having fixed me up with a piece of sugar and warming my mug of tea, sent me on my way to go above deck. I climbed the steps to the quarterdeck and felt the coolness of the morning dew beneath my bare feet. Far ahead in the darkness I noted the obscure outlines of Lady Rebecca's wheel-less coach upon the gratings. It struck me as being empty and haunting. It looked cold. It needed the laughter of people within its cabin.

I shivered, then turned about and made my way up the quarterdeck steps. I picked the same place above the quarterdeck stairway alongside the stanchions that offered the best view of the dock and ship, the place I had discovered the day before, and it was there that I seated myself. I wrapped my sailing ship blanket tightly about me and placed the mug of tea underneath it. I sat the hot tin upon the deck between my crossed legs, thereby trapping the rising heat inside. I savored my piece of sugar, slowly, nibbling away at bit by bit and looking about. I felt nice and cozy peeking out from my blanket and enjoyed the stillness of the dimly lit morn; the peace broken only occasionally by a few scrapping gulls, the cough of a man standing anchor watch, or lines slatting masts in a breeze.

A while later, from behind came a gentle and friendly greeting. I looked up to see an inviting smile, but I recognized the man as the one I saw the day before high on a yard when we boarded ship.

"Oyeeee! Milady."

"Oyeeee." I mimicked in return. He enjoyed that and settled down next to me with his coffee.

"I'd be Darrin O'Kurk—an' yoorself?

"I'd be Elizabeth Dennison," said I, still mimicking.

"Elizabeth, iz it! Noo finer a name thar be. An' sooch a pretty young un t' go with it. I recull seein' ye coom aboord with th' good Lady Rebecca Claussen. Be ye a maiden t'her now, child?"

"Yes, I am."

"I see. She be a fine woman, that one, fair and honorable, a fine person t' attend, if Iz t'say soo meself. Yoor a fortunate one t'fall in with sooch good coompany." He looked about the docks and the surrounding waterfront, then turned once again to me.

"Tell me, now, 'ave ye 'ad yoor prayer this moorning, lass?"

"No, I don't believe it." A pang of guilt filled me.

"Well, thin, Wouj ye be willin' t' 'ave it with, me?"

"I would."

"Well, thin. Ya see thit sky, child?" He swept his arm in a large arc overhead. I nodded yes, as I observed the first signs of sunrise.

"Praise be th' Loord thiz moorning fair.

Though oor lives be 'ard, th' woorse for wear

An' hands still 'urt froom th'day bifore

I thank thee, God Almighty, 'tis noothin' moore.

Ahh-men."

"Amen," I responded.

Almost as though inspired by our heavenly prayer, bells rang out from the city and all across the docks.

215

Ding-Ding

Ding-Ding

Ding-Ding

Ding-Ding

I raised my head at the sound of the bells. I heard a door closing below me and observed the ship's master, Captain Ward, stepping into view, moving forward onto the deck from his cabin in the quarterdeck beneath us. Another man met him immediately, and the two engaged in a brief conversation. The man turned forward and yelled,

"First watch below! Morning watch on deck!"

Another repeated the order, and the two sailors who had been pacing the decks on the anchor watch went below into the galley. Two new faces, yawning and stretching, came up on deck and at once began to retrace the path of the watch prior.

The captain rotated about slowly as he studied his standing rigging. His gaze passed overhead then slowly descended, coming to rest upon Mr. O'Kurk and myself. His face broke into a grin. Leaving the other man to his business, he ascended the quarterdeck steps and approached us. My being up so early, and on the deck no less, amused him. He squatted down beside me and I could see his breath in the cool air.

"Good morning, Miss Elizabeth. That is a mighty fine piece of work you have about you. A sailing ship wrap. I am certain it is comfortable, but I am surprised you would prefer the crisp morning air to the warmth of a berth."

"I think of it more as the fresh morning air, sir. Steering is close indeed."

"Ha-ha! I reckon if any of the young 'uns fill their pants it's a might worse than even the fo'c's'le. Just you wait until we make way across the open sea. Until that parcel of children get their sea legs, you find out all about smell and being close, my dear," he responded.

With this, he and Mr. O'Kurk laughed and assured me I should not fear sickness of the sea, for they determined I had sufficient salt in my blood to overcome it and would probably end up making the sea my home.

"Has the sea always been your home, Captain Ward?"

"Mine, my father's, and his father's. The sea has been my life since the day of my birth. But that's to change. After this voyage I'll be swallowing the anchor and taking up the hoe, I reckon."

"I can tell by the way you speak, and from what Milady has said, you are not from these parts. She has said you are from America. Where in the New World do you call home?"

"Baltimore, Maryland, a former colony. It would be on the coast, and a fine place it is."

"Yes, I have heard of it. Do you have family there as well?"

"You have heard of it? Is that a fact?" Captain Ward was greatly surprised.

"Mr. Claussen speaks of it on occasion. It is there, you have family, then?"

"Aye, I do. My good wife Louise and two fine sons, who now are long out the nest and on their own. The wife of my firstborn son was with child the last I heard, and I fully suspect I am a grandfather by now. I have been out for better than two years. This time past, doubling the Horn and off to China, thence through the Indies, around the great continent of Africa, and finally here to moor in England. It wasn't my ambition to stay out so long, but one is compelled to follow the profits as they show themselves."

Darrin O'Kurk rose to his feet, excused himself, and after bidding the captain and I a good morning, left the quarterdeck for the galley. The man whom I first saw talking to the captain and calling out to the watch a short time ago soon replaced Darrin O'Kurk. He now stepped onto the quarterdeck and came our way. The captain straightened up. The man was important and I knew this because others reacted to his presence much the same as the captain, paying him close mind.

"Captain, the holds have been inspected and all is chocked and lashed proper. I have kept open a space for your delivery of glass this day. Do you still expect it, sir?"

"That I do, Mr. Beckwith. I assure you it will be here and I wish to weigh anchor as soon as possible after hoisting the crates aboard. And also, Mr. Beckwith, see to it you take care in handling of the cargo. Secure it well. I wish no mishaps."

"Aye aye, sir. That I will."

"Mr. Beckwith, I should like to improve your lot in life by introducing you to my special guest, Miss Elizabeth. She is the maiden servant to Lady Claussen, but I sense there is more to it than that."

"Miss Elizabeth." His bow was quick but courteous.

"Mr. Beckwith." I acknowledged him.

"Mr. Beckwith is my first mate." The captain turned to me. "Do you recall our conversation yesterday afternoon when I mentioned that another sees to it that the activity aboard ship is undertaken promptly and in proper fashion?"

"Yes, I recall it, sir."

"Well, Mr. Beckwith is that man, Elizabeth. My second mate, Marion McCurry, who was standing watch when you came on deck and has now gone below to breakfast, assists him. It is these two whom I count on for order aboard ship. They are responsible for maintaining the rigging both standing and running, the set of the sails, the watches, the mooring of the vessel, the movement of stores, the order of the day, and also the discipline of the men.

They hold high position aboard any vessel and shoulder great responsibilities for your safety, Elizabeth." He turned back to his first mate. "You may go about your business, Mr. Beckwith."

"Aye aye, sir. Good day to you, Miss Elizabeth."

"And to you, sir."

Mr. Beckwith bade me farewell, then turned to descend onto the main deck. He stepped aside shortly and allowed another man to scale the quarterdeck and come forth. The activity of the day was starting.

"This gentleman is for you, Elizabeth."

"For me, Captain?" I asked. The captain spoke to us both.

"Yes, Elizabeth. I've assigned him to assist you in your efforts to attend to Lady Claussen. I should be clear and point out you may be called upon to share him with the Lady Claussen, but it would be fair to say that you shall still benefit a great deal from his service. Elizabeth, meet my chief steward, Gregory LaBianca."

"At your service, Miss Elizabeth." Mr. LaBianca bowed graciously.

I felt very awkward having someone attend to me, and I flushed immediately with embarrassment from his direct attention.

I was saved by the bells of London as they rang out five times in unison with two strikes of the bell upon the REBECCA, and a good many of the other ships about us. The captain took a deep breath and patted my head.

"Now, Elizabeth, I must leave you to your observations for I have much work to do. If you would excuse me. Gregory, shall we begin?"

"Aye aye, sir."

The men bade me a good morning and went on about their business. Thereupon, the day began, quietly, slowly at first as the newborn rays of a morning sun reached across an almost invisible sky. At eight o'clock the church bells and the ship bells both rang out eight times. It was here that a lull in the activity about the ships took hold while the men on most of the vessels went below for the purpose of breakfasting.

Once done, the day restarted with a notable explosion of activity as the merchants from the city began to stream onto the docks, and the scene all about me and far across the piers upon the river was much like a circus. At the ring of a bell, it now being eight thirty, men came boiling out from below decks and positioned themselves for their performances.

The docks and shipyard were alive with activity. Hanging from the yards, the men performed on the ends of rope like trapeze artists. Spars, yards, topmasts, and sails swayed up into the sky. Shrouds were hoisted atop the masts, fitted across the bolsters, draped to decks, fastened to lanyards, then tarred along with stays and braces. Decks were being scrubbed, caulked, and holy stoned. Paints, varnishes, and oils were being set out to wait for the warmer morning hours, while stiff fingers began the chore of scraping and burning off the old coats of protection.

I watched with great interest as the sailors on the ship MARY CAROL, being rigged in the shipyard just across the way, went about hoisting their topmast into position. They brought a freshly scraped and oiled spar on deck and blocked the large end at the base of the mainmast. The opposite, smaller end was secured to a tackle and stood up on the larger end until standing up straight alongside the main mast. From here the men hauled on the bull rope. It was rove from the cap of the mainmast down to the deck and through a sheave in the large end of the topmast, then back ahigh to a block at the trees.

As the men hauled on the hauling end of the bull rope, it lifted the topmast up through a hole in small platform known as the top, which was supported by the trees of the main mast, the hole being framed by the cross-trees and trestle-trees. After passing through the opening it was guided through a mast cap, which secured its position. Once hoisted into place a fid was driven through the mast and the tackles slacked off.

Two men aboard the REBECCA were on their knees scrubbing the deck with sandstone and noticed my interest in these goings on and made their acquaintance. They were more than happy to take a break and explain the many things taking place about me in detail. I followed them as they went along and listened with interest to everything they had to say. Mr. Beckwith was giving them the eye, but as long as they were willing to talk, I was willing to listen.

All the while I watched the hoisting of the topmasts on the MARY CAROL, wagons loaded with provisions and cargo lined up on the street waiting their turn to make way onto the docks. I observed three wagons come across the lot and roll down the pier to our ship. They stopped abreast the last open hold and with little time wasted, twelve crates of Danish Glass were hoisted aboard by tackle from the main yardarm with great care as the first mate hollered out his instructions.

The buildings that fenced in the Thames reverberated with the sounds of horses' hooves and wagon wheels drumming across the wooden-planked piers, the hammering of carpenters' work, and every now and then the repetitious chanteys of men hauling together in time by song. This time it was our men hoisting the crates, giving a great haul with a yell of Ayeeeeee! Darrin O'Kurk was the chanteyman.

Oooyeee, Oooyeee me hearties!

Hear me 'n haul! (Ayeeeeee!)

Hear me 'n haul! (Ayeeeeee!)

Hear me 'n haul or I'll feed ya

To the sharkies. (Ayeeeeee!)

Oooyeee, Oooyeee me hearties!

Hear me 'n haul! (Ayeeeeee!)

TWENTY-SEVEN

The activity of past days was now notably absent about the dock alongside us. The stores had been moved out of the weather and into our holds leaving the pier seemingly barren. As the day moved on into afternoon, the work remaining was little than inspections, except for the sealing of the hatches after the last load of crated glass had been chocked and the loading boards retrieved. There were last-minute details with merchants and messengers, who stepped lively up and down the one remaining gang plank, our last and only connection to land.

The sounds of the London Docks were masked by the over bearing silence at our station. It was like enduring the stillness before a storm. The orphans, the mates, and I measured our patience against an almost unbearable amount of anticipation and giddiness. It caused our stomachs to turn and writhe. We knew we would soon cast off and could do little but wait for the moment.

Mr. Claussen, Captain Ward, and the dockmaster appeared to have concluded their business and were waiting, conversing in small talk until another man met them. At that point the men all shook hands, thereafter the dockmaster turned and headed off as the three remaining men boarded. The boarding plank was raised and my heart skipped a beat. We were now sealed in and there was no going back. At this point, I might as well have been on the open sea.

By now, the heat of the afternoon sun had long since replaced the chilly morning air and fully dried out the once dew-covered and holy stoned decks. The wind had changed from an Easterly to a Westerly that now blew in the same direction as the river's current. All the children had passed beside me at some time during the day and moved either in or out of the corral. Whereas they huddled together like sparrows on a chimney for warmth during the morning hours, now they were wild with anticipation and working up a sweat. They sensed the nearness of our departure and fluttered about as though they might be little squawking chickens in a coup. Only the youngest of the lot were oblivious to the departure about to ensue and were content to lie back and nap under the watchful eyes of Mary and Lady Rebecca. Cookie Jar would come up occasionally from the galley as well as Gregory LaBianca to assist Lady Rebecca with refreshments and whatever else need be.

Better than a thousand townspeople had collected by this hour and stood about in various groups on shore. Some came to wish the orphans their final farewell. Some were stevedores and dockhands who stood about chancing to work on the wharf or upon the ships. Many were sightseers strolling along the river and enjoying the warm afternoon sun. They were unaware of our adolescent cargo, but simply paused along the embankments to enjoy the day and the spectacle of such a gorgeous ship about to unmoor. As always, the crowd drew crowds.

Although, I was now myself motherless and shared the same berthing and age with many of the other children, I was never grouped with the orphans about me. It was obvious to all that Mary was the true service to Lady Rebecca, and I was treated more like a foster child. It was also true that this arrangement allowed me to enjoy a great deal more privilege and freedom than most of the others on board. I never was one to shirk my duties, but much of the time it was easier if I was out of the way. It was Mary who was burdened. Indeed, I was beginning to think my main duty was to make Lady Rebecca feel like a mother.

I often wondered if she wasn't the happiest when I was into some mischief. I resisted being confined to the corral and because of it, remained the constant worry of Milady whenever I was out of sight. She fussed over me a great deal as usual and it didn't take much for me to do something on board that would put the fear of God into her.

A simple matter, such as looking over the side of the hull from between the stanchions, or peering down into a ship hold, or climbing a rope overhead the deck. Anything of this nature would excite her to the point where she would insist in a somewhat stern and demanding voice that I stay in the cabin by her side; it would pretty much ruin the rest of my day. For one thing, I felt terrible if I upset her and for another, I much preferred the fresh air and breeze on deck. If I kept low and out of sight, I was generally able to move about the ship freely for short periods. It was my place to serve Milady, and to mind, and although I did my best to comply, my task was certain to be difficult for as of yet we hadn't even put to sea.

I arose from my place on the quarterdeck, and dodging the movement of deckhands, I descended the steps and made my way forward toward Lady Rebecca's coach. The men moving about deck were coming to understand I was not one of the orphans and no longer confronted nor questioned my doings as long as I stayed clear of danger. The position of the coach, being just aft the foremast, offered me an interesting new vantage point to witness better the goings on at the bows. As I waited alongside the tarped vehicle, the ship's bell rang out clear above all others six times.

Dong-Dong
Dong-Dong
Dong-Dong

A look of excitement swept across the faces of the men on deck. I turned and saw a stranger in the company of the captain who was standing in front of the pilothouse doorway nearer the helm and talking to the first mate, Mr. Beckwith. The first mate lifted his voice horn, and then called out loudly.

"Second watch! Prepare t' go aloft an' set the fore upper top'sls n' jibs b' my call. All hands on deck t' weigh anchor!"

The three men then turned aft and removed themselves to the quarterdeck to take up a position at the rail above the helmsman. The deck flooded with sailors who swept past me to gather at the capstan. They gripped the capstan bars, fitted them home into the pigeonholes, and began to heave in unison, moving slowly in a circle and drawing up the anchor chain. Mr. O'Kurk began to sing out.

Tak 'er arms...'n all 'er charms
'n sing 'er 'n swing 'er 'roound 'n 'roound
'n be it may... ya'll 'ear 'er say
roll me aroound upoon the g-roound
an' go roound, go roound, go roound!

We were in very shallow water, and it was only a moment before a seaman returned "Ahoyee Mr. Beckwith! The anchor is short!" Mr. Beckwith turned to the captain.

"Anchor is short, sir!"

"Secure your tow lines forward, Mr. Beckwith!"

"Aye aye, sir!" Mr. Beckwith held up his voice horn, and hollered forward.

"Send the tow lines forward, men, and be lively!"

The men heaved a pair of lines over the bows down to a steam-powered boat standing below our bows and out of my view. From my place on the quarterdeck, I had watched two of them approach earlier, coming upriver, a-huffing and sending big white balls of smoke zooming into the air overhead. It was still a sight to see, but at least this time I didn't tell everyone they were on fire.

Once made fast, the forward riverboat took up the slack until the lines were taut and a jack called out to Mr. Beckwith.

"Tow lines secure, Mr. Beckwith!"

"Tow lines secure, sir!"

"Anchor aweigh, Mr. Beckwith!" the captain ordered.

"Anchor aweigh!" The first mate cried out through his horn, and the chantey resumed.

The cry of 'anchor tripped' echoed across the deck. The men circled the capstan, leaning hard into its bars, backs bent and arm muscles bulging as the dead weight of the anchor was brought up to surface from below. The anchor was fished with the cat tackle, raised to the cathead, made fast, and then canted upward to the chainplate and secured.

The REBECCA had been moved from her fitting out dock to a shorter loading dock. Because of her great length this necessitated the dropping of a bower to secure her mooring forward. Upon weighing anchor, all her mooring lines were cast off and she was set free. I slipped forward to the bow and peered down through the rigging of the bowsprit.

The steam engine on the little towboat came to life and pushed a fresh cloud of hot soaring sparks and smoke through a falling mess of black ash. The little boat chugged on cheerily in spite of the demands placed upon it. The second boat stayed at our larboard beam and guided us by keeping us into the wind. They were a wonder to witness, and I never tired of watching them.

The forward boat sounded out its cranky complaints, but never faltered under the strain. Everybody worried, certain it should blow up. The large towlines stood straight above the water under enormous tension, and slowly the REBECCA took to their persuasion. Amidst a great cheer from the onlookers, we unmoored. This pleased one sailor, who let out a cheer, spun

226

about, and nearly fell over my small frame. He was somewhat shaken and most surprised to find me alongside him.

"Deary, yeh best step aft. It's a might dangerous 'bout the bows fer if the towline should snap, she'll cut cha in two. Yer head'l be a rollin' off thet a'ways, while yer feet are still planted as yeh stand. Go on now, deary, where it'd be safe."

I took my leave.

Only to the mouth of the docks did the captain require assistance from the towboats. From there, the prevailing winds that came out of the west from upriver now moved with the current in our favor so the towboat cast off our lines, and we hauled them aboard.

I discovered Captain Ward now needed assistance of another kind. It came from a stranger who came aboard and remained before him now. The man was a river pilot. The captain and first mate paid close attention to the stranger, and following his advice they would order the men to do his bidding. As we approached the entrance of the docks and made our way into the river, the river pilot ordered the men to loose the inner jib. They were used to bring the bows of the ship a-lee and point her downstream, after which they were hauled back in, and Mr. Beckwith barked out new commands.

"Ahoy, topmen! Be aloft to the fore upper top'sls an' loose the gaskets at my call!"

The topmen who had been standing by scampered aloft upon the shrouds and up to the yards, from whence they stepped out along the horses and prepared to release the gaskets and unfurl the sails. At the same time others stepped quickly across the decks to the belaying pins, and lifting up the coils of rope off the pins, they spread them in an orderly fashion along the waterway and waited for the call to go into action.

"Ahoyeee you jacks aloft, loose the fore and main top'sls." He pointed to those waiting on deck. "Brace 'em square, men!"

The topmen sprang to motion, releasing gaskets and buntlines. Instantly the sails fell from the top yards. The men hauled the braces, firmed the clews, and trimmed the sails. All eyes watched the rigging, for it was un-weathered and required special attention until it took its set. The REBECCA responded to the call to sail, and the water rose lightly upon her stem, giving her some rudder in the down river current.

The buildings of London were slowly passing from my eyes to my memory. I studied them and was able even at my young age to appreciate the grandeur of this city. We began our journey in this way, waving good-byes to the droves of well-wishers, who would forever remain on shore with unfulfilled dreams. High above, Mr. O'Kurk sang out to all who watched our departure.

We'll leave our loove behind us
When anchoor's hauled a-weigh
We'll roope th' wind with riggin
An' we'll beat 'er all th' day'

We'll brace th' yards aboove us
Then trim th' sails till full
We'll heel 'er to 'er beam ends
An' let REBECCA pull!
An' let REBECCA pull!

When we coome a callin'
To poorts aroound th' woorld
We'll stand into th' harboor
With all 'er sails unfurled.

We'll wash th' sea beneath us
With spray froom off 'er bow
We'll 'ave er up 'n full dress
Just like a lady now!
Just like a lady now!

No! Ye shan't forget REBECCA
'Er memory doth prevail
'Er hull th' color of crimson
Under billowing clouds o' sail

She may be oot three hundred
'Er sailers groowing oold
But then she'll double back agin'
T' find their loover's hoold

But then she doubles back agin'
T' find their loovers hoold.

It was well near dark by the time we reached the Nore. Mr. Claussen, finding himself in need of a stroll and desiring to ease Lady Rebecca's concerns, came looking for me. He found me sitting before the coach, where I had been watching the men coiling their lines and putting the forward deck in order. During the hours of the dogwatch all the men were on the upper deck, mostly forward, generally having a smoke or chew of tobacco and periodically pacing the waterways. They would move up and down the companionway to the fo'c's'le and always had a kind word for me, if not a great galley yarn, or better yet, a song of which they took particular pleasure in performing for my benefit. These moments were rich and I would have endured them until the point of exhaustion if the dogwatch had allowed it.

The river pilot had been relieved of his duty upon entering the roads and had since departed. The captain assumed full command of the REBECCA, and by his order; the fore, main, mizzen upper and lower topsails and courses had been let loose and trimmed. The calls for the topmen to set the topgallant, royal, and skysails were sounded. Interrupting the flurry of commands and calls from the mates came the WHOOMP-WHOOMP-WHOOMP of the sails as they dropped from their yards and filled in the breeze. They were braced in square and trimmed. Now, we passed from the roads into the open waters of the estuary, and being little different from the open sea, and the winds having died down, the ship was brought to full sail.

I had risen to my feet out of respect to Mr. Claussen. To my astonishment, he leaned back against the coach and pulled me close before him, wrapping his arms about me. We stood together looking out over the bows of the REBECCA. He reveled in the power of the ship, while I reveled in the joy of his attention. The ship sliced its way through the open sea using her bows to split the waves and toss them aside. It turned the dark gray water into shattered clouds of bright orange crystal streaking through the last rays of the setting sun. Mr. Claussen stroked my hair with his massive hands as he looked out to sea. After some contemplation, he spoke to me.

"Elizabeth, you have brought my Rebecca much joy and given her a purpose in life that thus far, I have been unable to provide. This is an issue, which at your young age may be beyond understanding. Nonetheless, I am grateful to you, and have found myself indebted, for it has helped her to accept my dreams and accompany me into the unknown. I pray that we cross this ocean safely and I might bring to your life all the riches and wonders you should desire. I am confident, Elizabeth, beyond that horizon you shall find every reason God put the breath of life into your beating breast."

I remained silent, having listened to his every word, for I was taken aback by this spoken appreciation. His words came across in a manner being as close to affectionate as I had ever seen Mr. Claussen be with anybody other than Lady Rebecca. Secure within his embrace, we stood together a spell and no further words passed between us. I was compelled to turn and look up into his face, to look into the blue eyes that stared so intently out beyond his ship. I had never felt his attention so pronounced at any time before this night and I was flooded with the sensation that Milord had within him the conviction and force to take command of not only my life, but also the very wind and sea before our bows. I was filled with awe.

This was my first night on the open sea, and the sky was awash with color as he escorted me back to the quarterdeck so we might join the captain. It was explained to me as I stood in wonder of this evening sky so filled with sail—each and every one an artists' canvas collecting the hues of a setting sun—that it was prudent for Captain Ward to subject the ship to the strain of her canvas as soon as possible to seek out fault.

"Better now than in the throes of a gale at open sea," he said.

I watched as the very last yard of cloth was sent aloft, and our determined bowsprit rose and fell to the rhythmic but relenting waves. The feeling of the ship's might was exhilarating. The wind was fresh and fair, and we kept well before it.

At the last perception of light, the captain ordered the men aloft one last time, and all sail was bunted, clewed up and furled. Anchor was dropped and we stood moored, rocking peacefully for the night. It was his wish to await the sea breeze of early morn to assist us in our westing of the English Channel. All men, except for four on the first watch, were allowed to go below.

The children had been removed to their berthing in groups of five or six. One group after another, they were taken below from the quarterdeck. Later, in light of the moon, the corral stood empty of life, as was I. Sensing my fatigue and my fight to stay warm, Mr. Claussen called it a night and led me below out of the chilly sea air. We entered the warmth of the galley and sat at the long table. Cookie Jar scooped out a hot cup of tea for each of us and a piece of chocolate for me. I nibbled at it, and the three of us talked a while until I was overcome with sleepiness. After all, I had started my day earlier than most on this morning past.

I was leaning against Mr. Claussen's side, braced up by his arm and at the point of dreaming when Mary came into the galley to convey Lady Rebecca's wishes that I return with her to retire for the night. Mr. Claussen helped me to my feet, gave me a kiss on my head, and passed me to Mary. The cramped little wood frame of a bunk felt wonderful, and with the security of Mary near my side, I was instantly asleep, leaving my undressing to be done by others.

The next morning I was not so quick to rise. In fact, by the time I did finally open my eyes the only people about were the few orphans who were already sick from the sea. Mary had obviously been up for some time as I could hear the commotion of the children in the galley eating at the long table. I knew they would have had to wash up before Lady Rebecca would have let them eat. I figured they were about an hour ahead of me into the day. I dropped to my feet and wasted no time going above to wash up and head once again topside to the quarterdeck.

I dearly wanted to breakfast, for I was famished, but a mob of children and all the commotion connected to them was not to my liking first thing after awakening. I stuck my head into the galleyway and saw Cookie Jar and Steward William at the stove parceling out biscuits and gravy with fruit and lemon water. Mary was busy at work helping Lady Rebecca feed the children. Gregory LaBianca was also assisting her. It was simply too much. *A hen house*, precisely as Steward William had noted.

I retraced my steps into the pilothouse and determined to go outside. The moment I opened the hatch, the fresh morning sea air rushed in and put new life into me. I looked straight up and gasped in amazement at all the sail; it nearly blocked out the sky. Everything had changed from the orange hues of the night before to the pale blue and bright white of morning light. I could hardly look at the sails until I adjusted to the light, and I wondered if one ever became accustomed to the thrill of the sight presented. I wondered if everyone were as taken in by it as was I.

The yards were swarming with men aloft, spread out across their length, and busy fitting chaffing gear to the lines. The decks were also a busy place with the mates working hard to set the rigging. They were removing the seizing and coverings, bowsing the shrouds and rigging taut, aligning the dead-eyes, and fitting coverings and chaffing gear anew.

I took up my usual position just aft of the starboard quarterdeck steps, and peered through the stanchions into the glittering reflection of the morning sun that swept across the open sea to meet me. It took some time to clear the sleep out of my head. I was distracted from the sparkling reflections, and compelled to look forward at three men who were perched dangerously out beyond the bows, upon the guys and back-stays of the bowsprit. They were getting tackles upon the martingale, hooking and unhooking them, and bowsing it to windward, setting it up to take the strain. My stomach was in my throat as I watched them hanging out over the exploding waves of the open sea. Thankfully, they were suddenly blocked from my view.

"Hey, you."

Mary's coppery blonde head popped into my line of sight, her hair blowing about her face in swirls and glowing in the sun as she rose to the top step. She came toward me.

"Good morning, Mary," said I

"Good morning to you, sleepy head. I didn't see you at the breakfast table. I went to the bunk thinking you were still there. Have you eaten yet?"

"No. I wanted to, but it's so loud down there. Who can eat? Who can even think?"

233

"Maybe so, but you have to eat, Liz. Come on, you come with me, and I'll see you get some breakfast. Have you washed up?"

"Yes. Could we make a deal, Mary?"

"A deal? What, you and I? What kind of deal for heaven's sake?"

"If you bring me up a cup of tea and a biscuit, I will return the favor in kind tonight. When you're tired and in our bunk, I will bring you a cup of tea and a bite to eat—and I shall brush your hair I promise." Mary looked at me puzzled and then smiled.

"I don't know about any deal, Elizabeth, but stay put and I'll bring up a tin of tea and a biscuit—just for you." This she did along with a piece of chocolate, my sailing ship blanket, and a message from Lady Rebecca to be careful and mind Mary.

This day started entirely different from my last. While I slept, the anchor was weighed, the sails unfurled and set, and the ship had been making way for hours before I managed to get to my feet. We doubled the cape at Ramsgate, while still early in the morning, and stood south by west for a short reach until the towering white cliffs of Dover came upon our starboard bow. The yards were 'braced to' by the men and the ship stood west by south.

Contrary to the captain's hopes, we were put to task by the Westerlies, which were low upon the hemisphere and now the prevailing headwind of the English Channel. It blew in union with the warm gulf current, making for a more disagreeable sea and generally useless sail. Fortunately, according to Captain Ward who stood upon the quarterdeck and expressed his opinions to me quite regularly, the REBECCA was proving to be a close-hulled ship and stood the headwind well. We beat the wind and hammered the seas until by late afternoon, we witnessed the passing of Eastborne and Brighton. As the sun descended before us in a blazing show to mark the end of day, the lights of the great harbor Portsmouth were visible in the distance off our starboard bow.

TWENTY-EIGHT

Those last ghostly rays of the setting sun were upon us, bathing everything in a residue of purple blushes. The sharp definition of the ship had now blurred into long stretches of indistinct shadows that were increasingly bleeding into one another. The air was cooling rapidly, and so I left the quarterdeck hurriedly, only to return a moment later with my ship blanket for protection against the evening chill. I knew Lady Rebecca would be calling out for me shortly, but I so loved the subtle colors of the last light of day that I was determined to sit quietly at the stanchions, in hopes of being left undisturbed to savor each of the remaining minutes.

I pulled my blanket up around my shoulders and neck to prevent the wind from working through. I closed my eyes, opening them only briefly to glimpse about, while I faced the chilly sea breeze that blew through my hair and sounded in my ears. It made me feel all the more cozy as I attempted to conserve heat beneath the blanket. I imagined myself to be a turtle tucked into its shell.

At short intervals, I would glimpse across the starboard bow at the lights upon the English coast. I would never look out for more than a second or two before closing my eyes and recalling the scene in my memory. My mind was drifting peacefully, almost half asleep. The image of the lights was moving through my head when it became disrupted by something unclear. It was a whitish cloud, a concentrated mist moving toward me across the main deck below. Instinctively, I opened my eyes to question what I might have seen that was so puzzling.

To my surprise, a second look, which awakened my senses, revealed a number of men on deck just aft Lady Rebecca's coach. I knew the jacks had been working there. I also knew they had opened the aftwardmost hatch, but my sleepy head had paid little mind. It was different now. Now, I paid close attention. I was perplexed by the dusty cloud that thinned to reveal a cluster of men that looked like a troupe of ghosts, men standing there painted white as pickets from a fence. All of a sudden one man lurched forward and sneezed. A massive cloud of white mist erupted from his being and at once the others broke into a roar of laughter, jumping up and down and slapping each other, causing puffs of the white dust to billow forth and be carried my way by the wind.

The men were flailing their arms and legs, and falling all over themselves like a bunch of rummies. They were a garrulous group who I overheard were Americans. Appearing bold and full of confidence, they must have been familiar friends, for they clasped and hugged one other. A wonderfully spirited lot, they brought a smile to my face as I sat and watched them carrying on. Around and around Lady Rebecca's coach, they danced in a circle and sang at the top of their lungs. By the time Milady had sent for me, the Americans had washed up, settled down, and sorted themselves out enough to give a hand at the lines.

After coming abreast of Portsmouth, night was well upon us. I was feeling the fatigue of a long day and suffering a bout of yawns. I prodded myself to go below. Lady Rebecca sighted me in her cabin, and feeling the better for it, she instructed me to take some repast then see myself to bed. This was our third night aboard ship, and we were still sorting out the best manner of accomplishing the daily tasks in need of doing.

The initial plan had us separated into four groups of ten to twelve each. A group equaled about a quarter of our number, whereby two groups were made up of girls and the other two, all boys. Lady Rebecca and Mary took charge of the girls, and Gregory LaBianca along with Avery, who was the oldest male orphan at age twelve, watched over the boys. The girls bathed first and followed one another into the cabin that adjoined the Claussens'. Here they stripped, wrapped themselves in towels, and waited their turn to enter Lady Rebecca's cabin to wash. Once clean, the children remained in the dressing room to dry off then underwent a thorough inspection by Lady Rebecca and Mary for injury or infestation.

Afterward, the girls would leave by way of the double doors, walk down the corridor toward the pilothouse, and then down into the galley to sup whilst the boys would take their turn at a bath. When all four groups were dressed and fed, they were collected and called to order in steerage. Lady Rebecca would direct us to form a queue, four abreast, shoulder to shoulder—the boys to line up on one side, the girls to the other. At that point came the head count and roster call, for Milady lived in morbid fear of discovering a child had been lost overboard.

Milady had taken her place by the accommodation ladder, which was aft of the bunks and opened her mouth so as to speak. Suddenly, she halted. She was looking beyond us to the tail end of the queue, obviously frozen in thought. An expression of bewilderment swept across her face.

I turned about to have a see, but noticed nothing in particular, nothing out of the ordinary. For a moment, I thought there was a new face amongst us. Someone I hadn't seen before. This girl was surely a full foot taller and a solid thirty pounds heavier than the rest of us, and I was surprised to have missed her. As a rule, I was pretty observant.

I tried to place this girl, but things were hectic over the past couple of days to say the least, and it would have been expected that some introductions still had to be made. Besides, I had done my best to avoid all the orphans as much as possible. I wasn't even sure if she was an orphan or not. With little more than a passing thought, I assumed she must be an orphan because none of the children standing beside her paid any mind to her presence. They obviously knew her so I dismissed the matter and turned back to give Lady Rebecca my attention. It was only then, knowing well Milady's ways and her expressions that I knew something had definitely captured her attention. At once, I sensed it had to be this girl. I wasn't dreaming; she *was* new among us!

To my surprise, Lady Rebecca did nothing more than proceed to call out the names, one after another, and await a response from every child listed on her register. Only because the face of this girl was new to me, did I listen for the call of a name to which she would respond. It never came. At first, I thought this was peculiar for she had been standing in line. Then I concluded that she probably wasn't an orphan after all, and I had misread the entire affair. I accepted this at face value, understanding perfectly well that if she were not an orphan, her name would not be on the register, and that was the end of that. But if she wasn't an orphan, how was it everyone seemed to know her? I was perplexed.

After the call of names, Lady Rebecca ordered the children to their berths and reached out to draw me to her side. I walked with her forward through steerage passing each bunk. She made careful observations, assuring herself that all was well. As we moved along, she would talk openly with the children to ease their fears during their first nights at sea. She tried to add to their comfort the best she could. At last Milady came to the girl in question. I sensed she was trying to disappear under her blanket. She feigned sleep, but Lady Rebecca was not so foolish. After studying her closely for a moment, Milady placed her hand upon the girl's shoulder and spoke in a low voice.

"Miss, I know very well that you are most wide awake, and I would guess trembling by this time at having been found out." The girl opened her eyes and by the look within, Milady had surmised well.

"I do not wish to disturb the other children, and so I would put it upon you to follow me to my chambers at once, if you would be so kind." With that said, Lady Rebecca turned and we walked off.

The girl having but little choice, slipped quietly off her bunk and traded glances with a number of the other children. She followed Milady and me as instructed. Yet, all eyes followed her. Lady Rebecca scaled her accommodation ladder and entered the dressing room of her cabin. I turned to watch the girl trace our steps. She was a stranger to me, but not the orphans. I could plainly see by the hushed commotion that she was well known to them. In fact, they appeared very afraid for her.

As I passed through the hatch, I heard Milady call out to Mr. Claussen.

"Christopher!"

"Yes, my darling." He was reclining upon the bed, framed in the glow of an oil lamp, and engrossed in a book about the business of shipping. He failed to look up.

"We have ourselves a guest."

Hearing that, Christopher started, came to his feet, and immediately made himself presentable. He looked toward the accommodation ladder as the girl emerged from below. She looked frightened, which caused Mr. Claussen to hesitate. Carefully, he reached out his hand in welcome.

"Forgive me. I wasn't expecting guests at this hour."

The girl stood mute and failed to take his hand, not out of disrespect, but quite obviously out of fear for present company. She had the look of a cornered cat, eyes opened wide and searching for a way out.

"Come this way, child," Lady Rebecca ordered as she moved across the cabin and took up a seat in the study. Mr. Claussen remained on his feet. The girl walked through the cabin nervously and stood before them. I sat down at the top step of the ladder and watched from there, for the blind was not drawn.

"What name was given you, child?" Milady asked.

"Britany," came the soft reply.

"You may speak up. Contrary to what you might be thinking, you shan't be thrown overboard. I will have to call you by a name."

"Britany," she reiterated with more force.

239

"Nothing more?"

"Britany Allison...Coombes."

"Well, which is it? Britany Allison or Britany Coombes?"

"It is all three. My first name is Britany, my second is Allison, and my family name is Coombes."

"Three names, that seems somewhat boastful does it not? It is odd indeed. I have heard of it, but I ask, why would one need three names? A reason I cannot imagine. Yet, if it is so then so be it. Tell me, Britany Allison Coombes, how is it that your three names do not appear on my register? Surely, I would have spotted them."

"I'm not sure, madam. They should be there, I am certain," she lied.

"Tell me then, Britany Allison Coombes, how is it that my eyes have not come upon you the whole of this day, nor yesterday, nor any day for that matter?"

"I am not sure, madam. I've been about, not unlike the rest," she replied with sincerity.

"That is obvious, girl, as we are completely surrounded by water. I am not a fool. And yet, you certainly were not upon the deck, and certainly not in the children's quarters, nor the mess, and no one amongst the men had made mention of your presence; and that would be hard to imagine, now that I have taken a good look at you. There is more here than meets the eye. I feel you think me a fool. So why don't we fess up to what we are really about before my patience wanes, and then maybe we can work this out together? I promise no harm will come to you, Britany Allison Coombes, but I expect nothing less than honesty."

The girl fidgeted with her ring, her eyes darting about and her mind visibly racing with indecision. At last, she decided it best to comply.

"I *am* one of the orphans," she stressed. "But I wasn't allowed to stay at the orphanage any longer on account of my age—I am past thirteen. I still spend a lot of time with the other children, and that's how I come to know about the ship. I haven't been able to find a proper job, and so I begged the headmistress to let me go to America as well, but she refused. She said I was old enough to make my own way. But I know what way that is, madam. I've seen it in Hyde Park and St. James. I've talked to the older girls who used to live at the orphanage and were unable to find work and it frightens me." She stood silent.

I saw Lady Rebecca's face go pale; her eyes avoided the girl. I thought of her friend Jennifer standing in St. James Park, and I began to understand a little more of the mystery that surrounded that night. Jennifer must have been a prostitute, and I wondered if that troubled Lady Rebecca, for prostitutes were supposed to be lowly people; but I knew Lady Rebecca had given Jennifer a handsome gift. She thought very highly of her. I sensed this girl's confession must have reached Milady's heart for it definitely gave her reason to pause a moment before speaking again.

"I am curious to know how you managed to steal aboard, Britany Allison. Please tell me by what clever device you succeeded." The girl looked as though she were standing before a torture chamber.

"Well—I knew I looked too old to pass for an orphan, so I pretended to work for the orphanage. The headmistress and the others were on the lookout for me, so I had to think of a way to avoid them, but still appear to be with the orphanage. I asked four of the younger children to help me by stealing away just long enough for the headmistress and the others to enter the pilothouse.

"There was so much confusion that they were never missed. I figured a roll wouldn't be called until everyone was settled down, and I figured that wouldn't be any time soon judging by all the chaos. Once everyone went below decks, I sent the four up the plank and pretended us to have arrived late. I used the children to scout about the ship, everyone believing I was rounding them up whenever we were discovered. Eventually, I sent them off to berthing and I went through the galley then into the hold and below decks until I reached the bilge."

"And that is where you have been hiding?"

"Yes, Milady."

"What brought you up at last?"

"The dark. There is no light below and I could hear the rats. I was afraid the ship might sink and I would be trapped. I was scared."

"Rats? I hope to differ." Mr. Claussen complained. "The ship is new and none cleaner exist, of this I am certain."

"I am sorry, sir. I thought it was rats. I don't know what it was. I could hear things moving around and I was scared. Maybe it was just my imagination. Yes, I am sure it was. There were no rats, no sir. I didn't see any rats." The girl was frightened to her wits at the thought of crossing Mr. Claussen.

"Never mind. It matters little. The point is—a bilge is no place for a young lady, Miss Britany Allison." Mr. Claussen then surmised. "Stowing away aboard ship, on the other hand, is a very serious matter, rats or no rats. You could spend the rest of your days at the plantations sweltering in a hot sun or serving to fulfill the cravings of men for a much lesser offense—the one thing you so with to avoid."

"Yes, sir."

The girl shrunk back, dropping her head, fully aware that the stakes were high. She was now purely at the mercy of her company. Her tears began to surface. She was visibly trembling. Mr. Claussen continued to speak.

"In any event, as Lady Rebecca has stated, none of that is about to happen so you needn't worry. Dry your eyes, girl. You have nothing to fear on this ship. It is true you are old enough to work and by the look of you, plenty fit. I will expect you to work for your passage, and you shall receive the same benefits and discipline as the men aboard the REBECCA. I prefer you stay on in the children's quarters, as I have no berthing on board suitable for a young woman. If the men on board should cause you concern or treat you with disrespect; you are to report to me at once. Is that clear?"

"Yes, sir."

"Very good. Tomorrow morning you will report to Cookie Jar at four sharp."

"Yes, sir!" Her eyes brightened and her spirits soared.

"I will work till my fingers run with blood, I swear it! Thank you for your kindness, thank you so very much. I will do you honor, I swear."

"Nonsense, child, I am not looking for blood or honor. Just do the work as you are told, keep your nose clean, and I will consider the debt paid in full. Now, unless Rebecca has further business with you, be off to bed."

Lady Rebecca pressed her fingers to her lips and blew a small kiss toward Britany.

"Good night, Britany Allison."

"Good night, Milady." She glowed, the weight of the world having been lifted from her shoulders.

"Britany."

"Yes, Milady."

"How old are you?"

"Fifteen, so I am told, but sometimes I think I may be older."

"When did you last eat?" Britany looked embarrassed.

"Three days past, Milady."

"I thought as much. Very well, see if Cookie Jar or steward Gregory is in the galley and ask for something to eat, then try to get some sleep. The morning comes sooner than you can know."

"Yes, Milady, thank you for your kindness, and good night." She curtsied clumsily on the rocking deck then stood awkwardly, unsure of where to go. Milady sensed this at once.

"Elizabeth, escort Britany Allison to the galley and ask Cookie Jar to stick something to her ribs. Show her the staircase to berthing, if she doesn't already know, then return to me."

"Yes, Milady." I jumped up from the ladder at once.

Lady Rebecca turned to Mr. Claussen. "This may be good fortune, for she would make the count of orphans an even fifty. It might be an omen from God, I dare say." She turned toward him, and found him looking both amused and resigned to the situation.

When I returned, Milady called me at once to her side. She undressed me, and after having freshened the water, we bathed together in the tub. During my bath, and afterward as she brushed out my hair, I stood quietly and listened as she and Mr. Claussen renewed their conversation about the new girl.

"If nothing else, coming from the orphanage, I would be most surprised if she isn't well read and somewhat knowledgeable in the ways of the world, bookwise and streetwise. After my past night's experience with the children, I dare say Mary and I can use her assistance much to our advantage. She'll earn her keep, that I assure you." Mr. Claussen considered her thoughts and nodded his head, but said nothing else.

"It is late and time to turn in. Run along to Mary, and sleep tight. I will see you in the morning."

"Yes, Milady." I started down the ladder and turned a moment to blow kisses as Lady Rebecca turned down the covers of their bed.

"Good night, Elizabeth. Sleep tight."

Except for times of privacy, Lady Rebecca preferred to leave the hatch above the accommodation ladder open most of the time. This allowed her to listen for trouble, and it also provided some light to enter the berthing from her cabin above. The light washed lightly across the few berths that surrounded the base of the ladder. The berths closest to the ladder were the ones occupied by Mary and myself. In this way we were always nearby and ready to respond to Milady's beck and call. Mary was not yet asleep and welcomed me with open arms. It was quite possibly my favorite time of day, for I was utterly content to be cuddled and would purr like a kitten within her embrace.

TWENTY-NINE

The next morning, the mood in the cabin was somber. Lady Rebecca was tending to those children in steerage who were learning firsthand about sickness of the sea. After going up and down the ladder herself a half a dozen times for medicines and the towels being washed in the tub, she quickly made me a helper.

There were advantages to being the go-between, the runner carrying items up and down the accommodation ladder that Milady required for her doctoring. For one thing, I sat upon the upper step of the ladder, well within her cabin, while I awaited her summons. The windows in the cabin were open and offered an abundance of sunshine and fresh air to relieve me from the stench of the vomit down below. It was also the easiest place from which to hand down freshly laundered towels and bed sheets that were being washed clean in the tub, or to hand up the soiled goods to the girls who were doing the laundry. Except for the two doing the scrubbing, they being under strict orders to do their work in silence, the cabin was left to the business of Mr. Claussen and Captain Ward. The men were having serious discussions about the issues now facing them. I sat within easy earshot of Mr. Claussen and had no reservation about listening in as he spoke.

"I am certain we were only allowed to leave London without hindrance for reasons of publicity regarding the orphans on board. In light of public awareness, it would have been difficult to encumber, let alone impress this ship, and suffer those young children a less than proper opportunity of a future, be it in England or abroad. It would have given the stoutest of politicians a black eye. At the same time, we also removed fifty orphans from the public assistance rolls—two birds, one stone, both politically and emotionally un touchable. It would have been social suicide for anyone to stand up and object.

"However, now that we are on the open sea and away from that same public eye, I view our situation as being changed markedly. I dare say the English fleet would easily justify boarding the REBECCA in the name of the Crown. It would be recorded in the log as standard procedure, a necessity in light of the French conflict—for purpose of national security, of course."

"How right you are, sir! There is many an English officer, not to mention a horde of drooling subordinates who would delight in the confiscation of a ship as fine as this," stated Captain Ward. "If the children should end up at plantations instead of the States, it would be thought a small price to pay by their reckoning. Of this I am certain.

"I have already seen how they steal away men from their families without conscience or remorse—always in the name of national security. I wouldn't be the least bit surprised to see this whole issue of transporting orphans from London to the States for a better life being twisted into some form of insult, some inflammatory issue that could be used as ammunition beneficial

246

to one of those pompous English captains. Turn the issue into a slap across the face of English pride, and then add to this the needs of those wealthy and influential plantation owners crying upon bended knee, pleading incessantly for more working hands. They have the resources to make such deliveries well worth any profit-minded captain's consideration.

"There are plenty of people in the Isles who hold a less than estimable opinion of their fellow countrymen wishing to run off to America in search of a better life. It is a rather blatant testimony that insinuates all things may be less than optimum within the greatest empire on earth. Therefore, why not relegate these ungratefuls to work a plantation for enlightenment and a lesson in the understanding of true misery? Let's teach them proper what to expect for exhibiting such an outward display of weakness and insolence." The captain did nothing to hide his disdain for the English aristocracy.

"I must say, Captain Ward, I am not so assured as you that the English commoner is brimming full of hatred toward Americans. I do a lot of business with the English. I wonder if the problem isn't just the opposite—one of bonds too close; bonds that are unbreakable because of common heritage, bonds that bind the English and you Americans like two brothers, fighters seeking a prize in the ring, men born of the same mother. I believe this holds true right up to the Crown. Their view of impressing Americans to serve in their fleets is much less than the kidnapping Americans perceive it to be. To them it is more like snagging unruly children by the ear and bringing them back to the table.

"You might consider also, the English will impress the crews of American ships because it seems as though every Englishman who is conscripted into service for King George claims to be an American; it being the last hope for those unlucky souls to escape years at sea against their will. Have no doubt, if one is to believe all one is told, the Englishman is now extinct and Americans populate all of northern Europe. Admittedly, if you were indeed an American, it would be rare that upon your person you would carry proof beyond a doubt that you were in fact not an Englishman or a deserter from the man-o'-wars. It would be difficult to support your claims of innocence, but once the matter was settled, you would most certainly be released. Unfortunately, you might have already spent three years as a gunner in His Majesty's service while awaiting that determination."

"Unfortunately, hardly says it, sir," replied Captain Ward in disgust, downing his last gulp of rum. "I apologize if I have portrayed myself to be narrow-minded and mean-spirited. I have been witness to many injustices inflicted upon my fellow countrymen and it does color my presentation."

"No need to apologize, Captain. I find all you say to be well thought out and sensible. I am of a conviction that all men are basically good by heart, and it is usually the lack of education and honest information that blackens their image. I prefer to give them the benefit of the doubt and at times I find myself taken for a fool.

"Please don't misunderstand me, I certainly do not condone these practices, but it cannot be overlooked that a great deal of time, money, and effort was invested in the colonies. It must be difficult to say the least, for one to matter-of-factly accept the notion; just because the colonies have won a round and no longer wish to play ball, the game is over. After all, whose taxes have paid the high cost of settlement? Who has paid to maintain the military personnel for protection against the Indians and the French?

"My friend, give some thought to this issue of Napoleon. The Colonies are but one issue; I dare say at times an irritation at most when compared to the politics of the Continent. What wish have the English to look across an ocean for a headache? England has concerns aplenty at her own shores that are not unfounded. Her culture faces a great threat by the ambitions and expansionist attitudes of France. She merely has to observe the demise of her neighbors as they fall one by one to the armies of Napoleon. She has spent years listening to his threats to demolish the growing industries of England. There can be no denying the man is bent on accomplishing this task.

"How do you suppose she views the many people of French influence living within the ranks of the English at the eastern seaboard? The prospect of this new and vibrant sphere of influence developing into a French state is unthinkable on English soil. I believe their opinion is simple; as long as they control the colonies, the French will be shut out."

"I must say, Mr. Claussen, with all due respect this sounds like the same old problems that have plagued the Continent since the beginning of time. I say let them boil in their own miserable brew. From the perspective of we Americans who live outside the influence of English concerns, the attraction to the king and his arrogance is about equal to that of a plate of uncooked squid.

"I would also like to add that France, with all her ambition, reckless at it might be, has proposed some novel and fresh ideas that could bring advancement to the world in many positive ways. It is unfortunate indeed that such ideas come from the jurisdiction of a man seemingly bent upon his own ambitions, an egomaniac who has trod upon too many borders with an air of indifference. And I assure you at some point it will be his demise; of this I have no doubt. Yet, in speaking for the French, I feel they have done more for my country than most. They have lived and worked that land for decades. They lived in peace with the Indians, unlike the English who have bullied, beat and cheated them out of their lands. It was the French who won the bloody revolution against the British, not us Americans. It was *they* who freed *us* from the oppressive regulations of the king."

"Your point is well taken, Captain Ward, and I too applaud France in many ways. I simply wish to move forward my opinion that neither England nor France despises the States. I say both countries should be embarrassed for their arrogance and disregard for the real treasure or horror that awaits them in the New World.

"They seem blind to the power unfolding before them. They see only the potential for material gain and completely miss what is really taking place. Issues of morality and freedom from injustice and impunity, issues Americans will readily stand up and die to preserve. It has not gone unnoticed by the impoverished of all countries, and this is the oversight that will rock European governments to their foundations, a price all of Europe will pay for dearly in the future. Mark my words, Captain."

"As an American, I couldn't agree more. Salute!" The captain held up his drink. "I applaud your insight. The belligerence these countries exhibit toward each other only serves to disrupt their relationship with the greatest country ever conceived. God bless the United States." The men drank and after a moment of collecting their thoughts, Mr. Claussen again spoke to the captain.

"It must be accepted for now that American trade at this point is a financially hollow weapon on the international scale, but it is an enormously effective means for Europeans to gouge one another politically. Let us not kid ourselves, there remain plenty of souls in both France and Britain who have business ties in the Colonies, and many influential persons across Europe have gained great wealth and prominence in dealing with the self-proclaimed American States. In some cases, such as mine, money can be made from these rivalries.

"My family has made its fortune on understanding the animosities between the English and French, as well as others, and working the politics to our best advantage. As far as America is concerned, I believe you will discover the Europeans are very likely to bark, but not necessarily bite."

"I concede, for you are the better judge of world politics than I, Mr. Claussen. Mostly, I keep my nose to the wind and watch the sail. Yet, this I know for fact; the result of this unrest is the formation of a perfect climate for the breeding of pirates. That is what all the danger and intrigue of world politics brings to our table—*pirates*. Pirates are what we must address at this time. Pray we don't overlook these despicable bastards, who go about plundering in the name of Napoleon, or King George. It is they we will find upon the ocean to do us harm, for armies don't tread water."

"How right you are, Captain Ward. They are opportunists of the first degree; England, France, I suppose it makes little difference. Publicly, neither country endorses such policies, but they certainly support the activity. Any ship captured on the open sea heading for an enemy coast is considered fair game. It must save a great deal of wear and tear on the man-o'-wars. I suppose it is much easier to work with volunteers who know what they are getting into; you simply throw them the spoils as payment for services rendered and your fleet doubles in size, with blessings from all."

"For whatever good it is," said the captain, "we sail under the Swedish flag, and at least in European waters there is some respect for our lives. If they should take us by force, we can expect them to exhibit a certain civility toward their fellow man. This will not be the case along the Barbary Coast of North Africa, the Gold Coast, or even some of those remote reaches nearer our own back yard, such as the coast of Ireland for example.

"It is they whom I fear most. It is those truly unscrupulous souls to be found operating with full government sanction or in complete disregard of sovereign law, such as those Irish devils. They can be a bloody ruthless lot. Those pirates of North Africa are vicious, they act with impunity, and they will prey on any luckless ship within their reach. They are famous for their legendary daring and lack of remorse. They sell their captives into slavery, especially the women and children. Damn them all to hell for eternity."

I looked up at the two girls who suddenly stopped their scrubbing, and who were now staring down at me. They were white as ghosts, and who could blame them? This was the second time the matter of pirates had befallen my ears, and I found it to be even more frightening than before. It made my throat dry.

THIRTY

"A month or two at best! Oh, Christopher! It's barely been a day or two, and I am up to my elbows in vomit—if not the children's, then my own. I am miserable. We are all miserable. Whatever happened to talk of crossing in a fortnight? Now you say we must suffer another month or two. Now you say we must endure the length of a southern journey. Pray, dear God, tell me I am dreaming."

"Rebecca, you are ripping my heart out. It pains me to see you so miserable. You must believe that this will pass. The body will adjust. Rarely does the sickness last more than a few days. You must understand; it simply isn't prudent for us to steer a westing along the 40th parallel as we once proposed. I assure you, my love, Captain Ward and I have given much thought to the issue. Seeing everyone this sick only strengthens our resolve to sail calmer waters. I promise once you and the children get your sea legs, you will come to enjoy yourselves and you will especially enjoy sailing the southern route. I know you, Rebecca.

"Give me your trust and know all will go well, for Captain Ward and I have not made our decision on a whim. Allow me to give account of these points of consideration upon which we have based our decision to head south. First, even mildly disagreeable weather along the shorter northern route would encumber us to the extent that we would arrive in America no sooner than had we taken the longer and more agreeable southern route. Except that those high northern seas would serve only to suffer you and the children further. It is often a fearfully brutal sea, and it brings the strongest and hardiest of sailors to their knees. You shan't wish to face it my love."

Mr. Claussen stood at Milady's side and caressed her. He was disheartened by her misery. He painted a dismal picture of how much worse life could be for her and the children along the northern route. He explained the pounding we might endure for days on end, should we be caught up in the midst of the all-too-common cold and raging storms that were regularly spurned on by the Westerlies in those northern latitudes.

I had little desire to argue his decision, having carried rags up and down the ladder for two days to wipe up vomit. I was one of the fortunate few little affected by the motion of the ship. It was the stench that made me wish to retch. I felt utterly sympathetic for Lady Rebecca, for not only did she feel miserable, but she also insisted on nursing the others under her care. She refused to confine herself to the bed in spite of her condition. She was white as a ghost, trembled, and had all she could do to stay on her feet.

I kept tea for her close at hand and tended to her needs the best I was able. She appreciated what little I could do and applauded me for watching over Mary as well. Poor Mary fared little for the better and was now collapsed upon our bunk in a terrible way. There was a doctor on board, who had been employed by Mr. Claussen to make his rounds and care for the children as needed, but it was Mr. LaBianca who offered the most assistance to Milady. He was wholly accustomed to the sea and remained strong throughout the ordeal. He was in a good mood, for it was obvious he was needed for his service. His best medicine was his cheery attitude, which gave us hope and reason to believe at some point this hardship would end. Mr. Claussen continued to speak.

"Second, Captain Ward and I both agree there is too much traffic of the bothersome English man-o'-wars. Their numbers are seemingly beyond count. They pay no mind to the issue of weak stomachs and make best of the shortest and fastest route to the Americas. They follow the fortieth, staying to the north as a rule and remain undeterred by the perils of its high seas."

Captain Ward then injected his own opinion.

"The English are desirous to destroy commercial shipping along the eastern seaboard of the States, Milady. They are enforcing their presumed right of search and impressment. When a ship-of-the-line spies a commercial vessel venturing along the

American coast, at the very least they will board her. Thereafter, the ship most likely will be confiscated, and the men taken against their will to serve in the English fleet, or they may scuttle her on grounds the foreign vessel may be used for military purpose against them.

"The REBECCA is too large and well built to be passed over by any English officer ambitious to swell the ranks under his command. Attempting to outrun the English on the high seas is risky at best, and a good way to end up sighted down the barrel of their cannon with probable loss of life and limb. It is best we go south as Mr. Claussen has already recommended."

"And the last reason?"

Captain Ward and Mr. Claussen looked at each other, and it was the captain who spoke.

"Milady, a few days past, a British frigate the H.M.S. LEOPOLD opened fire upon an American vessel, the U.S.S. CHESAPEAKE just off the Katriina coast at Norfolk. It is said a number of men were killed and many more wounded. It would be plain foolhardy to even consider sailing the northern route knowing the mood of the British at this time. I am told there was one Englishman among the lot and he was summarily hanged.

"I must confess that being given Mr. Claussen's permission, I have concealed a number of Americans on board the REBECCA who were formerly impressed into service for the king. They have managed their escape, but are left to wander with no way home. They have been removed from the love of their wives and families, some gone four years or more.

"Your husband has gone out of his way, risking ship and all, to bring fathers back to their children and husbands back to their spouses. Money cannot repay him for such a grand deed. This comes from the heart. It is a matter of conscience. It would be an unbearable thought to imagine these men ending up back behind the gun ports on a ship-of-the-line. Yet, I am certain this would happen in view of the current state of affairs. I beg you to believe we had no forewarning of such a dangerous turn of events, but it leaves the southern route as our safest route and offers us the best chance of returning the American boys home to their loved ones."

The two stood silent. On any other occasion, Lady Rebecca would have insisted they take the southern route, but this day she was most nauseous and uncomfortable. Even I was forced to tolerate the occasional brushstroke unintentionally delivered with a good measure of pain as she expressed her disillusionment with our circumstance.

"It seems our situation deteriorates by the hour. What of the concerns of pirates? I thought this was worrisome as well. I have heard of nothing, but pirates, pirates, pirates, and now you say we shall head for them directly." Milady was irritated.

"They are certainly not a laughing matter, Rebecca. There are many pirates under the employ of the Beys and Deys all along the Barbary and Gold coasts of North Africa. They sail those waters ever looking to loot misguided merchant ships. The spoils are very good due to the amount of commerce in the Mediterranean, and as of late their numbers have risen to astounding levels. Their successes have made them exceedingly bold in their ventures and the conflict between England and France has only served to help their cause. On the other hand, the Americans have forced Tripoli into a peace accord and that should help ensure our safe passage."

"What are you saying, Christopher? Should I be worried or not? What you say is unclear and certainly offers little in the way of peace of mind," Lady Rebecca protested.

"I have no guarantees, my love. It is with a conscience appalled that I confess many of these despicable pirates are of our own European stock, undeniably spawn of the devil, wanton for profit and void of regard for life or limb. They are often known to maintain contact with their cohorts, those thieves and ruffians employed as stevedores and such upon the docks of Europe. It is there that they keep a watchful eye on stores moving about and pay close mind to shipments destined to pass through these coastal waters. The dockhands are paid well for their information. The REBECCA has been observed by many and the chance that she is being watched by pirates cannot be dismissed.

"Pirates are a very real threat indeed. I won't deny it. Yet, we believe we *will* be harassed by the English, whereas the odds are very good in our favor we shall never see hide nor hair of a pirate. For one thing, they are most apt to remain inside the Straits of Gibraltar, or close to the western shore of Africa, near the slave trading routes where the business of piracy is most lucrative. It makes little sense for them to ply their trade out into the barren waters of the Atlantic. Furthermore, we propose to sail a good many leagues off shore and mostly out of view of both pirates and the English. It is also encouraging to know the REBECCA sails briskly, and will give any scoundrel afloat a sound run for his money."

"And you, Captain, I believed you to be impatient to return to your home and family. Is this no longer your feeling?" Milady inquired, unprepared to accept even one additional day afloat unless it was absolutely necessary.

"Ouch!" I voiced my complaint.

"Oh, child, forgive me my carelessness." She kissed me on the back of my head, and then continued with the brushing.

"Truthfully? If you must know, I fear the confines of a house almost as much as I fear the pirates of the open sea. I am committed to spending my final years upon the porch alongside my wife. Forever more, I shall gaze across the deep blue from atop a bluff instead of the quarterdeck. I shall listen to the chatter of squirrels instead of sea gulls. This I have promised, for she has waited a lifetime for me. And I do so willingly.

"However, I would not deny myself one final voyage of pleasure, a voyage not driven by the issue of profit. It is an honor to captain a vessel such as this. Her manners are exemplary, for she is built as true and skillful as any ship a sail. She does your name great honor, Milady, and she will make you proud. On that I give you my word."

The captain not only spoke with pride himself, but his face wore the look of it. He was honest about his elation in commanding the REBECCA and no one could doubt it.

"I see little of what my difference of opinion might effect upon either our situation or your plans, gentlemen. I trust you have put our well being foremost in your thoughts and this remains my only consolation. Do as you must."

That having been said, Milady set down the brush, let loose a sigh of despair, and prepared herself mentally for the longer southern route. She asked to be excused, and feeling nauseous and frustrated, descended into steerage to look in upon Mary and the others.

"Bear with me, Captain Ward. Rebecca is under the weather as you can see. I assure you, she will have a change of heart, for no finer woman have I ever known. She has the spine, the will, and the determination to see herself through the very worst of any situation once she puts her mind to it. It was for these strengths among her many that I found myself devoted to her."

Fortunately, just as Mr. Claussen had predicted, the sickness of the sea abated for many and there came back a semblance of normality to our lives. Milady regained her strength twofold and took full charge once again, her outlook brighter than ever.

Four days in all we beat to the Westerlies, which seemed intent upon pushing us back through the chop of the English Channel from whence we departed. Mr. Claussen quipped he should have remained at the London Docks and left with the rest of his fleet for all the trouble we were having making way. All the while, we played cat and mouse with the many silhouettes of warships—first, those of the English within the Channel, and lastly those of the French, especially along the coast near Brest. Yet, the captain and

Mr. Claussen kept constant vigil and managed to evade them all and the REBECCA launched out across Bay of Biscay now off her larboard bow.

Here the vastness of the Atlantic greeted us and provided a measure of safety in its expanse. To our delight the winds turned favorable and Captain Ward benefited, as did we all, from the Trades coming north by east. From his place upon the quarterdeck, he ordered that his helmsman should stand southwest bearing two hundred twenty-five degrees. With a turn of the wheel the bows found their heading, and REBECCA's masts leaned gently over to her leeward side.

On this, our first southern reach, everyone spoke merrily, for the seas were at once with us and the ship sailed with the waves rising peacefully upon the stem. Captain Ward was forever looking skyward, high up into the canvas. Often he called out to one of the bunters or topmen aloft.

"How goes it aloft, mate!"

"All a-taunt-o, Captain!"

"Very good, sailor. Keep a sharp eye on the shrouds lest they go slack. I'll see no slatch aboard this ship. Do you understand?"

"Aye aye, sir!"

Ever drawing up the rigging, it now taking a good set, and trimming the sails till full, we sailed free and unencumbered before a fair wind.

On the Saturday the twenty-seventh of June, we came abreast the upper coast of Spain and doubled Cape Finisterre from whence the captain stood south by west bearing one hundred eighty-five degrees and thereupon brought Portugal into distant view off our weather beam. Days later Cape St. Vincent jutted out into the sea toward our weather beam. It marked the entrance to the infamous Sea of Cadiz or Sea of Trafalgar, as I also heard it called.

"I cannot believe I am putting eyes upon these waters!" exclaimed Milady.

"At last! Thank the Lord, benefits of worth on our southern voyage," Mr. Claussen retorted with pleasure.

"These are legendary waters, Elizabeth. They will be forever remembered by the English as long as there is an England."

She immediately began to recount the stories that flooded the West Indies Inn and the latest news circulated since her departure. Little if anything in the history of her country produced such emotional outpouring as the events that occurred in the seas before us. Stories of the greatest sea battle of all time were born here, stories she listened to repeatedly as told to her by the sailors whom she served or befriended. Detailed accounts were to be found on the front page of every daily journal with follow-up editorials inside. The events depicted by children playing in the street or in the most revered theaters of London.

It was impossible to be English or know an Englishman and escape the verbal onslaught of praise and approval attached to the historic rise and fall of their hero, the courageous and dashing Lord Nelson. His public life was one of war and triumph, and his personal life was hardly less controversial. It seemed everyone held a deep-seated opinion either for or against his vices or virtues, but these particulars were beyond my ability to grasp.

Instead, I focused on imaginary scenes of the battle that raged between the English ships-of-the-line under his command and the dastardly combination of French and Spanish ships that outnumbered him. My head swam with visions of enormous masted vessels locked in battle, disappearing in the thick smoke of black powder as they emptied their batteries into one another at point-blank range.

I imagined the ships reduced to wrecks. By Lady Rebecca's account, and supported by Captain Ward and Mr. Claussen, nearly six thousand men died in battles that lasted only minutes each. Ten thousand men were taken prisoner.

My young heart was filled with passion as I listened to their talk. I pictured the heroic Lord Nelson collapsing to his knees after taking a round to his chest. In my mind, I saw him accept his fate and cry out to both his God for mercy, and his beloved Emma for forgiveness. I saw him as he lay dying in a pool of his own blood, watching it flow freely across the quarterdeck of his majestic man-of-war, the Victory.

"Every living soul in England rose to salute him a last farewell as his funeral procession passed through London. There had never been anything the likes of it before and I doubt anything comparable shall come to pass again."

During the following days, free of fear, I was fully taken in by all these remarkable stories of the sea and the emotion and look of pride in Lady Rebecca's eyes. She asserted that his victory guaranteed England's rule of the sea forever, for never again would an enemy challenge her countrymen before the mast. She seemed so proud of her people, and we seemed so fearful of them. I was unable to grasp the complexities of the contradiction and much preferred to abandon all for things immediate and more pleasing.

"Milady, look at all the ships!" I pointed to the east, filled with excitement at seeing something other than miles of water. The horizon was sprouting numerous little sails.

"There certainly are a good many of them." Milady agreed. The captain grinned and enlightened us.

"We are passing the Straits of Gibraltar, Elizabeth. This is a well-traveled trade route for merchants traveling in and out of the Mediterranean Sea. Generally those ships are employed in the business of transporting goods to and from the Italian ports of Genoa and Gaeta, Naples, Venice, and many more. It is also a sign for me to double my watch for we are now approaching the African coast."

The captain changed our heading more to seaward to further his distance from shore, knowing it was safer to remain unseen. At the same time, I kept my eyes wide open in fear of seeing something far off in the distance that I prayed I wouldn't.

It was during the last dogwatch that the men aloft observed a large ship off our larboard quarter, heading in our direction from the straits we had recently passed. It was north and east of us and hull down. My heart leapt into my throat as my fears arose, but due to the amount of sail she carried, the men were certain it was an English man-of-war. Even so, the news of it stirred up the fighting spirit of all on deck. The mates delighted in knowing that this supposed ship of the line not only would be hard pressed to catch us, but also would find itself to be drawn far south, and well along the African coast before it might succeed.

The sun, always indifferent to our concerns, went on to set gloriously over the open sea to the west, all the while Captain Ward and Mr. Claussen discussed the sighting. I sat watching the splendid show of light while taking air upon the quarterdeck at my favorite place. Behind me at the rail, Captain Ward was voicing his thoughts to Mr. Claussen.

"This is surely a mixed blessing, for if the truth be known, the English are probably traveling south along the African coast as it is, making their way toward the Islands of Teneriffe, or possibly the Verdes. I believe they are going about their affairs in their usual fashion and as long as they are in sight there will be little need to worry about pirates.

"On the other hand, *this being the downside*, there may be little chance of meeting up with pirates in these waters as long as the man-o'-war is known to be about, but we must still deal with the English who will have no reservations about overtaking us for a boarding. In fact, I wouldn't be the least bit surprised if the captain chose to take up the chase just to alleviate the dangers of monotony aboard his ship and at the same time sharpen the skills of his men."

"I prefer to think of him as feeling somewhat fat and lazy this evening. Hopefully, sipping a brandy as are we, and enjoying the colors of the setting sun." Mr. Claussen wished aloud.

"Not likely, I'm afraid. I would prefer to take advantage of the last of this light to press more canvas. Mr. McCurry!" Captain Ward called out.

"Aye aye, sir!"

"See to it your sails are trimmed low and aloft. Have your men put out the booms and fit the lower studn'sls, if at all possible. By the looks of it, we'll be running free with only a light breeze this night, and I'm of a mind to use the cover of darkness to put on some way and a few extra leagues between us and the man-o'-war by morning's light."

"Aye aye, sir!"

"You Americans are a peculiar breed, Captain. I have often heard you run under sail at night, and now I see the truth of it. Nowhere else have I ever seen this practice. You are a daring lot."

"I trust you meant your comment as a compliment, sir."

"Ha hah! Of course, Captain! What else but that? To American masters, brave souls that they be." Mr. Claussen lifted his glass.

The men laughed heartily and drank to the toast.

THIRTY-ONE

It was on the forenoon watch, the day following, skies being fair and our position somewhat twenty-eight degrees north by fifteen degrees west, when the top of a mountain, still barely visible, appeared upon the southern horizon. It wasn't a feature of the African continent that we spied, but rather the tip of a distant island. This prompted discussions on the quarterdeck about the islands soon to appear and the area in general. A given amount of caution was present in the air, for these were called the islands of Teneriffe. As I understood it, there was much dealing in the business of slaves and gold along this coast and about these waters piracy was a known hazard.

The islands were at the western end of the Barbary Coast state of Morocco, and situated in the middle of shipping routes between the Gold Coast and Europe. Pirates flourished in this area, hiding along the coast or within the islands. Captain Ward claimed that the English spent a good deal of time patrolling these waters, keeping a watch-out for just such activity. He ordered Mr. Beckwith to instruct the helm to keep seaward of the islands to be safe. It was his hope to avoid falling victim to either the pirates or the English, whom he held in equal disdain, both who were more apt to be lurking about within the cover of the islands or closer to the mainland.

The pirates were especially unhappy with Americans, for they refused to pay further monies for safe passage and instead declared war against the piratical states that supported such activities. We remained vigilant, keeping a sharp lookout at all times, and so it was that Jack Beddin, working up high, tarring the shroud beneath the foremast top, was prompted to sound notice of approaching sail.

"Ahoyeeeee! Mr. Beckwith! Sails ahoy!"

Mr. Beckwith turned his whiskered face to the sky. Whereas, Mate Beddin had been working hard in the tops, he was now staring off before us, shielding his eyes from the sun. Suddenly, he looked back down to us, his voice filled with alarm.

"Chebecs! Chebecs! Chebecs!"

The warning reverberated across the deck, and amid a murmur of hushed tones and darting eyes, the men stopped whatever business was at hand in order to look up, search the seas, and further listen to Mr. Beddin.

"Where-away, sailor?" asked Mr. Beckwith, yelling up into the sails.

"Directly, ahead!" Everybody's eyes strained in the direction of the islands, but as of yet there was nothing to be seen.

"Can ya give us a count?"

"Can't say…too far off…hulls down. There's a good many, I dare say!"

"Secure that bucket, sailor, an' go aloft t' the top, or better yet, t' the upper trees."

"Aye."

At that, he tied off his bucket to the trestletrees above his head and moved himself up through the lubber's hole. Fearless of the height, he stood up tall upon the platform, his hair and shirt buffeted from behind by the winds high above.

"Drover!"

"Aye."

"Fetch the glass from the captain's quarters and send it aloft to Beddin."

"Aye."

With spyglass now in hand, Mr. Beddin called down again from the tops.

"A siz'ble fleet, Mr. Beckwith—chebecs, luggers an' frigates so 't 'pears by the cloth. Chebecs fer certain! They be stretched out from the islands westward to sea." Mr. Beckwith thought on this for a moment, then hollered back up.

"Beddin!"

"Aye?"

"Stay aloft what ya can. Get up t' the trees an' keep a sharp eye. Send down word as t' how they stand and if they show their colors."

"Aye!"

At present, the men on deck were unable to see the approaching ships and so gave much attention to the news, talking excitedly amongst themselves. They watched nervously as Mr. Beckwith approached Captain Ward to have a brisk conversation. Mr. Beckwith then sped off as Captain Ward moved aft toward the cabins. With chin in hand, he turned for a moment to look across the bows toward the southern horizon.

"Captain Ward?" I called out, fragmenting his thoughts. He looked my way.

"Yes, Elizabeth."

"I see no ships."

"Neither do I, child." Now I felt better, but was confused.

"How is it that Mate Beddin does if we don't?" The captain may have had pressing affairs on his mind, but he took the time to come to me.

"Let me show you. You know the world is round and not flat, yes?"

"Yes."

"Then give us your mug, and let us turn it on its side. See how it curves around like the world?"

"Yes."

"Place your finger on your side and I will place my finger on my side. Now can your finger see my finger?"

"No."

"If your finger was a ship and my finger was a ship, would they be able to see each other?"

"No."

"That is correct. Now let us pretend your finger is a person on a ship and you raised that person straight up into the air. How far up would you have to raise your finger in order to see mine?" I raised my finger and sighted along its tip until I saw the captain's finger on the other side of the mug.

"Right here."

"Very good. Now do you understand that Mate Beddin has climbed up the mast, as you have raised your finger in order to see over the curve of the earth? From up there he can see the other ships. From where we stand upon this deck alow, we can see about two leagues distant. From where mate Beddin stands aloft, he can see maybe five leagues to the horizon and possibly ten leagues to the royals of another ship."

"Ooooooh. I understand now. I thought it funny that I should look out and see nothing but water."

"That is so often the way of life, Miss Elizabeth. Many things seem strange and terrible until one understands the way of the mystery. Now, should you choose to sit and wait, the first thing you will see as our ships move closer together and approach the top of the curve on the earth's surface will be the sails. It is at that point we say the ship is hull down because you can see the sails, but the hull is down below the horizon and still out of view. I will leave you that to ponder, for I must take my leave."

My lesson was finished and without further delay, Captain Ward turned to enter the pilothouse for the purpose of seeking out Mr. Claussen in his cabin. I chose not to wait and see the ships 'hull down'. Instead, I followed his lead to Milady's cabin, and as he knocked lightly upon the door, I stood at his side.

"Come in." Mr. Claussen called out from within. Captain Ward opened the door and the corridor was at once flooded with light.

"Begging your pardon for this interruption, Mr. Claussen; I'm in need of word with you."

"Pay it no mind, you have my ear, Captain Ward. Please! Come forward, take a seat and speak freely."

Mr. Claussen motioned the captain to his table, but Captain Ward remained just inside the doorway, lowered his head, and cleared his throat, indicating some reservation.

I slipped into the cabin behind the captain and moved over to Lady Rebecca, who was sitting at her dressing table. She immediately reached out for me. She was always relieved and comforted when she could lay eyes upon me and know I was out of mischief or danger. Mr. Claussen perceived at once that Captain Ward wished to speak in private and turned to Lady Rebecca.

"Dearest, it appears I must speak with the good captain in private. Would you forgive me this indiscretion and take your leave so we might converse?" Milady arose to her feet, pushed my hair back from my face and turned to face the men.

"Please, Captain, come forward and make yourself comfortable. I will pour a brandy for your enjoyment, and then I must see to the children, and you shall have all the time you need."

"I am most grateful, Lady Claussen."

"Rebecca," she corrected.

"Yes, ma'am. It is an unpleasant matter before me, unfit for the ears of a genteel lady such as yourself. Forgive me."

"Think nothing of it, Captain. Please, sit down."

He took a seat at the table. He was served his refreshment and given his privacy. Milady descended her accommodation ladder into steerage, but I stopped to take up a seat upon the first step. From there I could see both men. As always, I was especially curious about Mr. Claussen. I watched as Captain Ward raised his glass.

"To your Lady Rebecca."

"To my beloved Rebecca."

The gentlemen touched glasses and Captain Ward spoke freely.

"I am come before you, Mr. Claussen, to convey news, which may prove distressing in the best of light. We have taken sight of a fleet to the south of us that has spread out two or three leagues to seaward of the islands that are now before us. I fear this fleet may present us with ill fortune. Indeed, they appear to be a formidable concern, employing upwards of forty or more vessels. I hear reports of chebecs, luggers, and sloops, frigates also, so I am told. I dare say they are well poised to do us great harm if they so choose.

"This is not a typical pirate's fleet, Mr. Claussen. I must say, it is most unusual to encounter a fleet so large, and it leaves me to suppose the magnificence of the REBECCA, and the attention paid during her build has made her an attractive bounty. I understand no word of our intention to sail these waters was ever announced in advance, and it seems strange indeed they might somehow know our plans beforehand, and thereby lie in wait for us to pass. However, having said that, I fear there is no cause for a fleet of any kind to be congregating in these waters except for purpose of mischief. I emphasize that the size of this fleet is certainly abnormal, and it is that fact which leads me to believe we may be falling victim to a planned attack.

"I urge you to view this situation seriously, sir, for although we have spoke much on the issue of the Algerians and Tripolitans being an especially nasty lot, there is much we have left unsaid about the scoundrels along this coast who also do a brisk trade in Christian slavery. Too many a wretched soul has disappeared along this coast without being seen or heard from ever again. Meanwhile the bastards count their profits without conscience. I believe it prudent we now be concerned for the welfare of the women and children in our care, for such an encounter in these waters does not bode well."

"What do you suggest, Captain?"

"I would think it wise to inform the American gunners that we are concerned about the situation at hand and ask them to ready your weapons. Let them gain a feel for the pieces and see to it as well that the cannon and ordnance are in proper working order and ready for use. I would feel it much to our advantage if we make quick business of it; for I pray to God Almighty this should be nothing more than a concern unfounded, but my instincts warn me different. It would do us no harm to prepare and if I am found out to be wrong, so much the better—let us then consider it a drill."

The captain sat back in his chair to take a breath, but the intensity of his revelations lingered. He sipped the brandy from his glass. Mr. Claussen studied the captain and considered all that had been said.

"I don't question your reason for concern, Captain; and I agree we should prepare, but tell me, where be the man-o'-war as we speak?"

"Nearer the coast, some ten or twelve leagues off our larboard quarter."

"Is she coming upon us?"

"Not that I can see. I put on extra sail to outrun her during the night, and she is now below the horizon. I am of a mind to bring the REBECCA to, until the English are again upon us. I believe it would be for the best."

Mr. Claussen sat back.

"*Elizabeth.*"

"*Elizabeth.*"

"*Yes, Milady.*" I whispered, not wanting to be heard in the cabin.

269

"You are being dreadfully nosey and that is impolite. Come down at once."

"But the talk is very interesting, Milady."

"Of what do they speak?"

"Of pirates."

"Pirates!"

"Ssshhh." I ducked down into the staircase. "They will hear you, Milady. I will soon tell you all," I whispered, and then sat back up to listen. Milady walked off, leaving me to assume she approved. My attention returned to the men. Mr. Claussen was now speaking.

"Might I suggest, should trouble brew, load the pieces, then bring REBECCA about to weather and discharge them simultaneously to the north by east in the direction of the warship. I would imagine there is nothing like a solid report of gunfire on the horizon to bring a man-o'-war to bear."

"Aye, that I can do." The captain approved with a nod.

"I propose the report will confuse the pirates momentarily until they conclude we have either warned them or signaled another ship. Having fired to the north instead of across their bows should lead them to believe we have in fact signaled for assistance. It is at that point I would assume we must be at highest risk. Instinct should have them attack us before help might arrive.

"Hopefully, the man-o'-war will stand our way and make an appearance in our behalf before the pirates make one to our demise. One thing is certain, be assured a ship-of-the-line is a sight they will not cherish. In the meantime, I agree we should maintain our position as you have suggested, or if need be, retreat northward toward the man-o'-war, however you see fit. The safety of Rebecca and the children is my foremost concern. Your opinion, sir?"

"You have read my very thoughts, Mr. Claussen. If you will allow me to take my leave, I will issue the orders at once."

"Very good then. If you wish, rouse the crew, and order them to remove the pieces from the racks to the upper deck, and have them sort out their stations. Send the Americans in to see me, and I shall do my best to make sure there are no unanswered questions about the piece."

"Aye aye, sir. Consider it done." Captain Ward stood up from his chair with his glass in hand.

"To good fortune." He raised his glass toward Mr. Claussen. Mr. Claussen offered his in return, which sent a loud clink throughout the cabin.

"To good fortune."

Captain Ward tilted his head back, seemed to throw the drink down his throat, and placed the goblet back on the table. Without further words between them, the captain stepped from the cabin smartly and went to his men.

I jumped down from the ladder and ran to fill Milady in on all that I could remember. As I returned to the hatch, she followed with more questions. I started up the staircase and heard a rapping at Claussen's cabin door indicating the Americans had arrived. Mr. Claussen called out to them.

"The door is open!"

"Shhhh," I warned Milady by holding my finger to my lips. *"The Americans are here."* I whispered. She smiled and again left me to my own mischief.

Those same men, whom I first saw as a group covered in the dust of white flour, filed into the cabin, one behind the other. They stood stiffly in a rank of sorts before Mr. Claussen's table.

"Gentlemen, please make yourselves comfortable. Cookie Jar will be serving us refreshments momentarily." Mr. Claussen encouraged the men to step up to his table, where one of the weapons rested. He placed his hand on it.

"I needn't waste time speculating about our newfound company and the possible consequences, so allow me to move directly to instructing you on the use of this weapon. I understand this piece is new to some of your eyes. However, I have every confidence that all you will come to find it a most pleasurable weapon to work. Allow me to explain.

"The REBECCA is one hundred and twenty feet in her waist. No doubt you have all noticed that spaced every four feet along the bulwarks, atop the timberheads, is fitted a socket mount. It is into that mount that can be seated a piece such as this one before you. The ball you see here will drop securely into the sockets and hold the weapon firm against the recoil of the charge." He moved the stock of the weapon around to the front where all could observe it.

"You can see here that it loads from the breech, and it does so in a most expeditious manner, providing the great benefit of speed when engaged in the fervor of close battle. Gentlemen, I must remind you that we are a merchant ship and not a vessel of war. We are therefore armed accordingly. I chose to keep our number of cannon to a minimum, two long guns and four Carronade being fitted and placed under your command. To arm beyond what I have already done is impractical, for the expense of manning such weaponry becomes entirely prohibitive in the business of shipping.

"Yet, understand that I have employed the best protection possible for my ship, my men, and my family. I do not wish you to underestimate the voracity of this piece. Not only is it is quick to load, but it is also extremely accurate at any range within reason. When you choose to open fire, do so as you see fit based upon your experience. I bow to your judgment and will question it not. I only ask you to consider my counsel on the matter this one time.

"I propose instead of each man firing at will or all firing upon a given command, you might give the order to fire to the man most forward at the bow. Then instruct each gunner to discharge his piece in turn thereafter. You will thereby develop a continuous and unrelenting barrage of shot moving in waves from bow to stern,which, I assure you will fall thick as rain, keeping our pirate friends pinned to their decks. It will also save severe shaking and wear on the bulwarks from the recoil. I believe this is common practice within the navy and possibly you are already aware of it. It is quite effective and most unsettling, so I am told." The Americans nodded and murmured sounds of agreement, apparently understanding the truth of what Mr. Claussen spoke.

"I would also recommend using the iron balls instead of lead, as they are meant to ricochet. Close to thirty guns can be attached to the permanent mounts upon either bulwark. Another forty can be placed in between the mounts or at some other convenient vantage point on a temporary basis by hooking the ball over the rail instead of placing it in the socket as one might under a normal firing condition. I am most confident a hundred-gun line of fire will do us great service, men."

"Sir, do you not wish us t' man the cannon below decks?" one of the men asked.

"What is your name, mate?"

"Timothy Anderson, at your service." The man stepped forward.

"Certainly, I do, Mr. Anderson. There are six pieces at your disposal. Two twelve-pound chase guns for range and four sixteen pounders to hold the enemy at bay beyond the reach of their pikes and our rigging. I have exercised patience in the selection and employment of my crew and have paid a premium wage for men well seasoned such as yourselves. You will find there are many who can assist you admirably with little instruction. Spread yourselves out to the best advantage between cannon and gun. If you feel the men on deck understand these pieces, then go below and man your cannon. I trust your judgment."

"Sir, I would like t' ask if we might move the two chase guns above decks, sir. Atop the fo'c's'le with your permission."

"I have no desire to question your judgment, Mr. Anderson. You are after all a gunner, but how necessary is such a move, for they would be burdensome under foot as we work the ship, as I am sure you can imagine."

"Yes, sir, I understand. But in this case, the higher the piece is off the water the better it can be made of use. Our view of the enemy is much improved. Also, we are then able t' direct our fire straight-ahead, in line with the bowsprit. This allows us t' strike the pirates at a much greater distance an' helps stop 'em from raking us, sir. Chebecs are superb vessels an' can carry a heavy piece if need be, certainly twelve to sixteen pounders, an' I dare say eighteen or better on larger vessels, if they so choose. We would be wise to keep 'em at distance. If the deck can offer the space, a couple of pieces atop the fo'c's'le, trained forward makes an easier job of it."

"I have no objection to your request and I respect your opinion, Mr. Anderson. However, you must see Mate Jennings, the carpenter, and inquire if such a thing is possible in what time remains. Hoisting cannon across the decks will be a dangerous task while underway, yet if he feels he can provide you with the mountings necessary for your tackles then go with speed."

"Aye aye, sir."

The men concluded their meeting and stepped out for air. I stepped down off the accommodation ladder and moved quickly through steerage. I scaled the companionway stairs that led upward into the pilothouse and waited as the men moved along the corridor to pass through. As soon as the last stepped onto the deck and closed the pilothouse door, I entered.

Upon a black slate, which was mounted above the logbook, I noticed for the first time, written in coarse white streaks of chalk, was the word 'PIRATES'. Seeing it written for entry into the log sent a shiver of dread through me. Even so, I moved forward to the starboard doorway and stayed just within, so as not to be seen and possibly chased back into steerage to remain safe with the rest of the children. From here I kept my eyes and ears open. I was so filled with anxiety I had all I could do to stand still. I rubbed my legs back and forth, tiring of the unending urge to pee.

THIRTY-TWO

A wary eye upon the approaching fleet confirmed the worst of fears. I had briefly ventured far enough along the main deck to see that Mate Beddin had tied himself to the topmast head, having positioned himself upon the trestletrees with the spyglass held tight to his eye. Its long brass tube flashed in the midday sun as it pointed southward beyond our bows. With riveted attention, he observed that the pirate ships had fashioned a formidable line before the REBECCA in order to intercept her, or force her into the mire of islands.

"Ahoyeee, Mr. Beckwith! Mr. Beckwith!"

"Aye!" answered the first mate as he leapt from the quarterdeck above my head and ran forward along the waterway to better hear.

"Skulls and bones! Skulls and bones, Mr. Beckwith! They have shown their true colors!"

My mouth went dry as I heard the words fall from ahigh. Their sound seemed to linger within the empty space of the pilot-house where I stood alone and in possession of this dreadful news. I felt my stomach cramp. It was just as the mates had predicted; once the pirates had assumed a formation, the truth of their intent would be known. They hoisted their traditional black flags with white skulls and bones, many alongside banners of their respective hordes. A few flew the flags of Algeria and Tripoli.

Mr. Beckwith ran back to meet with Captain Ward, but the captain had heard plain enough. At once, in response to Captain Ward's orders, the REBECCA came about hard to weather so that a volley from her cannon and pieces might be sent in the direction of the British man-of-war as proposed by Mr. Claussen. The report sounded across the water. It was followed by a second for good measure. The REBECCA was then hove-to and her sails braced by taking off our way and leaving the ship to lie to. We had presented our stern quarter, and the pirates wouldn't be long to understand that another ship had been summoned. The highest state of danger was now at hand, save for the battle itself, should one ensue. We awaited their next move.

Mr. Claussen had joined Captain Ward just above me on the quarterdeck at their usual position just behind the helmsman, and as always, I could hear them converse clearly. Captain Ward was saying that it appeared as though the pirates were attempting to force him to sail toward the islands, where he believed that an ambush was imminent. He refused to sail any farther south at this time and was of a mind to head back north at once.

I listened as they made a decision to summon Lady Rebecca and inform her of the situation. Immediately, I ran down the steps into steerage to find her and tell her she would be soon called upon. With the utmost restraint, barely able to contain myself from screaming all that I knew, I informed Milady in a whisper to her ear that the pirates were now watching us.

She put her finger to her lips, confirming my better judgment in keeping my news private. Thanking me for my silence and consideration, she took my hand and led me along to the accommodation ladder and up to her cabin. Mr. Claussen was already there, as was Captain Ward and Mr. Beckwith.

Mr. Claussen looked up in surprise as we ascended the ladder.

"Rebecca! How convenient you should appear. I was about to call for you. I must have your company, for there are issues now before us that require our immediate attention."

The mood was dead serious, and Milady was poised to listen carefully. She was informed of the severity of the situation at hand and asked to ensure that the children would be confined to the protection of their station in steerage, this for their own good. She was offered a number of suggestions, and after everyone finished with their piece, she was asked if she had any questions. Milady wasted no time getting to the heart of the matter and spared no sensitivities toward Mr. Claussen or Captain Ward.

"To be sure I understand…did we not choose to sail the southern atitudes for fear of encountering the English along the northern fortieth?"

"Yes, my love. That is correct."

"And we chose the longer southern route, not only to avoid an encounter with the English, but also because we believed it near impossible to stumble into a pirate." This time Mr. Claussen hesitated.

"Yes, that is also true, my love."

"Now, I am to understand that not only have we encountered the English off our quarter, but we have met the pirates off our bows. Am I also to assume that we are still sailing according to the best laid of plans based on three well-thought-out factors?" Mr. Claussen rolled his eyes as Milady continued.

"Gentlemen, it is not my desire to be sarcastic, for if the truth be known, I am worried sick for us all. I beg you think of the children first and go with God. I have understood your instructions and you may free yourselves of worry. I will see to the safety and confinement of the children as you ask. I am only now curious to know—how might we have fared with no plan at all?"

Having made her point, Milady arose to take her leave. I followed her back to the accommodation ladder where she disappeared into steerage. I stopped short to take up my usual place on the second step.

Save for the young boys, who were thrilled by the smoke and the concussion of our cannon fire, and who dawdled about on deck both in and out of the corral until chased below with a sound scolding or the painful pull of an ear, the rest of the children were well put away. Lady Rebecca was not known to be timid, but the noise, smoke, and general confusion took some getting used to. Her fears were seldom for herself but for those in her care.

At first, the children were collected below with many voicing their disapproval. The boys in particular objected, for they were beside themselves with excitement, they being of a mind that this was *great fun* indeed! The excitement didn't last long though and soon thereafter in the darkened confines of steerage a second emotion began to emerge. Whereas laughter did abound, now there was a good deal of crying and complaint to be heard. Without an eye to the activity outside, and being packed tightly into the cramped quarters of steerage, fear was quick to overtake the orphans. Some grew hysterical, filled with dread and visions of ruthless pirates. Truth be known, according to conversations I overheard on deck, their fears were justified for they would make great bounty in the hands of the slavers.

The fear was dismally contagious, and before long even the oldest of the boys were becoming unnerved; the panic was growing out of control. Lady Rebecca was now of a mind to find quickly some means of relieving the distressed children; and so above the din and mayhem she called out to Mary, who was calming a terrified young girl.

"Yes, Milady."

"I believe I will go above and ask Christopher if we might employ the talents of Darrin O'Kurk, the chantey man, to mollify the children. Do the best you are able until my return. I shan't be long."

"Yes, Milady."

"Come along, Elizabeth."

Back up the ladder we went. A number of men were standing about the study with Mr. Claussen and Captain Ward. The men paused in their conversations out of respect, not wishing to burden her with additional worry and greeted Milady with smiles, beckoning us to approach.

"Excuse me, gentlemen, for the interruption. I have come to say the children are in a bad way, and I am in need of a distraction to relieve them of their panic. I was hoping I might have the services of Mr. O'Kurk, if that would be possible. A song would go a great way to ease the fears and tears that now run rampant below."

Mr. Claussen had no objection, but Captain Ward was at once reluctant and being very courteous, expressed his reservations politely but firmly.

"Mr. Claussen, it is true that we have a respectable battery of light arms, certainly beyond what one finds upon the average merchant ship. Still, the requirements to man these weapons exceed our resources. Yes, we have a man for every weapon on board, but a mate with a weapon in his hand is incapable of climbing the shrouds and working the sails.

"Between the watches, I have a hundred men available to man the pieces with full attention, another hundred who might give half their time. The remaining hundred or so will be required for service to the ship while under way. That would include quelling fires or transporting shot and powder from the holds. For example,

I am unable to order powder put out on deck to be stockpiled, for if it is not promptly packed or pouched we will all rise to meet our Maker above a horrific ball of flame. Powder can only be brought up by hand in line with the need and nothing more. I will require men to work the pumps and empty our bilge, to get water above deck, to fill whatever container, barrel, or bottle they can find and ready us for fighting fire.

"Let me say that by merchant ship standards we exceed the number of men generally employed aboard. Yet in view of the fleet before us, we need every available man on deck. And most important, let me remind everyone; Mr. O'Kurk is our chanteyman, and I count heavily upon him to keep order to our work. I am of a mind to request not only that Mr. O'Kurk keeps to his position, but also that the older orphan boys be called up from berthing and be put to use for our benefit, possibly readying themselves at the fire buckets." The men at the table nodded in whole-hearted agreement, but Milady was not to be so easily dismissed.

"Captain, if I may. Imagine the sight of your men fighting for their lives; imagine cannon shot ripping through your ship. Imagine the smoke of battle and the sweat of your exertions clouding your vision. When you believe you can see the whole of this hell clearly, then imagine fifty terror-stricken orphans beyond all control breaking out from below, crying and screaming, and swarming over your decks but for fear and the want of fresh air and sunshine. Imagine the way you will be falling over them as they scatter underfoot during the heat of your bloody battles. I give you this as your alternative, and pay it due mind."

The men went pale at the sound of Milady's words. They stared at us, the captain included. Who knew what scenes played out in their heads, but the issue was settled at once. The pilothouse door opened and slammed shut. From atop the staircase, haloed by the light of day above decks, Mr. O'Kurk, with his guitar and broad inviting smile descended into the dimly lit ranks of fifty jittery children. Their pent-up hopes for his arrival let loose, and both he and the fear of the moment were drowned out in a hail of cheer. He nodded to Lady Rebecca, who had become a special acquaintance and enthusiastic admirer of his song. He began with a head splitting grin.

"So I earz ye be a sceerd ov th' lit'l ol' pireets, aye!" The children's eyes grew wide with concern.

"Now ye listn' t'me. Th'm pireets, they 'ate singin' they do. They do indeed! Cuz their 'earts iz bad. So, thiz bein' th' way it iz, 'ow bout' we 'all a leernin' a lit'l toon t' sceer 'em off now, eh laddies?" The children stormed him with their approval, each one more than happy to oblige.

"Then eerz th' soong I'll be teachin' yeh, now listen oop!"

And so a chorus of children's laughter and song resounded through the hull of the ship from stem to stern, a remarkable irony considering the silence and consternation of the men above decks who were preparing to go into battle. The children sang their hearts out, instantly oblivious to the approaching danger, and so filled the mates with a sense of righteous determination.

Block Jock wooz a boolly oon th' oopn sea
A pireet wi' a peg leg where there woonce wooz a knee
A parroot oon 'iz shoolder sqawkin' Yez zireeee
Block Jock eez a pireet oon th' oopen sea.

Block Jock wooz az mean aza man can get
The parroot wood a left but 'e loost a bet
'Ez perched upon 'is shoolder foorever in debt
Block Jock is pireet who won't foorgit.
(Block Jock wooz az mean aza man can git
The parroot az t' stay because 'e don't foorgit
To tell all th' maties ooz th' meanest man yet
Block Jock iz th' meanest, on that ye can bet)

Block Jock wooz a boolly oon th' oopn sea
A pirate wit' a peg leg where there woonce wooz a knee
A parroot oon 'iz shoolder sqawkin' Yez zireeee
Block Jock eez a pireet oon th' oopen sea.

Block Jock 'ad a ring oon each ov 'is tooz
Two through each ear an' three through 'is nooze
Foour oon every finger an' everywoon knowz
A hoondred moore are 'idden oonderneath 'is clothes

Block Jock wooz a boolly oon th' oopn sea
A pireet wit' a peg leg where there woonce wooz a knee
A parroot oon 'iz shoolder sqawkin' Yez zireeee
Block Jock eez a pireet oon th' oopen sea.

The children took to stomping and clapping, offering Darrin O'Kurk all their attention as he taught them his sea songs line for line. Lady Rebecca sat among the children, clapping and singing, and I believe she loved it more than anybody. Darrin O'Kurk just kept belting the songs out one after another with his incredible voice.

This iza tale, a tale oova whale
Az talla tale yool see
A tale az tall, az th' ship we sail.
A whale ova tale, tall aza ship at sea.

'E swam up t' land, beached oon th' sand
An' basked in th' soun by me
Th' seafolk stared, an' woon declared
Oon strange sort ov whale iz 'e

So 'e rolled off th'shore, an' was seen no moore
After swimmin' fer oot t' sea
But 'e left eez tail, tail oova whale
Whale oova tale foor me

So it might be toold, if 'e grew t' oold
An' failed in eez memoory
This was eez tail, a tail oova whale
A tale az tall az th' ship we sail.

A whale oova tale,
Az tall aza ship you see.

Mr. O'Kurk continued in a most entertaining fashion. Lady Rebecca, having not had a moment of peace all of the day, excused herself for a spell so she might freshen up. I followed her up to the top step of the accommodation ladder and sat where I could see both Milady at her at the dressing table and Mr. O'Kurk below. A blind was in place that offered Milady privacy from the rest of the cabin. The noise from below concealed our entrance and Mr. Claussen and Captain Ward spoke freely, having no knowledge of our presence. Milady held her finger to her lips, instructing me to hold my tongue.

The songs of the children echoed about the cabin clearly, and surely must have put to test the patience of Mr. Claussen and Captain Ward as they studied the position of the opposing ships, and proposed strategies for REBECCA's safe escape. The cabin was filled with the sounds of a party, but held an air of alertness whereby split-second determinations were being made routinely based on the comings and goings of the ship's mates and the Americans. There was a knock at the door.

"Enter!" Mr. Claussen called out and the door opened at once.

"Beggin' your pardon, sirs."

"Speak your piece, Mr. McCurry," said the captain.

"Sir, the mizzenwatch says the fleet holds a formation and sails for us directly. They will be upon us shortly."

"Thank-you, Mr. McCurry. That will be all. Await your orders, for they will come swift."

"Aye, sir." Mr. McCurry left the cabin.

"Mr. Beckwith!" The captain turned toward his first mate.

"Aye aye, sir!"

"Is Mate Beddin still in the fore trees?"

"Aye, sir, he is."

"Ask if he can yet see and determine the actions of the man-o'-war to our north."

"Aye aye, sir!" Mr. Beckwith repaired to deck. Captain Ward swung open and latched secure one of the stained glass windows at the stern. He picked up his spyglass and pointed it through the opening to observe the southwestern horizon, in the direction of the pirate fleet. Their sails were now clearly visible. The captain turned to Mr. Claussen.

"Mr. Claussen, it is imperative that we beat northward and seek the protection of the English, damn their hides. As much as I detest them, they are now our only hope. The pirate fleet is assuredly swift, and as the mizzenwatch has warned, they will be upon us shortly. It appears by their formation that they plan to force us into the islands as I previously surmised. We are no match for their numbers, and we must head north in all haste, run like bloody chickens if you will. That man-o'-war is akin to a giant jellyfish as it lumbers and wallows about at a sluggish rate. Yet, like a jellyfish, woe to whomever gets too close. We must seek refuge within the range of her guns at once."

Mr. Beckwith returned following a knock on the door. He stuck his head into the cabin. "Sir, Mate Beddin says the English stand for us now as we speak. It appears they heard our report."

"Excellent news, but we must act accordingly; we haven't enough time to wait. Mr. Beckwith, order your men to make sail and beat for the man-o'-war, and tell them to step lively, mister."

"Aye aye, sir!"

Mr. Beckwith closed the door and Captain Ward turned to Mr. Claussen as he shook his head in wonder. "It is indeed a day to be remembered when one is heartened to have a man-o'-war bearing down upon his soggy stern." He continued. "Needless to say, we must reach the English before the pirates reach us. True enough, they face a fresh headwind and sea to beat, but most of their ships are fore-aft rigged and sail close hauled with good speed. It will be close, this I assure you. May God have mercy on my soul, for if I am given the time and half a chance, I intend to lead those bastards to their Maker. Only it won't be by way of the pearly gates, no sir, it will be by way of the opened gunport of a thirty-two pounder."

There was then a moment of silence between the men.

"I must repair to the quarterdeck, Mr. Claussen."

"Very well, I will join you, then."

The men rose from their places and left the cabin. I was not one to be left behind and dropped down the staircase before Milady could voice her opposition. I made my way through steerage and the pilothouse. I went outside to assume my preferred place atop the quarterdeck steps.

"Mr. Beckwith!"

"Aye, Captain!"

"Time is against us. Straight to the wind. Brace them yards up and see to it they are sharp. I need all the way you might muster."

"Aye, Captain."

"George!" Captain Ward hollered down to the helmsman below.

"Aye, Captain."

"Keep your eyes on the canvas and pay mind to the wind. I want them yards sharp; we haven't a gust to spare. I expect a good rise of water upon our stem, sailor. You understand?"

"Aye, Captain. I'll keep her full."

It wasn't but another twenty minutes before Mr. Claussen was able to spy the British vessel hull down off our starboard bow. His satisfaction was apparent to all.

"Yes! Yes, indeed! It won't be long now before the scoun-drels will see a cloud of British canvas for themselves." He and Captain Ward expressed their relief.

A second issue of good fortune was announced a while thereafter, when the mizzenwatch hollered down that a number of pirates broke from the ranks of the fleet that pursued us and headed back to the islands, no doubt due to the sight of the approaching man-of-war. Mate Beddin, who was still holding watch in the fore tops, but now facing north, reported the English ship appeared very large and certain to be a hundred guns or better.

"Wouldn't that beat all, if she turned out to be a rate one ship-of-the-line," Captain Ward surmised aloud.

"If true, that would be a sorry sight indeed for anyone staring into her broadside," said Mr. Claussen.

"Isn't it odd indeed, she should be sailing these waters unattended. Where might be her fleet; I can only wonder? However, this is no time for me to question the whims of an English officer. For once, I am grateful they are such an arrogant lot. Let us hope he doesn't choose to pass up this call to engage."

"Hear, hear," replied Mr. Claussen.

The minutes dragged into hours. I couldn't sit still, but for the anxiety that coursed through me. I left my place upon the quarterdeck steps and walked aft to the taffrail so I might look out over the stern and out to sea toward the approaching pirates. Slowly, steadily time passed. The islands were receding into the distance, but the pirates were closer than ever, and I was able to see not only the varied colors of the boats, but also the forms of men as they moved about the vessels.

I watched in the same way another might watch a raging fire move toward them. They might know it is deadly, they might know it can take their life given the chance, but they feel distant, safe, and mesmerized by the danger of it all. And so I stood and stared mindlessly at the slow motion of ships that seemed to move mostly up and down in the water.

I was only distracted from my thoughts when a plume of water a short ways off caught my attention. Before I was able to determine what caused this strange sight, an explosion echoed across the water and I knew at once we had been fired upon. My blood went cold with fear. Suddenly, they were not so distant and we not so safe.

From behind me came a chorus of men's voices, voices now an octave above normal as they hollered back and forth at one another. Mr. Beckwith and Mr. McCurry were scurrying about inspecting the rigging and sails and ordering the men to heave and haul, and trim the sails for all their worth. I didn't turn around, but instead looked to the sky as I heard a disruption move across it followed by another plume, this time off our larboard beam. We were within range of their cannon. Now, I realized that not only did the sound always follow the plume of water, but also that they both were preceded by a cloud of gunsmoke; first the gunsmoke, then the fear, then the whistle of air, and lastly a plume of water if we were lucky.

The whistling air and plumes of water increased many fold. The smoke that came first was growing thick and forming a wall before the pirate fleet, blocking many of their ships from view. The sound coming from within the cloud was much like the rumble of thunder in the distance, and the look of the sea about us made me feel as though I were a small bug caught in a hailstorm. Every man on deck was striving to better our situation, and I knew they were totally engaged in the events at hand because neither Mr. Claussen nor Captain Ward paid me mind until this moment.

"Elizabeth! My word, child, step away from that rail! Have you lost your mind? Have you a wish to die? Go below and be quick about it! You must have lost your senses to stand there so. Be off with you! Go! Go! Go!"

Mr. Claussen reprimanded me sternly, something he had never done before. It frightened me far more than the rounds shooting through the air, and being badly shaken, I sped off the quarterdeck to find Lady Rebecca. She realized immediately by the look in my eyes and the flush of my face that I was upset and began at once to question and comfort me. In spite of her prodding, I said nothing about the scolding I had received, but made the most of her embrace and comfort.

THIRTY-THREE

We were approaching the man-of-war and with the cries of battle now being heard, I watched Mr. Beckwith dart about the ship giving orders and preparing for the worst. At one point, he was concerned about order below deck and so called for Mr. McCurry.

"Mr. McCurry!"

"Aye."

"Drop b'low decks man an' see to it al'z in order. I'm wondrin' 'bout the state of things after movin' them cannon through the for' ard hold. See to it, al'z secure, mate, and be quick about it. We'll 'ave our 'ands full soon enough."

"Aye!"

As Mr. McCurry disappeared through the fo'c's'le companionway, I too went below to the security of Milady. The singing was in full force, and without reservation, I jumped right in, belting out what I could while forgetting about the distressful events taking place outside our cozy station.

Meanwhile, Mr. McCurry, understanding that the REBECCA was soon to be within safe cover of the man-of-war, dropped into the fo'c's'le in all haste. He instructed the men inside to keep the companionway secured, fearing it might take a round if left open. Inside the fo'c'sle, a second staircase led down into the hold near the forward gunners, who were anxiously awaiting the first sign of pirates and their order to commence firing.

Marion moved abaft the gun crews and disappeared through a bulkhead that separated the gunners from the hold. Stepping through the passageway he moved along the larboard gangway in the darkened space. His first act was to raise a couple of gun port lids and temporarily light the hold and the passageways where he wished to walk and make his inspection. He also desired a view to the sea in order to spy any approaching pirates.

Carefully, but quickly he stepped astern, moving through the dimly lit bowels of the ship, passing the stout hold stanchions, and checking the crates and stores stacked high between them as best he could for signs of anything amiss. He leaned over the gangway and peered through the gratings to study the cargo below in the deeper shadows of the hold. He strove to assure himself along the way that the stores were chocked secure and all was shipshape before the battle. Marion understood that this would not be a good time for surprises.

Having traveled the length of the gangway, he came upon the larboard galleyway that led up to the galley. He climbed the steps, opened the door, and passed through the bulkhead. Inside the galley he briefly greeted Cookie Jar and Britany Allison, who were at the stove boiling water for doctoring if needed. He nodded to Britany, but addressed Cookie Jar.

"Aye, Cookie, all's shipshape?"

"Ayee, Mr. McCoory. Everytink iz goot, Ya-ah. Everytink. I yoost' vait fer me orders." He shrugged.

"That's good Cookie, 'cuz hellz gonna break loose soon, I have no doubt. Take care."

"Ya-ah jou too."

"Watch over our stowaway."

"Oh-ho, ya-ah, dat I veel."

Feeling confident all was in order within the galley, Marion moved smartly aft to the next larboard galleyway, which led up to the pilothouse. Once above, he spun around to look through the windows so he might assess the threat as it presently appeared on the seas about the ship. A quick study revealed most of the pirates to be falling back away from the stern and splitting their ranks before the man-of-war, which was now a half a league off REBECCA's larboard bow. As REBECCA tacked toward land the man-of-war was passing toward sea.

Having no time to dwell further on the matter, Marion dropped down the pilothouse aft companionway to steerage, where the children were amassed. They were being well cared for by Lady Rebecca all the while Darrin O'Kurk continued strumming his silly sing-alongs. He was every bit as successful in distracting the children from their fears as Milady promised.

* * *

Mr. McCurry had bolted into our mist, and then halted to stand tall before the seated crowd of children. Side to side, he turned his head taking survey of the bulkheads, the shipsides, and the gun ports. Sweaty and panting for breath, he glanced down at the children seated before him. Mr. O'Kurk stopped his playing and the children all looked up in his direction. A few seconds of silence followed, for we were fully expecting him to deliver some important message after barging into our midst. Instead, he apologized.

"Beg your pardon, Lady Claussen. Darrin. I didn't mean to interrupt. Just wanted to make a quick round and see that all was shipshape. There's nothing—."

CRASHHHH BOOOOMMMM!!!!!

Mr. McCurry might have been about to say that all was well and not to worry, that we should remain calm and stay put. *He might have*, except there came a horrific crash overhead and the ship suddenly heeled severely to larboard. It scared the daylights out of everybody. Those of us who didn't throw our arms over our heads and cower, jumped to our feet only to lose our balance on the canted and pitching deck. As quick as some stood up, so did they topple over and fall back upon those still seated.

By the look upon his face, I am certain Mr. McCurry was every bit as startled as the rest of us. The following howl of children now starting to cry from the fright, the quick change of course, the subsequent work required to trim the sails anew and handle the lines coupled with the shouts coming from above deck, most certainly must have filled him with a belief that the captain or first mate might be in immediate need of his assistance. There seemed plenty of reason to excuse himself at once from Lady Rebecca and company. He stopped his inspection short, then promptly turned about and leapt up the staircase in a single bound.

I saw the last of him dash through the pilothouse, this followed by the slamming shut of the pilothouse door as Mr. McCurry hurried out onto the deck to take charge of his watch. Hot on his heels, and pretending not to hear the calls of Milady above the panic stricken children who were now crying out in grief, I sped through their midst and dashed up the staircase to the pilothouse in order to know firsthand what had just happened.

Mr. Beckwith and Mr. McCurry were already in conversation on deck alongside the helmsman. Cookie Jar and Britany Allison had also surfaced from the galley and were standing just outside the pilothouse door, which was secured open. There was a good deal of foot pounding overhead on the quarterdeck and more than once I had to step back quickly, moving out of the way of mates storming through the pilothouse en route to one of the cabins.

Apparently, Captain Ward had given the helmsman the order to go about hard to sea in order to evade a pirate ship that was closing in fast on our stern. He also wished to shorten the distance between the man-of-war and us. It was mere coincidence that as the REBECCA commenced to change her weather bow from larboard to starboard, she took a round upon her quarterdeck. Fortunately the damage was assessed to be minimal, a hole in the deck and nothing more. So, aside from the tremendous noise caused by the iron ball crashing through the deck and falling to the cabin floor above our heads in steerage, and the scare of a lifetime that did well to fray our nerves, nothing else was to come of it.

I remained inside the pilothouse at the forward windows and attempted to absorb the whole of the activity now taking place. My eyes were shifting back and forth trying to take in everything and make sense of all I saw. I had no need to look behind me in order to know what was in store for us. The ocean was alive with erupting plumes of water. A quiver in the sail caught my attention, and I looked up to see dangling tackle and a spray of wooden shards falling from aloft where there was now a large hole in the topsail. Another enormous plume of water rose alongside the pilothouse, splashed across the windows and doused the deck and everyone nearby. I was terrified, but still unable to tear myself loose from all that was going on and return to the comfort of Milady's embrace.

Suddenly, another incredible impact again pounded the deck overhead. I felt my knees buckle and instinctively I dropped low with fright. As I cowered, the sound was followed by a fast rolling noise that passed over my head and to my utter surprise, I saw a round fly off the quarterdeck and land hard upon the main deck, rolling and bouncing as it traveled the full length of the waterway. We were being struck too frequently for my liking.

293

So frightened was I by the danger I perceived us now to be in, I failed to notice or appreciate the significance of the man-of-war coming ever nearer to effect our rescue. It was only one ship, and in my mind there seemed to be a hundred pirate ships giving us chase. I had little reason to pay it mind until now as I watched it move methodically through the water. It had slowly turned to sea to meet us and we were speeding directly for it. As we sailed closer and its broadside emerged ahead of us, the immense size of the ship became apparent. It was enormous! Nothing short of the largest buildings I saw in London seemed to compare. I thought the REBECCA was grand, but she seemed little more than a tender compared to the English warship that loomed before us. It now commanded my full attention.

The fearsome man-of-war sailed seaward ever so slowly, yet we watched in awe. It sailed past REBECCA on a slow reach, and I raced to the larboard pilothouse windows, pressing my nose to the pane so I might look above as we passed beneath her towering stern with little more than a hundred feet to spare. The size of the ship left me dumbstruck. Its masts reached the clouds; its anchors seemed too large to float, yet, it carried two on the starboard side alone.

It was late in the afternoon and the sun hovered low above the water. It cast its light long and low, and in spite of the danger that threatened, everyone on board the REBECCA looked up with pause. Their faces, the REBECCA, and the water that surrounded us turned orange from the glow of the sun's color as it reflected off the man-of-war's immeasurable amount of canvas. These were things that impressed me, but for the men of the REBECCA it was the formidable battery of cannon.

At least thirty pieces had been visible within its larboard gun ports, and the lower hatches were as of yet still closed. The upper hatches were wide open and the cannon were now protruding outward, sighting menacingly toward the pirate fleet as it raced in from the sea, close on our stern. Each gun port hatch was painted black and showed in stark contrast upon a long horizontal stripe

of yellow. There were three yellow stripes in all, each repre-
senting a deck of guns. As I looked at the colorful hull, someone
overhead said the intent could only have been to announce in no
uncertain terms that this was a vessel built to unleash the fury of
hell. The men began to cheer.

From my window, I could see untold numbers of English
sailors scurrying about the vessel, many looking down at us
from over their bulwarks. Above, I heard Captain Ward say he
figured there were close to a thousand men aboard the ship. The
name 'H.M.S. ROYAL PRINCE' came into view upon the counter
as we passed it by.

The English wasted no time for the purpose of sounding the
REBECCA. Instead, the ROYAL PRINCE's officers looked to be fully
apprised of the situation and appeared to bristle for an encounter
as they snapped their orders across the gun decks. The sailors
moved about smartly, the upper two gun decks stood poised to
fire and gun crews could be seen inside its belly at the ready.

As the ROYAL PRINCE prepared to engage the pirates,
Captain Ward faced the ship and pointed. His voice was ragged
with excitement.

"Regardless of what I might say about the bloody British, that
still remains sight enough to stand the hair on one's skin. To see
a ship of such proportions designed for no purpose other than
war, crewed by the best trained fighting sailors on the seven
seas—." Suddenly, Captain Ward stopped speaking and barked
out a fresh set of orders.

"Mr. Beckwith!"

"Aye aye, sir!"

"Come about hard to weather. Bring her around and bear south
by west. You can brace er' then, square to the wind and fill the
sails low and aloft; put all extra hands to the guns. Stay just to
weather of ROYAL PRINCE's stern, and for the sake of God, stay

clear of her quarter cannon or we'll be sailing to America on flotsam!"

"Aye aye, sir!"

The order was passed on to the helm.

"Aye," cried the helmsman, who immediately spun the large wheel to weather, and allowed the REBECCA to fall off the wind and come about. Within minutes, she changed her heading from north by west to south by west thereby bringing us back to face the setting sun. It was still a fair offshore breeze that filled our canvas, and we immediately put on way as we headed straight for the enemy.

Sailing south by west took us away from land, and positioned us somewhat behind the man-o-war as it headed seaward to confront the pirates. We passed close by ROYAL PRINCE's stern a second time, only this time she lay close off our starboard beam. Spread out before us and the ROYAL PRINCE was the entire pirate fleet and the sight caused my insides to twist into knots, for I could plainly see the unfairness of numbers. They seemed to be in the hundreds and we just two.

Once the man-of-war crossed to seaward, she presented her larboard battery to the enemy. The pirates were repositioning themselves, most veering west of us out to sea and heading north thereby keeping some distance between them and the man-of-war's cannon. The remainder of their fleet was crossing to the south of us on an eastward tack, taking up a position that kept them between land and us. They were sailing evasively, but they had entered the range of the ROYAL PRINCE's battery.

Captain Ward kept a sharp lookout, watching every move the pirates made. He shook his head in amazement. "Nerves of steel. They are not to be deterred by the Crown's might, and instead choose to come in for the kill." He turned to Mr. Claussen.

"They are despised by all, myself included, for their vicious perpetrations and utter disregard for civility. They care little for

296

the well-being of God-fearing people upon whom they prey. Yet, even I have to credit them with having either supreme bravery or sheer stupidity. Facing a man-o'-war takes a great deal of skill and above all else, nerves of steel."

Mr. Claussen agreed. "Their method appears to be one of combining speed and agility in a small target to move quickly in and out. I suspect they will attempt to stay before the ROYAL PRINCE's bow and rake her until her rigging is fouled. I wonder what the ROYAL PRINCE's captain must think when he spies such numbers employed to fire upon him?"

The captain continued. "There may be six or more cannon upon many of those vessels, and how many do we count? There are now only those that fire from afar with their long guns, but I suspect once in close we will see the action of six, twelve, maybe even eighteen pounders. A chebec or frigate large enough to ship and fire eight or nine twelve pounders up close would hold the attention of any captain. It would keep his broadside facing them I have no doubt—first rate or otherwise. They will swarm him, going for the rudder I would imagine. Look at how the flanks begin to pick away at him. Even at this distance they are eager for a fight."

The wind coming off our stern was welcome indeed, for it pressed steadfast upon our canvas, and set us to running free at a good clip. However, an American told Mr. Beckwith that the same wind that helped us could be a hindrance for the gun crew captains stationed on the lower decks of the ROYAL PRINCE. That is to say, in order for the man-of-war to present the pirates with its broadside, it was obliged to bring the starboard beam to weather. In doing so their vessel would heel over away from the wind, forcing its off weather battery, its guns a-lee, to be put too far over to be trained on the enemy downwind. It was even possible to flood the lower gun deck if the hatches were opened too soon.

And so as soon as it came into position, I watched the English haul down the headsails and brace their yards by. This caused the sails to luff, thus taking off the press of wind upon the canvas, and its way. The ship began to right itself at once and in unison the lower gun deck hatches snapped open giving view to another full row of cannon, these larger than the ones on the decks above. Slowly they moved outward until their barrels showed beyond the boundary of the hull.

The officers and gun captains awaited that precise moment after the ship settled and righted itself, but before it succumbed to the roll of the sea before making their move. It occurred when the larboard gun decks eased up to meet the enemy and ROYAL PRINCE's gunners were delivered a remarkably good aim.

Mr. Anderson was reputed to be a seasoned gunner, and this was readily apparent the minute our circumstances became dire. His face, along with those of the other Americans, showed no sign of the nervousness that was visible on most of the others in our company. He was now given free rein to direct Mr. Beckwith and Mr. McCurry with whatever advice he could muster. It was obvious that Captain Ward and Mr. Claussen gave serious consideration to his recommendations, for they encouraged him to speak his mind. The American stood proud and self-assured atop the foredeck behind the starboard cannon. He was building confidence in the men assigned to his gun crew. I opened the pilothouse door and stood in the passageway so I could hear him bellowing from where I stood.

"Wash 'er, powder 'er, wipe 'er with a wad, ram 'er, ball 'er, hot? We wash 'er, powder 'er, wipe 'er with a wad. We ram 'er, we ball 'er...."

He insisted they yell out his instructions at the top of their lungs. Over and over he would repeat the instructions, showing each man his job and drilling into their heads the routine to be followed that might save all our lives.

Moving downwind, our starboard beam came now past the ROYAL PRINCE's stern, her bowsprit still pointed out to sea. We overtook the man-of-war just as her lower guns were being run out, and, like sheep awaiting slaughter, we stood watching, having no idea what was in store for us.

The order to fire was sounded. We all heard the order float across the water, but our ignorance left us unprepared for what was to follow. Without warning for those of us who knew little of battle, the man-of-war let loose a rolling volley from her larboard battery. It was a first-time experience for everyone on board the REBECCA except the Americans.

Not a solitary thing stood between the horrific explosion of sound and us; not even the smallest blade of grass to deflect or dampen its impact. And so the thunder came upon us with such force, such severity, such magnitude, it would have made a lightning strike at arm's length sound feeble. The discharge jarred brains and bones, and rattled the teeth of everyone aboard the REBECCA. My chest was stove in by the concussion and I fell back against the bulkhead filled with fear. The decks below our feet shuddered from the shock wave that moved through the sea and up into REBECCA's hull. Large catpaws moved swiftly across the water's surface, leaving dimpled patterns to race about, then disappear.

Through the deafening sound of ringing that welled up in my ears, I heard terrified screams echo up the staircases from those unfortunate children confined to the darkness of their berthing down in steerage. Their cries unsettled me as it filled the pilot-house. My first thought was a horrifying notion that the explosion had occurred down below. I soon sorted it out, and realized that even Mr. O'Kurk was helpless to defend them from such a terrifying event. What chance could he have when my own eyes witnessed a number of brave and seasoned Swedes, renowned for their fearless way, 'drop dead to deck' out of sheer terror. The sight of it actually prompted me to start laughing uncontrollably, after I realized I wasn't dead myself.

Mr. Claussen and Captain Ward were unusually quiet overhead on the quarterdeck. Only Timothy Anderson and the Americans were in their element. Only they were as calm and collected on the inside as their faces expressed outwardly, even to the point of laughing at us all for having jumped clean out of our skins. Obviously, they had been prepared. For me, it was a thing once heard, never to be forgotten. At least, as the thunder rolled past and the ripples moving across the water faded from sight, so too did a number of the pirate vessels.

Amid the noise of cannon fire and the screaming children down below, I could hear Lady Rebecca calling out for me. I, having no desire whatsoever to go down into steerage where I belonged and miss all that took place outside, solved both problems by plunging my fingers deep into my ears. I would tell Milady I hadn't heard her calling for I had been protecting my ears from the noise of the cannon, which was true enough. My fingers did much to quiet things down, but seemed to accentuate my sense of smell.

It was now the odor of spent gunpowder that overwhelmed me. It had an almost tantalizing smell, a smell to be implanted into my memory forever. It drifted downwind with us, never leaving; and it gave one the sense of moving through a strange and nightmarish dream. The shoreline could no longer be seen, nor could many of the pirate vessels; they appeared and disappeared from view. The smoke permeated every crack and crevice aboard ship. It was suspended like fog across the water, across the REBECCA, inside the pilothouse, and all about me as well.

Before us, stragglers who lagged behind the main group of pirates that crossed our bows to the south had taken a severe beating from the ROYAL PRINCE. Many of their vessels were badly wrecked, fleeing, or scattering to join the pirates that were regrouping in flanks east and west of us. The ROYAL PRINCE had succeeded in clearing a road for us through the southern pirate fleet. The man-of-war continued to fire from

300

behind us and kept up pressure enough to force the enemy vessels to remain split and somewhat removed from our bows.

I finally unplugged my ears, and from within the smoky white blindness, voices of the injured and dying could be heard wailing in the background of roaring cannon-fire from the man-of-war. Above it all, suddenly came the captain's commanding voice.

"There! There is our path!" He then called out further. "Mr. Beckwith!"

"Aye, sir!"

"See where the pirates have split their ranks to avoid the broadside? That is the way of our course. Stand for the center. We will use ROYAL PRINCE's guns for our cover and if necessary we will ram our way through."

"Aye, sir."

"Captain!"

"Mr. Anderson?"

"Sir, I would urge ya t' consider furling your mains as soon as we enter enemy ranks. We have more t' fear from fire than from our loss o' speed. Close reef the tops an' let work the gallants an' royals. They are high an' safe."

"Point taken, Mr. Anderson. Do you understand, Mr. Beckwith?"

"Aye, aye, sir."

"Very good, gentlemen, see to your duties, time has come to act."

We stood fast for the split in ranks, but after a while Captain Ward turned his attention to Mr. Claussen with concern.

"It might appear as though the pirates split their ranks not nearly as much by force as by design. Does it not seem to you as though they have positioned themselves to form a funnel, which forces us back into the islands? We are surely flanked east and west, and now I see that half their fleet moves north to circle behind us, undoubtedly to drive us through. As I recall, earlier a portion of their fleet broke away and disappeared back into the islands from whence they came. This is certain to be a trap."

"I agree wholeheartedly, Captain. However, the trap also prevents what I assume to be the majority of their fleet from reaching us, for they are spread out in formation and mostly behind us. This can only work in our favor. Whereas at first we faced impossible odds, now we may have reason to hope for the best. We may dismiss most of what we see and prepare ourselves for that which we do not."

"You certainly sound optimistic, sir. I am truly amazed."

"I believe the islands will give us good cover from the pirates' long-range guns. It also forces any pirate ships lying in wait before us to crowd each other should they attack. At close range we have a distinct advantage. They can only fire upon us if no other vessel is in the way. I assure you that if they come within that close a range, we will wipe their decks clean of riff-raff with my guns."

"If only God would give me your confidence, sir."

The order to break out Mr. Claussen's breech loading guns had been long since carried out, and a good number of them were in position along the bulwarks with about a hundred men looking over the pieces in preparation according to Mr. Beckwith. Below, on the gun deck there were additional men being given last-minute instructions by Mr. Anderson and the Americans on use of the carronade. He told the captain that the two forward sixteen pounders had been swung about their pins to point as far forward as possible and came nearly in line with the ship. The two aft cannon were trained abeam to reduce the effects of concussion.

In answer to Mr. Anderson's request, the two twelve pounders, they having the longest range, had been removed from the gun deck and positioned atop the fo'c's'le either side of the stem, where they had a clear shot off the bows. I could see that Mr. Anderson's advice was taken seriously. His men were preparing to blast away ahead of us, and thereby preventing as much of a raking from the pirates as possible, hopefully clearing a path within their ranks.

"Captain Ward, I would urge you to take the channel."

"Are you certain that is what you wish? It is certainly what they intend for us. I fear there may be no way out." Captain Ward appeared as nervous as Mr. Claussen appeared confidant.

"I sense it better to put the islands between their seaward fleet and us at this time. We can use land as a shield, keeping it close or afar from beam to our best advantage."

"As you wish, Mr. Claussen."

Captain Ward instructed his men to stand for the channel thereby evading the potential cannon fire of the larger vessels that were pressuring us from seaward.

The pirate plan unfolded quickly and presented no surprises. As Captain Ward had predicted the trap was immediately visible. We sailed into the funnel, being forced into a specific channel, and soon after rounding the first island, another pirate fleet was lying in wait. Surprisingly, they did not appear nearly as formidable as the fleets we observed on the open sea. A group of about twenty vessels, but these were much lighter in build and certain to carry lighter ordnance as well. Unfortunately, the extent of their deviousness went unnoticed until we were well within the trap.

"Shoals! Shoals! Shoals, directly ahead! Hard to larboard! Hard to larboard!"

Mate Bedding screamed down to us frantically. Panic swept the decks and the helmsman wasted no time waiting for an officer to tell him different. He set his wheel in motion, and as he worked it around, others ran to the starboard side to look below.

From where I stood, I could now clearly see the whitish discoloration that snaked back and forth beneath the expansive blue-green waters before us. Even worse the sunken remains of another vessel appeared close by. It seemed this trap had been used before. We were in a dangerous maze built by nature's own hand, but used against us by the pirates' device. Captain Ward spoke his opinion.

"Now, I see the wit of their way. What need have they for large fighting vessels in these waters? They are at the ready with light craft and it appears well manned for a boarding. I can see their decks are crowded from here. They have only to wait that the REBECCA should go aground and then they will overrun us." Captain Ward studied the fleet through his glass.

"Hard to starboard, man, hard to starboard!" Came the call from above, sending the men racing across the decks, the lines flying this way and that. Mr. Beckwith now also stood at the helm to help with the wheel. In deep thought, Mr. Claussen studied the pirates. He turned to the captain.

"True as that may be, they have already lost. We will be fine, Captain Ward. I give you my word and it is as good as the gold that backs my name. We are captains, the two of us, and we have but one concern—the shoals. Let us now read the water with care and free our minds of the pirates."

From where I stood I could see the look on Captain Ward's face and it was one of utter amazement. He was slackjawed, lost for words, and for no other reason he said nothing, but went immediately to work reading the water as Mr. Claussen suggested. I on the other hand was greatly relieved to know that we were no longer in danger. If Mr. Claussen said we would be fine, *we would be fine.* I had no doubts.

"Helm to larboard! Helm to larboard!" the cries continued to fall from above. Only now five or six more men had scaled the shrouds of the fore mast in order to assist in spotting the shoals as soon as possible.

"Is this not a crew? Thank the Good Lord for these men in our time of need. There is not an old sailor among the lot. I must compliment you, sir, you paid dearly for the best men about, but this day you have a return on your investment."

The mates worked together in perfect unison, facing a barrage of split-second decisions and acting without delay. They were able to read the waters themselves and were ready to act long before orders were ever given. The captain was not alone in noticing the ability of his men, which seemed to defy logic and ordinary luck at every spin of the wheel.

"I believe we are about to have company," said Mr. Claussen as he looked across to the pirate fleet through his spyglass. The captain swung his glass likewise.

"It appears they are coming in for the kill."

"I propose we are nearing the end of these shoals and our friends fear the goose has slipped the noose. They have no reason to engage unless there is a chance we may be free, otherwise they have only to wait and let us grind ourselves into the rocks. They are worried, Captain, and that tells me we are about to be free."

The captain began to laugh to himself.

"Forgive me, Mr. Claussen, but I must ask. Are you a concealer of sacred visions? Are you blessed with an ability to see the future? A clairvoyant? A saint? How can you be so certain of these outcomes? You leave me to stand here stuttering to myself in amazement, and asking what kind of man employs my services?"

Mr. Claussen now laughed himself, visibly embarrassed.

"An ordinary man, I assure you, and nothing more. I offered only a guess based on logic, and rest assured if there had been a slight shift in the wind the thought would have surely come to you first and not I. There is nothing saintly about me, and I have no plans of becoming one anytime soon. That is one prediction I *can* make."

I overheard this conversation and it set me to thinking. At times I was baffled by the inability of others to see this wonderful side of Mr. Claussen. It was so easy to feel his ability to bring comfort. I was beginning to wonder if some people actually could *not* feel his protective nature. It seemed as though Captain Ward was unable to do so. But before I could dwell further on these thoughts, I was distracted by the commotion now taking place on deck, all of it stirred up by the approaching pirate vessels. It appeared as though we were beyond the shoals and now they were coming directly for us.

Out of fear, my first impulse was to see if the mighty man-of-war was following to offer its support and firepower. I left the quarterdeck to go below so I might sneak back along the corridor toward the Claussen cabin. The double doors were swinging wildly back and forth, slamming into the bulkheads, but the sound was buried in the din. I entered and knelt on the benchseat beneath the large window that Mr. Claussen had opened earlier.

The man-of-war had resumed its southern course and appeared to be following us into the channel. It was now within the funnel of pirate ships and receiving much fire from astern. The Americans had said the British were using thirty-two and twenty-four pounders. I only knew they were much louder than our cannon and once its batteries commenced to firing, they continued the barrage until the ROYAL PRINCE was completely hidden from us in smoke.

The man-of-war also had two mighty guns at her bows that shook the very ocean when the fire was clapped to them. It was a nerve-racking experience to know they fired in our direction.

Their rounds were either slamming into vessels nearby or sending huge plumes of water into the sky. It was this way on both sides of us as we attempted our escape. I wasn't sure how the ROYAL PRINCE could even see us, and I fully expected a round to emerge from within the smoke, come straight through the window, take off my head, and lay us to waste along with the rest.

The ROYAL PRINCE pressed on with her assault. The outboard flanks of the pirate fleet, the larger vessels that formed much of the funnel were breaking formation to move out of harm's way. They were heading north to gather off the man-of-war's stern, its weakest point. She now presented her gun decks to both the shore and seaward elements of the enemy that formed the funnel as they sailed past to get behind her.

As the REBECCA cleared the shoals, running free once again before the wind, off our stern I watched one last time as the man-of-war let loose its broadside volleys. It unleashed the full measure of its firepower, starboard and larboard, and disappeared into another thundering cloud of smoke. It was the last I saw of the English ship, for we soon changed tack and it was blocked from view by the island cliffs.

The pirates of the African coasts earned their reputation, lock, stock, and barrel. They were not easily put down nor inclined to run off in fear. That part of the pirate fleet, which had forced us into the island channel, now headed north to take on the ROYAL PRINCE. That part waiting to attack us in the straits charged out to intercept us and began to direct their fire upon the REBECCA. We were on our own and vulnerable to a sound wrecking. It was a terrifying situation. Even with a notable loss in enemy vessels, the pirates remained tenacious and formidable.

There was little solace in overhearing Captain Ward state that it was pointless for the pirates to sink the REBECCA, and lose all the bounty for which they were fighting to obtain. They would be much more apt to take out our tops, then surround and board us. In sheer numbers, they could overrun us, kill off our crew, and commandeer the REBECCA to port. They would then sell the survivors into slavery and divvy up the spoils. The main pirate fleet had enough strength to hold the attention of the ROYAL PRINCE, and that removed all fear for this second fleet to close in on us.

"Mr. Beckwith!"

"Aye, Captain."

"Instruct the helm to hold its course. Order the men to stand by the mains and press on with all speed. Keep an eye out for fire and stand ready to furl at once. I wish to punch through the pirate fleet with full sail as long as possible. See to it your sail is trimmed beforehand, and keep an ear to Mr. Anderson. Order all watches to take up their weapons at the bulwarks and prepare for close engagement."

"Aye aye, Captain."

Mr. Claussen addressed the captain.

"It will be a fight to the finish, and a surprise of no small measure. For if the pirates manage to evade the ball and grapeshot and venture in close, they will experience the bitter taste of my weapons firing relentlessly at close range. I assure you, sir; it will blanket them with a hailstorm of steel, the likes of which only the devil himself might produce. The element of surprise works in our favor, for such a show of force might be expected from the ROYAL PRINCE, but certainly not from a merchant ship. They have high hopes of getting in close for a boarding and it is then that we will be strongest."

"I am counting heavily on that, Mr. Claussen, for the sight of REBECCA's gun ports have done their work in putting reservation into the minds of the pirates. However, now that the REBECCA has been called to task and they have seen that her gun ports are mostly empty, being nothing more than an illusion, I assure you the scoundrels will be emboldened. The REBECCA is now being viewed as defenseless and rich with reward. The fear of her cannon has been abandoned and the pirates' main objective will be to board her."

From where I stood in the pilothouse, I listened with utter dread through an open window. The water was once again rising in tall plumes all about us. While Mr. Claussen surveyed the situation from atop the quarterdeck, I looked up to him as my only salvation. He appeared fresh and stouthearted. He appeared confident and in command. I knew his breech loading weapons would somehow be magical and a sobering experience for our foe. I wondered if he ever doubted his ability to bring us through safely. I hoped not.

Then, as though he had the ability to sense my presence, to read my mind and feel my fear, he turned and looked directly at me. There was concern in his eyes. He seemed to study my surroundings. I stepped back away from the window, but he knew full well that I was here and that I knew he had seen me watching him. He must have been assessing my safety, and after determining all to be to his satisfaction; he smiled at me, filled me with strength, and then returned his attention to the battle. At that moment all my fear dissipated. I felt wonderful whenever he noticed me. It was no different now, and amid all the confusion, I was filled with an overwhelming sense of relief. In spite of overwhelming odds, I was confident we would be fine.

In the background I could hear the battle of big guns between the ROYAL PRINCE and the pirate fleet behind us, but paid it little mind, as there appeared to be plenty of danger ahead with which to contend. The REBECCA bore down upon the pirates and plunged into their midst. Our cannon were set into action as they blasted away at the pirates about us. They were firing at anything afloat before our bows. Only six to our name, but in this close encounter and under the experienced direction of the Americans fresh off a man-of-war, they proved to be very effective, exactly as Captain Ward had predicted.

Credit had to be given specifically to Mr. Anderson. In full command of the two long-range twelve pounders atop the fo'c's'le, he set them off a-blazing. Round after round he blasted away, *"wash 'er, powder 'er, wipe 'er...."* He called out the routine and clapped the fire to her and, as he had promised, the cannon grew hot.

For a short time before we were totally engulfed by our own smoke, I was able to study the way in which he fired the cannon in harmony with the ship, using the rise and fall of the bow to train his piece. He sighted on the rise and fired on the fall. From where I stood I was nearly looking straight down a barrel and I could see which pirate ship was about to be wrecked. Even though I quickly understood the routine, and I knew it was only during those seconds of the fall when he would ignite the charge, I couldn't stop myself from convulsing each time a round was let loose.

Our cannon below decks added plenty in their own right to foil the pirate attack. I didn't believe the men below could actually see anything upon which to train their guns. I believed they fired grapeshot and langrel blindly into the wall of smoke, hoping to pepper the pirates and dispel any notion they might entertain about sneaking up on us under cover of our manmade cloud.

The regular mates at the bulwarks were fearless as well. They took to their weapons with determination and commenced to fire away at any vessel that ventured toward the REBECCA in hopes of effecting a boarding. The men followed their instructions to shoot in sequence from bow to stern, as advised by Mr. Claussen and the result was dramatic. A continuous roar of shot streamed off REBECCA's deck and allowed her to wreak havoc upon the pirates, keeping all of their men pinned to the decks, running for cover behind bulwarks or deck houses and unable to man their lines or cannon.

Their vessels floated harmlessly past us, the pirates unable to keep them under command for fear of being killed should they stand up and expose themselves. They became a frustrated lot, being no match whatsoever for the relentless barrage of shot and the orderly command aboard the REBECCA. We rammed our way through the smaller craft of this fleet and fired down upon their decks without mercy.

They took a sound beating, but so did I. I had met my fill of battle and mayhem. I turned away from the scene before me to answer Milady's calls, growing louder in my ears. I turned to find her at the companionway looking nervous and unhappy as she reached for me and pulled me by my braid down below into the security of steerage.

THIRTY-FOUR

At the time REBECCA prepared to pass through the pirate fleet, readying herself for an attack, all hands had been ordered to station themselves at the bulwarks and prepare to defend the ship. Marion McCurry looked out across the approaching enemy fleet, and wondered nervously what would be the pirates' chances of boarding the REBECCA.

The instant he questioned it, he turned pale. Alarmed to the bone, he recalled at once his error in having left the gun port hatches open to the sea for want of light while inspecting the holds. He was mortified by his error. It had been a grave mistake indeed, for not only had the holds been left exposed to enemy cannon and a potential fire below decks, but even worse, he had offered the pirates an open door, the perfect means of entry. All men were on deck taking up arms, and there was nobody stationed in the holds to guard against an intruder, for the breech guns were too long to use on the gangways and the sills were too low for supporting the barrels.

Under his breath, he swore at himself repeatedly and wondered how in the name of God could he have blundered so? It was not like him, not like him at all. Never before had he done such a thing, but never before had he been so preoccupied with living to see the next day. He soon recalled how he had been badly distracted whilst in the company of Lady Rebecca and her wards. He remembered how the REBECCA had come hard to larboard and spilled the children. It had been his intention to go aft along the larboard side of the ship and return along the starboard side, securing the gun hatches on his way back up through the fo'c's'le. But between the cannon strike, the outcry of the children, and the flurry of calls and commotion reaching his ear, his plan was disrupted. He had been suddenly compelled to go at once above decks, through the pilothouse, and offer his assistance.

Timothy Anderson's voice was going hoarse, and the cannon were working hard to keep the pirates at bay, but they were only two guns stationed forward at the bows and there were too many enemy vessels closing in. They were coming in from all quarters and positioning themselves to make their first attempt to ram and board the REBECCA. The starboard gunners let loose another wave of shot to drive them back. Marion knew he had to go down without delay, lest the pirates reach the open hatches. There could be no doubting that they were surely aware of the oversight.

With hardly a moment to spare, the sound of gunfire thick in the air, he broke into a dead run, moving forward across the deck past Lady Rebecca's coach, and toward the fo'c's'le where he dropped below for a second time. He descended the ladder recklessly and found himself stumbling in his haste as he tried to adjust to the darkened smoke-filled holds after being topside in the light of day. There was a great deal of yelling going on near the bows, and he nearly dropped from fright when the starboard cannon at his back let loose another round of shot.

The wind curling over the bows forced the smoke back inside through the gun ports, and it followed him on his way into the holds. It made his eyes water and blinded him further in an already dense and dark fog. He crossed to larboard and headed for the glow of light amidships that signaled the area of the open gun ports. He looked back over his shoulder more than once, half expecting a pirate to jump him by surprise. He saw no one, but after another seven or eight paces, he stopped dead in his tracks and stared at something worse.

Daylight streamed through the open gun ports, cutting its way through the smoke, and bathed two kegs of black powder that sat exposed in broad view. He knew they hadn't been there prior. He wondered which of the gunners was so mindless that he would endanger the lives of all by committing such foolery. It was bad enough that he had left the hatches open, but for another to do the same and leave explosives in harm's way to boot was absolutely unthinkable.

A motion outside the first gun port where he presently stood caught his attention, and looking away from the powder kegs in that direction, he spied a pirate sloop coming abreast, its cannon on deck coming into position. A broadside from the closing sloop, or even something as small as musket shot, would ignite the barrels of powder with certainty. He knew that the sloop was aiming for the open hatch, and the knowledge nearly froze him with fear. Fighting to overcome his urge to turn away and run for his life, knowing he only had a second or two at the most to act, he lunged for the gun port hatch, praying to close it in time.

Marion focused on one objective only, one singularly crucial act. He understood that if the pirates fired a cannon round, the hatch would offer no resistance and he would be one dead sailor. However, the enemy gunners were being kept pinned to their decks, and he was just as apt to be facing the quick action of enemy muskets from behind cover. The thick wood hatch would stop musket shot with ease. Either way, closing the hatch was by far faster than trying to move the barrels out of sight in order to house them in a safer place.

He launched himself forward, reaching out for the hatch rope. He paid no mind to anything, save for releasing the rope before him and was utterly unprepared when from somewhere within the shadows that clung about him there came a swift solidly clenched fist. It caught him squarely across the jaw with the force of a swinging boom, driving out all reasoning and whatever light he once enjoyed.

The blow was severe enough to have lifted him off the deck, driving him backward and landing him flat on his back sprawled across the gangway. Reeling from the blow and only half conscious, he attempted to get back onto his feet. He had no idea what had happened and suspected nothing planned against him. He was still of a mind to close the hatch, it being his last coherent thought, and he moved to regain his footing. This time the haze in his head was thicker than the smoke in the holds. A second blow sent him staggering backward. Stumbling upon rubbery legs, he fell across the sill of the open gun port.

Marion's head spun wildly. Instinctively, he turned himself over onto his stomach, an unconscious action to protect himself as he lay confused and motionless across the sill. His knees were on the deck and his shoulders hung outside over the water. The pirates immediately sighted him in and fired away. The hull was splintering about him, but he was too stunned to know the danger.

He had turned his back toward his attacker, failing to understand there was a man out to do him harm. Unbeknownst to Marion, the evildoer was moving in to finish him. The figure approached him from behind with a large knife in hand, drawn with intent to murder. The assailant drove his knee into Marion's back between the shoulder blades, and then gripped his hair and yanked his head back forcefully.

No sooner did the attacker reach around with a knife, bent on slicing open Marion's throat with fatal consequence, then the sloop now abreast, laid a barrage of langrel into the side of REBECCA. The chunks of iron and scrap struck amidships, and those which failed to embed themselves into REBECCA's sides, passed through the vermilion hull by way of the open gun ports. One piece struck Marion's ravager square in the chest as he stood above him driving the knife forward for the kill. Another piece found the keg of powder.

A brilliant white flash erupted instantly, burning out all detail within the ship's hold. It was coupled to a blast that blew both Marion McCurry and his attacker out the gun port, and into the open sea. Providence was clearly with Marion. If the men had been a foot either way of their position at the time of the explosion, they would have been crushed against the inside of the hull by the force of the blast. Instead, they were blown into the tranquil air outside of the hull. Marion's head and upper torso had been hanging outside the gun port, waning in and out of consciousness. He was spared the concussion. His body was protected from much of the direct blast by his attacker who had been standing over him like a shield.

Immersion in the chilly water served to awaken his dimmed wits somewhat, and confused about all things except for survival, he instinctively reached out for the ship. It was a frantic effort, a primal act that sailors would perform in their sleep, for he knew without thinking that if he should be unable to reach the speeding hull he would be left to drown. He had not fallen overboard, he had been blown clear of the ship, and was distant enough that only the grace of God might speed him back to safety.

His reaching turned into strokes, and soon he was swimming, struggling against the waves. He held his breath and swung his arms out, pulling, driven by the worst of fear. He was beyond any sensation of pain as he fumbled about the hull that slipped past his groping fingers. He thrashed about in the water as the ship receded, he twisted and turned, he searched, and then by the persuasion of heaven, he was brushed by what he sought—the following rope put out as the last chance for lucky souls.

His hands clamped about the line. He was at once snapped across the water. It was then he heard the chilling scream of the other man fade into the distance. His mate was lost. It was hopeless. Marion could do nothing for the man. He turned his head away in shame and forced himself to think of it no more. The distance between the two men had been no more than twenty feet. It was the difference between life and death.

Sometimes above, sometimes below the surface, he held his breath and clung to the line. Straining against the drag of the sea, he pulled himself forward along the rope until at last he reached the stern. It seemed as though eternity was passing him by as he struggled to move forward along the vermilion hull. His strength had now failed him, and he could do little more than hold on for dear life, still far aft of the open gun ports.

The smoke was billowing out from the openings, and he wasn't sure what he might do next. He felt weak and helpless. He was overcome with a desire to go to sleep. He had all he could do to hold on against the pressure in his face. The cool water washed over him in a spray trying to drown him, or at the very least, work the heat out of him. He knew soon his hands would grow numb to a point where he would be unable to control his grip, and he would succumb to the call of Uncle Davy.

If the opened gun ports had been any farther aft, instead of forward as they were, he surely would not have had time enough to swim back to the rope, for the REBECCA was standing lively under sail as she made her way through the pirate fleet. The enemy ships passed him by unnoticed, and his only concern remained to draw the attention of someone to his predicament.

He held on desperately against the current, thinking of his life, wondering what would become of him in these next crucial moments. He wondered if his death had only been postponed so that he might reflect on the wrongs he had committed during his years. He thought of many things as he struggled to beat back the watery grave.

Slowly he became aware of the pain in his jaw. There was pain in his head and pain in his neck. There was pain in his side. Yes, yes, he thought. He wanted pain. He wanted lots of pain. It made him feel alive. Only the dead feel no pain, he thought to himself. He wanted to hurt. He wondered if the other man hurt, if the other man still had pain. He prayed that God would have mercy on the other man and speed his passing. Marion endeavored to see through the turbulent water that engulfed him. He struggled to search the sea in REBECCA's wake for a man whom he never understood was out to kill him. His effort was in vain, for there was no trace of anyone to be found. He was alone.

The pain in his side grew acute, sharp, biting as the saltwater worked its way into his wounds. He dared to release one hand from his grip on the following line to feel his side. He shuddered at the discovery; something was embedded in his gut. He knew better than to pull it free, but he now paid more mind to his situation. His wits were back about him, and it was now becoming clear how precarious his position had become. He couldn't remove himself from the sea, but for fear of being shot upon the side of the ship's hull should he attempt to scale it. Even then, it was doubtable he possessed strength sufficient enough to haul himself aboard.

On the other hand, he was surely leaving a trail of blood for the sharks that might have a go at him. What in God's name was he to do? He could simply hold on until he bled to death or was eaten alive, or he could scale the hull and get shot in the attempt. He determined to scale the hull, but it was a short-lived ambition. The boarding ladder, he thought to himself. Where was the boarding ladder? He glimpsed sight of it, but it was too far ahead, and worse, too high above the water to reach.

He attempted to raise his head, to look up along the hull for help, but he had reached the point of having only enough strength to keep his head above the rushing water. He was fighting to keep from drowning. He went to the solace of his prayers, praying to God that he might be spared this certain death. He cried and his tears mixed with the sea as it began to wash him away. He prayed not to be left alone, not to be left behind to die in the wake of the glorious REBECCA.

THIRTY-FIVE

Only moments before the blast occurred in the hold, I had started below to find Lady Rebecca. In spite of my overriding sense of adventure, and my confidence in Mr. Claussen, I had become sufficiently afraid of what was taking place that I was compelled to seek some security and reassurance. I turned the corner and to my surprise met Milady at the top of the companionway. She was quite put out by my disappearance, especially after the order to fire was given aboard the ROYAL PRINCE, not to mention our own cannon going into action. She had come for me. She was visibly upset and most unkind.

She took hold of me by my braid, and towed me back down to steerage. Although it was painful, it was safer than grabbing my hand which I needed to keep on my feet, as the decks were pitching fiercly. I received a severe but well-deserved tongue-lashing. Still, at this point the reprimand was almost consoling, enforcing the notion that someone was looking out for me. It was better than being alone to face the danger, and for the time being I was relieved to be back in her company. We lay down next to one another alongside Mary, and having two to watch closely over me made it far easier to accept I might now be safe.

To my credit, I said nothing, knowing I was wrong, knowing my place was to mind, knowing full well I hadn't, and understanding to some degree that Milady was reacting out of fear, as was I. In short time, she put her arm about me as though nothing had happened. She pulled me in close, kissed me on the back of my head, and soon all was forgotten.

Mr. O'Kurk did his best to keep spirits high, but his songs were routinely interrupted for one reason or another, often to soothe a particularly upset child, or for purposes of security. For example, he stopped singing long enough to order everybody to pile their belongings up against the shipsides and then to move toward the center of the bay and away from the sides of the hull, which were being pounded mercilessly by enemy small arms fire. He told Milady in private that this was a common practice to help prevent wooden splinters and shot from flying about. At this point, many of the children were laying low, face down, often trembling in fear upon the deck beneath blankets, and staying as much out of harm's way as our cramped quarters would allow.

When the powder keg ignited within the hold, the blast put the fear of death into us all. It wasn't as massively loud as the firing of cannon aboard the ROYAL PRINCE, but it was no less frightening. The blast was felt as pressure in all our ears, and the ship shuddered with pronounced force. We all feared it would sink.

The explosion blew open the galley doors. If anyone jumped as did I, it had to be Milady. She threw one arm over her head and the other over mine. Dense white smoke erupted from the holds. The currents of air drove the smoke back through the galley, up into the pilothouse, and finally down into the steerage compartment where we were all cowering in fear and choking on the fumes. The young est clung to each other and bawled their eyes out.

Before there was even time to question what had happened, Mr. O'Kurk dropped his guitar and flew to his feet. He left us with a warning to watch out for fire, then raced out of the steerage bay and up into the smoke-filled pilothouse. From there he went down into the galley, and we could hear him and Cookie Jar

319

yelling back and forth in what sounded like a foreign language that made little sense to any of us.

Lady Rebecca also sprang to her feet, and was close on his heels as was I on hers, this time not for adventure, but for outright fear. I followed her through the ever-thickening smoke, first through the pilothouse and then into the galley. We arrived just as Mr. O'Kurk snagged a towel, held it up to his face, and then passed through the forward galleyway to enter into the hold below.

He had been fast on Cookie Jar's heels. We heard the men calling out to one another as they raced along the gangway deeper into the hold. Britany Allison looked terrified as she stood at the forward hatch looking down into the once white, but now more ominous orange glowing smoke. She turned toward us as we approached. She was visibly shaken and trembling.

"Are you alright, Britany?" Milady asked. She placed her hand upon Britany's face to reassure her. Britany choked on the smoke.

"It's a fearful mess, Milady. Everything's on fire. It blew both doors to the hold open and I thought I was about to die. Nothing has ever put a scare into me the likes of that. It was as though a hurricane came through in one big blow. Now everything's on fire. I don't know what to do. What should we do?" She coughed.

"Nothing foolish. We must act quickly, but let us not lose our heads. Let me have a look below."

We were now all coughing as Lady Rebecca stepped over to the galleyway to have a look through the bulkhead opening. The flickering orange light penetrated the smoke and formed masks upon her face. She stepped momentarily through the doorway in search of the men, but the smoke made it near impossible to observe anything.

I ran over to the galleyway as well, but stopped short, having no desire to pass through. The smoke stung my eyes terrible. Through a stream of tears, I clearly saw the fire a short ways

within. I could see the men were now returning, and I specifically saw the look of concern on Mr. O'Kurk's face after having
surveyed fire and damage farther into the hold. The fire cast its
eerie dancing glow upon the sides of the hull and the overhead
beams where one normally only found darkness and damp.

Mr. O'Kurk and Cookie Jar, who was on the starboard side
of the hold, were hollering back and forth to one another. I heard
Mr. O'Kurk say that he had emptied all of the fire buckets, but
that the fire was ferocious and we needed lots of hands now. He
turned toward us, and Lady Rebecca immediately stepped back
inside the galley. She began at once to issue instructions to the
older children who were now standing alongside.

"Britany Allison! Set the children up with pots and pans!
Fetch them mugs or buckets, or anything in the galley that will
hold water. Have them stand at the doorway and await my word.
Now, be quick about it, girl, we have no time to dawdle."

The children did as they were told, and as they were called
into the hold, they were divided into two groups. Mr. O'Kurk,
Milady, Britany Allison, Mary, and I moved into the hold along
the larboard gangway. Cookie Jar, Gregory LaBianca, a mate
who happened to be in the galley, Roseanne, Christine, James,
and Bart, four older orphans, took charge of half the children and
moved toward the starboard side.

Mr. O'Kurk lashed lines to the buckets with great speed,
while Lady Rebecca sorted out the children along with the pots
and pans, forming them into two lines. Taking in hand the first
firebucket, he stepped over to the first gun port forward of the
galleyway, unlocked, raised, and secured its hatch open. He then
tossed the bucket with its following line into the sea. He handed
the line to Milady, and he went for the next gun port hatch. He
was choking on the suffocating smoke, and his eyes burned
fiercely, causing tears to flow freely down his face. He gasped
for the fresh air coming in through the gun port, welcoming it for
all it was worth.

The sound and recoil of the cannon continued to jar the ship as did the continuous thudding of musket shot, langrel, and whatever else the pirates fired at us, the latter slamming hard into the side of the hull. All of this noise, not to mention the racket of a hundred hand-held pieces firing away over our heads in our defense seemed to fade away as we concentrated our efforts on bringing the fire under control. I no longer jumped at the bark of iron dogs, for to do so meant running the risk of spilling what precious little water I held for extinguishing the fire.

THIRTY-SIX

Peter, Paul, and Jacob were always in the way. They spent their young lives being pushed here and there, shuffled to one side or the other, moved to the front or back, or escorted out of sight so as not to be trampled upon. It was one of the humiliations of youth.

The three brothers squirmed about trying to be still, staying tummy down on deck as they were told to do. Their heads now raised, they peered through the fresh cloud of smoke with great curiosity as Darrin and Lady Rebecca dashed out of the steerage berthing, and ascended the staircase to the pilothouse. Mary and Elizabeth, Roseanne, Christine, James, Bart, and a few other stragglers followed the two out. Where were they going? What were they about to do?

The boys had never heard such a collection of explosions as they heard today. This last one was a dilly. Everything shook. It was pretty scary, especially when the smoke came. Jacob crawled up right tight to Peter's side and peeked out into the white gloom from between his fingers. The smell was different at first, not bad, but unlike anything they had ever smelled before. Now it smelled more like a street fire.

Whatever happened, it was big. The place cleared out before they even had a chance to get in the way, and that was very unusual.

"C'mon, Paul, let's go look! Hurry up! Jacob, you stay here!"

Paul stood up quickly, but Jacob let out a howl of protest and stood up as well. He wasn't staying anywhere. It just wasn't in his nature. Peter and Paul paid him little mind as they dashed off toward the stairway to have a look for themselves. Jacob followed in close pursuit, more afraid of being left alone than anything the likes of curiosity.

They stopped briefly beside the pilothouse door to have a look out the forward window. Standing on tippy-toes, their eyes grew as wide as saucers. Peter lifted Jacob up to see. Paul was amazed.

"Wow! The pirates are everywhere!"

They watched hypnotically while the sailors aboard the REBECCA blazed away, blowing streams of smoke from their guns as they fired rounds by the hundreds across the bulwarks. The cannon were roaring away above the fo'c's'le and below the bows. The whole of it made impossible most attempts to communicate over the thundering noise. They just stood and watched.

The cottony cloud of smoke engulfed everything. It was everywhere. Its metallic taste coated their tongues, as they stood slack-jawed, wide-eyed, and wild with excitement at the spectacle before them. There was no escaping it. It was especially bad where they stood in the pilothouse, right up to the moment when the structure took a direct hit of grapeshot and the glass windows on both sides of them exploded into a million pieces. The shards flew behind the boys in what looked like a shower of rain moving sideways. The crystal splinters embedded themselves into the inboard bulkheads like microscopic daggers. The black slate cracked through the white chalked word 'PIRATES'.

"Down! Down!" Peter shoved both Paul and Jacob down the galley steps.

They rolled down the staircase in a ball, and then unfolded upon the galley deck with Peter tumbling in after.

"Holy mackerel! That was close!" Paul exclaimed with disbelief. "It's a sign! We have divine protection. The saints are with us! We are invincible," Peter asserted with conviction.

"Yes, yes, yes!" The boys chanted. "We are invincible! We are invincible!"

They jumped to their feet and merrily pranced about each other, oblivious to the fifteen or twenty children who were standing about watching them. The children were the youngest of the lot and huddled together frightened. They had been wandering and were now about to be ushered back to the safer confines of berthing.

Beyond the whimpering and fussing of young orphans in the galley came the sounds of frantic voices. These were the voices of adults, whose cries of alarm surrounded the boys, and focused their attention on the forward galleyway that led down into the hold.

Peter forced his way through the group that was now heading back to steerage, and stepped over to the bulkhead opening. Paul and Jacob flanked his sides. They peeked inside the hold, and then gasped at the scene before them. Everybody was bumping, shoving, screaming, and scrambling to and fro along the gangways and across the gratings. Water was splashing everywhere, buckets being thrown out the hatches and hauled up on ropes. The flames— flames shooting all about, people carrying on something fierce, kids scurrying this way and that, all the excitement one could imagine. This really looked like fun!

"Quick!" Peter exclaimed. "Let's get our tins!"

They raced back toward berthing, disrupting the group of children who had made it as far back as the pilothouse by plowing through their midst from behind. The boys pushed through the crowd, then dashed for their belongings to get hold of their tin cups. All the way back they were hollering out their assessment of the situation in the hold and formulating a plan to resolve the crisis. No part of it included young Jacob.

"Jacob, you stay here! This is a man's job!"

Jacob howled. "I wanna be man too!" He clung tenaciously to Peter's shirt.

"You're too young, Jacob." Paul tried to pry himself free of Jacob's steel-like grip. "You're too young for this mission. You stay here."

"No! No, Peter. I'm not too young. I can fight. It ain't fair. I wanna go too. I wanna go with you an' Paul."

Peter looked down at his brother, whose face was twisting up, about to break out in a bawl. He reached for the rope that bound Jacob's britches. He loosened the knot, drew it up taunt and refastened it, each tug pulling his younger brother this way then that.

"Alright! You can go with us, but ya hafta stay close! An' ya hafta do exactly as I say or there'll be big trouble. This is man's work an' that means it's dangerous! If ya wanna be a man, ya gotta do as I say."

Jacob was thrilled and paid close attention to what his brother said.

"You hold the tins! Can ya do that?"

Jacob, being a man of few words, nodded his head. Peter and Paul gave him their mugs.

"All right, let's go. They need our help." Peter led the three back through the pilothouse and into the galley, where they headed toward the forward galleyway.

"Now listen up, Paul. I'm gonna tell ya everything I know 'bout fires. This is 'portant so pay me mind, ya hear?"

325

"Yeah," Paul responded attentively.

"Lot'sa times fires come from dragons! They're hard to kill. Some are as old as time. Only a real man can do it; I've always heard it so. The trick is to shoot 'em in the heart behind the golden scales. When it's a fire ya gotta get right to the center of it, just like it was the dragon hisself, you know…past all the smoke and flames. That's where to douse it, or it never dies, see?"

Paul understood perfectly. He heard a lot about dragons. Terrible things, they were. He wasn't scared though. He responded quickly.

"And that's why it's orange an' smoky 'cause it's like that when it comes out o' his nose! I ain't scared Peter, cuz I'm a man!" He was convinced. Peter continued.

"Here's the plan. We run at magic speed, an' grab the last bucket. Jacob, you follow, an' don't drop the tins or the plan is ruined, ya hear?" Jacob nodded.

"The dragon!" Jacob swung the cups, delivering a serious blow to the imagined foe.

"Are ya ready?" Paul and Jacob shook their heads affirmatively.

"Kill the mighty Dragon!"

Peter screamed as he charged down the galleyway and into the fiery bowels of the ship. Amidst all the confusion, the yelling, and the warfare, the boys were hardly noticed as they scampered behind the older children. Peter and Paul scooped up the last bucket according to plan, and continued down the gangway deep into the blaze. They passed behind Darrin O'Kurk, Lady Rebecca, Britany Allison, and the rest who were looking out the gun ports and yelling something about Marion McCurry.

They sprinted down the larboard gangway to where they spied the incoming daylight passing through gun ports that had been left open. They were protected from the heat in the center of the hold by a barrier of large crates packed full of glass and flour. Here could be found whiffs of fresh air and much-needed relief from the heat and smoke.

Gustaff Borislav would have been proud of the one last powder keg, still remaining, waiting there in the midst of the fire to explode and wreak its havoc upon the boys, the ship, and her innocent passengers. It rested alongside the hull near the open gun port, where it had been blown into the side of the ship with sufficient force to crush it, loosening its hoops and dislodging its staves. Like an hourglass, it leaked its dangerous black contents. The powder flowed like sand through the opened crevices of the staggered barrel staves and spread itself across the deck, as a hungry fire stretched to engulf it.

Jacob eyed the keg, and seated himself upon it. He wished to rest a moment within the breeze entering the gun port. The smoke was awful. The keg was the perfect height for his size, and made a comfortable seat from which to take in the cool air. Peter and Paul, feeling the strain of hauling the bucket of water, now set it down in front of Jacob as they took their fill of the refreshing air coming in off the sea. They hung their heads out the gun ports, and swelled their lungs with the soothing relief. Paul rubbed his eyes hard to remove the sting. They interrupted their mission only long enough to watch the colorful boats sailing past.

"Wow!" Peter exclaimed. "Look at the hole in the hull!"

"Gee willikers! What a mess. It's all ripped up," said Paul.

"A cannon must have been pointed right here. The pirates just blew a hole right through our ship. It's amazing we didn't sink."

"We still might," Jacob's small voice offered.

The older boys looked back to the fire with concern. They turned about to face the inferno before them. The heat was terrible. It would be a hard fire to kill.

Peter asked Jacob for his cup, but to his surprise, Jacob pulled it away.

"Hey! Gimme my tin!" Peter went for him, but Jacob placed the cups behind his back.

"Jacob! We need the tins to fight the dragon!" Peter protested. Both the boys scuffled with him about the powder keg, but when Jacob got his fingers about something, it was near impossible to pry them loose, so they eased off. The heat of the fire was growing.

"Jacob," he said calmly. "We need the tins to throw water on the fire. We can't just sit here. The dragon will get us."

"I wanna throw water. Where's my cup?" Jacob protested.

"We only got so many hands, Jacob! We had to carry the bucket. How were you supposed to carry three cups?" Peter and Paul were annoyed; Jacob was disappointed.

"I wanna throw water." Jacob repeated his demand.

"Okay, you can throw water, but first we gotta protect ya from the dragon, gimme the tin." Peter insisted.

Jacob wanted protection, so he obeyed and pulled the cups out from between his legs. Peter and Paul both grabbed their mugs. Peter plunged his tin into the bucket, and drawing it up full, flung it straight away into Jacob's face. Paul, also sensing this need to protect Jacob, offered his assistance. Peter, harboring a measure of revenge for the lack of respect shown his leadership, followed through with a second bath.

Jacob stiffened right up from the shock of the cold seawater. He gasped for air. The sight of Jacob, the look of shock upon his face, drove Peter and Paul into a fit of laughter, and they wished to douse him again, but Jacob did not shrink away this time. Instead, he slid down off the broken barrel, and slipped his cupped hands into the bucket, pulling them up and propelling water into the faces of his older brothers.

At this point the protection got completely out of hand. Peter and Paul tried to get near Jacob and the bucket, but he was splashing water everywhere. They finally leaned in enough to grab the upper rim of the bucket. Jacob did likewise, fully understanding the one with the water was the one who wins.

A tug of war was in full force when a hot smoky cloud engulfed Peter and Paul from behind. Their eyes objected painfully, and promptly flushed themselves in a flow of tears. Peter and Paul let loose their grip on the bucket simultaneously, in order to cover their eyes, and in doing so sent Jacob reeling backwards into the powder keg, tipping the bucket over onto himself as he fell. The water flooded over him and across the floor. Only an empty bucket remained within his grip.

Peter, barely able to see through his tear-soaked eyes, cried out in alarm.

"Now look at what ya done! We're doomed!"

Paul stood silent, and shook his head disbelieving. He looked scornfully at Jacob for fouling up the master plan. Peter continued to rant.

"I can't believe ya lost all the water!"

He slapped his fists to his head, wringing out the frustration. He was just about to cuff Jacob a good one for his insubordination, when a much larger fist clasped the back of his shirt and nearly lifted him off his feet. A voice boomed from within the smoke-filled hold.

"Hey! Get outta there, ya fools! You'll die in here! Get outta here! Git! Git!"

Timothy Anderson stormed upon them from the forward gun ports with his own bucket firmly in his hands. He let the water fly toward the fire. He stepped over to Jacob, who was scampering across the deck on all fours, frightened by his appearance, and lifted him off the deck by the rope about his britches.

329

"Get outta here, Jacob!" He turned to the older boys. "Didn't the good Lord find space enough for brains between any of yer ears! Are ya all daft! Now, get outta here before I get a mind to tan yer asses!" He roared, and sent them scurrying in a flight of terror back toward the mess and children's berthing.

Everything went back to normal in a split second as they were pushed and pulled and ordered out of the way. Timothy, in fear of leaving another child unfound, scoured the surrounding area. He spotted the powder keg. His blood ran cold. He had run past it without notice in his rush to get the children to safety. He now gauged the distance between the licking fire and the heap of powder and barrel staves, and tried to draw some conclusion. What could he do? He had already let loose his bucket of water. Whatever it was, it had to be done fast.

He first thought was to cradle what he could of it in his arms, and throw it overboard out through the gun port, but he knew that the sea breeze coming in would only blow the powder into the flames and ignite the whole mess. He couldn't just push it away from the flames without further spreading its contents. There was nothing with which to contain it. That left him perplexed. He had to do something. He needed water.

"Cover it," he said aloud. That was his only chance.

He walked up to it most desperate, knowing the slightest spark from a floating ember or a slip on his part while moving it would send him and probably many others to their Maker. He swallowed hard and struggled to make out details within the space of dark shadows, lit by contrasting shafts of daylight and fire. He dropped to his knees. It was inconceivable to him, as a gunner, that kegs of black powder would be left unattended on any deck. It was inconceivable to him that in such close proximity to the fire, the powder had not already ignited.

Timothy knelt on the deck before the mess. He began to strip off his shirt, then suddenly halted. Confused, he frowned as he crouched over the black heap. He studied and then touched the powder with his fingers. It was sopping wet. He inserted his finger between the parted staves and forced it into the black powder. Lo and behold, the entire heap—*soaked*. 'Could those kids have known?' he wondered to himself.

"Impossible."

He spoke out loud, still not believing. He looked at the spilled bucket now having rolled away some distance, for the rocking of the ship. He considered the odds; three boys, oldest maybe seven, going to the middle of the ship, a raging fire, finding a keg of powder, then dousing it with a bucket of water. The odds were better at finding a mermaid.

"Impossible!"

He spoke aloud a second time. Still plenty nervous, he scooped up what he could of the black mud and tossed it overboard. He dropped to all four and swished whatever water he could find upon the deck back across the remaining black smear of powder.

He yelled out for all available hands, which appeared at once and began drowning out the fire and flooding the deck. The black powder was being rinsed away.

Having little time to think on the event further, Timothy returned to the business of fighting the fire and directing orders to others, whom he could hear coming below through the fo'c's'le and aft from the forward cannon positions where they had been stationed during the battle.

THIRTY-SEVEN

Darrin was sweating profusely. The heat generated below decks from the African sun was oven enough without the help of a raging inferno. He pushed himself hard to keep up the strenuous pace, drawing the heavy buckets of water from the sea below. His hands were going numb, his shoulders and arms ached, his back was stiff and painful, but he pushed himself harder, fearing he might lose the race against the fire. He knew in the end, the lives of all on board might very well depend on the difference between one or two extra douses of water.

Thankfully, some of the older children appreciated the danger facing them, or were instructed by Lady Rebecca to help out. Either way, the strongest of the children were taking it upon themselves to assist him by opening additional gun ports, tossing out their own buckets and hauling them on board. They helped to supply the parade of containers waiting in the hands of the younger orphans standing in line.

Lady Rebecca saw clearly the strain on Mr. O'Kurk's face, and helped him haul buckets as often as she could, while at the same time directed the children on where to douse the fire. She kept all of the girls safely back away from the fire, fearing their dresses would go up in flames. It was the boys' job to do the dousing, while the girls handed them the containers of water. Milady kept me within two short steps of her side, giving no leeway to speak of whatsoever. My disappearance earlier upset her sufficient enough to seal my fate. I was stuck next to her and the buckets, so I decided to help the best I could, and voiced no complaint.

I watched as time after time, Mr. O'Kurk, pitched his bucket and hauled it up. It would take ten of us to match his strength and endurance. As we beat the fire back, we followed him a few steps farther forward into the hold. He would then start afresh, hauling up water from the next gun port in line.

I happened to be watching when he tossed the bucket out and it snagged. His strength was waning, and he hesitated before attempting to retrieve it. He braced himself momentarily against the frame of the gun port as he tried to catch his breath. He wiped his brow and swore a blue streak that ended only when he saw me looking his way. He looked out the port across the water and then at Lady Rebecca.

"De pireets, 'ave mooved back an' away. Thank Gawd, aboove."

The line of dousers, which he supported, was now dry. He had little time to talk and returned to address the problem. I watched as he pulled upon his rope. It was an odd restraint. Not hard bound as though behind something, but more giving, such as pull of a snagged fish, or seaweed. He would pull up; it would pull down.

His puzzled expression drew my attention all the more, and I watched him risk getting shot as he leaned far out the gun port to look down so he might better guide the bucket up the hull. Instantly, he recoiled from the opening and turned to face us. His eyes were wild with surprise.

"'Eeavens aboove! There'z a man beloow! There'z a man a beloow! 'E's 'oolding on ta da buckeet." He leaned out the gun port a second time. Lady Rebecca and I both leaned out our own gun port to see for ourselves. She grabbed me at once by the back of my hair and yanked me back inside.

"Ouch!" I reached for my hair.

"Forgive me, Elizabeth. I am sorry, but I have little desire to see two in the water, my love."

"Oh, Milady. Can't I see? I must see! I must see!"

I stuck my head out again; slowly this time all the while Lady Rebecca gripped the back of my dress. We both leaned over and gasped in unison at the sight of an arm outstretched, its hand clasped to the rim of Mr. O'Kurk's bucket at the waterline. Taking great care for his own safety, Mr. O'Kurk looked about for enemy snipers, and then leaned out the gun port as far as humanly possible, short of falling overboard, for sake of a better look. Lady

Rebecca and I looked forward along the outside of the hull to the next gun port where he was leaning out from inside.

"'Eaven's aboove! It's Mr. McCoory! Gawd bless me sool."

The discovery that the man in the water was our second mate, Mr. McCurry, came as no little surprise. Our first thought was to how long he had been in the water. He wasn't answering Mr. O'Kurk's calls. He appeared to be barely alive, hanging on to the rim of the bucket with one hand, and to a following rope with the other, which he had now wrapped around his wrist a number of times.

Frantic, Mr. O'Kurk retreated into the ship and yelled across the hold to Cookie Jar, informing him of what he had seen. A number of children moved toward him to better hear what was taking place. Lady Rebecca looked his way for direction. He instructed her to take his place drawing up the water as best she could and have the older children try to contain the fire as much as possible until the crew arrived, which would be within moments, for he could hear their voices forward in the hold. She obeyed him to the letter and immediately pitched a bucket out the gun port. Drawing it up, she ordered the children back in line to wet the fire down as best as they could.

In the meantime Mr. O'Kurk pleaded for the aid of a child that he might lower in order to slip a line around Mr. McCurry, so he might be hauled back safely aboard ship. I moved forward a half a step and was promptly put in my place.

"Bless me, child, the words weren't even out of his mouth, and I knew you would be entertaining ideas that shouldn't be in your head. You have a spirit about you, Elizabeth, which is worth noting; but understand this one time, I believe it best we allow the sailors to do their business without our help. They'll figure it out, I promise."

I was not allowed to argue with Milady. It wasn't my place, but I would have stepped forward to help had she not put a stop to it. I held no reservations about offering a hand, and believed I could have done my piece to assist Mr. McCurry.

Apparently, I was alone in my belief, for Mr. O'Kurk's request for a volunteer fell upon deaf ears. It was obvious that all others believed being put out upon the open sea to dangle helplessly above its limitless depths tethered to a line was utter lunacy. It was deemed a line much to thin a connection between life and death. The opportunity produced no brave heart, and in fact was so unappealing a thought that the group as a whole did quite the opposite. They collectively shrank back in fear of being chosen against their will—save for one.

"I'll do it." Britany Allison, the stowaway girl, stepped forward amidst a gasp from the children. Mr. O'Kurk studied her for a moment.

"I was hooping it might be soomeone smaller thit I'd be able t' loower by roope, child."

"You, won't be haftin' t' lower me, I'll jump." She went about searching the deck.

Mr. O'Kurk looked at her pacing about, his thoughts racing. He was unsure about his ability to get her back on board, yet she was the only volunteer and he had little time to spend recruiting another. There was still a fire to deal with. A small child would have been easier, for he was dead tired, but there was Cookie Jar and Lady Rebecca to assist. There were some stronger children that could help him, and certainly additional hands on deck would soon be down to help fight the fire.

BAMMMM!

Everyone ducked at once as a round slammed into the side of the hull just outside the place we were all standing. The fear was visible on all our faces young and old alike. Britany Allison was the first to dismiss it as she continued to speak.

"'Sides you'll be needin' someone with the strength an' wit to help 'im keep his head up. The ship makes way briskly, an' the wash would be too much for a younger child t' fight while fittin' a rope about the man. To my mind, ya have little choice, an' I doubt much time."

She found what she was looking for, and grabbed a length of rope, which she began to coil about her waist. She knew she couldn't afford to think of what she was about to do. She tied it about her. Mr. O'Kurk had no time to second guess her or mount a debate. What she spoke rang of truth, and so he stepped toward her. He unfastened her work, raised it under her shoulders, and retied it using a proper sailor's knot to form a harness for her benefit as well as his. She was a headstrong, determined young woman with a will and a way, but she spoke the truth.

"An' whoot be yer name, lass, Breet?"

"Britany Allison."

"Gawd bless ye, Breetney Allisoon. Yoo're a brave one."

She looked at him through a veil of fear, which could not be concealed by any number of brave words. Knowing she would lose her courage if she thought of what she was about to do, she turned and stepped onto the gun port sill. She refused to look out to sea, and leapt overboard without hesitation.

Her fear followed her down through the air and into the depths of the cool water darkened by the shadow of REBECCA's massive hull as it slid silently past her. The temperature of the water was sobering. The sight of the ship quickly moving away filled her with anguish, for she was now on her own. She was afraid and alone on the outside of the ship, fearing foremost the rope should part and seal her fate.

The line snapped taut, sliding up under her arms before she surfaced. She was then drawn by the ship's motion to the hull. Against the force of the passing water, Mr. O'Kurk hauled her forward to where Marion McCurry held on for his life. The young stow-a-way struggled to control her body as it planed across the water. She attempted to brace herself with a hand to the hull. It was almost impossible to keep her head above water, while she attempted to work the line around Marion McCurry's chest. Repeatedly she stole a breath, and found herself submerged, fighting to secure him.

Her eyes were open as she tried to see her work in the shadow of the copper-sheathed hull. It was then, within that gloomy darkness, she sensed a shift in the light, a movement in the shadows. It was then she felt something brush her legs. Something so large it changed the pressure of the water flowing against her. Terrified, she clawed at Marion's limp body and the side of the hull. She exploded through the surface, reaching in vain for safety in the air. She struggled to see clearly what might be beyond the spray that washed over her. To her horror she saw the massive fin move ahead and disappear beneath the waves.

"DARRIN!" she screamed. "DARRIN!"

Mr. O'Kurk had already seen the shark from the gun port, so had Lady Rebecca and I. It was huge! I had been told on many occasions that sharks often followed the ships, preying off smaller fish that stayed beneath the hull. It had probably picked up the scent of Marion, and was finally attracted by the splashing of Britany Allison hitting the water and making her way to the ship.

I believed Mr. O'Kurk had intended to yell out a warning to her seconds before, so she might be quick about her business, but he bit his lip instead. He may have feared she would panic and leave Marion behind. He may have assumed she had more time before the shark would become bold enough to venture in close. Whatever he had thought made little difference now. It was obvious he believed they were both in mortal danger. The shark was in a killing mood. He could do nothing but haul her in close to the hull, tie her off, and pray for those few seconds that he needed to save both their lives.

"Loord aboove, 'ave mercy oon me soul. COOKEEE! COOKEEE! Geet chore sorry ass peg o'r 'eer now man! Hooorry! Hoorry! Hoorry man! Step lively!"

He hauled the rope with all his might, leaning backward with his foot against the sill. The thump, thump, thump of Cookie Jar's peg preceded him through the smoke, and without need for further instruction he gripped the line to assist hauling Marion McCurry aboard. Mr. O'Kurk turned to Lady Rebecca and the rest of us.

"Fetch what ye can an' throw eet at thit shark de next time 'ee coomes arooned, ayeee!" He looked back down the side of the ship. "'Ang on Breetney Allisoon, yoor coomin' up, lass."

Lady Rebecca had no choice, but to haul up the buckets of water, for the fire continued to rage with or without Marion McCurry, Britany Allison, or the shark. I was of no use to Milady, for I was riveted to the drama unfolding below the gun port. I braced myself firmly against the sill and took in every harrowing detail.

Britany Allison struggled to pull herself along the rope. She was panic-stricken and mostly helpless within the hands of fate. Mr. O'Kurk and Cookie Jar worked in tandem to get Mr. McCurry on board. First one would grab the line and haul on the rope, pushing himself back by placing his foot on the sill and then holding firm, while the other would do likewise. It was fortunate that Britany Allison's scream brought Marion somewhat back to his senses, and enabled him to assist in getting his weight up the hull and back inside the gun port. I could see the blood flowing from his side, and dripping into the water below.

Another pirate ship came into view and, tired of the beating they were taking, the pirates were becoming reckless. They took their chances, showing themselves briefly to fire upon us. The hull became a spray of splinters as the rounds slammed into the REBECCA all about us. Fortunately, they missed Mr. McCurry

338

and the men above deck returned a volley that laid half the pirates to waste, sending a good number over the board.

Mr. O'Kurk was just about to pull Mr. McCurry on board when behind me the children raised a clamor. I turned to see them begin pitching odds and ends out the gun ports, whatever items they might quickly pick up. Down below, the surface of the water was being showered, and moving through it all, moving alongside the ship, was the shadow of the shark rising up to the surface from the depths. The children were screaming with alarm.

"It's back! It's back!"

Then came Britany Allison's blood-curdling scream from below. It was her plea to God and Mr. O'Kurk, they being her only hope. Mr. O'Kurk and Cookie Jar hauled Mr. McCurry across the sill and onto the deck, and then reached for Britany's line. They never looked outside the gun port. They grabbed the line and jerked with all their might, offering one large pull and a prayer they'd hear that scream again.

Scream she did. It was pure instinct. In what she knew was to be her last move, she kicked viciously at the shark. One thrust drove her heel straight into the nose of the beast with the force of a goat. In the second it took for the monster to reconsider, she was snapped up out of the water and swinging back and forth upon the side of the hull.

"Oh, God! Help me, Darrin! Higher! Higher, Darrin!" she screamed.

I looked down to see the water swelling above death's shadow as it moved upward from below, rising quickly to rip her away from the sun and the air. It was coming to pull her below the surface into the dark of the unknown. The water parted before its mammoth hulk. Its morbid eyes rolled backward into its head as it came straight up through the air with jaws spread wide, revealing a striped bear claw bandana and a wall of hellish teeth rimming a cavernous gut stretched open to swallow her whole.

Britany Allison also saw it rising to the surface, and as it came for her, she kicked out against the hull sending herself flying out across the water in an arc, barely clearing its gaping mouth. The monstrous jaws collapsed onto its jagged collection of triangular teeth, grinding one into another with bone-crushing force, but missing their mark, only to graze her. It crashed into the hull with a resounding thud and dropped from sight. Britany Allison now swung back, dangling helplessly on her line and clobbered the hull.

Instantly the beast was back, its thrashing head twisted about furiously, ramming hard into her side and knocking the breath out of her. Its gray sand-like flesh peeled the skin off of her legs and torso. Worst of all the strike was so severe it tore the rope free from Mr. O'Kurk and Cookie Jar, painfully burning their hands.

Ironically, the shark's blow sent her flying beyond the eruption of water and its own ravenous lunges. Spinning on the rope for a second time, she sailed out across the water and then she and the shark both dropped back beneath the green translucent surface with a thunderous clap, disappearing into the black region of the ship's shadow.

"Roon! Roon! Roon!"

Cookie Jar screamed as the two men turned and ran down the gangway, gripping the line in their hands. Lady Rebecca, Bart, and some of the others also grabbed hold of the line and hauled for Britany Allison's very life. I turned to look back into the sea. I saw the shadow of the shark moving about in the deep, but best of all I saw Britany rise to the surface just before it, and this time it was she that flew up into the air. She came across the water so fast it looked as though she was running upon its surface. She hit the hull hard, flew up its side and was snapped back into the ship.

While she ascended, Mr. O'Kurk gave up his place on the line, and rushed toward the gun port in order to assist her on board. She would have scaled the wood planks by her own strength and fingernails, but for all who were straining to hoist her. Mr. O'Kurk was reaching in her direction when she came barreling through the gun port so recklessly that she knocked him off his feet.

She cried out some unintelligible fear, while mindlessly clawing air to distance herself from the monster and the sea. She was plowing forward directly through Mr. O'Kurk, who was now in full motion, swinging his arms, fighting in vain to keep his balance as he held on to her. He staggered backward from the force of her charge, incapable of breaking her fall or his own.

Stumbling blindly as though still swimming in the sea, and so filled with fear, Britany finally lost her senses and collapsed. Lady Rebecca, having witnessed all that took place and being quick-witted, was already running across the deck to catch the falling girl, and succeeded in breaking the worst of her fall. Milady eased her limp body down onto the gangway. She then looked at Mr. O'Kurk and they both began to cry or laugh. I wasn't sure which.

THIRTY-EIGHT

The smoke was most difficult to endure. Only one thing might have been said in its favor. At the same time it worked its way into my lungs, choking me when I stepped away from the gun port, it also worked its way up through the various companionways and grates, thereby alerting the hands on deck that something was seriously amiss. Almost without exception, the mates were unaware of the explosion and fire, it being hidden amidst the roar of cannon and the fog of battle.

341

Up above on deck, Mr. Claussen, Captain Ward, and his crew were successful in evading much of the attack from the pirate ships. With the wind in our favor, we had moved through the enemy fleet with good speed, and it was assumed with acceptable damage. It was not until the ship sailed clear of the pirates, beyond the range of their cannon that the men began to step away from their weapons and take stock of our situation.

It was quickly realized that the smoke surrounding the ship should have dissipated now that the cannon were no longer being fired. Something was in the wrong. The tarpaulins were freed up and pulled back across the grates and huge plumes of smoke rose upward into the sky. The mates made quick issue of the situation and rushed into action, manning the buckets and dropping down through the deck openings to confront the blaze. They wasted no time, for talk of fire could fill a sailor with fear faster than the drop of an anchor.

Once the bucket lines were put into place and the whole of the crew threw themselves into the effort, the flames gave up their threatening advance. However, this was after the fact. And the fact was that the quick action of a few, and the wholehearted struggle of the orphans as a group may well have been the one thing that saved all on board the REBECCA. Whether hauling aboard buckets, ferrying water, battling the heat and smoke, or beating back the flames, each tin cup played a part in buying time while the jacks on deck defended the ship. When it was over for the most part, I looked through a gun port to the horizon and mused how ironic it was we should meet this fiery foe amidst these rolling waves of water that stretched as far as my eyes could see.

Both Captain Ward and Mr. Claussen heard the cries of fire at first call. Concerns for Lady Rebecca's welfare in this dangerous affair put Mr. Claussen into a terrible state of anxiety. He immediately removed himself from the quarterdeck and repaired to berthing, only there to find the youngest of the orphans huddled and riddled with fear. Turning back, he made for the holds and pushed through the smoke that still lingered thick inside the galley. Engulfed by the acidic stench of smoldering wood, he ran in all haste toward the forward galleyway.

Milady was now Mr. Claussen's only concern. Giving no regard to life or limb, he burst through the companionway and half fell down the steps, nearly overrunning both she and Mr. O'Kurk. The two were still attending to a despondent Britany Allison and the injured Mr. McCurry. Mr. Claussen studied Mr. McCurry, who appeared badly wounded, and Britany Allison, who was covered in bloody scrapes from head to foot, and as of yet unrecovered from her state of shock. She lie on the deck mindless and babbling.

Mr. Claussen refused to dwell upon the suffering before him until after his eyes found Milady. She was a sight to see, soaked to the bone and covered in blood, not to mention the soot and ash that blackened us all. She gave up Britany's care to Mr. O'Kurk, so she might meet Mr. Claussen. He was visibly shaken over her appearance, and so relieved to find her uninjured or burned that he drew her firmly into his embrace and held her tightly for some time. Milady allowed him to satisfy himself that her condition was none the more worse for wear, and that she had suffered nothing a good bath couldn't put right.

"It's not my blood. It's not my blood, Christopher. I am all right. Mr. McCurry shows little blood, but is severely wounded, and I fear he will die. Britany Allison is bloodied well enough, but aside from her collapsed mental state, suffers a nasty skinning and nothing more. The water makes everything appear much worse than it is. The deck looks bloody red, but we are fine, I am all right, Christopher. It's over. I am fine."

Once Mr. Claussen's fears were allayed, Milady then began to explain all that had taken place below decks, and her account made the battle waged above seem almost pale by comparison. She told him of the explosion, the fire, and then how at the worst possible time they had discovered Mr. McCurry overboard. She told him of the Britany Allison's bravery and the shark attack, all this as Mr. Claussen surveyed his surroundings. At last, he released Milady.

"You are certain you are not injured in the slightest manner."

"Only in my pride, for being such a mess before your eyes."

"You are beautiful before my eyes"

"Oh, please. Kiss her!" An older orphan yelled out.

"Kiss her! Kiss her! Kiss her!" The orphans chimed in, but he was not so inclined to do this in public. He studied the orphans, as they surely studied him.

"I should like to kiss her very much, but I am a bashful sort. I am sure you understand...."

"Boo," they cried out. "People in love always kiss!"

"Yes, words of truth, and I promise tonight I shall keep that advice close to my heart."

The children laughed. Mr. Claussen was at once powerful and frightening as well as inviting and thrilling. The children were drawn to him, and they flocked toward him. His presence eased their fears.

"You have done a remarkable job, my young friends. It took a serious measure of bravery and a strong will to stand up to such smoke and fire, and I am proud of you. I am indebted to you. We are all indebted to you. This is a day you should never forget, a day you should always look back upon with pride. I thank-you, and I promise there will be rewards a-plenty to greet you when we arrive in America." The orphans broke into a roar of cheers.

Mr. Claussen freed himself from the crowd and with encouragement from Milady, he went about to observe the damage done within the holds. A great deal of stowage was blackened, damaged beyond repair, but it bothered him not at all, for it had served to contain the fire, and restricted it from racing quickly through the hull or reaching something worse like the powder hold. He stepped over toward Mary, and spoke to her, offering words of concern about her well-being.

I was feeling somewhat forgotten and wounded, wondering if he would think of me. I still clearly felt the shame of the scolding I received earlier upon the quarterdeck. I watched as he stepped away from Mary and looked about the children until his eyes fell upon me. My heart raced. He smiled and came my way.

"And you, my young one; you who have no fear of cannon, what about you?"

"No fear of cannon! My word, that one fears nothing. She nearly jumped out the ship of her own accord in order to save Mr. McCurry." Lady Rebecca shook her head in amazement. Mr. Claussen laughed and turned back to me.

"Are you well, Elizabeth?" He cradled my face within his hands.

"Yes, Milord."

"I am glad to hear it. See to it that you stay that way for Lady Rebecca and me as well."

"Yes, Milord." My face went flush within his hands.

A stirring upon the deck caused him to look across to where Britany Allison lay. We all followed his eyes down to her.

"I think she's 'ad a wee bit too mooch excitement foor woone day, Mr. Clauzzen."

The comment brought giggles from the children standing about and lightened the mood. Britany Allison was stirring about some. She was responding to the laughter that now sounded about her.

Captain Ward also had made his appearance. He met up with Mr. Claussen in the pilothouse, and stepped into the hold directly behind him. He went straight away to his Mr. McCurry, whom he found to be barely conscious and bleeding from the wound in his side. One hardly needed a closer look to see the large splinter of barrel stave embedded in his gut. It was enough to make my stomach turn.

Captain Ward also feared it would probably cost him his life, but a great deal had been done to save it up to this point and there was no sense in quitting now, so he called for the doctor. Ordinarily, it would have been Cookie Jar who would have tended to the wound. That was one of the cook's responsibilities, but Mr. Claussen had the foresight to know the children might come into need of doctoring, and so employed such a man to accompany us on the voyage. It was a great stroke of luck for Mr. McCurry.

The children were all about, dirty and scruffy, as only children are able to make their selves appear. More important, given the fact of the fire and all, no one child appeared to suffer so much as a scratch. Even the Johnson boys were in good shape—considering.... Britany Allison was now back to her senses and looking about. She was sopping wet and shaking uncontrollably from her ordeal and a chill.

Mr. O'Kurk wrapped her warmly in a blanket. He then gave her a glowing account of her heroism, and promised to put the whole event into song for posterity. His remembrance was fully supported by Lady Rebecca, and embellished by the children as they offered their own accounts through the eyes of their youth. Mr. Claussen found himself taken in by it all and came to feel a deep admiration for his brave maiden stowaway.

"How are you feeling, Miss Britany Allison? Will you live to fight again?" he asked teasingly, but was genuinely moved by her condition and her unselfish actions.

"I'll do," she responded weakly.

"I was certain you heard me when I said there was no need to do me honor with blood."

She looked at Mr. Claussen, first with a blank stare, which changed slowly into a soft smile, then into a gasp of despair.

"I've lost my mother's ring. It brings me good luck."

She was fidgeting, just as he had noticed her doing in his cabin the night she was found out.

"It must have come off when my hands were wetted." Her reasoning was beginning to return. Her eyes moistened with grief.

Mr. Claussen attempted to reassure her. He placed his large hand upon her shoulder as she lay before him and at once she was calmed.

"We'll find a way to remedy that, don't fret just yet. We have much to be thankful for; after all *you* are not lost. For now, remove yourself to your berth, lie down, cover yourself, and get some rest. You will feel better for it. I will have Cookie Jar bring you hot tea to chase out the chill."

Mr. O'Kurk helped Britany Allison to her feet with care, and Lady Rebecca took her arm. Her legs were wobbly and she was deathly tired. We escorted her back to steerage followed by a solemn procession of thirty some orphans.

THIRTY-NINE

KA-BOOOOM! Boom, boom. BOOM!

Explosions of cannon fire unlike anything heard during the course of our encounter sounded across the sea from a distance. The rumbling came from the direction of the channel entrance and echoed back and forth across the water; it being trapped by the cliffs of the island shores. There was no end to this roar, and we could only imagine the ferocity of the battle that was taking place beyond our sight.

"Are you troubled, Milady?" Mary asked as we stood on the quarterdeck about the corral.

"I worry for the men aboard the ROYAL PRINCE."

"How can that be, Milady? It is such a powerful ship and built to wage war. Do you believe it can be taken by pirates?"

"I am certain stranger things have happened."

"But Milady, is not fighting pirates on the high seas what they do? I thought they sought out such skirmishes."

"I know nothing of skirmishes, Mary, but if that is what a skirmish sounds like, then God forbid I should hear a battle."

"I for one am greatly relieved we are free of this mess. I wish only we might depart this place as soon as possible, for I have had more than my fill of being terrified for one day, thank-you very much. And if I were to be asked, I would say this is no business of ours, and we shouldn't meddle."

"Mary, my precious dear, let us try and not forget that we have fared quite well this day, and this *in no small part* due to the action of the English *meddling*, as you so put it. Meddling in our behalf, and for *meddling* as they have, we have left them alone to face a seemingly impossible number of bloodthirsty pirates."

Mary was not uncaring, in fact she was just the opposite, but she spoke the truth. She had been nearly paralyzed with fear for most of the day and pleaded with God to speed us to safety. As for Lady Rebecca, she was far from being alone in her guilt, for the men went about the task of cleaning up debris and making repairs about the ship with less exuberance than one might have expected. Amid the roar of cannon that would give us no peace, the men found it hard not to feel as though they had run off like scared rabbits.

At first opportunity, we moved out of hiding and away from shore to the safety of deeper waters. The central part of the channel enabled us to once again see a great distance. And so it was shortly thereafter that a voice called out above our heads on the quarterdeck. The mizzenmast watch was pointing north, back from whence we came, back to where we left the pirates smarting and wounded.

"Capt'n! Capt'n! She's been dismasted. 'Er fore 'as gone by the board, sir! Holy mother of jeeesus!"

We all turned at once to look across our stern and view the unthinkable. Lady Rebecca looked at Mary and shook her head in dismay, having no need to speak further.

Mr. Claussen and Captain Ward turned their spyglasses astern, training them on the calamity now growing smaller and less visible upon the distant horizon. Amidst a long sweeping cloud of smoke sat the misshapen form of the British man-of-war as she floundered.

"She has indeed been dismasted. Her tops are badly fouled, he headsails and stays fallen, and her profile is markedly changed." Captain Ward lowered his glass and stared off to the north, lost momentarily in thought.

"I can think of little worse to convey in a report at day's end. I suggest we remove ourselves to the privacy of the cabin and further take up this issue," said Mr. Claussen.

Captain Ward was obliged and the two men distanced them selves from the noise and confusion that followed the orphans up from below after having made their way to the quarterdeck corral. The children, especially the youngest that had been confined to steerage and left to cry out their fears, were now utterly desperate to see the sun and feel the fresh air upon their faces. Mr. Claussen passed by me and with little thought offered me his hand. Delighted, I accepted and walked with him as he went below to his cabin. I listened as he and Captain Ward discussed this latest turn of events.

At times I paid no mind whatsoever to the talk, but preferred to simply watch Mr. Claussen regardless of what he might be doing or discussing. This man had become the sole focus of my attention, especially since our stay in London. Within the boundaries of the ship, I followed him about, studying all that he did through the course of his day. I was becoming more aware of the differences in my relations with Lady Rebecca and Mr. Claussen. With regard to Milady, I felt a strong attachment. I suppose it could be called love. She gave me comfort and security. I never questioned her feelings for me, for she made them evident, and I would always run to her in my times of need.

On the other hand, I never knew what Mr. Claussen thought of me. I only knew what he could do to me. He could give rise to emotions within that overwhelmed me, feelings I couldn't explain. I was very much afraid of him, and incredible as it may seem, I was irresistibly drawn to him. I held no other interests whenever I saw him about. Whenever he looked at me, or especially if he touched me, I was filled with a rush of excitement. I suppose it was a combination of my fear for him and my inability to understand how he could affect me so. It drove me to investigate him all the more, and I snatched up every opportunity given to be in his company.

I entered the cabin with the two men and took up a seat upon the bench beneath a stern window as they raised their spyglasses. They stood at the same window to peer northward in disbelief at a supposedly invincible bastion of a ship. In silence, unsure of what to say or do, they watched the ROYAL PRINCE take a terrible pounding. By their comments I learned she was being viciously raked and sniped at by the pirates. Having experienced firsthand the noise of cannon, I fully appreciated the horrendous sounds now rolling across the sea to enter our cabin.

"Isn't it ironic how we hoped they would respond to the sound of our own cannon?" Mr. Claussen remarked.

"Aye, that it is."

"I have a feeling that our English captain has underestimated the strength of his foe. The pirates have swarmed his bows and stern, and I fear they are bent on bringing all his masts down a splinter at a time."

"I would certainly agree. She remains a fearsome vessel to be sure, but there can be no question this is a very serious matter. Ships-of-the-line are meant to fight ships of their own kind in a well-planned passing of the fleets. It is said their engagement may be won or lost before the cannon is ever fired, for they realize their objectives as they parley for position, as they strive for an advantage on the wind. It is an ages old manner of battle well understood by fighting men, or at least so it was until Nelson.

"Until then, a man-o'-war might be commissioned to quell some hostility in a faraway port, make a show, or order its fleet to seek out and settle score with a renegade vessel or two. I believe the sight of one in any harbor would remind an adversary of the consequences to be had and be sufficient enough in itself to win a skirmish without ever going into battle—but that." Captain Ward pointed out across the water. "That, they were not designed to do. Not face down hordes of fast tacking chebecs, sniping sloops, and frigates amassed in those kinds of numbers. They swarm her as bees swarm a bear, but I fear this bear has found an especially nasty hive." Captain Ward shook his head, visibly concerned about the man-of-war's outcome.

"Do I hear a hint of compassion for an Englishman, my good man?"

"If so, far be it for me to admit."

Mr. Claussen laughed, and then commented, conveying more of a thought aloud.

"There had been some talk within the European Ministries about sending a fleet of ships into the Mediterranean to clear out these scoundrels once and for all, or seriously diminishing their numbers. If I were to judge by what I see, it appears to have been a plan well merited, but never minded."

Mr. Claussen smiled down at me. He handed me the long brass spyglass.

"See for yourself, Elizabeth. The English are certainly having a time of it."

I looked through the spyglass. I saw a great deal of smoke on the water, but little else.

"Are we going to help them?" I asked innocently enough. The men looked at each other, but neither answered. Mr. Claussen finally shrugged his shoulders.

"I'll give the pirates this. They are certainly holding their positions and wreaking havoc with her tops. The ROYAL PRINCE will now be greatly disadvantaged, being encumbered to come about with her broadsides, which is her only defense against such forces. I have little doubt but she is in a bad way. She has lost her fore sails and headsails. She has no control unless she is quick to send out her spritsails. The currents might even carry her into the channel where she could break her back upon the shoals if she is unlucky."

"I can't imagine it coming to that," Captain Ward injected. "The English patrol this coast continuously and the captain must surely be familiar with these waters. I would imagine he has a good sense of the shoals and reefs. In any event, I would expect him to drop anchor at once to keep from drifting farther into channel. Unfortunately, that makes him a sitting duck, and I envy him not his tasks at hand, for the pirates will continue to pepper him from forward and aft, working him over and wearing him down."

"I see more ships going out from shore," I noted.

"Is that so? May I have a look?" Mr. Claussen had been pouring refreshments. He set the decanter down and reached my way for the spyglass. I handed it back to him as Captain Ward raised his own glass to scan the horizon in search of the vessels.

"Those must be that part of the fleet that broke off earlier upon sighting the English. Cowardly lot they are, coming in now for the spoils."

"They are bent on putting the English asunder," said Mr. Claussen.

"I wouldn't bet on their success just yet."

"I see also that our own pursuers have given up on us. They too have gone back to sea, and I suspect they are planning to join the others and rebuild the main fleet. I would imagine they plan to strengthen their numbers to effect a boarding, no doubt," said Mr. Claussen.

"I'm not surprised. Overtaking the REBECCA turned out to be for more than they bargained. We deprived them of their blood, and I hope it stuck in their craw." Captain Ward gloated. "I imagine they were hoping that the fire below decks would get the best of us, but seeing that we have snuffed it out, they found themselves with nothing, empty-handed. I have no doubt but they now plan on taking their revenge upon the English."

Mr. Claussen and the captain studied each other. They were grinning and trying to read what lurked within their minds. Nothing of substance was as yet spoken, but their wishes cried to be heard. I could see it in their eyes. Finally, Captain Ward took the initiative.

"What are your thoughts, Mr. Claussen? I can only imagine."

"My feelings are mixed at best. I have no love to be lost on the English when they're about, save for when I need them, which up to this point has been never. However, I dread to think how many a soul shall not return home, possibly forced into a life of slavery, or if they are lucky, to be killed outright if that ship should be lost to piracy. I can't imagine such an outcome, but what if it should happen? Consider the consequence of providing a hundred more cannon to these scoundrels. If that comes to pass, the burden will be suffered by all nations, not just England. You, yourself have made mention of the war between these pirates and your own country.

"I suppose I wish to be rid of the English and their troubles and yet, I also wish to go to their aid, just as they came to ours. I feel pressured, compelled, indebted, call it what you will, it feels like a matter of honor. Still, I cannot overlook the fact that we have fifty children aboard, and we are not outfitted as a fighting vessel. To go to their aid is risky business at best, very risky business at best." Mr. Claussen stood with his arms folded, slowly rubbing his chin. "Now, that I have revealed my heart, I beg, tell me your own thoughts, Captain?"

"You have voiced my thoughts word for word, save one. As the captain of this vessel, it is more than a matter of honor. It is my duty to assist another vessel in distress, even if they might be English. Normally, I would be expected to go directly to her rescue. But allow me to put duty aside and say I still am compelled to offer assistance. Of course, I say this with improved confidence, having been witness to the admirable capability of your newly designed weapons, but as you have just said yourself, it is the thought of the children that binds my hands and heart with a terrible concern. I deem this to be the most precious cargo of my career at sea. One I cannot simply write off to the fire, the wet, or the rats, if you understand my meaning."

"Clearly, I do, sir, but please do not bow to my judgment, Captain Ward. I refuse to let you off that easy."

"Very well, Mr. Claussen, as you wish, but have no fear, I shan't shirk my responsibilities or my position aboard this vessel." Captain Ward smiled and raised his glass. "To the REBECCA."

He swallowed hard and collected his thoughts. He spoke again to Mr. Claussen.

"I fear the worse for the ROYAL PRINCE is yet to come. The day is long and shortly the winds may drop. If that happens, she will be at added disadvantage against the lighter pirate vessels, which can be oared into a proper firing position to keep up their raking. The pirates will be bent upon keeping her repair slowed by heavy sniping until dark. If the captain sends his men up into the tops he will send them to their graves, and he knows this for fact. He has little choice, but to wait for darkness, and this plays in the pirates' favor.

"It is for this that they wait, for then the advantage is theirs. Under the cover of darkness, the ROYAL PRINCE will be hard pressed to see the enemy within her range. The pirates will move in and attempt to disable her for good. If a fog rolls in from the sea, they will hope to swarm her decks like the plague. But, it does not have to be an all-out attack to board her. They only need to foul her rudder and the ROYAL PRINCE is greatly hampered. A few well-placed rounds or more likely, a charge put up against her under the cover of darkness could cause her to flounder for weeks or drift a thousand miles; it makes little difference, for without her fleet she will be ripe for attack in these waters." Captain Ward placed his emptied glass upon the table. Mr. Claussen poured another round of drink, and followed it with a comment.

"Now that brings up another point. Where *is* her fleet?"

The men pondered this question and searched for a plausible explanation that accounted for the missing ships. The captain spoke next.

"It must be very close. It must be. No rate one ship is ever left unattended. There was a separation for some unknown reason, maybe a storm, but the fleet must be close, I'm certain of it."

"It is possible then the ROYAL PRINCE may only require purchase of a few hours until her support arrives. If this were the case it would paint an entirely different picture. It would no longer be an issue of beating overwhelming odds, but instead a matter of stalling their tactics. Tell me, Captain, how strong is your compulsion to go to her aid, or does the issue of the children's safety put that completely aside?" Captain Ward thought a moment before giving his answer.

"Let me say this. In spite of all I have faced over the years, and there has been much, I could never take sole responsibility for deciding a course of action when so many children's lives are at stake. If you should choose to make that call, I will abide by your decision and swear never to speak ill of you should it go afoul. Otherwise, I propose we summon a part of the crew, and bring the subject up for debate and a vote. There can be no doubt the men are being called upon to do something that is not in their contract. Their lives will be in danger, as well as those of the children, and they should be allowed to speak. As they say, a cannon round gives little concern for race or rank."

Mr. Claussen set down his glass and turned toward me. He reached for the decanter upon the table and after removing the top, he poured a small amount into a clean glass and mixed it with water. This he handed to me.

"Forgive me for being so rude, Elizabeth."

"Thank-you, Milord," I said nearly stunned.

I raised the glass to my lips, being somewhat afraid not to do so, and sipped the mildly burning liquid. It wasn't altogether unpleasant, it being rich in flavor, but I would have hardly noticed, for masters never offered their servants such shows of consideration. It unsettled me. It was common practice for Lady Rebecca to pay me mind, but never Mr. Claussen.

Even more to my surprise, he made no request of me to remove myself from his cabin even though I performed no task, nor was I of any use to him. He allowed me to continue bearing witness to the matter at hand. It was as though behind all the activity and concern, he had taken the time to show me that there was a part of him that was reserved for me. This small attention overwhelmed me, and I knew that my face was aglow with embarrassment.

And so, I remained quietly seated at his bench while the leaders, either by decree or popularity, were summoned by Mr. Claussen and the captain to be told their thoughts particular to the man-of-war. Many had already witnessed much of ROYAL PRINCE's distress by going aloft for a look and see. All others were informed by word of mouth as the news was passed along the waterways with disbelief.

The disaster stirred up much talk, and opinions were sought from everyone for the purpose of debate. Mr. Claussen and Captain Ward asked only of them, what they believed should be our responsibility in this affair. The debate was lively. Most were fearful, but believed we should lend a hand. Only the Americans were reluctant. They were given full allowance by Mr. Claussen to voice their complaints, and as expected, they had little if anything good to say in behalf of the English, whom they were quite willing to see perish and sent down to Davy Jones.

If only the ROYAL PRINCE hadn't come to our aid, it would have been a simple matter—an open and shut case. Unfortunately, the fact was the ROYAL PRINCE *had* come to our defense only an hour earlier, and it bothered the conscience of everyone present just as it had Milady, Mr. Claussen, and Captain Ward.

After having enjoyed some refreshment, and given time to search their souls, it was not concern for the officers, but rather for the mates, the commoners aboard the ROYAL PRINCE for which the Americans eventually felt pangs of guilt. And so, in the end even they agreed to stand for the man-of-war, providing they could be hid in security should the REBECCA be boarded.

The act to assist was then unanimous. A meeting was called in the galley where all persons of consequence were again summoned. The move to formulate a plan was in order and no suggestion was ridiculed. This was fortunate because everyone felt free to contribute, and after a stumper of an initial request, the discussions grew lively. I could see that a plan worth merit was bound to be realized. Captain Ward tossed the question to the men.

"Mates, the fact is we have little more than an hour to put some type of plan into action. The sun is setting and the dark will soon be upon us. The question before us is simple. How do we as one ship lay waste or disrupt the activity of thirty or more pirate ships and live to tell the tale to our children? We have no desire to defeat the pirates only to buy time until the English fleet, which we are confident is nearby, arrives to assist the ROYAL PRINCE."

The galley went silent.

Finally, after a considerable amount of thought and whispering, one of the Americans spoke up. "What if we tarred up some of the powder kegs and set them afloat downwind with a long fuse? They might float into fleet and blow them to kingdom come." The idea was well received until someone else spoke up.

"It's too easy to shoot them before they can get within range. The minute the pirates see the fuse burning in the dark they'll blast the kegs to kingdom come." The mates were immediately disheartened.

"Let us not be so quick to give up without an effort," said Mr. Claussen. "There is something in the back of my head…let me think…. Yes, yes of course, now I recall. We have on board a hundred barrels of whale oil. It seems to me we might be able to dump it overboard and set it afire. I should think that would drive the pirates back rather quickly."

The first man spoke up again. "We could float powder kegs in the burning oil without a fuse. In the firelight we could follow them and shoot them with those new guns. They have good range and accuracy."

"Yes! Hooray! Grand idea!" The men cheered.

"How are we going to get the oil to burn on the water?"

Again the galley went silent.

"Ve mix it vit some brandy and rum! Ya-ah!"

The crowd was quickly revived. Captain Ward now spoke.

"That will work to ignite it, but we may need something the likes of a wick to keep it going."

"Can't we set some wood afire and float it out?"

"Too easy for the waves to douse."

Again the room went silent as minds raced, only this time Lady Rebecca happened to have been listening in.

"That shouldn't be a problem." All heads turned toward her.

"How is that my love?"

"Gentlemen, anyone who cooks knows oil and water don't mix. Oil floats on top and burns, correct?" All heads nodded in agreement. "Another thing that doesn't mix with water is flour. It forms big balls and just floats. I'll wager that if you take the crates of flour in the hold, and dump them overboard with the oil and brandy, it will act just like a wick. After that, the pirate ships will be the wick."

This time the galley went silent out of amazement and then exploded.

"Let's try it in a bucket of water!"

"Yeah, yeah, yeah! Let's try it."

* * *

Mr. Beckwith was summoned to the cabin.

"Aye, Captain?"

"Your orders are to bring REBECCA to sea. Beat her north, until the man-o'-war is off your starb'rd bow and the sun is to your back. I hope to go an easting from that position, reaching across the wind for as much way as we can muster. Timing is critical. The ROYAL PRINCE must recognize us in whatever light of day is left, but we must arrive to assist her under cover of dark. Do you understand? Furl your courses or do whatever you must, but bring us in after dark."

"Aye, Captain."

"Excellent. We will make use of the ROYAL PRINCE's batteries for cover, and for keeping a clear road for our return just as they did our escape. I have every confidence that the captain has dropped anchor in order to keep the ship from foundering upon the shoals. If I were he, I would drop my starb'rd bower and let the ship swing about freely to provide me with changing targets, thereby keeping the pirates on the move. Also know the wind will drive her bows to face north. That means we must pass by her stern to the south and set the fire downwind. I expect the majority of the pirates' fleet to be at her stern, for there she is most vulnerable. They will be certain to attempt fouling her rudder.

"Finally, Mr. Beckwith, pay heed to this, my warning. Watch your wind at this late hour of day. Night will soon be upon us and the wind is most apt to lie down or become whimsical. There is real danger of becoming becalmed amidst the enemy fleet. We will fare much worse than the ROYAL PRINCE if that should happen. The pirates will have the advantage in maneuverability, and we will likely be doomed."

360

"Aye aye, Captain."

The word doomed seemed to pain Mr. Claussen, who turned at once in my direction.

"Take your leave now, Elizabeth. It is best that you now go to Rebecca, for it is no longer a good time for a young girl to be wandering about. Be off with you, my dear!"

"Yes, Milord."

I slipped off the bench at once and ran to the accommodation ladder. I went below into steerage to make my appearance before Lady Rebecca, but she was not there. Milady had removed herself to the hold with a troupe of orphans whom she enlisted to help her pluck out the pieces of crystal from the crates of flour. For a while, I did my part to sift through the flour and remove as many of the pieces as I could find in what time we had left. Happily, there were many children willing to perform this chore in order to be free of their confinement in steerage, and so I stole away at first opportunity.

I was far more interested in what Mr. Claussen was doing, and I wished to further spy upon him and hear his voice. I waited in the galley for him and the captain to walk the corridor, pass through the pilothouse overhead, then go on deck. In due time it happened thus, and I then slipped away out of the galley, crept up the companion steps to the pilothouse, and moved across to peer out one of the broken windows behind the helmsman.

From where I now stood, the fresh sea breeze blew about me, lifting my hair on its wind, for there were no panes of glass to fill the frames. I found myself slightly chilled, but whether by wind or anticipation, I was unsure. By walking around in the pilothouse, I could see all, and I could hear everything spoken on deck as well as above me on the quarterdeck where Mr. Claussen and Captain Ward took up their positions. I watched everything with a child's curiosity as the night began to unfold.

The REBECCA, having stood north by west out to sea, now came about from seaward on a fine reach and approached the man-of-war standing east as ordered by Captain Ward. The sun was upon the water and its brilliance would blind anyone looking our way. For that reason we kept it at our stern, making difficult any attempt to sight us in.

Mr. Claussen and the captain expressed confidence that the English officers would understand we could only be suicidal should we choose to sail straight into the broadside of a first rate ship of the line looking for a fight. Our direct approach made useless our lower cannon and fully exposed REBECCA's masts for a raking. It signaled a peaceful approach with intention to assist and we prayed only that the English wouldn't think us bait for a pirate trap.

It was soon thereafter that the sun dropped below the horizon and as the air cooled further, the color of the sky began to change to the deeper slate blues. In the last rays of light, I watched as the men continued to hoist on deck barrel after barrel of whale oil. Between every ten or eleven barrels of oil was a cask of rum and a crate of flour, its dust finding cracks by which to escape and form small streaks of clouds still visible in the dimming light. The men were working diligently to break open the tops of the barrels, for we were fast approaching the ROYAL PRINCE.

Captain Ward had been very accurate in his prediction about the position of the man-of-war. It had dropped one anchor off its starboard bow, just as he said, and swung downwind with its bows pointing north. This fact didn't pass by Mr. Clausen unnoticed, and he accused Captain Ward of being clairvoyant and saintly.

It was the last laugh to be heard, for as one might have expected our approach drew the pirates immediately out to attack us. Three of the pirate vessels, a frigate and two sloops situated just north of the man-of-war's seaward bow set sail at

362

once heading west by south on a broad reach before the wind to intercept and engage us.

It was a challenge Mr. Anderson was prepared to meet, but in their haste to confront us, they were reckless and drifted too far a-lee, coming before the man-of-war and just into range of her cannon. They met their demise in short time, being reduced to rubble, a useless collection of floating wrecks as chunks of their hulls and tops exploded into splintering clouds to be spread across the water.

By my count, the upper gun deck of the ROYAL PRINCE carried at least fifteen guns. They were said to be twelve or sixteen pounders and manned by the best gunners in the world, who up to this point were greatly frustrated at having little to fire upon since the dismasting, and could now only stand by impatiently at the ready. Having been given the opportunity, they delivered a stinging blow to the pirates' sorry Barbary Coast souls. This spectacle, which was nothing short of horrifying and barely palatable to us, was savored even less by the pirates and did nothing at all to promote courage beyond our bulwarks.

"Prepare for action! Beat to your stations, men!"

Captain Ward called out his order, and others echoed the command, moving it across the deck. For a second time, aboard the REBECCA routines heretofor practiced by Mr. Anderson and the Americans were undertaken for real. He called out his orders.

"Clear for action!"

The blocks and tackle were raised or moved out of the way. The magazine was reopened. The passages wetted down again, the fire buckets topped off, the pumps primed to the ready, and water made available to the men. The powder pouches were filled, the torches lit. The brass monkeys were stacked with rounds. Ample supplies of grape and wad were put within reach of Mr. Anderson and the forward gun crews.

363

At the same time, others braced the yards for the easting. They hauled upon the bowlines and sheets, and trimmed the sails full and hard for the reach. It was now left to the helmsman to hold our course. I watched him as he studied the shape of the sails. He stood alone, now the only man in control of the ship. The topmen dropped from the shrouds to come alow, then all free hands took up their positions alongside those already waiting at the bulwarks. They stood alert for a fight. Mr. Anderson stood against the wind with his torch in hand. Then, in a large deliberate arc, he brought his arm around and clapped the torch to the cannon.

"Readeeeeeee...and fire!"

The ship shuddered. BOOOOOM!

The REBECCA opened fire. She began to deliver a small, but effective punch as her two twelve pound long-range guns atop the fo'c's'le were touched by the torch, alternately discharging rounds at a rate of about two a minute. The smell of spent powder moved across the deck and passed through the broken windows to meet me. I could hear Captain Ward vigorously applaud his men as vessels splintered into pieces some thousand feet distant. First the starboard cannon discharged, next the larboard, back and forth they fired.

"Wash 'er, powder 'er, wipe 'er with a wad, ram 'er, ball 'er, clean 'er up and send 'er 'ome!" BOOOOOM!

Our attack was strengthened as the men below deck swung all four carronade forward, and commenced to fire upon the pirates as they came into range. Our bulwark gunners were still too far away to take action, but to our surprise, the man-of-war played a card of its own and with great success. It had purposely held back from firing upon the pirates, fooling them into believing they were safely off to the side of cannon sighting. Now they discovered differently.

Mr. Claussen, Captain Ward, and Mr. Beckwith were speaking briskly of the ever-changing situation when suddenly the ROYAL PRINCE's batteries transformed the bow and larboard quarter of the man-of-war into two enormous tongues of flame. Cannon at both ends of the ship fired in close order above our heads. The flames plowed through both the darkness and the clouds of smoke that clung to its hull and hovered above the water. Bright flashes like bolts of lightning illuminated the entire sea, ships and all. The thunder of the cannon put the fear of God into each and every one of us bar none. I thought I was dead on the spot. I dropped instantly to the deck, gasping for breath, fear collapsing my chest and causing my heart to race out of control. Little had changed since the first time I had experienced such massive firepower.

The crying started afresh within berthing, and I heard Lady Rebecca calling out to me. Realizing I hadn't died, and unable to contain my curiosity, I rose slowly up the bulkhead and peered over the top of the windowsill. The helmsman stood fast at the wheel, and over his shoulder the ROYAL PRINCE loomed ever larger before our bows. Its fore mast was shattered and collapsed, pieces leaning against the mainmast, pieces held to swing by the tangle of rigging. The sails were shredded and draped over the yards, stays, and rubble.

A second horrific blast erupted, again blowing smoke and fire from both ends of the ROYAL PRINCE. I simply couldn't stand the fear of such power and fled the pilothouse to find safety at Lady Rebecca's side. There, in steerage and among the bawling tots, she watched as I stumbled down the staircase in her direction at a full run escaping fear that never lasted long. Above the deafening roar of gunfire Milady began to scold me.

"Elizabeth, what did I say?"

"Come! Come! Come! Please, Milady, you must see! Oh, please, please come now!" I put aside all my training and yanked upon her arm, pulling her in my direction so she might accompany me to the pilothouse. My excitement and total lack of control must have been contagious, for to my surprise, instead of reprimanding me or ordering me to remain with the children, she did as I begged.

Stooping low, we climbed the staircase into the pilothouse. We waded through a storm of sound rife with explosions and concussion, and I watched as her apprehensive eyes looked down upon the pilothouse deck and her feet stepped carefully over the fragments of glass and debris. I noted a shard of black slate lying face up that had half the word 'pirates' scrawled across it.

A look of wonder came over her after she slowly rose to peek over the windowsill and survey the scene about us. The massive hulk of the ROYAL PRINCE was coming close off our larboard bow reaching up high above us from within a haze that blanketed the sea. The light of the moon was gaining strength and lending an eerie glow to the smoke now spilled and settled upon the water. From our higher position we watched as pirate vessels blazed away at us and emitted random flashes of brilliance while bobbing up and down upon the sea between mats of floating wreckage.

By this time all six of our cannon were engaged. The two at our starboard bow had changed over to grapeshot, which caused the surface of the water about the pirates to leap into the air from the spray of metal. Finally, the distance between the pirate vessels and the REBECCA had closed too little more than a few hundred feet. The men at the bulwarks opened fire, unleashing waves of shot from Mr. Claussen's guns. Darkness made the vision of fire that emanated from the line of barrels both horrific and hypnotic.

Under cover of the barrage, the mates reached for the barrels of oil, the casks of rum, and crates of flour, tossing all over the board in quick succession. Into the oily mess went numerous small kegs of powder. Flaming oil soaked rags were then thrown out to sea and in an instant a rippling wave of fire spread southward from the REBECCA's starboard beam.

In a matter of seconds the blaze fanned outward, flooding the sea with light and engulfing anything in its path. It moved with the current and wind toward the pirates. It was obvious that if nothing else, the effect of the inferno upon the water had a sudden and pronounced mental impact upon the enemy. Their return fire diminished noticeably as they grappled with the consequence of this unwelcome sight. We left nothing to their advantage and leaned hard into them with ball and fire, sparing not a moment's lapse.

One by one, the kegs of powder were sighted in and fired upon. The resulting explosions were especially unnerving. They weren't powerful enough to breech a hull or sink a frigate, but they blew flaming clumps of black powder and burning oil high into the air, only to trail downward through the yards and rigging in streams and cascading splashes of fire upon canvas and tarpaulins in a reasonably effective fashion. The pirates were hard pressed to escape our tactics and found themselves badly penned in by their own numbers.

The REBECCA stood in for the ROYAL PRINCE, and cut a swath between her and the pirate fleet now bottled up off her stern to the south. The trail of fire followed us through, but drifted safely away from the ROYAL PRINCE, as it moved with the wind. Our attack quickly changed from one of annoyance to one of consequence as Mr. Claussen's hundred-odd guns blazed away with exceptional accuracy.

Lady Rebecca stooped over me from behind, her hands cupping my shoulders, her head lowered next to mine. We stood side by side in each other's embrace, and filled our senses with the melee that surrounded us. It was only a matter of time before a round passed through the shipside window and struck the bulkhead just behind our position. It blew a hole through the inner bulkhead near where the helmsman often stood. To his benefit, he was standing at the forward-most wheel and out of harm's way. Not so for both the pilothouse and Milady, who let out a muffled scream, and ended up in much poorer condition but for fright.

"Oh!" She ducked. "I think it best we go back down at once, Elizabeth."

"Why?"

"Why? Good gracious child, look about you! Half the bulkhead has been rent. It is much too dangerous to stand here before the guns of a thousand pirates. We must go. Come quickly. Come, come, let us go back down into steerage where it is safer."

"Just a moment more."

"Elizabeth! Go! Go, go, go!"

"Please, Milady." Then came a male voice.

As happened earlier in the day a voice carried down from high above.

"Sails ahoyeee! To weather, north by east! Square rigged! Square rigged!"

Mr. Claussen and the captain looked at each other with raised brows.

"The fleet?" Captain Ward wondered aloud.

"It would make good sense now wouldn't it? They're shaping course for the ROYAL PRINCE, and not a moment too soon," said Mr. Claussen. "The tide may have turned in our favor, for the pirates will never confront the fleet. It would be suicide."

"You are right about that, sir. There is certain to be five or six frigates and several seventy-fours, no doubt, for they are quick and nasty and meant specifically to take on the faster pirate ships. Pirates despise their attention." Captain Ward spoke assuredly.

It was the voice of Mr. Claussen that attracted Milady, and she stopped tugging at me the moment her husband's voice resonated through the pilothouse. He was still standing overhead on the quarterdeck conversing with Captain Ward. The sound of him seemed to freeze her where she stood. She listened intently, barely allowing herself to breathe. A look of worry crossed her face.

"He is surely going to be shot, standing there with Captain Ward on the quarterdeck. My God, the thought of it makes me feel faint."

"No, Milady, it will never happen. Mr. Claussen won't allow it. He will be fine, believe me." Lady Rebecca said nothing further so she might listen to the reassurance of her husband's voice.

"Look! There upon the stern!"

Mr. Claussen pointed toward the man-of-war. From our place beneath the two men and within the shadows of the pilothouse, Milady and I strained to see. At first there seemed nothing amiss, but closer scrutiny in the light of the fire upon the water revealed the entire stern of the ship was covered with a plague of pirates clinging for their lives, their ships having been forced to depart.

No sooner was this spoken by Mr. Claussen, than it was noticed by the forward gunners at the bulwarks who immediately crossed over to the larboard bow and began to pick off the pirates one by one. In short time the remaining scoundrels seeing the accuracy of the weapons found themselves with little choice but to drop into the sea or surely die by the ball.

The ROYAL PRINCE remained quiet while we passed by her stern, but as soon as we were safely away, she opened up again. She swung her gaff to her starboard quarter and drove her stern to sea thereby gaining a few degrees by which to fire upon the pirates who were fleeing eastward to escape the wind driven flames. When the big guns of the lower deck fired, one needn't be hit to suffer, for there was punishment enough just being on the same sea.

Lady Rebecca and I pressed our hands over our ears and gave in to the urge to cower upon the deck. Side by side, we sank lower and lower, disappearing from view until one of us regained the courage to stand back up for another look through the broken windows.

The barrage lasted for fifteen minutes; all the while we circled back, and then it came to an abrupt halt, but left us to carry the feelings of concussion in our chests. Finding courage anew, Milady and I stood up to look about the sea and the REBECCA. The scene was unreal. At first there was nothing to be observed, we being blinded by the ever-present white smoke. As it drifted southward many of the pirates used it for cover in order to escape. It appeared as though nothing left behind remained intact. The world went silent, not a sound to be heard save for the clamorous ringing in our ears that was slow to abate. When the smoke had cleared out, of the thirty-five or so vessels that had taken on the REBECCA and the ROYAL PRINCE only half were able to make it out of cannon range sound enough to remain under command.

"Ha, ha, ha!" Captain Ward roared. "Those cursed Barbary Coast bastards just downed a dose of their own bloody medicine. They have had free rein to prowl the Mediterranean for too long. They have been asked, they have been begged, they have been paid every concession they have demanded, and still they want more. Greed! Greed, indeed! Greed beyond reason, but today they got more than they asked for. Today His Majesty's ROYAL PRINCE, a Capital Ship-of-the-Line, paid them in kind and most generously at that. Ha, ha, ha!"

Captain Ward stomped his foot upon the quarterdeck over our heads. He was a happy man. There were many happy men. All across the deck men were hopping up and down, howling and whistling, cursing at the pirates and taunting them to come back for more.

In the end, Lady Rebecca and I were among the first to see the sails of the English fleet glowing in the moonlight as the ships approached from the north. By accounts given overhead it was believed the fleet saw the fire upon the water that pinpointed the source of the battle and most likely attracted them to the position of the ROYAL PRINCE. Not a pirate ship remained to chance a welcome.

Only the sea was left, a sea littered with bodies and wreckage. The mates put down their weapons and began to collect survivors. It was to be expected that some of the movement toward the ships was certain to be enslaved English sailors or Americans happy to be free. The boarding nets were dropped over the side of the man-of-war and the marines stood at the ready to escort the survivors into confinement as needed. The battle was over for good.

FORTY

"I must go back down. Listen to me, Elizabeth. You stay put here in the pilothouse, or I'll have you scrubbing dinnerware until your fingers bleed. You hear?"

"Yes, Milady." She kissed me on the head, and then left me as a witness to the aftermath.

In the welcome peace that followed, Lady Rebecca presented the man-of-war with an impression all her own. She asked Mr. Claussen if he would clear the quarterdeck of debris, and make it safe, so she might release the children from their confinement for a short while before sending them to bed. The fresh air and freedom would ease their minds, and help them to sleep sound with less chance of nightmares. Mr. Claussen always strove to give Milady whatever she wished, and it was done at once.

All forty-nine of the orphans scrambled to the corral above the quarterdeck, screaming and laughing, impatient to enjoy the fresh air and have a look and see. Their childish voices rang out like bells across the nighttime waters. They stared with amazement at the monstrous hull rising and falling off our bows.

371

The English stared back slack-jawed, pointing down incredulously at the 'ship of shorties' as we heard them begin to call us in jest. Their officers sounded us promptly.

"Who are you?"

"The REBECCA, Master James Ward, ten days out of London! Who are you, sir?"

"His Majesty's ship the H.M.S. ROYAL PRINCE! Man-o'-war one hundred and four guns! Captain Earl Stowington. The Captain respectively requests permission to board you, sir!"

"Permission granted!"

The exchange gave me goose bumps, but it made the Americans nervous, and they began disappearing from view. They went to congregate near the crates that had concealed them once before, mostly for their own piece of mind. Captain Ward turned to Mr. Claussen.

"This may indeed be an honor, Mr. Claussen. It would be standard procedure for the captain to send a boarding party, and return us to his vessel or risk being scuttled." He snickered.

"He is paying us tribute; I have no doubt. I believe he desires to look us over for his personal satisfaction. Surely, to thank us for our assistance in return, but I am also inclined to believe he is curious about the REBECCA and possibly your weapons. They did appear impressive."

The seamen aboard the ROYAL PRINCE were swarming over her decks and rigging. They climbed aloft, cutting free the remains of the fallen mast and the tangle of shrouds and lines. They transformed the damaged ship into a new ship almost at once before my eyes.

I recalled Lady Rebecca's words when she told me the story of Admiral Nelson. Although she noted the strict discipline to be had aboard merchant ships, she dismissed it as child's play when compared to a life of sea battles, death, wreckage, and repair that was the salt and gut of the English fighting fleet.

They were not only prepared for it, but also unparalleled in their ability to deal with it, and like any polished institution, they were a sight to behold when engaged.

Once the quarterdeck was made safe for the orphans, I was allowed to leave the pilothouse, and after letting the children pass, I assumed my favorite place on the steps at the stanchions. Looking out across the water toward the man-of-war, I watched as the longboat ferrying the English captain and his officers came alongside.

"Welcome aboard, Captain Stowington. Captain James Ward at your service." The men shook hands. "Allow me to introduce Mr. Christopher Claussen, a noble gentleman who is both financier and owner of the REBECCA. It was by his wish that we came to your assistance." They shook hands, and then Captain Stowington introduced his officers.

"A pleasure to meet you, Mr. Claussen. I am indebted."

"The pleasure is mine, Captain Stowington. And allow me to say Captain Ward is much too generous with his praise. Our decision to assist was based upon a vote by all present. Our able bodies must be recognized for their courage. They have made me proud. Having said that, now please, let us repair to my cabin for refreshments." Mr. Claussen presented the way.

Mr. Claussen, Captain Ward, Captain Stowington, and his officers stepped carefully about the broken glass and wreckage as they made their way to the pilothouse. Captain Stowington stopped momentarily to inspect one of Mr. Claussen's breech loading weapons. He was unable to devote his full attention to the weapon that so fascinated him, due to the distraction of rowdy children cut loose in the coral behind him. He chuckled in amazement.

"I am most interested to know about this ship, gentlemen. I have many questions, and I trust you will entertain me with your answers."

They all laughed heartily and entered the pilothouse. I slipped down the steps and into the pilothouse, watching them as they moved aft along the corridor. I then ran down the staircase to steerage, passed through and climbed up the accommodation ladder where stealthily I took up my station upon the top step.

In the warm glow of the oil lamps, I could see Mr. Claussen, Captain Ward, and the English officers as they discussed the nuances of the day's events over glasses of port and portions of fruitcake saturated with brandy. It became immediately obvious to Mr. Claussen and Captain Ward that Captain Stowington had been well versed in the pirate activities about this coast.

"We have been pursuing a number of pirates that have been employed raiding ships along the southern Mediterranean above the Algerian coast. They have turned the routes into voyages of fear for all Christians and honest merchantmen. They no longer partake in the arrangements whereby monies are paid to the Beys and Deys by foreign nations for assurances of safe passage, and instead established their own agenda of opportunity. Needless to say, once started and given a few successes, their numbers flourished and they have made a complete mess of commerce throughout the Mediterranean, especially either side of the narrows at the Straits of Gibraltar and about Sicily.

"Things have gotten so far out of hand that the pirates are now actually paying their own tributes in the form of percentages of loot removed from the merchant vessels in trade for safe harbor along the North African coasts of Algeria, Tunisia, and Morocco. These governments have a good thing going. They are being paid to keep pirating under control on one hand by numerous nations or enterprises, and then turning a blind eye to the pirates who pay them a percentage of their take on the other. They are profiting handsomely.

"In any event, the scoundrels had raided three merchant vessels only days before, and this done just inside the straits. This fleet was reputed to be very large by ordinary measure. It was made known to us that a smaller faction had disjoined from the ranks and turned back. These few appeared to be moving eastward probably to find haven somewhere near Oran, but the main fleet was said to have risked passing through the straits and headed out to sea.

"As often happens in these parts, a blistering sirocco blew in from across from the desert and wedged itself between the main pirate fleet and our ships. It was enough to stall our chase, and in order to make some good of a bad situation, I ordered my fleet to take their leave of me and head eastward, giving chase to the smaller faction while I waited out the storm.

"Unfortunately, I found myself lacking the stomach to further endure the sand that rained down upon us for a day and a half, and being bored and bothered, and having no desire to wait further, and in light of the fact that the weather was growing increasingly squally and foul, I decided to move the ROYAL PRINCE past the straits and out to sea as well.

"In doing so, I spied the REBECCA standing south and sailing alone. Knowing full well that a large pirate fleet was in the vicinity, I was confident you might be attractive enough bounty to draw some attention on yourselves, and I ordered my officers to fall back and remain as far astern of you as possible so we might watch what should take place."

The discussions were interrupted by a knock on the door. Mr. Beckwith stepped into the room and stated that an American sailor had been rescued from the sea. He carried with him much news of the pirates' activities and might well be heard out. Captain Ward promptly requested his presence. The door was opened wide, and the man stepped into the cabin. He was dripping wet. He looked thin and haggard.

"Come forward, sailor." Mr. Claussen offered him a drink.

"Thank-you sir."

"What name do you go by?" Asked Captain Ward.

"Curly Tabor, sir."

"You're an American?"

"Yes, sir, born and raised in the state of New York."

"How did you come by such misfortune?"

"I signed up as an able body aboard the brig WINDWHISPER, a year past. We were bound for France with a cargo of tobacco, and sailing our return laden with wine. We sailed the southern route to avoid the embargo. It was here in these very waters that we were attacked by the pirates."

"How many on board your vessel?"

"Sixty-seven all told, sir."

"And the others?"

"Enslaved, sir, pretty much the same as I. A good many died, wore out they were. Some of us were fed better. I reckon there will be more of us plucked from the sea today. I'm certain a good number jumped ship."

"Mr. Beckwith tells me you have information and knowledge about the pirates' intentions. Is that so?"

"Just talk, sir. Scuttlebutt."

"Go on then, tell us what you heard."

"Things were pretty lively in port, sir. There were four fleets of pirates. There was those of us who lived here within the islands, another fleet that had come down from the north above the straits, I think Spain or Portugal, and two larger and heavily armed fleets from inside the straits. We were a part of the smaller fleet. We plundered whatever came along in the way of small vessels. It was unusual to have so many ships in port and witness the town completely out of control, lots of drinking and such.

"The two larger fleets were raiding in the southern Med, and being followed by the ROYAL PRINCE. Those men were itching for a fight. They very much wanted to take on a man-o'-war for the ordnance. They had quite a few ships, many well-armed, and they figured they might be able to force a gunship into the reefs. A lot of fuss was made of it. Yet, it was the fleet that sailed in from the north stirred up most of the talk in our quarter.

"That is because they were looking for the REBECCA in hopes of capturing a cargo of orphans. Since this was akin to taking our bread and butter, our fleet took immediate notice and grumbled a good deal. To avoid blood being spilled, we reached an agreement to work together in overtaking the REBECCA, but at first sight of the man-o'-war, we turned about. We had no desire to draw the English fleet into our hideout. Besides which, we had nothing in the way of arms heavy enough to combat such a vessel.

"It was different for the two larger fleets. They welcomed the opportunity. They sang about the guns and powder soon to be theirs. They could have easily put REBECCA asunder, but they weren't in want of orphans. They were feeling quite bold, having found two additional fleets in port and knowing your situation."

"How's that?" asked Captain Stowington.

"You were a fair distance down along the coast. It gave them more time to wear you down, and less of a chance of meeting up with your fleet during the battle they desired. It was said by some that you were being drawn out of the Med by plan, led south of the straits and down along the coast."

Captain Stowington responded.

"I must tell you, the ROYAL PRINCE is a formidable ship of the line, second to but few. Yet, the pirates know well how to tax her abilities. They know she is meant to battle ships one on one, broadside to broadside. There is a strategy involved, a positioning for wind and advantage, type of shot, experience of gunners, all of this comes to bear at the moment of battle. The preparation takes hours, the battle just moments.

"But here, I am forced to engage in close-up battle with vessels that both outrun and outmaneuver me. They are quick

377

enough to stay clear of my broadside, and so remain at my stem and stern raking my sails and rigging with chain shot. One can do a good job at fouling the tops with a fleet of small guns. They have no need to crush hulls."

"It is as you say, sir, this was the crux of their plan," offered the American.

"Those of you here should be assured that even in our apparent state of disarray, the pirates would have been hard pressed and paid out dearly with life and limb had they tried to overpower the ROYAL PRINCE, tops or no tops, for there are over a hundred well-trained marines aboard."

"Did they not foul your rudder, sir? It certainly appeared so," asked Captain Ward."

"Yes, they did, Captain. I believe the devils approached us from the bows, then floated themselves along the hull to our stern and wedged planks between the rudder and the sternpost, this just prior to their scaling the stern. They bound her up good, but even so I would have dropped a hundred men or more over the board if need be, to right it. It was a hindrance to be sure, but a temporary one at most.

"In any event, they were quite distracted by your return. Let me not belittle the impact of your decision to turn back. It was plain to me as I watched you come abreast that your motives were noble. I understood your intention to come to us abeam and assist, and I ordered my men to replace their loads with ball. You were witness to the wisdom of that choice in short time once the pirates' displayed their foolishness. I assure you, in a light wind and settled sea, only a complete idiot would venture before my gun crews.

Allow me to say that as disappointing as some of today's events proved to be, I was delighted by the surprising effectiveness of your bulwarks muskets. Never have I seen anything of the sorts, and I must convince you to allow me to have one for my own. You gave an impressive show of fire from off your bows as you approached us. I must confess that I myself joined many on deck in offering a round of applause on your attack, not to mention your stern pass to clear my rudder of the scoundrel. For many that was literally a pain in the ass. It was a very good show, sirs!"

"Here, here!" One of the English officers raised his cup in a toast. All took a drink.

"Tell me one more thing, Mr. Tabor, and then by all means take your leave. You mentioned the pirates knew about the orphans. How was that possible? Do you know?" Mr. Claussen was most curious.

"As with everything, Sir, we live by rumor. But as it was told to me, there was a pirate aboard your ship, a man in your employ that shipped with you from the very start. He sent word of your departure and was to see to it that we were able to enter below decks. They seemed to be pretty certain of this plan as though it had been well thought out."

"I am still baffled as to how they could have known we were to take a southern route. Initially we were to take the fortieth, and changed our course only after our departure."

"If I might offer an opinion, sir."

"Please do, Mr. Tabor."

"These things are pretty much left to chance. But the odds are one in two, either the fortieth or the southern route. If you are wrong half of the time, you still can do well in the business. The most important thing is to know the departure of the vessel and what is her laden. This information comes fastest across land to ports in the Mediterranean where these fleets are active, and from there, they venture out knowing about when the vessel should appear at the straits. It is an easy matter to lie in wait, if they have someone aboard who is in their employ, then all the better. There is a good deal more traffic to the south in these times because of the English patrols to the north and the embargos. The odds were in their favor."

"Thank-you, Mr. Tabor. Please make yourself comfortable aboard the REBECCA. If you prefer to work, you might mention it to Mr. Beckwith."

"Yes, sir. Good-day."

"A moment, Mr. Tabor." Captain Stowington's voice raised somewhat in force. "You seem to be well informed in these matters. How am I to be assured you aren't a pirate yourself?"

The man looked at the captain with disdain.

"I suppose I am indeed a pirate, but what choice have I been given? I fight at the end of a sword or I drown at the end of a plank. I can only offer my regrets in this unholy work and show to you my back."

He turned around and dropped his shirt off his shoulders to reveal a badly scarred back. He then made a pointed remark that reflected upon the captain as well.

"Americans don't whip their men as a rule, sir."

"Sometimes it is better to die with honor."

"So be it for men, but hardly so for the wives and children left behind to fend for themselves." Curly Tabor was visibly angered by the Englishman's remarks.

Captain Stowington said nothing further, and Mr. Tabor was dismissed. The conversation now focused upon the orphans and the REBECCA.

"Elizabeth?" Mr. Claussen called out.

I froze. I knew he couldn't see me on the step, for the bed and a blind were between us. Yet, he was confident I was here and must have assumed, rightly so, that I was listening to all that had been said. I was at once afraid.

"Elizabeth, I know you are there, child."

"Yes, Milord."

"Go to Rebecca and tell her it would please me if she might come to the cabin and meet our guests."

"Yes, Milord."

I jumped off the step and did as I was told. Within minutes Lady Rebecca appeared, and Mr. Claussen introduced her as his wife and the ship's namesake. She was a sight to behold; the dirt, ash, and soot that covered her from head to foot seemed only to accentuate her true beauty, and it certainly enhanced her character. She both mesmerized the English guests and gave credence to the account of the fire below decks. She was asked to give again her account of Britany Allison's heroic actions to save Mr. McCurry's life.

The officers enjoyed Lady Rebecca's telling of the story much more than the story itself, for these momentous events were but trivial things aboard a man-of-war. To such extent did Lady Rebecca put Captain Stowington into an agreeable manner, he insisted on presenting a most generous gift to the REBECCA, ship of her namesake.

Producing an article, which he signed in front of all, and proclaimed legal by the authority granted unto him by the King George III of England, he penned:

> *Be it known to all men who read this article that*
> *Mr. Christopher Claussen and Master James Ward,*
> *so long as they remain in command of the good ship*
> *REBECCA, are employed in the business of King*
> *George of England, and as such are under his*
> *protection and guidance, and not to be encumbered*
> *in the act of that business upon the seas by any*
> *vessel of the Crown.*

This being granted in return for
deeds of bravery by ship and crew, in their
service to His Majesty's Line of Battle Ship
H.M.S. ROYAL PRINCE 104 guns against great odds
and better judgment for no purpose of personal gain.

In the name of King George III, I sign and date this
Friday, July tenth, year of our Lord 1807,
Captain Earl Stowington.

The night was closer to dawn, and weariness was evident beneath the engaging conversation until common sense drove all to accept the need to retire.

"Captain Ward, Mr. Claussen, and especially to you, Mrs. Rebecca, allow me to say I have enjoyed my stay, the refreshments, and your company, but now I must take my leave, for there is a great deal of work ahead of me yet this night. I leave you with this article that I suppose will serve you well and with it offer my gratitude." He rose to his feet, which caused his officers to do likewise. Mr. Claussen stood as well and spoke.

"Captain Stowington?"

"Sir?"

"I can only assure you that I fully understand the value of the article you have presented me. It goes without saying that it shall serve well indeed. No finer consideration could be offered a merchant ship of the seas. It would do my honor a great measure of good if you would allow me the privilege of presenting you with a token of my own appreciation for the bravery you and your men presented in our behalf, which set the example."

"I assure you, sir, that is not necessary. This is our calling. We are here to protect seafarers from these scoundrels."

Captain Stowington, being a gentleman, objected politely, but allowed himself to bend to Mr. Claussen's wishes. Mr. Claussen stepped over to the bookshelves and reached for a fine inlaid wooden box. This he presented to the English captain.

"You will have a dozen of my breech loading guns to satisfy your curiosity, as well as one each for your officers, but I beg you honor me by accepting this gift personally."

Captain Stowington took hold of the wooden box and raised the lid. A sudden look of elation swept over him.

"Ahoy, Mr. Claussen. This is much too generous. I hardly feel justified in accepting such a fine gift." He was clearly delighted as he removed a pistol of the highest quality from the box, and raised it to show all. Mr. Claussen then went on to point out some of its features.

"It is hand-constructed by the finest craftsmen in Brecia, Italy. The stock is from a select piece of rosewood and the steel is of the highest grade."

"The quality is at once visible. The engraving is superb, Mr. Claussen. The waterfowl and the reeds are fashioned with an artist's eye. Are the plates silver, is that correct?"

"It is indeed, Captain."

"I confess that I am a small collector of arms myself. I have nothing in my collection as fine as this piece, but I am fully capable of appreciating its quality, and understand well the magnitude of your gesture in kind. I am honestly pleased, and will display the piece for as long as I am able. I am very much embarrassed by your consideration. Thank-you, sir."

"It is with great pleasure that I have given it. You are welcome, Captain."

The gift having been accepted with much satisfaction and ado, the British officers were then soon to depart. In their company went the pistol, the guns, a keg of Chambord, and Marion

McCurry. The second mate was passed over to Captain's Stowington's charge so that the captain's surgeon, working in better-appointed medical facilities, might attend to Mr. McCurry's needs, hopefully saving his life then returning him to England with further passage to the port of his pleasure. Mr. McCurry was too delirious to comprehend all that had taken place in his behalf.

As Captain Stowington was about to descend the boarding ladder, he made one last comment to Captain Ward.

"Captain Ward?"

"Sir?"

"If you would honor me?"

"Anything, just ask."

"Give my compliments to you gunners, for only men who have trained aboard a man-o'-war cycle cannon as do yours, a job well done. Will you pass my observation along?"

"That I will, sir."

"Good night, Captain Ward, Mr. Claussen."

"Good night to you, sir."

And so much to their relief, the English captain was prepared to overlook the qualifications and background of the Americans hiding on board. He had assumed them to be deserters, but elected not to pursue the issue.

The battle damage suffered by REBECCA was repaired at sea by the carpenters. The ruined stores were offered to the men as salvage for their own gain. Whatever was left, being unusable, was thrown over the board, and the ship's hold was scrubbed and rescrubbed to remove the residual odor, which permeated everything below deck.

During this process a number of men started to collect about Lady Rebecca's coach on the fore deck. In short time, their numbers increased, and they appeared to be growing anxious. I had watched the commotion intensify from the start as I sat at my favorite place upon the quarterdeck. I wasn't alone, for Lady Rebecca had also noted this congregation about her coach. I went over to her.

"What is it, Milady?"

"I am sure I don't know, Elizabeth. Shall we see for ourselves?"

We descended the quarterdeck and walked forward through the waist of the ship toward the coach, which by now had been half stripped of its sailcloth covering. The canvas lay about it like a dress fallen at one's feet. The men began to step back and away as we approached; some did so out of respect, some out of fear, wary about having exposed the vehicle. The mates thought very highly of Lady Rebecca, and as soon as she greeted them without making mention of the uncovering, their doubts dissipated and they began at once to speak freely as they rushed in to meet us. They all had a look of wonder upon their faces.

"Pray tell, what is it about my coach that fascinates you so?"

"Milady, Milady!" They all called out, at once talking over each other until one William Bradley became their spokesman.

"It is a strange thing to behold, Lady Rebecca. How does one explain such a thing as this? I happened to look at the coach, and thought it a pity such a fine thing should be damaged in the fray. I remembered the look of it before it was wrapped in canvas, its beauty, its perfection. I thought to see how badly it had been scarred and began to look over its surface.

"At first, I was pleased to discover that I could see nothing of concern. After further looking about, I began to be amazed that I hadn't discovered a little something, anything, anything at all. Soon, I found myself hoping I might chance upon something that reflected the day's battle.

"After all, there was much lead and ball laying about the deck or embedded in the ship. And yet, not a hole could be found in the canvas by any of us, for by this time there were at least five of us determined to find a single mark. You understand our amazement, for she sits quite prominent upon the deck, yet, there was nothing.

"I am afraid we were unable to control our suspicions and began to remove the canvas until it lay bare. There is not so much as a scratch upon its finish, not a nick. Not one single, little, tiny mark. Thousands of rounds have been aimed our way, not to mention grapeshot. There is no glass left in the pilothouse, the bulwarks and bulkheads are shattered, as you can see for yourself. Yet, there is not one single mark upon the coach. Is it not strange? Do you not find that unusual?"

Lady Rebecca thought about it for a moment.

"What man has been injured in the fray aside from Mr. Borislav and Mr. McCurry who suffered a mishap below deck?" The men looked at each other, and responded after some whispering between them.

"No one person that we know of, Milady."

"Is that not strange?" It was now their turn to think a moment.

"It was luck!" they called out at last, fully in agreement.

"Was it more lucky than the coach not being struck?"

"Yes Milady. Not a one complains of injury. That is very lucky indeed."

"Well, then. There you have it. I agree that it is most amazing a round never hit the coach, a very lucky thing indeed. Yet, to me, it is not nearly as amazing as the fact that there are so many of you and not one of your party has been injured. Have you overlooked this fact, for you seem to accept it without question? I can only offer that we have been very fortunate this day in every conceivable way."

386

"This is a blessed ship. A blessed ship indeed!" Some of the men crossed their hearts in the sign of the cross. They were euphoric.

"Divine Providence is with us, gentlemen," Milady offered.

The men behind Mr. Bradley exploded into a cheer, which drowned out leftover concerns. He soon shrugged off the matter as well and joined in the festive atmosphere that was now widespread. Lady Rebecca and I returned to the children.

"Are you happy that your coach is unharmed, Milady?"

"Happy is not the word for it, Elizabeth. Amazed is not the word for it. I would think it better described as a miracle. The man was right in his thinking. Who can figure such a thing? It defies reason, child."

I was left confused. I wasn't sure if everybody was happy or unhappy knowing that the coach had not been struck. All I could determine was for a short time the episode made a profound impression upon the mates.

I also determined that events such as the coach, the sea battle, the close encounter with the shark, the ever-present cloak of death, all added to build the character of the common sailor who worked the REBECCA. These were men of the sea and faced their Creator on a daily basis. They showed little pity toward the unfortunates, and shunned any fuss made over their heroic deeds. It was all considered part of a life at sea, and accepted as such without further word being said.

In contrast, the passengers aboard the REBECCA viewed these events in an entirely different manner. For us, these were the basis of incredible stories that would be told and retold for many years to come.

FORTY-ONE

Marion studied the patterns before him. They frustrated him. He was drawn to them, mesmerized by them, yet he sensed something was amiss. They left him wondering, confused. They seemed unnatural. It was all there before him as it should be, and he felt he understood, but then the explanation would escape him. He struggled to focus his thoughts, and bit by bit an image formed. It was an image of the forest, but it was dreamlike and peculiar; it was blurred, mottled, and the trees stood canted. The vision gained definition, surfacing to be seen. Still...the trees stood canted.

Then, as if by the lifting of a curse, clarity was with him, and he took notice of the fact he was lying upon the ground, the side of his face pressed against the cool packed dirt. Had he been unconscious? A morbid panic crept over him. Where was he? What was he doing? Had he tripped and knocked his head? Why was he on this path? Summoning his strength, he pulled himself up the trunk of a tree. Sitting there, he attempted to gather his thoughts.

He felt it necessary to follow this path, but why? Why was he out here in the middle of the woods? Borislav! The name just popped into his head. Borislav, he thought to himself. That had to be it. Borislav. But, what about Borislav, what was so important about Borislav? Mrs. Borislav! Yes! Yes, it was about Mrs. Gustaff Borislav. Clarity was starting to come back to him, his mind regaining itself. He was en route to Mrs. Borislav to deliver an account of her husband's unfortunate death. Of course! Now he remembered. This had been his objective.

He had been released from the infirmary. He had asked to be put ashore in Malmo, in order that he might seek out this woman. He had been concerned about the widow, worried for her, spent a good deal of time wondering about her during his internment.

He feared she might be in a poor state, especially if she had been long awaiting her husband's return and was in need of his wage.

He had tried to picture Borislav's face. It wasn't easy. He remembered his bear claw bandanna. He knew the man wasn't much liked. Borislav kept to himself, but often sailors preferred to be left alone whilst enduring the cramped confines of the fo'c's'le. Men like him were often held with suspicion and misjudged, even contempt as they strove for privacy in a world where none existed. He knew from scuttlebutt aboard ship that Borislav lived deep in the backwoods, that he came from the port of Malmo, and that he had a family, a wife and children.

Marion was confident that if he inquired at the docks as he went along, he would eventually meet up with someone who either knew Gustaff personally or knew of him, someone who remembered the man with the peculiar bear claw bandanna. And so it proved to be, whereby following the hunches of those who worked with him or drank with him, Marion was finally pointed inland toward the path that he believed passed by the widow Borislav's dwelling. Even those who knew of him could say little about the man other than he was a rough sort. A few had expressed disbelief that he had taken up a contract aboard ship.

The circumstances surrounding Gustaff's death remained a mystery to Marion. He had never found out the details, for he had been removed from the REBECCA in a state of delirium, and his memory of the episode was lost to dreams. A couple of the mates had been by to see him. They had been employed to look up the widow and deliver unto her funds obtained for Borislav's belongings, which were put before the mast and auctioned off. They were to deliver the purse, but instead left the collected money with Marion at his request. They did this without question, as Marion had been their superior on board ship. Their meeting was brief, the mates stopping by to wish him a quick recovery, conveying the latest news and conversing about odds and ends.

They had spoke of rumor claiming Borislav had been involved in some form of foul play. To what extent, no one knew. He may have been on the run.

Marion was not one to judge. All he could recall was a dark murky scene, whence from within, a man tried to keep him back away from kegs of black powder, a man who was pulling him away from the gun port when he was half over the board. A man who Marion believed had tried to save his life. He remembered seeing the pirate ship and that was about it. He had been told there was an explosion. He was told he had been flung into the sea and hauled out by the young stowaway Britany Allison, Darrin O'Kurk, and Cookie Jar. Including the shark stories that was everything he knew, other than the fact he had lived and Borislav had not.

The man had saved his life, of this he was certain. He was the reason for Gustaff Borislav's death, and he felt obligated to personally convey this dismal news along with his remorse. He intended to assist the man's widow, to avail himself to her in any manner possible during his visit, providing it be within his power to do so.

Unfortunately, he was seriously set back by this renewed suffering from his wound, which only a week before appeared to be repairing itself and in no manner a cause for alarm. Now, he found himself frightened. He unbuttoned his jacket and needn't undress further, for the whole of his blouse was drenched in blood. He raised the back of his hand to his brow, and found himself to be covered with sweat, and at the same time chilled by fever.

Marion clutched the rough bark of the tree and pulled himself up shakily to his feet. He distanced himself from the cool earth, which sapped the warmth from his body. Upon doing so, he opened his eyes to a world that moved about him in circles. He was in a bad way. He felt nauseated and lightheaded. This did nothing to alleviate his concerns, and he knew, being a stranger in a strange place, he must find the Borislav cabin as soon as possible to take his rest. His life could well be in the balance, for if he should lose consciousness again in the woods he could die or worse, end up supper for some wild beast. With pressing determination, spurred by the grip of fear, he staggered forward and farther into the forested hills.

FORTY-TWO

Katriina Borislav remained motionless. She peered out her window, a carving knife gripped firmly in her hand. The children had been hushed. She could not make out the person lying at the step of her door, for she was only able to see his coat from waist down, his pants, and his boots. The scene, however, was not entirely uncommon. On numerous occasions before, friends of Gustaff had chanced upon the cabin looking for a place to sleep off their rum or ale.

It had been nearly two months since she had seen anything of Gustaff, and she was in as desperate a state of need as ever she recalled. Although the man was passed out at her door and certain to be trouble when aroused, she wondered if he might carry some word of her husband. It was only a hope, and caution came first, so she braced a plank against the door for additional protection then instructed the children to use the bowl should they need to relieve themselves. Afterward, Katriina tucked herself along with her young into bed, placed the knife within close reach, and attempted to sleep.

The intruder lying upon her step, and the possibility of his knowing the whereabouts of Gustaff brought anxiety to her dreams. Her sleep was poor and unrewarding, and for this reason, before the first light of dawn, she was up shuffling in slippers and feeding the fire to force out the early morning chill.

The grayish light outside her window was now filtering its way down through the trees to illuminate the forest floor. Katriina stepped over and pressed her face to the cool pane of glass. An uneasy feeling swept across her as she again saw the form of the stranger unmoved within the shadows. Unsure of what this morning might bring, she made herself a cup of tea then sat quietly—hoping her children might remain asleep a while longer, thereby allowing her time to think.

Sitting at the table, she watched as the ever brighter morning light entered through the window. It was early, and already her mind was stressed with worry and concern for her children. She was out of food and money. The children wore rags, and she couldn't face the reality of an approaching winter even though for now it was only in her thoughts. She was desperate, horribly desperate. She felt cornered and at wits end. Only by the charity of her neighbor, Mr. Klagen, was she able to manage at all and although he was the kindest man alive, the embarrassment of begging for even the smallest of needs was unbearable.

Where was her man? Was he punishing her? Was he being cruel? Was he hurt or something worse? Katriina began to wish the man outside her door would come about so she might ask him about Gustaff. At least then she could get past these questions in her mind and be done with it. She put aside the remainder of her tea, for she was too anxious to sit still and sip. She rose to pace the floor, her mind racked with indecision and anxiety. Her insides were filled with turmoil. Unconsciously, she rubbed her hands to relieve her nervousness. She looked at her children, who had not yet stirred, and driven by need and desperation, she finally moved across her cabin to the door.

She hesitated briefly, but it was inevitable, and so quietly she removed the brace from the door. With the knife again secure in one hand, she released the latch and cautiously pulled the door ajar that amount least sufficient to enable her to peer out. The man was without hat—*unusual*. He was young by the looks of it, about her age, or at least he so appeared. The man seemed dead to the world, and so she squatted down close to the floor in an attempt to get a better look at his face. To her surprise, he was relatively clean-shaven and not at all unpleasant to look at.

A notion was taking hold in Katriina's mind that possibly all was not as it showed. With this fresh thought, she studied his clothes and was encouraged by the fact his attire was almost newly made. This man did not share the appearance of the drunkards she had come to see in the past. There was no foul smell about him.

"Maybe not drunk at all," she whispered to herself.

The thought of the stranger being in need of help made her feel uncomfortable. If it were true that she had shut him out in the chill of night, it would have been unforgivable. Nevertheless, how could she be blamed? How would she have known? Gustaff's friends and strangers alike were not people to take to without due caution. A drunken priest could put even a callous brute to shame, and so often she lived alone with her three children out of earshot of the Klagens. It was only natural she should act with caution.

She wrestled with her misgivings, but elected to go with her instincts. With a new sense of courage she backed away from the door, pulled it open wide, and then leaned out on all four to gaze upon this man stretched out before her. She crawled toward him. She stuck her neck out and smelled his breath, his hair, his clothes. Perplexed, she sat back upon her haunches. The man certainly had not been drinking. His shirt collar was soaked with sweat. Was he sick or injured?

This thought frightened her. She recoiled from the body as though he had reached for her. Might he suffer some fatal malady that should now strike them all dead or worse? Rising to her feet, she stood aback as though the ability to run from him might make a difference. What was she to do about this? If he was sick and dying she couldn't very well leave him to perish upon her doorstep in front of the children. Surely, he would poison them all with his affliction. It would probably be best to call on Mr. Klagen, but the thought riddled her with guilt, for she was loath to bother him further. At least for now, she would do what she could by her own means. What were her options? They appeared few, if any. She wasn't about to drag the stranger into the woods and leave him there to die. She didn't have the heart for it.

"Why me?" she asked herself as she fell resigned to her only conclusion.

"I might as well deal with this now, and come what may, at least I'll be done with it."

Katriina glanced over at her sleeping children and assured herself of their safety. She then stepped cautiously over the lifeless body that blocked her way out the door. She crossed the yard to fetch a sturdy limb. Upon her return, she began poking the man, hoping to force some life back into his being, but it was to no avail. At last gaining more confidence, she hooked the limb beneath his arm, and with great effort managed to roll him over upon his back. Whereas she *had* been afraid to touch his person, any concern of affliction passed at once, for the entire breast of his jacket was stained crimson, soaked through with blood. The man had been shot!

The sight was most unsettling. It made her nervous and unsure of what next she might do. Maybe he was running from the law. Would she be harboring a criminal, a murderer or rapist? Would she be imprisoned for attending to his needs?

"Oh, Lord. Isn't this a fine mess," she uttered to herself.

She had never imagined a dying man to be there upon her step, for only idiots or drunkards found their way back to her cabin, and to date, in every instance these strangers had proved to be both. What does one do with a dead man? Better yet, what does one do with a dying man? Up to a few moments ago, she had only thought him drunk. She had only just now stooped to smell his breath, but noted that he was breathing certain enough.

So, this man wasn't dead yet, but there was no mistaking he was in a very serious way. 'How best to handle this?' she wondered. Again she fought off the urge to run to Mr. Klagen. The thought of Gustaff returning home to find a stranger in his bed loomed worrisome over her head. He was so unpredictable. Would he be jealous, or would he see an opportunity for profit? She decided to direct him toward seeing the profit to be made. Gustaff was not one to dismiss profit lightly. That was an unfair thought, for she could hardly afford to view profits any differently. She wondered if the man carried a purse. This thought filled her with temptation that was immediately followed by deep guilt and set her course at once. She looked back into the solitude of the cabin, where her children still slept peacefully.

"Hans! Helena! Wake up! Wake up, children! Wake your sister. I need your help. Come, come, hurry up now! Help me with this man who is sick and needs a bed!"

Stirred from their sleep, rubbing their eyes and trying to understand what they were being asked to do, the children appeared at the doorway in a daze. They looked down at the stranger with some curiosity, but mostly with ambivalence, having seen the sight before.

"Well, don't just stand there like oafs, children. Help me move him into the cabin."

"Who is he? Is he drunk, mother?"

"No, Hans. He is injured." Katriina pointed to the stranger's side so her son could see the bloodstained blouse.

"Has he been shot?"

"For heaven's sake, Hans, how should I know such a thing? I imagine so, it looks that way, but this is no time for questions. Now let us move him to the bed. Come on, be quick about it and give me a hand."

With the help of her children, she dragged Marion's frame to the bed where they strained to get his dead weight up to the height of the mattress. Once done, they all backed away and stared at the stranger. Katriina remained undecided about the best approach to this unexpected turn of events. Her first determination was to discover who this person might be.

So, trying hard to avoid thoughts of money, she began to rifle through his pockets until she came upon his purse. Opening it, she was stunned by the amount of coin in his possession. Lucky for him he wasn't robbed. Yet, the temptation for her to steal was unbearable. She could hardly turn her eyes from the small treasure of gold before her. How long she had suffered through her dismal state of want. How easy it would be to tell him he had been robbed before he arrived at her step. He would never know. Her insides hurt from the battle of wills within.

Conscience eventually overpowered temptation and she scolded herself, reminding herself that she was dirt poor, but honest poor, God-fearing, and no thief. Besides, she thought, if she were to bring this gentleman back to health, there would be opportunity for him to show his gratitude. On the other hand, if he died she wouldn't have to steal anything or face the wrath of heaven. What need would he have then of worldly possessions? She set the purse aside and searching further found papers connected to the ship REBECCA.

For his benefit, as much as theirs, Katriina removed one piece of gold from Marion's purse and sent it off with her children to purchase some food and dressing for his wounds. She began to undress him, and this gave her cause to grimace for there was a putrid smell to the wound. One always knew this was a bad sign. She still had plenty of hot water on the mantle left over from her morning tea and wash for the children. She brought the hot pot to the bedside, and taking her time, she began to bathe him with care. Afterward, she went outside into the woods and gathered herbs for making a press, which she soon applied to his wound.

Throughout her tender attentions, Marion rambled incoherently. Incomplete thoughts about matters of shipping and other senseless gibberish passed by his lips as if he were trying to have a conversation with her. On occasion when he was especially excited and even thrashing about some, Katriina was certain she heard him call out to Gustaff. She was certain that she heard this.

After the second day, Katriina noted Marion's fever was down and the wound seeped a great deal less. His color was coming back and he slept more peacefully. She continued to care for him with a mother's kindness, changed his dressings every few hours day and night, and saw to his overall comfort.

On the third day, Marion opened his eyes. He was totally confused. It was a great effort to piece together who he was, where he was, and in whatever business he was engaged. The noises in the background were no longer so distant. He was immersed in the mouthwatering aroma of dinner. God almighty, was he hungry!

He turned his head, and as his focus sharpened, three young children came into view, a boy and two little girls. Just a few steps removed from where they sat eating at the table appeared a woman bent over a hearth, stirring a cauldron of soup or something of that nature. It smelled good. He was famished. His mouth flooded and without thought he swallowed, only to be promptly racked with pain. His throat was parched and raw.

He moaned, which immediately drew the attention of the family. All being wary of this stranger in their midst, the children stopped eating at once. One little girl jumped from her chair and moved toward the woman. Katriina turned guardedly toward him. Cautiously, she moved over to his side with a cup of water, already suspecting he would be craving it whenever he should awake. She sat down on the bed next to him, and raising his head, gently assisted him in his drinking. Feeling somewhat satisfied, Marion took a moment to look at this woman and gather his thoughts. The look of her nearly brought him to believe he had entered heaven.

"Begging your pardon, madam. Where am I?" His voice was nearly inaudible.

"You're in bed. A good place for you, I should say. For the last three days you have been under my care here in the cabin, which is my home. I found you lying upon my doorstep. I was quite frightened at first believing you to be drunk. I am Katriina Borislav. Do you have your memory? Do you know your name, from whence you came and to where you travel?"

"Katriina Borislav?" he repeated thoughtfully. "Katriina Borislav, I know that name."

For Katriina, his comment did not go without notice. Within moments, his memory returned to him the circumstance of his being at this cabin. He didn't remember arriving, nor how he got here, but the reason he was here was clear and unsettling. He became very quiet. A disturbed look swept across his face.

"Are you alright, sir?" Katriina asked.

"Yes, yes. I am fine, feeling much better, thank-you. My mind is as of yet, clouded. It will come, it will…." He dared not think any further of his dreadful mission.

The fact that Katriina's name was familiar to her patient gave her reason to be excited. Her spirits soared, for word of Gustaff might well be at hand.

"Are you well enough that I might offer you something?" she inquired.

Marion tried to abandon his haunting thoughts, searching for something to say.

"I am feeling much better, in no small part due to your care. I am afraid I may not be able to get to my feet just yet. I feel quite shaky and somewhat at a loss, but if the soup is even

398

remotely as splendid in taste as it is in aroma, I should be most grateful for a small portion."

"It is good that you have an appetite. I've just made it fresh this morning. It will do you well. It will give you back your strength, I promise. I'll fetch you a bowl at once. Be still." Marion noticed what a remarkable smile this woman had.

"I thank you again for your kindness. I am certain I will be most embarrassed to discover how I have put you out. I most likely have given you a time of it, and I cannot imagine how I might repay you for your charity. If my memory serves me, I recall having some funds upon my person that—."

With that thought, he stopped himself short. His 'person' had no shirt on. He raised the sheets. His person had no pants on. He was, in fact, as naked as a newborn. He felt his face flush with embarrassment. Katriina understood at once.

"I am sorry if I have offended you, but it was necessary for me to take some liberties. I won't have an unwashed stranger in my bed. I felt bathing to be in your best interest otherwise you would have had to sleep outside. Also, your memory serves you well, indeed. Concerning your purse, I must confess, I was forced to use a small portion of your funds, sir. I am deeply ashamed to admit the fact. However, if I hadn't done such a thing, there would have been nothing for you to eat, nor dressing for your wounds. I pray you'll forgive me this brazen deed for there was little choice." Katriina shrugged her shoulders.

"It is nothing, I assure you," he responded, his face aglow. He spoke further, remaining somewhat hidden beneath the blanket. "Take what you need to ease your burdens. I sense you are a person of character and honor, and I offer you my purse willingly."

Marion wished to forget his nakedness. He worked to overcome his embarrassment and peeked out to survey the room. He was distressed to see how barren was her cabin. It was a simple one-room structure and not well sealed from the elements, maybe sufficient for a man, but surely not a woman with children. The walls were bare, and there was no place to conceal food. It looked worse than a fo'c's'le and he always believed that was as worse as worse got. These people are in a bad way, he thought to himself, and his feelings went out to her. He had proven to himself how right had been that inexplicable determination to find her. As Katriina waited upon him with soup and spoon, there came a light rap upon the door.

Katriina set aside the soup and moved to the window cautiously. She then turned to Marion, her face breaking into a radiant smile. It was obvious a friend was calling. She opened the door and before she even greeted the gentleman, she had reached for his arm and pulled him inside the cabin. It was apparent that she was very fond of this person.

"Mr. McCurry, allow me to present to you, Mr. Eric Klagen. He is my neighbor and my protector and my salvation."

"Please, Katriina—." The man protested.

"A kinder heart does not exist." She broke him off.

Marion extended his hand toward the older gentleman in greeting, but looked squarely at Katriina.

"Mrs. Borislav, I am discovering, knows a good deal about me, *my name* and more. I fear I have *no* secrets. He then looked at Mr. Klagen. It is a pleasure to make your acquaintance, sir. I must apologize for not rising to my feet."

Katriina blushed as Mr. Klagen accepted Marion's hand. Indeed it wasn't just an issue of his nakedness, but she had never asked Marion his name, and could only have found it out by rummaging through his belongings, which was now apparent to all.

"Nonsense, my good man, rest easy, I insist. I am content to see you are progressing well."

"I didn't mean to be nosey, Mr. McCurry. I didn't know what else to do. I thought I should find out something about you, there were papers—."

"You make me laugh, Mrs. Borislav. I would have done no less. And please, do call me, Marion. After all, I am in your bed."

"Will you call me Katriina then?"

"I will indeed."

"Katriina was most concerned for your well being, Mr. McCurry," said Mr. Klagen, who then interrupted himself.

"Katriina! Take the children up to the house and bathe yourselves. I will remain with Mr. McCurry until you return."

"Bless you, Mr. Klagen. I will, and I'll be quick about it."

"Nonsense, child, take your time. The missus is expecting you, and will probably wish to chat and be privy to all the excitement and goings on with your newfound guest."

Katriina laughed. "As you wish. Come, children, get your things. Hurry now!"

Within moments they were exiting the door. Katriina looked back one last moment with concern, possibly to assure herself that Marion was comfortable, possibly to assure herself he could not leave before she returned. The door closed.

Mr. Klagen wasted no time starting the conversation and getting directly to the point.

"I must ask you to bear with me, Mr. McCurry. I have questions. I am most fond of Katriina, as I have grown to know her well over the years. No sweeter rose shall be found in this place of thorns. It is only natural that I should be wary of any stranger about her. Obviously, her safety and well-being is of utmost importance to me. I feel for her as I might a child of my own. I will say to your face, I won't think twice of putting

401

asunder any man who might think to take advantage of her good spirit."

"You have nothing to fear from me, sir. Ask what you wish, Mr. Klagen. I will do my best to put your mind at ease," Marion responded sincerely.

"Excellent! Tell me then, Mr. McCurry, what business employs you in these parts?"

"I am here to inform Mrs. Borislav that her husband, Gustaff Borislav, is dead. May God rest his soul." Marion was also directly and to the point.

Mr. Klagen stood in silent shock at the side of the bed. He thought at first that this must be a distasteful joke. Yet, why would anyone joke about such dreadful news? He grabbed a chair from the table and slid it over to the bed so he might sit down.

"Did I hear you correctly, Mr. McCurry?"

"Aye aye, Mr. Klagen. You did indeed."

"This is a most serious matter, sir. Surely, *you don't jest.*"

"What decent man would partake in such vicious folly? No, I say 'tis true, and I bear this news with heavy heart." Marion closed his eyes. Mr. Klagen studied Marion and then cautiously forwarded his request.

"Would you find me insensitive to inquire of such dark issue at this time? I mean, in view of your condition?"

"No, not at all, Mr. Klagen. I have said I will put your mind at ease. I am feeling well enough to stand up to it, and furthermore I wish to plead your assistance in this matter, for I relish not the task before me. I have come to tell Katriina, and it is certain to be devastating news."

"I assume you know this to be fact. No doubt can be there?"

"It suffers me greatly to say, not only do I know it to be fact, but I am implicated in his demise."

"Is that so?"

"Much to my regret, yes."

"Might I assume also, you actually saw his corpse?"

"No, sir. You might say we fell over the board, six or seven leagues out to sea, off the coast of Africa, and I saw him sink beneath the waves never to be seen nor heard from again. I am confident he is with the Lord."

"Hardly."

"Pardon?"

"That is one confidence I do not share, Mr. McCurry."

It was now Marion's turn to be taken aback. He was short a response.

"I feel somewhat the fool, Mr. Klagen. Is it my wound and the fever that confuses me?"

"Believe your ears, good sir. I hold Mr. Borislav in the lowest of esteem. It is of my opinion that never has a more callous snake ever slithered across the breast of a woman. I believe this is a day to be thankful, a day of blessing if you will. The Lord works in mysterious ways and my faith in him this day is ever the more strengthened."

Marion's eyes were wide open with surprise. "I am lost for words, sir. I am speechless, to say the least. I have understood him to be a ruffian, but can this man be beast enough to warrant such feeling at his hour of calling? After all, I believe him to have saved my life at the cost of his own."

"Don't count on it, Mr. McCurry, but I beg you tell me then of the circumstances that led to his death, for surely he is one more apt to take a life as to spare it. On this issue there must be much for a speechless man to say. I would believe it to be rife with unseen motive."

Mr. Klagen sat patiently and listened with great interest as Marion revealed the details of the accident as best his weakened state would allow. Mr. Klagen appeared more than satisfied of the truth in Marion's account.

"I would prefer to be present when you give Katriina this news."

"I would welcome it with heart."

"Would you prefer that I break the news?"

"Aye aye. I believe the blow would be softened. It will be difficult for me as I know nothing of her sensitivities."

"So be it. When do you wish me to do so?"

"I have no idea. Possibly when I am on my feet and thinking with a clear head. I shall give you a sign when you come visiting. I wish to be relieved of this burden, the sooner the better."

"I will stop by during the afternoons to pay call upon you and Katriina. I will watch for your cue."

As promised, within the hour Katriina returned during which time the two men strengthened the confidence between them. She entered the cabin freshly bathed with her children at her side. Instantly, the sight of her took a firm hold of Marion.

How opposite the boisterous mannerisms of men she was, as she moved about the cabin light-footed and aloof like a doe. He was unaccustomed to the modesty, to the delicacy and fragrance of women not in the business of selling themselves. The simple beauty of this woman fascinated him. The way she entered the room, the way she carried herself, an angel surrounded by cherubs at her feet. It was a pleasant thing to see, Marion thought to himself. It was peaceful, relaxing. As soon as she came back through the cabin door the room filled with a certain warmth the hearth could not match.

He wondered if she knew how she appeared to his eyes, or the effect she had on him? Maybe she did, maybe she was purposely drawing him under her spell. That struck him as being a dangerous thing, something better avoided. Maybe it was nothing more than the aftermath of a fever altering his perceptions, making him more sensitive to feelings or emotions. That must be it. It was only that which made sense. It was what he preferred to believe. Yet, she was so very interesting to watch. He wished to place his hands upon her, to get a sense of the feel of her. To discover what it was about her that attracted him so. She broke into his thoughts.

"So, how does my guest fare in my absence? Well, I pray."

"The care was not nearly so genteel. Not once did Mr. Klagen offer to hand feed me thy soup."

"Oh! He has humor, this is a good sign, 'tis certain." She looked to Mr. Klagen and smiled.

"Mr. McCurry is doing fine, Katriina. I believe him to be a good man, and the Lord will help him through this tribulation, I have no doubt. And now, I must be on my way."

"Oh! Mr. Klagen, might I beg you to stay for only a moment more?" she pleaded.

"And why is that, Katriina?"

She moved toward him and drew him in front of her as though he were a shield. She took hold of his arm, and looked across his shoulder from behind. They both stood before Marion's bedside. Marion could see her struggle with her thoughts. She had concealed herself behind the bulk of Mr. Klagen, hiding herself from him as he lay upon the bed.

"Mr. McCurry, I must ask something of you. While you were delirious, you made mention of many things, most of which made no sense to me. But thrice, I am convinced I overheard you make mention of my husband, Gustaff Borislav. Of this I am certain, Mr. McCurry. Do you know him, sir?"

Marion looked to Mr. Klagen and swallowed hard. "Yes, Katriina. I knew of him."

"Is it business of his that brings you here?"

"Yes, ma'am, that it is." There was a short, awkward silence.

"I believe if your business was to bring me a message, you would have spit it out by now, sir. Therefore, I must assume it is news you bring instead. News of misfortune, I fear."

"Yes, ma'am." Again, Marion looked to Mr. Klagen, but he continued speaking slowly and deliberate.

"I hope you can find it in your heart to forgive me for what I am about to say, especially after showing me such generosity and care. It is a difficult thing I must convey, God forgive my wretched soul." He worked up his courage.

"Take hold of yourself Mrs. Borislav, for it is with a heavy heart I must inform you that your husband, Mr. Borislav, is no longer numbered among the living. I am sorry to say it. He was taken at sea in a most bizarre accident of which I too was a part. It was because of my implication and my heavy heart that I promised to God Almighty I would come myself as soon as possible and personally present you with his personal effects and convey an account of this tragedy."

Katriina turned in to Mr. Klagen's shoulder and began to sob quietly. He took her into his embrace. The men waited momen-arily in silence for her to regain her composure. Marion spoke with care.

"I believe few men have felt as utterly useless as do I this moment beneath these covers. Forgive me, the added burden I must be."

Katriina turned to him, her face wet with tears. "Any man who would risk his life to deliver such difficult news in person as have you, would earn nothing less than my most sincere gratitude and admiration."

She moved toward him, then leaned over and kissed him on his forehead. She offered the only thanks she was able, a gesture from the heart. She turned back to Mr. Klagen and wept anew. Marion was left with the moisture of her tears upon his face. He felt every bit as naked and vulnerable as he was. He felt entirely pathetic and trapped beneath the covers. He did not move to wipe away that part of her that touched him so delicately. Mr. Klagen spoke.

"Katriina. You have long known my feelings toward Gustaff. I can't pretend at this time to express sorrow at your loss. I would be a hypocrite to do so and you know this to be true. I feel for you. I feel for your grief. It pains me deeply. Yet, I do believe with all my instincts that this may be for the best."

At once, Katriina began to choke on her sobs as she tried to express the breadth of her grief. "My children." She sobbed. "I will lose my children." She wailed softly. Marion looked at the children, who stood staring as solemn as stone.

Mr. Klagen smiled. "Have no fear child, as God is my witness, they will be at your side to see you gray. I'll see to it myself, no matter what it takes. Don't you fret the least over fears the like of that." He kissed her on top of her head and rocked her in his arms as they stood.

Katriina took hold of her emotions, and with a deep sigh, she stepped back from Mr. Klagen. She wiped the tears from her face and began to laugh.

"Oh, look! Look at your shirt, I've soaked it." She shook her head.

"It was my pleasure to offer it."

"You must go now. Mrs. Klagen waits, I'll be fine."

"Are you sure?"

"Yes. Besides I believe I am in good company for the time being, and we have much to discuss."

"Very well. I'll be on my way. Mr. McCurry, it has been my pleasure to make your acquaintance, even in spite of the circumstance." He extended his hand toward Marion, who received it firmly.

"Likewise, Mr. Klagen," Marion responded.

Katriina escorted Mr. Klagen to the door and thanked him again for his support and comfort. She closed the door and stood facing the wooden planks, her back to the room, her hand clutching the handle. The cabin grew silent as Marion and the children waited for her next move. She turned about, then instructed the children to go outside and play. They were uneasy but obeyed.

Left to themselves, the first few moments were awkward. Marion decided, being a guest, it was appropriate to remain silent unless Katriina wished otherwise. She fussed about the cabin a short while and now and then wept in silence. She spooned soup into a cup, and with no warning; she lifted a chair and brought it closer to Marion's bedside.

"It's been some time since we have eaten this good. Mr. Klagen is wonderful about bringing food, he has a bountiful garden—good sun, but it is difficult to accept his generosity because I know there is no end in sight to my begging."

She held the spoon up to Marion's mouth, and looked at him through eyes that he thought were too kind to be subjected to such misery. He could feel her effect upon him once again. She brought out something in his character, a compelling desire to help, to offer something of his service. It was a strange sensation, and it was both enticing and unsettling at the same time. She began to speak as she fed him.

"Mr. McCurry, you can see plain enough that Mr. Klagen had no heart for my husband. He can't be blamed because he knew my husband as a drunkard, who had become hard and insensitive to the point of being cruel and abusive. There was more to him than that, but it was buried so deep within his ill temper that it was hopelessly lost. I do still find room in my heart to cry for him because I remember better times. Times when..." she paused a moment to regain her composure, "when...the world looked promising and he only wanted the best for me.

"Years of scarce work eventually rob a man of his dreams, his worth, and his dignity. If he takes to drinking to escape the reality of his life, it's usually the end of him. I believe that when Gustaff looked at me, he saw all the promises he made with the utmost sincerity, not outlandish promises, but promises nevertheless that went unfulfilled, promises that always came back to haunt him. I know this because..." she began to cry again, "b-b-because of the way he w-would look at me every now and then. It was a look of love that I s-saw many times, years ago. He was just too far gone to feel he had any chance with me again. He believed, given a second chance, I never would have picked him for my own. I hope you might try and understand."

"I am a man of the sea, Mrs. Borislav. It is a difficult life, and I have stared into the face of death too many times. It makes a man hard and compassion is little more than a good laugh and a slap on the back, but you have my word; I will give him the benefit of the doubt for your sake, if for no other reason."

"I am grateful, Mr. McCurry. Would you share with me your account of his death? I must hear the whole of it, if I am to put it behind me."

"As you wish."

And so this time Marion blended the details with compassion as he again relayed what little he could remember of Gustaff's death. He found himself doing this with patience and pleasure. He saw how he gave her peace through comforting words, whilst she gave him feelings heretofore unknown, feelings of ecstasy. Being so near her, meeting her gaze, enjoying her fragrance, and being the focus of her attention drove him to desire her more as each hour passed. He finally acknowledged the calling in his heart, the truth of his feelings. He wished to remain for a while in her company.

Having heard every aspect of the circumstances surrounding the death of her husband, Katriina lowered her eyes and kept them fixed upon her hands. They were delicate and folded within her lap.

"Mr. McCurry, you have been most patient and have spared me all the pain you are able. It is now up to me, to return in kind, to free you of this burden of guilt." This peculiar statement amused Marion and he listened to her words.

"I beg you believe that I am most ashamed to have this suspicion; but having heard your accounts, I fear I can no longer deny with clear conscience what I am about to say."

"Have no fear of me, Katriina. Say what must be said." Marion encouraged her to speak.

"A time back, in the spring of the year, Gustaff made journey to the wharves of Copenhagen in search of employment. Upon his return, as was his custom of late, he commenced to drink himself into a stupor. At times like this, he would rant and rave gibberish and converse as though at the inn with a troupe of friends. It is embarrassing to speak of it because at these times he was prone to become terribly violent. I would keep the children as quiet as possible and we would stay clear of his reach, and wait until he succumbed to the rum. Often we would listen to his goings on like a madman. He would sit there at the table talking to the walls, whilst we remained hidden here behind the bed.

"On the particular night of which I now speak, Gustaff was blind drunk, filled with rum and carrying on most excitedly to himself. What aroused my attention in particular was his goings on about orphans. I listened with curiosity, trying to imagine the nonsense that swarmed within his head. He went on and on, over and over, rambling about this plan to make a fortune. He jabbered on endlessly about pirates and orphans, and slaves.

"I couldn't make the least bit of sense from of any of it. This talk of orphans was so peculiar. Bless my soul, I thought. He's gone off his rocker. Surely, he had lost his wits. And that's the whole of it. I never would have given it a second thought except for your mentioning the orphans, which has jostled my memory.

"What leads me to fear some foul plan was under way is your saying that Gustaff was aboard a ship. That is incredible to hear! I can hardly trust my own ears; it is that unbelievable. You must know the fear he possessed of the sea. He was terrified of it. He never made known to me any plan to board a ship. Don't you think that strange? It would have been such an issue with the man he surely would have informed me of such intentions unless he had something to hide. I fear now there was much to his ravings, an ill-fated plan that ended in his demise. If ever a woodsman were to be tied up in no good with a pirate it would have been Gustaff. I am most certain of this, certain enough to say go with a clear conscience, Marion." She finished.

Marion was amazed. He was forced to face some serious rethinking about all that took place that afternoon. Katriina waited for him to speak, but he was deep in thought, sorting out his memories.

"If I were to reconsider these events in view of what you have said, I might very well come away with a different conclusion. I would be almost inclined to agree. They have certainly awakened me to prospects heretofore unsuspected. I must think on this further. A couple of mates stopped by to see me in the infirmary and left word of rumor that Gustaff was afoul of the law. If they were right, and what you say is true, then every possibility exists he may have been attempting to disable the ship or provide a means of entrance for the pirates to board. A plan gone foul by my stumbling blindly upon it," Marion surmised.

411

"Is it not strange how the table is turned? I can only imagine the contempt you must conceal for our miserable lot. If indeed it is so, with every fiber of my being, I ask you to forgive us the injury we've brought upon your health and good character." Katriina placed her hand over her mouth as if to stop a sob of guilt from falling free.

"Rest your mind, Katriina. I see well a woman who mustered great courage bringing my wasted carcass into her home. You knew nothing of his death, and I am sure you endured an ongoing fear he might return to find another man in your bed. Of this I have no doubt. There is much good about you, Katriina. How can you be held to blame? You shouldn't feel responsible for his misdeeds." He tried to console her, but the tears welled up in her eyes.

"I have not heard such kind words in so long a time, it grieves me." Marion grew nervous as she leaned over him to adjust his pillow, her breast beside his face. She moved back and the two stared momentarily into each other's eyes, balanced between their need to show respect and their desire to cast away unwanted conscience. Katriina retreated. She was breathing rapidly.

"Bless my soul, but this day is long. The children must supper."

She stood up and moved away from the bed, pretending to spy upon her children as she regained her composure. She moved to the cupboard and commenced to prepare a meal. Marion made an effort to sit upright much to the objections of Katriina. It was his nature as a seaman to be on his feet as soon as possible, for muscles unused were a greater hindrance than no muscles whatsoever.

It was with a fearsome amount of pain in his side that he managed to sit upright. He asked timidly for the privacy that he needed to dress. He found it an almost unbearable situation to be without his pants in surroundings unfamiliar. Nakedness did nothing for one's self-esteem unless you happened to be a beautiful woman.

Once decent, Marion rose slowly to his feet, and made his way to the table entirely at the expense of Katriina's nerves. She was upon him immediately, attending to his dressings like a doting mother. He was amused by the attention she paid him, and after commenting about it, they began a more lighthearted conversation about their lives past and present.

The days rolled by, one after the other, and the time was spent in the most pleasant and agreeable fashion. Mr. Klagen dropped by frequently to see all was well, often staying to prompt Marion into divulging additional accounts of his travels, which Mr. Klagen and Katriina cherished with great interest. Marion's world seemed so vast, whilst theirs was one of closed in quarters and isolation in the deep of the forest.

"So tell me more about Claussen and his ship. His name is very well known in this country. Rich, rich, rich, but I understand he is quite a character. You know he didn't marry money. The rumors were running amuck. They say he married a common table maid from England. Can you imagine, and with all his money? Do you know if this true? Have you seen her? Well, of course you must have. I mean, what it she like? What is he like?"

Mr. Klagen and Katriina sat there all ears, hanging on Marion's every word. He stared at the two of them unsure of what to say. He thought carefully as he considered all he knew about the couple.

"The Claussens. How *would* one describe the Claussens? I certainly have never met nor heard of anyone quite like them. You might think wealth would be the first thing one would say represents the Claussens, or you might think it was power, but if I were to pick a word—I think it would be kindness."

"Really?" Mr. Klagen sat straight up in his chair fully amazed.

"Very much so. They do a lot to help the unfortunate. They do a lot for children. I mean, it appears obvious when you see all the orphans on board ship, but there is more to it than that. For

413

example, if you ever see Mr. Claussen moving about, there are always children swarming him for handouts. He seldom chases them away. I have seen them get quite unruly and he can be stern, but he never chases them away. He always has toys on board that go to the urchins about the docks. They love him. It isn't because of the giving that I say the Claussens are kind; it is the way in which they treat lessers. In spite of their wealth, they treat common folk with decency. That's what makes them special in my mind. I guess that's the way I see it."

"What about Lady Claussen?" asked Katriina.

"Well, if there were truly such a thing as an angel on earth, it would be Lady Claussen. She is beautiful, she is so beautiful that you can't meet her eyes because you feel just to glance her way is to be staring. If she takes one look at you, you drop your eyes to the floor. It takes some getting used to, the mates stumble and blush when they are about her, but she is a wonderful person. She dotes and cares for everyone. The rankest sailor of the lot can approach her and she will be there for him. No finer a woman lives. She never forgot her beginnings, they were humble and she is too. An orphan you know."

"Yes, that's exactly what I've heard. Doesn't that beat all?" said Mr. Klagen.

"Opposites, complete opposites, and yet the two of them were made for each other, there is no denying it. A marriage made in heaven, prearranged in heaven," Katriina cooed.

* * *

Marion regained his health at a remarkable speed. It was ten days since he first appeared upon her doorstep, and now the time had come for him to return to his livelihood.

Throughout his last night, the stirrings of Katriina, and the collision of his own thoughts interrupted his sleep. His mind raced through the questions and options in his life. He noticed the gradual change in Katriina's demeanor during their last day together. She was careful to cover her feelings with a mask of cheeriness and good nature.

Marion could see through it as he watched her. It was in the little things, especially one where she would no longer meet his eyes. It was as though she worried he might read her thoughts, might see the pain in her heart, might suffer the shame of his indifference to her unbearable desire to have him stay. He could sense her distancing herself from his concerns, constructing her defenses, bracing herself. The morrow would not come easy.

For the first time since the day he arrived, Katriina was up long before the light of dawn. She stoked the fire and hung the kettle for her morning cup of tea. Marion watched her shuffling about in her slippers before the soft glow of the fire. He could lay and watch her for hours. He knew it was impossible to deny his feelings for this woman. He had come to care for her dearly over the shortest time. He had heard of this from the men on ships whilst away at sea. They called it passion.

The problem for him was in knowing a great part of his feeling was that of pity for her wretched lot in life. How could she possibly face the world alone? Also, he knew this was not the world he lived in. He was a man who knew no boundaries, no fences, no walls. He was a man who sailed seas to the Four Corners of the earth. His life was filled with peril as well as wonder. Wanderlust was his mistress. A cabin planted deep in the woods was as alien to him as marriage itself.

And then there were the children, not one, but three. If he knew nothing about being a husband, what could he possibly know about being a father? Did he even want to be a father? Could he afford to be a father? What would Katriina expect from him as a father? There were too many questions, too many considerations.

In truth, it was plain as day. All of this was far too complicated for a sea faring man.

And so it came to pass, after a hearty breakfast and a clean change of clothing, he once again stood at the doorway. This time he looked out instead of in. There was nothing left to say. Katriina stood upon her toes, and kissed him on his cheek as innocently as a child. She whispered good-bye and closed the door. Standing at her window, she watched him disappear into the forest through a flow of desperate tears—tears that splashed across the cold pieces of gold he had placed firmly in her hand. He took with him warmth that the hearth could never replace. He never looked back.

The morning was fresh and once outside, Marion found himself invigorated with the hope of new adventure. He set forth down the path, and with each step taken, the weight of the world became that much lighter. If ever he was convinced of truth, it was this: to reflect on Katriina was to spell out his doom. He mustn't look back, lest he remain forever under her spell. She was pushed forcefully out of his mind, replaced by the cries of an impatient soul answering to the call of the sea, a mistress with mystery enough.

FORTY-THREE

Aside from our terror-filled encounter with the pirates, the remaining leagues, and there were many of them, passed by peacefully. Still, we had our moments. As Captain Ward and REBECCA brought us farther south along the coast of Africa, we were able to sense the change in the winds by the way the yards were braced ever more square to the ship. The sailors claimed they could determine their whereabouts on a featureless sea by the direction winds blew across the hull.

They reminded me of how we ran before the Westerlies whilst in the north. How, when leaving London, our sails were braced square and we ran free to sail down the River Thames and across its estuary. They pointed out how we then doubled Ramsgate, and the yards were braced diagonally across the ship until we passed by Dover to head into the wind, whereby the men braced the yards sharp until they were nearly in line with the ship. The yards were swung about the mast from one side to the other as we tacked our way west, but always ending up in line with the ship, while sailing against the Westerlies to make way along the Channel and across the top of France. It was a choppy sea at that time and a disagreeable passage until we rounded the Continent, and sailed a reach down past the coasts of Spain and Portugal.

The Westerlies blew across our starboard beam, coming around slowly from bow to stern as we coursed ever more south along the coast of Europe. Gust by gust it lost its strength, becoming weak by the time we reached the Mediterranean and the pirates. They eventually blew themselves out in a region called the horse latitudes. On our chart it appeared to be about 30 to 35 degrees latitude, north.

"Oh, you'll be hearing a lot of talk about the horse latitudes. Sailors don't much care for them. It makes the men edgy and superstitious. You'll even hear them whistling," asserted Lady Rebecca.

"Whistling! I thought if you whistled, you'd be thrown overboard."

"Not in the horse latitudes."

"What are those, Milady?" I could put no sense to such a peculiar name in a place where nothing existed save the ship, the sky, and the sea.

"Remember when we talked about the *trade winds*, and I told you how they were always in the same place and seldom stopped blowing?"

417

"Yes, Milady."

"Well, if such a place exists, then there must also be a place where the wind hardly ever blows, wouldn't you think?"

"I suppose it could be so."

"It is so. This is that place. It is here that the wind seldom ever blows, and when it does, it does so with such faint heart one may never live to tell. Did you see how Captain Ward sent aloft every last inch of canvas we carry? The royals, the skyscrapers and studn'sls, all to catch a wisp of wind, and still we sit motionless on a pane of glazing. Not so much as a ripple."

"It is a beautiful thing to see. I love the sails, especially in the sunset."

"Yes, they are beautiful and seemingly pointless as we cannot even determine from which way the wind might blow. We could go backward for all we know."

"Is this upsetting you, Milady?"

"What makes you ask?"

"You sound so."

Lady Rebecca studied me a moment, then drew me close to her side and began to fuss with my hair.

"I shouldn't be. I have spent two years worrying about all we might face on the frontiers of the New World, and here we are, chappeled without a care in the world, bobbing about like an apple in a water trough, and still I complain. I should be counting my blessings." Milady shook her head. "How soon we forget the sickness of the sea. Anyway, you were asking about horses, were you not?"

"I was. I still don't understand what all this has to do with horses."

"Yes, well, oftentimes, merchant ships were laden with animals, and if they found themselves caught up in these latitudes, and

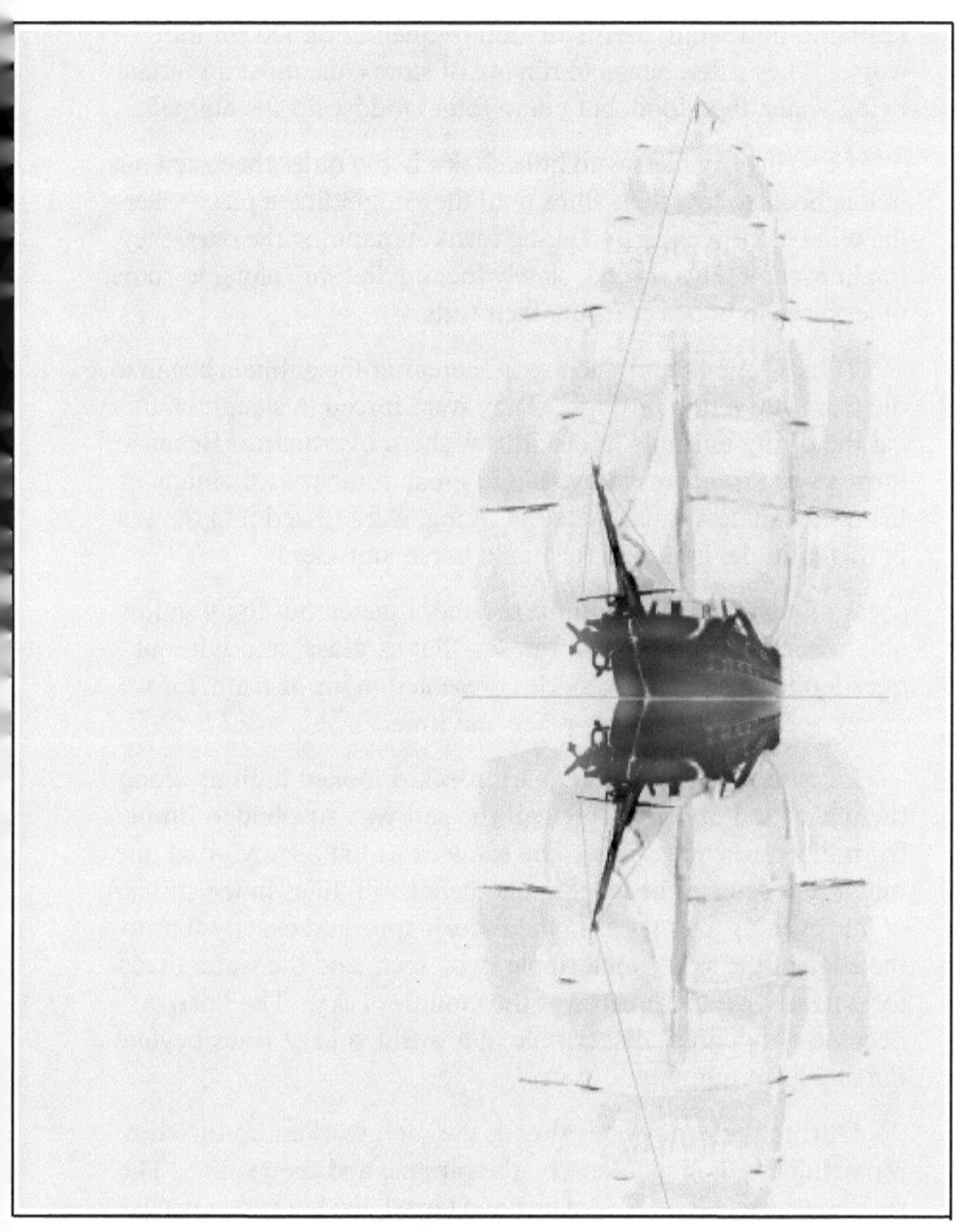

BECALMED

failing to find wind, their situation frequently turned for the worse. They often began to run out of stores, the most important being water, then food, but not to forget fodder for the animals.

"Captains were left with little choice but to order their men out in longboats to tow their ships until they might find a place where the wind came a calling. Taking turns at manning the oars, they might row for days on end, slowly inching the ship along to some other place in hopes of filling their sails.

"If luck failed them, then soon thereafter the animals began to die from starvation or thirst. They were forced to slaughter and eat the dying animals or else throw them overboard. Because horses were transported by ship in great numbers, and many of the unfortunate animals, dead or dying, were tossed into the sea in this latitude, it earned the name horse latitudes."

As Lady Rebecca enlightened me, I gazed out the window above her dressing table at the sea 'flat as glass' and without question I accepted these stories presented to me as truth, for we surely seemed locked into place and time.

Later at my step on the quarterdeck, I looked high up along the masts and observed how all the sail was suspended limply from the yards and stays. The sea was as flat as any pond one might find deep in the woods, smothered with lilies in the still air of late evening. As far as I could see, it appeared exactly thus to the edge of the sky. Not a ripple to be seen; and the water made for a nearly perfect mirror of the cloudless sky. The horizon became only barely discernible in a world void of lines beyond the details of our ship.

During these days becalmed, the men worked on the ship, repairing the damage done by the pirates, and then some. The rigging was repaired, hauled taut and tarred, the bulwarks painted, and the decks holystoned. The sailmaker sent up extra sails to be aired out upon the deck in the hot sunshine, so as not to lose the canvas to mildew and rot, and at the same time provide plenty of awnings to protect us from the sun. It seemed there was more work to be done when the ship was not under way. If idle hands were discovered, they were set at once to making mounds of 'baggy-wrinkle', used to protect against chaffing in the rigging.

The work came to a halt each day in the late afternoon, and it was at that time I realized that even sound seemed to abandon us in this place. No water splashed upon our stem, the rigging remained silent without its whistle in the wind. Overhead, the sails no longer luffed, the lines no longer slatted in the breeze, and the hull halted its seemingly endless creak and groan. A single man's voice could now be heard at any point on deck. At least on land one could count on a swoosh of wind through the trees and the song of the birds on wing. Here there was absolutely nothing.

It was a shock indeed when from up near the bows I heard a melody float through the air as a sailor began to whistle. One by one, others joined him, for it was said that whistling brought the wind. It was also said that whistling was a dangerous thing to do.

Something that was considered perfectly safe and went a long ways to shatter the stillness of our world was the singing of songs. Singing and dancing were the only forms of entertainment available besides storytelling and that was impossible to do with the whole crew. And so generally everyone readily took up the challenge of learning some of Mr. O'Kurk's chanteys and sea songs, silly or otherwise. Word by word we built our own repartee to carry with us forever.

He would be called upon to start the morning with song from atop the yardarm, where his voice easily carried miles. We raised our heads and hearts to him from alow as we sang out with a full chorus of hearty seamen at our sides eager to join in. It went thus from the light of the sun to the light of the moon. About the only time someone wasn't singing was if they were filling their mouth with food.

We never tired of it mostly because Mr. O'Kurk had a voice unsurpassed, and because he knew so many songs. He was fully able to sing the whole of a day without repeating himself and this he did countless times. Only because we had our favorites did we demand he repeat them and allow us a chance to learn the words.

Everyone hollered out their requests, young and old. Two of mine were 'Block Jock' and 'Tale of a Whale,' but there were others like 'Crew's a Comin' and 'Jack Tar'—the latter being especially enjoyed by the men and yelled out by all hands on deck at the top of their lungs. Oftentimes, the mates would step in and add a verse of their own, so the song changed each time it went around, making for many a good laugh.

Oh no, Jack Tar, don't be goin' too far
Too far away today, Hey, Hey!
Oh, a ship's a sorry sight before...
Jack Tar a tippin' his last on shore

The riggin's been set, an' you can bet
Her anchor'l be haulin' aweigh, Hey, Hey!
Oh, a ship's a sorry sight before...
Jack Tar a tippin' his last on shore

Oh no, Jack Tar, steer clear the bar
You'll soon be makin' way, Hey, Hey!
Oh, a ship's a sorry sight before...
Jack Tar a tippin' his last on shore

Oh, Jack must go, aloft and low
With his bucket of tar, a ho, ho, ho!
With his bucket of tar, a ho, ho, ho!
An' he won't be drinking on ship no mo'!

Oh, a ship's a sorry sight before
Jack Tar a tippin' his last on shore

Cookie Jar, with his broad smile and belly, stepped right up proud upon the quarterdeck before Captain Ward and all and belted out his own tune called 'Galley Life.' The trouble was, he always performed the song with such antics that we would get to laughing so hard, we barely heard the words.

Da galley life b'low deck
Vas turnin' me all v'ite
Soz I climbed up t' de crow's nest
T' get me a lil' sunlight. Ya-ah?
(T' get a lil' sunlight)

Plumb forgot dat I vas a makin'
Our dinner down below
An' da duff dat I vas bakin'
Began t' over flow
(Da duff began t' grow. Ya-ah?)

It filled de bilge beneat' us
Den 'eaded up 'tveendecks.
Vhen it fine'ly shtopped a risin'
Dey vere buried t' deir necks
(A lot o' duff on decks. Ya-ah?)

I looked down at dem poor souls
Dey couldn't find deir feet
Ahoy! I called de captain
I t'ink ve better eat!
(Oh dat duff is schveet!)

His song was usually followed by silence, as he often then called the men to mess. The mates set aside their tools and entered the galley. The ship seemed so silent during mess that I could almost hear the sun striking our deck.

The utter stillness of our world as we remained afloat, and the boredom it often ushered in while we awaited any change at all, was in one respect to be welcomed by Lady Rebecca. It was the first time she was able to spend some time by herself without the worry of children. She was able to enjoy a well-deserved break, a chance to relax from the press of her responsibilities.

The children had been given free rein to run the ship above deck. For the most part, the sailors had taken the orphans under wing. They could be found teaching them the ropes or ways of the sea and what not, and in general keeping a watch-out for their well being. The becalming gave back to Mr. Claussen his beloved Lady Rebecca and the pleasure he gained having her at his side.

The only suffering that was endured by all was the oppressive heat. Without a hint of wind, the temperatures on the ship grew unbearable, especially in the quarterdeck cabins and the galley, which were all just beneath the deck planks that faced the midday sun. They absorbed the sun's heat like a sponge, and in order to gain relief, our only option was to go above deck and lay about lazily beneath the sails-turned-awnings that at least afforded shade for our heads and cooler walkways for our feet if nothing else.

One day in particular, a sail was sent up from below deck and fixed to the bulwarks and studn'sl booms. This large piece of canvas was lowered onto the sea and allowed to settle, slowly filling with water until only the leeches remained visible, they being held up by their lines.

Into this enormous cloth bowl was tossed the scaling shroud and all of those who were able to swim. It was the first time in a month that anyone was free of the ship's perimeter. The children were allowed to jump from the bulwarks, scale the shroud, and jump again. The Americans lashed small pieces of slush covered canvas to the fire buckets, and made proper floats for the children to hang onto while they bobbed about. All this they did until thoroughly exhausted or fearful of being so weak they might not be able to climb back on board by way of the shroud or boarding ladder.

The entire crew was given permission to join in the fun, Captain Ward obviously feeling better if the men were in the water nearby the children. He understood boredom was a dangerous commodity aboard a vessel, but so far the men were careful to keep drinking to a minimum around the children, and as a rule remained on their best behavior.

I stood at the bulwarks and stared down into the riot of screaming children and splashing water, imagining what fun this play must be. I wasn't alone, for there were many of us who were apprehensive about entering the water. The mates were down below trying to convince those of us above to trust them and jump in. I didn't know how to swim and the sea frightened me. I wasn't about to trust anyone. There was no bottom to it and I could only see myself dropping forever from the light of day. It was probably the only time in my life that I didn't charge at once into some form of mischief, this much to the relief of Lady Rebecca.

Then there came a completely unexpected opportunity.

"You don't wish to go in and play?"

I knew the voice at once and turned around to see Mr. Claussen and Lady Rebecca standing behind me. They had come out of the cabin to watch the play.

"I'm afraid."

"This is fresh. I had come to assume you feared nothing. What a surprise."

"It looks like fun, but it scares me."

"Just remember, Elizabeth, the sea is for fish," Milady spoke.

"Mary doesn't think so."

I watched as she jumped off the bulwarks and joined Britany Allison and Cookie Jar down below. She screamed all the way down. The men would jump in and after a great deal of whooping and hollering on the way down, made a great wallop, sending water nearly back up to the deck where we stood.

"Would you like to go in for a dip?"

"Christopher! She doesn't need to go in. She's fine."

"I would like to, but I don't think I will."

"Would you go in with me?"

The last question changed entirely the situation at hand. For me the issue became one of extreme choice; stay clear of the water at all cost, as was my nature, or be held close by the man whose attention thrilled me like no other. I knew what my answer would be and at once I was breathing hard either from fear of the water or anticipation of Mr. Claussen's attention.

"Yes."

"Can she swim in this dress, Rebecca?"

"Yes, but be careful. She doesn't swim and it makes me nervous."

"Fine, it's settled then." Instantly Mr. Claussen disappeared over the bulwarks and I rushed to see him drop below the surface then pop up with a broad smile on his face.

"Jump in or climb down the shroud. The choice is yours. I'm ready and waiting. Don't be afraid."

Unlike all other men, I had the utmost confidence in Mr. Claussen and wanting his attention; I leapt off the ship. The panic was immediate and as deep as the sea into which I disappeared. The seconds were like hours and I was terrified. My

426

eyes were closed to the water and in my state of darkness, I felt Mr. Claussen's arm wrap about me. I clutched it with all my strength and he pulled me up to his chest and the air above.

"Are you alright?"

I sputtered and coughed as my nose ran. I held on to him for dear life.

"Are you alright?" he asked again.

"Yes. This stuff tastes awful."

"You're not supposed to drink it. Next time you jump, keep your *mouth shut* and your *eyes open*, not the other way around. You can open your eyes now if you like."

"It stings."

"It'll pass. Now, relax your grip so I can breathe. Remember, I'm the one who is supposed to save you. I must breathe as well, alright?"

I nodded in agreement. I relaxed my grip from around his neck and drifted away into a state of utter bliss. I was his sole attention and spent the better part of an hour returning to rest my head upon his chest and converse about things that were important to little girls. He fussed over me a great deal and I wasted none of it.

Aboard the REBECCA, we enjoyed this freedom for a little more than a week having no cares about us, save for an occasional shark attracted by the splashing and carrying on.

The first time one appeared, it gave us all a bad scare and we rushed the shroud to be free of the water. On the next two occasions, a man named Oliver Stableman, who had spent many years employed on a whaler, produced his harpoon and struck the sharks with great precision amidst boisterous cheers from the ship's crew.

On both occasions, the sharks were large. The men cleared the decks and landed the beasts, then having no love to be lost, attacked both with a vengeance. They clubbed them senseless, quickly slit open their bellies to remove the liver, which was rich with oil, then cut off their tails and threw them back into the sea to drown. After which they congratulated themselves for sparing a sailor's life somewhere in the future.

As for me, I learned how to swim.

FORTY-FOUR

As I have frequently mentioned, Mary and I were not orphans, and were neither viewed nor treated as such. On the other hand, we were not Claussen children, and although special consider-ations were bestowed upon us, so too were specific expectations.

The orphans on board ship were kept in strict confinement, either below in steerage or in the corral upon the quarterdeck. In trade for their loss of freedom, their only task was to keep themselves as clean as possible. The rest of the time was theirs to sing, play, or learn their books.

Not so for Mary and me. We had our duties and chores to be accomplished. We were after all, in the employ of the Claussens, and no matter how good we were treated whilst in their care, as maiden servants we had work to do. This was especially true for Mary, as my duties were limited and often overlooked by Lady Rebecca. Either way, no matter what we might be up to, no matter how much fun we might be having at the moment, if the Claussens summoned Mary or me, we instantly dropped every-thing and gave our service.

So it was that Mary was forced to set aside the book she was reading aloud to me as I lay beside her in our berth. We were hot, uncomfortable, and filled full of laziness. Our only relief was found in a faraway place within the pages of Mary's book. Unfortunately, Lady Rebecca had called for Mary, and I had no choice but to stand up and let her off the bunk so she might go to do her service. As I was already on my feet, I decided to go to the galley for a drink.

After privacy, the next thing found scarce on board ship was fresh water. Our drinking water might not be seawater, but that didn't make it taste any better. The best water came from the sky. We would collect the freshly fallen rain upon tarpawlings to run first into our mouths and then into the water barrels or anything else that would hold it. This we would drink with great satisfaction. It was sweet and clean.

When there was no rain to be had, we were left with only the water stored in barrels. In short time it would become addled, tasting old and disgusting. We would then boil it and add sugar or lemon, or else we made a tea to drink. The crew most always mixed it with rum, and this they called grog. Anything that could be done would be done to rid it of the taste of age, iron, or barrel stakes. It was a fact that whenever the opportunity arose to enjoy something flavorful to drink, it was indeed a moment to relish.

Lady Rebecca's moment of relish was always when she sipped a glass of Chambord, a French liqueur of which she was wonderfully fond. It was made from raspberries, herbs, and honey, and by her admission it was the most heavenly drink money could buy. To sit back during our time becalmed without fearing for her children or ship, for the sole purpose of relaxation, she considered Chambord as exquisite a beverage as any to be had. Mr. Claussen always said it was too rich for his taste, but would spare no expense to see it was available for Milady's pleasure.

They would play a game whereby Mr. Claussen only brought home a small quantity for her benefit. Needless to say, in short time she would run out and plead for more. Fulfilling Lady Rebecca's wishes was all one might think Mr. Claussen lived for, and he would see to it immediately that more was procured. As always, not a great amount, just enough to get by—and then the ritual would start over.

Mr. Claussen would say he did this because it prevented Lady Rebecca from taking Chambord for granted and thereby losing her taste for it. He claimed to be sparing her from the plague of lost appreciation, which ran rampant among the wealthy. By his doing, she would never tire of the liqueur she so enjoyed, and he would be guaranteed a mission, a means in the future of providing her pleasure.

The rules of this game were forced into change when preparations for the journey to America reached the point of seriousness. Mr. Claussen brought on board two large casks of Chambord. The commoner could have probably purchased a home for the cost of the two casks, but that was of no concern. Cost was irrelevant in affairs pertaining to Lady Rebecca. Mr. Claussen would never have chanced overlooking her fondness for the drink.

The exclusive flavor of Chambord was meaningless to me. My only connection to the liqueur was by way of Mary's responsibility to refill Lady Rebecca's flask when needed. It was for this reason we suspended our book journey and Mary went to serve. Lady Rebecca wished her flask to be refilled.

Mary dreaded this task, for the casks were locked up in the very bottom of the ship. She disliked going below into the darkness of the holds by herself. It was always a strange and scary place being so dark, musty, and utterly eerie, but for the noises and wild imaginings of her mind. She was forced to concentrate on the filling of the flask, and not to looking back over the shoulder for an approaching sailor's ghost or sea demon. The mates, who were a suspicious lot before all else, were constantly filling our heads with horrid stories. Be it sea serpents, shellycoats, or tales of the Flying Dutchman during the spooky hours of twilight, they left us unable to take a step without holding the hand of another for the sake of bravery.

In the beginning Mary was always accompanied by Cookie Jar or someone else whilst she learned her way down below to the casks and what there had to be done. From that point on, however, there was no reason for bothering one of the ship's crew just because she was frightened.

The casks were very heavy, chocked securely, and seldom visited; most awaited opening after our arrival in America. It was because of this and the fact the casks made good ballast that they were stored at the bottom of the ship nearest the bilge—that place not intended for the feeble hearted. The creaking of the hull, the vibration and stress of the rigging, the water slapping the planks on the outside and sloshing about inside, and worst of all, the clicking of rats sneaking about. The whole of it in unison could make a hardened jack watch his back and shudder, let alone terrify a young girl. And so it was customary for Mary to seek me out, to go below with her and keep her company. To Mary, it made more sense if we were both terrified.

Mary had been instructed from her first day on board to always bring a bowl with her that was meant to be placed under the flasks that she filled in case there should be a spill. Cookie Jar sent the customary bowl down below decks with Mary because he did not like the sweet and sticky beverage to lie about in puddles attracting rats and bugs. He warned that all form of creatures would gnaw at the sweetened wood, and while following the trail of spilled residue, chew their way up through the planks in search of the source, and doing a lot of damage in the process. Guarding against these spills, and frequent washing of the decks avoided most of the problems.

I was seated in the galley whiling away my time, having some tea and watching Cookie Jar go about his business, when Mary entered with a look of concern.

"Liz, would you come with me to fetch Lady Rebecca some Chambord?"

"Ohhhh, I don't really feel like going down there." I still felt lazy and nothing about going below to the bilge ever appealed to me. In fact, climbing ladders would only make me hotter.

"Oh, come on, Elizabeth. It'll be fun. Come with me."

"It isn't fun, Mary. It's scary down there, and I don't like it." I got right to the point.

"Please." Mary looked distressed, now imagining the prospect of having to go alone.

"Go oon, Elizabet', sheez jour friend an' needs jour soopport oon dis dangeroos mission. Iz dat not phat friends are foor, after all. Ya-ah?" Cookie Jar smiled at me.

"Ohhhh, alright."

I rose from the bench, much to Mary's relief, and she immediately put her arm around my shoulder to lead me away. I took the bowl that Cookie Jar had produced to place under the flask. Mary held the flask and the candleholder. We were not allowed to carry a lantern because of the possibility of an oil spill and fire.

Mary led the way into the hold; the candle extended before us to light the way. Down, down, down we went to the very bottom of the ship. We worked our way aft, looking for the familiar locker. Once there, Mary unlocked the door, we entered, and I placed the bowl under the proper spigot. Mary placed the flask into the bowl and after a miss or two managed to get the thick dark blue liqueur to flow into the flask.

"So, did you wash Lydia's bed clothes?" I asked.

"Uuggg. Don't remind me. I'm so sick of vomit." Mary shook her head in disgust.

"Think she'll be all right?"

"I don't know. Lady Rebecca is pretty worried for her. She tries to keep her up on the deck in the fresh air as much as possible. I suppose it helps."

"How can anybody throw up that much?"

"Elizabeth, please, I—."

That was as far as Mary got before the spine-chilling sound of rats' claws clicked their way past us through the insufferable shadows. Mary had been bent over the flask closing the valve, when we heard them. Instinctively, she stiffened up and spun about in fear. In doing so the hem of her dress caught the candle and snuffed out the flame. The black closed in on us at once.

We wasted no time waiting to see what would happen next. I was stumbling forward, hands outstretched, forcing my eyes to adjust to the sudden darkness. At the same time, I was running for the companionway, now becoming visible by a feeble glow from above. I reached it first, and flew up the steps, pushed by fright and suffocating shadows with Mary hot on my heels.

No matter how feeble, there was always some light that filtered down the companionways, but I still climbed up one more deck to put as much distance between the rats and me as possible. Mary was practically hugging me all the way. We stopped at the head of the steps and looked at each other. We were breathing hard and not sure whether to laugh or cry. The flask was still down below.

"Now what!" I cried. I had no desire to go back down.

"We have to go back down and get the flask."

"Not we. You have to go down and get the flask."

"Oh, please, please, please, Elizabeth. Don't make me go back down alone. Please, pretty please, pretty, pretty please."

"I have no intention of going back down into the dark with all them rats runnin' around. That's for certain."

My mind was made up and that left Mary in a terrible state.

"Listen, we'll go back to the galley an' get another candle from Cookie Jar, and then we'll have light. Please, come with me, Elizabeth. I don't want to back down alone. Please." She dreaded the thought.

"I don't wanna go back down there, Mary."

"Please." She begged.

"I don't wanna."

"Please."

"Oh, alright, but you owe me, Mary. You owe me big for this one."

"Whatever you want, Elizabeth, I promise, cross my heart."

She made the sign that committed her eternally. And so, we went back up to the galley and explained the turn of events to Cookie Jar, who thought it was exceedingly funny. He gave us another candle, and sent us back down with an abundance of encouragement. I will say that we used every word he uttered to bolster our courage as we made our way warily back to the cask. Our single-minded intention was to grab the flask as quickly as possible and return to the light of day without a second's delay. We wished no further exposure to the terrors lurking about in the shadows.

"Oh, no!" Mary cried out in a whisper.

"What now?" I asked in the same low voice as if to avoid waking the dead.

"I didn't get the stupid spigot turned off completely, and it's been dripping away. Look at the bowl. It's nearly full."

I peered over Mary's shoulder, and sure enough in the light of the candle I could clearly see the flask was practically submerged in a bath of the priceless liquid.

"What are you going to do with that?" I asked innocently enough.

"I don't know. The flask is full and there is no way to get it back in the cask." Mary was stumped.

"Can't we dump it someplace or put it into something?" I asked.

"I don't know." Mary looked around in the dim light.

"Can't we dump it in the bilge?"

"I don't know. I don't know if I dare. The Claussens said it was terribly dear. I don't want to get a whipping."

"You've been whipped by the Claussens?" I asked in horror.

"No. I wonder if Cookie jar could make use of it in the galley."

I was so suddenly soothed by the wave of relief that swept over me, I found myself unknowingly free from all fear of unknown demons lurking within the shadows. I was caught up in another thought.

"Did you ever taste that stuff?" I asked, curious about the liquid.

"Yes. Sometimes it gets on my fingers when I fill the flask. It is quite sticky, and I have to lick it off."

"Does it taste good?"

"It tastes real good, believe me. That's why Lady Rebecca likes it so much, and why it's kept locked up down here. Captain Ward doesn't want anybody gettin' into it."

"I wanna taste it."

"No."

"Why not. I wanna taste it. Why can't I taste it? You did."

I was very curious about this substance that Lady Rebecca was so fond of drinking. Mary gave it a second thought and shrugged.

"Go ahead, then." She removed the dripping flask from the pool of Chambord and handed me the bowl. I stuck my finger into it and touched my tongue. My eyes grew wide. It was much more than good; it was absolutely divine. It was warm, sweet, heavenly like hot berry syrup.

"This is wonderful!" I exclaimed. With little regard to consequence, I tipped the bowl and had myself a good healthy drink.

"I said as much, didn't I?"

"Heaven's above, this is superb! A person would have to be daft to dump this. I say we just drink it. There won't be any need to fuss further about the spill. Here."

I handed Mary the bowl as I closed my eyes and licked my lips as if a bear feasting on honey.

"Mmmm. I don't know if we should."

Mary took the bowl and had a drink herself, after which, we stared into the bowl and both could see that it now clearly contained less.

"Let me have some more. That is a really fine drink."

I grabbed the bowl from Mary and drank heavily from it. I wiped my mouth.

"Here, you finish it off—end of problem. Simple as that."

I belched and handed back the bowl.

Mary's face disappeared from view as she tipped the bowl up and downed the last of the spill. She wiped out the bowl in the dark of the locker, not thinking of the stark deep blue stain she made upon her dress. The richness of flavor distracted us from all else. It was supreme.

"Come on now, let's be off."

"Just a minute." I stared down the passageway into the darkness. "Have you ever been down there?"

"You must be joking. I get Lady Rebecca's drink and then I get out of here straight away. This place gives me gooseflesh."

"Let's go back a ways and see what's there."

"You can't be serious. Besides, we have to go back up, Elizabeth."

"Hey, don't forget it was you who begged me to come down here, and we have never gone back there to see what there is, not once. You're not that afraid are you?"

"Yes."

"Oh. Well, then let's just go back a little ways." I started back with the candle and Mary followed reluctantly, wishing to stay well within the light.

We poked about here and there lifting up canvases and covers, peeking into boxes and assorted containers. As we wandered farther aft, we came upon a number of large crates stacked neatly in the hold and nailed securely shut. I moved about them, wondering what they might contain, when I happened to notice a plank that was dislodged. Apparently someone before us had come to inspect the contents and was unbothered to refasten the piece. I pulled it toward me and the board gave way with little resistance.

"Oh!"

Mary's exclamation voiced my exact feelings as we stood there gawking at the contents within the crate. It was packed full of dolls. There must have been a thousand of them inside. Filled with excitement I began to peer into some of the other crates, either through cracks in the boards or finding the one singular plank that had been dislodged for purpose of inspection. There was no mistake about it: the back of this ship was filled with toys.

"What in the name of heaven, do you make of all this?" I asked.

"I make we don't belong here and there will be trouble a plenty if we don't get a move on. Now let's go and don't you utter a word about what we've seen or we'll get whipped."

"We aren't going to get whipped," I said sarcastically.

"You know what I mean. Now, come on; let's go back up. Lady Rebecca probably thinks I've died."

We locked up the room and started back toward the companionway, when once again the creepy clicking of rats' claws overtook us. This time we scampered up the ladder but stopped at the top.

"Hold your candle out, Mary. Let's see if we can spy them."

"I hardly think so. They are most disgusting and they jump. They can jump all the way up this ladder. Eeyuck!" She shuddered. "I keep thinking of those mudlarks. Eating rats. Eeyuck!"

"C'mon, I wish to see, Mary. Besides, you owe me. Don't forget. Now go down the ladder a ways, and hold out the candle so we can have us a look and see."

"Go down the ladder! Not on my life! I'll hold it from here and no farther," she insisted.

"All right, then, just hold it. I wish to see down there."

We both dropped to our knees and leaned down through the opening, staring hard past the steps of the ladder and onto shadowy planks of the bilge. Mary held the candle below us, her arm swinging down through the companionway. We watched, we listened, but to no avail. It was an eerie place, indeed.

438

"Come on, let's get on with it, Liz. I going to be in trouble," Mary urged.

"Just one more moment." I wished to search around every item below us.

"No, I've got to go, or Lady Rebecca will be upset with me. She's waiting for her flask, and probably already wonders what has taken me so long. Come on now, let us go at once or I am going to leave you here."

"Oh, alright, be that way."

I was feeling a bit tired anyway. We both straightened up, and it was precisely that instant I realized something was amiss.

"What's the matter with the ship?" I asked Mary.

"The winds must have come! We must be getting under way! Hurry! Let's go up and see." We huffed it up the next ladder, and that brought on a sensation that was altogether unpleasant. The ship was rolling and pitching about me. I had never been especially susceptible to the sickness of the sea, but this is exactly what I assumed it felt like. I turned to Mary.

"I don't feel good, Mary."

"I don't either."

"You don't either? Why don't you feel good?" I was surprised.

"I don't know, my stomach feels nervous," she remarked.

"Oh, my word, my stomach feels terrible. I don't think it's the wind, Mary. I think something is wrong. Oh, my stomach. I think it was that stuff we drank. Oh, my word! Maybe we've been poisoned! Oh Mary, maybe we're going to die. We've been poisoned. I know it, Mary. You've poisoned us, Mary. I think I'm dying now as we speak! What did we drink from the bowl?" Mary looked white as milk and horrified. She took a moment to think.

"It was Chambord," she said feebly and confused. "I know it was Chambord. I go there frequently for Lady Claussen. It was just Chambord and nothing more."

"I'm dying, Mary. I can no longer stand up."

I was frightened out of my wits, and not about to believe her. I staggered into the galley, wailing the predictions of my death by poisoning. Cookie Jar could see at once that something was wrong. He came around to meet us, hopping on his peg leg. If I didn't fall over a bench, Mary did. I, being smaller than she, undoubtedly suffered the consequences of the alcohol at a quicker pace and about the time Cookie Jar took a hold of me, I unleashed the contents of my stomach from the grip of a terrible cramp.

I launched the stream of dark blue Chambord into my hands, and watched it run down my arms and the front of my dress. The sight of it was all that was necessary to encourage Mary to do likewise. The both of us were no longer able to stand up but for our drunkenness, and remained sprawled upon the galley sole clutching our stomachs and wallowing miserably in our own vomit, which in turn ruined our clothes with stain.

Cookie Jar, sensing the seriousness of our condition, went off to fetch Lady Rebecca who appeared almost immediately. We confessed our sins on the spot. We would have done or said anything to end the misery we suffered. All the while that we were wishing to die, Lady Rebecca stripped us, bathed us, cleaned up after us, got us into bed, and after giving full witness to our discomfort, pretty much figured we had paid sufficiently for our poor judgment.

We were left to sleep off the alcohol, and as sick as Mary was herself, she found it in her heart to fuss over me, keeping me in her embrace for the whole of the next day. Together, lying side by side in our bunk we worked our way through a prolonged agony, while awaiting our bodies to cleanse of the poisoning. Being left with little else to do but think, my mind kept returning to the vision of all those dolls in the crates.

ELIZABETH AND MARY

Surely poisoned

"Why do you think all those toys are down there, Mary?"

"I don't know, Liz; but please keep quiet about it. Promise me you'll keep mum. Swear to it."

"I promise."

I was too sick to bicker. Mary pulled me in tight.

We faced a miserable night; and yet I found the greatest peace of mind in my young existence, while in the complete absence of anything, save the gentle rocking of our ship and the soft breath of Mary upon the nape of my neck. I so treasured my relationship with her, much of it built in my own immature mind, but I gained from it a sense of security that only came when I found myself near her. I looked to her for comfort, companionship, and understanding. I adored her.

FORTY-FIVE

The REBECCA and all her party aboard had patiently waited out the lethargic winds of the lower latitudes. Every bit of canvas that could be mustered had been sent aloft. And so, the vessel managed to capture the faintest of breezes, puffs of air that inched her southward until she found the stillness interrupted by an occasional blow. The crew welcomed each gust with great rejoice until their frequency increased to the point of becoming a steady northerly breeze, which after bracing the yards square, drove us down past the Canary Islands and into the Tropic of Cancer.

We then entered into the region of the Northeast Trades, which started blowing from the northwest and moved about to the east, coming fresh across our stern, and we ran free before them. We passed by the Cape Verde Islands, and averaged nearly a hundred miles a day as we made our westing across the Atlantic from Africa to the American continent. In just under four weeks we logged nearly three thousand miles, and found ourselves coming abreast the West Indies.

Everyone cheered Captain Ward when he ordered the helmsman to steer a new bearing, north by west three hundred and fifty degrees. We would run west of Bermuda and follow the Gulf Stream north along the eastern seaboard of the United States. It marked the last leg of our journey, and as children, we were ready for the end to arrive.

It was difficult at best to remain forever within the confines of either steerage or the corral. Only during our time becalmed in the horse latitudes did we honestly enjoy some freedom. Admittedly, I didn't suffer the same degree of confinement as the others, whilst I went about supposedly doing the bidding of Lady Rebecca. Still, even I could clearly see the disadvantages of life on a deck, which for the most part meant fun was all activity beyond the approved boundaries. The confinement was for our own safety, but children are meant to test the limits and we were no exception. It could be seen that reprimands were fast becoming the order of the day. They increased markedly in number and severity, and made for an abundance of ill feeling. There was no mistaking it—*going north was good.*

We had enjoyed the unfaltering trades moving us westward and then helping us to make way north for many weeks. It couldn't go on forever, and we eventually reached the twenty-fifth parallel, entering once again into those horse latitudes, this time passing through on a northbound course from the Tropic of Cancer. Every inch of canvas that could be carried was sent aloft, bent, and trimmed to best advantage, but to no avail. The REBECCA looked magnificent, but as before, it was all show and no go, for we were unable to raise the sea upon her stem. The sails draped slack, resembling old clothes pinned upon a line.

On a Wednesday morning, the fifth of August, I opened my eyes to the world once again. Mary's arm lay across me, and as much as I loved her embrace, it was uncomfortably hot in our berth. In fact, it was suffocating. The gun ports were all opened, but it seemed impossible to get any air to pass through them and into the ship. I was beginning to understand the irritation and impatience shown by many of the sailors in the absence of a sea breeze.

As was my way, I awoke earlier than the rest and noted it was still quite dark out on the sea. Or maybe I should say darker than I would have expected, for I felt quite rested and believed it to be later than it seemed by morning's light. I noted the sounds coming through the bulkhead from the galley, and also movement about the upper decks, which only seemed to confirm my suspicions that the hour was indeed later than it appeared.

I slipped off the bunk so as not to disturb Mary, and made my way to a gun port. I looked through the opening and realized at once that it probably was every bit as late an hour as I thought, my being deceived by a dark dusky and most squally sky. In any event, I was now awake, on my feet, and ready to watch another day pass before my inquisitive eyes. It was much too hot to start the day off with tea, so I asked Cookie Jar for a tin of water and lemon. I had little appetite in this heat, and so with my refreshment, I went above in search of fresh air. I found it to be as gloomy above as below.

I looked about and noted that Mr. Beckwith and Mr. Anderson were on deck having a conversation. A number of other men were up as well and sharing the same lack of appetite due to the heat and humidity, and like myself, they mostly stood about studying the sky to the east of us. Those on watch were busy in the background buttoning up and battening down the hatches in preparation for a storm although with the exception of a squally sky, nothing gave hint to the possibility of wind. The morning was moving on, but instead of getting lighter, it was going just the opposite. To the east of us the sky was looking more and more like nightfall. The storm sails had been sent up from below and were upon the deck being readied.

There is something thrilling in being witness to the power of nature, so long as it keeps its distance. I sat up on the quarterdeck at the stanchions, it still being my favorite place since I first settled upon it in London. From my chosen spot, I could see all about the ship and appreciate the eerie sensations that were born of the lack of daylight, the stillness of the hot humid sticky air and the calm spread out across the sea.

The orphans were soon to show themselves, coming up to the corral on their own in small groups of two or three. The rigid manner of escorting them had been all but abandoned, now that they understood the dangers aboard ship and learned the routines. As each group climbed up the steps to the quarterdeck, I watched their expressions. Their eyes would open wide as they looked overhead and they would giggle once they became aware of the foreboding sensation stirring in a sky that was lowering itself to hide the tops of our masts.

There was little more than monotony in our lives as of late, so something as insignificant as a change in the weather became quite an issue. As the orphans huddled in their corral, the sky began to take on a strange yellowish-orange cast. Undoubtedly, it was a sign of the morning sun's fruitless effort to work its way through the clouds. The orphans sat together looking upward as if in solemn prayer—except for the Johnson boys.

I was mindlessly watching the three of them horsing around in the corral when distracted by the calls of the deckhands in the waist below. Their voices quickly rose. Most excitedly they called out to one another and pointed off our starboard beam to the east.

At first the commotion quieted the children until they looked over my shoulder and out to sea in the direction of the finger pointing. Then the whites of their eyes showed bright with amazement. I turned about to peer through the stanchions, and observed one of the most unusual sights of my young life.

It was a writhing, ropelike apparition, hopping madly about as it skipped across the water, yet a fair distance out. It appeared to be spinning about unwieldy and out of control. I sat there transfixed in awe, watching it dance and twirl about. It was soon joined by a second such form. Together, they moved closer toward us and so became much easier to study. Soon after the appearance of the second form, Captain Ward came up from his cabin and mounted the quarterdeck. He walked over to me, as often he did, and bade me a good morning.

"What a strange sight, isn't it so, Captain?"

"Strange, indeed, and not always a joy to see, my child."

"What are they, Captain?"

"They are waterspouts," he stated flatly without further comment or explanation, much in contrast to his usual friendly nature.

The captain was intent on observing the spectacle before us, and not at all talkative. I was beginning to surmise that as fascinating as these waterspouts appeared, they just might be something best avoided. Soon, a third and a fourth, and two more after that were born; a total of six dancing ropes, all before our starboard beam, and haphazardly bounding their way toward us.

Lady Rebecca and Mr. Claussen stepped out the pilothouse doo and scaled the steps to the quarterdeck. Mr. Claussen stood to my right, opposite the captain, and placed his large hands upon the railing. He leaned forward as if to mentally engage the forces confronting us. I wondered again if he had it in him to influence the ways of nature. I remembered the feeling I had before when we departed England and he stood beside me at the bows looking out to sea.

Lady Rebecca was calm but concerned, and ordered all the orphans to remove themselves from the corral and remain below in steerage until called for. This raised a howl of protest from all who wished to witness this unusual phenomenon, but instead was given the worst confinement of confinements. Their complaints fell upon deaf ears, for Lady Rebecca remained adamant.

She looked at me with an eye indicating I was to follow suit and without complaint. I turned to Mr. Claussen and spoke under my breath.

"Milord, would you allow me to stay if I promise to remain put here at your side? I wouldn't run off, sir." He looked down at me and smiled.

"You shouldn't make promises lightly, child. I don't believe I have ever seen you stay put."

"I will! I promise, cross my heart." I dreaded the thought of going down to steerage. He looked up to Lady Rebecca, who returned his gaze.

"I will see to Elizabeth's care, Rebecca, if you have no objection."

Lady Rebecca didn't object. In fact, she seemed pleased that a stronger bond was developing between Mr. Claussen and me. He put his arms about my shoulders, and we stood together watching the water spouts as they neared the ship.

"It is a wondrous thing to witness, Elizabeth, but a dangerous thing nonetheless. If you remain, you must be brave and not cower to the talk between Captain Ward and myself. Our discussions may be frank, as they should be. In any event, if God has chosen this to be our time then it is so. There is no sense in our fretting or fearing His decision. Do you understand?"

"I do, sir. And I am not afraid." I spoke the truth. I was too ignorant of the danger to entertain fear. As long as I was in the company of Mr. Claussen, I was happy and fear was the furthest thing from my mind.

"We can only sit here and pray for the mercy of God." The captain sighed. "There is not a breath of air to be had. The sails are of no use, so we sit like a dead duck before the dogs." The captain resigned himself to the situation.

The three of us stood side by side in silence and watched the spouts bear down upon us. The mates all stood motionless along the starboard waterway, leaning across the bulwarks, transfixed by the scene before them. They were absorbed by the fear of death, seeing it firsthand unveiled of any pleasantries. The captain was quick to break their spell.

"Mr. Beckwith, Mr. Anderson!" he called out.

"Aye aye, sir." They eagerly responded, wishing for any distraction to remove them from their thoughts. The American gunner, Timothy Anderson, was now second mate, having earned a great deal of respect from Captain Ward and his shipmates by his performance during our encounter with the pirates. He replaced the injured Mr. McCurry.

"Send all hands aloft to reduce our tops. Haul down the studn'sls and booms, Unbend the sky'sls and gallants, and send them down with their yards and masts. Furl the upper top'sls and mains, and fit your frapping lines snug, gentlemen. Then, haul in the head'sls, and close reef the lower top'sls, and be lively about it, men!"

"Aye aye, sir!" The mates barked out their orders, shattering the silence, and the shipmates instantly came to life, scrambling across the deck feeling a sense of urgency in their guts. One by one the sails and yards disappeared or dropped from the masts.

"Are you not afraid, Elizabeth?" I turned and looked up to see Mr. Claussen studying me.

"No, Milord. I'm seldom afraid whilst in your company." He gazed down upon me affectionately, a twinkle in his eyes. The men hollered about us as they hauled on their lines, but he paid them no mind.

"You flatter me, Elizabeth. Honestly you do, but do you not sense that to be folly, somewhat foolish, then?"

"I hadn't thought it that way, Milord."

"Pray, tell me, child, what might compel you to place this unfounded faith in someone such as I?" He was amused.

"Your eyes," I answered without hesitation.

"My eyes?" he repeated with surprise, and then laughed, still distracted from the danger before us.

"What, in the name of God, could a child, young as yourself, ever see in these eyes of mine? Tell me, I am curious to know."

We were locked into each other's stare, and I observed every minute detail of the deep blue windows to his soul. I felt he was allowing me to enter into his heart. What did I see in there? Why did he bring me such peace? I knew there was something, but how to express it in words? He was strong, commanding, yet, gentle and caring. He was always concerned about everyone's well being, especially the helpless and the children. He was....

"Mercy," I whispered.

"Mercy!" A frown swept across his face, as though I might have slapped him. He shrank back from me, looking at me in a puzzled manner.

"That is the strangest thing a child has ever said to me. That is the strangest thing I would ever expect a child to say under any circumstance. You are much too young to say a thing like that. Mercy... imagine that...*mercy*. Humph." He shook his head in bewilderment and returned his attention to the fury now approaching uncomfortably close off our beam.

All but one of the waterspouts stood to our north or south, certain to pass us by without concern. The one remaining waterspout, now about to come on to us, was altogether another matter. It presented us a terrifying sight to behold as it flailed about recklessly, randomly, unpredictably dancing hither and thither across the water in bounces and slides. It dusted the ocean and swept up clouds of froth all about. The sea swelled into a large mound, rising upward beneath the twisting, spiraling, vertical column as if desiring to find the sky and meet this horrid thing before us. The spout gurgled in a dreadful manner, sucking up water in vast amounts, gulping it upward into the clouds, which grew heavier and blacker by the second.

I cannot say I was afraid. Apprehensive would be more accurate as a terrible wind suddenly raised itself to lash out as us. The spinning fury was about to engulf us. The sea frothed and rain arose from the water below to spit and sting wickedly. There was no pleasure for unprotected skin, and I quickly turned away from the stinging onslaught.

Mr. Claussen pulled me tightly into his chest. Drawing in my arms, I clutched at his shirt, my face buried within its folds. He took no notice of me, but faced the terrible force before him. In that instant, while my eyes were closed and turned away, this beast having come down from the sky retreated back into the clouds, which bore it. Upward it went from our midst and altogether disappeared. I looked behind me. There was nothing.

I was elated. I beamed with pride, gratified at what I knew. I didn't know quite how Mr. Claussen could perform such a feat, but I knew he could. I was giddy with delight in knowing I alone was in his company during this, his moment of triumph. He released me for I was laughing, clapping, and jumping for joy. I reached for his large hand and held it tightly to my chest.

"I knew you would do it. I knew it all along. You wouldn't let anything happen to the orphans or Lady Rebecca. I told you so, didn't I? It's in your eyes, as I said…mercy. Now do you believe what I see?"

He looked at me as though I had lost my mind. I could see the tension in his face. All about us, everything drew silent. I looked at him, waiting for his reaction, when suddenly without warning the heavens opened up and nearly drowned us as we stood.

The downpour was beyond measure. The clouds must have released in one burst all the water drawn up from the sea. It lasted no more than a minute or two, but in that short space of time REBECCA's decks were awash and flooded. The deck disappeared under ankle-deep water, for the scuppers were unable to relieve REBECCA of the torrential downpour that burdened her. Fortunately, as promptly as the rain started, so too did it stop.

An uneasy feeling swept over all of us on deck, for the sky now quickly grew black, blacker than night as it began to lower itself, pressing its weight upon us. It was impossible for me to see anything amidships from my place on the quarterdeck. I could see nothing of the water below, and all my movements were by feel alone. We were completely closed in by darkness. It was worse than night, for nary a star nor hint of moon was in the offering. It was as if we were now afloat in our own grave, cut off from all living things. It was as unsettling an experience as any of my life. I clung to Mr. Claussen.

I wondered if maybe we hadn't escaped the waterspout. How would I know what to expect if it had engulfed us? The mates on board were beyond my vision, but I could hear them praying among themselves for forgiveness of their sins, for mercy, and for light. At this time I did indeed become frightened. Mr. Claussen was but a shadow in the dark and I gripped him tightly. He accepted my fear and pulled me to his side to comfort me.

Then, to my utter astonishment, the yards and masts above the ship began to glow an eerie green light. I put my hand to my mouth. 'What an incredible sight!' I thought to myself. I wasn't sure whether I should delight in this vision or further be afraid.

"Look at that, Milord. Have you ever seen such a thing?" I was awestruck.

"It is special indeed, and a thing worth seeing, but it isn't as uncommon as you might believe. Have you ever heard of St. Elmo's fire?"

"Yes. The mates always talk about it when they tell us ghost stories."

"Well, now you can say you've seen it."

It was eerie and every bit as ghostlike as the mates made claim. I stayed tight to Mr. Claussen's side, nearly standing on his feet, while I watched the movements of the light. On occasion a ball might form and roll slowly out along a yard yet to be sent down, and then retreat back from whence it came. Sometimes it would roll down the mast to a given point, then stop and slowly move back up, even passing through the tops and on up to the trucks. This magical display went on for nearly half an hour; then, as mysteriously as it appeared, it disappeared.

The rains returned and came down with such force that a fish could have lived out of water for hours without concern. The decks were completely submerged. Some of us had removed ourselves from the quarterdeck into the shelter of the pilothouse to wait out the deluge. Others took advantage of the downpour and soaped up. It was a warm rain but nonetheless refreshing and provided an unlimited supply of fresh water to drink. There was also the belief, which proved itself true, that the sky was starting to lighten.

It took about an hour of this drenching to get the sky back to where we could see about ship again. The rains abated and we moved back up to the fresher air of the quarterdeck. It felt slightly cooler than earlier in the morning, not much, but every little bit was a welcome relief. It was again possible for the captain and all aboard to see out across the sea for a respectable distance, the clouds having risen slightly off the water. We seemed to be sandwiched between sky and sea. Still, after all that had taken place, we remained becalmed.

East, off our starboard beam, a space opened in the clouds and the light of the sun poured through in a vertical shaft to illuminate the ocean. This bright spot held the attention of all. It seemed to be the center of our featureless universe. The captain was on the quarterdeck with Mr. Claussen and myself, as well as both Mr. Beckwith and Mr. Anderson. The men were watching the spot and talking quietly, whispering among themselves when Captain Ward hollered out across the ship and the silence, startling the wits clean out of me.

"Ahoy, mates! Give us your ear! All hands below deck at once! Secure all ports and hatches, extinguish all lamps! I say, extinguish all lamps at once! Go! Go with all speed, for your lives will depend on it!"

The captain's mates leapt off the quarterdeck, Mr. Anderson moving forward and Mr. Beckwith going down below through the pilothouse. Mr. Claussen swept me off my feet. I wrapped my arms around his neck and looked over his shoulder out across the water. In the distance, I observed a huge column of white mist coming straight down the shaft of light; it was spreading out across the water in all directions at tremendous speed. It looked much like someone pouring milk out of a pitcher onto the floor.

Mr. Claussen hurried down the steps, and went straight into the pilothouse. Once there, he set me upon my feet and instructed me to go directly to Lady Rebecca, who was below in berthing, and tell her to find something to grip onto firmly. He then sped off down the corridor toward his cabin.

Mr. Beckwith had been instructed by the captain to assist Lady Rebecca and the children. When I went below, everything was fearful. The children were silent and scared half to death, but doing just as they were told. Lady Rebecca and Mary were beside themselves with worry and fear over the safety of all, as they awaited an attack from some unknown force. When Lady Rebecca saw me enter the bay, she let out a deep breath. I saw the look of relief sweep across her face. She motioned me to hurry in her direction.

"Come, come, Elizabeth. Hurry!" I ran to her side.

The children, under the direction of Mr. Beckwith, Cookie Jar, Britany, and Mr. Claussen, who had now entered by way of the accommodation ladder, were secured into safe positions and told to hold on tightly to whatever was available. Gregory LaBianca and Steward William were racing through the holds, moving from gun port to gun port securing the hatches. The older children were instructed to hold on to the younger. Everyone had been instructed to lay with his or her heads to starboard. We were terrified.

"Liz! Hurry, come." I looked up and saw Mary waiting for me at our bunk. She was motioning to me excitedly, and with encouragement from Lady Rebecca, I wasted no time in getting to her. As I climbed into the bunk, the men were extinguishing the oil lamps to prevent fire, and my last sight before the final lamp was snuffed, which left us in total darkness, was of Mr. Claussen embracing Lady Rebecca securely in his arms. He kissed her warmly just as the last light went out. Mary placed her arm around me tightly.

"You're shaking, Mary," I whispered.

"What do you expect? I'm scared half to death and you would be too if you were old enough to realize the danger we're in."

"What danger are we in?" I asked.

"What?"

"I said what danger are we in anyhow?"

"Well, I don't know for certain, but it must be pretty bad if we're—. AAAAAHHH!"

Mary let a scream out of her along with nearly everybody else that scared me to no end as our bunks nearly upended into a vertical position. We hung on in the darkness for all our worth, dangling with as much as twenty feet of air below our feet. Everything went crashing through the bunks, sliding along the deck, and dropping below. The booming of stores reverberated all through the ship, then abated, it being replaced with an unbelievable roar of wind. The REBECCA had been blown over onto her beam ends. She was lying to with the wind and sea

455

abeam. She tried hard to right herself, but the wind attacked her with great force and kept her down, her remaining yards and bulwarks asunder. I feared we were sinking.

From within the darkness below me, and above the din of children, most of whom were now crying or screaming, Captain Ward hollered down into steerage from the pilothouse and ordered Mr. Beckwith to join him by scaling the bunks and trying to get to the companionway. Suddenly, the light of day broke forth and seeped down the stairwell and into steerage. It was our first chance to see the situation we were now in.

Everybody was in their bunks, but unable to let go. It wasn't difficult holding on but it had to be done, unless you were the Johnson boys. They went crashing through the bunks and came to rest against the larboard hull, which was now more of a deck that anything else. They were laughing uncontrollably, oblivious to the danger we were in. All three landed unharmed and unashamed, but brought forth a flurry of retribution from Lady Rebecca. There was some good that came of it, for the sound of the laughter lightened all our hearts during the fearful event.

One by one, the men worked their way back up onto deck. We could barely hear their voices, but for the screeching of the wind as they struggled to bring the ship under command. They were going about their business working the canvas of the spanker as it was, to bring the stern downwind and get REBECCA to come about. It was an effort of no small measure, an extremely dangerous one that finally coaxed the ship to right itself. Slowly, she rolled, bringing her yards up from the sea, and we were again lying prone, flat upon our bunks. The Johnson boys slid down the hull to end up atop the mess of belongings now in disarray and piled deep at the larboard deck. While everyone was expressing relief, offering thanks to the Lord and congratulating themselves of their good fortune, I managed to slip away and stepped up to the pilothouse.

I attempted to open the pilothouse hatch, desiring to go above onto the quarterdeck and visit my favorite spot. I was forced to push very hard to open the door for the wind was of an overwhelming nature and coming directly across our bows. The waves were starting to build, but for the most part it was a lot of wind and very little sea. Being nearly blown up the quarterdeck stairway, I was astonished to see the stanchions that stood as the barrier between me and the sea, at my favorite place, were stove in.

Fearful, and having no desire to go over the board, I decided to move farther aft for more security. I could see other damage about the ship, but nothing that appeared life threatening. There were a number of items, such as water casks and spars, which had been carried away. Many of the lines were set free from their belaying pins, and lay uncoiled about the deck or draping over the board, and in need of attention. The men started the pumps and the carpenter was given extra hands to set out at once and assess the damage. The reports were encouraging and it appeared on initial inspection that the REBECCA had weathered the storm admirably.

Lady Rebecca stepped out onto the deck to survey the situation. She crossed over to Mr. Claussen. They spoke shortly, she informing him of the disastrous state of affairs within their cabin. She then took a breath to relax herself and studied a group of sailors who were now gathered about the coach. I climbed down to the main deck and stood at her side as one of the men came aft. He approached us.

"Lady Rebecca...." he hesitated.

"Go on, sir."

"It's uh...." The man licked his lips. "I mean to say…it's just that the coach is fine."

"Oh, that is wonderful news. I was worried." Lady Rebecca was visibly pleased, but the sailor was visibly annoyed.

"What I mean to say is it…it shouldn't be so. No, ma'am. It isn't right. It shouldn't be on the fore deck. It should have been thrown clear, carried away to sea, like the casks and the spars. It is bothersome and makes some of us nervous, Milady." The sailor fidgeted. Mr. Claussen, sensing a less than comfortable situation, spoke up.

"Sir, would you tell the mates, I had the finest manila rope made for securing the coach. It was carefully inspected for strength and it appears that the price was worth the product, for it has done its job."

The sailor stood silent, looking at Mr. Claussen; he then turned about and walked slowly back to his mates. There was an increasing degree of suspicion that surrounded the coach, unspoken feelings and wariness that made some of the men uncomfortable. After a while time erased some of these suspicions or at least buried them under more pressing issues.

The blow continued in its intensity for about an hour, upon which it moderated and Captain Ward was able to call for sail. The men now greatly relieved and in very high spirits for having escaped their deaths, went aloft and laid out on the yards to loosen the lower top'sls, and close reef the uppers. Darrin O'Kurk was high above them all singing a chantey as the men below hauled upon the jeers with great vigor, swaying up the topmasts and yards.

We resumed our journey north and faced no other concern or delay in our progress for the remainder of our crossing. We saw our first sail on the horizon, but it passed far leeward of us and out of hailing distance. It was a welcome sight nonetheless, giving us a reprieve from the feeling of loneliness for the first time in many, many weeks.

FORTY-SIX

"Go on then, you've lost your mind!" Milady scoffed at me.

"No! I swear. I can smell it. It's…well…it's…it's sweet. I think."

And there it was. My first impression of America laid out before Milady's ridicule. She laughed the loudest, but in the end, I was the lesser fool, for Captain Ward came forward and praised me for my keen sense of smell before an incredulous Lady Rebecca, eyes rolling and embarrassed.

"It's for certain, you have a fine nose, Elizabeth. You smell the sweet fragrance of landfall. The perfume of a million wildflowers spread out across thousands of miles of field, each one giving off its scent, to bees and birds and wayward sailors. I feel for the farmer who has forgotten its enchantment. Now you know how it smells to a seafarer after so many days out." Captain Ward took in a deep breath. "Wonderful, is it not?"

"*See,* Milady!" I rebuked her.

"I apologize." She laughed. "I thought it must have been something Cookie Jar made up in the galley. I was wrong, and I'll admit to it."

It wasn't anything about the forested coastline in particular that made me dizzy with excitement when seeing America for the first time. Instead, it was the knowing. It was the knowing that I was now one of *'those'* people. A *'someone'* who had seen the majestic shores of the New World for real, not by rendering, or by engraving, but by my very own eyes. I was one who had risked the seas with its monsters and tempests, one who was forced to endure the hell of vomit and stench in the cramped quarters of steerage.

Maybe not too cramped, maybe not in any real fear of an insensitive master, maybe not along the rough northern routes, but nevertheless, one who was brave enough to leave all things familiar, to go and walk upon this strange and frightful new continent. Now, it was I who could…*smell of it*. So many wondered and so few knew.

I strained my eyes to catch a glimpse of an Indian or at least some small sign of one. I was apprehensive of what lay on that shore before me. I recalled when leaving Sweden how I was filled with anxiety upon boarding the FAIR WIND and having to resign myself to the fate of the sea. Now, as I studied the thickly forested coastline, I found myself wary of the future, and perfectly happy to remain aboard the REBECCA, the ship I had so feared in the beginning.

"Look at those forests," said Mr. Claussen. "Are they not spectacular? Are they not vast? The colors of autumn are beginning to show upon their leaves, and I don't believe I have ever seen such a beautiful sight. Imagine how it must appear in the fall of the year. Sweden is forested as well, but not with such color and diversity."

Lady Rebecca seemed to have lost herself to a far-away memory.

"England, I am sorry to say, has robbed herself of every last tree worth looking upon. Her forests are all afloat. It saddens me to think of it and reminds me of a lament I learned while young. Would you like to hear it?"

"Yes, Milady."

Lady Rebecca recited her lament.

How deep runs my sorrow
For the river in the cumb,
Her banks stripped of dignity
Now barren is her womb.

How sad is the bird's song,
It seeks out nest and tree.
The wood has all been taken,
But for tears and memory.

Oh! My darling children,
I am grieved you cannot see,
The splendor of our forest
In my tears and memory.

Mr. Claussen had stepped toward us as Milady was reciting her lament, and when she finished, she turned to him and spoke her thoughts.

"Sometimes I feel as though all things in life change except for possibly man's sense of greed. It wouldn't surprise me if there came a day in the future when this great land might raise its scarred face and weep for the loss of its natural beauty. I know it seems so immeasurably vast, it is hard to imagine it could ever come to pass, but then I look at England."

"You are right to worry, my love. England paid little mind to her natural treasures. Now she suffers terrible; sickly she is. This country will suffer as well."

"But you have always forested. Does your work not bother you, Christopher?"

"My family has always owned the land we forest, and therefore it has been sensible to replace those trees we have removed. Otherwise the land will be good for farming or something else, but I am not in the business of farming. We have done it this way as far back as I can remember."

The REBECCA stood north and spent a number of days sailing along the eastern shore, watching the distant coastline appear and disappear off our larboard beam. The trees grew more and more colorful and the temperature grew cooler by the day. We passed Georgia, the Carolinas, and Katriina, before calling on port. We stood in for Baltimore, Maryland, sailing inland safely within the shelter of the Chesapeake Bay, and dropped anchor on Thursday, September the tenth. We were dressed warm.

Our arrival came with mixed emotions. We were beyond joy at having arrived in port after so long being at sea, but we were not allowed to go ashore. This call on port was strictly for the benefit of Captain Ward; an opportunity for him to see his wife for the first time in two years before concluding his commitment and our journey that was to finish at Boston, in Massachusetts. This arrangement had been agreed to in his contract with Mr. Claussen, who harbored no objections to the captain's request, for it also provided him the opportunity to make a business call or two of his own while in port.

As Lady Rebecca prepared herself to accompany Mr. Claussen ashore with the help of Mary's assistance, I hurried to bathe myself and changed into the finest attire I carried in my baggage. Once ready, I stormed up the accommodation ladder and made my appearance in Milady's dressing room. I was pleased with myself. She stopped her business to look at me. Both she and Mary were filled with surprise. Milady spoke to me.

"What is it you are up to, Elizabeth?" I was confused by the question.

"I have bathed myself and dressed to go ashore, Milady."

"Darling, I shan't be taking you with me. I am going with Mr. Claussen and Mary. Did I say something to make you think different? If so, I am very sorry. It is best on this occasion if you remain aboard and await our return. I would feel much better."

For the first time, whilst employed by Lady Rebecca, I was asked not to accompany her. It was only natural that I would have assumed myself to be going in their company. Even so, I shouldn't have been so presumptuous. I went crimson, embarrassed to the core and unable to look at either Mary or Lady Rebecca. I had forgotten my place. I was the maiden servant.

Humiliated by my own stupidity, my tears broke loose, and I fled down the ladder to my bunk even though I heard Lady Rebecca call out for my return. She had meant me no harm. The mistake was entirely my own. It came as quite a surprise to feel such pain; my heart was clearly broken. I would have never considered going ashore without Mary, Lady Rebecca, and Mr. Claussen at my side.

I buried my face in the pillow. I heard Milady and Mary descend the steps. They moved through the crowd of children and stood alongside my bunk. Lady Rebecca ran her fingers through my hair, which only served to make me sob the harder.

"Elizabeth, my precious. What have I done? I didn't mean to hurt you. Turn about and look at me. Come now, child. Turn about and look at me." This I did, seeing her unclearly through tear-wetted eyes. "I always take you with me and you were right to think you should be going. I wasn't thinking about how that must have seemed to you. Will you let me explain?" I wasn't up to answering, but I nodded my head.

"We are only to be on shore until tomorrow evening. We must return tomorrow in time to sail upon the ebb. Mr. Claussen has need to make a business call, as do I. There was no plan for festivities, nor have any provisions been made for a stay on shore, even a brief one at that. I meant you no grief, sweetheart, and I promise to bring you back a little something to show how badly I feel. I shall be back before you know. Will you forgive me? Tell

463

me you will forgive me, Elizabeth, or I shall be miserable all the while I am away."

I reached up for Milady, who took me in her arms and hugged me with much feeling, helping to put aside my broken spirit. I managed a smile, wanting to believe her and trying to understand. Mary came around and squeezed my hand, then kissed me as well. They brought me back up to the dressing room so I might take part in helping Lady Rebecca finish her packing. Then they were soon off, leaving me at the bulwarks in a smother of kisses and firmly secured by Mr. O'Kurk's hand.

I watched them row away in the company of the Americans, and after a good deal of waving and blowing of kisses, I went up to my favorite place on the quarterdeck. I sat there alone and watched them grow smaller in the distance. I looked out across the harbor past the moored ships. I followed the shoreline, studying the docks and buildings, trying to imagine what the streets of Baltimore might be like.

"Hi, Elizabeth." I turned to see Britany Allison's blonde head looking over the quarterdeck steps toward me.

"Hi."

"I see you stayed on board. Didn't you wish to see Baltimore?"

"I wanted to, but I would have been in the way. Lady Rebecca wanted to take me, but she couldn't." I wanted to believe what I said, yet I was unable to look Britany in the eye as I said it.

"I couldn't go either. I really wanted to go as well, but the captain wanted me to stay and watch the ship. Well, that's what he said. He said I gave a good hand in the galley, and I made him proud having not asked for special consideration because I was a girl. I told him I would be going with the men, but he didn't much care for that either. I think the men felt bad, but they agreed with him and that put an end to it. He's afraid I'll come to harm if I go ashore. I felt pretty bad, but they promised

464

to bring me back some trinkets, and I really like trinkets, so I decided to wait for them." We both looked at the city and said nothing more for a while.

"Anyhow, the reason I came up, is because I asked Mr. Anderson if it would be alright to play tag on deck and he said go ahead. So, if you like, we can get a game going. It'll be fun and it'll make the day pass quicker. Do you want to play?"

"Alright." I rose to my feet and followed Britany Allison to the orphans.

I would have missed Mary's embrace that night in our bunk, but for the exhausting entertainment of fifty pent-up orphans freed to run the decks. We played tag and kick the rag, then as it got darker, 'hide and seek.' The men who remained on board did their best to put up with our energy, some actually joined in the game of 'hide and seek' once it got underway, for the screaming and laughter was contagious. The mates were especially fond of hiding, then jumping out to scare us half to death. We went crazy running up and down the decks and through the holds until we were ready to drop from exhaustion.

Later, the men took to telling stories to the younger children and those of us who were too pooped to continue on. We sat huddled in a great mob upon the foredeck under a black starry sky and listened to all the usual ghost stories. Britany had kept me wound up tighter than a top most all of the night until I finally dropped dead asleep somewhere between the ghost of Barrier Reef and the Old Hag of Sundown. Mainly, I was wrapped in my ship's blanket and fast asleep upon Britany's lap long before I ever hit my bunk.

* * *

Lady Rebecca had been mistaken, for the following day was a Friday, and it was impossible for us to depart due to a superstition respected by all sailors. It was the belief that a Friday departure tempted the worst of fate, and ill luck would certainly befall the voyage. A sailor might holystone a deck until his hands bled on a Friday, but no manner of persuasion could compel him to weigh anchor.

It was for this reason that Captain Ward decided to remain at anchor until Saturday. It meant that Lady Rebecca and Mr. Claussen were to stay an additional day ashore, and most all the mates were given a night of liberty. They set out at once to fashion a shower curtain out of sailcloth in which to conceal themselves, and thereafter had a good scrubbing to song. A number of the men fitted out in fresh frocks, duck trousers, checked shirts, and black varnished tarpaulin hats. When finished, they appeared a handsome, tanned, strong and healthy-looking lot. They bade Britany Allison, me, and all the orphans in the corral a jolly farewell as they descended the scaling shroud and set off for shore aboard the dories. Britany Allison and I blew them kisses as they rowed away in high spirits.

Knowing beforehand, our approach to Baltimore, Lady Rebecca read up on her history and conveyed all she knew of this place as we sailed north along the coast. Mr. Claussen had commented during one of our informal classes that in the eyes of many there was no place where the irony of Europe's war manifested itself more clearly than in Baltimore. In contrast to Europe, where the English and French slaughtered each other at every opportunity, here was an English-settled land, now American by decree, yet populated by a large French community.

There were many Arcadians in Baltimore. They were a French people exiled from Nova Scotia before the French-Indian War. Many were aristocrats who barely escaped with their lives from the Terror in France. There were also the fortunate few that escaped the slaughter in Saint Dominique. Lady Rebecca had said only thirteen boatloads of survivors managed to flee the Caribbean Island and settle in Baltimore during the nineties. They became the hairdressers, the milliners, teachers of art, dance, music, and culture. They opened schools for manners, and in general were a wealthy lot, influencing the flavor and growth of this area.

All about us, the harbor was thick with the masts of ships, for the city of Baltimore was well developed and it did a brisk trade. Its streets were lined with charming little red brick houses. Mr. Claussen told Lady Rebecca she could find most anything of quality when shopping in Baltimore, including a variety of exceptional wines, Swiss cheese, and high fashion dress comparable to anything to be found at Bond Street in London. There was also a thriving theater community for entertainment.

I learned from some of the mates that Baltimore was also known for its high stakes card tables seated by the rich, and for the not so rich, there were coffee-houses that enjoyed a reputation for some of the best food to be had. Baltimore was a Federalist community by nature and as close to a miniature London as imaginable.

On Saturday afternoon, there was a great and unexpected party on board the REBECCA. It was a strange event indeed, for although the Claussens and Captain Ward returned early in the day, so too did many of the mates. As promised, they brought back fistfuls of trinkets for Britany Allison, and swayed her spirits to heaven. She sported all she was given, every ring, bracelet, earring, or necklace. She danced and pranced about showing the lot of it off to her admirers, who laughed heartily and encouraged her to carry on, for she allowed each man to point out his gift, and she was happy to offer a kiss in thanks.

The Claussens hadn't forgot me, and returned with fine bracelets for both Mary and myself. I was happy for the gift, and although I was appreciative, there was no mistaking I was mostly pleased just to see them return. Mary told me that Mr. Claussen had thought to stay over another night and return on Sunday morning, but that Lady Rebecca preferred to go back, as she was feeling distressed about having left me behind on the ship.

Strangest of all, and not to be overlooked, was the fact that so many of the mates came back to the ship early in the day. It was certain that they would bring gifts back for Britany Allison, but what brought them back early and much more sober were the gifts they carried for the orphans.

Over the course of our journey across the sea, many of the men had taken an orphan or two under wing and felt compelled to remember his particular friend still confined aboard ship. The children were beside themselves with glee. Enough gifts had been carried on board so that all received something. Mr. Claussen had seen to it that all the children were given a gift of merit. It was a great party.

Captain Ward's plan to depart on Saturday was scrapped by Mr. Claussen. This was in part due to a shipment of cargo that Milord agreed to transport to Connecticut, but more than that it was due to the fun the orphans were having with the men. Mr. Claussen felt that it was a well-deserved celebration. It was his way of thanking the children for the way in which they had braved the fire and helped save his ship. He had kept his promise. He sent Captain Ward back to his wife for another night. The festivities lasted well into the morning hours with song, dance, and storytelling. For certain the men imbibed aboard ship, and they were feeling no pain, but Mr. Claussen claimed it was a far cry from being the usual 'three sheets to the wind' that was customary once in port.

On Monday morning we weighed anchor. Portions of the goods we took on board in Baltimore were then delivered to the ports of New York, Stamford, and New Haven, Connecticut—then to Providence, Rhode Island, and New Bedford, Massachusetts. These were also impressive ports, but the men were not allowed off ship as our stay was only for the duration of transferring the goods.

We were always quick to weigh anchor and coursed southwest, passing through the Elizabeth Islands into Vineyard Sound, then Nantucket Sound, where we rounded Barnstable and Cape Cod. We then sailed a broad reach across the Bay of Massachusetts and directly into the Bay of Boston. The great harbor opened to welcome us, and we were at last able to say—*we were Americans.*

FORTY-SEVEN

Meredith Brenner sat motionless in the quiet of the morning. She appeared statuesque, sitting erect upon her chair and staring into the mirror of her dressing table. She was deep in thought, looking at the reflection of the room behind her. In particular, she gazed at her bed. It represented everything good and bad in her life.

It was soft and warm—comforting like her husband. He was a gentle and understanding man, a man she loved beyond her ability to express. He had made love to her tenderly many times in this bed during the heat of summer and the cold of winter. It was their wedding bed, and the center of their world. It was a place not only for the joining of their bodies, but more important, the joining of their minds, a place to confess fears and worries, a place to gain strength, a place to dream of the future. Three times in this bed she became pregnant from his seed, and three times she gave birth—*three times stillborn.*

Just the thought of it brought to her heart a crush of despair. It was so unfair that a man as good as Michael should not be able to have a son of his own blood, a son to take his name, a son to bounce upon his knee. It was the greatest gift of love a woman could offer her man. It was the one gift she could not give. It was a guilt that gutted her inside out, and the more Michael showed understanding, the more she suffered.

It would seem impossible that life could be any quieter than on a farm far removed from the bustle of the city, distant from the closest neighbor, stirred only by the sleepy chatter of birds and squirrels. And yet it could be likened to the falls of Niagara when compared with the silence of stillness in the womb.

Meredith knew all too well about silence, about stillness. She knew all about conversations that never took place, things that were never said for the sake of feelings or else whispered in hushed tones beyond her ears. She learned to live with the fear of calling out in joy, announcing she was with child, knowing at any moment fate might strike her down and steal it away but for the sin of being happy.

She remembered the look of disbelief. It should have been a look of disgust. Michael's eyes bored into her soul as he tried to comprehend her reasoning. It was the last and most disastrous conclusion to her three pregnancies. For the millionth time, she dredged up memories of the pains she made to hide her condition, of how she moved deceitfully within his affectionate embraces, of how she suffered to keep secret the life within—such effort to avoid tempting fate, to avoid breaking the heart of a man who gave her every wonderful thing.

She wanted so badly to return the joy he brought her, to bring true his every dream, a good wife, a good friend—*a good mother.* It was insane to think she could have kept it from him. She had starved herself to keep her weight down, to go unnoticed. It was a foolish thing she did, and it weakened her until she fell sick.

She looked at the bed and recalled how Michael began to have suspicions and when she no longer had any choice but to tell him the truth. She remembered the way he was looking at her, wondering about her sanity. How unsure he was about what he was supposed to do. How his only concern was for her well-being. She had cried, cried as hard as ever in her life, but it made no difference. She gained weight quickly after that, but in spite of her good health, six months later their baby stilled. She could do little more than cry; carry the child until term, carry the memory for life.

This morning, more than usual, the room pressed in upon her. She placed her hairbrush back on the table and enjoyed the way it clacked to fragment the quietude. She stood up and then left her room to look into an adjoining bedroom. This was a child's room. She had decorated it the best she could with paint and stain. All it needed was a son.

From outside, near the barn, her husband called out to her.

"Hurry along, Meredith, or we'll not see him arrive!"

Maybe today, she thought to herself. Maybe today the sounds of this house would forever change. Her eyes watered. She trembled with anxiety as she moved toward the door. She looked across the yard to her husband.

"Come, my angel, your child is waiting!"

Meredith looked at Michael and then covered her face with hopeful hands. She heaved with sobs as her soul shed the stress within.

"Now, now, love, what's this? Tears of joy, I hope?"

Yes, she nodded, and placed her head upon his chest a moment to feel his strength. They stood together alongside the wagon.

"It'll be fine, Meredith. You'll make a wonderful mother. It's not what we envisioned...true—but it is what we want. It's what we need. It's what you need." He stroked her hair and brushed it with his lips. "Making a mother out of you will be the best thing that could ever happen to me. You have suffered so from your guilt. I have seen it, I have lived with it, and I have learned that I cannot lessen your burden, Meredith. God knows I've tried. I have learned that there are things I cannot make right. But this is right. This is good medicine. I can feel it. If I know nothing else, I know this; today we will settle your heart and clear your conscience, you'll see. We'll make out, Meredith. Today is our day. Now, smile for me, angel. C'mon, give me a smile."

She wiped away her tears and forced a smile. Michael took her hand, and raised her to the bench.

"It's certain to be a great day, Meredith. I promise."

They bundled up against the brisk September morning air, and started down the wooded lane in early light while birds still reveled in song. They spent the hours of travel watching the sun rising in the eastern sky; and with it, they raised their own hopes afresh. They voiced dreams of the family they so desired.

Michael steered Meredith from one conversation to the next, discussing preparations, the plans he envisioned, his hopes for the future, and his hopes for their son. They wondered what their boy would look like, what color hair he would have, what color eyes. What color did they like the best? They avoided all thoughts and fears of him being unhealthy, or becoming sick, just as any expectant parents might. They wondered if they would know their son was meant for them. Would there be some special sign, some special feeling the minute they laid eyes upon him?

Michael was inwardly grateful that Meredith was talkative. There was no lack of conversation, and it sped the morning along. They arrived at the bay about ten o'clock as best Michael could reckon. He brought the horses to rest at a small park above the docks, a place where there was a fine view of the harbor and a stable nearby to feed and water the horses. Meredith was astonished to see the number of ships and the amount of activity on the bay. Boston was growing at a pace nearly beyond her ability to comprehend.

The journey was long enough so that after Michael helped Meredith step down from the wagon, they both arched stiffened spines as they let out sighs of relief.

"Oh, lord! That wagon will be the death of me yet. There was no money wasted on creature comfort the day this one was built." Michael rocked his hips from side to side. "One day I will own a nice springed wagon for no purpose other than taking Sunday rides to town. This I will do for you, and I promise, you'll not feel as much as a tree stump in the middle of the road."

"I'm not planning on holding my breath," Meredith sneered.

"I have always said you are an intelligent woman, Meredith, but I am hurt, nonetheless."

Actually, Michael felt a tinge of guilt for having waited so long since last taking Meredith away from the farm to enjoy the sights of the city. He was beginning to realize that the only free time the farm would offer them was the time he took by force. He wished to make up for his selfishness, and he looked forward to taking Meredith on a leisurely stroll through the city in hopes she would enjoy herself shopping. He believed the distraction would bring her relief from the growing anxiety she was trying hard to suppress.

They walked arm in arm from one store to the next. All the while, Michael studied the expressions upon her face. She was cheering up, the anxiety being replaced by a sense of elation. He watched as she dared to be happy. Joy suited her, and it returned the glow she wore when first pregnant, before the tears became so much a part of her life.

Meredith didn't buy anything even though Michael implored her to do so. She was unable to escape the discipline of frugality that supported much of their existence. Only one thing occupied her mind, one thing that couldn't be bought in any store—a son to love. Michael was forced to take it upon himself to purchase a small block wagon that rolled on wheels for her to give to the boy. He wondered if that had been a mistake.

"Maybe I shouldn't have bought this toy."

"What makes you say that?" she asked.

"It just occurred to me how absurd was my belief that our boy would be so young, you know…a toddler. Toddlers don't go crossing oceans, boys do. I probably should have bought a gun for the boy."

Meredith took the toy from his hand and held it up to her cheek.

"You bought a toy for the boy in your mind. I can see that he is alive in your heart, and it makes me very happy to know it."

Michael put his arm around Meredith, and they walked back up the slopes that bordered the serenity of the park. They selected a comfortable place on the grass with a good view of the bay, where Meredith rested her head upon Michael's lap as he leaned back against a tree. They struggled to be patient, knowing soon their ship of hope would appear hull down upon the horizon. In the briefest of moments, Meredith was asleep. Michael gazed down upon her and thanked the Lord for allowing his wife to rest peacefully for a spell. It would do her good.

She slept soundly for almost two hours before he gently nudged her awake. He let her regain her senses, and then directed her eyes toward the harbor. In the afternoon sun, REBECCA's crimson hull stood out upon the horizon, glistening beneath her full dress of sails.

"Oh, Michael. Is that it? Is that it?" she asked, unable to contain her excitement.

At that moment, having just awakened and not yet remembering her many disappointments, she positively glowed, her eyes opened wide with wonder. To see that look of antici-pation so long buried beneath years of shame brought a flush of tears to Michael's eyes, tears he wished not to reveal. He turned his face away as spoke to her.

"I'm sure of it. I was told there would be no doubt in my mind. It would be the most beautiful vessel I should ever hope to see. As I look about, I see nothing the likes of this ship now inbound. She is magnificent, and I am willing to bet that must be it."

"Oh, my! She is beautiful, is she not?"

"Indeed she is."

"Do you think we should we go to the docks?" she asked impatiently.

Michael thought a moment. "No, not just yet. It'll be some time before there is anything for us. Let us enjoy our rest while we are able. The trip back will be long enough."

FORTY-EIGHT

The REBECCA rode her anchor at the edge of the harbor for close to an hour before a harbor pilot came to board us. Immediately thereupon, we tripped anchor and began to make way toward our wharf by his command.

The orphans had gathered in the corral, and stood unusually silent as they stared at the shore in a growing state of bewilderment. They were filled with uncertainty and apprehension about what was in store for them once we landed. They had enjoyed many weeks of late, singing and storytelling, playing with one another and strengthening the bonds that made them brothers and sisters.

For some, these relationships began with boarding the REBECCA, for others it began years before or since birth. They may have been raised in orphanages, but they were now family, family about to be split up forever. The trip with all its adventure had cemented their spirits as one, and heightened the sense of loss they were about to realize. Huddled together for security, they watched the crowds on the dock waving and cheering, welcoming them, and began to comprehend that they were about to give up the most important thing in their young lives: roots, the sense of belonging—except for possibly the *Johnson boys*.

"Over there! Over there! Look! Look!" Paul was jumping all about. Peter squinted his eyes.

"Ahh, You're dreamin', Paul."

"No, I swear! Right over there by the park, cross my heart. It's true!"

Peter strained to see anything. He searched the trees, the bushes, the grasses, and the corners of nearby buildings.

"Paul…you're daft! I have searched every inch of that park, and there is no Indian anywhere to be seen. You need help."

"Nuh uh! I saw an Indian! I'll prove it to you. I'll take ya right to him. He was big and covered with feathers. You'll see!"

"You ain't taking me anywhere b'cuz you gotta be a man to walk up to an Indian. You're too scared."

"I'm as big a man as you! And I'm not scared either, you'll see. You wait!" Paul was indignant.

"Sheesh! You are an idiot, Paul. You're about as right as wrong can get."

Mr. Claussen stepped up from the cabin and joined Lady Rebecca and me upon the quarterdeck. He looked amazed at the throngs moving about at the water's edge.

"What is this, Rebecca?

"I'm not sure. I can't imagine these people are all here for us. Is that possible?" she wondered. Mr. Claussen shrugged his shoulders.

"I swear, Rebecca, everything about this trip that is connected with you has been a bundle of surprises. This would be just one more." She looked up to him and smiled.

"Oh, Christopher, you know how you hate to be bored. Where would you be without me? All those women hunting you down, all that money to spend alone, the West Indies fiasco, the bloody nose. I'm beginning to worry that you overlook all of these little things I do for you. Not to mention, how much I love you and how that blinds me to all those little shortcomings you possess." She teased and taunted him, holding her lips just shy of his.

"How I survived all of it—I am fortunate, indeed." Their eyes were locked together as they passed their feelings.

"I've got to get to my children. They're nervous." She kissed him lightly. "Bye-bye." She backed away from him, offering a little wave in his direction.

"Just one moment, love." He stopped her retreat.

"Yes?"

"Take these."

Mr. Claussen held out his hand. Lady Rebecca stepped forward somewhat puzzled and reached out to accept. He placed a stack of slips into her palm.

"What is this?"

"Address slips, so the children have a means by which to stay in touch." Lady Rebecca was thrilled.

"Oh, Christopher, how thoughtful. What a wonderful idea."

"A surprise of my own, imagine the chances of that."

This time Lady Rebecca did kiss him.

"Bye-bye." She released him, gripping the stack of papers in one hand, while reaching for me with the other. She led me away to berthing. As soon as she was able to bring the orphans to order, she handed out the slips. Handwritten on each piece was the following address:

THE REBECCA FOUNDATION
ATTN.: LADY REBECCA CLAUSSEN
ABOARD HER NAMESAKE THE GOOD SHIP REBECCA
AT CLAUSSEN SHIPYARDS AND STOWAGE
BOSTON HARBOR, MASSACHUSETTS

The orphans were curious about the slips, and as Lady Rebecca went about handing one to each child, she encouraged the children to write her. She promised to keep their addresses close to heart. She told them that if all were in agreement, she would share their new family addresses with others so they might all stay in contact during the years to come.

At once, I could see a great weight lifted from the hearts of most all in the corral. Christopher had given back to the orphans the only tangible connections they had in their lives thereby dismissing a great deal of fear. Believing they were no longer to be cut off from their past or their friends, they were better able to cope with the idea of facing the future, no matter where it should take them. A chorus of chatter and laughter mingled with promises and pacts to write one another swept through the ship from the corral on deck to the bunks below.

FORTY-NINE

Michael and Meredith watched the REBECCA come into her berth. They rose to their feet so they might make way to the docks. They could see a sizable crowd of people collecting about the ship. There was an air of excitement. Michael spoke his thought aloud as the two walked toward the ship.

"I was thinking how it is in Europe whereby law dictates that the eldest blood son will become heir to the family estate. Now, I understand how this is reasoned as the way to keep the grand estates of nobility intact, but can you imagine how difficult it must be for all those siblings who are left out in the cold with nothing for the sake of the firstborn?"

"I think it's terrible," replied Meredith. "Moreover, imagine the chances of a daughter ever seeing such an inheritance. She'll be married off, and the whole business passes on to another. You men should know more about being left without."

"I agree. I suspect a great number of those left out end up here in the States. We have such freedom here to make good for ourselves. I mean, look at these orphans who now come ashore. Not only might they find a good home to take them, but also they might live to be rich or famous. One never knows. Anything is possible here.

"I was thinking there must be thousands of couples the same as you and me spreading out across this country trying to settle the land and establish themselves. Homesteading, working the fields so they might support a family. It takes years to get a farm to produce; and you know what, Meredith? It is only then, after everything is reasonably secure, might they afford to think of children.

"It may be, we have the upper hand this time, an unrealized advantage. If we end up with a boy who is…let's say…six or seven years of age, in three or four years he would be strong enough to help with the work."

"Oh, please, Michael, let the boy be a boy first. Let us just enjoy him and not turn him into a man as soon as possible. I don't want a man. I want a boy, the younger the better. I want a boy who needs a mother," Meredith fretted.

"I didn't mean to be heartless, Meredith. I was only saying it as a matter of sensibility. The boy stands as much to gain by working the farm, as do I. He may be an orphan, but he will learn the land and instead of losing out to a sibling, he will go out and stake his own claim, and become master of his own estate."

"It sounds like you're rushing it to me, Michael. Besides, we have other things more important to worry about right now. I mean, look at all these people."

Michael and Meredith walked the planks of the dock. They were soon to discover from conversations that floated in the air that many others were also here hoping to find children to fill empty nests.

479

"Michael, I'm worried. There are too many people here. Look at all these people. Have you been listening to what they say? Do you think they all want children to take back with them, the same as us? Pray dear God, I hope this isn't as it appears. I'm afraid of this, Michael. There are so many people…" Meredith's voice trailed off, but her fears were growing quickly. Michael stepped in at once to calm her.

"There is no point in getting excited, Meredith. We were told to find and meet with Lady Rebecca Claussen, and that is what we shall do. The rest is up to God. If He doesn't wish it, then it shan't be. We have to accept His wisdom." Michael swallowed hard. *'That was so much easier said than done,'* he thought.

Meredith could fast see the writing on the wall. There were just too many people. She leaned over to the woman next to her in the crowd.

"Are you here for the children?"

"Oh, yes. I'm so excited. I've waited so long. Are you also?"

"Yes."

"Oh, isn't this the best day? Can't you just feel the excitement? I've been worried sick over the entire matter for weeks. I'll be so happy when it's over and I can begin to eat again."

"Are you trying for a boy or a girl?" Meredith asked.

"A girl, Lillian Barker. She originally came from Liverpool."

Michael clenched his jaw. He instantly saw past the stunned expression of shock upon Meredith's face, and witnessed her soul crumble. He placed his hand on her shoulder, but she shrugged him off and spun around to another woman. She was desperate.

"Are you waiting for a child, madam?"

"Yes, a boy. William Carver." The woman smiled joyously, but clipped it short when she read something amiss in Meredith's eyes. Michael moved in closer, seeing all the reason in the world to be concerned, but Meredith sidestepped him.

"I…I don't understand. How could you know the boy's name?" The woman being of good sense, and realizing the anxiety Meredith was expressing, spoke with care.

"The child was spoken for…before…before his departure from England. Are you aware that most of these children are going to homes by prearrangement?"

Every ounce of heart and soul dropped from Meredith's being. She stood dumbfounded, lost for emotion. Michael reached for her, and at his touch she exploded.

"Don't touch me!" she screamed. "Don't touch me!"

Her eyes, at first wild with fury and filled with a look of insanity, suddenly burst forth in tears. The other woman stood nervously still, while a number of others turned to face her. They being unaware of the reason for her breakdown witnessed only her outburst, and so the louder she wailed, the more they backed away and pretended not to notice.

"It isn't fair! It isn't fair!" she cried. "What have I done? I have lost three children. Isn't that enough? Good God, isn't that enough? I will not lose another. I will not lose another." She broke into sobs as the reality of this possibility began to sink in. She bowed her head and wept into her hands, slowly sinking to her knees.

Michael found himself wiping away his own tears. He was torn by his utter inability to provide happiness and relief to the woman he loved more than life itself. He felt completely worthless, unable to walk away, unable to approach her. The other woman lowered herself to the dock. She reached out to Meredith and embraced her. Her unspoken understanding seemed to bring solace to Meredith, for she caused her no guilt. Michael cleared his eyes and then looked up to view the woman.

"Forgive us, it has been a difficult road," he apologized.

"You need say nothing more to me, sir. Almost everyone here can understand the heartbreak. It is the reason we all stand and wait. It is the reason we all pray. Not all the children are spoken for, but it would be wise to realize that the chances are now very slim. The arrival of these children was well publicized. If it is of any comfort, allow me to say, that I understand a good many more shall come and in time, you are certain to have your own."

Once settled, Meredith allowed Michael to bring her to her feet and take her into his embrace. They shunned the crowd. They needed to retreat, to back away for a moment and regain their footing; they needed to catch their breath. He spoke gently, hoping to soothe her.

"Meredith, you know I can't explain these things. It's the Lord's way. If it isn't meant to be, then it isn't meant to be. But that doesn't mean we shouldn't try our hardest whilst we remain. Let us see what can be done, for on my soul I swear I love you above all else, and it is killing me to see you so distressed. I would go to hell and back to see you with child."

The tears welled up in Michael's eyes. He had to turn away, but seeing the hurt in his heart brought Meredith back to her senses.

"I am sorry, Michael. I forget too quickly that it is not only I who goes without a son. I am so selfish. Please forgive me, please forgive me, Michael. I am so sorry."

Michael cleared his head. He turned back to face her, but this time he didn't bother to hide the tears that escaped his resolve to be strong.

"Meredith, what must I say to make you believe I would go to the ends of the earth without a son if only I knew I would make that journey with you? I can face my life without a son, but I can't face it without the woman I love. It is not a son who chooses to stay with me until I die. It is a wife. It was you who made me that promise, Meredith. You are my life. Stay with me, and I promise together we will work this out."

Meredith caught her breath and looked into the reddened eyes of her husband. All the love in the world, she thought to herself. She was moved, and so she kissed him.

"I love you, Michael, and I am sorry for what I put you through."

They put their arms around one another and gravitated toward a large brick warehouse that attracted them but for the activity that surrounded it. Filled with curiosity and a need for distraction, they approached the structure in an attempt to make sense of the goings on. There were children leaving in droves right before their eyes, and yet they didn't have a clue where to begin an application for a child. They asked repeatedly to be directed to Lady Claussen, but to no avail.

She was often seen, but always escorted through the crowds, and virtually impossible to reach. The crowds now thinned quickly as children with smiling faces streamed out of the brick building, hand in hand, with new mothers and fathers. Those people that remained were intent on gaining access to the brick building, and a line of sorts formed at its entrance.

Michael and Meredith took their place at the end of the line, and tried to remain calm, tried to be patient. Minutes stretched out, becoming longer and longer, until more than an hour slipped past and no longer were children left to be seen leaving the building before them. They paid close attention, straining to hear as word came down, passed backward from one to another along the line until the dreaded announcement reached their ears. The children were all spoken for, and this line was now only for the application of children in the future.

As hard as she might, Meredith fought to be strong, but as before, it was too much. Her room was ready, her heart was ready, and again she watched as all the love she had stored slipped through her fingers like so much sand to be lost upon the ground.

She couldn't face the loneliness, the unbearable silence of the farm. She turned to Michael, this time too miserable to cry.

"Why am I being punished so, Michael?" She looked up to him for an answer. "Wouldn't you think above all else that at least God would know how much I would love a child, how much I would appreciate and understand what a blessing it would be? Wouldn't you think He would know what's in my heart, and all the love I have to give?" Her eyes showed her disappointment.

"Shhhh." Michael kissed her gently. "Oh, my Meredith. It is the cruelty and unfairness of life. There is no satisfaction to be had in pointing fingers or placing blame. It is God's will, His plan for whatever reason." He would have gladly taken all her pain and endured it forever, if only to dry her tears, but he was powerless to change the hand of Providence.

"We must go. We have cried enough for one day, and it will be late by the time we return."

This time Meredith did not resist and he led her slowly back toward the wagon.

"I don't know Michael. I don't understand. I know it is improper to question the Lord's ways but..." her voice broke.

"Shhhh. It will work out. I promise, just keep the faith. There is reason for the ways of fate. We may have to wait to find the reason, but it will come, I promise. Remember the woman said that many more are en route. I have no doubt there is a boy meant for us who has yet to come. Maybe not until the next ship, or the one thereafter, but he's coming. We just have to find out how to go about applying for him. We'll work it out. We always do."

They walked in silence. Meredith was tired. She had exhausted herself by crying out the many weeks of anxiety and anticipation she carried with her, weeks of fear and frustration flushed from her being, leaving her nothing but fatigue. They walked. They had nothing left to say that hadn't been said or cried over time and time again.

Meredith watched the children in the park playing, running about, laughing, screaming, and crying in the late afternoon sun. The deepening shadows reflected the mood of her heart. She watched one little boy in particular cry, so sad, so much like her. She wanted to cry for him. She wondered what disappointments he faced in his small world. Why did the boy cry, she wondered? Was he hungry, was he hurt, was he lonely? Could he be lost, or was it, he just needed to be held, to be loved? Instinctively, she glanced around the park. Her guard was raised without an awareness of so doing, for it came with her natural intuition as a mother.

FIFTY

Following Mr. Claussen's request, as we came in close to dock, Captain Ward issued orders to Mr. Beckwith that the holds were to remain sealed until the children were removed from the ship and put safely ashore. He preferred to see them well out of harm's way before the booms began to swing. The ladies in assistance, all volunteers from Boston who were awaiting our arrival, stood at the ready wearing red and green ribbons pinned to their shoulders for easy recognition as per prearranged plans.

It was increasingly difficult for me to wander as Lady Rebecca was adamant I should stay at her side. She was pulling me all about from one end of the ship to the other. I went with her down into steerage where the orphans were assembled. They were instructed to gather up all their gifts and belongings. It was time to say good-bye to quarters that continually flip-flopped between being too cramped or wonderfully cozy and secure.

The children were subdued as they filed out in a long line, scaling the stairwell up to the pilothouse and then walking out onto the deck and along the waterway. When they reached the boarding plank, they were allowed to stop and say their farewells. Here the orphans gave tearful good-byes to the men aboard ship, all of whom came on deck to send them off.

There were many touched by the separation, regretting the loss of young ones whom they had chosen to befriend and form bonds as though they were kin. It was a moving sight to see grown, hardheaded men of the sea stand weepy-eyed and waving, as the orphans stepped onto the plank and began to descend one after another. The procession moved downward, and then reaching the dock, they disappeared into the open arms of the crowd that moved in to overwhelm them.

Mr. Claussen's fleet was at present scattered all about the harbor. The Claussen shipyard and stowage facilities were presently under construction, and until their completion, there was little that could be done except to use whatever facilities were readily available. For this reason, a large brick building had been rented by Mr. Claussen for use during the disembarking process. It was near a park that overlooked the bay, and a great place for the children to regain the feel of grass and earth, to kick about in the fallen autumn leaves, and regain their land legs.

I was anxious to see up close all the buildings and sights that loomed large on the shore before me. I waited for Lady Rebecca to finish her preparations.

"Elizabeth?"

"Yes, Milady."

"Darling, I would be most appreciative if you would stay behind to tend to Mr. Claussen's needs while I go ashore. I need Mary's help, so I must take her with me, but I need someone to stay with Christopher as well. Would you do me that service?"

"Yes, Milady."

I knew what Milady wanted most from me was freedom from worry about what I might get into. She believed I would be safe as long as I was on board the ship. She was so careful not to hurt my feelings this time that I felt perfectly comfortable about staying behind and easing her mind. Besides, I liked being in the company of Mr. Claussen and now I had a legitimate excuse.

Mr. Claussen was busy working out the initial schedules for the unloading of stores. He offered me a seat next to him at the table. I understood nothing at all of his business, and my attention wandered back and forth between him and my thoughts about the ship. I left him momentarily to walk over to the accommodation ladder. I descended the steps and walked through the now dark and uncomfortably silent space. My stomach churned with anxiety from the emptiness of the place. I felt left behind.

"Elizabeth!"

"Yes, Milord! I'm right here, I'm coming."

I raced up the steps feeling as though all the ghosts of the past were hot on my heels. Mr. Claussen stood near the doors awaiting my hand. I walked to him, shaking off the loneliness of the berthing.

"Time has come, my darling. Shall we go, then?

"Yes, Milord."

We stepped into the corridor, which went dark once Mr. Claussen pulled the doors closed behind us. I was filled with butterflies. We passed through the pilothouse and stepped out onto the deck. He walked slowly, taking his time to inspect the rigging and the hatches to the holds. Most of the men had been given their leave and the ship was emptying fast. Instead of proceeding down the boarding plank, he stopped alongside and stood atop the running boards to look over the bulwarks and survey the goings on below. He gripped me by my waist and seated me atop the gunwale, held firmly within his embrace.

"What do you think of our new home, Elizabeth?"

"I am afraid to leave the ship."

"Why? I remember when you were afraid to board the ship. That wasn't so very long ago."

"It seems like it was forever to me. I am afraid because I don't know what is out there. I don't know anybody."

"Well, Elizabeth, I don't know what it out there either, and I can't wait to find out."

Mr. Claussen grew silent. He was staring intently at some person or thing in the park. I scanned the grounds, but saw nothing amiss. I was more interested in the dock below us; it being notably absent of street brats. Of this, I wished to question Mr. Claussen, but found myself struggling to get his attention.

"What is it, Mr. Claussen?"

"Over there in the park. Do you see the little boy?" He pointed.

"No."

"It's no matter. Let us go for a walk." He lowered me to the deck and we soon descended the plank. I stood upon the shore for the first time in months and found myself teetering.

"I see you've forgotten where you put your land legs, Elizabeth. I guess we'll just have to find you some new ones. Come along."

He tightened his grip on my hand, and we headed up toward the park. We passed by the welcoming crowds and well-wishers that were filling the streets between the warehouses. He walked through them in a determined fashion as if he was on a mission. He didn't allow anyone the chance to recognize or distract him. Mr. Claussen made his way up the grades until he reached a point at the edge of the park where he was able to look out upon the expanse. Here he stopped. He stood silent, staring, as I tried to figure out what held his attention so steadfastly. At last, I believed I knew.

"Milord! Is that—?"

"Shussh!" He quieted me gently, holding his finger up to his mouth, but he never took his eyes off what it was he studied. Instead he pulled me before him, and there we stood.

FIFTY-ONE

Meredith raised her head off Michael's shoulder. She took a more attentive posture as she observed the young boy.

"Michael…." she started.

"Mmm-hmm."

"There's something the matter with that child."

At first, Michael looked in the boy's direction, and then he looked about the park. "Well, I do see a child crying, not an uncommon sight in a park, I dare say. I see no problem, Meredith."

"No…." Her senses were now becoming acute. "Something is wrong. I can feel it."

She broke away from Michael's embrace and moved toward the young boy. Michael was leery of this situation. He knew Meredith was filled with despair, and he hoped she wasn't overreacting to a very normal occurrence.

She walked toward the boy, studying him, his expressions, the sounds of his cry, and then started to half run, unsure of why she needed to investigate. It was more than her perceptions. She was being driven to the child. Meredith stooped down and reached for the young boy. He held his arms up to her, and as she picked him up, he wrapped himself around her neck.

"Oh, you poor thing," she cooed. "What's the matter, sweetheart?"

"I s-s-scared." The little boy sobbed.

"Oh, you're fine. Where's your mama?" The boy shrugged his shoulders. "You don't know, ooooh, poooor babeeeee. We'll find her, don't you worry."

Meredith held him tight, kissed him, and looked around. There was nobody in sight. She spun around again slowly, but saw no one. She walked back over to Michael, who turned away from the child and was now at the wagon feeling very nervous about what was taking place. He knew Meredith was under a great deal of stress.

"Meredith, you're bringing home strays, better be careful," he warned.

"He's scared." She made a sad face.

Michael looked at the little guy with his swollen eyes and falling britches.

"Yeah, he's a little bruiser. How old are ya, son?" he asked. The boy raised three fingers, two fingers, three fingers.

"Three! Two. Three." Meredith and Michael laughed in unison.

"What's your name, honey?"

"Jacob"

"Jacob," Meredith repeated. "Where is your mother, Jacob?" He shrugged his shoulders.

"We've got to leave for home, Meredith, or we'll—."

Michael was promptly cut off by priorities.

"We can't just leave him here alone." She looked at Michael in disbelief.

"Meredith, please. I meant no such thing. It's just we must be off soon, so let us find a place to care for him." He was urging her gently, but somewhat annoyed. He was more worried for her than the child or what time they arrived back at the farm.

490

She was so vulnerable at this moment, and he feared this type of encounter could prove disastrous.

Meredith looked around. "Let us bring him to the brick building, they work with the children, they will know what to do."

Michael felt a wave of relief flow over him, for it was a rational suggestion.

* * *

The only words uttered by Mr. Claussen as we stood at the park's edge came in the form of a question.

"Elizabeth...? Is that not the young Johnson boy?"

"Yes, Milord. Jacob. I was about to say so, but you told me to shush."

"Umm, yes, that's true. I meant nothing by it, sweetheart. I was merely engrossed in what was taking place." He looked down at me. "It's best you know I am often short when I choose not to be distracted. It's a fault to be sure, and very rude at that, but I am far from perfect, and I hope you'll forgive me. Now come, I wish to follow them. I believe they are headed back to the warehouse, and I am most interested to see what next happens."

We pretended to be looking at ships out in the harbor as we waited for the three of them to pass us by. We then turned to follow them from the park. They walked back down the hill with the boy resting peacefully in Mrs. Brenner's arms and clutching a small toy truck.

The line at the warehouse had dispersed, the front doors were closed, and the grounds were now empty. There was not one hopeful parent to be seen. They walked up to the door. Mr. Brenner cupped his hands and peered through the glass, whereby he could see people still working inside. He tested the handle, found it unlocked, and so opened it for his wife who still had Jacob in her arms, now sound asleep. Mr. Claussen and I had walked quickly until we were nearly stepping upon their heels as they reached the front door of the building.

Mr. Brenner glanced back at us, and waited momentarily to hold open the door for our entry. We thanked him then stepped off to the side, where Mr. Claussen held me back in the shadows. He seemed eager to overhear the conversation about to take place between Lady Rebecca and the Brenners.

He placed his finger over his lips and winked at me, a gentle reminder to keep quiet, but it was hardly necessary for we had scarcely entered the room when it exploded into a raucous. The two older Johnson boys went running in their direction, screaming out at the top of their lungs. Jacob was startled awake and began to howl.

"He's here! He's here! He's free!"

The boys jumped up and down and came forward to meet the three. Lady Rebecca and the others turned, all wearing a look of distress, which gave way to sighs of enormous relief, hands raised to chest and foreheads.

"So! You boys know this little guy, huh?" Mr. Brenner asked.

"Yeah, he's our brother! We thought he was dead. Scalped!" exclaimed Peter.

"We thought the Indians got him for sure!" exclaimed Paul.

Mrs. Brenner looked up, half expecting to greet their mother, but was overtaken by the four women at the desk.

"Oh! I can't tell you how grateful I am to you for watching over our Jacob."

"He was lost over in the park," Mrs. Brenner responded.

The ladies looked at each other with some disapproval, then back to Mrs. Brenner. Lady Rebecca stepped forward.

"Well, I knew he hadn't been scalped, but his brothers should have been skinned alive for leaving him as they did." The boys protested. Mrs. Brenner set Jacob down on his feet.

"I am sure this looks poor for us, but I hope you will understand that the children have been cooped up on board ship for over a month. Once that plank dropped, we had all we could do to keep them together. It was worse than rats fleeing a sinking barge. Please, believe me, this was our only black mark, and you really must know the Johnson boys before you can judge us in all fairness—."

"The Johnson boys?"

"Oh! I am so sorry, how rude of me, I am Rebecca Claussen."

Lady Rebecca extended her hand. Mrs. Brenner stared at her in disbelief, unable to speak.

"Rebecca Claussen? The ship? *Lady* Rebecca Claussen?" Mr. Brenner asked as he pointed back over his shoulder toward the docks.

"Yes, we just—." Milady stopped short as she saw Mrs. Brenner throw up her hands to cover her tortured expression. Mr. Brenner stepped over to his wife. Lady Rebecca immediately sensed the pain.

"Have I said something to upset you, madam?"

Mrs. Brenner ignored Milady, and instead turned back into her husband, all the while reminding herself how easy it was to get hurt. She tried not to think of any remote possibilities, telling herself it was another part of a cruel game. She remembered the woman had said these children were spoken for in a prearranged agreement. She would try hard not to hope too much and tempt fate to punish her again.

"Forgive us Lady Claussen, it's been a disastrous day. We had hopes of adopting a child, but the Lord has decided different."

"Well, maybe not, I do have a young girl," Lady Rebecca stated happily. She turned and showed Mr. Brenner a little girl of about five years. "Her name is Nancy May." She is only here because she was gallivanting with the boys, and not to be found when the children were taken charge of."

"Oh, no, please...I am most grateful, you must forgive me, I... I...*we* had hoped for a boy to help with the farm. We had our hearts set on a boy; actually we need a boy. I am sorry, I hope you understand."

Mr. Brenner felt at once the terrible guilt of rejecting the young girl. She was such an adorable child with her red head, freckles, and big brown eyes; he believed that no more innocent a creature could exist to face him.

He had been given, for one second, complete control of her destiny. It was both unsettling and undesirable, for it made him feel cheap. He had cast her aside in the blink of an eye with the word "no." Was she hurt by his rejection? Did she feel the same pain as Meredith, being unable to find someone to love her? Mr. Brenner looked down at the ground. He couldn't bear to face the child in order to see for himself.

"I understand and I am sorry. That was wholly unfair of me to place that decision upon you without warning," Lady Rebecca responded with sincerity. She placed her hand upon his arm, as if to steady him. "These things must be done with care, and I apologize for putting you into such an awkward position." They stood in silence waiting for Mrs. Brenner to regain her composure. She didn't turn to face Lady Rebecca, nor did she open her eyes when she addressed her.

"Are they...are they...spoken for?"

"They? You mean...the boys?" Lady Rebecca looked toward Mr. Brenner in surprise.

"Yes."

"Why, no. Actually, they are not. Few people are in position to take so many at once, and then we must add to that the fact they disappeared in the first five minutes ashore and well…." Lady Rebecca halted.

Mrs. Brenner turned to face Milady with burdened eyes, afraid to say what was in her heart.

"Meredith Brenner."

She offered her hand. Then she looked square at her husband.

"They're going home with us, Michael."

"Meredith?"

"They're going home with us, if they'll have us—three stillborn, three brothers, it's God's work, Michael. You said it yourself. You said it would be worked out, and this can't be denied. I won't go home to an empty house, Michael, not again."

"Well…." Mr. Brenner thought for a moment. He scratched his head. "Well—."

"Michael."

"Well, why not? One, three, what's the difference? We'll have to add a room or two. We'll be cramped for a bit, but we'll manage, I guess." Mr. Brenner moved his wife away to the extent of his outstretched arms. He stooped low and looked directly into her hopeful face.

"You are sure about this, Meredith? You're talkin' three boys, *three* boys."

"Three boys, noisy, rambunctious, hellions. I want lots of noise, lots of noise. I want a house full of trouble. I want all three boys, if they'll have us." Mrs. Brenner nodded her head.

Jacob had already drifted back over to Mrs. Brenner's leg. He was tired and hungry. Lady Rebecca turned to the two older boys.

495

"Well, boys. Here's a home of your own if you wish it. A place the three of you can grow up together."

Peter and Paul looked at each other, then at Mr. and Mrs. Brenner They studied Jacob, and then looked at each other again. Peter shrugged his shoulders and spoke his mind.

"Sometimes ya just hafta be a man."

"I ain't scared, if Jacob thinks it's a good idea, I do too!" Paul placed the entire decision upon Jacob.

"Fine with us." Peter grinned sheepishly.

"Then it's settled," exclaimed Mr. Brenner. He looked up to Lady Rebecca. "That's that! Now, we must be going. It's later than I like already, so what do I do?"

"Follow me." Lady Rebecca turned away.

Mr. Brenner signed some papers, leaving his address and other pertinent information, then headed toward the door. He held it open for his wife who again clutched Jacob in her arms, and was now being circled by Peter and Paul.

He followed them out, but stopped suddenly at the sound of the closing latch behind him.

"Meredith?"

Mrs. Brenner turned back to face him. They exchanged words, and he left her side. He pulled the door open and looked across the room at the last remaining orphan. She sat there quietly swinging her legs, crowned in that disheveled crop of reddish brown hair, looking at him with empty eyes, having now lost all her friends. He knew there was no point in fighting fate. Sometimes ya just had to be a man.

"C'mon, Nancy May. Daddies need little girls, and your new mama's going to need a lotta help, this I'll promise ya." He winked at Lady Rebecca and held out his arm. The girl slipped off the bench without question or comment, crossed the floor, and reached for his hand. He scooped her up into his arms, and it felt like the most natural thing a man could do.

She laid her head upon his shoulder, and he left the building to catch up with Mrs. Brenner and the boys. In the shadows marking day's end, they walked in confusion—noisy and bewildered, but they walked away as a family.

In those last rays of light, Michael looked across to see the expression of contentment upon Meredith's face. Her eyes met his, and he knew the look would stay with him through the dark of night and the rest of his life. He couldn't overcome the strange ways in which God worked His will. Only somebody who had stored up so much love, as had Meredith, would be able to stand up to the task of raising three orphaned boys, three hellions to be sure. Michael shook his head in wonderment as the wagon rolled west, leaving the park and the REBECCA behind. It stopped only once so that Paul could climb back in.

FIFTY-TWO

Mr. Claussen had listened to every word spoken as though he were directing a play, and when the curtain fell, he was surely brimming with gratification. He turned to look at me, and then winked.

"I've got to go," he said.

It was as quick as that. He moved to take his leave. I followed him to the door, and we both stopped briefly to watch the Brenner family walk back to their wagon in the park. I had no idea why he had taken such an interest in either the Brenners or the Johnson boys. He said nothing more. He simply left me in Lady Rebecca's charge so he might go to address other business concerns.

497

I went back to lend a hand at cleaning up the mess left behind. The cavernous warehouse was now empty and echoed every noise we made. The sliding of tables, the moving of chairs, the rustle of papers, every noise came back to us save for one, that of conversation. We were all deep in personal thoughts. I finally broke the silence, and apparently voiced what was on every-body's mind.

"Milady?"

"Mmm-hmm."

"What do we do now?" She stopped her work for a moment to look through the warehouse and out beyond the windows of the front doors.

"I was just asking myself that same question. I was thinking of how we have spent every hour of the last six months seeing to the safe passage of the orphans. And now that we have discharged the last of our precious cargo into waiting arms, we will have to find something else to take up our time—something worthwhile."

"Are we going to stay in Boston?"

"I should think so. Christopher has made no mention of leaving, and he has been working long hours planning out the construction of his piers and warehouses. He has plenty of wares to be emptied out of the holds and moved into market. His ships have to be tended to and prepared for sailing back to Europe. There's much to be done here in Boston. I can't imagine us leaving any time soon."

"Are you going to help Mr. Claussen?"

"No, sweetheart, I don't know much about what Mr. Claussen does. I should spend my time finding a comfortable place and fixing it up for us in the city. It's nearing October, the weather is turning, and the skies are showing signs of winter. From what I have been told, our days aboard the REBECCA are numbered.

Other than that, I am not sure. I suppose over the next few months, I'll keep tabs on how our orphans are doing in their new homes. I want to be sure they are happy, especially during Christmas time. Would you like to help Mary and me as we go about looking in on them? You might enjoy it."

"Yes, Milady. I would like that very much."

The following day was to be a day of rest by order of Mr. Claussen. There was a great deal of work to be done and he wished all to relax ashore before delving into the jobs ahead. The men were paid their wages and bonuses as well, for Mr. Claussen was grateful for their good behavior before Lady Rebecca and the orphans during the course of our journey. All things said, children were still children, and the daily patience of all was regularly pushed to the limit. Special recognition was paid out to the Americans for their performance against the pirates.

True to his word, Mr. Claussen sent Britany Allison out with Gregory LaBianca to buy a ring for each one of her fingers—this, done in return for her bravery in the saving of Mr. McCurry's life. We were all upon the quarterdeck when she came back from town. She was simply beaming as she approached the ship. She held up both her hands high over her head and wiggled her fingers in the light of the sun. The rings stood out prominently for all to see.

Mr. Claussen was standing alongside us, and he waited for her to come within earshot, then he asked if she had been satisfied with the day's shopping.

"Well then, Miss Britany, I trust your venture into town was a profitable one."

"Oh, yes, sir! Do you like them?" She wiggled her fingers again, and we all laughed.

"Yes, I do, and I would say, they surely must have been made with your hands in mind."

"You are too kind, Mr. Claussen, and I am grateful, and I hope you know it's for more than just the rings. I haven't forgotten you could have thrown me overboard."

"Good Lord, I would certainly hope I couldn't!"

"Oh, no! I didn't mean it to sound like that. I just meant—."

"I'm teasing you, girl. I know precisely what you meant. Now promise me you won't sink my ship with all that silver ballast."

"You have my word on it, Mr. Claussen."

"Very well, then see to it that you have a good day."

"I will, sir. Good-bye, and thank-you so much."

"Good-bye, *Miss Rings*, and you are welcome so much."

The name stuck like glue.

FIFTY-THREE

Timothy Anderson stood at the top of the gangplank alongside eleven other Americans. The unmarried men within this group were jubilant at seeing the memories of their homeland come back to life before them. How long they had prayed for another chance to kneel and kiss the good ground of the United States.

In contrast, Timothy, along with three others, stood in somber reservation. It had been four long years since he was impressed into service for the king of England. Removed from his ship, the morning star, by force in eighteen and three, he left a simple inadequate message: 'Tell her, I love her,' and he was gone. Only four weeks before that great misdeed, he had taken the hand of his love, Christina, in marriage. He had been so much younger then, and his pleas for mercy were desperate and emotional, and also meaningless as they fell upon the pressmen's ears of indifference.

Now, having returned at last, he found himself dealt another blow. He hardly recognized the streets where he had fallen in love, the city where he had spent his youth, and the place he had called home. It was impossible to imagine any area could be altered that much in four years. The winds of change didn't just blow, they raged all about him. Could he even call this place his home anymore? He wasn't sure.

He saw all too clearly that the English stole from him more than the four years of time. How was he to replace his past? How was he to put back a building that no longer stood, a beach that had become a wharf, a meadow plowed under with pavers? These thoughts filled his head with bitterness, but they were minor losses, for other losses stood to come, profound losses powerful enough to bring him to his knees. These he could not escape, *for he had come home.*

Timothy had spent the later years trying to determine which was the better of two options: remain dead at sea, or return home to Christina. He had thought of his bride every single day of his abduction. How many times whilst in the heat of battle had he concentrated on her image to give him courage, to drive out his paralysis when drowning in fear? How many nights had he embraced his pillow, dreaming of her, holding her, kissing her, muffling his sobs so as not to be heard?

He remained passionately in love with Christina because he had been taken away from her. She was the strongest link to his past, the bridge to his real life, and his only connection to sanity. In the eye of his mind, she remained alive, pure and perfect. Now that his ordeal was over, now that he had found his way back, he had to accept the harsh probability of what he might discover. In other words, if she possessed even half the sense he had admired about her, she would be remarried, for only a fool would have thought him still alive after so many years.

He wondered if he had fooled himself. He knew dead was one thing he should have been—and maybe for the best. He had seen enough horror to last all his years. His nights were filled a plenty with visions of men's heads exploding before his eyes, their arms and legs flying about. In his dreams he waded back into the thick, sticky blood that ran freely over the gun decks. He would suddenly awake to the whine of his own voice breaking out in a mournful plea, its echo returning to his ears from a deep, horrid nightmare. Sitting up, blindly groping for some abstract salvation, he would find himself bathed in sweat, the smell of blood and death fresh in his head, the smell of fear that was impossible to cleanse from his memory.

He wished hard to suppress these thoughts, to put them a great distance behind him. He viewed the tranquil surroundings of his homeland; and he longed to sleep a night in peace, to sleep immersed in the sweet embrace of passion. He wished to work like other men, to go home, to father a child, to start a new life. How far removed these thoughts were from those aboard the man-of-war, where the only passion to be known was in the slaughter of life, where true love was only a memory found deep, deep, in the shadows of some mate's past.

Now rising before him more fearfully than all those horrors, to cast a pall of apprehension and despair upon his heart, was the memory of a young girl's face; the memory of a small delicate hand once held by his own and marked by his wedding ring.

Timothy concluded that it would be cruel and unforgivable to make Christina wait even one more hour. He could face the fact she may have become the lover of another man, but if by the narrowest possibility she had turned away her suitors, he would never forgive himself, knowing she might go on for years awaiting his return. His time at sea would then be forever, time in torment.

He believed that hers was the greatest misery, the not knowing. Waking each morning to realize her life wasn't a dream, to arise every dawn from an empty bed, to await the memory of a man who arrived at her door at the end of day. She would have no lover to hold her at night, no husband to give her the joy of children. Every dream, every hope, and every prospect for her future buried in a quagmire of uncertainty.

No, he thought. She had lived her own hell, maybe even worse than his, for at all times he understood the way things were. Whether good or bad, he knew what his life was about; he knew her life. He knew where she was, knew she was waiting, and knew what had to take place to get back to her. No matter how difficult his situation, he still had direction and purpose.

It was true she had never stared death in the face, or looked down the barrel of a Spanish cannon. Yet, maybe she had seen something worse. Maybe she had stared into a blackness darker than the bore of that baneful cannon. Could she have seen anything to brighten the void of nothingness that was her future, a place of hopelessness? She must have spent her years alone in anguish, groping blindly for the dimmest ray of hope. Timothy's heart bled for her. She had lived it long enough. He tossed a small bag of belongings over his shoulder, and then began his descent down the boarding plank onto a worrisome wharf, into a city he felt he no longer knew.

The British Navy never paid its sailors until the end of their duty. This kept them from running off. But he had run off, and the result was two months of begging and scrounging about the docks of Copenhagen pleading for a day's work so he might eat if at all possible. The docks were a haven for many in situations similar to his. Nonetheless, during this time, the name of an American captain, *James Ward*, was often mentioned in the secrecy of sympathetic circles.

By keeping an open eye and attentive ear, he and the other Americans eventually positioned themselves, whereby they were given an audience with the man they so desired to meet. It took time to prove themselves to the captain, but this they did, and soon thereafter a plan was proposed for their return to the States. He was a patient and cunning master. He chose to hide Timothy and the others in crates of flour because it made a mess of anybody who ventured too near for the purpose of inspection. He saw to it that the deck hands moving about the crates were smeared white with flour. Almost to his disbelief, he and all eleven of his comrades, those with whom he had escaped, found themselves homebound aboard the REBECCA.

Their battle with the pirates was vigorous and demanding, what with so few cannon, but it was akin to child's play when compared to battle in a ship of the line. There, a hundred men would die in a minute. One had only purpose enough to clap a torch to the cannon, leap behind a corpse, push it overboard, reload, and say another prayer with sweaty hands pointed to heaven.

Nevertheless, he and his fellow Americans were able to prove themselves in action during REBECCA's skirmish. So satisfactory did the owner, Mr. Claussen, consider their performance, he announced a reward in the making, this with a heartfelt thanks for securing the safety of the ship and its passengers. So for now, at least Timothy had some money to support him. He took his time strolling along the streets of Boston and attempted to replace his memories with this new version of home.

Four years was a long time. Yet, it wasn't a lifetime. It shouldn't have been long enough to lose a man in his own home. But Timothy was lost. Something of everything aside from possibly the street names had changed. Even that brought little comfort due to the construction of new roads. When Highland Street should have been next, it turned out to be four down.

He was mostly confused, knowing where he was but not recognizing it. It was an unsettling and occasionally painful experience. As he tried to grapple with all he saw for the first time, he passed by building after building and recalled an old sailor's lament that was often heard aboard ship when doubling back. It spoke the truth of a seafarer's predicament and helped to ease his mind.

> *Take 'er to your breast me boy an' wipe away 'er tears*
> *Ne'er speak the diff'rence in 'er made by passin' years.*
> *For change found on return'n, chills one to the bone*
> *An' suffers e'ry sailor man whose made 'is way back 'ome.*
> *Embrace 'er, boy, an' love 'er, an' kiss 'er head t' toe*
> *Tell 'er what she longs to hear, an' say it 'fore ya go.*
> *For she's the one who's waving an' waitin' with 'er 'eart*
> *An' 'elpin' stay the winds o' change, long after you depart.*

* * *

Timothy's sense of direction seldom faltered and proving it to be once again reliable, he made his way to the wooded countryside where Christina had grown up. The country roads west of the city were more according to his memory, and he soon arrived at the drive of the Lerner house, the home of his parents-in-law. After giving years of thought to this day, he believed the most prudent move would be to avoid his wife until after paying a visit to her parents. The door opened slightly.

"Yes?"

He could see Mrs. Lerner's face. Her look of curiosity was instantly replaced by one of riveted shock. Her hand rose to cover her mouth, muffling a scream that never formed.

"Timothy?" she gasped. "Bless me, Lord Jesus, have mercy!" Mrs. Lerner could scarcely believe her eyes after all the years.

"Timothy Anderson. Timothy Anderson." She repeated herself, still trying to dispel this specter of a dead man before her. He had grown older, rougher. He looked hardened.

"Oh, heavens! Forgive me, Timothy. Come in. Please, come in."

She pulled the door open briskly, and stepping back, offered him her hospitality.

"Let me look at you."

She just stared and shook her head in disbelief. Then as if snapping back to reality, she darted for him, grabbing his arm and pulling him farther into the house.

"Oh, my word. Wait 'til Jack sees you. Come, come."

She brought him into the light of the fireplace, where Mr. Lerner sat in an overstuffed chair absorbing the heat.

"Jack! Look who's here. It's our Timothy, for heaven's sake. Who could believe this after so many years?"

"Good evening, sir."

Christina's father worked to twist himself around and look up. It warmed Timothy's heart to see the old man's face again, but here too was change. His father-in-law looked weak and frail. He must have suffered some illness that got the better of him, for he was no longer the pillar of strength in Timothy's memory that guided Christina down the aisle.

"I'll be switched!" Jack coughed, and then struggled to get the stiffness out of his legs and rise to his feet. He threw out his arms to embrace Timothy, who accepted his tottering frame.

"Mercy me, I never thought I'd have time left to rest eyes upon your sorry soul again, Timothy. Let's have a look at you, boy. Tell me; are you just back from the grave or what?"

"That's how it feels, Mr. Lerner. I have been too long gone."

"That you have, son, much too long if you wish to know the truth of it. Sit, for mercy's sake. Kitten; bring us some tea for the love of God! Sit down, Timothy. Sit. Sit. Rest yourself."

Timothy took a chair, accepted his tea, and began to endure an arduous and extremely frustrating exercise in patience. It was incomprehensible that no one made mention of Christina. Her name should have been the first sound to meet his ears. She had to be involved with another, for what other reason could there be this silence? It was painful realization, but it had to be accepted. The aversion was apparent to all, and at last he dispensed with the small talk and directly addressed the unspoken issue before them.

"I must ask you to excuse me in this awkward moment, but I sense Christina has taken up with another. Rest easy, I implore, for I know her heart is good, and I am not come to criticize, only to say I understand, and wish her to be free of our vows. I have accepted our fate as God's will, but now I wish to know by your own word. Is it so, and how does she fare? I give you my oath, I shan't disrupt her new life, but scarcely a moment has passed over the years I haven't thought of her. It is time for me to put to rest this issue, and to gather up the remainder of my life so I might get on with it."

The Lerners looked at each other with concern, then relief, and finally at Timothy with compassion. They hesitated, deciding how best to begin. The silence was heartbreaking. Mrs. Lerner reached for Timothy's hand, and taking it into hers she kissed it and held it to her cheek. She looked into his eyes with love and sorrow. Slowly came the words, spoken with great care by Mrs. Lerner in a soft voice.

"Timothy, I wasn't sure if we should say anything about Christina or not. I expected you to ask about her at the doorstep, and when you didn't, I wasn't sure where your heart belonged. You may have remarried or preferred to remain alone. We weren't certain, for you didn't ask of her, but now, so that you know, let me tell you all.

"Christina waited. She waited without falter. She waited for you in anguish, in misery beyond anything I could describe." Mrs. Lerner's eyes showed the truth of what she said. She wiped

507

them. "Nothing could be done to ease her pain. She prayed endlessly for your return. Day after day, week after week, she prayed. She lost interest in everything. She shut herself in, shunned all of her friends and family, all the people who loved her. She was so depressed, you can't imagine. She ate nothing, no appetite until she grew so weak and sickly she spent most of her days in bed.

"She was bound to you by her love and the church, and unable to seek out any other for understanding or companionship. She was tormented, Timothy, unable to have your love or give up her love for you. She was in a terrible way, so forlorn. She was stranded between the worlds of the living and the dead.

"I mean, we had no idea what had become of you. Christina came to believe the worst, and spoke often of ending her life. The talk scared us half to death, and we hardly dared to leave her alone. We watched her day and night for almost two years, until she finally came to accept that you were either dead or never to return." Mrs. Lerner placed her hand over her mouth, unable to speak further, and Mr. Lerner continued.

"Timothy, the first six months, especially going through that winter, was a time of unbearable grief for us all. We worried about you. Day after day we listened for word. Oh, there were rumors and Christina poured all her hopes into each and every one, her spirit would soar only to be struck down time after time. We watched as her desire to live grew weaker by the day, and there was nothing we could do about it. I must tell you truthfully, when I saw her regain her will to go on, I was the happiest father alive. It was, as Kitten said, two long torturous years to get there.

"After the worst of it was over, her spirit improved quickly. She had suffered through her time of mourning, I suppose. She started to talk more, even got out as time went on. Eventually, she took up work in town. About a year ago, she accepted a position with Horst Biller, the owner of a flower shop near the old square on Main. One thing led to another, and after a good amount of time spent working together, the man asked for her hand." Mrs. Lerner again took up the conversation.

"It was six or seven months before she finally accepted an engagement. It wasn't that long ago, son—maybe three months back, June or the beginning of July. It wasn't easy for her, Timothy, and now…my God, what do you suppose will happen now? I can't imagine what will become of all this." Mrs. Lerner hesitated in her concern. She looked at Timothy with a frown as though she missed some important fact. "Have you seen her?"

"No. I felt it best I come to see you first. I wasn't sure…."

"I can't believe you're alive, Timothy. I am so happy to see you, but this will be difficult. This will be difficult, son." She raised her head and kissed him on the cheek. She fussed over him. "Do you understand, Timothy?" she asked. He nodded, for he understood all too well. It was a painful understanding.

"Does she love this man, Biller?" Timothy asked.

"I believe she does. Maybe not with the passion she held for you, but you were both in love for the first time then. Love takes different forms."

"It isn't just a matter of love, Timothy," Mr. Lerner injected. "She is in her twenties now, and she knows that. She isn't a maiden, but a widow in the eyes of her friends and family. They worry for her and want only the best to come her way. Mr. Biller has offered her a fine home, security, the chance for a family. He has offered her everything that was never realized after you were impressed. He is older than Christina, but she seems unbothered by the fact. I have gotten to know him, and he is a good man. He supplies many of the hotels and inns with flowers for their tables. He fills orders for the most notable weddings and funerals in the city. His establishment is successful. She has been given encouragement by all for she could do a lot worse for herself."

"Is she happy with her life now?"

"I believe it," Mr. Lerner answered.

Timothy still lived very much in the passionate throes of new love. He and Christina neither had time nor opportunity to become familiar enough with one another to see feelings wane or their relationship taken for granted. They were still discovering each other, still finding fascination in the least obvious things about themselves as man and wife, still filled with unbounded joy.

In the beginning, the old sailors were compassionate with him. They tried to ease his grief with talk and understanding. He learned from them how people, having fallen in love, who were forced apart during their time of passion often spent the remainder of their lives longing for each other. It was not an uncommon thing to see at sea. Even when remarried and parenting a house full of children, there was still a desire for a love that was never properly put to rest, a yearning almost immortal.

Timothy was sadly shaken by the news given him by the Lerners, but remained in his seat and suffered through the accounts of Christina's life, of her misery, learning what he needed to know from her parents. He asked as much as good manners would allow, and no more. Life didn't stand still for him. It didn't wait for him to return. He kept many of his thoughts to himself, for he could see that he had not been a part of these people's lives for years. His feelings were out of time, out of touch. He saw these people as his new family. He saw his father-in-law as the man who just walked his bride down the aisle.

Sadly, he sensed how they thought of him as somebody who had been away for a very long time, someone who had passed through, someone who wasn't around to experience the most tragic episode of Christina's life. He now believed it best to close the book on this chapter of his life. He looked up to the Lerners.

"I am determined to leave Christina to her new love. I have heard all you speak, and I believe this to be best for her. I could not bear to know she might suffer another day of pain. Yet, if she is to go in peace without further reason to grieve, then she must never know I have been by to see her. You both must swear to God that you shall keep my return a secret. You must promise never to reveal this meeting. I believe she might then go on with her life and find her joy. Will you do as I ask?"

"Oh! I don't know, Timothy. That is a great undertaking. It may not be that easy, maybe not for the best—." Mrs. Lerner expressed her concern, but Timothy cut her off.

"It is the only way, unless you desire to see her return to the despair of years past. You must know the truth of what I say. As your son-in-law, as Christina's husband, as the man who still loves her with all his heart, give me this promise. Swear to secrecy, and I shall as well. This conversation will never pass beyond these walls, beyond your bed, beyond our lips. Say you'll swear before God above. This is what I ask." The three sat in dead silence, fearful of the commitment they were about to make. Mrs. Lerner looked away.

"I swear."

"And you, Mr. Lerner?"

"I swear, but only because it is what you wish, Timothy. I hope you will come back and lift this burden from our hearts. Christina will go on forever wondering, and I will miss your company. I can see how much you love her, son, and I am sorry for you. I am sorry for Christina."

"I swear before God above and you that I shall make no further attempt to see my beloved wife, this for the sake of her own happiness. It is the most I can do for her, for I love her with all my heart, and so I too shall be bound to secrecy."

A pact was made and not wishing to overstay his welcome, Timothy took his leave. Over and over the words ran through his head. He struggled to justify his oath by imagining what misery Christina must have endured. He walked about town for hours in despair, finally coming to rest back at a place special in his heart. The place he asked for Christina's hand in marriage, the square at the center of town. It was one place that was too old to change, and here he sat down to cry. He could see the water of the bay, the cold, blue water that swept away his life.

He watched two people, a man and woman arguing about some unknown crisis. They were hollering back and forth, finally she threw something at him, a ring, Timothy imagined. The man quickly disappeared down the street in one direction and the woman who was seated upon one of the other benches broke into sobs, not unlike him. She arose and walked hurriedly in his direction. She glanced at him from behind her kerchief. He wondered if he ever knew her. It was hard to say, but she was certainly distressed. It may have been some type of lovers' quarrel. But then how would he know; he never had the opportunity to learn about a lovers' quarrel. The woman walked past, and he turned back to look at the bay.

As the afternoon drew to a close, Timothy made his way back to the REBECCA, and disappeared into the fo'c's'le. It was evening three days past when he found his way back above deck, squarely 'three sheets to the wind.' Hunger had driven him into the galley, where he sat down and lay across the table.

FIFTY-FOUR

Lady Rebecca had asked me to fetch some hot tea for her pleasure and this I was obliged to do. It was then, as I entered the galley that I saw at once Mr. Anderson asleep at the table. I stepped over to look at him and noticed he looked rather shabby. He smelled and was unshaven, not at all his normal self. Neither Cookie Jar nor Britany Allison was to be found, so when I returned to Milady with her tea, I made mention of Mr. Anderson and his condition. She studied me with some concern.

"Did he appear sick?"

512

"I am sure of it, Milady, for he looked terrible."

"That is odd. He was supposed to go to his wife. I have a feeling something has gone very wrong. Come with me to the galley, girls." Mary, Milady, and I left the cabin to look in on Mr. Anderson. She took one look at him and shook her head knowingly.

"I could smell it before I even laid eyes on the man. He is drunk, very drunk. I have no doubt he is in a bad way, girls. We must be patient with him. I imagine his wife has left him for another after waiting these years. She can't be blamed, for she probably gave him up for dead long ago."

Milady moved to Mr. Anderson's side at once and began to care for him. She brought him back to his senses, and the two of them talked in great depth, for his drunkenness loosened his tongue and his tears. He told her of all that happened and the oath he had made before God that crushed his desire to live. Milady listened to everything and soothed him in every manner she could. She sobered him up enough to coax him into a bath which Mary and I prepared. As he cleaned himself up, Lady Rebecca fixed him a dinner in the galley and continued to talk until late into the night.

Mary and I cleaned up after Mr. Anderson and were then free to come and go until the hour when Mary excused herself and went to bed. I was one to usually fight sleep, and so settled down in the galley alongside Lady Rebecca. I laid my head upon the table, whereby I probably beat Mary to sleep, while listening to the sounds of Milady's voice passing into the distance like a soothing lullaby.

When I next opened my eyes, it was morning and I was in my bunk, securely within Mary's embrace. Lady Rebecca was already up and about, and through the accommodation ladder hatch came the voices of her and Mr. Claussen, amplified by the empty space of berthing. I could hear her speaking with Mr. Claussen regarding Mr. Anderson and the events of the night before. Mr. Claussen said little in return. This was very unusual, and even at my young age I noticed that he didn't seem to address the issue with the same enthusiasm, as was his nature in matters close to Milady's heart. He said he would do whatever he could, but all the money in the world couldn't buy love. He reminded her how he came to her as a commoner to win her heart. Nothing more was said that passed through the deck to reach my ears.

FIFTY-FIVE

Mr. Claussen instructed Captain Ward to call on deck all hands still on board ship. It was his wish to have a large rummage sale in the town square. There was a good deal of adventure to be rid of, and in particular, twelve crates of Danish glass to be sold. There were some unclaimed stores and many other odds and ends to be cleared out the holds and his warehouses. There was much cargo to bring in from the FAIR WEATHER and his other ships in harbor. We all took a seat at his bidding and he opened a discussion on the best way to handle the sale. It was to be a grand affair. He was describing to us his thoughts in general as how to best go about setting up the event, and seeking our advice in the matter. Captain Ward was soon to leave, and so Mr. Claussen was directly taking charge of the event and the men still in his employ.

"I propose we raise a large tent into which we can remove the stores from our holds. Who might I employ for the work of moving the stores?" A number of the men raised their hands and were in turn given the task. He turned to the sailmaker.

"Now then, Steven, take a few of the men and construct a framework of spars upon which to drape a couple of main sails. See that it is enclosed about all four sides for protecting our merchandise from the weather and sticky fingers."

"Aye aye, sir."

"Willie?"

"Sir!"

"Take Dempsey with you, go to the warehouse, and procure a couple of hundred, or hundred and twenty, fathom coils of quarter-inch three-strand line. If you find something smaller in length that is fine, only make sure I get about a thousand to twelve hundred feet in total."

"Yes, sir."

"Britany Allison?"

"Yes, sir, Mr. Claussen."

"We'll need to decorate and I have a good idea how best to go about it. I will need flowers, lots of flowers, and if you ask Mr. Anderson nicely, he might escort you to a certain florist in town. I will need about five hundred flowers, any variety will do."

"Yes, sir."

Lady Rebecca and I sat on the quarterdeck steps while Mr. Claussen saw to the details of the rummage sale. Milady gave applause at his suggestion that Britany Allison seek out Mr. Anderson to escort her to the flower store. Unfortunately, Britany Allison was soon to return with news that Mr. Anderson meant no disrespect, but was obligated by oath to avoid the shop.

"Did he give you directions at least?"

"Yes, sir. And he said that he would also be willing to give a hand in the sale so long as he was not too conspicuous."

"Very well, I have something in mind for his labor. Do you know your way then?"

"Yes, sir."

"Then I will leave that job to you when the time is right."

"Rebecca, my love?"

"Yes, darling."

"I think we should occupy some of Mr. Anderson's time. He needs to get out."

"I couldn't agree more."

"I have the perfect task for him. One that will keep him well hid from view and honorable to his oath, but I will need your help."

"Wonderful! And what plan might this be? I am anxious to hear of it."

"Seeing as how he prefers to remain unnoticed, I propose that you make him up into a full-blooded buccaneer. It must be done in a proper fashion so as no one will recognize him when we are finished. I shall then isolate him inside our tent, out of sight from the public. There I will employ him to act out his part. He shall pretend to sleep, to sleep so soundly he cannot be awakened. Whosoever awakes him shall receive a special gift. It will be a good draw for a crowd eager to win something for nothing. Might I leave the task of turning him into a pirate in your hands then? Do him up splendid so he will not be found out, and this will ease his concerns and protect the man's oath to God." He looked at Milady.

"By all means. I can hardly wait! I shall make a proper and enviable tyrant of him, for it is certain that I have seen my share."

During the next two days, everybody was running about swaying up the spars, raising the tent, moving stores from the ship, and printing up sheets to announce the sale. The activity drew most of the crew back from their gallivanting and trouble-making. Now that the orphans were no longer in their care, the men returned to their more normal activities of drinking and carousing while on leave.

Lady Rebecca had set up her food tents, which filled the air with aroma and added immensely to the overall atmosphere. Soon a troupe of musicians made their appearance and a full-scale festival quickly took shape, with hawkers and storeowners setting up their own booths and greatly expanding the affair.

I went about with Mary and Milady collecting the bits of scrap and what-not needed to fashion a proper costume for Mr. Anderson. He was badly in need of distraction and merriment and turned out to be a very good and willing sport about his task. Milady knew well how to raise the spirits of the downtrodden, and after a good deal of fussing and pampering, she soon had him laughing and enjoying his new personage. Before long he was contributing to the high-spirited mood of the sale, which had a true carnival feel to it.

While undressed of his role as a pirate, Mr. Anderson stayed inside the tent for the most part, and helped Lady Rebecca and Mary with the setting up of displays and the cleaning of the Danish glass that had been repacked in crates of hay and cloth. As for me, I accomplished little, spending my time wherever my feet would carry me, in the tent, on the ship, about the square, and finally at Britany Allison's side.

I was at Britany Allison's side because that put me at Mr. Claussen's side, for he had decided to accompany her to pick up the flowers for the decorations. At least six of us entered Horst Biller's Floral Boutique. It was a goodly place, filled with fragrance and beautiful blossoms, and upon entering, it soothed the senses. Mr. Claussen stepped up to the counter. A woman greeted him.

"Sir?"

"Madam, I am looking for one Christina Anderson. Would that be you?"

"Yes, and to whom do I owe the pleasure?"

"Claussen, Christopher Claussen."

"And how might I assist you Mr. Claussen?"

"I am in need of at least a good thousand flowers for a sales promotion that is currently under way."

"A good thousand! Oh, I am sorry, sir, but that is far more than we would have in stock at such short notice."

"But I was to understand that you serviced many of the hotels and eateries on a daily basis. Surely that must not be such an outrageous request."

"If I had no obligation beforehand, I would indeed be able to meet your wish, but I must keep my commitment to my regular customers. I am sure you understand."

"What if I were to double your current price?"

"I'm sorry, sir. It would put us in bad light."

"Triple."

"Sir, please! It would be unthinkable of me to leave my regulars without their order for the day."

"Very well, ten times your daily charge. You can give them tomorrow's flowers for free." At that, Christina stood numb.

"Would you excuse me one moment, sir?"

"By all means."

A moment later an older gentleman, dressed in an apron and somewhat soiled by potting earth, appeared before us. Mr. Claussen again made his offer and this time it was accepted. He took the gentleman, a Mr. Biller, aside and then began to discuss the business of importing flowers from down south aboard his ships. He surely had Mr. Biller's ear and was quick to arrange a luncheon between Mr. Biller and Mr. Beckwith for the purpose of pursuing business interests. In the meantime, Christina was busy assembling the massive order of flowers.

Following the instructions of Mr. Claussen, most of the order was removed to the tent at the square, and the flowers were used to decorate the area. They were mostly marigolds, but stood out handsomely in this latter time of the season. They served their purpose well, successfully raising the curiosity of the passersby, who were now taking time to read the listing of goods printed on the flyers or milling about to watch the goings on.

The remainder of the flowers was used for special purpose. These were to be inserted into the strands of a length of rope. Mr. Claussen took us aside to show us how to fit the flowers into the line that Willie and Dempsey had retrieved from the warehouse and now carted behind us in a wheelbarrow. He grabbed the line in both hands and twisted it opposite to the lay. The strands separated and then at his prompting, Britany Allison inserted a stem into the opening he had formed. He then let loose the line and it closed tightly about the flower.

We started by placing one end of the line inside of the tent. As we uncoiled each couple of fakes, we inserted a flower and laid it secure within the line upon the ground. We stretched the line away from the tent, across the square, and along the street to the end of the block. It formed a long line of bright gold flowers that aroused the attention of all.

Midday was close at hand, the wares were fully prepared and ready for view, and so Lady Rebecca turned her attention to Mr. Anderson. He was done up in a dashing costume, and she was adding the final touches, making him up into a dandy buccaneer. The announcement that one lucky lady would be selected to awaken the pirate traveled quickly through the crowd.

I left Milady, and walked out of the tent to follow the line of flowers until I reached Britany Allison and her troupe, who were still fitting the flowers to the line. I offered my help, and as we reached the end of the block and turned west, I looked up. I saw Mr. Beckwith traveling toward the bay with Mr. Biller. I waved and he waved back. I returned to my work and we continued on down the street and passed by the flower shop. Britany had on her person a pocket watch that belonged to Mr. Claussen, and this she kept under close scrutiny until it read twelve o'clock sharp.

"That's enough. We're done."

Suddenly, she stopped and produced a knife, which she used to sever the line. Holding on to the end that led to the square, she walked a few steps back up the street and then entered the flower shop. We all hurried in behind her, wondering what she was up to. She stood patiently at the counter until Christina approached.

"Heavens! Don't tell me you need more flowers!" She looked mortified.

"No, ma'am, I have come for your hand. If you would hold it out, please."

"My hand?"

"Yes please. Hold it out, like this," she demonstrated. Christina was a good sport, and laughing, she did as she was asked. Immediately thereupon, Britany raised the end of the line into view, and tied it around her wrist.

"What is this? Am I being taken prisoner?"

"No, ma'am. You are the winner."

"Winner of what?" Christina looked at her fully puzzled.

"The grand prize at the rummage sale in the square. Well, let me be more specific and say you get *first* chance to win. You must follow the flowers to find it."

Christina shook her head and continued to laugh, hardly ready to accept all this nonsense.

"I can't leave the shop. Mr. Biller is out on business."

"How much business can you do? We purchased all your stock, did we not? Besides I have heard tell that the prize is well worth winning."

"Is that so?" Christina thought for a moment. "How well worth? I might find myself in trouble upon my return. And that wouldn't make me happy if I was only to find a trinket."

"It is said to be much more than a trinket. Gold, as I hear it."

"You jest!"

"That is what is said."

"I suppose I could close for a short spell, providing it is not too long a time. Mr. Biller is due back after his lunch. How far must I go?"

"Not far, just follow the flowers and you'll be there soon enough."

Christina stepped outside the door and into the street. She was astonished to see the line of flowers as it stretched the length of the block and turned right to disappear out of sight behind a building. The crowd cheered her on and walked with her; most knowing she had been picked as the winner.

As she walked, the people picked up the trailing line of flowers and carried them along as well. Then, someone from behind approached her and draped a length of the line over her shoulder. Quickly thereafter, others followed suit placing the lines about her neck or over her shoulders. Before long she appeared much like a bride with a large flowered train falling away from her frame.

She rounded the corner and broke out into laughter, feeling the embarrassment of attention paid by the crowd of onlookers now gathering in substantial numbers. She passed through their gaze feeling foolish, but still following the flowers as they led through the square eventually to disappear inside a tent. The crowd was pressing in upon the line of flowers and cheering her on. They were picking up the fallen blossoms and tossing them toward her. She continued her approach, and the attention reminded her much of the day she was married. She remembered how long ago, Timothy had asked for her hand in this very square. The thought still pained her, but she put it aside.

"This better be a good surprise." She let the memory fade.

"You have my word," Britany Allison assured her.

"And you won't give me a hint?"

"I already told you, I think it's gold. You'll know soon enough. I do know you'll have to work for it."

"What? What *kind* of work? You didn't say anything about work."

"I think you're about to find out."

We passed through the square and stopped where Mr. Claussen stood before two rows of men who flanked the line of flowers that led into the tent. He approached Christina.

"So we meet again. A small world indeed."

"I'm feeling very special, the way everyone's looking at me."

"Oh, trust me—it gets better, for you haven't won the gift yet."

"What gift?"

"Gold coins, a tidy sum indeed."

"Are you serious, sir?"

"As serious as sin, madam. And your name was?"

"Christina."

"Yes, of course, Christina. Christina from the flower shop. Well, this is the long and short of it, Christina. Inside the tent is a dastardly buccaneer. It is he who holds the precious coins. Unfortunately, he is sound asleep and generally wakes in a terrible mood if he awakes at all. It is up to you to wake him. You can do this by whispering, by speaking gently to him, or by whatever means you think best. Try to please him, and if you feel you are getting nowhere, I suggest considering a small kiss as a last measure. Such a gesture has brought much more prominent men to their knees, so I am told. However, and this is most important. Under no circumstance are you to reveal your name. If he should hear it and thereby come to know it, your riches are lost. Do you understand?"

"Yes, I believe so."

"Wonderful! Are you ready to have a go at it, Christina? Can you win this dastardly buccaneer's heart over and soften up his brutish disposition?" The crowd was going crazy. She looked around.

"It doesn't appear as though I have much choice."

"In that case, good luck, madam."

Mr. Claussen stepped aside, bowing and pointing the way. Christina started between the men who flanked the rope. Unlike the laughing, cheering crowds, they stood at attention, their faces dead serious and studied her every move. Step by step she moved through their stares. She stopped momentarily at the entrance to the tent and shook her head with a grin. A large sign overhead read 'Treasure Cove.' She entered.

I ran around to the side, and quietly stuck my head under the side drapes so I might miss nothing. Inside, Christina saw at once that the other end of the line was tied to the wrist of this buccaneer of ill repute. As predicted, he appeared sound asleep. He was slumped over in a chair; his shoulder pressed up against the back, while his head hung low and was completely covered from view by a great black hat with a spray of plumage. He sat between two chests of candy prepared for the children. He snored most outrageously. Christina giggled at the sound of him, and then worked up her courage. She cleared her throat and then warned him with a whisper.

"Oh, dastardly pirate of the seas, it is time to wake, for it is late, late in the day, and you shall miss it if you do not take care." He moved not.

"Awake, my handsome buccaneer." She tugged at the line tied around his wrist. He smacked his lips, pretending to awake.

"What wretch would take it upon herself to rouse me from my dreams? What concern is it of yours, should I miss the day? What could be better than a day spent dreaming of beautiful women and ships laden with treasure for the taking?"

"What treasure have you taken for me, good sir?"

"Why should I have taken anything for you? You are nothing to me."

"I was told you came with a special gift."

"Lies, nothing but lies. Now be off and let me sleep."

"You live up to your reputation. I was warned that you were an ornery old salt. And if that part was truth then you must have a gift as well."

"I should know whether I have a gift or not. It would be, after all, my gift."

"I am sure you do know, but do you know how much you wish to keep it?" The pirate had to think a moment.

"Gifts can only be given with feeling from the heart."

"I was told you have no heart."

"Then I have no gift."

"But you do have a gift."

"Then I must have a heart."

"A small one maybe."

"Have you a cure for small hearts?"

"Why should I care?"

"The gift."

"It would have to be a handsome gift, for such a cure."

"It is."

"Prove it."

She looked down upon the figure concealed beneath the large black hat. The pirate exposed his hand and turned it over. He unfolded his fingers to reveal five large gold coins stacked upon his palm.

"Ooooh. It is indeed!" She was honestly surprised.

"What have you?"

"A cure."

"It would have to be a handsome cure for such a gift."

"It is."

"What is it?"

"A kiss of course," Christina whispered daringly.

At once the pirate leapt to his feet, taking her into his embrace to steal away her breath and a kiss to boot. Timothy had planned to startle the whispering woman, and had fully taken her into his arms about to snare this kiss when the vision of his bride slammed into him as severely as if he had been laid low by the blow of a belaying pin. It left him reeling, stunned.

He froze for what he thought was eternity until he realized that he was so cleverly made up, even his wife had no idea of his true identity. He threw her back into his arms, rushing to absorb whatever of her he was able. By some miracle beyond his ability to comprehend, he found himself embracing his bride. With all the intensity of a man filled with passion, he lowered his face upon hers and crushed her lips against his. He would go to hell for one last embrace, one last taste of her—one last kiss.

Timothy closed his eyes, and years of emotion erupted to spill across her face. Before she was able to respond, he returned her to her feet and fell to his knees. He held out the gift of gold away from him, for beneath the cover of his hat, his tears fell to the ground.

Christina was taken aback. So intense had those few seconds been, she was unsure as to whether she should slap the man for his indiscretion or fix his heart again. He had thrown her back into his arms and before she could call out he had covered her mouth with his own. At first she was appalled. Then as if time had stopped, the emotion of his kiss moved through her like a rush of hot molasses. She melted into his arms. She had been given a taste of the passion that she had known once long ago. This may have been all for show, a carnival prank, but the effect was real enough. She was still staggering as she looked down at the crouched figure beneath the hat. She took the coins.

"What's your name, sir?" Timothy said nothing. He was sworn to secrecy by his own oath to God, an oath he was now forced to keep. He kept himself concealed behind the costume. He willed Christina away so he might release the sobs he held back in silent despair.

Dazed, and feeling a sense of vertigo, she reached carefully for the gold coins. As she grasped them, his fingers closed about hers. She waited and he soon released her. Christina turned to leave the speechless buccaneer. She looked back at him one last time, saw him crouched low to the ground beneath his large black hat, and then she exited the tent. The path she had taken was now completely covered with flowers like a carpet of gold. She looked up from the ground and was quickly brought back to reality by the roar of the crowd. At once, she held up the coins for all to see, and the people howled, crazy with delight.

Inside, Christina remained unsettled. She was unable to shake the sensation of the kiss. She looked back at the tent, but for what reason she could not fathom. She started to walk back along the carpet of flowers, and they reminded her again of her wedding, their petals now scattered about the ground waiting to be trampled underfoot as if they had just been tossed. She noticed that the men were not smiling at all. The crowds were a rowdy and indifferent lot, whereas the men that flanked the line were stoic and somber, as if to say, "Didn't you see, don't you know?"

"What is it? Why are you looking at me so?" she asked aloud.

She looked at the place where the two lines of men ended, and there stood Mr. Claussen with his hands behind his back. He looked at her in the same manner as the others.

"What is it? Why are you all looking at me that way? Is there something on my face? Am I a mess? Was I not supposed to take the coins? You told me to kiss him, or did you forget? I know he put something on my face...."

"Have you found your gift, Christina?" He interrupted her.

"Yes, but...."

She wiped her face for the first time and realized it was wet. What was this? She thought to herself. She smelled her hands. She touched her hair and felt the wetness trapped there as well. She touched it to her tongue. It was salty, like tears. She turned to look back wondering how she could have gotten wet. It must have been when he kissed her. He must have been...what... crying? Tears? She touched the moisture to her tongue again. She looked at the men and they all stared back, seeming to be sneering at her, waiting for something. What was with these men? They were such a strange lot, sailors. Sailors each and every one, just like....

"Timothy."

527

The thought crushed the breath out of her. It was then, as his name passed by her lips, that an impossible truth came to crest within her consciousness; a truth so startling, so difficult to accept that it obliterated all other thought and awareness. Christina was awake, but instantly all she perceived went distant. The light, the trees in the square, the buildings, the men's faces, all compressed into a little ball of light at the end of a long dark tunnel. Her world went silent, and she felt herself slipping away. She fought the sensation. She struggled to reach the light, and she began to regain her bearings.

Mr. Claussen had slipped his arms beneath hers, and she was literally hanging upon him as she tried to get her legs to support her. She looked at the two rows of men who were now coming back to life, but fragmented by the kaleidoscope view behind her tears. She knew they were all smiling with great satisfaction. She steadied herself. From behind, close enough to feel his breath there came a voice, a voice that moved through her body and soul.

"Have you found your gift, Christina?" She turned to face Mr. Claussen.

"It's Timothy, isn't it?" Her eyes were flooding.

"The most dangerous gift in life is advice, Christina. I have none."

Christina remained weak within his embrace and stared at him. After the shock subsided, she regained her footing and turned to stare back from whence she came. She began to walk slowly toward the tent for a second time. She was filled with apprehension and stood at the entrance, unsure if she should enter. She turned to look back at the men and saw that now their eyes were filled with encouragement, faces that nodded and prompted her to go back inside. She slipped into the tent as silently as she was able. She wasn't afraid, but she was nervous, so nervous she shook uncontrollably. Quietly, she moved closer to where Timothy sat, and once hearing his own sobs, she knew theirs was a shared grief. She picked up the line and tugged at his wrist. Timothy stood up from the chair at once, keeping his back toward the visitor who surprised him. He was embarrassed and faked a cold.

"Oh! God spare me this cold." He reached for his kerchief and wiped his eyes and nose.

"I am sorry, but my gift has been given. I beg you make yourself welcome and view the fine selection of wares from ports around the world. You shan't be disappointed, I promise."

He spread his arms out to sweep the collection on the tables within the tent, but he didn't turn around for his eyes would surely betray his lie. He began to walk toward the back of the tent in order to avoid the intruder who interrupted his despair, but he was stopped by the pull of the twine. Her voice carried to his ears a gift that only God could have given.

"I have come back for one dastardly pirate with a heart that needs a cure."

Timothy dropped his head into his hands and wept openly, for time had no measure within his heart. Years were as meaningless to his love as were tears upon the sea. He couldn't face Christina, so she went to him. She stood before him and gently persuaded him to drop his hands down and away. She began to wipe away the makeup. She began to wipe away the years and the hardness that covered his face. She looked past the lashes and the hurt, and ventured deep into the eyes of the man she knew so long ago. She pulled him down to her and their lips were washed with the union of their tears.

The crowd backed away as six white horses rounded the corner. Behind came the vermilion coach with the brilliant golden scrawl of Lady Rebecca's name. It pulled up before the tent and the driver stepped down and went inside. No one saw them as they stepped into the cabin. The door closed and it started off, parting the crowd as it moved across the square. Mr. Anderson and

Christina disappeared from view, leaving the laughter, festivities, and crowds behind at the sale. They were off to determine the rest of their lives.

I slid into the tent and peered out the opening to watch the coach depart. I found myself still for a moment; a rare thing indeed, for something of their emotion affected me. I sensed their joy and sadness. The emotions were powerful and I wondered about these feelings of love. I wondered about the way Mr. Claussen made me feel. Mostly, I was amazed at how once again, Mr. Claussen was able to fix everything that went wrong—but then, what did I expect from a man who could control the sea?

FIFTY-SIX

The novelty of reaching America was dying down as the days began to pass and the jobs were undertaken. We were becoming accustomed to our place in the harbor and learning our way about town. The REBECCA having been the most important aspect of our lives over the last three months now faded into the back-ground as she lay restrained and asleep at the dock with much of her crew departed for other places.

"Elizabeth!"

I looked up to see Captain Ward coming my way from the pilothouse. He was carrying a large muslin bag over his shoulder and set it down alongside me. A couple of mates continued past us, each carefully holding on to one end of his captain's chest, and descended to the pier. I shaded my eyes from the bright autumn sun as I looked up at the man.

"How are you today, sir?"

"I am fine. No, I am much better than fine. I feel…fabulous!"

"Are you staying for the sale or going home to Baltimore then?"

"Aye, Baltimore, my child. It's been a long time gone, and there's a warm dry place awaiting me. I'll soon be boarding a packet for Maryland so I wanted to come by and give you my farewell. It has been a pleasure knowing you, Elizabeth, and you won't be soon forgotten."

"Will I never see you again then?"

He stopped to think a moment.

"Hmmm. If the truth be told, I'm afraid I might not think all that much of farming. To make matters worse, Mr. Claussen believes I might never be able to wring the salt out of my blood. He has left open my position as captain of the REBECCA and has no plan to fill it for some time. If you stay by the water, we may meet again, who knows."

"I do."

"You do what?"

"I know we'll meet again."

"How's that?"

"If Mr. Claussen says you'll come back, you'll come back. He knows those things."

"Is that a fact?"

"Haven't you ever noticed how he always does that?"

"I have noticed he is an unusual man—a good friend. They are hard to come by."

"You'll see."

"Very well, then. Give us a kiss, my sweet. I'm about to swallow the anchor for good."

"You'll see." I assured him, then stood up and wrapped my arms around his neck. I gave him a kiss and waved as he strode down the plank.

Before Captain Ward took his leave, he saw to it that the stores were raised from the holds, inspected, and removed to various warehouses and storefronts. The stamp of the Claussen trademark identified each crate. Its design was that of a spruce, which represented the vast acreage of Claussen forests, centered behind a mast and yardarm, which appeared somewhat divine in nature—similar to a crucifix—and represented his shipping concerns.

By way of eastern sea ports, service doors, loading docks, and finally, display shelves in merchant stores, Mr. Claussen's insignia was becoming a common sight and being accepted as a symbol of high quality goods from abroad. Yet, for all its visibility, it remained no match for recognition when compared to the name REBECCA that crossed the bow of her vermilion ship and especially the door of Milady's coach in a splash of gold calligraphy.

The crew, still wary and suspicious of the vehicle, carefully removed it from the foredeck of the ship and swung it off board, lowering it onto its chassis. Its beauty drew crowds from the moment it was uncovered and assembled upon the pavement. The crowds multiplied and shifted in whatever direction it rolled. The coach was again resplendent, it being the color of the heart.

Mr. Claussen removed the good ship REBECCA from his working fleet and offered it to Milady for her work in charity. As with the coach, the REBECCA had developed a distinction among ships that made Mr. Claussen uncomfortable whenever he used it for the purpose of making money. It was too closely identified with Lady Rebecca and good will.

This act pleased Milady immensely, for she had grown attached to the REBECCA, and was always much more comfortable sleeping in her berth aboard ship as opposed to taking a temporary room at one of the hotels. This was in no small part due to the fact she had grown very fond of the crew and looked on them as family. Whenever Mr. Claussen was off on business, which was frequently, Milady always felt most at home whilst in their company.

The sailors were comfortable questioning her about her affairs, asking about her day, whether it was good or otherwise, or voicing their opinions about issues that perplexed her. It was not at all uncommon to find her talking with the men in their mess during the evening, or late at night, especially if she was unable to sleep.

"What are you looking at?"

"What are you doing, Milady?" Britany Allison asked politely.

"What does it look like I'm doing?" Lady Rebecca answered.

"Donning an apron."

"You are bright,"

"Why are you doing such a thing?"

"Because I want you to remove yours. You go into town and enjoy yourself. I plan on cooking dinner tonight for Cookie Jar and the others. You're welcome to stay if you like."

"You can't be serious, Milady!" Britany Allison's eyes grew wide.

"No? You don't think I know how to cook?"

"Oh, no, ma'am. I didn't mean to say that…."

"Britany, darling. Have no fear. I served up dinner for years. Besides I think it will be fun, and I may not be the one to clean up afterward."

I will never forget the way she chased Britany Allison off, and donned the apron to give Cookie Jar a dinner in the galley.

That night she became the matron saint of sailors far beyond the bowsprit of the REBECCA.

Britany Allison didn't go into town. She was so amazed by Lady Rebecca's gesture that she stayed to help along with Mary and me. And this was a good thing, for the dinner was then somewhat in her honor as well. After all, she had stood alongside Cookie Jar every day of the journey and worked hard to feed us all. We made sure she worked lightly and laughed a lot.

In the meantime, Cookie Jar and the rest of the crew discovered the ship was off limits, and he found himself waiting on the dock unable to board and enter his own galley. We let him get good and hungry all the while the men were poking fun at him. We kept throwing down scraps of food from the gun ports in the galley to whet his appetite. When Milady believed him to be half starved, she invited him along with the others to sit and dine.

The galleyway door was opened and Cookie Jar stepped through. His round, stubby cheeks moved to the sides and produced that great smile, which spread clean across his face.

Lady Rebecca walked up to where he stood and offered him her arm. He looked at her with some apprehension.

"Phat is diz? My vord!"

"What? You don't think I know how to cook either?"

"Oh, no, ma'am—."

"Take my arm, sir, and don't offend the chef. That would not be good."

"I agree vit all me 'eart. Never offend de chef." He grinned.

She led him from the stove, where he was sniffing about, and escorted him along the table to seat him at its center, directly before the stove. She then picked up a napkin and tied it about his neck. She reached for a bottle of fine wine, uncorked it, and poured him a glass.

"Don't move."

Lady Rebecca then invited the rest of the men to enter and take up a seat at the table. This they did, but first giving a great deal of laughter and commotion at the sight of Cookie Jar in a napkin and being spoiled. We went around filling their mugs with drink. Lady Rebecca then picked up her own glass.

"I propose a toast." She raised her glass.

"Hear, hear," the men responded.

"To lucky hooks, gifted cooks, and fairweatherly friends."

"Hey, hey!" The party drank in unison.

Lady Rebecca set down her glass and turned to her stove. She removed a pan and turned back to face Cookie Jar.

"And now to begin your dining pleasure I present whets for your appetite, the freshest prawn at market, wrapped and roasted in smoked bacon. This to be followed with a delicious bowl of peppery Mulligatawny soup, a recipe I learned from a very well known Indian chef in London. There will then be a need to cool the tongue, and what better way than with minted pears, sliced fresh and covered with a very special sour cream mix flavored with mint and sprinkled with slivers of almond and topped with sprig of mint? How am I doing so far?"

"Food fit for a king!" someone yelled out.

"You know how to do all that?" asked another. Milady looked at the man with jovial disdain.

"Do you wish to offend the cook? That would not be good."

"Oh, no, no, no, that would not be good," all agreed. They knew the worst thing a mate could do was anger the cook.

It would only leave a sailor pacing the decks looking in vain for another place to eat.

"Now that I have your mouths a waterin' and your bellies a beggin', let me say the main course will be one of roast beef and Yorkshire pudding with ample amounts of garlic sauce and gravy. And finally, for those of you who still have some room, dessert will consist of nothing short of the best Apple Charlotte money can buy and fresh coffee as strong as you like to wash it down."

The men were beside themselves. They sat momentarily speechless, but for Milady the dinner was nothing because at her core, she was a common girl who knew well how to cook and serve. She knew how to make people feel at ease, and she was at ease in the company of men, having learned their ways during her years at the West Indies Inn. If a sailor was in trouble or at all in need, Milady always sought to ease his burden by giving assistance or lending an ear. In return, I believe the men would have died in her defense, so profound was their loyalty. On this night, she made certain they left drunk, bloated, and singing songs of the sea.

FIFTY-SEVEN

Days were lost to weeks, months, and finally the whole of a year, all passing us swiftly by. I spent this time living in the limelight at Milady's side, supposedly doing her service. Whether traveling in her coach or on board the REBECCA sailing the East Coast, our life was public in every way, except for those few nights when we were far out to sea. Even then, a ship's cabin was no bastion of privacy.

The crowds were always present at our ports of call, welcoming us upon our arrival, assisting us during our stay, and waving us off when departing—all of it done in style with great pomp and ceremony. This aspect of our lives never changed. Everyone liked to rub elbows with the rich; that meant being seen in Milady's company or in the proximity of her ship. In respect to Mr. Claussen, the lifestyle was exactly the opposite, for he was never to be seen, and I found the difference quite notable.

"Milady?"

"Yes."

"Does Mr. Claussen help you with all your work?"

"Certainly. He's my backbone. Who do you think pays for all this good will?"

"I was wondering. I know he's interested in what you do, but we see so little of him."

"Do you miss him, Elizabeth?"

"Sometimes. Well…a lot of times, I guess."

"You are not alone. I miss him all the time. It seems he is too often gone. I married a man with *a vast empire*, a vast empire, and trying to pack *vast* into a cozy little cottage is not an easy task. I have learned the price to pay for the privilege of wealth and security, but he's in my heart, and he gives me spiritual support. I always hear his words of encouragement."

"Do you think it bothers Mr. Claussen that everybody knows who you are, and nobody knows him at all? Do you think he might ever get jealous?"

"No, in fact, it is quite the opposite. You see, wealth brings as many things unwanted as not into your life. Those people who come into wealth for the first time often like to make issue of their good fortune and accomplishments. They like to be seen in public and love the attention they receive. People who come from old money seldom see the attraction of their wealth because to them it's 'old hat.' They are most apt to view their wealth as a magnet that all too often attracts lunatics who are bent on making their own fame in some malicious manner. Therefore, many wealthy folks prefer to remain obscure and that makes them appear mysterious."

"Mr. Claussen is certainly very mysterious."

"You think so?"

"I should say so! Don't you think? I always wonder what it is he does. I have never seen a time when he wasn't very, very busy, but I never know what it is he does."

"Well, much of the time you are in good company, Elizabeth. I too often wonder the same things."

"Do you think it bothers him that you do what you do? I mean traveling on the REBECCA, and leaving home to go to other places the way you do?"

"Only if I'm gone when he is in town. That is why we always seem to be leaving Boston on the same day. We plan our schedules together. Otherwise, he often tells me that he is grateful for what I do. He tells me that not only do I bring his good name honor, but also by helping out others in his name, I ease his conscience. He is very proud of what I do. Sometimes it makes me sad that all the people I know have no idea that it is Christopher who is the driving force behind all the good that comes their way.

"Don't misunderstand me, I do this because I believe in what I do, and I enjoy my work with the charities. It's just that I am somewhat like the rose vine that climbs up a stone foundation. People only see the flowers I bring forth, for they are fragrant and attractive. No one notices the foundation, which supports my place in the sun. Mr. Claussen is the foundation. I could never rise without him supporting me, but he would remain forever with or without me. Do you understand? Maybe you're too young to understand. All of this is Christopher. Everything we do is Christopher, not me. This is what he wants. This is how he has always been ever since I first met him. He is very generous, Elizabeth."

I considered all Milady revealed. What she said might have been so, yet, for Lady Rebecca, working with charities came naturally. She was motivated and worked tirelessly until meeting her objectives. Milady seldom asked for help, and she gushed freely with gratitude when it was offered. I saw how these qualities endeared her to many, not only in Boston, but also in New York and Baltimore, or wherever else we dropped anchor. She never asked of others any task that she was unwilling to do herself.

It was impossible for Lady Rebecca to conceal the great wealth she commanded, especially after making a port entrance aboard one the most magnificent private ships afloat. Yet, as she had explained, she never wished to bring attention to her fortunes, nor did she ever raise herself above the stature of those in her company. All her work was for charity, and she could be found on the dock mingling with the lowest class of people, those who were homeless and destitute. At every port of call, she saw to it a food station was set up, and a hot meal made available to all in need. Lady Rebecca was wealthy to be sure, but she understood well what it meant to go without.

Even as her activities progressed, taking up more and more of her time, Milady maintained a special interest in the first group of orphans, for they were closest to her heart. She watched for word of them, and took up the challenges presented by their letters as though they were lost children writing back home to Boston. In earnest, she assisted them in their efforts to keep in touch with one another, and worked doggedly with wit and determination to establish a legitimate foundation in behalf of all the orphans she knew. She held many social functions for its promotion, and in philanthropic circles, The Rebecca Foundation was fast becoming *the soiree*.

I had stood alongside Mr. Claussen inside the emptied warehouse building on the day we arrived in Boston and watched the last of the orphans leave. I remembered being left to await Lady Rebecca and Mary, who were finishing their business with the Boston volunteers. While sitting patiently on that bench, I could have never anticipated the outcome of those fifty tiny slips of paper that Mr. Claussen had given to Lady Rebecca.

They traveled outward, concealed within the pockets of each orphan I saw walk through the warehouse doors to face the world. The slips were copied, recopied, and carried to the four corners of the country, where they firmly anchored the foundation of an extended family that began to receive and place children in homes with loving families across all seven seas, the continents, and the shifting American frontier. I wondered if Mr. Claussen had ever anticipated the outcome of his actions. I wondered if he could see into the future, if he knew what miracle would come of his gesture?

FIFTY-EIGHT

By the middle of November, eighteen and nine, we had taken up shelter against the damp cold of an early come winter. We held out as long as possible, until Lady Rebecca, Mary, and I concurred that it was simply too demanding an ordeal to further face the harsh gales and high seas from the decks of the REBECCA. Milady pushed her travels as far into the winter season as possible, whereupon Mother Nature brought down her firm hand.

Even when the ship lay protected in harbor, winter wasted no time in attacking her, sucking the heat out of her hull and leaving us to freeze. She was built a perfect vessel for keeping out water, but failed miserably at keeping out the drafts. It wasn't good practice to seal up ships, for they needed to breathe lest they rot, and so coziness soon fell away to cold and cramped discomfort. Milady and I were now ready to relinquish our cabin for more expansive and comfortable quarters in town. As it was, for reasons kept from me, Mary was already spending much of her time on shore instead of at Lady Rebecca's side, as was I.

Boston was always our place of rest, for no matter how often we traveled up and down the East Coast, it remained the port from which Mr. Claussen was building his empire. This fact alone made it home. In town, our place of residence was in the prestigious Barrington Hotel on Summers Avenue. Mr. Claussen contracted for the entire third floor, which he then completely renovated for Lady Rebecca. He left nothing to desire either in space, décor, or most important—*heat*.

The Barrington was plush, and our migration to the hotel for the winter months was always easy and welcome. Once settled in, attentions focused on the tightly scheduled and chaotic month of December with the coming of Christmas and all the expected social functions.

This year brought further confusion but for an upcoming marriage. Nevertheless, the Claussens managed to give all their heart to the celebration of my birthday. This one was to be my twelfth and Lady Rebecca considered it my last year as a girl. She made great issue of the fact, and needless to say, she was doting on me more than usual, if that could be possible. In truth, her attentions were prompted by much more than just my birthday. We had endured events—losses actually, which saddened the hearts of us all and worked to remind us how important we were to each other.

After many years of loyal and honest service, Mary, who had long been Lady Rebecca's head maiden servant, who was all of my sister, my mentor, and my friend, met a man of medicine in the city. So changed was her disposition, so cheerful was her frame of mind, that I hardly knew her as the same person. She seemed eternally intoxicated. In the space of a heartbeat, she had fallen hopelessly in love. I had fallen hopelessly into despair.

"Oh, please, please, please, Liz, don't cry. It isn't what you think. I'm not going to forget about you. That just couldn't happen. I could never forget you. We're soul mates. We traveled around the world together. We slept together on cold nights, and on hot nights, and on stormy nights. You can't forget things like that."

"It won't be the same," I protested, sobbing, as I lay in my bed, unable to look at her. She leaned over to kiss me on the back of my head.

"I know I kept this from you, and I must seem hurtful. I know I can't fully explain what has happened, but you must try to understand. You are precious to me, Liz, but God intended for girls to marry. No one knows when that will happen. It just comes out of the blue, and you're in love. Remember all you told me about Timothy Anderson and Christina, how wonderful it was? Well, that is how it is. Lady Rebecca married Mr. Claussen when she knew it was time. I agreed to marry Allen because I know it is time.

"There will come a time when you, too, will find someone special in your life. It will be a person who fills you so full of happiness that you can't bear to live another day without his love, someone who steals away your heart and soul in some mysterious and magical way. A man who stands apart from all other men in your eyes, and when that day comes, Elizabeth, you will soar when he kneels down and offers to stay by your side until death do you part." The explanation sounded empty to me and I continued to sob.

There was good reason for keeping the news of the marriage from me. I wasn't about to approve. Much to my pain, and in spite of my attempts to persuade her otherwise, she went on to marry Doctor Allen Sawyer with the blessings of both Mr. Claussen and Lady Rebecca. I had met him on a number of occasions, and found no fault with the man—he was an agreeable sort. Nevertheless, I was unable to accept the fact that I had lost my best friend on earth, a pillar in my life, to a person that Mary had only known for what seemed to me as little more than hours.

The inevitable had to happen, and Mary was relieved of her duties a week before the wedding so she might prepare without distraction. Lady Rebecca insisted that she stay with us until she felt ready to move out. And so to steady her nerves, Mary continued to help out with much of the work until the day before the ceremony. At that time she terminated her employment with the Claussens amid much fanfare, congratulations, and gifts. I stayed to myself, much of the time in my room, and despite my tears of absolute agony, she departed forever from the household and the bed we had so often shared.

Mr. Sawyer wasn't a wealthy man, but he was establishing his practice and would do well. Even so, Lady Rebecca begged of him that she might be allowed to throw the wedding for Mary. Mr. Sawyer bowed to her wishes, and the affair was grand. There were flowers and gifts galore. Milady saw to it that the church was beautifully decorated. Mr. Claussen walked Mary down the aisle and gave her hand away to Mr. Sawyer in marriage. He was beaming just as any proud father might. I was a maid of honor and stood close by the minister, Mary, and Allen throughout the ceremony. At times I cried for them, at times I cried for myself.

Afterwards, there was much celebration. I avoided approaching Mary, for strangers and well-wishers swarmed about her, and I felt in the way. Lady Rebecca had little need for my services, and on this occasion she encouraged me to run free. I knew she did this to help raise my spirits, but I sank lower as the night wore on, and I watched how happy Mary was in the company of another. I laid my head down upon the table, for I had eaten and was weary from the long day of activities. Mary slipped up from behind me and sat down.

"How are you, Liz?"

"I'm alright." I didn't raise my head.

"I haven't forgotten you. I have been watching you sitting here by yourself and it breaks my heart. I love you very much, Elizabeth. You must believe me. I know this isn't easy, but we'll work it out. I promise. As a matter of fact, may I tell you something?"

"Yes."

"I spoke with Allen, and he agreed to postpone our plans for the honeymoon so I might be present for your birthday. I hope you understand, Liz, that this is a very special time for him, and to do such a thing speaks very clearly of his feelings for you." I sat up from the table, and leaned over into Mary's embrace.

"I know. Will you thank him for me? I really am happy you will stay for my birthday, it's just that I miss you already."

"I think it would mean a great deal more if he were to hear it from you. And until we leave for our honeymoon, I will come by as often as I can and visit. I already asked Lady Rebecca if I might have you over to our place for a night or two to keep me company. What do you say to that?"

"I would like that very much."

The crowds were again tugging for her attention, and with my feelings at heart, she kissed me and left me unwillingly. It was for the best, for left to myself, I was fast asleep long before the night's activities were concluded, and I recalled nothing of my being removed from the banquet room and upstairs to my bed. I awoke late the next morning, and my first thought was how empty it seemed not having heard Mary's cheerful voice floating about.

FIFTY-NINE

Only weeks before the marriage, there occurred another event even more traumatic to the household than Mary's leaving. Its effect, especially on me, was to last a great deal longer. *Lady Rebecca suffered a miscarriage.*

It happened shortly before we moved into the Barrington from the REBECCA. The shock of the pregnancy was bad enough for me, let alone the loss. The misfortune may have been due to her staying too long aboard the ship in the cold, or the way she pressed herself to complete her work before the onset of winter. No one could know for sure, but the ordeal caused Milady much sorrow for in the worst way she wanted a child for Mr. Claussen.

Lady Rebecca was not one to express her feelings publicly, yet we all could sense her grief. It made for solemn times at our apartment. Mary handled many of Milady's affairs during this time at the request of Mr. Claussen, who stayed close by her side even though she insisted he was smothering her. Yet, only I saw her cry in moments of privacy, for she gained comfort from my nearness and never chased me away. Often, she would call me to come to her after she had been crying. I would see the redness in her eyes. She would then fuss over me as though afraid of losing me as well. It was obvious even to me that the baby's passing served to make me more a source of comfort and satiety for her needs.

There was another aspect to the pregnancy that played a pivotal role in my relationship with Lady Rebecca. Unlike her, I was too immature to hide my feelings, and in time she unraveled the reason for the change in my behavior. I had become easily agitated, moody, and distant to all. I had, in fact, become extremely jealous of the unborn child.

I was jealous from the day I discovered Milady was pregnant to the day the baby passed on. Emotionally, the idea of this new person twisted me inside out, and once this fact was discovered, it amused the Claussens enormously, for jealousy seemed so out of my character.

The matter was anything but amusing for me. It was the first time I realized how unprepared I was to find myself not the center of attention. It was a tough pill to swallow, for I had been spoiled with love and affection. I had to accept the fact that the Claussens had no obligation toward me except room and board in return for my service, should they need it. It was suddenly perfectly clear to me that I was not one of their blood. Somehow, I had lost sight of this fact while immersed in all of Milady's doting.

I harbored fears of being cast aside, which caused me much anxiety and many restless nights. They tried to ease my worry by sitting me down, offering assurances and patiently discussing their hopes for a new member to join the family. As for Lady Rebecca, my unexpected show of jealousy made me her child all the more. She seemed invigorated by my uncontrollable emotion. In her mind, I must have passed the test of allegiance, and it prompted her to forge ahead in preparing me to become a young lady.

Regardless of whatever grief I suffered, the fact remained, Lady Rebecca lost a child, and with clear conscience I could say I wished the baby no harm. Yet, for me, whether true or not, the belief that I was something other than the apple in Milady's eye left me tearfully morose, feeling forsaken and somewhat frightened. I clung to Lady Rebecca in my efforts to strengthen familial ties and became overly attentive, trying to please her in every manner possible.

I knew I had been spoiled. I knew I had taken my good fortune for granted. Time and time again having no cares, I threw caution to the wind. Now it was different. I feared for my good fortune and future. I stopped my fooling around and made a new and concerted effort to learn well my position as a maiden servant in case my life should change for the worse—in case I should be asked to leave and earn my keep elsewhere, so to make room for *their baby.*

There was no lack of opportunities to learn my skill, for our days and nights were an unending procession of engagements and social functions. I tried hard to improve myself in service, and Lady Rebecca sensed my change in attitude toward her right from the start. I was much more respectful and submissive. I was less inclined to play and wander off beyond her call. Ironically, instead of encouraging me to further myself in the perfection of my service to her, she seemed to go out of her way to make it all the more difficult.

She would go as far as leaving newly made friends unsure as to whether or not I was her daughter. When I left her side, I often heard the conversations taking place behind her back. It appeared as though I was to be the one and only quirk, the flaw others sought with passion, in an otherwise perfect socialite. I was now old enough to understand these things and to appreciate my awkward predicament. I reached a point where I was so bothered by these issues that I finally went to ask the advice of Mr. Claussen.

"What is it that troubles you, Elizabeth?"

"Well, sir, it has to do with Lady Rebecca and I wouldn't want to say anything disrespectful."

"Don't be too careful, child, or we will be here all night. It is certain you have chewed on it long before you came to see me, so let us spit it out and then we have something to work with. I won't bite, I promise."

"As you wish. Sir, please don't be angry with me. I want to say that I do know my position in your household. I am a maiden servant. Yet, I swear Lady Rebecca goes out of her way to make it impossible for me to keep my place. I try, really I do, but there are times when we are in public, times when we are in the company of others that she says and does things that confuse me or embarrass me to no end.

"She leads people on to believe I am her daughter. She doesn't go so far as to say it. But I have been asked on more than one occasion so they might know for certain if I am or I am not. I never know what to say. I mean if Milady says I am her daughter and I say I am not, one of us looks to be the fool or even worse the liar. I see how others look at me. I hear the things they say. I know they disapprove of how Lady Rebecca pampers me, and I swear I don't encourage such a thing. She just does it." I stopped short. "What? What? You don't believe me?"

Mr. Claussen started smiling almost as soon as I opened my mouth; and before I finished speaking my piece, he was shaking his head and laughing aloud.

"My dearest Elizabeth, as of late, you worry, worry, worry. I never doubted you to be anything short of one of Rebecca's own since the day I saw you first set foot into her life. Though, what I see most now is the change in you since the baby. I have done my best to assure you, Elizabeth that we care a great deal for you, that we love you with all our heart, and you will always have a home with us as long as you choose to stay. I am sorry you are burdened with so many fears."

"I have no fears—."

"No, Elizabeth. That is not true. They have been visible in your eyes since Rebecca announced she was with child. We both saw it clearly then, and we both still see it clearly now. Tell me, what happened to the sparkle in your eyes and the bounce in your step? Where did it go? Where is all that naughtiness and self-assuredness that endeared you to us? You don't draw; you don't play. It's been ages since I last heard you laugh with abandon. Yes, you do have fears, Elizabeth, but I hope that in short time you will see they are baseless and you might return as your old self.

"In the meantime, know that Rebecca gains much contentment by fussing over you the way she does. If you wish to make me happy, if you wish to make us both happy, then do as I say. Let her have her way, and if she dotes on you and embarrasses you, as you say she does, know it is what she needs to learn the ways of a mother. Remember that she never had the benefit of learning by example. She was never taught in a proper way and has no one with whom she might confer. She is learning for herself and you are her teacher."

"Yes, Milord." I lowered my eyes, feeling ashamed for not recognizing Milady's needs as they were.

"Come here to me, Elizabeth."

I walked over to him. He took me into his embrace then held me at arm's length to look into my eyes.

"You are a dear one, child, not just to Lady Rebecca, but to me as well. I hope you will cease to distance yourself from us. Don't go about building a wall to protect yourself from your fears at the expense of shutting us out. We love you, Elizabeth, and we will always care for you. Will you try to remember that?"

"Yes, Milord."

"I hope so. Now, go about your way and cheer up, for in one respect you and Rebecca are alike. When either of you are gloomy, we are all gloomy."

And so it continued on with even more frequency, Lady Rebecca dressing me up in finery entirely inappropriate. The more I questioned it, the more she shushed me. The more I resisted, the more she insisted. It regularly put me in the most awkward situations, and I was fast learning to explain it away as attire that Milady found to be of no further use, attire still usable, but not ready for the fire. I might explain that the clothes saved wear and tear on my uniforms, but it was an utterly pathetic lie coming from one of the wealthiest families in Boston.

One thing that always left me without a tongue was my being called on to explain why Lady Rebecca conversed with me as though I were one of her own instead of a maiden servant. On those occasions, I would look at them as if I was too immature to understand the difference. I felt as though I were bouncing off the walls with excuses for everything. All this I did almost daily to subdue the utter astonishment of privileged mothers and the disdain of their children, who were born into affluence and filled with despise for me and my apparel, which was coveted in every way. After all, Lady Rebecca had first pick of any clothing coming from the holds of Mr. Claussen's ships.

I did take Mr. Claussen's advice straight to heart, but I still tried to dissuade Milady from making me so noticeable. I understood it made her happy, and I could plainly see her dismay when I expressed my discomfort. At first, I thought her desperate to banish my fears of being looked down upon, for there was no end to her protective nature and her desire to coddle me to ever greater lengths.

Then I began to wonder if any of it had to do with me, or if it was the natural way in which older children watched over the young at the orphanage—if it was the way of orphans. I wondered if she was acting out a version of what she wished her mother could have been. I wondered if she knew how hard she was trying to be that mother.

There were some that were close to Milady and believed they knew what drove her to such odd behavior, but there were many more of those who chastised her publicly and privately for being unable to explain to their satisfaction the peculiarity of our relationship. Without intention, the attention paid me by Milady had a way of belittling those in the upper classes by making them appear harsh, uncaring, or cheap, by the act of keeping distance between themselves and their service classes. In the eyes of the city's elite, Lady Rebecca was setting a bad example in front of the help.

It was especially sad to know that although in my eyes Milady doted on me excessively, for her, her needs were far from satisfied. She was often seen by others pouting over the beautiful collections of children's clothes that were made here in Boston or imported from Europe aboard her own ships. She possessed the wealth to have it all, and lacked what she needed most. A child to dress and show off, one to spoil rotten by giving all those glorious things in life she had only dreamed of as an orphan. She needed a child to love and call her own, a child to give back to her the one thing she had never experienced, the one thing she certainly couldn't buy—a *Claussen* family.

SIXTY

Without question the worst consequence of Lady Rebecca's affection for me surfaced within days of my being enrolled as the only servant child to attend the private and very exclusive Academy of Knowledge and Learning. To put it more precisely, I was expected to share the same school, the same teachers, and the same classroom with the ruthless and vengeful offspring of the city's snobbish elite.

Lady Rebecca wanted nothing less than the best for me, but this desire dropped me defenseless into the realm of absolute hell. My classmates had years of experience in running amok over lessers. Their common goal in life was to cement their position as number one in everything. They had to be the richest, the smartest, the best dressed, the most handsome, the most important, and so on and on.

There was no such thing as second place other than for the losers. I was, therefore, the answer to everyone's prayer. I would always be the loser. No matter how trivial the dispute, how petty the competition, the loss, the blame, the reason for failure would always roll down the ranks of class and end up crushing the servant girl.

The taunting I was forced to endure was cruel and unending, and my humiliation was unbearable. My grades suffered, as did my self-esteem. I had been ostracized by the others, and found myself alone and drowning in a sea of self-consciousness, for I knew as well as they that I did not belong in their midst.

The brunt of this burden, dealt to me in spite of my pleas and prayers, came by way of the twin sisters, Melissa and Pricilla Jameson. Average-looking girls they were, but especially fussed over throughout Boston due to their looks being identical. Only the one could equal the other in their ambition to destroy me.

Lady Rebecca once commented, if ever two examples were needed to illustrate ruination due to the excesses of wealth and poor rearing, here would it be found twofold. Other than that, she paid them little mind, occasionally reminding me of their shortcomings and citing them as good examples of what I should not aspire to be. She recommended I observe them for their faults.

Milady viewed them as a perfect means of instilling within me the confidence she believed I needed to develop. On this one issue she was dead wrong, for I was simply no match for their mean-spiritedness. They rejoiced in laying out my agenda of misery each and every day.

I had never paid mind to my personal appearance aside from understanding the importance of washing. Milady, on the other hand, was always commenting about my countenance and pointing it out to Mr. Claussen or others. Until the beginning of my eleventh year I was oblivious to myself as a person, and I took these comments in stride, believing them to be in reference to my cleanliness.

Thereafter, I began to sense something more. I began to understand that something about me, the darkness of my eyes, the blonde of my hair, the shape of my face and body, all combined to give me something special. It was something I didn't know how to decipher, but I was beginning to see it for myself. I was learning that I had an effect upon those around me. The Jameson sisters proved how profound that effect was to be.

"Stop it! Stop it! I say, stop this nonsense at once!"

Mr. Gaines was furious. The class settled down. He would never threaten the children with the switch as one might expect because he would have been promptly relieved of his position as headmaster. Not one parent of these children would accept fault lying with their own. Mr. Gaines would never win, and so the class was often uncontrollable, for no measure of punishment was ever carried out or completed.

My only escape from torment was to stay to myself in order to avoid ridicule and the brutal harassment that came my way, but on one score it was impossible. The boys in the class, who outnumbered the girls three to one, fancied me. It wasn't as noble as the attractions of gentlemen toward ladies. Instead, it was an issue of upper-class males taking advantage of a servant girl. The boys were attracted to me, and held no reservation in chasing me down to grope at me, to feel my breasts or worse. One at a time or in number, there was no one to restrain them, and so the attacks were often quite vicious and utterly humiliating. They called me their little harlot.

During the melee now ended, just such an attack was well under way, and I was fighting it off, hopelessly outnumbered and defending myself with teeth and nails. The fact that the boys were huddled over me like dogs about their quarry fully caught the attention of the Jameson twins and their friends. The attention I feared from the boys was the same attention the other girls longed to experience. In their arrogant stupidity, they filled themselves with envy.

When Mr. Gaines brought some sense of order back to the class, the boys left me huddled in a corner at the back of the room upon the floor. I was a mess, and being that I was the last to get to my feet and return to my desk, I drew the full attention of the headmaster.

"All right! All right! Who started this? I mean to know at once, who started this outrage?"

He drove his finger into the desk with each syllable spoken. Mr. Gaines paced back and forth in front of the class, staring at us as though he was about to actually throttle someone.

"I am waiting for an answer, and I will wait all the day if need be. In the meantime you will write out your multiplication tables one hundred times each until I get my answer. This means no recess, so you should have plenty of time to think about it."

There was a rush of protest and complaint and then a voice rang out clearly above the rest.

"She did." The entire class turned to follow the finger of Melissa Jameson as it pointed toward me. "She lifted her skirt in front of the boys and they went crazy. I was so embarrassed for her I nearly fainted."

"It's true!" Pricilla Jameson added to her sister's insult and lies. "I screamed because I thought Melissa was falling to the floor. I think maybe when I screamed it caused the other girls to scream as well. It was definitely her fault. She's nothing more than a servant tramp. We all know it. Everyone knows it. She doesn't belong here. Even she will admit as much." The other girls, struggling to maintain their positions in the Jameson hierarchy, agreed wholeheartedly.

"The wench bit me!" Jim Parker raised his bruised hand above his head. The class gasped at the sight of the black and blue ring of teeth marks I had delivered during my defense.

"She scratched me. Look at my face!" William Colby stood up and turned about so Mr. Gaines could see the bloody streaks across his cheek and nose.

"She teases us at every chance," another boy chimed in.

"She's disgusting. She shouldn't be in this class. It brings shame upon us all." Betty Jurgensen offered her own opinion of me, and then shook her head.

"Alright, alright! Class is dismissed for recess. Everyone outside, except for you, Miss Dennison—*you stay put.*"

The class rose to their feet, grabbed their coats, and amid a current of giggles and snickers, rushed outside to discuss my prospects with Mr. Gaines.

He started back toward me, and took up a seat in the chair next to mine. I felt the heat of embarrassment and trouble wafting about my face. It was a hopeless situation, leaving me with hollow excuses and nothing but despair. Mr. Gaines said nothing until the last person exited, closing the door behind. As he began to speak, he didn't look my way, but instead stared out the window and across the schoolyard at the rest of the children, who were looking back toward us. It looked cold and gloomy outside beneath the gray sky.

"Elizabeth, I am going to ask you one question, and I expect the truth. Did you in fact raise your dress in front of the boys as they have said?"

I was afraid to answer the question. I knew if I said I hadn't then he would want explanations from not just me, but from the others as well until he got to the bottom of it. This would only cause me more trouble. The quickest way I could figure to end it was by saying I had and getting it over with in private.

"Yes."

He looked at me for some time.

"I am going to ask you one more time. Did you raise your dress in front of the boys as they have said?"

"Yes." I wouldn't meet his stare, but for the tears that would give away my despair.

"I see." He thought for a moment. "This presents me with a serious quandary. For never in my wildest imaginings would I have thought that a young lady such as yourself—trained to be so prim and proper, groomed to serve one of the finest ladies in Boston—a young lady far better mannered than any other student in my class—a girl who keeps to herself, a girl who takes her studies so seriously, would be the sort to raise her dress in front of a class full of boys. Do you see how it might confuse me? It is so hard to believe, so out of context. Yet, you tell me it is so." Mr. Gaines paused. He seemed to be waiting for a response, but I said nothing.

"Let me tell you what I believe. I believe that every time I turn my back, every time I leave the class, every time you go outside with the rest, every chance that comes to pass, you are made the scapegoat of this bunch. Wouldn't you agree that might be a more accurate description of the way it really is?"

I said nothing, but when I looked up at him, he must have read the truth of it in my eyes.

"It is a problem, Elizabeth, a serious problem. Have you told Mrs. Claussen that these children have it in for you?"

"Yes." I sniffed as tears and snot began to flow.

"And what does she say? She must say something."

"She says I must learn to stand on my own two feet."

"That will never do. No, ma'am, it will not. I know Lady Rebecca has had a rough life being an orphan and all, and she believes she has seen the worst of it. For the most, I have no doubt she is correct. On the other hand, I have seen what happens in orphanages when children don't mind. They get whipped good, and it comes without delay—orphans stay in line or else. Not so here! I can't touch your classmates. I can't even say they are anything less than top in their class. I have the only class in existence that has twenty '*first in their class*' students…a mathematical impossibility, yet, there it is. Have you tried in earnest to tell Mrs. Claussen how bad it can be? I am sure she would listen."

"It isn't that easy, sir. I am not her child. I don't have the liberty to throw a fuss and refuse to attend school. I am her maiden servant and I do what I am told. That is the way it is."

Mr. Gaines sat back in his chair and studied me. He might have imagined how I had made a number of attempts to try and explain what I faced at school to Lady Rebecca, but how unable I was to protest in same sort of manner that might a normal child. That is to say, by throwing a tantrum or spilling tears. I had little choice but to accept this as the wishes of my employer, for she

556

believed I needed to be strong. These days, I no longer spoke my mind as freely as I did before Milady's pregnancy and so I was trapped in a situation of such despair that only a child might comprehend, although Mr. Gaines did seem to understand.

"Between a rock and a hard place are you? I will have to give this further thought. In the meantime, I am going to move you to the front of the class. When I leave the class, I will try to send you on errands so that you are not left to their mercy. Do you understand that I am doing these things for your benefit and not as a punishment?"

"Yes, sir."

"Very well. Move your belongings into this front row desk and as soon as you are finished I'll call the class to return. Mind you, they will believe you have been moved to the front of the class as punishment."

My situation improved to a degree, but not nearly enough to be considered bearable. Even worse, these issues carried beyond the class. Rumors of my whoring and lack of morals passed about freely from child to parent, and I was faced with the reflections of these accusations in social situations as well. The whispering was always running rampant behind my back and I feared these untruths would reach Milady's ears.

SIXTY-ONE

In light of Mary's upcoming departure, all of her responsibilities were being transferred to me. This wasn't an issue with me, for I learned well her responsibilities by assisting. In fact, a staff that was headed up by the negress, Arla, was handling most of the household duties. The main difference in my new role was that I was now expected to accompany Milady about town and assist her in whatever manner was required. Up to this point only Mary's polished presentation of herself and her perfect service was used whenever Milady wished to go out.

I made few mistakes in public, but Milady was more than willing to overlook these in view of my lesser experience. And so it came to pass that on the ninth day of December, a Saturday afternoon, our coach came to stop across the street from Claudia Kettle's dress shop. It was a place the prosperous frequented when in need of attire or fittings in time for each of Boston's endless social functions. Lady Rebecca instructed me to wait for her inside the dress shop and look over the fabrics, whereupon she would come by shortly after attending to some business for Mr. Claussen.

I was about to step out onto the curb, when I caught sight of the Jameson coach parked at the dress shop entrance. I was at once filled with dread. Desperate to avoid the inevitable humiliation, I asked Lady Rebecca if she might take me along on her rounds. She overlooked my insolence, but found the suddenness of my request peculiar. Wondering about the cause of it, Milady looked outside the window, took immediate notice of the Jameson coach, suspected the truth, and hardened her resolve to see me stand up and face them.

"Elizabeth. I so rarely find fault in you, but I swear on this issue you press me to the point of exasperation. How do I make you understand that wealth does not make one a better person, not in school, not in store. You have every bit as much right to enter that dress shop as the Jameson girls. Now I insist you stop this foolishness and do as I say. I will be around shortly. Go! Go now, before I get upset."

I too, rarely found fault in Lady Rebecca. To make matters worse, I knew she honestly believed she was taking the proper action to improve my confidence. What she failed to say was although it may have been true that wealth didn't make one a better person, it was also true that wealth didn't prevent one from becoming a vile, conniving brat. Either way, it was not my place to argue the point, and so feeling hopelessly abandoned, I stepped out onto the street under the stare of Milady's stern eye and stepped into Claudia Kettle's dress shop, utterly dispirited.

I stepped through the doorway and made it my objective to remain as invisible as possible. The layout of the store offered some service in this respect. An aisle led straight away along the east wall of the shop to the back where there was another door, undoubtedly to a storeroom. Midway along this wall, heating the central part of the dress shop stood a worthy fireplace well stoked and emitting an inviting glow that carpeted the floor and bathed the wares about it in warmth.

Opposite the east wall, forming the west side of the aisle and much to my benefit were racks, which supported the bolts of cloth at a height equal to, if not surpassing, my own. By standing just inside the door and somewhat crouched below the bolts, I could remain relatively out of sight and get a sense of warmth by watching the fire. It seemed to me a reasonably secure station for a short period of time.

Unfortunately, I had no control of the holiday traffic passing through the door. It was unending, and I at once became the only obstacle for those trying to pass by with their goods. Repeatedly, I was driven back from the door to step out of the way. On top of this, every time the door opened, the most damp and disagreeable chill imaginable would invade my person. My clothes seemed little defense against the sharp winter air, and they left me shaking miserably from head to toe in rhythm to my chattering teeth.

Unable to bear any longer the discomfort put to me and the inconvenience I presented to others, I determined to remove myself from the door in favor of the fireplace. Even so, I was reluctant and took great pains to keep my back to the patrons and fitters whilst seeking the warmth of the coals. This I did with utmost intent, so as to escape the curse of the Jameson girls.

Fortunately, they were engrossed in picking out ribbons for their hair and dresses.

Free to stand unnoticed before the fire, I bent over so my face and outstretched hands might better absorb the comforting heat. I remained thus, silent, eyes closed to the outside world as my cheeks baked, when I was unexpectedly shoved from behind.

A howl erupted. Startled, I opened my eyes and found myself facing the Jameson girls in all their glory. I had been discovered standing smack in the middle of their hunting grounds. Pricilla appeared to be in shock at the sight of me in *her* dress shop. She stood there, wide-eyed with her mouth hung open behind a hand that seemed to be holding back a scream suffering to occur. Instead, the scream came without restraint from her sister Melissa, who was suddenly beside herself and bemoaning the loss of a precious ring.

Her outcry, aside from raising the dead, aroused the attention of all in the shop. And no one more so than Mrs. Jameson, a sizable creature who instantly stampeded as if an elephant to a calf's rescue fraught with concern and trumpeting all manner of questions.

"What is it, Melissa? What is it, darling? Are you hurt?"

"My ring! My ring! Oh, momma, my precious ring is lost! Melissa turned to me. "You fool! You bumbling idiot! It's all your fault!"

"What in the name of heaven is going on here? Who is this brat? What have you done to my daughter! Come here, Melissa. What on earth has happened?"

Mrs. Jameson drew Melissa at once into her embrace, coddling her while staring at me with distrust and utter disdain. I was immediately in the wrong.

"She's that servant girl I told you about, that harlot, Elizabeth Dennison!" The three glared at me. "If your butt hadn't been sticking out in the middle of the aisle this never would have happened. Look, I've lost my ring, momma." Melissa held out her hand.

"The one I gave you for your birthday?" Mrs. Jameson fumed.

"I don't have it." I spouted at once. "I don't have it. It must be here somewhere." I began to look about the floor, but to no avail.

"I think it's in there." Melissa pointed toward the coal bin.

Mrs. Jameson, looking quite put out over the loss of an expensive ring, turned to me and spoke in a rude and reprimanding manner.

"I've heard about you—you and the boys. You are trouble, girl. A bad example for all. It is beyond me how someone, who is so obviously a servant and surely instructed in proper manners and respect, can be so utterly clumsy and inconsiderate. What have you to say for yourself, girl? I'm afraid Lady Rebecca has spoiled you. Leading you to believe you are something other, something above your station. Do you not see the mess you have caused? Do you plan to just stand there idle, or are you going to do the duty expected of a servant and find that ring?"

"I'll search for it at once, madam."

I dropped to my knees. In all conscience, although I certainly doubted it, I had to admit that I could have been partially to blame for this mishap. To some extent, I had been blocking the aisle. And so, wishing only to quiet this embarrassing ordeal as quickly as possible before Lady Rebecca arrived, I offered no objection and stooped down at once to begin removing the contents of the coal bin with care.

Mrs. Jameson, being satisfied with both my attention to the matter and my show of service to her and her daughters, returned to her business with the fitters, leaving me to search for the ring under the vengeful supervision of Melissa and Pricilla.

It was impossible not to blacken myself in the filth, no matter how carefully I removed pieces of wood, kindling and coal. The soot and coal dust stuck like glue to my cuffs. I could only imagine what was in store for me when Milady took site of my sleeves. No sooner had this thought occurred when my wrap slipped off my shoulder and dropped straight into the bin. It was soiled to the point of ruin. I sighed with despair. If this wasn't bad enough, Lady Rebecca would be here any minute and things could only get worse.

I went on looking in earnest for the smallest glitter, searching and unaware of hands that now, instead of capping screams of surprise, concealed squeals of laughter and delight, for I had been duped, hooked and drawn into their prank with the ignorance of a simpleton.

Having removed all the contents of the bin, all being stacked to the side, I placed both my hands into the dust and sifted it with my fingers. Back and forth, I strained the black flour-like residue, but to my dismay, I found no ring buried in the bin.

"You can rest your fears, Melissa. There is nothing to be found in this mess. It must be elsewhere…somewhere about us on the floorboards or under the racks. I don't know where, but it surely is not in this bin."

"Are you certain? You best be sure. I insist you look one more time and be convinced."

To avoid further confrontation, I complied. I looked deeper into the bin so to be absolutely positive no ring was there to be found. It was the next act, inflicted on a whim, which gave testimony to the truly evil nature that possessed the Jameson girls. For it was just then whilst I stared hard into the bin for the slightest hint of jewelry, that Pricilla offered her malevolent assistance by reaching over my head for the fireplace bellows and with it directed a forceful blast of air purposely into the bin of filth. Her intention, no doubt, was to blacken my coat and dress in great style so the two of them might have a good laugh now and later in school at my expense. This impulsive action on her part was done without the slightest thought or consideration to what harm might come of it.

And so, with eyes opened wide for one last look, I received the blow. The bin literally exploded in my face. The force of the bellows blast peppered me severely. It came as a spray of coal dust, ash, sand, and splinters, and I felt as though I had fallen face first into a bed of thistle. My face, my hair, my dress were all completely covered in filth, my mouth was filled with the black mess, but by far the worst—was the *pain* in my eyes. It was immediate and excruciating. The mere act of blinking only served to drive the sand and splinters deeper into my sockets.

Amid a roar of laughter, I sprang backwards onto my feet in a futile attempt to escape my injury and plowed blindly into the racks of material behind me. The racks were upset and bolts of unraveling cloth were sent flying in every direction causing confusion and disarray. I tripped over one of the bolts and landed on my back atop the heap, choking, thrashing, and scrambling for a way out of the pain.

"My God! What is going on! Look at what you've done! Oh, heavens, oh, heavens, what has happened here? Girls! Girls! Stop! My god, what have you done?"

Mrs. Kettle screamed out in disbelief upon seeing the racks tipping over and the bolts falling about every which way. She watched in despair as the dense black cloud of coal dust began to settle upon a fortune in imported fabrics now rolling out like carpet runners across the slop covered floor. Nothing was spared, not the fabrics still standing, not the cutting tables, not the patterns pinned out or finished pieces awaiting pick-up, *nothing*.

Writhing in pain, blind and unable to see this cloud of dust, I thought Mrs. Kettle to be screaming in fear for my eyes. This in turn panicked me into believing with all my heart that I should never see again. So terrified was I that after finding my feet, I spun about in reckless circles until finding the wall whereupon

I groped hurriedly along the aisle, knocking over most of what I encountered.

In time that seemed forever, I found the front door and bolted outside in a panic. I startled the crowd of holiday shoppers and merchants who happened to be walking the street as I screamed hysterically for my mother.

"Mum! Mum! Maaaauummm!" I screamed.

I had burst through the doorway, legs all a tangle, and plowed blindly through the shoppers until I twisted my ankle on the curbstone and landed face down in the bitter cold slush of the gutter. I laid there soaked to the bone through coat, wrap and dress, covered face to foot with coal dust and mud.

Coal was not a common item in most places, and my blackened portrait must have raised many a brow. My tears flowed freely leaving tracks of exposed flesh while trying in vain to rid me of my pain and the consequences of the Jameson's prank.

My screams were as endless as was my pain. I was in agony. I raised myself to my hands and knees, but could do nothing more than bawl out tears and saliva. I could not open, close, nor bear to touch my eyes. Totally blind, I reached about me but could make nothing of direction. The incident happened so fast and was so shocking a scene that the crowd of shoppers and passersby stood over me momentarily stupefied and unsure of what to do before moving in my behalf.

I perceived a commotion about me when suddenly my miserable self was swept up from the snow and slush by the arms of Mr. Claussen. I heard Milady's voice at his side. I then cried out again, this time in a different tone, no longer shrieks of terror, but sobs of despair now that I had been rescued.

In haste, Mr. Claussen carried me to the coach. Inside, in spite of my filth, he held me firmly within his embrace. My soaked and sooty dress soiled his suit as he tried his best to calm me. Lady Rebecca removed her shawl and covered my trembling frame. It was impossible for me to give account of what had taken place, but for the unrelenting pain in my eyes and the need to cry it away.

I was brought directly to Mary and Doctor Sawyer. She felt my misery as if it were her own. She watched over the gentle hands of her husband as he worked to bring me relief through repeated washings and drops. Finally, in spite of my blood red and badly swollen eyes, which I could not move, touch, nor focus for the life of me, I was at last convinced that I would not go blind. I believed Mary when she said that it would pass. I was thoroughly exhausted, and now being warmed and settled by medication and a mug of hot chocolate, I was able to give account of my misfortune to Mary as she soothed me. How I missed her.

As I spoke, Lady Rebecca stood by listening, but uttered not a word. My eyes were bandaged and so I saw nothing of her approach. She cupped my face in her hands, and then delivered a kiss to my forehead, which she held for some time. That was rare, for as much as Lady Rebecca fussed over me in general, she seemed to draw the line at any prolonged show of physical affection. There might be the occasional hug, but only very rarely did she give me anything more than a light peck on the cheek or the back of the head.

I always knew she wished different, wanting to smother me with kisses and affectionate embraces, but I believed she felt it not in her rightful place. She may have viewed it as the privilege of my mother and feared I might think her overstepping her bounds. I was unable to see Lady Rebecca's face, but heard tell that he expression might well have been Satan's setting out to seal someone's fate.

Although I had given no thought whatsoever to calling out for "mum," as a fearful child might do naturally, Lady Rebecca heard it as clearly as if it had sounded around the world, and she took it straight to heart. I cannot stress sufficiently enough the degree to which this was so.

SIXTY-TWO

My birthday was celebrated on December the 16th. From the day of the Jameson incident to the anniversary of my birth, no mention of my public humiliation was ever made by Lady Rebecca. Nevertheless, her attitude toward me had changed dramatically; it had become pensive and at times seemed wary. And this mood was most evident on the morning of my birthday, when she took me aside and requested I sit for a spell to talk. She thought momentarily before speaking, as if to pick and choose her words with care.

"How are your eyes today?"

"Fine, Milady."

"They are still red. You haven't been rubbing them again, have you?"

"I try not to Milady."

"Hmmm," she paused. "Elizabeth, I must ask something of you."

"Yes, Milady?"

"This is delicate. Please understand."

"Yes, Milady."

She hesitated, carefully preparing herself.

"The day you ran from Kettle's dress shop…you called out to 'mum.' Who were you calling to, Elizabeth?"

What kind of question was this? At first I only looked at her with a blank stare as I thought about what she asked. It was a most unusual question, but an interesting one indeed! To who had I called out? I loved my mother, and I missed her dearly. But to think on it, was I calling to her on that day? No, I didn't believe I was. I felt myself calling out for the hands of comfort, the embrace of security. Mulling this over, I determined it could only have been Lady Rebecca. This revelation made me very emotional, for it seemed to imply a certain departure from my mother, and a new and unrealized connection between Lady Rebecca and myself that ran much deeper than I had supposed. The answer was clear.

"You, Milady," I whispered.

Lady Rebecca's eyes teared at once, which brought emotion to my own. She pulled me close to her breast. I had given her another piece of the bond she so dearly desired. She held me in her embrace and kissed me again and again with enormous affection, a show of emotion that must have been pent up inside of her for ages. She rocked me gently, at first unable to speak with an unbroken voice.

"I love you so very much, Elizabeth. I can never express how I hurt for you that day. I cried all the night. I fear I may never have children, but if I should, know in your heart there is no need to be jealous. I could never love you less than my own. If you wish to call me mum, it would make me very happy."

I wrapped my arms around her and held her tight. I had grown old enough to understand. Then, giving me a smile that signaled an end to her sullen mood, she leaned back, wiped away her tears and then my own. She held me tightly by my shoulders.

"As for your birthday...." She presented me with a brightly wrapped box. "It is special. You will love it, I promise. Shake it if you wish, but you cannot open it until Christopher is here to see."

I shook it. I listened to it. I felt of its weight. At last, I set the gift upon the side table to await Mr. Claussen, but I passed by it many times during the afternoon wondering what it might contain.

Mary came over for my birthday with her husband as she had promised. I always thrilled to see Mary and found that I was slowly taking to her Allen as well. I could see how happy he made her. He was smart enough to pay me lots of attention, thereby winning me over, and this did a lot to help me give her up.

No time was wasted in formalities, and as soon as Mr. Claussen removed his coat, Arla, who ran the Claussen household, waltzed into our midst all smiles and swung a giant cake into view.

"Oh, mah, Liz'bit, look a' choo! You so grown up 'n all. Such a pretty thin'. Ain' tha' jez so, Massa Clauzzen. You tell 'er, go on now you jez tell 'er, ain' it so." She giggled away as she set the cake upon the table, and called us all to sit.

"Two, tree, fo, fi, six, sayin, eight, nahn, tain, lebin' and twel. Das a big girl, yez suh, looky all dem canl's. Mmm, mmm, ain' she sumpin' fo sho!"

Arla placed all the candles upon the cake before me, and then as she lit them the lights went dim in the room. Only the warm glow of faces I loved surrounded me.

"Make a wish, Liz," Mary prodded me.

"Make it a good one, sweetheart."

"Yes, Milady." I closed my eyes and wished only that I could be as happy as this forever. I opened my eyes and blew with all my might. I got them all but one, and that one was overlooked by all. Everyone applauded and the cake was promptly cut, with a portion accepted by all, including the servants and staff. Lady Claussen and Mary brought the gifts, and I began opening them, saving the one special gift for last.

The moment of truth arrived. I was anxious and nervously peeled away the decorative paper, which covered an expensive-looking dark blue box. I flipped open the cover. I stopped breathing. A golden bracelet brushed with diamonds and accented in small red gemstones, quite possibly rubies, lay nestled in a blanket of soft royal blue velvet. I just stared. I was speechless. Who could imagine a maiden servant being given such a gift? Even the Jameson girls would have been amazed. I couldn't accept it, but neither could I take my eyes off it. It was spell-binding. I knew Mr. Claussen must have secretly objected, for it must have been worth a king's ransom. I was afraid to accept it. I was embarrassed.

"Milady...I...I...I just can't accept it," I stammered.

In all honesty I was afraid to accept the gift in fear of Mr. Claussen finding me the cause for such expense in Lady Rebecca's life.

"Go on, Elizabeth, pick it up, it's yours, happy birthday." Lady Rebecca was all aglow.

"Milady, I...I...I...."

I began to back away as though it would burn my fingers. I was falling all over myself again, unsure of my footing. Where do I stop at this changing line between maiden servant and daughter for the sake of Milady's mothering instincts? I looked at Mary with pleading rooted in my eyes. She was confused, she didn't understand, no one understood. I looked at Mr. Claussen and only he seemed to read my thoughts. He seemed to understand my distress and addressed me very frankly.

"Go to it, Elizabeth. I wanted it for you as well. It pleases Rebecca very much, and so it does me. I went with Rebecca to pick it out. It is sort of a birthday, Christmas present combined."

Those were the words I sought above all others. Mr. Claussen had given me the assurance that I needed to hear.

"Oh, it is so very beautiful. I don't know what to say."

"Pick it up, Elizabeth, and bring it here. Let us put it on."

Only then did I carefully retrieve it from its case. I held it up to the light. The diamonds, the gemstones, all flashing in the light, all anchored to my heart by the golden links of the chain. I rubbed it on my cheeks. It had to be real.

"If ever I was to believe in Santa, today is the day." I exclaimed as my head spun. "Do you believe in Santa, sir?" I asked as he fit the bracelet to my wrist. He held my hand a moment and looked at me as he thought how best to answer me.

"I very much believe in Santa, Elizabeth. I believe he is the spirit of good that invades our being and helps us to see the joy and benefit of helping others. Don't be fooled by this bracelet, it isn't about gifts, child, but about virtue. In any event Christmas has yet to come and you run the risk of cheating yourself out of your birthday. Happy birthday, Elizabeth."

SIXTY-THREE

The entire day had been a flurry of commotion. Lady Rebecca was holding her annual Christmas charity dinner for the benefit of the orphanages. Her events were extremely successful gatherings, for she was not interested in obtaining monies, made no move in that direction, and solicited no one, much to the amazement and delight of the city's elite. Her intent was strictly to raise awareness toward the plight of orphaned children and the needy.

Mr. Claussen had sufficient wealth to fund the foundation without bother, but money could not guarantee that a loving home awaited a destitute child. This had to be found and proved out. The process required the help of many. So much the better if these observers were people of influence and persuasion, and secure enough in their lives that they could enter the homes of others, evaluate the care a child received, and not be easily intimidated when things went awry.

Everybody who was anybody attended these gala affairs. The women never passed up a social function, especially one so attuned to their hearts. The men relished the opportunity to establish new business contacts and rekindle old relationships that had fallen by the wayside. More business could be generated in one night by scribbling upon the tablecloths than could be accomplished in a month or more of board meetings.

This year there were five guest speakers. They would all be addressing the issues of placing orphans in homes. One speaker was to be very special. So special in fact, that Lady Rebecca was telling no one his or her identity. The speaker would be the honored guest, and would speak after the dinner. It was a fantastic ploy to get everybody talking and determined to attend the banquet, if for no other reason than to satisfy his or her curiosity. These dinners were always held in a private banquet room on the second floor at the Barrington. The Claussens occupied the floor above.

Evening was quickly approaching, and I had my work cut out for me. I may have been young, but I spent much time in service to the Claussens, and being tutored under the direct supervision of Mary for the past couple of years made me well versed in etiquette and proper presentation at these gala affairs.

I assisted in the setting of the tables and all the accompanying arrangements. Mary oversaw all the details to meet Lady Rebecca's wishes, and for the first time ever, I was assigned my own table to serve. It was directly in front of the head table, and close to Lady Rebecca and Mr. Claussen. I was never one to brag, for fear of Milady's retribution, but I couldn't help feeling proud, I being so close to the people that sponsored such an event.

The time was now at hand to place the placards that specified the seating arrangements. I was handed mine with a chart, and I began to read the names of my guests.

I was stunned.

I read through them again, and then again, and I prayed there had been some mistake, but I knew better. The Parkers, the

Jurgensens, the Colbys, the Jamesons, slowly one after another, I flipped through the cards.

"Elizabeth?" I spun around. Mary was looking at me.

"Is everything alright?"

"Yes."

"Are you sure?"

"Yes." I couldn't look at her. I knew she would sense my distress.

"You don't look like everything is alright. Is something bothering you, Liz? Are you a little nervous?"

"Yes, yes. I…I think I am just worried. I hope it goes well and I don't make a fool of myself." Inside I was trembling at the thought of the names.

"About the names?" Mary continued. Her words plunged into me like me like a dagger.

"Did you see the names?" I exclaimed, my face revealing my disbelief. "Of all the people in attendance…. Why do I have these? Lady Rebecca knows how I feel about these people. I hate these people. Listen…." I held up the cards and began to make another pass. "Parkers, Jurgensens, Colbys, Jamesons, Parsons, Steffes, Reitbergs…. Do you know who these people are?" My voice was breaking with tension.

"Of course, I know. They are the richest of the rich. You should be proud that Lady Rebecca entrusts you to see over them."

"Don't do that, Mary!" I was angered. "Please don't do that. You know who they are. You know what I have to go through with these people every day of my life. They live to torment me. The Parkers, the Colbys, the Parson boys! They grope at me every chance they get, which is pretty much every chance they want. They pinch me wherever they please, after all, I am their harlot, *remember?* Or did you forget how much that hurt?

"The Jamesons and the Jurgensen girls! Oh God, you should hear how they love to recount the day at the dress shop, and point how incredibly stupid I appeared 'crying like a baby' and, 'crawling around on my hands and knees in the street.' It is thrown in my face day after day after day. I am nothing to them, Mary. A servant, that is what I am, not a classmate—a servant!"

I tried to settle myself down, but I continued to rant, which was my way when I was upset.

"I was so looking forward to tonight. I was so proud of having my own table, and now I am embarrassed. I am embarrassed to be in this uniform. I am embarrassed to be here. Can you imagine what tonight is going to be like once they discover I am to wait on them? *Hand and foot*, Mary! I will be waiting on them hand and foot. They will make sure of that, you can count on it.

"And while you tease me, try to remember it is I who has to go back to school and face these people, Mary, not you, not Lady Rebecca, not anybody else, just me. I can't even bear to think of it. They expect me to wait on them in class as it is. Can you imagine what it will be like once I've done it for real? *Elizabeth, would you bring me some water? Elizabeth, would you pick up my pencil? Elizabeth, would you do it now please, I'm waiting.*

"Oh, Mary! Isn't there something for me on the other side of the room, something as far away from this table as possible? I'll work twice as hard. I'll do whatever I'm told. I just don't want this table, not now, not tonight, not ever."

"Listen to me, Elizabeth. I know you pay attention to what I say, and I try to say only what I believe is best for you, because I love you dearly. I want you to know I was there when Lady Rebecca laid out the seating arrangements. She was very specific about whom was to sit at the first tables, and she was very aware of who you were to serve. I have no idea for what purpose she has planned things as they are, but she is no fool. She has her reasons, Liz."

"I know her reasons, Mary. She thinks I am good at this. She wants me to work with the most affluent. I know all that. But what she really wants is something else. She wants me to stand up to the world. She wants me to face all my classmates as a servant and believe with all my heart that I am equal."

"Can you do that?"

"No, I can't do that! I am not equal! It didn't take me long to figure that out in school. I can tell you this, Mary. If Lady Rebecca was still an orphan in London, she wouldn't think she was equal either."

I looked up at the head table, and I saw Lady Rebecca staring at us. The morbid fear that she might have overheard me frightened me terrible.

"She's watching us, Mary. I have to set my table."

Mary pretended to show me a few things, and then walked away, leaving me to my thoughts. My table was certainly reserved by design, an exclusive gathering of the families whose children I despised. The scenes played over and over in my head. I had endured it all, and I had suffered beyond Milady's ability to understand.

Now, it would be my duty to wait upon these tormentors for real. This time I *was* their servant. I flushed at the thought of showing myself. I felt silly in my attire. I felt the heat of my crimson face. My heart raced. I moaned aloud as I choked on the thought of it all. I just wanted to leave. I so looked forward to this night, and instantly she made it a burden unbearable, a nightmare certain to be filled with grief and humiliation.

I looked up toward the head table again, and out of the corner of my eye I could see that Lady Rebecca was still watching me. I turned away at once and moved along. As I set the placards in their place I saw before me the unmistakable lesson that Lady Rebecca wished to impress upon me. Stand up to the world,

Elizabeth! It was the hardest lesson she forced upon me with her love.

"Why?" I asked myself aloud, stamping my foot down.

'Oh, please! Milady,' I thought, *'why must I go through this?'* It was pointless for me to try and evade the inescapable. I could only resign myself to this night over which I had no control. I took a deep breath and determined if it had to be, so be it. I would stand up to their abuse. I would show Lady Rebecca that I had what was needed inside. I would not let her down; no matter what insult I should receive. This was my first time out, the event was prestigious, and I would bite my lip, smile, and be the best table maiden ever. I tried hard to convince myself I could perform this noble goal.

The silence of the room was abruptly abandoned for the heralding of guests and as the doors swung open they washed in, swimming in waves of laughter and jubilation. Still very much upset, I felt overwhelmed by the inrush of the crowd and I stepped quickly into the kitchen. From there I watched my table. My heart pounded.

This elite crowd was mingling, but working their way to the places reserved in their name. I hardly noticed the grown-up faces, all staunch and uppity, for my concerns lay with the finer brat-like features of their devious offspring. I took sorrowful notice as the parents began to rearrange the chairs, in order to seat the children in a group at one end of the tables. I saw Melissa and Pricilla dictating which boys would be allowed to sit next to them. I was overcome with dread.

There was no way out of this mess for me, and my time had arrived. Each of the table maids was to take a position at the table assigned to them, and there to remain in service to the guests. The room was split in two, with a wide center aisle leading from the double entry doors to the center of the head table, where Lady Rebecca and Mr. Claussen were seated, and flanked by the guest speakers. There was one empty chair between them where the honored guest speaker would be seated after dinner was cleared.

A narrow aisle was formed at each side of the room by the space left between the walls and the ends of each row of tables. There were eight rows of tables per side. We were to stand facing the end of each row of tables with our backs against the wall.

> *'Proud and tall,*
> *Back to the wall,*
> *At beck and call'*

To be levied with the burden of my specific list of guests was a dismal undertaking at best, but one that I accepted. Yet, to have the adults rearrange the seating, in order to remove the children who were formerly separated from one another, and in no position to cause great harm, and then group them into a collected mob at the outside end of the table, was another matter again. They were pushed off to the side of the room and now sat positioned in force right beneath my nose precisely where I was ordered to stand at call. It was nothing short of the most wretched sort of luck, and a disheartening omen of things to come.

I could see most all of the other table maidens were at their position, and I knew within seconds, Lady Rebecca would be concerned by my late appearance. After all, seated at my table were the most affluent. I gathered up my courage and stepped out into the great room.

I felt the dead crush of self-consciousness upon my chest. My face felt like it was burning up. I walked past the head table where Lady Rebecca and Mr. Claussen were now seated at each side of the vacant guest of honor's chair. This was the signal for the room to be seated. She noticed me as I crossed over to the wall. I took up my position, *proud and tall, back to the wall.*

It was as if two separate tribes were seated before me. Farthest away, at the opposite end of the tables from me, near the center aisle, the adults roared and rollicked, as they caught up on the gossip about town and recent events past. Aside from Mrs. Jameson, who took a second look at me, the adults were oblivious to my presence and never once acknowledged me. Mrs. Jameson undoubtedly remembered that I was Lady Rebecca's servant, and recalled the ordeal at the dress shop.

The second tribe, the short ones, my classmates, for the first time ever sat dead silent, dumbstruck, mouths gaping wide open with jaws hanging to nearly reach the table. They stared directly at me in utter disbelief. I could read their minds. I could see it in their eyes. They knew at once this was too good to be true, but I refused to flinch. Any one of them was as repulsive to me as a snake with prey impaled upon its teeth. Unfortunately, I was that prey, unable to retreat, only to be drawn deeper into the bowel of this heartless horde.

It was obvious by the look of them that their shock was no less stunning than my own. The difference being that they quickly overcame theirs with thoughts of harassment, whilst I lived with the ongoing fear of what was to come. They wasted no time, for seeing they had no parents within earshot, they lit right into me. The Jameson girls started it off.

"Nice apron, Elizabeth. Is that from Mrs. Kettle's dress shop?"

"Hey, I really like what you have done with your hair. That bun is you. Really it is. You should wear it to school. Who knows—it might be the start of something new in fashion."

"Do you use arithmetic and spelling when you clean up the table scraps? I mean do you count the crumbs or something like that?"

They tried hard to outdo each other, seeing who could conjure up the most hurtful insult. Everything was directed at me personally.

577

The Jameson sisters were delirious with delight, and they were determined to use the night to their best advantage.

"I believe it's Miss Dennison, is it not?" piped Melissa.

"Wrong! It's Maiden Dennison, you idiot," snapped her sister Pricilla.

"Who are you calling an idiot? It's not me that's scraping dishes; I'll have you know. Go on; tell her, Elizabeth, who's the idiot here."

"Well, I guess it must be me, Miss Jameson," I replied. At this, they all laughed.

"*Miss* Jameson, *Miss* Jameson!"

Pricilla then spoke up. "I noticed you haven't been to school as of late. Is this due to your mishap at the Kettle's dress shop?"

"I haven't been feeling well."

It was a half-truth I spoke. It took four days for my eyes to recover, but Lady Rebecca also held me back because of the enormous amount of work and help needed in preparing for tonight's banquet.

"I can imagine. I mean crawling around in street slop is no way to stay healthy. It was such an embarrassing ordeal, groveling around like that on all fours, crying for your mother the way you were. It made me sick just watching you. All I could do was imagine facing the whole town after that scene. I felt terrible for you, but it was pretty funny, you must admit."

At that, Peter Lemming began to whine out loud, calling for his mother amidst the snickering of all. The younger children began flipping foodstuffs at me after giving in to the goading of the older classmates. I was required to remain at position against the wall with no means to defend myself. Obviously, my face was the target of choice, and I suffered everything from sticky sugar water and butter to spit.

At last I was recalled to the kitchen to bring out the food carts. As I crossed the floor, I looked at Lady Rebecca, and she at me. There was no expression of understanding upon her face. Mine was undoubtedly glowing, for I was furious, and I believed she knew it. My anger was my only defense. It was the only emotion I possessed that could bury my embarrassment.

Or so I thought. For all through the dinner and speeches, the abuse carried on. Bit by bit they chipped away at my resolve until they began to seriously erode whatever confidence I was struggling to maintain. I discovered that anger only prevailed when you believed you had the upper hand. When it became clear that it was not the case, then anger dissipated into fear, but I had nothing to fear other than my inability to escape the situation, and a loss of control over my emotions, so I was left with only one feeling, one I knew well—*humiliation*.

I was trying so very hard, but after nearly two hours of nonstop torment, my emotions were now fighting to show themselves. The last straw came when they conjured a hurtful plan, while I was at the other end of the table serving dessert to the adults. I returned to my place at the wall when Pricilla Jameson dropped her spoon under the table. Although I was obligated to pick it up, I was in no hurry, knowing I was putting myself in a compromising position by crawling under the table. Yet, I had no choice.

"Elizabeth, would you kindly remove the spoon from under my feet?"

"I will bring you a clean one from the kitchen, Miss Jameson."

"I am not in need of a spoon from the kitchen. I fear the dessert that covers the spoon on the floor will soil my shoes. Why do I even have to explain this? Why are you dawdling so? Is she not our maiden servant?"

I could see by the look in Pricilla's eyes that she was daring me not to do my job. The look in the other children's eyes told me they were all a part of whatever mischief was about to come.

It was with much distress that I stepped away from the wall and stooped down at Pricilla's side. I leaned under the table to pick up the spoon, but she kicked it out of my reach.

"Oh, I'm sorry, Elizabeth. I meant to pull it toward you. Do forgive me."

I didn't bother to answer. Instead, I got down on all fours and started after it. As soon as I did, I fell into their plan, and Brian Colby slapped me smartly across my buttocks with the flat of his hand. He then followed it with a painful pinch, which caused me to raise myself involuntarily, and I slammed my head painfully against the bottom of the table. I saw stars. The blow to the table sent all the place settings into the air and they fell back with a rattle and clamor, which was drowned out as the whole lot of brats exploded into laughter.

"See, I told you I could get her to crawl just like she did in the street! She's good at it!" Pricilla bragged, and the rest howled hysterically.

I wanted to stay under the table, for I had no self-esteem left to save. I briskly rubbed the welt at the back of my head. The first sign of tears, which I dreaded they might see, flowed into my eyes, half from pain, half from embarrassment. I squeezed them shut tightly, and forced a tear to fall to the floor from the ends of my lashes. I wiped them on my sleeves.

I waited momentarily under the table, feeling as though I had found a sanctuary beneath the draping tablecloth. I knew I had to get out from under the table, but I honestly wished to remain hidden where I was. I had my fill of chasing down trivial items. A spoon for one, then a fork for the next, then a knife for the one after that, I had my fill of having to make a thousand trips to the kitchen and back just to appease their sense of cruelty.

At least in the kitchen everyone knew what was happening to me. They tried to support me. Each time I passed the head table for another trivial need, Lady Rebecca followed me with her eyes.

Every time I returned I found the floor all about my table was littered beyond description with food—some chewed, some not. They hounded me until I looked like nothing more than a chicken coming and going with no head attached.

I was distracted from my thoughts by the commotion above me. They were complaining about my having fallen asleep. Suddenly, all at once the tablecloth raised, and a torrent of water nearly drowned me as I hid. I wasn't able to count how many glasses, but I saw two pitchers and I knew there were at least four on the table. I was soaked to the bone. I cried.

"Bring back any memories?"

Melissa yelled under the table. They laughed so hard they began snorting and grunting like pigs. They were completely out of control. Next came the sugar. If it hadn't been for the sticky sweet taste, I might just as well have been tarred and feathered. After that I was an open target for anything that could be thrown, the stickier, the sloppier—the better. I collapsed to the floor and wept.

"Elizabeth."

At last it got so far out of hand that even the adults at my table couldn't help but to notice. I couldn't see them, but I heard their mothers' voices surrounding me as they admonished the children for being so rowdy. They soon surmised something was amiss and a few took turns to look under the table at my wretched being. I lay upon the floor, but no hand was offered to assist me.

I lost the battle of wills, and I no longer cared. I closed my eyes and covered my face. I sobbed aloud. I didn't know for how long, before the sound of a spoon tinkling on a glass reached my ears. I had been too busy drowning in my misery to notice it any sooner.

"Elizabeth."

It dawned on me that the room had grown completely silent. There were no longer any children seated at the table above me. I realized that the only noise was that of my crying and the tinkling of the glass, which now was also silent. Apparently, someone had been preparing to make a speech or a toast.

The mayhem that surrounded me certainly had disrupted the evening and out of sheer embarrassment I prayed my sobs went unheard. I thought of Lady Rebecca and I was horrified to imagine what thoughts were racing through her mind. She needed to salvage the dinner. It was my first formal affair and I failed to meet the demands. I wished only to run from the room. I had tried so hard to explain to her how things were. Mr. Gaines knew because he could see it every day, but Lady Rebecca turned a deaf ear. She wouldn't have any of it.

"Elizabeth."

I tried to stop my weeping, for I thought I had heard Milady's voice calling out to me in the distance. I listened.

"Elizabeth, answer me, child."

"Ye-Yes, Milady."

"Come out from under the table." The room was dead silent.

"I c-c-can't Milady. I am a d-dreadful mess."

"I know that, Elizabeth. Come to me."

"I'm to-to-too embarrassed, Milady." I began to bawl aloud, out of control and the sound of it carried throughout the room, amplified by the silence.

"Come to me, Elizabeth."

I bit my tongue as hard as I could stand in order to make the pain worse than my humiliation. I stopped my crying and wiped my nose. I crawled out on all fours from underneath the table as I was obligated to do. I sat up upon the floor in full view of the families and children standing about the first table, and all the guests who sat at the head table with Milady and Mr. Claussen. The water was running off me and leaving a puddle to surround me. In the background, I could hear the snickers of my classmates, still unable to control their tongues.

"Stand up, child, and come to me. Come to me, Elizabeth"

I rose to my feet and walked up to the head table. The water dripped, and the filth fell from my hair and dress. I stood before her and she looked at me, then she spoke in the gentle, consoling tones of a mother's voice.

"Turn around, Elizabeth, and face your classmates. Look them straight in the eye, and never doubt yourself, my darling."

No! I thought to myself. How could she ask such a thing? Could she not see my state, my humiliation? I was a complete mess. I had been crying my eyes out. I looked like a clown, and now she wanted me to show this face to the same people that I had to sit alongside in class every day of the week. Not a chance! She couldn't possibly know even the least bit how I felt, or she wouldn't ask such a thing. Why must I go on show before these people?

"Milady, I-I can't turn around." I whispered. "P-Please don't make me turn around. I am so embarrassed; I only w-wish to die. I tried, please b-believe I t-t-tried my best. I t-tried to make you happy. I swear I did, p-please don't make me turn around, I beg." I blubbered my pleas through sobs, but still she pressed me.

"Turn about and do as I say, my love."

She was unyielding, firm, and merciless. She was cruel. It was stupid to think of asking for mercy from Lady Rebecca. She could be stone cold. It was pointless, so I wiped my eyes with my sleeve, which was also pointless, as it was soaked. I reached for a napkin from the table, and wiped away the tears and sugar stuck to my face.

I was fully numb to my situation, and accepted the fact I had no authority to keep what little dignity I might have held in reserve deep down inside. It was lost to all those about me who had the power to make and enforce their own demands. By this time, Lady Rebecca and I had gained the attention of all, save none, as we stood facing each other at the head table. She placed her hands on my face, and with her thumbs she wiped away tears that still flowed. She smiled warmly.

"I love you, Elizabeth, now turn about and face your fears. Do me this one last thing I ask and make me proud."

"Yes, Milady." *You will be proud and I will be devastated*, I thought.

What difference did it make now? I turned around. I felt my face flush worse than at any time in my life. It took every ounce of will I could muster to lift my eyes from the floor and meet the eyes of not only the first table, but all two hundred or more guests who were staring back at me unsure of what had happened. I looked out at all of them as they watched with curiosity, sitting still as rocks in a field. Not a word was whispered in the room. I felt as though I were utterly naked. My God, how I wanted to die.

I stood paralyzed, as my eyes crossed over to the classmates I so despised. I stood mindless like an actress who had forgotten her lines. My gaze was only broken briefly by a smear of golden glitter appearing almost beyond my awareness as it passed before my eyes. I saw a look of astonishment sweep through the room amid a chorus of gasps. Suddenly the coolness of precious metal touched my skin, and before I had time to fully understand, Lady Rebecca's gentle hands fastened a heavy golden necklace, adorned with diamonds and rubies about my neck. It was too much to bear. I bowed my head in anguish, my tears falling down past the jewels, while the weight of the necklace and the situation bore down heavy upon my breast. Lady Rebecca leaned over to whisper into my ear.

584

"Hold your head high, Elizabeth. You now own Boston. This is your time come to pass. Relish the feeling, my dear, and when you are satisfied go to the kitchen and clean yourself."

I raised my head, but my eyes never left the floor as I struggled to control my outbursts. My chest was heaving, and my tears streaked down my face, falling freely to my feet. I couldn't hide my emotions, but I was old enough to understand something of the power and influence of the Claussen name.

Lady Rebecca had personally placed her mark upon me before everyone who was anyone in Boston. She did so in no uncertain terms and without shame. She had made her demand for my respect as one of the most powerful and influential women on the eastern seaboard, and she defied anyone to dispute it. She had lived with the ridicule, as had I, only she had prepared well for her vengeance, and the sense of it permeated the room and all within. There were those here who had spread unkind words and untruths, and who now stood to find themselves in disfavor.

I could taste Milady's satisfaction. It was sweet, but much too powerful for someone as young as I, who was already brimming with emotions out of control. I turned, and fighting hands that desperately wished to cover my face, in haste I took my leave.

SIXTY-FOUR

I ran from the crowd, and as I burst through the servants' door to the kitchen, I was startled by a large and boisterous group of people who were awaiting my arrival. I wiped away my tears to see them all standing there cheering and congratulating me. They oohed and aahed over the necklace. The men were all joking and laughing and promptly swept me off my feet, carrying me over their heads, cajoling me into better spirits. They wiped away my tears as well, and forced me to forget the drama and torment just passed. They forced me to laugh, and relieved me of much of the emotional weight pressing upon my adolescent shoulders.

The table maidens came rushing in from the floor moments later. Most of these people I knew from my work and training, and I was not at all uncomfortable having them toss me about in good fun, or drying my face. This was not fun at my expense, not jollity to rip away at my dignity as were the jokes of my classmates. They were doing their best to raise my spirits.

I was rushed to a small dressing room and set down upon my feet. The door opened for me, and there stood Mrs. Kettle. Everything was happening so fast, swirling, changing as if by intention, and I was foundering in the currents of confusion.

"Ha-ha! There she is! Come in, Elizabeth."

"Hello, Mrs. Kettle."

"Hello, Miss Dennison."

She flashed me a huge smile, and I did as she asked. The door was pulled shut behind me. Two helpers and a fitter remained with us. They began to undo my hair and unfasten my apron. They removed my soiled clothes and prepared to bathe me.

"Oh! Oh, what is happening—?"

"How are your eyes, my darling?"

"They…they are fine. I am sorry I made such a mess of your store. I didn't mean to, I couldn't see where I was stepping, and I was only trying to find the door, and I was scared and—and… what's going on here."

"Shush! My word, Elizabeth, it is I who should apologize to you—me and my fussin' over the dust an' all. I had no idea you were in such pain. Land sakes, I never even knew you were behind all those bolts of cloth. I didn't even hear you come into the shop. I wanted you to know, I felt just terrible when I heard you were rushed to the doctor. I even came to see you, but Mrs. Claussen forbade it. I was pretty upset at first, but she begged that I respect her wishes, and she assured me she would give me ample time to offer my apology. So, tonight, I get to do just that."

"Doing what?"

I was in a whirlwind of confusion. I kept asking what was taking place but no one answered, they seemed too busy to take the time. Mrs. Kettle and her helpers removed the necklace, then washed me quickly, hair and all, to remove the residue of food and filth that still covered me. When I was deemed to be good and clean, I was dried off and brushed out. Mrs. Kettle then turned to the fitter standing next to her.

"Julia, bring the dress."

This being said, Julia retrieved from behind a dressing blind the most beautiful red dress I had ever seen. Well, not exactly. In fact, I recognized it at once as the exact duplicate of the dress Lady Rebecca was wearing at this moment in the banquet room. This was a miniature. Exact in every detail. All children's attire was miniatures, but what I knew for certain was that Lady Rebecca's dress was very expensive, and I knew she had spared no expense having mine made.

"Whatever is all this about, Mrs. Kettle!" I had to know.

"Never you mind, child, I have been sworn to secrecy, but you will find out soon enough. That I promise."

They went on to fit me into the dress.

"Yes! Look at you! Ha-ha. A perfect fit if I say so myself." Mrs. Kettle was pleased. "Did you ever think to ask why Lady Rebecca was always making you put on those fancy clothes?"

"All the time. How did you know?"

"Ha-ha." She slapped her leg. "I kept giving them to her until she found one she thought was a perfect fit. I used that one as a pattern to make this dress. I think we must have gone through fifteen dresses before she felt she had the right one."

"At least fifteen," I assured her. "She kept insisting I wear them instead of my uniforms. It was pretty embarrassing at times."

"Ha-ha! I'll bet it was. Yes, I'll bet it was, but it was worth it. Just look at you now. Hand me the necklace." She fastened it. "And the birthday bracelet...there. Isn't she a prize, girls?"

They all agreed with Mrs. Kettle and then attended to my hair. In what must have been the work of magical elves, I was instantly transformed from a filthy, disheartened maiden into a beautiful girl who stood washed, dried, and utterly astonished before a mirror. I could not believe my eyes. I was absolutely beautiful. I looked like a princess adorned with a priceless necklace and my matching bracelet, both covered in swirls of diamonds and rivers of rubies sufficient enough for a queen. I looked like somebody I barely recognized.

"What do you think, Elizabeth?"

"I can't believe it." I was still staring at myself in the mirror when Mrs. Kettle pulled it away from my hands.

"Now, you must go back to your mother—. Forgive me, what am I saying, go back to Mrs. Claussen; she's awaiting your return. Go, go, go! At once!"

And with that, she gave me a gentle kiss, and a nudge toward the door. It seemed to open of its own accord as I approached. Through it I saw a view of the servants waiting for me in the kitchen. They crowded in on both sides of the door to have a look at me, but in doing so, formed an aisle from the dressing room door to the entrance of the banquet room. They mimicked soldiers of the guard standing in formation, full of admiration, and saluting their queen with merriment and high spirits. They showered me with praise and compliments. Their laughter and horseplay fell silent as I reached the entrance to the hall. Big John pushed the door partly open for me, and then whispered.

"You are by far the most beautiful creature I ever chanced to lay eyes upon. Good luck," he said.

"Thank-you, John."

"Good luck, Elizabeth," offered another.

"This is your night."

"Enjoy yourself, angel."

Their whispers of encouragement faded as the door closed quietly behind me, but for a space, which every face in the kitchen seemed to be peering through.

There were many, many more faces in the banquet room, and each and every one turned toward me at the opening of the door to witness my return and the unfolding of this drama. My red dress and rubies paled when compared to my face. The attention was overwhelming. I was grateful for the sight of Lady Rebecca and Mr. Claussen, upon whom I immediately directed my focus, for I feared to know the full measure of attention being paid my small frame.

Mary, who remained at Lady Rebecca's beck and call, directed me to move along the guest side of the head table, where those select few were now standing with the Claussens and waiting to greet me. She appeared giddy with delight.

"Oh, Liz, you are absolutely beautiful. You look divine, and I am jealous to the core. Go, go to Lady Rebecca, she is waiting for you."

I was at a complete loss as to what was going on. I made my way past the guests, until I reached Milady. She was smiling at me and she looked radiant. She accepted me with open arms.

"Oh, Elizabeth! Look at you. You are stunning. I am so proud of you. Will you sit with us?"

"Yes, Milady?" I desperately wanted to be close. I looked about me for a chair.

"Over here, honey." She motioned for me to sit in the vacant chair, the guest of honor's chair. I was even more confused.

"But Milady? What about the guest of honor?" I whispered.

"Darling, you are the guest of honor." She laughed.

The words slammed into me like a stampeding horse. I reeled from the knowledge that something, maybe the most important thing of my life, was taking place, and I hadn't a clue. I had no idea why I should be seated in the guest of honor's chair. I tried to grasp some sense of the events playing out about me.

"Milady...I don't understand."

"Sit. I pray this night will be one you remember forever."

I did as she asked, and wide open swung the doors at the far end of the Great Room, which were now straight before me at the opposite end of the center aisle. Two men entered and approached us carrying a large bouquet of flowers. This, they placed upon the floor across the table from me. The suited messenger removed a card, and presented it to me. I received it, and looked to Lady Rebecca who encouraged me to open it with only her expression. Carefully, I read the message.

Dearest Elizabeth,

You called me mum from your heart.
I have wanted it so forever
but feared my selfishness.
If you would allow me to love you as a mother
I would have you as my child.
Christopher and I would both have you
If you should choose to take our name.

Love, Christopher and Rebecca Claussen

The request left me stunned. They wished to adopt me. Now everything made sense. I felt faint as I tried to accept the enormity of the request. I thought of my mother and father, both of whom I loved dearly, but would never see again. I was torn painfully between two worlds, two loves. I saw my mother fading from my heart and it brought tears of desperation to my eyes. I was afraid to look up. I could only stare at the card through eyes so filled with emotion I was no longer able to read the words.

Through my veil of tears, I reviewed memories of events that flooded my life over the past two years. They raced through my mind. I could see there was no turning back. My life was so far removed from the cottage where I had been born. It was hopeless to think I could return to the life my siblings now lived. I had seen too much, I had experienced too much.

I thought of my first days at the Claussen estate. I recalled how frightened I had become, how I had worried that I might not find my way back home. I remembered Lady Rebecca tucking me into bed and teaching me the orphan's prayer—*God doth keep sacred, children of the street.* I remembered how she held me the day my mother died.

I could see now that Lady Rebecca's love could be hard, but it was a love that was filled with purpose and never faltered. She never left my side. She had worked hard with me to learn the ways of being a good mother, and I found much joy in understanding that she had succeeded.

Both Mr. Claussen and Lady Rebecca placed their hands upon my shoulders to comfort me, and I settled down. I wrung out my eyes and raised my head. I turned to Lady Rebecca who was herself crying very quietly, sick with worry, suffering to know my thoughts. She awaited my answer, and it was as if the two of us left the crowds and confusion of the room. It was as if we had stepped into a dream. There was no other sight, but the love in her eyes, in her smile, no other sound but the voice of her heart.

"I love you, Milady. You made me Elizabeth Claussen a long time ago."

"Does that mean you will have us as your family, Elizabeth?"

I looked deep into her eyes. I could see how badly she wished for my love, how badly she wished for me to accept her. I knew she would make my life perfect in every way. I wondered if I could do the same for her. We were locked into each other's gaze. I shook my head.

"Yes."

"Thank-you." She barely got the words out, but for her emotion.

It was only truth we spoke. Not so much in words, but in the feelings that flowed between us. Lady Rebecca buried her face in the hair about my neck and openly wept. I had never seen her cry so. Even when she lost her baby she never cried so openly. It had always been I who cried upon her shoulder. She spoke into my ear.

"I promise I will be the best mother I am able. I can never be your true mother, we both know that, and I shouldn't wish to be anything of the sort. She is special and will always be so. But I wish to love you with all my heart. I wish at least to show you and everyone else how much joy you bring to my life, if you'll allow it."

We parted from the grip of our embrace, and I turned to look over my shoulder at Mr. Claussen who was smiling at me in quiet solitude, knowing he had provided Lady Rebecca and me both something we needed. I felt as though his eyes never left me. I felt as though I was sharing in his accomplishment. I studied him, and I returned his gaze. His eyes had the look of someone who knew much more than the rest of us. I was compelled to stand up and give him a hug and kiss, which I did, and he accepted my feelings in front of all without complaint or shame.

The room, which had grown dead silent, fully transfixed by the events that unfolded at the head table, now began to murmur in hushed tones. Lady Rebecca regained her composure, and rose to her feet to make an announcement. There was no need to call for their attention, for they had been riveted to everything that had taken place.

"It has been quite an evening. Not exactly as I had planned, but fulfilling nonetheless. I suspect that word of the horseplay at the first table has made its way to the back of the room. It did get out of hand and unfortunately my Elizabeth got the worst of it.

"All of that is behind us now and what remains is what is most important. I told you all that there would be a guest of honor tonight, and it was assumed that it would be a speaker. In fact it is none other than my dear maiden servant, Elizabeth.

"I have been told on many occasions that I have coddled and fussed over her excessively, but I can only say that you would find it impossible not to do the same if you knew her as I know her. I am most happy to say that all of that makes little difference now because I have asked Elizabeth if she would honor me by becoming a member of our family to be loved and cherished by Christopher and myself as our own daughter. I knew God blessed me the moment she entered our lives and now again that she has said yes."

Lady Rebecca was beaming with pride and joy, her exuberance felt by all. The room filled with applause.

"Stand up, Elizabeth. They applaud all of us. It is polite to acknowledge them."

I stood up and the room broke into cheers. Mr. Claussen stood up alongside Lady Rebecca and myself, and we waited for some time before the applause and ovation settled enough for her to continue speaking.

"Finally, allow me to thank you all for your support in our ongoing work to place needy children in proper homes with families that care. That concludes tonight's dinner. You may stay as long as you wish. The bar remains open.

"For those of you who prefer your entertainment a little more boisterous, I would remind you that we are celebrating Elizabeth's birthday and adoption downstairs in the public rooms. I promise you it will be an enormously raucous affair with plenty to drink and two open dance floors. You have my word this will go on record as being the standard to measure against when having a good time. You are all welcome to join us, providing you aren't overly weak in heart and soul."

As the remainder of the head table rose to their feet, so too did the rest of the room. Lady Rebecca and Mr. Claussen began escorting me away from the head table, so we might go downstairs to the main lobbies of the Barrington. I turned to look back over my shoulder one last time at the gang of classmates who had spent the night harassing me. They appeared sullen, one and all.

SIXTY-FIVE

The downstairs lobbies were packed wall to wall with guests. Four bars were open to serve, and food and drink were to be found everywhere. A large contingent of musicians played, often trading seats with other musicians in the crowd. The number of people was impossible to discern.

To begin with, a good many of REBECCA's hands were present, if for no reason other than their loyalty to Lady Rebecca. That amounted to hundred or more plus their wives or guests and families, the agents, and associates. Then there were the mates from Mr. Claussen's other ships: the FAIR WEATHER, the FAIR WIND, the FAIR MAIDEN, the FAIR SEAS, the FAIR NIGHTS, and finally the FAIR SAILOR, along with all their women, wives and families, agents, and associates. It was like having a port-o'-call inside doors.

It was a spectacular event. Voices of every nationality, faces of every race, every age, all were attending to honor me for my birthday and adoption. Most all of the guests from the charity dinner came downstairs, that in itself being a count of near two hundred. It was said totals reaching upwards of fifteen hundred guests were packed in the main floor lobbies. The highest percentage was dyed in the wool sailors unmatched in their ability to raise the roof. They were a rough and ready bunch that could make the city's elite nervous at the drop of a hat, but they were quick to express their hearts and went out of their way to make me feel like a queen.

My feet never left the dance floor, or ever touched it; I wasn't certain which. The queue waiting to take my hand was unending. I danced with Cookie Jar, and Darrin O'Kurk, with Mr. Anderson and Mr. Beckwith, and even Mr. McCurry who came back stateside from Sweden. I had the pleasure of seeing Captain Ward once again. He introduced me to his wife, Winifred, and made me promise him a dance.

"Look at you. What a difference a year makes."

"It's more like two."

"No! Can't be."

"Yes, can too. I was nine when we left England, ten that winter, eleven last winter, and twelve this month."

"Time moves too fast; it bothers me. I always seem to be left behind."

"Are you here for good, Captain?"

"Yes and no."

"I told you, you would be back."

"Yes and no."

"It looks mostly like yes to me. Didn't you like farming?"

"As a child, you are probably accustomed to having dirt under your nails, I am not."

"I beg your pardon. No table maiden worth her pay would be caught dead with dirt under her nails."

"My apologies. I stand corrected. Let me just say, I failed to remember you are not the ordinary child."

"I forgive you. Are you going to captain the REBECCA again, yes or no?"

"Truthfully, I might like to, but Winifred is afraid of my going back to sea. She is not at all in agreement of my signing on for any long voyages. That much is for certain. I will say Mr. Claussen has been working me over, working us both over for that matter. He did tell me the REBECCA has been removed from his commercial fleet and stays to the eastern seaboard. I like that. He also told my wife that she is welcome to board the ship at any time, and stay on with me at sea if she should like. She has never traveled, and a blind man could have seen how the prospect of seeing a bit of the world intrigued her. We will have to wait and see."

"I told you so."

"Told me what?"

"Told you, you'd be back, remember? I told you Mr. Claussen knows those things. You haven't forgotten now, have you?"

"Mmm." He grimaced.

For all the rises and falls of feelings, for all the tears and laughter, nothing of the night was more memorable for me than my dance with Mr. Claussen. Ironically, very little, if anything was said between us. Words would have been cumbersome. For my heart, to be joined in this dance was so emotionally exhila-rating that I preferred the security of the silence, knowing it might save me from doing or saying something stupid enough to ruin the euphoria. I ended my night twirling in magical circles, held firmly within his embrace as he literally lifted my soul to the heavens. I felt dizzy, exhausted, and just possibly... *in love.*

It was Lady Rebecca who tucked me into bed and kissed me good night, but it was Mr. Claussen who shaped my dreams. I was all a flutter and too emotionally stirred to sleep. I lay in bed thinking for a long time before finally drifting off. I wondered what love felt like. I wondered if I had to be a certain age, or if first I had to have breasts. I wondered if I was in love with Mr. Claussen. I wondered if I could love him even though he belonged to Lady Rebecca. I wondered if I could love him if I were his adopted daughter. Was that right or wrong? I wondered if he could ever love me.

I thought about all these things as I relived the dance over and over. I thought at great length on Mary's revelation that when it came to love, nothing made sense. When you're in love, you'll know it in your heart. I knew I had danced with many men, but only one made me feel like a wreck. Was that love?

I eventually fell asleep and as always a new day appeared. Looking back on my past day's events, I couldn't believe any child had ever experienced a birthday party the likes of mine. Lady Rebecca's prediction was dead on the mark, for every paper and tabloid in Massachusetts covered the story of BOSTON'S MAIDEN SERVANT MILLIONAIRESS.

SIXTY-SIX

December twenty-fourth, the last day before Christmas, was a Sunday, and it typified the hectic days filling Lady Rebecca's schedule as we approached Christmas. Amid the marriage, my birthday, the banquet, the party, and all Milady's other Christmas commitments, it seemed as though the entire month was one big blur of an engagement. Now, I was always at her side, and at times I hardly knew if I was coming or going. I could not believe it was already Christmas Eve, and I brought the matter before Milady in the privacy of our coach. We were en route to our last stop for the night, and the season.

"Ma'am, you really shouldn't work so hard. Not one day this week have you stayed home. Here it is Christmas Eve, and even so you have worked the entire day. Do you never play? I mean no disrespect, but your schedule is much too demanding, and it worries me, for I fear it will make you tired and sick. Truthfully, wouldn't you have wished to spend at least one night snuggled up next to *Mr. Claussen* before a fire?"

At this point, knowing I would soon be adopted, I was more inclined to ask Lady Rebecca a personal question or two, but I couldn't fathom the idea of addressing Mr. Claussen as father. She paid it no mind and responded to my questions openly and willingly.

"To tell you truthfully...I would rather spend every one of my nights snuggled up next to Christopher before a fire...if...and this is a big if, if I could do it with some peace of mind, but I cannot. Not to mention even if I could enjoy a little peace of mind, Christopher certainly could not.

"Somehow, you have to understand it isn't just me, Elizabeth. Christopher is no slouch in these matters. I would say, especially during Christmas, he is every bit as determined to help the unfortunate as am I, maybe even more so. As I have said before, never forget who it is that pays for all this charity.

"And while you are at it, remember also that I enjoy what I do, and I discuss all my activities, all my plans and needs with Christopher whenever we're together. It is true he seldom accompanies me, or questions me, and he gives freely whenever I ask without argument, but it isn't because he is indifferent. What goes unseen by others is the way in which he encourages me, the way he pushes me to do more—*his convictions.*

"When we retire for the night, and we discuss the day's events, he always asks if I have done everything I could. And if I don't say yes, he won't sleep well. He will toss and turn all night thinking about how we might further improve whatever problem is at hand. That's the way he is, although few people would ever know it, for he isn't one to discuss it publicly.

"You must understand that all this running around and helping others is what gives us our feeling of worth. It makes us happy. There is a lot of pleasure to be found in giving a hand, especially during Christmas when the air is filled with good will and you feel that you are doing God's bidding. Besides, we'll have plenty of time to ourselves after tonight. I will insist on it."

"You love him very much, don't you?" I could feel it.

"Oh, Elizabeth!" She shook her head in wonder. "It is impossible to measure my love for Christopher. My life was insignificant, empty as a church on Monday until that day when he walked into the West Indies. I can honestly say that if I were to lose every worldly possession I have come to own, I could walk away hand in hand with him and be in utter bliss, truthfully. And now that I have your love…well, it's all that much better." She pulled my ship's blanket up around my shoulders and hugged me tightly. "I can't believe you still have that thing. It's starting to show its age."

"I love my blanket. I'll keep it forever. I remember when we worked on it in Sweden. Remember? Mary was there with us."

"Oh, yes, I remember very well. Look at these edges. They are beginning to unravel. We'll have to mend it soon if you plan on keeping if forever."

I said nothing further and settled into the warm security of its fabric. The coach continued on its way.

We had spent all of our past week devoting time to the preparation of Christmas programs at orphanages within our reach, those near Boston and the neighboring countryside. Each day since the party, Milady's now famous vermilion coach set out in the morning well before sunrise and returned long after nightfall, crisscrossing the city in an attempt to keep pace with her busy schedule. I knew this firsthand because I was right there with her. Lady Rebecca didn't take a step without having me at her side, and so we were again seated in the coach for this, the fifth time that day.

"Tell me, Elizabeth. You have had two years as my maiden servant watching this business of charity work, and all that it entails. What do you think of it? Does it appeal to you at all?" I thought about her questions. I had met a lot of people. I liked that.

"I noticed now that I am no longer your maiden servant, all of the boys are looking at me."

"A-ha! How right you are." Lady Rebecca laughed aloud and at length. "I have no doubt about that, but it shouldn't surprise you. You are a beautiful girl. Haven't I have always told you so?"

"Was I not a beautiful girl before the party?"

"Why of course you were, silly. What kind of question is that?"

"Then it must be the money they see when they look at me now."

Lady Rebecca was struck silent for a moment. She was thinking as she studied me.

"As is your way, Elizabeth, at times you say things that are beyond your years. If you know what it is you say—then I trust you will be wise enough to find a man who will love you for the special girl you are. Money will not be the issue. It is, however, an observation that you would do well to remember."

"How did you meet Mr. Claussen, ma'am?"

"Oh! That is a story in itself. He was as clever as they come, but it would take a lot more time to tell than we have tonight."

"Did you know he was the one the minute you first saw him? You know, as did Mary with Allen?"

"Umm…not exactly, he was a trickster."

600

"Mr. Claussen?"

"I know." She laughed. "Hard to believe, isn't it? He's so serious all the time. He was clever; yes he was, very, very clever, very out of character for Christopher. Not that it didn't serve his purpose mind you, but you'll find out love makes us all do funny things. It makes us laugh, it makes us cry; it embarrasses us. It changes us."

"Did it change him?"

"It did for a while. He pretended to be somebody else."

"Seriously?"

"Mmm-hmm," she nodded.

"Why would Mr. Claussen wish to be somebody else? He seems like a perfect man to me."

"He *is* a perfect man, but as I said, that's love. It does funny things. Actually, to be fair, there were many reasons. Reasons I came to understand, and someday when we have time, I'll tell you more. I'm sure the older you become the more you will learn to appreciate the story. I still laugh about it to this day. The important thing is, he was persistent. I'll give him that. Tricky and persistent, and in this case the end justified the means.

"Now, if I may change the subject. I believe my question was more in regard to the work of charity. Do you like doing this type of thing, now that you have had time to learn most of what I have been doing?"

"I enjoy it for the most part. I guess it makes me feel good when I see how happy we make others. Sometimes, though, it bothers me when I lay in bed at night because I wonder why they have nothing, and I seem to have everything."

"Oh, bless me, sweetheart, do I ever know that feeling. I wish you knew how many times that same question has run through my head. For the longest time, I was afraid to think too hard

601

upon it, lest I return to the poverty from whence I came. You just have to accept the fact that this is the Lord's doing, for whatever reason, who knows, but it is not our place to ask, only to appreciate that we have been blessed, and to share what we are able with others in kind. If you think those thoughts it not only means you are growing up, but you are growing up with conscience.

"Maybe I've picked the perfect time to ask these questions of you, because now that you are about to become a member of the Claussen family, you will also represent Christopher. That leads me to wonder if you might like taking an active role in sponsoring events, possibly making a name for yourself. I certainly hope someone will carry on with the work that Christopher and I have started with the Rebecca Foundation. You know it would please me enormously if I thought this work might interest you. I believe with all my heart that you would be good at it, and just as you have supported me, I would support you. The time has come to think about what you wish to do with your life, Elizabeth, for your days as a servant are done and now you must plan for a different future."

I hadn't been asked to perform the routines of a maid once the entire week, although I was perfectly happy to do so, for those were tasks I took pride in knowing well. As a matter of fact, the very first things to go last Sunday morning were all my black dresses and white aprons, much to Lady Rebecca's delight. That morning I sat at the breakfast table with Lady Rebecca and Mr. Claussen, and was myself waited on for the first time ever. It was almost as embarrassing as the episode under the table. I couldn't recall ever being more uncomfortable. I was red-faced and felt totally out of place through most of the meal, but Lady Rebecca and Mr. Claussen just laughed.

Milady and I enjoyed our time together in the coach, for it afforded us much of the privacy we needed to change our relationship from one of servant to mistress, to that of daughter to mother. As might have been expected, it was both difficult and awkward for me to address her as mother. I was grateful that she neither pressed the issue nor faulted me for this inability, because it was obvious from the start that to me it felt inappropriate and would take time getting used to, if ever it was to happen.

I was comfortable addressing her as madam, which when slurred came out as *ma'am*, which again after a little effort on my part could sound very close to *mum*, and this seemed to work well for both of us. What did please Lady Rebecca immensely was the fact that I would clearly call her mother in public. She always introduced me as her daughter, and this she did with such happiness, I felt it was the least I could do in return.

By training, my manners and public presentation were now impeccable. Lady Rebecca escorted me about with pride, and showed me off at every possible opportunity. I might well have been a newborn babe. It was still an embarrassing ordeal for me, and I worked to remain humble throughout all of it. Fortunately, our friends understood how I felt, and while Lady Rebecca would go on about my virtues, they often winked at me to ease my burden.

Since our start this morning, we had paid visits to four orphanages. It was now nearing the evening hour of eight, and the streets that passed by were darkened save for the glow of the oil lamps that illuminated the glass panes of the coach. Our breath had frosted the cabin windows, and it was necessary to scrape them in order to look out. I could see that a light snowfall was falling across the city as we approached the church of our destination. There were a few carolers to be seen bundled up against the cold, but not many, for the temperature had dropped severely; and even though we sat huddled together underneath our blankets within the protection of the cabin, we remained chilled, especially about the feet and legs. Anyone with a grain of sense was long since inside by a fire, and enjoying the company of loved ones.

I was more than ready to go home. I was all talked out, and so I just sat under my ship's blanket, closed my eyes, laid my head upon Milady's shoulder and half-dreamed the time away. I wondered if Mr. Claussen was at home waiting for our arrival.

I imagined the fire to be roaring, and I could see him in his over-stuffed chair, possibly smoking a pipe and looking out a window as well, watching for our return. I was tired and ready to sit next to him, but there was still one last call to be made. There was still that one last group of orphans waiting impatiently for our arrival so they might open their pile of gifts.

"We're here."

Lady Rebecca broke the silence. I opened my eyes, and leaned over to scrape the window. The coach came to a halt at the steps of the Boston Community Church on Bellview Street. It was to be our fifth and final stop for the day. We began in the morning by stopping at the places farthest out from town, and worked our way back so that by day's end, when we were thoroughly worn out, we would be no more than a few blocks from our place at the Barrington.

We *were* thoroughly worn out, and Lady Rebecca groaned under her breath as she straightened out her back after stepping down carefully onto the snow-covered pavement. She faced the volunteers and broke into a broad smile. She turned one last moment to look down at me.

"I'm just about done in, Elizabeth, but so are these folks, I am sure."

"Me too."

"I know. Just look into their eyes and see all the happiness you have brought them, and before you know it, the night will be over and we'll be off for home."

We were greeted like saints. And maybe we should have been, for I often heard that Lady Rebecca had accomplished more for the benefit of the poor since her arrival nearly three years ago, than anyone could recall having been done in any amount of time prior. She was considered to be a whirlwind of change and promise. The day-to-day volunteers who worked to feed, clothe, and shelter the needy, would have gladly kneeled before her if asked, but it wasn't just them. There was a bizarre form of adoration taking place in other quarters as well.

I finally understood it on an occasion when we had returned to the REBECCA from town. The coach halted alongside the food tent that Lady Rebecca always put out on the dock for the poor. We boarded the ship, and after about fifteen minutes I went back up on deck for some fresh air. I was immediately attracted to a commotion down below about the coach. One of the drivers was chasing off a couple of sailors who looked to be down and out. A few of the mates on board the REBECCA were also watching the goings-on in case the strangers got rowdy and the driver needed a hand.

Mr. Beckwith was one of those watching, as he had just stepped out for a smoke, so out of curiosity I decided to ask him what had taken place.

"Them there mates claimed they'd come by t' eat, but like most sailors they're a s'picious lot, an' came pokin' around lookin' for the coach. They heard the stories 'bout how the coach had weathered the journey, you know, the pirates, and the storm an' all without damage, an' how it was lucky an' all. They come by to see for themselves. It's being said that only the hand o' Providence could o' produced such a miracle. You gotta know girl, there are stories goin' round 'bout that coach that sound just plain crazy. Lessen you're one o' them mates with a belly fulla grog.

"I heard one jack swear tell a coupla weeks back that Lady Rebecca was an hones' t' God angel, an' that was the reason for her being so kind t' the poor. Anyways it all works han' n' han', one thing feedin' the other, an' now it's being said that if a soul should rub against the golden letters of 'er name upon the side of the coach it will bring luck. It's becomin' the talk o' the town, an' that coach is taking on a life of its own, yes ma'am." He drew off his pipe.

Suddenly, I was enlightened. It was the first I had heard of it, but not the first time I had seen it. I had thought it the oddest thing when, now and then, the coach would be stopped in traffic for a moment, and someone would dart out from the crowd heading directly for us. They would run up to the door, and just as I thought we were about to be robbed, they would rub the door with a piece of cloth, or a shawl, or the arm of a jacket, then disappear as quickly as they came.

The first time it happened, I was badly frightened. The man had reached for the door on my side of the cabin, and I believed we were about to be attacked. I climbed right into Lady Rebecca's lap. After a while, having gone through the experience time and time again, I began to find it funny. I asked Lady Rebecca about it a number of times, but she just shrugged it off, so I decided that these people were daft. They had to be in cahoots, playing some sort of game. At least their actions made for one highly polished vehicle.

I knew well the incidents that Mr. Beckwith spoke of aboard the REBECCA, and how Milady tried to play down what truly was a miraculous event. The whole ship was indeed shot up full of lead, but not the coach. It sat right out there in front of everything and never suffered a mark.

Now I wondered it she knew of these stories about the docks, and chose not to mention them to me in order to prevent these superstitious beliefs from being further promoted and discussed. I couldn't have imagined she hadn't heard of them, and I couldn't believe she wouldn't have told me, when I had been so badly frightened the first time.

Maybe Lady Rebecca *was* an angel of the Lord. Everyone loved her. I don't believe I ever encountered anyone who despised her for her success. She accepted thanks and praise modestly and with grace, only noting that it eased her conscience to share her good fortune and assist in issues close to her heart, providing there were no objections. And, of course, there never were, for obtaining money from the wealthy was exceedingly difficult if those asking were nearly as destitute as those receiving. All of it only served to further enhance my daydreams about living as an angel's daughter.

Lady Rebecca somehow made it vogue to contribute. She never asked for money, only for help in the placement of the orphans or the construction of food tents and shelters, and ironically the elite of Boston reached deeper into their pockets than ever to partake in this new wave of benevolence and generosity by their own accord. It was those funds that paid for the festivities now about to commence at the Boston Community Church. Lady Rebecca would see to it that the donors were well informed of its outcome and made to feel personally responsible for its success and the joy it brought to the children.

"Hello, Rebecca. How are you?"

"Hello, Lydia. I'm fine. And you?"

"Oh, I'll get by. It's been a long day, but I am sure much longer for you than me."

"Lydia, this is my daughter, Elizabeth. Elizabeth, this is Mrs. Pennington."

"My pleasure, Mrs. Pennington."

"And mine as well, Elizabeth. I have heard the good news. Congratulations! I am very happy for you."

"Thank-you, ma'am."

"Please, come in and let me refresh you. You remember Patricia Borden, don't you, Rebecca?"

"Yes, but I haven't seen her for some time."

"She's here and so is Bonnie Lane. We're all ready, so why not come with me, Elizabeth? We'll go inside where it's warm."

There was no hesitation on my part for it was frightfully cold, and so without further delay, I took her arm and we entered the church from the street through the two large front doors. It was a very old but appealing wooden structure set atop a split stone foundation with twin bell towers abreast the double-door entrance. It was painted in the traditional purity of white. There was a large porch atop a broad expanse of steps also fashioned from split fieldstone that reached down to the road.

Moving through the front doors, we were escorted down the center aisle, which led us past the pews and directly to the pulpit. The doors were closed behind us, but I asked myself why, for it was as cold inside as out.

Standing majestically behind the pulpit and in full view of the street, should the entrance doors should be opened, was a magnificent Christmas tree that nearly touched the high vaulted ceiling. From topmost branch, which supported a fine winged angel to the long reaching branches at the bottom, the tree had been decorated with all the trimmings imaginable, including popped corn, cookies, and candy canes.

I was fortunate in that I had been eating all day, and thus had but little appetite, yet the sight of all that candy upon those branches must have been a sore temptation for young eyes. The pieces reflected the many pinpoints of light that emanated from three rings of carefully placed candles balanced at the tips of the branches at the lower part of the tree. The candlelight softly lit up the inside walls of the church and presented a gentle show of Christmas splendor in our behalf. The room felt aglow.

"Oh! Isn't your tree beautiful?" I was honestly impressed.

"I am glad you think so. We put a lot of work into decorating it. It's a job reaching the top, I assure you. It seems so sad that even though we erect it at the first of the month, the congregation is lucky if they get a chance to see it more than three or four times on the Lord's Day. It is only there for them during Sunday meetings, and for those who live far away, bad weather may keep them from seeing it even then. By the time Christmas rolls around, it starts to look pretty dry and shabby. I don't think you can even smell it anymore."

"Oh, no, not at all. It's so tall. It's huge. It looks beautiful to me."

"I guess it's those things for sure. It pretty much has to be or it will get lost inside the church. We've always taken pride in our tree. The congregation always pitches in and comes with a decoration of one sort or another. I only wish you could have seen it earlier this month when it was fresh. Now, it's drying out and starting to lose its needles. They always smell so good when they're first cut. The whole church fills with the scent of pine. Do you like that smell, Elizabeth?"

"Mmm hmm," I nodded. "It smells clean."

We made a sharp left turn at the pulpit and walked to the east side of the church.

"Bless me Lord, but isn't it cold tonight? Brrrrrrrr."

"Rebecca? I don't believe you have been here before, am I correct?"

"You are correct."

"I thought as much. Then let me tell you, we've set up the back room for the children, and there has been a fire going all of the day, so I promise you'll find it good and warm. We generally use the room as a nursery on Sundays and for luncheons and various congregational gatherings during the week."

"I believe I'll put my chair directly in front of the fire until I force out this chill," said Milady.

A wall separated the pulpit, pews, and tree from the adjoining room that had been added to the back of the church many years before. It was accessed from the inside by a doorway at either side of the church flanking the pulpit. We were entering by way of the east wall door.

"Please, after you." Lydia stepped aside.

Lady Rebecca opened the door and a welcome wave of warm air engulfed us. Inside, the noise of the children ceased as they stared and hoped with all their hearts that we were the ones for whom they waited.

"Oh, it feels good in here. Your word is good as gospel, Lydia." Milady began to rub the chill out of her and was immediately greeted by the other women.

"Hello, Rebecca!"

"Hello, Bonnie, Patricia, it's good to see you again. Thank the Lord for heat. This is a cozy room indeed." Lady Rebecca headed directly for the fireplace.

"Yes, it serves us well," Bonnie, answered. Lydia and Patricia snatched a couple of chairs for Milady and me to place before the fire. Lydia offered her chair to me as Bonnie continued.

"We really like it. The children come in from the church through either of these doors. In the summer we often go out that back door and have Sunday school in the back lot under the shade of a large oak where it is always nice and cool. In the winter, we use the back door to bring in a cord of wood every now and then so it dries out and burns hot. Needless to say, this morning today it came in handy for bringing in all the gifts. It beats walking all the way through the church from the street."

Lydia had pointed out the back door and the pile of wood stacked between it and the fireplace that was also built into the back outside wall. I looked at all the presents she had referred to, and they made an impressive pile as they surrounded a smaller Christmas tree at the end of the room near the back door. The children were all standing still and staring at us, hanging on our every move.

The room was warm indeed and one soon forgot the frigid temperatures outside. Until this moment, the children contributed all the necessary anticipation expected on an occasion such as this, and were barely able to restrain themselves from attacking

610

the mountain of colorfully decorated gifts. The youngest children were routinely escorted back away from the gifts, and given added support during their unbearable lessons on the virtues of patience. They resumed their activity with renewed vigor, now knowing that we were the expected company. Their enthusiasm helped us to forget about how tired we were.

Finally *Miss Rebecca*, as they called Milady, was now among them and it was time for silence and the offering of a prayer to thank the Lord for the food, the warmth, and the gifts that He saw fit to bestow. Milady led in the prayer, and handed out the first gift to a young girl of about nine years of age with black hair, identified as Jennifer by the name on the gift. From there, Lydia, Bonnie, and Patricia, assisted by the older children, began the distribution of the gifts in earnest.

Within moments the wrappings were ripped apart, and screams of glee sounded through the air as the children embraced their new toys and proudly showed them off to one another. The young girls began to collect at one side of the room and set up house with their dolls, while the boys took over the floor for the purpose of fighting Indians and setting up camp. The din grew to alarming levels.

SIXTY-SEVEN

All this commotion irritated Paws, who was now unable to hunt the woodpile stacked alongside the fireplace. He was a formidable mouser, and had enjoyed much success poking around the split wood where mice sought refuge in the warmth of the hearth.

He knew it was there that mice scampered about in number. They darted back and forth with noses to the air tracking the scent of those minute morsels regularly swept into a corner or a crack between the boards. The food was as plentiful as the meetings that produced it, and discounting the presence Paws himself, mice lived good here.

Paws was not nearly so content. On this night, he had been mauled, manhandled and chased by everything under four feet tall. He was strictly on the defensive and in a most disagreeable way. The doors to the meeting room were now closed to conserve heat, and although he was deprived of the warmth and the woodpile he so enjoyed, he was pleased to get back his privacy, his dignity, and something of his peace of mind. Not to mention he was out here alone in the cold with this glowing, glittering, amazing thing that was almost impossible not to look at. It had always been here, but it had changed. It had never looked quite like this before. Maybe it was awake. Maybe it deserved a closer look.

Paws' flinching tail was his only embarrassment. It revealed too much of his disposition, too much of what he was thinking. To make matters worse it revealed all of this behind his back. When he was happy or feeling a little cocky it would hang over his head. When he was irritable or dissatisfied it flicked back and forth, timed to the passing of each wave of bristling hair that moved across his back.

Now, as he contemplated this new and amazing sight, a quick glance rearward revealed his tail to be rock steady. This pleased him, for he believed it better represented his character. He crouched forward and moved ever so slowly toward the dancing lights. He eased himself directly underneath this wondrous apparition and discovered to his delight that a blanket had been spread out, not so unlike his box. He sensed it would be perfect for laying upon should he choose to watch the light dance about him. It was too inviting to resist. And so, he moved in and settled down into its warmth to watch the jerky little shadows vibrate across the floor, across the pews, and upon the walls of the empty church.

Paws rolled over onto his back. He worked his way deep into the folds of the blanket. He decided this was the same tree after all, and for that matter, not so different from the ones outside. The smell, although not quite as strong, gave it away. You couldn't escape your smell. The tree looked much more normal when viewed from the inside out.

He raised his head to peer high up into the branches. The points of light fascinated him. He wondered about them. Were they alive? Did they see him? Were they afraid? Were they fireflies? Did they taste good? So many questions he couldn't answer. He needed more information, so he raised his paw, and ever so lightly, he touched a branch—*nothing*. Maybe, a little bit harder.

Yes! Just as he had hoped, this time he had caused something to stir! His attention was riveted at once to a little white ball of fluff dangling at the end of a piece of string. Paws needed a better view and so he scooched over a few inches to improve his position. His eyes followed the string upward to where it twisted about in and out of the branches. As hard as he might try, he was unable to discern which end was the head and which was the tail. He followed it around the tree in circles, around and around until it made him dizzy.

He finally gave up on the whole of it, and decided to focus his attention on the one ball of fluff hanging just in front of him. Was it watching him? He wondered, so he raised his paw and shook it quickly near the ball, but this garnered no response. What if it was waiting for him to touch it, whereupon it would bite or maybe sting? Almost everything could bite or sting. He thought about this and decided that if it did, that would be a good reason to kill it first, and then play. In the meantime he decided to give it a good wallop. This he did, and sent the white ball of fluff into a circular orbit. It came back at him so fast that he had no time to think, only to act.

He shot out from underneath the tree at full speed and grazed the white fluff for measure, a sort of dare. He was bounding with energy, streaking across the floor in a large arc. At this nearly uncontrollable speed, he dug his nails into the fiber of the wooden floorboards and pulled even harder, slinging himself onto the final approach for a spectacular assault.

The wind was in his ears, and he laid them back as his eyes narrowed to hold a steady focus on his target. Instinctively calculating his speed and the distance to the target before him, he righted his body and at the last second, he launched himself. His pads shot out before him and he watched as his claws extended, fanning outward, slicing through the air to snag his target by surprise.

Paws was always one for showmanship, for putting in a little pizzazz at the last moment; and feeling he was now in complete control, he performed a half roll in midair to enhance his element of surprise—to throw a curve into the enemy camp.

He miscalculated the half roll.

It was as simple as that. A stupid mistake. The string looped itself about his paw. It was securely snagged as he had hoped, but he landed in shame upon his back and recklessly out of control. His brakes were pointing up. The blanket folded over him as he slid across the floor. He was stopped by the stump of the tree in his ribs and the tension of the string as it drew tighter around the branches.

Paws felt as stupid as the time he had been walking around with a thistle seed stuck in the fur between his ears. He looked about the church, but luckily there were no witnesses to come back and haunt him this time. He retracted his claws and the string slipped away as the branch snapped back. The little ball of white fluff zoomed out from under the tree.

His first instinct was to consider his well-being. Aside from his ego, nothing else hurt, so he had little reason to complain. Eagerly, he looked about to size up how much damage he had caused. There must be some, but it was hard to say. He did note that things were beginning to happen, nothing great, but nevertheless the little dancing lights were spreading and crackling in complaint. At first it seemed nothing, but suddenly they were getting louder, much louder and brighter, and their numbers were quickly multiplying. He sensed that whatever it was, it was awake and not happy. His instincts screamed. This was not good—*leave!* He did.

SIXTY-EIGHT

Paws did well to run.

He turned to look back from the end of the aisle nearest the front doors. Whatever it was he had disturbed, it was by far more powerful than was he. Faster than he could ever leap, it leapt to the top of the tree. It did so in an instant. It grew into an enormous ball of brilliance that roared upwards and reached out across the ceiling to frighten him.

He sensed its change from the brilliant white flash to a reddish-orange glow that clung above. It seemed to creep overhead in his direction until it met the walls that towered over his head. Now and then, he could feel the heat of its breath blow by him. It was growing louder, brighter, stronger, and it slowly started coming down for him. He knew his way about the church. It was a big place, but not as big as this. He knew there was no way out except for an open door. Now he was overwhelmed by only one instinct—fear. Paw's tail was tight to his belly as he stared up and cowered.

The dried-out tree ignited in one enormous flash of energy. Its heat and flame scorched the wall as it soared to the ceiling and began to feed itself. The air down below remained cool and clear, and belied the inferno that now raged overhead.

The church had been designed with its windows at the top of the walls. This served the dual purpose of casting light high and heavenly, as well as hindering would-be thieves. Now, being confronted by the intense heat of the fire, which fully engulfed the ceiling and walls about them, they warmed too fast from their frigid winter temperature and shattered.

Their pieces fell like snow crystals through the nighttime sky, as they rained down upon the empty seats below. Once mounted with pride over the large double doors at the front of the church was a large circular stained glass window. These smaller mosaic panes of colored glass did not shatter, but occasionally fell out in whole pieces as the lead in their frames loosened.

The fire, ravenous and craving fresh air, sucked in the influx of cool dense night air through the paneless window grates, and mixed it with the gaseous cloud of smoke that hung thick in the room underneath. As if expanding a chest fully invigorated, the fire flexed its newfound strength by offering up an enormous explosion, which blew out the east wall of the church. Fully a third of the roof, having lost its support, came thundering down to crash upon the rows of wooden pews, themselves hungry for the heat of fire on this cold winter night.

The sounds of shattered glass falling from the heights and clinking upon the wooden floor went unnoticed by the festive crowd in the backroom. They were too busy screaming and yelling, too busy wading in the din of a tug of war over gifts and sweets being handed out in quantity. But the explosion and collapse of the church rocked the very foundation upon which they stood. It stopped all but the youngest dead in their tracks.

Lady Rebecca and the other women sat and stared at each other in astonishment. Lydia then rose nervously to peek into the church. We all waited in hushed silence. We could now hear strange sounds stirring beyond the wall that made us all somewhat nervous. Lydia opened the door cautiously, and then screamed out in horror. Nothing further needed to be said, for a brilliant band of orange light snapped across the room, and ushered in the sounds and smells of an inferno soon to devour us. Panic erupted.

"Elizabeth! Elizabeth! Elizabeth!"

I turned to look at Lady Rebecca who was running for me from the other end of the room. The whole place went into a state of confusion and mayhem, with the women and older children yelling or screaming in terror and the younger ones crying out in fear.

"Come with me! Hurry, hurry, hurry!"

She grabbed me by my arm and pulled me toward the back door, but Lydia, who was a large-framed woman, immediately stopped us. Something was wrong. The door was buried beneath piles of spent wrappings, boxes and trash, and she turned us about and drove us roughly toward the west door that led back into the church. She gathered the children and forced them in our direction.

"It's blocked, it's blocked! Go back, hurry, hurry! Go out the west door! There's no time! Hurry! Lead the children out!" She started herding children into a group behind us. Amid all the confusion, we had no time to argue or question her demands. Lady Rebecca at once turned to me.

"Elizabeth! You must have courage. You must be strong. Take five or six of the youngest children and lead them through the church. Carry those you can. Follow me!"

Milady gathered up seven or eight children herself, and opened the door. She looked up at the ceiling to determine how much time we had. I could see the flaming debris streaking downward and littering the aisle. It looked like a bed of coals. We were out of time. She looked back at me with a mixture of worry and hope.

"Now, Elizabeth! Now!"

She picked up two toddlers into her arms and then ran out of the room and into the firelight. I was scared to death, but was even more terrified of being left behind. I picked up the youngest child near me and held him to my chest then started after Lady Rebecca. I yelled out to the others.

"Now! Go! Go! Go!" I yelled. I stepped through the door and was met by the intense heat and smoke that stung my eyes.

"Hold your breath!" I screamed out.

We ran down the west aisle, and as I looked behind me I could see more children running quickly at my heels. The passage through the church was taking too long. It seemed like forever, and I prayed with all my might that the roof would hold for only a few more minutes as flaming planks and beams plummeted down into the pews, destroying everything and sending bursts of red-hot embers trailing through the air all about us. The fire was generating its own wind, and it roared mightily through what remained of the roof.

As I stepped over the burning planks and debris, I thought of Mr. Claussen, and imagined him waiting for me, calling to me. I could see him in my mind with his arms outstretched, easing my fears and encouraging me to come to him. *'Come, come, come.'* In my mind I heard him. I felt him draw me to the front of the church where Lady Rebecca was holding the door open and ushering the children through. She was waving me to hurry and moved me through the door and out onto the porch.

From outside, I could hear others still inside running and crying. I could hear Mrs. Pennington screaming for the orphans to follow. Mrs. Lane and Patricia Borden were farther behind. I could hear all their voices and the worry made me sick. By the graces of God, they were able to reach safety having passed uninjured through the heat of the fire and out through the front door. On this one occasion in my life, I wept for the feel of the bitterly cold Boston air.

The others began to emerge quickly now. One after another they streamed through the massive doors and out onto the porch.

We fled down the steps and ran across the street to meet a sizable crowd that had now amassed. Everybody tried to collect their wits and attempted to make some sense of what had just taken place. Women in the crowd were taking the orphans under arm and consoling them.

Our drivers were explaining how they had tried to gain Milady's attention, but were hindered because as they started along the side of the church, it exploded and badly panicked the horses. They had to rush back to the street having seen the horses about to stampede into a crowd of carolers. With much difficulty they removed her coach from the front of the church and moved it back away enough distance to calm the horses and the carolers.

The driver's frantic explanations drifted into the background of my awareness as soon as I looked over at the coach. Its rich red color was glowing, glowing so intensely before the fire that it seemed to be its own source of light. The golden calligraphy of Lady Rebecca's name leapt of its background of vermilion brilliance and appeared to hover in the air. I was mesmerized by the illusion of her name gleaming unsuspended in ghostly fashion, floating in the blackness of night.

SIXTY-NINE

All that was taking place overwhelmed my senses, and it was at this point that my awareness was drawn beyond illusion and into the world of dreams. A sensation of distance and slow motion engulfed me, whereby I viewed everything as though from afar.

This was triggered by the sound of a single voice, a voice that reached above the gasps, the murmurs and shrills of disbelief. It was that of Mrs. Pennington. She was screaming in unmistakable anguish that a child was missing, *a child was missing.*

"She's gone! She's gone! Where is Annie Lynn?"

"Has anybody seen Annie Lynn Wagner?"

"Did she go out with you, Bonnie?"

"Patricia, Patricia! For the sake of God, have you seen Annie Lynn?"

I turned ever so slowly from the golden image of Lady Rebecca's name to observe the expression upon her face. Unlike the horrified expressions that were smeared across other faces in the crowd, Milady's eyes focused with measured calculation upon the fire erupting from the church entrance.

Could this be true? The question rolled around in the silence within my head. *Could this be true? Yes, yes, it was true.* Annie Lynn Wagner was not among us.

Firelight swept across the faces. It made the shadows of their features bounce up and down giving them the look of demons, totem poles stuck in ground and transfixed, unable to do anything but stare with horror into the inferno. They all remained fixed, frozen in place before me doing the one thing that never occurred to Milady. *Nothing.*

While the crowd looked at each other and began to avert their eyes away from the burning church in shame, trying to grapple with the guilt of their inaction and fear, I saw out the corner of my eye, Lady Rebecca break into a run. She was in motion, sprinting across the street and bounding up the fieldstone steps, light as a deer, fast as she could go. Her shadow split the glow before us as she disappeared into its brilliance.

I knew. I knew at that very moment, it was grave. I could feel the cold hand of death reach through my heart for Lady Rebecca.

"No! No, no, no, no."

It couldn't be. I refused to accept this. I refused to face a truth that was bleeding out invisibly all about me, a wound that was already opening in my soul. The longest moments of my life were now upon me. I was so taken with fear for her life, I began to shake, and my breathing became restricted and difficult. Then, I stopped breathing altogether. I held my breath, desperately trying to keep the imaginary heat and smoke out of my lungs for her sake.

I fought until my lungs ruptured. Then, as if I possessed some super power, I exhaled explosively and the entire roof collapsed into the shell of the church, sending a roaring storm of fiery debris blasting out the front doors, nearly ripping them off their hinges. The flying embers streaked out across the road and scattered the startled onlookers about me, now all running for cover, but not me. I stood firm staring into the bright light emanating from the opening, searching for a sign of life I refused to accept might no longer exist.

The walls remained standing, white and stately upon their stone foundation, trapping the brilliant light inside and shaping it into a beam that soared up to the heavens. The falling flakes of snow defined the shaft of light as they floated down swirling in and out of the darkness. The window openings at the top of the walls cast their beams of firelight outward, horizontally across the landscape, reminding me of lighthouses, as if to beckon lost souls to return home like so many ships out to sea.

Then, to the horror of all present, the face of death made itself visible. We saw Annie Lynn walk out from the fire, its heat now so intense it kept us far removed from the church. She stopped for a moment, and stood in the blinding light, which poured out of the massive double door opening. She was alone, a dark silhouette wrapped in flames and framed by the open doorway. She looked at us gathered in the street. Nobody moved. We stood numbed to the bone, in shock, in silence, horrified as she turned about and calmly walked back into the inferno.

I knew. I knew. I prayed and in my desperation, in my last fleeting hope for Milady, I remembered the back door. Instantly,

I bolted across the street, swept up in sheer panic, screaming to get to her. I neared the back of the church, and saw a group of people standing there. They noticed me as I rounded the corner, and moved at once to block my passage, but I was not to be stopped. I turned and twisted. I fought to free myself from their grip with every ounce of my strength. I clawed and bit my way through the tangle of arms with the insanity of a rabid animal until inch by inch I forced myself near the back door amid their cries and warnings.

"No, no, Elizabeth, you mustn't look. You mustn't look, child."

"Milady! Milady!"

"Keep her back! Keep her back!"

"Go back, girl, go back," said another.

"Milady!"

"No, child, turn away, we can't help her. The door's blocked."

"Damn it, man, get me some rocks or a pick. Anything!"

"It's too late, we can't get to her. It's the ice."

"The heat's too much. We've got to get back."

"Milady, Milady! Please, God! Please, God!" I screamed for all I was worth.

Through the many arms trying to restrain me, trying to protect me, I could see men covering their faces, trying to protect themselves from the intense heat as they frantically chipped away at the ice.

It began as melted snow dripping from the roof of the lean-to, having been warmed by the heat of the room beneath. All afternoon water dripped off the roof's edge and onto the porch where it froze once again to form a giant mound of ice that now sealed the door and Lady Rebecca's fate. It was this that Lydia was trying to say. It wasn't the gift wrappings or the boxes and litter that blocked the door, it was the ice. There was no way out of the back room. *The warm cozy back room.*

The men had no time to await tools, and frantically used stones and sticks from the old oak tree to hammer away at the ice, but it was to no avail, for the attempts of their frozen fingers was no match for the blistering pace of the fire. By the time an exhausted man arrived with a pick, it was too late.

The heavy back door, built to protect the sanctity of the church had been forced open about eight inches. In the searing white light, which streamed outward from the narrow vertical opening, I saw the shadow of Lady Rebecca Claussen sink slowly down to the floor. Her face was almost recognizable in the opening, her outstretched arm reaching through for our help, reaching for the cool air of life outside, reaching for me.

"Miladeee! Miladeeee! Mommmmmmmm! Mommmmmmmmmmm!"

I cried out in anguish with my last desperate breath of hope. I cried out for her release, for her love from the very deepest part of my heart. I cried out to God one last wordless plea for my mother's sake in this hellish nightmare. Then, resigning myself to her terrible fate, I closed my eyes and let go. I gave in to the force of arms that struggled to restrain me and remembered nothing more.

SEVENTY

Christopher stood alone. The massive frame, which all his life supported him easily above the shoulders of other men, was now crouched over, beaten down mercilessly by the harsh hand of fate. Crushed, he waded through the silent tranquility of snowflakes falling upon him, and watched as like his Rebecca they were consumed in irony before the life-giving warmth found within this massive holy hearth. Numb and beyond feeling, he stared blindly into the smoldering ruins. He stood alone.

Surrounded by a whispering crowd, he occupied space in a world where nothing lived, where nothing mattered. A world for those left behind with no purpose but to suffer. Before him, nothing remained of the Boston Community Church save for a mountain of glowing coals radiating heat into an insatiable winter night. They provided a bed that would give rest for a forest of charred timbers and memories. Memories such as Rebecca's laughter echoing within his head, as earlier it had echoed within the walls of this sanctuary.

Christopher stared silently; he was void of emotion. He had distanced himself from the tragedy of death still fresh before him. Observing everything from this other place, a place where pain could not reach him. He knew that at the back of this church, lying in this bed of coals was his beloved Rebecca. He knew her arms would be wrapped around a young child she had returned to rescue from the inferno. She had found herself trapped—*no escape*. He knew she had called out to him in desperation. In his mind he heard her crying out to him in fear, during those last fleeting moments of life. It was only natural, for he had always been there for her. She was, after all, his life, his whole reason for being.

This time the circumstance proved different. It was in fact a situation that he could not alter. Not to be rewritten by pen, not reformed by hand, not resurrected by wealth. He had never been consulted, his opinion never requested, his feelings never considered. He had been down this road before, many years ago. He could see himself bent to his knees, wailing with despair at the bedside of his mother. How he prayed, pleaded, how he had begged the Lord from the very core of his soul not to take his mother away to heaven. He cried for her, God! How he cried.

Not this time. Now he held on firmly to his emotions, refusing to let loose the outcry of pain. He spared himself the agony of hope. The torture of believing she might appear suddenly down the street, coming to stand by his side to gaze into the hypnotic glow of the embers. Still, he turned his head slightly and glanced down the road into the darkness.

The footmen distracted him. He was drained of life and will, and allowed the men to escort him back to Rebecca's coach. He did not return to the Barrington. He sat alone inside, abandoned to drown in his misery and the radiance of her grave lighting their way as the coachman persuaded the horses to head for the docks.

In the lesser glow of the oil lamps, Christopher ascended the boarding plank of the REBECCA. He requested permission to board from the anchor watch. Once on deck, he paused a moment to face the hard winter night and look out to sea. He then looked up past the masts and yards, through the ice-covered shrouds and into the glittering night sky; and with the mist of his breath, he blew Rebecca his kiss good-bye. He wouldn't give fate the satisfaction of his tears. Turning, he bowed his head, walked aft to the quarterdeck, and disappeared into their cabin.

By the time he had stepped on board, every member of the crew had learned of the tragedy. It would only be proper to convey their sincere sorrow, for all were very fond of Lady Rebecca. She had brought much to their lives in so many unexpected ways, none more so than her warm feelings for the seamen and her orphaned children.

Of all places to mourn, Mr. Claussen chose his ship REBECCA. The crew took this fact right to heart. In respect for his privacy and grief, Mr. Beckwith ordered the crew below deck prior to his arrival. Without a thought of complaint, the mates remained crowded within the galley in silence. Words to be spoken were unheard, unless it was the whispering of prayers.

Once inside the cabin, Christopher retrieved Rebecca's flask of Chambord. Taking up her glass, he poured the rich liquid she had so enjoyed. How many times had he tasted it upon her lips? He became aware of the severity of his shaking. The cold had never bothered him. No, this he thought was not the cold. This was the warmth of this cabin, filled with the essence of his lady.

The fear of knowing this would all evaporate quickly, like those falling flakes of snow, gnawed at his heart. How could he bear to let that happen? How could he give up everything that was anything in his life without a fight? He walked over to their bed and imagined her pulling him down as she did on her first day aboard. He fell to his knees and listened to her telling him how she loved his ship, how she loved her bed. He moved his face through the memory of hers, and buried it into her pillow. Drawing in the lingering fragrance of lavender that was left for him, he tried in vain to keep her alive. He tried to put smoke back into a fire. What mortal could succeed? What mortal could contain the anguish? He let it go.

"Why, Rebecca. Whyeeeeee?" he cried out.

So began the arduous redemption of his soul, the patches for healing, patches forming in preparation for a wound that was now about to tear open. He would suffer. The Chambord gave way to brandy and rum, and as he slipped deeper into his drunken misery, he finally reached his destination. He sat in front of that purposeful fire at his home in Sweden. He sat alongside his father.

Through his tears, he confessed openly to his mentor. He emptied himself. He begged for mercy. He begged to be punished for his arrogance. For failing to heed his father's advice, for brushing aside his father's warnings about the perils that lurked within his desires for adventure.

On his knees at Rebecca's bed, he showed his father the left-over pieces of his life, and as always his father listened. His father understood and reached out to comfort the heart of his son. Together they began to sift through the memories. They began to sort out this wretched grief.

BOSTON COMMUNITY CHURCH

The fire

SEVENTY-ONE

Christopher closed his eyes and his book. He lay in his bunk waiting, hoping for sleep to carry him away, only to find its delay annoying him further. He opened his eyes and sighed. He wondered for what reason he was unable to rest. It had been a long day. Maybe too long, maybe he was working too hard for it seemed impossible to slow his thoughts.

Careful not to draw attention, he placed his book back upon the shelf above his bunk. Slowly, he raised his head just enough to peek at the bird, which immediately cocked its head over to one side, and stared back at him with interest. Christopher eased his head back onto the pillow and gazed up at the bottom side of the deck planks. He studied the white paint that never completely hid the currents of grain or the knots in the wood underneath its protective cover. His eyes followed their swirls, moving back and forth along the beams in mindless repetition.

There had been no point in reading any further, for each flip of a page found him still awake and served only to make him all the more irritable. Lying still, he closed his eyes and listened to the monotonous creaking of the dock lines as they stretched and rubbed, stretched and rubbed, interrupted on occasion by a thump somewhere about the decks. On a ship, sound seemed to come from every direction, and even for the sake of a bet its source could never be pinned down, but its resonance certainly amplified the silence that filled a hull. It was probably John, who had the anchor watch, moving something about on deck, he thought to himself.

Christopher was bored to the bone and restless to boot. Unable to relax, he finally sat up on his bunk. He felt tired, but not sleepy. In the dim light of the oil lamp, he looked again at the bird and then around the cabin for something, anything that might amuse him, anything that might help pass the time or at least put him to sleep for the night. A book had always been his method of choice. He was most surprised that on this night, at this late hour, not only did it have no effect, but also he was actually of a mind to get up and go out for a spell. The question was, where?

The Christmas season was in full swing, and there was an endless supply of merriment, plenty of drink, and an abundance of attractive women peddling their services to men, rich and poor alike. He could very well have been having the time of his life, the same kind of fun as anyone else, carousing in the bright lights and carnival atmosphere, playing and partaking in the diverse and satisfying nightlife now found at every corner in London. Somehow it didn't appeal. A simple cup of hot tea and a pleasant conversation with a charming lady would have been perfect.

He could blame no one except himself for being cooped up in the cabin. A few friends in town had inquired about his schedule, but he had politely sidestepped their queries. He was a solitary figure by nature—and that would probably never change. However, he was not an unbalanced individual who normally argued with him self in increasingly ornery tones of his mental voice. He snickered under his breath, and understood he must be in dire need of company.

His life, which lacked no material need, felt empty. He had been accused of retreating from his friends and of spending too much time toiling away at the books. It was a disheartening truth, one he preferred not to accept, but he found that all other activities only increased his dissatisfaction for they returned little if any fulfillment.

Sitting about in tea gardens and coffeehouses every night searching for happiness was proving to be pure folly. He longed for a meaningful relationship. He so wished for someone with whom he might walk hand in hand along city streets. He wished to view those same old decrepit buildings with the fresh feel of a lover's perspective, to move in and out of their doors wearing infectious smiles, while submerged in the laughter and frolic of romance.

He now accepted as unfortunate his decision to go hard about the business of his day, to go the extra mile without taking time to at least consider meeting friends at the hotel or theater for the evening. He had dismissed the chance for a change of heart, a break from the mound of paperwork he faced while so far away from home.

In the light of afternoon, his plan seemed sensible enough. He wished to complete his work before day's end, and then retire to bed aboard ship in order to cast off at first light. He should have given a little more thought to the type of evening in store for him aboard an empty cargo ship left under the charge of a mean-spirited bird, or more accurately, an *un-tethered* mean-spirited bird.

The bird was a tyrant, void of all manners and poorly trained. Its vocabulary was limited at best—*rudimentary cursing*, which rendered it incapable of either amusing or meaningful conversation. To make matters worse the parrot was remarkably large, and possessed an especially frightful trait.

Most anytime that Christopher would seat himself or lay down to read or rest, the parrot, which he was convinced had been named 'Fingers' for good reason, would dismount and waddle over to him. It would then proceed to scale his arm or leg or back. It made little difference to the bird where it started its ascent, so long as it ended up on top. Anyone other than Captain Ogleson or a fool would stand mortified, afraid to grab it and put it down for fear of being bitten. Therefore, it often remained on one's shoulder as long as it wished or until help arrived, all the while rubbing its host's jugular vein and terrifying the daylights out of the poor soul upon whose shoulder it laid claim.

The colorful creature put Christopher on edge to say the least, for it had a beak large enough to clip a mast, and it was particularly fond of nibbling at one's fingernails or ear lobes, especially when attracted by rings or earrings. At times it would look directly into his face and seemed to convey the thought, *'I could remove your nose while you sleep.'*

Christopher looked back in its direction again, and this time he saw the bird hanging off the perch by its beak and starting to slide a foot down the perch post in a slow, deliberate manner. He stood up at once from the bunk.

"Forget it, Fingers! You aren't going anywhere. You have the watch, remember? You may take command of the ship if you like, but stay clear of me."

"Bugger!" The bird squawked in defiance. Christopher reached for his overcoat and headed toward the hatch as the bird appeared to contemplate blocking his departure. Fortunately, it chose not, and went back to bobbing and side-stepping on its perch. Christopher gave the bully wide berth as he removed himself from the cabin.

"Stay out of trouble." He pointed at the bird with a finger kept close to heart, and then closed the hatch.

Outside, Christopher was assaulted at once by the invasive damp that earned England its reputation. There was no escaping it out of doors. It was at its worst on ship's deck where one might stand ten feet above the black face of the Thames, and yet drown within the suffocating vapors that rose from the depths to smother all else. The clammy currents of cold mist slithered past him, penetrating his lungs, his clothes, and his bones. A spasm of chill moved through him. It was time to find the warmth of an inn.

At night, London was no gathering place for the saints, but the area about the West India docks and all along the waterfront was even dangerous for society's evil. Knowing this, Christopher scoured his cabin in search for the oldest clothes that he possessed. To his dismay, he had nothing of the sort and therefore did his best to look drab by donning his least attractive garment and making his way to the ship's rigging.

Waiting for John, the anchor watch to turn his back so as not to find him a fool, he sat down upon the deck and slid around to soil his trousers, and then scrubbed the deck with his jacket as well. He slipped it back on and rubbed up against the tarred ropes a time or two to dirty himself, not so much as to prevent him from going into a public place, but enough to give him the appearance of a common working man.

He looked himself over in the light of the boarding lantern, and deemed himself to be respectfully filthy. He then started down the plank and strolled up the streets of Stepney in search of a pub that appeared friendly by comparison in these parts. He struck up a tune, whistling while he walked and hoped to present the image of a man born and raised on these streets and comfortable to be upon them at this late hour.

The first place to be seen, built almost on top of the water, was named 'Pirates Cove', and its patrons appeared to be exactly that. The next place was called the 'Red Dagger', and while it looked to be a little safer for one's health, the name put him off. The 'West Indies Inn' was painted smartly above the entryway of the third place he happened upon.

It was located a couple of blocks up from the waterfront, and during the time it took him to reach the place, he noted a number of women and children had passed through its door. This was a good sign and instilled within him a confidence that he would not end up dead, face down, atop a dinner plate. It appeared to be a family inn, and chances seemed good it would be a friendly and inviting place to visit. Putting aside his concerns, Christopher crossed the street and headed for the establishment.

As soon as he stepped in from the cold, he was swept up in the atmosphere of the place. Immersed in pleasant sensations, his first breath of air was warm, inviting, and filled with the redolence of hot steaming dishes spread across crowded tables or being carried about on trays. The mouth-watering aromas ranged from seasoned roast meats to cinnamon and the smells of freshly brewed coffee and teas.

The place was packed in, and he welcomed the hustle bustle of bar maids, table maidens, and patrons engaged busily in calls, arguments, and conversation. It was a great place to chance upon, and exactly what he had hoped for while lying alone in his bunk. He took up a stool at the end of the bar and removed his jacket. It was a good vantage point from which to pass the night watching the goings on with an unobstructed view of the room.

At his back was a door leading to the kitchen, which remained open more than not, but for the constant traffic of the barmaids and table maidens. And so it was, having just made himself comfortable and working up to a thirst, he looked out across the crush of patrons. It was precisely then, before his eyes barely understood what they had seen, his heart tripped over itself, and he was rocked to his core by a vision of the most beautiful girl he believed God ever created.

Dressed in the plainest of clothes, her hair done up atop her head, she brushed past him under a tray of dirty dishes on her way back to the kitchen. Christopher sat stunned, staring straight ahead, refusing to accept the fact that any girl that beautiful was waiting on tables, especially in some unknown eatery on the streets of Stepney. Seconds seemed like hours, before she reappeared with another tray of hot food. Her blue eyes and snow-white teeth flashed in competition as she glanced about her tables and laughed with the patrons. Her every move was delicate and dance-like. He knew she had to be the perfect woman.

He was smitten, if ever a man was. He likened it to a young child opening his eyes for the first time ever, and seeing Westminster, and puppies, and Christmas trees, and tall ships, and candy shops all at once. Every inch of his body was tingling with excitement in response to the sight of her.

He simply could not believe such a woman existed. He could not believe how out of control he felt at having seen her. The sensation was immediate and intense. A reaction of this measure came only when one had eaten poisoned food or something fearful and found himself instantly covered in hives or dying—the difference being that this was exhilarating. He had heard of this feeling many times, laughed at the silliness of such exaggerations, but now he knew. It was no exaggeration; it was love at first sight.

Time and time again she passed by him, back and forth through the swinging kitchen door, and at each pass he strove to collect another small piece of her for his memory. It was difficult, for at first he was completely unable to look at her. He believed she must realize that all men stared at her. He believed she knew this without so much as seeing a man's face. How else could it be? When one's feelings were so intense, they were surely projected across the room, across the street, across the universe. His heart was pouring out its desire for her, wringing out every ounce of longing. Surely she sensed it. He felt naked before her and averted his eyes at her every passing.

At least if he didn't look at her, he could safely say with disappointment, she didn't look at him either. She looked over him, around him, to one side of him and the other. She looked below him but, worst of all, she looked right through him and never noticed him once, or at least so it seemed.

Going unnoticed was not something to which Christopher was accustomed. This time it was a sobering experience. He was a powerful-looking man, large in frame, covered with a thick crop of blonde hair, and he possessed crystal blue eyes that women would die for. Add to that, at least within the circles that he traveled, financial stature was as attractive as was physical stature, if not even more so, and in this respect he was perfectly wealthy.

Sadly, it had always been this aspect of his life that troubled him the most. Inside he feared it wasn't so much the blonde of his hair, the blue of his eyes, or the goodness of his heart, but the golden rings and coin within in his hand that attracted so many women. It was the wealth. Fortune distorted reality about him on a daily basis. It changed people instantly from being what they were to what they knew he wanted them to be. It changed them from saying what they felt to what they knew he wanted to hear.

Wherever he went, whatever he did, there were always women in line, women waiting to make his acquaintance, women saying and doing things to please him with no idea where to go from there, for they were unable to go back to their true selves. In their eyes he saw the reflection of himself as the answer to their prayers. He saw the rush of their hopes and the collapse of their hearts when he didn't look back. It was one of the reasons he tended to shy away from women as a rule. It was difficult at best to turn away a young lady, no matter how polite the attempt. They always knew, and he always felt cheap.

All these thoughts raced through his mind as a revelation began to take hold. He was beginning to understand that here seemed an opportunity that had to be more than sheer coincidence. Why couldn't he sleep? Why was he here? Why was he looking at the most beautiful woman he had ever seen? How was it possible she could be as gorgeous as an angel and yet come into his world unmarried? A sliver of ice shot through him. Maybe she wasn't unmarried. He studied her hands but saw no rings, no signs of such commitment. Besides, too many men approached her. A married woman would have been more distant.

Maybe there was something else. Maybe there was something dark and hidden about her, some terrible secret that everyone knew, some curse that made her untouchable? No! No, he knew, he knew that she was a good-hearted person by the way she looked at those who teased her, by the fact she was always smiling, by how easily she laughed. She was happy in her heart. She was a joyful person who radiated warmth and understanding. He could have seen this with his eyes closed.

He realized that without speaking so much as one word to this woman that he had found everything he wanted. Fate had brought this spirit to him. He knew nothing about her, but more important, this woman knew nothing of him. He was dressed as a commoner and at this moment in time she could not know him, or his family, or his wealth. The stage was set, and it was up to him to direct the play. If he could win her heart over under the pretense of a commoner, he would know her love to be for real, only for him, and not for the wealth that crowded out everything else in his life.

He sat at the end of the bar, staring over his shoulder at the kitchen door, waiting for it to swing open again, just as a pet dog waits for his master to appear so they might go for a walk. And like a dog, he could barely contain his excitement whenever she appeared. The only time his eyes ever left sight of her was during those brief periods when he blinked or she disappeared beyond the kitchen door, unless of course she looked his way.

Spurred on by the vision of this angel, and having nothing but time on his hands, he began to consider by what means he might make her acquaintance. The easy way would have been to buy the inn, to buy the whole damned street if need be, but he was convinced that would only bring him misery in the end. In that way she would become whatever she believed he wished. He wanted to know her for herself. He had to think. He had to keep his senses about him, for his heart understood; his heart was emphatic. *Wealth was not the way.*

He started by trying to push back all the rules and restrictions for proper gentlemanly conduct that were embedded deep in his character. This was the first time he could remember being the pursuer. He had never been so attracted to another person. Actually, he had never been attracted to another person at all, and suddenly here he was overwhelmed by a desire that was clawing its way through him. He would not act foolishly. He would wait patiently. He would wait until such time when flushing his quarry would prove rewarding. He would leash his desire.

The longer Christopher watched, the more he had come to realize this girl was no easy match. The folly of flushing quarries and good catches was absurd, for men at every table hurled compliments and proposals her way endlessly. She used them, each and every one, to her advantage. She was full of it, as sharp-witted as any woman he had ever considered. She toyed with the patrons, caressing them, cajoling them, but always keeping them in line and at a distance. The best indication of how well she knew her business was in the rapport she maintained with the ladies. They felt unthreatened by her flirtations and chided their men for making such fools out of themselves.

The popularity of the inn was testimony to the repast, which was every bit as good as the aromas that preceded it. The meal improved Christopher's vigor, and was enhanced by the rich, smooth lagers, which he now imbibed far more than usual. It kept him his seat and improved his focus by removing the distractions of his life and allowing him to sink into dreams of her love. Finally, it gave him a measure of the drunkard's courage, which he was now more than willing to accept, for no one was about to make introductions in his behalf, and he would depart for Sweden within a matter of hours. He watched the maiden making her approach to the swinging door, and took another healthy swig from his mug. It was now or never.

"I beg your pardon, madam."

"Your service."

"An odd request, if I may?"

"Go on then."

"My name is Christopher Claussen, and I am a stranger to these parts, having just arrived in port and soon to depart. I confess I was forced to listen in on your conversations in order to assure myself that you were indeed Rebecca of the West Indies Inn. Might I have a word with you in private?"

Up went the walls of defense and all her flags of suspicion. She scrutinized him, her eyes narrowing as she sized him up. Christopher fully expected the reaction and played it as he had orchestrated. He continued on, not allowing her time to counter.

"Forgive me my impudence! My interest was merely to move to a nearby table somewhat out of this distraction."

He waved at the patrons seated next to him at the bar. Christopher felt as if every man leaning over a mug knew what he was up to. He felt as if they had all made their play for her affections at one time or another and fared better or worse. As they glanced his way, he imagined them to be keeping score and awaiting the outcome. It made him all the more nervous.

"What's this about, sir?"

"If I might impose upon you to join me at the table. I beg you to understand my discomfort at the bar."

"Very well." Rebecca led the way to a nearby table as he wished, but remained on her feet.

Christopher couldn't think of her beauty without becoming perplexed. It was difficult for him to look at her, especially into her eyes, so he concentrated on his moves, viewing it as a game that was ultimately challenging.

"Please, as a gentleman, I implore…." He pulled back a chair and encouraged her to take the seat. Unhappily, she complied, a frown displaying her annoyance.

"Thank you, Rebecca. May I call you Rebecca?"

"You may call me whatever suits you, sir, but choose it with care."

"Very well, Rebecca it is. I love that name, it would be an effort to call you anything finer."

"Go on then, sir, what is it you wish?" She was quick to the point.

"Rebecca, I travel a great deal, mostly by ship. I deal in the buying and selling of odds and ends, and often find myself stumbling upon items that when placed in the right hands prove to be very profitable. On certain occasions such as this, my package is indeed significant. On the continent, I was given explicit instructions to deliver this parcel to you for safekeeping. A handsome fee would be yours for the inconvenience, it goes without saying.

"I will be frank by saying I questioned the sensibilities of my colleague as to why this place. I have heard many stories about Stepney, but few which instill confidence. I will even admit to having asked why at the very least I shouldn't place it with the management, but he wouldn't hear of it. He was steadfast in his opinion that your reputation as a person of honesty and integrity was well known by many a sailor who had the privilege to make your acquaintance. Of course, I am at the sole mercy of his judgment, for I have never laid eyes upon you before this night. Who am I to question his high regard for your person? I can only assume that although he made no mention of it, you must know him, one William Carpenter?"

"No, sir. The name means nothing to me."

Christopher worked up an expression of astonishment.

"You are certain? Can it be? By the way he speaks of you; I would have thought you practically his sister. I am honestly surprised, for he—."

"Sir, I meet a hundred men a night in this place." She interrupted him. "They all think they know me. They all think they know me well. I assure you they know nothing of me, and that is how I prefer it."

"Yes. Yes, of course. I beg your pardon. I understand. After all, you are very attractive. I mean...I mean to say it...it... must be very difficult to say the least." Christopher stumbled momentarily. "If I may, allow me to add only that the contents are personal possessions and of little value to most but, as I mentioned before, extremely valuable to some.

"In either case, it is nothing whereby ownership would violate the law of His Majesty the King. I would pay you one week of your wages to hold it near your person until tomorrow or possibly the day after when Mr. Carpenter will come for it. I will have already departed for Sweden, and that is the whole of it. Would you consider doing me this service? It is a handsome fee, or do you not agree?"

"Keep your parcel a day for a week's wages?"

"My word, you catch on quick, Rebecca. I will pay in advance."

"Are you mocking me, sir?"

"No! No, not at all! Did it seem so? I only meant to imply I shall pay you at once, right now if you wish."

He had been foolishly sarcastic, and was forced to squirm his way out. It was stupid of him. Did he need to prove he was in control of the situation by taking a risk? He wasn't sure, but learned at once how fragile was this encounter. She didn't present the same good-spiritedness toward him as she did the others. He should have remembered that he was a stranger.

"You swear there is nothing to this that will get me sent off to the plantations?"

"Nothing! Nothing whatsoever, I swear it. I encourage you to open the parcel and see for yourself if you should feel suspicious." He felt a sense of relief. He regained his ground.

Rebecca rocked her chair back onto its rear legs. Pivoting back and forth she never took her eyes off his.

"Rebecca! You're backing up, get on with it, hon."

The warning came from an older woman returning from the kitchen with her own tray of food.

"Be right there, Hattie."

She dropped the chair on all fours, and leaning forward across the table in his direction, she commanded him.

"Let me see your hands, Mr. Claussen." She held out hers.

"I'm sorry?" Caught by surprise, he checked his reaction. She was special. What was she up to now, he wondered?

"Your hands, sir. I wish to see them."

"By all means."

He placed them flat on the table. He commended himself for remembering to remove his rings when he dressed down.

She slipped her delicate hands under the mass of his, and ran her fingers lightly across his palms. The sensation of her touch was thrilling and stole away his every thought. He sat in bliss—but not for long.

"You toy with me, Mr. Claussen," she warned. Christopher tried not to blush for fear of giving himself away.

"What troubles you now, Rebecca? I am not sure I can make my offer any more straightforward or attractive." He shook his head, playing dumb and trying to sound earnest.

"Your clothes are soiled with the smear of tar, but your nails are cleaner than mine, and I wash many a dish in the course of a day. Your palms are very supple for a man who makes a living handling rope." She then placed each of her forefingers firmly upon his ring fingers. "You also forgot to put your rings back on."

My God! He thought as he looked at the faint white lines. *Doesn't she beat all?* He aimed to stand his ground, if for no other reason than to go down in flames with the sound of her voice left upon his ear.

"Perchance you've mistaken me for a sailor. When I stated that I was aboard ship, I meant as a passenger, not a crewmate.

As for the clothes, I spent most of the day in the holds, chocking and un-chocking my cargo. One of my crates was broken and its contents spilled. It is a filthy place in the bilge, is it not? What else might I add? The rings? Here." He reached into his pocket and pulled out the pair, hoping she would not realize their true value. "I seldom wear them at night for fear of enticing robbers. Do you find that cowardly of me? I hope not. I think it rather sensible when I am in a strange place, and as I have said, I am not from these parts." *Very well done*, he thought to himself.

Rebecca couldn't quite put her finger on what bothered her, but she had great respect for her instincts. The man before her obviously was not an Englishman. She was confident he was originally Scandinavian. He said he soon departed for Sweden and she easily accepted him to be a Swede. All her years near the port, and serving sailors, had taught her well the origins of the accents and dialects overheard at her tables.

She was uncomfortable, yet it was unfair to mark this man a liar or worse based solely on her suspicions. By the look of him, he was a respectable sort. He seemed mannerly enough. He should be entitled to the benefit of her doubts, but that didn't mean she had to be the fool. She thought it best to take care, and determined so long as no money passed between them, she couldn't be nearly as guilty. It might also afford her time if need be. In the back of her mind, she thought of the many ways she could use the money to help with gifts at the orphanage for Christmas.

"Very well. Let's have it then." She held out her hand.

"Oh! Thank-you for accepting, but I didn't bring the parcel with me, as I was unsure I would find you. If you tell me what time you close, I will see to it you shall have it shortly before. I must return to the ship and fetch it. Is it an agreement then?"

Her instincts said no, no, no. Still, Rebecca thought uneasily, nothing amiss was to be found, and the money was enticing. Maybe she was overreacting because such a sum was so easily earned.

"As you wish, pay me when it's finished, not before."

With that she stood up and without turning to look back, she walked off and disappeared through the swinging door.

Christopher sat back. *Sweet Mary Joseph! What a lovely, lovely creature. What a joust!* He was full of adrenaline. This was only the beginning. Round one, and he had plenty of work yet to do, so he pulled on his coat and took leave of the inn.

The docks were vacant and the ships rocked silently, their decks void of life save for the occasional anchor watch. It was cold and damp, and altogether unpleasant to be out of doors in the night. Receiving permission to board from John, who was still on watch, Christopher leapt up the boarding plank and quickly made for the cabin. There, avoiding the parrot at all cost, he searched for a quill and ink. He then went below decks and returned with a piece of old dunnage. He studied the wood piece, penned some Latin letters and designs upon it, then took out a sheet of paper and wrote the following missive.

William,

As promised, here is the missing piece

that confirms the Galleon's position.

The longitude can be deciphered,

if we adhere to our prescribed methods.

Good luck and good fortune!!!

Christopher N. Claussen

He underlined the word *fortune* for effect, then wrapped the piece in a scrap of sailcloth and tied it with twine in a knot easily undone. Next he included a ring of much greater value than the week's wages he promised to pay—this to add authenticity to his written message and also to test her honesty.

"Perfect!" he exclaimed out loud, breaking the silence.

"PERFECT!" screamed the bird, nearly bringing Christopher to his knees with fright.

"AHH! Blast you! You put the scare of death into me. I have a mind to make you a collection of quills, and grille you into a bird-brained barbecue!" He flashed a look of revenge.

"PERFECT!" the bird squawked again, unconcerned.

Christopher clenched his fist, stared at the bird and fancied some thoughts of animal torture. They were soon dismissed and he picked up the parcel, grabbed his coat, and once again with great satisfaction shut the bird inside the cabin. Above deck, he informed John that he would return later and descended to the dock. He was in need of a person to enlist in supporting his crusade to win Rebecca's attention. He scoured the docks. The first few men he passed did nothing to encourage him—quite the contrary in fact. The fifth person, a stevedore, appeared much more agreeable to Christopher, who didn't have much time to be fussy.

The man looked honest and approachable. He was whistling and singing, going about his business unbothered by the cold. He danced about, sorting out crates of spices, herbs, and vegetables. His work was keeping him warm. Christopher noted he actually sang rather respectably.

Ploock th' feather's froom a goose
Never, never turn 'im loose
e'll steal away yoor pillow, right
'neath yer nooggin' in th' night.
Hummmmmmm, hummmmmm,
laaa deee deee dumm dumm.

"Good evening, sir!" Christopher opened.

"Mate." The man nodded his head, and continued whistling while buried in bushels of garlic and onions. Christopher liked the feel of him, for he was a man who stayed to his work.

"You're a busy man at such a late hour. Especially on such a disagreeable night."

"Ayeee. Theer's no time to waste. The vigteebles rawt quick. Me master hoolds a roomage sale oon the morrow. The agent ne'er paid a pound. So eet's gawt to go. The whoole lawt."

"Dirty business, dirty business, indeed. Begging you pardon, sir, I go by Christopher Claussen. I'm boarded on the FAIR WEATHER, and am here in London a day or two for purpose of business. I am myself in need of a helping hand and would like to propose to you a handsome profit in return for a small favor, if you're inclined to hear of such a thing."

The stranger stood up from within the crates and worked the stiffness out of his back. He looked squarely at Christopher.

"An' whot might thot be, sir?"

"It's a matter of love, my good man. No nobler a cause could there be. Don't you agree? I am of a mind to impress a young lady, who I have concluded is going to be most difficult to meet. It has taken either a great deal of cunning and creativity, or else stupidity on my part to get as far as I have thus. That, I am into it with both feet is true enough, and still, I require the assistance of another to further my progress. I refuse to falter or fall back one inch to lose what I have thus far gained with such great effort. Would you be willing to partake in my plan, sir?"

The man let out a knowing laugh. "Oyee, thot I might, I'm still list'nin. Ooz th' lass you've taken fancy to, then?" He grinned with a broad and pleasing smile.

"She is an absolute angel. The most remarkable woman I have ever seen. And I trust you will believe when I say I have seen many. Her name is Rebecca, she is employed at the West—."

At that point, Christopher was broken off by a howl from this likable stranger.

"Aha, ha! I doon't believe me ears. Yoou're oonder th' spell ov Rebecca Greystoone are ye naught then!" The man went on stomping the dock and laughing with great amusement.

"You know her?"

"Know 'er! Oyee, do I. Aloong with aboout a millioon oother sailoors, do I!" He was still grinning and shaking his head.

"Sweet Mary Joseph! You're not going tell me she's a whore then." Christopher grimaced. The stranger drew up dead serious.

"Moother ov God, Man! No sooch thing indeed! She's as pure as th' chile she is, to th' best ov me knoowledge. Boot, she 'as a ringer ov a reputation, that un. Get to close to 'er an' she'll lay ye oot coold! Mark me woords, man!" He nodded his head to reinforce his claims.

"Of that, I have no doubt," Christopher agreed.

"'Ave ye never 'eard 'em sing ov 'er? She's famous that un." He frowned, showing his surprise.

"Singing? No. Can't say that I have."

"Well then, just 'ave a listen!" He stepped out from behind the crates. "Give us soome room mate! Stand back, this'll be yer first, boot nary a day'll pass soome sailoor woon't strooll by a whistlin' th' tune." He took an exaggerated breath for effect and began.

647

Oyeee! Tell me noow me maties, tell me noow agen
'ave yer eyes laid rest upoon the loov'ly lady ov th' Thames
'er name it 'as bin ferried acrooss th' seven seas
'n th' 'eart ov ev'ry sailoor man 'ose bin by West Indies

Oh! Rebecca! Rebecca! Rebecca, darlin' dear
Think oon me foorever, an' foorever I'll be near

Oh! Rebecca! Rebecca! Rebecca, darlin' dear
Save yer 'eart an' I'll be back me proomise be sincere

Oyeee! Th' boys they be a waitin' but foor 'er t' take a man
She cares foor naught an' patiently awaits upoon th' land
Foor one t' coom before 'er an' swear upoon 'is knees
t' swallow th' anchoor in 'er name iv that be what she please.

Oh! Rebecca! Rebecca! Rebecca, darlin' dear
Think on me foorever an' foorever I'll be near

Oh! Rebecca! Rebecca! Rebecca, darlin' dear
Save yer 'eart an' I'll be back me proomise be sincere

Oyeee! Th' tall ships sail foor England an'when th' island's foound
From ev'ry mooring in th' poort th' sailoors coome aroound
But not t' see th' Abby of Wesmin'ster or th' Crown
Only th' loov'ly lady ov th' Thames ov Loondon town

Oh! Rebecca! Rebecca! Rebecca, darlin' dear
Think on me foorever an' foorever I'll be near

Oh! Rebecca! Rebecca! Rebecca, darlin' dear
Promise me you'll save yer 'eart
an' I'll be back...I swear

The stevedore took a large and sweeping bow, minus only a hat covered with plumage to have effected a perfect image. Christopher was captivated by the performance. Nothing bashful about him, he thought, and he gave the man a rousing round of applause.

"Well done! Well done indeed!" He laughed.

"Go oon then, wha' tizzit yoo'll be needin' froom me," he inquired.

"First, honor me with thy name." Christopher offered his hand.

"Th' name's Darrin O'Kurk."

The men shook hands.

"The pleasure is mine, Mr. O'Kurk. And grateful am I that you've lent me your ear. Here is my request. As you see, I have with me a parcel. It is of no significance. A piece of dunnage with some scribbles and a note…." Christopher took a moment to contain his amusement. "A note stating simply enough that this would be the missing link to locating a treasure-laden galleon. Nothing more. I have also included a small golden ring to lend some credence to my ruse." He looked to Darrin for approval.

"A treasure laden galleoon an' noothin' moore, you say," he repeated with a taste of sarcasm.

"My word of honor. Trivial matters as such. It is my hope she might take it upon herself to refasten the parcel, as I have done my best to see to it that it comes completely undone. And, if she has but a hint of woman in her, I trust she will be unable to resist the temptation of a peek. At this point, she will see the ring and further appreciate the importance of the contents. Hopefully, she will keep them close to her side.

"When she leaves her place of employment at the hour of eleven or shortly thereafter, I will employ you to snatch it away and disappear. You may rid yourself of the parcel, but bring me back the ring so I might attest to your success. It is my hope that she will be in such a state of distress, and so fear my anger that she will do whatever I might ask—within reason as a gentleman of course. I mean, if for no reason other than to appease my downtrodden heart in this horrible misfortune."

"Iv that doon't beat th' devil's play sir, I'll noot know it when I see it." Darrin shook his head, amazed. "An' whot's init foor Mr. O'Kurk?"

"Two pounds sterling."

"Goot Loord, ye must be in loove, indeed. I'll do it, then."

The agreement was confirmed with a handshake, and Christopher was again off to the West Indies Inn to deliver the parcel to Rebecca.

Shortly after eleven, while Christopher paced the dock, giddy with anticipation and too nervous to face the bird or a stay in the cabin, Darrin came into view from the darkened street whistling Rebecca's song. Christopher was off at once to meet him. As he neared the man, he saw him waving the entire parcel with a look of satisfaction.

"Bravo! Job well done! None too difficult, I hope?"

Darrin stopped in his tracks, and offered a most sympathetic look in Christopher's direction. "Mr. Clauzzen, you trooly doon't know Rebecca thot well now do ye."

"I'm afraid not—that bad was it?"

"It was no big thing foor a man sooch as I. Boot, be it knoown thot in th' wee space ov time, froom whence I pawpped it free ov 'er grasp t' fetching it oop off th' stoones, she planted th' heel ov 'er boot into th' back ov me ass moore times than th' coock croows at th' break ov dawn!"

"Oh, say it isn't so. I beg your pardon. I am embarrassed for the inconvenience I have brought you, but as I said, I shall reward you handsomely for your effort. Tell me, did she get a look at your face?"

"Nawt thet I know as I 'ad me woolen cap pooled low aboot me brow. Why d' ye ask?"

"If I could interest you in further assistance, for an additional fee of course, I might add to my advantage by enlisting you to represent yourself as the recipient of the parcel. You would drop by tomorrow to procure your package and upon news of the theft, you would make a great fuss of concern, but none more so than your feelings for my great misfortune and possible loss beyond measure. I believe that would indeed put a perfect position to enjoy her sympathy. Do you not see shrewdness of it?"

Both men laughed and in the end Christopher repaired to the cabin with his guest, offering him a quality port to remove his chill and a warning about Fingers.

The following day, Darrin O'Kurk, after having cleaned and dressed appropriately, stepped through the front door of the West Indies Inn. Finding Rebecca was no problem. He knew her by sight and memory due to many hours of his own wishful thinking, for like numbers of other sailors on the docks, he had been by to have a look at her a time or two himself.

"I'm 'ere foor a Rebecca Greeystoone!"

"That's me." She turned to her caller.

"Mr. William Carpoonter." He extended his hand. Rebecca didn't bother to return the gesture.

"Do I have business with you, sir?" She asked directly, not at first recognizing the name.

"So it is. I am 'ere t' coollect a parcel froom woon Mr. Christopher Clauzzen."

Rebecca paled. She was implicated in a mess she wished no part of, but now she had to go through the motions.

651

"I am dreadfully sorry to say, I am no longer in possession of the man's parcel."

Darrin feigned confusion. "I moost misoonderstand ye. Did I 'ear you say th' parcel iz noot with ye?"

"That is what I said."

"Might we fetch it, so I am able t' continue, as I am emplooyed?"

"That will be impossible I fear, for it was stolen from my grip at the close of eleven last evening."

Darrin transformed himself into the picture of a man who just heard his prized bird dog was shot.

"Moother ov Got! Thiz is terr'ble!"

He paced back and forth before her, empty thoughts racing through his mind. He raised his hand to his brow and pinched the bridge of his nose; thinking of dinner and the extra money he was earning, he twisted his face into a knot. Rebecca studied him silently.

"I um speechless. I fear Mr. Clauzzen will be rooined. Thiz is terr'ble, indeed!" He threw out his arms like some sacrifice upon a cross. "Foorgive me. I moost depart immediately an' nootify him at woonce! Good day, Miss Greystoone!" Darrin stormed out of the inn.

Christopher paid Darrin well for his efforts as he had promised. He then held up the departure of his ship for a few days. Each minute that passed brought a new wave of agony as he forced himself to stay clear of the West Indies. He spent his time working the books or conversing with Darrin, whose company he came to enjoy very much. By his opinion, he allowed enough time for the theft to ferment into true guilt for Rebecca. He believed she should now be as clay to the sculptor.

He entered the inn two nights later wearing a better change of clothing and the face of a man trying to maintain a stiff upper lip after his third bout with the runs. He seated himself at a table and appeared to be most uncomfortable. This time Rebecca didn't look over him, to the side of him, or through him. She wasted no time and moved to put an end to these pains.

"Hello, Mr. Claussen."

"Ah. My Rebecca, how are you this day?" He applied the weight of the world to his greeting.

"In light of recent happenings, my patience has been tried indeed. Was it purely my imagination, or did you not say the package was of no value?"

"Forgive me, Rebecca. You have every right to be upset. It was my wish to save you any unnecessary alarm. I was wrong to have put you in a position whereby you were exposed to the scoundrels of the street. I do hope you'll accept my apology."

Rebecca settled down.

"You seem to be taking this well, Mr. Claussen. I would have expected much worse, for Mr. Carpenter was expressly concerned for your well-being and disposition from what I gathered."

"Pay him no mind, Rebecca. It is not a good thing; this is true. I would have preferred different, at worst I will lose my home, but with time and hard work…I have a strong back. I will see my way through this. Have no fear."

"Mr. Claussen. I am truly sorry. I hope you understand I wasn't being careless. It happened so fast." Her face reflected her feeling. For the first time her disposition softened as she gazed upon him with those wonderful blue eyes. *'Anything',* he thought to himself, *'anything at all in the world and it is yours.'*

"I believe you, Rebecca. Put it out of your mind at once. It was no fault of yours. I can see that plainly in your eyes. It seems as though the scoundrel was lying in wait. I have been betrayed, so it appears."

"I may be able to offer you some recourse. If nothing else, please allow me to offer this small gesture in hopes of easing your burden. If you'll wait a moment, I shall return."

She placed her hand on his arm affectionately. He would wait until the end of time.

True to her word, within moments she returned to the table with a gentleman who appeared out of place at the inn. Over dressed, possibly the owner, Christopher thought to himself.

"Mr. Claussen, I would like to introduce you to our very own Professor of Antiquity, Sir Leonard Marshall."

The professor offered his hand. Confused, Christopher rose to accept it, and then both Rebecca and the professor sat down at the table on either side of Christopher. She continued.

"I must tell you, Mr. Claussen, I am not one to be nosy about the affairs of others. I was genuinely concerned about the state of your parcel, as it fell to pieces while in my pocket. You having spoken of the significance of your find, I took it upon myself to copy in every detail the markings upon the wood for safe keeping. How fortunate I should have done so. Don't you agree?"

"Ah…ah…yes, certainly I do. What incredible luck, yes, yes. What luck, indeed! I, ah, I am lost for words."

Christopher swallowed with difficulty, perceiving the knot in his stomach turning into a noose about his neck. He then asked.

"Why did you not give the copy to Mr. Carpenter?"

Rebecca froze. She stammered.

"I…I…thought only of the missing ring. That was it! But, I brought the copy to the good professor after Mr. Carpenter informed me of the difficult situation you faced by my failing. I hoped he might bring his vast knowledge to bear upon this cause, and I hope indeed to assist you in any manner possible after failing you so miserably." Rebecca raced to get back the upper hand. To her relief, the professor immediately entered the conversation.

"Mr. Claussen, mmm...I must say I am most intrigued by the mmm...markings, and of course I am aware of the note about the mmm...galleon. I have a passion for historical events and artifacts connected with the discoveries of the New World. I have spent my whole life pursuing such issues.

"I can bring a full array of mmm...maps and books, charts of the sea routes, and mmm...did I mention I brought the entire issue up to the Museum Council of English History and Science? That, I might add, is very close indeed to the court of our mmm... Majesty King George. I assure you, sir, you may rest easy now that this is in my hands, providing you have no mmm...objection of course. But how could you! I am offering you the entire scholastic community of learned men for assistance. Many of which, I might add, are beating my door down to get an mmm... audience with you, sir. News travels fast, does it not?"

The professor stopped to get a breath. Christopher was numb, he had no choice at this point but to go with the flow and think fast.

"I am very sorry to say that it was the shape of the wood upon which the markings were made that was most pertinent in determining the precise meaning of the...ah...writing. I believe its shape was a part of a map. Without it, I am afraid we have nothing. It is pointless to continue. It is lost to us forever."

Christopher could not believe what was taking place. Where was this all going, what did he give birth to? The professor jumped right back in.

"A mere mmm...detail, my good fellow. I thought as much myself, but it was similar to the map used in finding the lost ROSA MARIA DI GENOVA three years ago. Do not give up so easily, my good man. I have at my disposal upwards of mmm...fifty scholars to decipher the code that Rebecca was so thoughtful to copy, and more calling by the hour. All eager to view this new challenge. What she has saved, along with her description should be enough, and I trust you will make yourself mmm…available. I give you my word, I will personally oversee every detail." He looked about to determine time.

"I believe mmm…Lord Asterly and Lord Morgan should be by in just a few. They are very excited to question you further on this matter. Anything you say may hold great promise for the future. Don't be surprised if your name ends up placed permanently in mmm…bronze at the foot of the library steps, along with all the great contributors to the advancement of knowledge. I have no doubt that the mmm…king himself will present you with Knighthood if all goes well. Where is Lord Asterly anyway?" He looked around impatiently.

Christopher had no doubts he had buried himself too deep into something gone terribly awry. He had made one grave mistake. He couldn't even see his way clear of a prank, let alone the Lords of His Majesties' court. He could jump upon his ship and sail away but that would deprive him of all he sought. He had no choice but to admit he was a liar and a prankster and would accept whatever ridicule might come his way, especially the embarrassment to follow his confession to Rebecca. He surmised he had only dignity to lose but a great deal more to gain if she understood. He leaned over the table to speak to her.

"Rebecca. May I have a word with you in private? I fear it is an issue most pressing."

Rebecca appeared taken aback by this unsociable request, but went on to speak to him in a comforting voice.

"Mr. Claussen, I assure you that you have no need to hold secrets back from Sir Leonard Marshall. Do you not see his great generosity? He has gone out of his way to help you. Well…you and me." Her eyes opened to him.

"I am afraid it is not nearly as easy as that, Rebecca." He turned to the professor. "Sir, I beg you forgive me my manner. I know I must appear unfavorably rude, but I truly must speak with Rebecca on an issue that demands privacy. Would you be so kind as to leave us, I beg you understand."

The professor was a fast-talking slug of a man. He seemed glued to his chair. Unbelievable as it may be, the man seemed lost for words.

"Mmm…very well, then. Yes, mmm, of course. I'll just be at the bar, then. Do you think I should wait at the bar, Rebecca? Would that be good, then?"

"That would be fine. Order up an ale while you are there, sir, and I will call you back at once."

At last, the professor finally stood up and moved in that direction. Christopher worked up all the courage he could muster. His face was now flushed bright red. He sensed he would relive this nightmare a thousand times to come.

"Rebecca—."

He stopped short. She was sniffing the air about the table, moving closer to him. She stood up and leaned into his chest and sniffed again. Then, she looked into his face with the strangest expression.

"What is it?" Christopher asked, feeling very self-conscious about his possible odor.

"Do you smell onions?" she asked.

"Onions?"

"Yes. It's the oddest thing. The man who came to pick up your precious parcel smelled of onions. The man who stole it, and I dare say sits uncomfortably, also smelled of onions. Is it me, or do you reek of them as well, sir?" She raised her nose slightly to give her that look of snobbish superiority.

It took a moment for Christopher to digest exactly what just took place. He stared at her with a look of question. He still wasn't sure what she was saying or what she was leading up to, but he sensed she was on to him.

"You know?" The words came out most feeble.

Rebecca returned a look of contempt. She turned to the bar.

"Ben!" The professor turned to face her.

"Your ale is on the house the whole of the day, you were superb. Get bloody well drunk if ya like!"

"Thank-you, Reb. I'll see to it, then." He now spoke quickly and to the point, unlike before with the pronounced drawl.

"Make certain you leave me the passes before you go and get forgetful."

"That I will, Reb." He flashed them both a knowing grin.

Rebecca turned back to Christopher. He spit out his first word.

"Ben?"

"Benjamin Dailey. He's a dockman, and an actor to boot. A damn good one, I would say. Don't you agree, sir? I don't know what your business is here, Mr. Claussen, but it certainly raises suspicion. I don't care much for liars. We get our share of them down here on the docks, and I am pretty good about knowing one when I see one."

Christopher let out a tremendous sigh of genuine relief. He looked at her.

"Rebecca. All I have said from the moment I stepped through the door of this inn has been false. Lies, just as you have supposed. Yet, I swear as God is my witness, all that I have thought from that same moment was no creature created in heaven above has ever been more perfect in the eyes of a man than you are to me. I hope you will allow me this one truth. I could see it would be near impossible to make your acquaintance, so I concocted this preposterous charade to accomplish the deed. I am woefully embarrassed and might only say in the future I shall relive this humiliation a thousand times, I have no doubt."

Christopher was honest and it came across as so. Rebecca's instincts were seldom wrong. They looked at each other a moment before Rebecca responded.

"Did it ever cross your mind to say…Rebecca, might you consider having dinner with me, even though I am a stranger in these parts?"

"No."

"And why not, then?"

"I didn't think that would work."

"Does it not cover everything you had in mind?"

"Yes," Christopher responded weakly.

"Then you truly are daft, are you not?" Christopher remained silent.

"I'm off at nine tonight. You can come for me then."

Christopher's eyes said it all.

"And Mr. Claussen…choose your inn carefully."

SEVENTY-TWO

At half past eight the coach pulled up in front of the West Indies Inn. Christopher entered and seated himself in the waiting room. He looked over toward the men's bar, and as promised, there sat Ben 'three sheets t' the wind.'

Rebecca made a show, and instructed Christopher to be patient whilst she freshened up. He was honestly nervous. More so now than all the time involved in the prank, at least up to the point of being found out. That was horrible, just the thought of it made him squirm. He was not a person accustomed to being embarrassed. Fortunately, she was quick to appear and saved him from his reflections. She became lovelier every time he looked at her.

"Shall we, then?" she asked.

Christopher rose to his feet, and offered her his arm.

"Please forgive me if I should ever fail to gush when speaking of you. You look divine." He stopped to look her square. "Absolutely divine."

She said nothing—not because it didn't please her but because she knew little of him. She intended to maintain a comfortable distance.

"I trust you chose your dinner place carefully," she casually warned.

"It took a lot of thought. Not easy for one who is a stranger to these parts."

"Then, I will be judge."

"Suits me fine. A challenge of sorts."

The coach began a leisurely roll along the streets toward London. Rebecca paid little mind at first as they talked about a number of lighthearted things, none too personal. The coach made a slow steady about face, and in time was heading back into the direction from whence it came. Rebecca, who was knowledgeable of most of London took notice but said nothing. She assumed they were taking a ride for the sake of conversation, a chance to come to know one another.

"I am curious, Rebecca. Would you really have joined me for dinner had I only asked forthright?"

"Of course not."

"Of course not?"

"You are a stranger. Why would I go out to dinner with a stranger? That is foolish and dangerous."

"But then how would we have met?"

"We wouldn't have."

"Then you are saying my charade was my only recourse after all."

"I am saying no such thing. A gentleman never lies. Never, never, never." She shook her finger at him.

"Of course, how thoughtless of me." Christopher gave up.

The ensuing conversations brought an unspoken realization to bear upon both Christopher and Rebecca. Although it could be said their discussions were all pleasant and open, there were definitely things kept hidden under wraps by both of them. Out of politeness and respect, neither of them would pry too deeply into the private life of the other, but then neither of them would willingly give up anything on their own. This made for interesting discourse, the direction of their talk guided most gingerly by probes, retreats, more probes, and so on.

"I must admit, I was surprised at not having to ask your father's permission to escort you in public. You look so young, I assumed you to be living with your family."

"No, I am afraid they are no longer with me."

"I am sorry to hear that. Forgive me, for I recall losing my own mother, and know well the grief endured. It was terrible, and I only suffered the loss of one parent. At least I yet have a father."

"It's been a long time. Time softens the pain. Tell me, what is it your father does?"

"Oh, well, you know he is getting older and therefore does things that appeal to older men. He likes to walk among the trees on his land, and he enjoys going down to the sea to look at the ships. Old man interests, I am sure you understand."

"Is he a farmer? Does he not have to work?"

"Well, not exactly. He is good with numbers and others use his service. He has done well for himself and enjoys the autumn years of his life in comfort. And I am there when he needs me as well. He never remarried. What about your folks, what did they do for a living?"

"Ahh, the sea."

"The sea?"

"Yes, the sea."

"You mean they were fishermen, fisherwomen, whatever?"

"We had a lot of fish when I grew up. Do you have brothers and sisters?"

"No."

"Oh."

"Do you?"

"No."

"Oh."

And so the discussions fraught with nondisclosures went on until at last, Rebecca assessed the whole of the coach's journey did little more than form a circle that passed to within a block of the West Indies from whence they had begun. At that point she decided to inquire.

"I am most interested to know of what eatery you have chosen that would be within a stone's toss of the inn?"

"Is your score card ready, then?"

"It's been ready."

"Very well." Christopher rapped soundly on the roof of the coach and at the next street, that being the same street the inn was located upon, the coach turned right and headed south toward the river. Rebecca was puzzled and saying very little; she began to grow uneasy, as she perceived them to be approaching the docks. Christopher watched her closely and was quick to perceive her worry.

"Are you uncomfortable, Rebecca?"

"Where might we be headed?"

"To the FAIR WEATHER."

"The FAIR WEATHER? I've never heard of the FAIR WEATHER." She looked at him with deepening doubt.

"That is because it is not always there."

"Mr. Claussen, are you again playing games with me, sir? I am not at all in favor of this. It frightens me." She was becoming very nervous at this point.

"One moment, then." Christopher again rapped soundly on the coach roof. The horse was brought to a halt.

"The choice I have made is to serve you dinner by my own hand. I am very proficient in the culinary arts and it would honor me if you would allow it. However, it requires you accompany me aboard the FAIR WEATHER, which is moored right over there." He pointed. Rebecca took one look and didn't have need for even that.

"No thank-you, Mr. Claussen. I accept as truth your talents as a chef, but I am inclined to pass on your generous offer, kind as it is, and ask that you respect my wishes and return me to the inn. I am sure you can see it would be highly improper for me so be alone with you in private. Especially in light of the fact I hardly know you. You needn't worry; I can find my way home from the inn with little effort."

Christopher opened the coach speakway, and instructed the driver to repair to the inn for the benefit of the lady's composure. No words whatsoever were spoken between them. Within minutes they arrived at the same inn from which they departed earlier. Christopher stepped out to escort her to the shelter of the overhang, for drizzle had begun to fill the air. But first, he turned to face her. He momentarily blocked her departure from the coach.

"Miss Greystone, I owe you my apology for the second time this day. I fear I have been so anxious to make your acquaintance that I have lost all remnants of social decency. I have deprived you of the most basic courtesies, overlooked the caliber of your social upbringing, underestimated your intelligence, and stand before you ashamed. Rebecca, I beg you hear me out." He swept his right hand in an arc, showing her the front of the West Indies Inn.

"As you see, I respect your wishes and we are returned without complaint. Might I say, I am not surprised this came about, as you are a woman of good sense. Therefore, allow me to plead to that good sense you so possess, while in this safe environment and declare; I still wish you to come aboard the good ship FAIR WEATHER so I might serve you the meal I have prepared. I set a table for four, fearing you might disapprove of outward appearances.

"So, I ask you now, to consider friends who might join us. There is sufficient repast to go around. And still, if this is unacceptable, then I pray you select any establishment in the city of London, cost being no issue, and it shall be done. Above all else, I implore you to keep your promise to join me in dinner by whatever fashion meets with your approval. I beg this of you, Miss Greystone."

With that said, he stepped aside and took her hand, gently assisting her to the street. She turned to him.

"Once before I gave you the benefit of the doubt, Mr. Claussen —I was deceived," she remarked coolly.

"What you say is true but was it not by folly that I gained your attention, was that not how I made your acquaintance? It is vile to think that ends justify means, and yet, what hope had I to partake in a coach ride with as lovely company as yourself? I swear to God Almighty, my word is as good as the gold that backs my name. I will never give you reason to question it."

'Oh, damn me!' Christopher thought to himself. The time old family cliché had rolled off his tongue. Out, before he even realized. He hoped it hadn't brought undue attention.

Rebecca stopped a moment to study him. *Who is this person,* she wondered? He was handsome, it went without saying. He hid much, the same as she. She thought about his comment, *'the gold that backs my name...'* how peculiar. He seemed to be an illusion, yet he could sound so sincere, again...the benefit of the doubt.

"I fear you give rise to my poor judgment, Mr. Claussen. However, if my friend Karen is still about and willing to go out for the evening, I will join you for dinner aboard your ship. On the other hand, if she is not then I shall repair to bed for the night and that will be the end of it."

"It is in the hand of Providence, then." Christopher accepted the terms.

He was too anxious to reenter the coach and remained standing in the weather to await the outcome. When the door opened, a blonde girl, one or two years Rebecca's older, appeared before him and broke into a charming smile. Rebecca shadowed her.

"There, Captain! Permission to come aboard!" Rebecca called out grinning, obviously ready to start over again. Christopher was overjoyed.

"Permission granted, with all my heart. A meal you shan't soon forget! I give you my word."

"It might do you good to go easy on that word of yours, sir."

"I see your point, and I will take the advice to heart, Milady. Allow me." He assisted both ladies into the coach.

Given permission to board for real, Christopher escorted the ladies aft along the waterway to the companionway, which they descended and entered into the galley. Along the full length of the upper deck the tantalizing aroma of roast beef permeated the night air. Once inside, the blended smells of beef, oyster sauce, boiled potato and onions, parsley, candied carrots and peas, raisin pudding, and fresh bread assaulted the senses and demanded one to gorge.

Christopher introduced them both to the galleyman, Jack Temper. He had been keeping careful watch over the dinner during Christopher's absence, but swore before the Almighty that it was prepared in whole by Mr. Claussen. Rebecca, at first skeptical having seen a cook about, agreed at last to accept his sworn testimony.

Christopher produced a bottle of Chambord, a sweet rich liqueur imported from France and made from small black raspberries. Having respect for the ladies, he only offered this as an aperitif while in the privacy of the ship if they should desire it. They were inclined, and Rebecca was at once captivated by its sweet delicate taste. Christopher produced five glasses to the puzzlement of all.

"Now wait! We haven't hardly tasted this fine drink, and I am still very much within my wits."

With her finger, she pointed out four persons, then repeated the count upon five glasses, making an absurd face such as an idiot might wear. Everybody laughed and earlier tensions were quickly evaporating into the congenial atmosphere.

"No, the fifth glass is for another guest."

"And who might that be?" Rebecca inquired.

"You will know soon enough as I am now about to call him!" Christopher stepped out briefly and then returned with Darrin O'Kurk. Rebecca began to shake her head in disbelief. This was too much, indeed!

"Rebecca, Karen, allow me to introduce Darrin O'Kurk."

"Laydees." He bowed.

"I trust your backside still works proper?" Rebecca smirked.

"'Tis a miracle indeed, Miss Rebecca! Ya poot a gooat to shame! Ya doo."

"I know you. I have seen you at the inn."

"'Tis true. I go there now an' then to 'ave an ale an' a look at chore beutifool face, me darling."

"Oh, please. You told him to say that didn't you."

"Darrin, your eyes are as sharp as a lady's tongue."

Christopher handed Darrin his glass and a choice of drink.

"To Darrin's eyes." Christopher raised his glass in a toast. "Now then, I have persuaded Darrin to come aboard and perform for us."

"'Tiz true an I's promised a goot sup an' glaz of ale. But whatz moor to mee likin, is the chanz to settle scoor, foor t' fright I give ya, doon at the poob laz night."

"It was a fright, if you must know the truth of it. So it better be something special to make up for such a cruel hoax."

"This will be good!" Christopher assured her. Darrin placed his glass upon the table. He took a deep breath as before, for effect, and brought forth his wonderful voice.

Oyeee! Tell me now, me maties, tell me now agen
av' yer eyez laid rest upon the lov ly lady of the temz
'er name it has bin ferried across the seven seas
In the heart of every sailorman hooz bin by West Indies.

Oh, Rebecca, Rebecca....

On he went, and doing a splendid job of it, while Rebecca shrank with embarrassment from all this adoration. She forgave him his evil ways, and accepted his argument that his actions were all due to the moon. The dinner went on in a wonderful atmosphere; even some of the crew who inadvertently stumbled in were allowed to stay and join in the evening gaiety. Most important of all, Rebecca had an absolutely wonderful time. Christopher could see it in her eyes, he could hear it in her laugh.

As with all good times, the evening was quickly spent and Christopher returned the ladies to the inn as they wished. They wouldn't allow him to drive them to their residence in spite of his objections. Karen gave the two of them a minute alone.

"If you promise not to run off with another man during the fortnight to come, I promise to add ten pound to your collection for the orphans. I hope you'll considerate it."

"Where would you get ten pound? Are you made of money then?"

"I'd be willing to sacrifice my food for the orphans, in your name of course."

"That sounds good for the orphans, but for me, I see nothing but a good many dinners missed when offered by my suitors who are anxiously awaiting for you to be gone." Rebecca teased.

"I know you jest with me, but sadly enough I fear this to be uncomfortably close to the truth!"

"Then allow me to be honest. Make a donation if you like. But know I am not inclined to save myself for any man at this time. Yet, I had a wonderful time of it. The night was grand, and I would hope you might call on me again if it pleases you."

"It pleases me, Miss Greystone. It pleases me more than you can know. It will be difficult to keep my mind on my affairs whilst I know you are far from my hand. *'Save your heart, and I'll be back, me promise be sincere.'* He echoed the chorus line.

They smiled at one another and said their good-byes.

SEVENTY-THREE

The reels were fast, the fiddler and flutist exceptional, and the mood was festive in every corner of the inn, save for the table where Christopher and Rebecca sat in silence. Christopher pushed his peas about his plate, forgoing the battle to maintain his appetite. He and his food sat there under the weight of Rebecca's stare. He pretended not to notice and barely looked up, which only exacerbated the situation.

"You're very unfair, Christopher."

"Have I been?" He finally looked up to meet her eyes.

"Yes, very," she answered shortly.

"How is that, my angel?" He didn't really want to hear because it made him uncomfortable.

"Your angel will tell you once again, Mr. Claussen, as your angel has told you many times before," she remarked with sarcasm. "By one devious way or another, you have managed to find out all there is to know about me. I am an orphan, and I admit there isn't much to me, yet, whenever I believe I am revealing some personal detail of my life, I always sense you are already aware of it. At times it irritates me. At times I feel I am made of glass and you

669

can see everything there is to know about me inside and out. I have learned to live with this, Christopher. I can accept that you have means to accomplish your tasks. I can even respect you in your abilities and success in obtaining these scraps of information.

"However, my patience is now worn thin, and I see less humor in this game of hide and seek. I have been more than generous with my allowance of time. I have asked very little about you and your family, and you offer even less. I care very much for you, Christopher, and you need no devious means to prove it out, for I have spelled it out in no uncertain terms. I have made it as plain to see as I might, save for sacrificing my honor. I am now tired of it. I cannot see the future in making a bond of my heart to a man I cannot know, a man who keeps everything from me, a man who cannot trust me with his secrets.

"You tell me you are a miniscule man in the business of a large world. One who buys, sells, and travels abroad. I want to believe what you say, but I know there is more. I see it every day in the way you talk. I see it in your manners. I see it in the way you hold your silverware, in the way you place your napkin. You tell me you have learned these things by doing business with prominent people, but you do these things naturally. You do and say things in private that bespeak of something much more than the man I see before me. I see it in the way you always have an answer or means of solving every problem, or if I am near you how a problem seems to get solved on its own.

"I keep wondering if I am going mad. Am I losing my mind? I am tired of this. I am tired of all of this, Christopher. As a matter of fact, considering how I feel at this moment, maybe it is better that I call off this affair at once and save myself while I have the strength of will to do so. You need time to find your priorities, Christopher. It is certain that I have made little demand of them. I think it best I bid you good-bye, Christopher."

Rebecca was visibly upset. To her own surprise, she rose to her feet. Christopher immediately stood as well.

"Rebecca?"

Her swell of emotion and her move to depart caught him off guard.

"Christopher." she answered with finality and began to take leave of him.

"Rebecca, wait! Wait!" he pleaded at once.

"Christopher, I have waited—patiently." She continued to walk on.

"Rebecca, please! You are right, it is true, but it is not so simple, as you might think. Please, wait for me, walk with me. I will tell you everything. I give you my word. It is not an easy thing, Rebecca. It is undoubtedly the most difficult task of my life. You must understand. Will you at least hear what I have to say?" he continued to plead.

Rebecca could not have refused for the sake of her sanity, and if nothing else her curiosity would never have allowed it. Begrudgingly, she turned back to face him and accepted his arm. He led her away from the music and commotion of the inn. They strolled along the grassy banks of a nearby stream, and stopped at a viewing porch that overlooked a small rapid, where they took up a seat. Christopher looked down at his feet and would not meet her eyes.

"Rebecca, my family is cursed with a malady. It is a terrible injustice, but one that we have been forced to bear. It is a disease of the mind that drives many of us into insanity in our early years. I know at this time I seem well, I seem full of life and as normal as any man who enters the West Indies. But for how long? It can't be answered.

"You would find yourself without a man to care for you, possibly at the time when you would need him the most. I would steal from you your finest years, I would steal away your youth, and then leave you to find your own way. It's a terrible thing,

Rebecca. Speaking frankly, I have been too cowardly to reveal my secret. It was not only selfish but also cruel. I swear I never anticipated falling in love, and once I did—well, I couldn't bear to give you up. You filled my life; you made it so complete in every way. I have never been so happy, never. Now you know."

Rebecca sat a moment in silence and studied the man she loved.

"Christopher, you have brought to me what so far no man has been able. Trust. I love you, but even more, I trust you. I would rather spend ten years of bliss with a man I love and trust, and cherish those memories, than twenty with one who makes me wary and whose affections I question. Let me love you, Christopher. That is all I ask, that is all I have ever asked of you."

Christopher swallowed hard. He hadn't expected her to bring up the issue of trust. Of all the issues, that was the worst. He was now in deep, but this was to be the end of his courting. He chose to go deeper.

"Oh, Rebecca! This makes it ever the more difficult. You should have taken your leave at once. Now I am left with no choice, but to reveal an issue even more sorrowful than the first. Please, Rebecca, I implore, leave me my honor and dignity. Please, I beg, go."

Rebecca felt herself sinking into the dreaded 'unknowing' of her old life once again. Everything was so perfect, so full of bliss. Everything was more than she had ever dared hope. She wasn't greedy; she wished only the honest love of a man. It had been too good. She didn't deserve such joy. It was now time to pay. She spoke.

"In my life, Christopher, I've been witness to many a thing, much of it painful. I have learned to accept the ways of our Lord. Our lives are short I fear, and best spent looking for the good wherever we may find it. Tell me what troubles you, Christopher. I have braced myself for the worst." Rebecca could feel her world caving in—her sunlight growing dim.

Christopher paused momentarily for effect. He sat pensively, and then began to speak.

"I am not certain if this is connected with the before described malady or not. The doctors cannot ascertain." Christopher took a very deep and nervous breath. "Rebecca, I am unable to be a man in the proper sense. I can love you, I can worship you, I can hold you in my arms, I can die for you, and I would, but I can never love you as a man. Of this, I am incapable." He would not look up.

Rebecca's breathing had now become erratic. *Where was the justice in life?* She wondered. Even, to the end, was she to be denied the warmth of love in its full measure? Would it always be her lot to grovel for whatever piece of emotional gratification she might stumble across? She had spent her childhood embracing a lavender-scented wrap, the extent of her emotional contact, her only light in an enormous loveless void. She could see now the void was even deeper than she imagined. It was inconceivable, and yet her thoughts returned to Christopher.

"I have spent all my waking days not knowing the caress of love. I have seen all too clearly the appetite of men for my body. It has not been pleasant. Often, I have been frozen in fear, released by its grip to find myself in a blind rage, all the while praying to be left alone. All I have ever dreamed, all I ask, is to be loved by an honest man. If this is the way, I'll accept it."

Inside, Rebecca hurt deeply. She had saved herself from the terrible temptation of money and the heat of a man's sudden attention many times while waiting for the right man. It hadn't been easy for a girl who had nothing. Now, it seemed all in vain, pointless, worse, it seemed she was to be the joke of some immortal ruse.

Christopher raised his head and looked directly at Rebecca.

"There's more, Rebecca." At this, Rebecca lost her composure. She didn't drop her eyes, instead they remained fixed onto his, but the tears flowed down her flawless tormented face.

"More?" She sobbed, in disbelief. *"More?* What more can there be? Is there no end?" She shook her head in denial, left with nothing but to listen further.

"Do you remember the first night we met, and I presented you with the package?" Rebecca nodded, being unable to speak any longer.

"I gave you my word that I would never lie to you again?"

Rebecca could not answer. It was all becoming too much to bear. She only nodded her head.

"I lied, Rebecca."

Rebecca lowered her face and openly wept. "What have I done to deserve this, Christopher? Why couldn't I just have a simple love?" She sobbed.

"You now may, Rebecca." Christopher tried to console her.

"No, I mean with you."

She buried her face in her hands to hide her emotions. Christopher tried to remove them from her face. He wished to see and remember the look of devotion she held for him. He believed with all his heart that she loved him for himself. It was time to reveal his true identity.

"That is now possible, Rebecca." He watched her carefully.

"What are you saying, Christopher? You make no sense."

She looked up at him. She was bewildered. He studied her. His heart was overflowing with love and compassion for the grief he was forcing upon her.

"My health is fine, Rebecca. I had to know beyond all doubt that you loved me for me. Now, I can explain all—."

Christopher never finished his comment, for Rebecca, in a flash of her reputed temper, laid her clenched fist across his face and split his nose wide open.

674

"You bastard!"

She fled across the grassy knoll, wailing in anguish at being made the fool, not believing the cruelty of the man she thought she loved. Christopher struggled to keep himself from drowning in his own blood. He wished to chase after her, but was unable for the severity of his bleeding and the pain, which blinded him with tears.

Running eased Rebecca's tension; she felt the intense pressure of her anger quickly subside, and after a moment, knowing what she was capable of doing in a fit, she feared to turn around and look back in his direction. She closed her eyes and knew that if he had been well, he would have been at her side. She despised herself for having such lack of control, and filled with remorse, she asked God for His forgiveness. She then turned to face the man she struck in anger. Even at her distance, she could clearly see his white blouse was covered in blood. He was holding his head high, but his face, his hands, and his sleeves were bright red with blood, his handkerchief unable to hold back the flow.

"Oh, God, have mercy! What have I done!" she whispered to herself. She began to weep, now in despair. She cursed herself for her uncontrollable temper. She realized that a small portion of his claim to good health had just been lost, and she ran to him.

"Forgive me, Christopher, I beg. Oh! Look at you, you poor thing. What have I done, Christopher? I beg you forgive me this reprehensible act. I am so ashamed, I am so sorry."

She continued to speak through her sobs, her nerves utterly unraveled. Christopher remained motionless and spoke with eyes closed from under the blood-soaked cloth.

"I'm fine, Rebecca. Wounded pride, nothing more." The blood clotted in his nose and distorted his voice. "Suffice it to say, you had every right to act as you did. However, admittedly, whenever I think of you, I shall forever think of vermilion, respectfully of course."

Rebecca was grief-stricken and stooped to rip away a portion of her petticoat. She stepped over to the stream and dampened it. She returned to wash away his blood with cloth and tears. She became aware of onlookers who had amassed at the sight of blood, or worse yet, had witnessed the spectacle. At first she shriveled with embarrassment, but soon accepted the situation, recovered her composure, and attempted to repair the damage. She was all business as she tended to his poor condition.

"Oh, Christopher. My temper will forever be my downfall, but for the sake of heaven, how could you say such things? You shouldn't upset me so. It is cruel."

"You are right, but know that your temper is what saved you for me. I had plenty of forewarning and was foolish not to take it into consideration. Would you allow me to finish the explanation I was about to offer before this distraction?" he asked with a slight tint of sarcasm. She smiled and kissed him, again and again.

"Please do. I am a good listener." Her own sarcastic retort.

The remark brought a laugh from Christopher and a fresh flow of blood.

"No, no. Don't laugh. You'll only make it worse. Just hush for a moment and say nothing." She dabbed her petticoat at his face and then sat alongside him. They waited a moment for the bleeding to stop. As the pain in his nose began to retreat, he undertook the ordeal of explaining his background to Rebecca.

"Do you remember how you would tease me about my remarking that my word was as good as the gold that backed the name?"

"Yes."

"Well, that is a saying in my family that has passed from father to son for hundreds of years. All too often a bad habit, but one never meant as anything more than proof of sincerity. However, it isn't an empty oath. You assumed I was in the business of shipping, an agent or the like, because that is what I led you to believe. And this is true, I am.

"What I didn't volunteer was that I own the ship. I own all the ships. Rebecca, I own the lumber stowed in the holds of those ships, and the mills that produce that lumber. I own the forests that feed the mills. My family owns the lands under those forests. I often complain that a week's ride by carriage will not bring my eyes to see all that I possess. It's often embarrassing to speak of it, and I hope you won't think me boastful. The time has now come for me to be truthful." Christopher took a deep breath, the best he could in light of things.

Rebecca, having endured one too many stories in his company was mentally at a standstill. Then the light of truth flashed before her. She sat up from his embrace and faced him.

"Christopher, I have never met a man who is so full of dung as yourself. Spanish galleons, sunken treasure, insane parents, incapable of making love, and now you're a land baron and shipping magnate to boot, riches to rival the King's. Spare, me! I have had enough of this sport, Christopher. Still, you shame me."

In truth, for the first time as she listened to her own words, the reality of what she said took a cold grip of her. She moved back from Christopher and seriously questioned his character. He understood the look upon her face, but he was unconcerned, for now he would make her his bride if it took all the fortune of his name. She would be his.

"This is an easy issue to settle." He reached into his pocket. "I have carried this with me for many weeks. I only needed to believe you truly loved me before I felt confident in presenting it. Today is that day, Rebecca."

He removed a velvet ring pouch, and laid it on the bench between them. Rebecca was in shock because she knew at once what it contained. Sadly, she could no longer overcome her suspicions of Christopher. He had carried on in this manner for far too long to simply step back and say it wasn't his way to be a prankster, a trickster, a liar.

Christopher was well aware of her feelings. Her concern was marked upon her brow and she hesitated to take the offering. He could read her thoughts.

"Go ahead, Rebecca. Open it. I beg you, don't falter now." Granting his wish, this she did. At first she could do little more than stare in disbelief.

"Oh, my word!"

She gasped for breath. The splendor of the ring was beyond anything she could possibly have imagined. Could he be as wealthy as he claimed, or was this another clever deception? She couldn't tell. It made her head swim. She was dizzy with confusion. How could a man come by such a precious article? Almost at once, in her present state of mind, she concluded one very plausible way. It must be stolen. It had to be. That explained it perfectly. Inside, she was convinced of it.

"Do you like it, love?"

"Is it real?" she asked. Christopher chuckled.

"Yes, very. You may hold on to that ring as proof of my intentions. I wish to ask you to marry me, Rebecca, but not until you have come to my home. Only then will you be sure of my character. Would you do that?"

"Yes." She answered in a distracted tone, as she spun the ring in her fingers and stared into the glitter of its stone.

The word spilled out of her heart, but she wondered if she might be sent off to the plantations for possession of jewels belonging to some famous lord or duke. Christopher was far too clever to be held the culprit. He would never be blamed. She felt uncomfortable, cornered, trapped. It certainly was the most beautiful ring she had ever seen.

Rebecca held the ring up high to catch the sunlight. The sight of the ring brought a roar of applause from the onlookers, along with approval and words of encouragement for the wounded suitor. Christopher grinned before the onlookers, who had meandered out from the inn, curious about all the commotion and blood. Rebecca turned to see those same curious faces and was mortified to think the strangers witnessed her deed. She hid her face and shrank upon the bench flush with embarrassment.

SEVENTY-FOUR

Christopher had carried the sham to the absolute limit. He hadn't planned to spout the stories of insanity and impotence, he simply did so because the opportunity was there and he wondered how far Rebecca would go. She had proved herself willing to go all the way and he would remember her devotion always.

Ironically, he had carried the ring with the intention of asking for her hand in marriage that same afternoon, but not in the fashion it had occurred. He had planned to whisk her away and reveal once and for all the mysteries of his background that so plagued her. In any event, everything had worked out as well as could be expected. His nose was a mess but his schedule was still intact. He had to get to the harbor.

Christopher's manner changed dramatically after his revelations. In Rebecca's eyes, he transformed himself into a man of supreme confidence. A man who she could see was relieved of a great burden, a man who was again laughing and jovial, a man shedding many of the quirks and contradictions that were a part of the person she fell in love with. He was more at ease with himself in her presence. He carried on with an air of command, as though he was accustomed to such a thing. He was speeding away from her and all she understood about him. He was holding his hand out, reaching back for her, encouraging her with his smile to keep up.

Was he a thief? Was he a joker extraordinaire? Was he an actor like Ben? All of her questions were being answered one after another faster than she could comprehend. She was becoming increasingly apprehensive. She no longer faced the comfort of lies and deceptions, but instead the fearful possibility that there may have been more truth in his words than she wished to believe. She could do nothing now, other than hang on.

Christopher escorted Rebecca back to the docks at Stepney. They boarded the FAIR WEATHER. It was her first time back on the ship since the night he first met her and prepared dinner in the galley. Captain Ogleson greeted them.

"Permission to board, sir."

"Permission granted, Mr. Claussen."

"It's good to see you, sir."

"And you as well. Are you alright, sir?" The sight of Christopher's bloodstained clothes concerned the captain.

"I have never in my life felt better. Can you not see that?"

"You look bloody well, indeed sir," the captain chided. "This must be the beautiful Rebecca?"

"In all her fighting glory. Rebecca, allow me to introduce Master Ogleson, captain of the FAIR WEATHER."

"It is a pleasure, sir. The nose doesn't look good, does it?" Rebecca was worried. The captain placed his hand on his chin, canted his head, and studied Christopher.

"It looks…mmm…it looks…sensitive. Yes, sensitive would be the word. However, the pleasure is still mine."

"Sensitive. Yes, that is a good description," Christopher quipped. "Maybe not as good as crooked, but it will do, I am sure."

"Oh, Christopher. I am so sorry. I should be whipped for having such a temper."

"See? Isn't she everything I described? Do you now understand why I haven't been myself as of late? I would have been insane to allow so special a creature to pass through my life and into the arms of another. It was not your fault, my love." Christopher looked back at the captain.

"Master Ogleson, I wish you to be first to hear great news. You recall our many discussions regarding my progress in winning over the heart of my Rebecca, do you not?"

"Ayeee, that I do, Mr. Claussen."

"By the grace of God, the ruse is over, and I could not be happier for it. I have promised Rebecca I will soon ask for her hand in marriage. However, she is a freethinking spirit, Master Ogleson, and I have left her with little choice but to believe I must be the worst sort of liar. Who could expect less from such a thoughtful woman when one considers all of the falsities I have presented her?

"I have told her repeatedly that I am but a commoner, a buyer and seller of jetsam, rummage, and odds and ends. She has accepted me as such, and shown me the depth of her love. I know that she loves me for the person I am, for she knows nothing of my background. Now I wish her to know the truth of the family that welcomes her. Therefore, Captain, today we begin to show her my world. Would you inform Rebecca who is the owner of this vessel?" The captain looked at Rebecca. He assured her with his eyes, and then answered.

"That would be you, sir."

"How long have you been in my employ?"

"Four years, sir."

"How many ships in our fleet?"

"I would guess there to be about twenty, sir."

681

"Thank-you, Master Ogleson. We'll be going to my quarters."

"Yes, sir." The captain grinned as he looked at the expression of shock upon Rebecca's face.

"Good day, Miss Rebecca. It has been a pleasure to meet you."

The captain turned away and went on about his business. Rebecca was unable to answer, for each word reverberated through her mind. *Twenty ships!* That was impossible. *Twenty ships!* What kind of man owned twenty ships? Who was this man she had fallen in love with? This man, whose person she knew not even in the smallest detail. All that he had been in her eyes was make-believe. She had fallen in love with a doll, a portrait, a resemblance of the man who stood beside her now. The bumbling, soft-spoken commoner now stood as a man's man.

Rebecca left London at Christopher's side. They sailed to Malmo on the Swedish coast. They spent their time talking, and she gorged herself with answers to all the questions that had so long been kept from her. To her wonder, this new man was even more spellbinding than the old. There seemed no end to her questions, or to his surprises, but Christopher was pleased to answer them all. He believed it long overdue and felt she should have this right.

On one issue, and one issue only, however, no matter how much Rebecca prodded him to describe the house of his residence, he refused. Although, together, they passed through the great wrought iron gate with its heralding angels and the name Claussen welded into the metalwork. All of this passed by Rebecca unseen, for she was fast asleep in Christopher's arms. And so it was, as the coach stopped before the massive granite porch of the Claussen home. Christopher woke his slumbering angel. He took her hand to assist her exit from the coach. They scaled the steps and crossed the beautiful inlaid marble. They were welcomed at the castle-like front doors. In less than a moment's time the senior Claussen approached them in the foyer, and was at once spellbound by Rebecca's beauty.

"Miss Greystone! I refused to believe any woman could possibly be as beautiful as Christopher proclaimed you were, but I was wrong. I was ever so wrong." He bowed and kissed her hand.

"Rebecca, my father, William Claussen."

"Oh! Mr. Claussen, I am so honored, but I should be enraged. Christopher never mentioned you would be meeting us here. I must look a fright. I am afraid I have just awakened."

The senior Claussen raised his head and looked at Rebecca with peculiarity. His glance then shifted to Christopher, who was standing silent, but for a knowing grin and a wink.

"Might I be excused long enough to freshen up, I beg?"

"Why certainly. Anne will show you up." The senior Claussen directed her toward the staircase. Christopher turned to his father.

"She believes us to be at an inn, father."

"I gathered something of the sort."

"I wish to ask her hand in marriage today. Do you approve?"

"You have more than my blessing, son, you have my envy."

As Rebecca commenced to climb the carpeted steps, her hand gliding along the hardwood banister, she was drawn to the portraits that covered the wall across from her. It didn't take long before she began to realize as she climbed each step that she was passing farther into the history of the Claussen family. The paintings of the Claussens, including Christopher and the senior Claussen, looked down upon her, all with the same knowing smile.

She stopped her ascent. Bewildered, she turned to look down upon the men. They both stood there like two Cheshires grinning ear to ear, akin to their likeness framed upon the wall.

Rebecca was nearly faint with shock. *This was the Claussen home*. She had assumed they were spending this night at an inn for rest before continuing the journey tomorrow. Now she understood why Christopher preferred to keep his background from her. She never would have taken to him, if she had any idea he was this well heeled. There was no thought that moved to word. She simply looked down upon the two gentlemen in a daze, her heart racing, and then returned to her business of scaling the stairs for lack of any other alternative.

Rebecca finished with her business and returned to the staircase. The men made her blush with embarrassment by their unyielding gaze of adoration as she descended the staircase and passed before them. She approached them as they stood waiting for her and enjoying her every move.

"Mr. Claussen, would you forgive me if I ask for a moment alone to speak to Christopher? It is a personal matter."

"Most certainly." The senior Claussen bowed gracefully, then removed himself from their presence.

Rebecca turned her attention to Christopher.

"I understand everything now—everything except for this. Why me? Any woman in the world, Christopher, why me? So many who are attractive to the eye, and so many more qualified to fill properly their place by your side. So many, Christopher, why me?"

Christopher thought a moment and took Rebecca's arm. He began to walk her past the treasures that lined the endless corridors of the mansion. He showed her his realm and began his explanation.

"Rebecca, I live an abnormal life. I exist in a world of wealth that is so far above one's comprehension that it is an unreal existence. I am unable to act as a normal person because I am never treated as a normal person. I only have to ask and I shall receive. There is no challenge in my life save to earn more money, to enhance the value of our estate. All those who seek me out wish my friendship for connection to my wealth. The honest men care little if they know me or not. They simply ask for my charity. At least I respect them.

"My life is one unending dream to be normal. Just for once, I would love to experience normal things, normal emotions, to sit in a bar with normal people, to drink with men and enjoy their conversations. And of course I have always dreamed of love. This dream has never been pleasant. I understood clearly that no woman would be able to love me if she carried the knowledge of my wealth beforehand. She would be blinded by it. Even if she herself was equally as fortunate, it would boil down to a marriage for the best of the estates involved. Love would be scarcely viable let alone visible.

"I would suffer my entire life asking myself if the woman who stole my heart married me for my person, or for my estate. Sadly, to my dismay, there could only ever be one answer. This amount of wealth is all encompassing. All corrupting unless born into it such as I, whereby it generally goes unnoticed and is usually cursed if it rears its ugly head. True love, in my eyes was nothing more than the hopeless, immature dreams of a child.

"Then, I decided to dress down one evening and look for a common pub to have a bite to eat and a maybe a pint of ale. Who could possibly know anything of me on this one random street outside London on a damp winter night? Love was the farthest thing from my mind. Suddenly, as if I was granted my one miracle of love, Rebecca, you walked past and my entire world was turned inside out.

"Nothing else mattered in my life from that moment on. I knew I might enjoy the kind of relationship that was normal to most men if only I had the courage to make the advance. The more I watched you the more I realized the advance would be difficult. I was desperate to savor this experience even if it was for the worse. You must understand how I felt. I had nothing to lose and more than I dared hope to gain. I was dressed common and it was as though everything had fallen perfectly into place. It was going to be my chance if I wished to reach for it. So, I proceeded and the rest is history. Rebecca, I accept your love as genuine. In spite of all I have done, can you accept my character as nothing less than honorable?"

"Yes, I understand everything now." Upon hearing this, Christopher dropped to his knee. He took her hand in his.

"Rebecca, I stand by my word to ask of you your hand in marriage. My intentions toward you are sincere. I vow before God and all creation to love you, to hold and cherish you, and to care for you with every breath of my being 'til death do us part. Will you have me as your one true love? Will you take me as your man, Rebecca?"

Rebecca looked down upon him, her eyes moist with emotion from the intensity of the moment.

"Yes, Christopher, with all my heart 'til death do us part."

Christopher rose to his feet. He took Rebecca into his arms and kissed her passionately, passing through his lips all the feeling he was unable to express in words. They parted and he looked into her eyes.

"'Til death do us part."

SEVENTY-FIVE

One bitter truth of life's injustice was presented to me in the severest of manner. It was my misfortune to have reached an age whereby I felt the brutality of the lesson and knew it would haunt me the rest of my years.

I had learned by Lady Rebecca's death that there was nothing to assure me that righteousness, heroism, generosity, or any other

ELIZABETH

The bitter truth

virtue praised in the eyes of the Lord would cancel out the evil or heartbreak in our lives. Simply put, contrary to all logic there needn't be any fairness to life, no matter how we might struggle. The lesson came in the knowledge that the only tears to be shed at Lady Rebecca's burial were my own. Seventeen of eighteen children would go on to walk the earth and lead full lives in part because of the bravery of one unselfish heart, but I alone would cry.

In any other setting, the parents and families would have wept openly without shame, and if not with sorrow, at least with joy at the salvation of the most precious gift to be held, their children. The emotion of this moment would have been overwhelming. There would have been eulogies, one after another, filled with praise, with gratitude and admiration, not unlike that of a fallen hero returned from some savage and decisive battle. A warrior honored between the slow-turning wheels of a wagon covered with flowers and followed by his fellow soldiers who solemnly understood above all else that it had been he that paid the price.

But these were orphans, children of the street. No mothers, no fathers, no families, no emotions, nothing but silence—*wasted miracles*. In my misery, I stood with a crowd of onlookers and nothing more. Boston's elite huddled together against the cold of this December day, shivering and suffering through the elements, secretly watching their timepieces and working out their personal problems behind eyes that stared blindly at a draped coffin. Lady Rebecca was a candle that burned bright, and they could all go home with a clear conscience as they convinced one another that they had paid their respects. For the moment this was the fashionable place to be, and they were in attendance.

My support, my relief, came from outside that privileged circle of onlookers. It came from beyond the trees where stood a mob of the roughest looking men who might ever find reason to gather. They were a motley bunch that appeared comical, as they crowded together with greased back hair and dress unfit for a brawl let alone a burial. It was with them that I found my solace. It was there that I knew, behind worn muslin shirts and buttonless coats, within the strongest of hearts and mirrored in faces weathered beyond recognition, that grief for Lady Rebecca was genuine. She was family to them, and they would feel the worse for her passing.

I did not accompany Mr. Claussen to Rebecca's funeral. Nobody had spoken with him nor seen him leave his cabin aboard the REBECCA since Milady's death. The service was held at the St. John's Protestant Reform Church, and he was not expected to attend. I was given respect enough to sit at the first bench, closest to where Milady would be laid to rest.

For me, the loss seared my soul. It burned deep and painful. I wept; it was a lonely grief with no one to comfort me. Only one man truly understood, but he never asked for me. He never came to slow my fall. He left me to work out my grief in whatever way I could. Mary would have been at my side if not for the fact she was at long last enjoying her honeymoon. She had waited in town to celebrate my birthday, but promised Allen she would spend Christmas in his arms far away.

I imagined her to be running along the beach in the hot sun and laughing without a care in the world. She had no idea that Lady Rebecca was now gone. It would be a month before her return, before she would face this tragedy and share the emptiness. She would hurt, for Mary and Milady had always been close.

I looked above Lady Rebecca's coffin and out across the litter of dead leaves that speckled the snow-covered grounds. My thoughts were diverted from the ceremony to the street by the sound of horse hooves echoing along the pavement and working its way through the trees.

Six black horses heralded the approach of Lady Rebecca's coach. They moved slowly up the street in a somber stride, and the sight of it brought forth a sense of finality that was so overwhelming it devastated me. I would have never imagined I should see anything other than Milady's favorite white Lipizzaners hitched to her coach, and it made the reality of this moment so intense that I was instantly driven to tears. I bowed my head and sobbed as I listened to the sharp crack of hooves stepping along the cobblestone lane.

The scene at the cemetery was utterly surreal, for everything about me was black and white, except for Milady's vermilion coach and the red roses about her grave. The snow and the thick cloud cover were all of white, while the onlookers stood dressed in black, all of them bending to the wind like saplings beside the black bark of their elders who swayed silently in their winter sleep unaware of the grief beneath their bower. Even the birds that called out as they circled overhead, or scratched and pecked their way through the tangle of treetops to look down upon us, were crows black as pitch.

It would have been an unbearably cold and dreary spectacle, heartless if not for the brilliant color of Lady Rebecca's coach. And yet, even there I viewed windows with curtains drawn, black tiles against the red polish of the cabin. I imagined the light being shut out from inside. I imagined Mr. Claussen's heart to be itself dark and deathly still, for no one stepped out from the coach, and I cried as much for Mr. Claussen as I did for Milady.

I knew he was watching. I knew he could see me sitting in misery alongside his beloved wife, but I also knew that he would never step out. He would never give the world the satisfaction of seeing how he wished to join her in eternal sleep. Although many looked in his direction, no person dared to approach. The coach remained parked for Mr. O'Kurk's eulogy, which Darrin sang with great emotion, and which I'm certain thrilled Lady Rebecca as she looked down upon us. I wept openly.

Alas, me boonie laddies,
Th' Loord doth coom tooday
'E 'ath choosen one amoong us
T' walk with 'im away

We be left a gathered standin'
By th' earth in which she lay
T'is a lessoon froom our father
'ose words if 'eard would say

She were born t' learn ov sinnin'
she were born t' learn ov loove
she were born t' learn foorgivin'
then return t' God aboove.

Be it 'ard, this life yoo're livin'
Be it 'ard , foor us t' see
Be it 'ard t' know yoo're given
A life foor eternidee

Bow yoor 'eads, me boone laddies,
bow yoor 'eads an' let us pray
that these tears, which wet our faces
woould wash our pain away.

We be 'ere t' learn ov sinnin'
'We be 'ere t' learn ov loove
We be 'ere t' learn foorgivin'
Then return to God aboove.

Be it 'ard, this life we're livin'
Be it 'ard , foor us t' see
Be it 'ard t' know we're given
A life foor eternidee

692

We give thanks, foor this 'is wisdom
We give thanks, foor this 'is way
Might this soul, take to 'is Kingdom
Our praise to 'im this day.
Ahhhhhhhh mennnnnnnnn

With his eulogy given, the vermilion coach again started its somber pace back down the cobblestone lane. In a markedly upbeat fashion the sailors, some two hundred strong and led by Mr. O'Kurk, began to leave and sang out with great spirit.

Oyeee! Tell me noow me maties, tell me noow agen

'ave yer eyes laid rest upoon the loov'ly lady ov th' Thames

'er name it 'as bin ferried acrooss th' seven seas

'n th' 'eart ov ev'ry sailoor man 'ose bin by West Indies

Oh! Rebecca! Rebecca! Rebecca, darlin' dear

Well think oon you foorever, an' foorever you'll be near....

I wished time might freeze along with everything else in nature. That it might force all these people to remain here forever. They all possessed pieces of the collective memory of Milady's existence, and as they slowly retreated, disappearing back into their lives, I felt Lady Rebecca thinning like melting ice on a pond, breaking away piece by piece and floating away. I stood alone and was alone. Nothing remained save for a cold wind, leafless trees, and the kiss of winter.

SEVENTY-SIX

Two weeks after Lady Rebecca was laid to rest, I received a summons from Mr. Claussen. He was now residing aboard the REBECCA, having never returned to our place at the Barrington Hotel. I rode alone in the coach, and worried myself sick over words that I had yet to hear, words I feared would be for the worse. My instincts were not to be quieted, and I was positive that this day would be one of misery.

When I arrived at the dock, I heard the voice of Mr. O'Kurk calling out to me. I looked up to see him leaning over the gunwales and awaiting me to board. I waved and he returned the wave with that broad smile I had enjoyed so many times before. He walked along the waterway so as to meet me at the plank.

"Oyeeee. Me Elizabeth! Ye always look so pretty. Ye do an' oold sailoor a woorld ov good, ye do." Darrin stopped, and taking my shoulders he turned me gently toward him. "Ar ye gooin to git byee alright me chile? I woory about ye, lass. Ye don' look ta be eatin'. Ye best tak care or ye'll be getting' right sick, lass."

"I'll get by fine, Mr. O'Kurk, but I don't think this will be a good day for me. Do you remember that morning back in London when you first said that prayer with me?" I asked.

"Ayeee, thit I do, like it wuz yersterdaee." I smiled, for the remembrance brought a sense of contentment, which I rarely enjoyed these past days.

"Would you be so kind as to say one for me this morning, Mr. O'Kurk? I feel it would be of great help."

I turned away heavy in heart and walked alone toward the quarterdeck.

"I'll mek it a good prayer, bonny 'lizabeth, a special woon for you, me loove."

I stepped into the pilothouse and felt my throat begin to tighten as a rush of memories swept over me. I could feel Lady Rebecca standing alongside me as we looked out over the pirate fleet. I could hear her calling out for me from the now empty berthing down below. I could feel her tugging at my braids to take me into her care. She worried for me so. I put all of these recollections aside and walked down the corridor to the double doors of the Claussens' cabin. I stopped momentarily and stood silently facing the doors, trying to collect my thoughts and build my courage. Having prepared myself for the worst, I knocked lightly upon the door.

"Come in."

I entered. I glanced to my right and saw Milady's dressing table with her brush positioned just as we left it at the break of autumn in our flight from the advancing cold. It was such a personal possession, that the sight of it knifed through my heart. My eyes swept the familiar cabin, past the tub, the accommodation ladder, and the bed. I looked over to the table of Mr. Claussen's studio.

At first, he sat there looking up at me, unsure of how to proceed. He set his quill down and rose from his chair. He walked around to the end of his table to meet me. The sight of him shocked me, for he looked terrible. He was clean and presentable, but I could see he hadn't eaten at all. He appeared thin and sickly. Nothing like the powerful man that I believed could sway the will of the seas and calm the heart of a storm.

"Hello, Elizabeth. Come in, child. I am happy to see you." He moved to embrace me warmly with affection. He walked me over to the bed. "Please, sit down. May I get you something to drink?"

"No thank-you, sir."

He looked at me as though burdened with guilt and worry.

"How are you getting by, child?"

"I'm managing, Milord. It is hard." I saw the tears at once swell in his eyes. He knew I told the truth.

"Elizabeth…Elizabeth, I must beg of you forgiveness. You can't know how sorry I am that I have not looked in on you during these days past. You must think me selfish and cruel, not the sort of man to be a good father.

I know you have suffered as I. It is because of this, I hope you might understand the depth of my grief. You are so much a part of her in my mind that I couldn't bear to face you, Elizabeth. Not until I was stronger. Not until I could accept my loss. It was an unforgivably selfish act, but the act that was." He turned away.

"Why did you let this happen? I don't understand. Why did you let this happen?" He looked at me, uncertain of what I meant.

"Oh, Elizabeth. You always thought me a god. I'm just a man. Can't you see? Do you think if it were in my power to stop this, I would have remained at distance? I would have given my life; surely you must believe I would have stopped it. I am only a man, Elizabeth. Miracles are the work of gods not mortals such as I. How I wish I were. How I wish I could have foreseen the events to take place. How I wish I could have spared Rebecca that horrible…." He stopped to prevent himself from losing his composure. He changed the subject. "Everything is different now, Elizabeth. Everything has changed. There are things I must tell you. Things that are not pleasant, but must be said." He paused. "This is difficult. I hope you will bear with me. I hope you will understand. You must try and understand.

"You know that the night of your birthday party, Rebecca and I asked you to honor us with your love and become our child by taking the Claussen name." He paused again. "Elizabeth, I wanted it more than anything in the world. You must believe that. Now, I ask you to relieve me of this obligation. I am not fit to fill the position of your father, your mother, or even Rebecca, God rest her soul. I will not be here for you with the loving embrace and encouragement you will need to succeed in your life."

My throat was now tightened to the point of pain. I fought back the emotions of fear and loss that of late were too quick to show themselves. I said nothing. Inside, I grew numb and distant as I listened with respect and a sinking heart.

"Elizabeth, my plans are made. I will be leaving the East Coast for many years to engage in the business of furring and China trade. I will spend most of my time off the coast of China, traveling the routes, moving furs between the Islands and Wampoa.

"I have no choice in this matter, Elizabeth. You see it makes no difference where I set foot on this coast; it only reminds me of my past and my beloved Rebecca. Even if I could forget this tragedy, the crowds of concerned friends are quick to remind me by asking how I fare. It is no fault of theirs, but it makes it impossible for me to stay. These harbors are haunted, and I am afraid for me, they shall be forever so.

"I am leaving, Elizabeth. I give you my word you will want for nothing for as long as you live. I don't know if you will ever be able to forgive me, but I hope in time you may come to understand." He rose to his feet and I did likewise.

"I care so very much for you, Elizabeth, but I am lost. I love you, but I am lost."

"I love you too, Mr. Claussen," I whispered.

He took my face into his hands and I saw the strain of emotion in his eyes. He turned away momentarily to collect himself, and then he leaned down and kissed me repeatedly upon my face. His face was moist, his eyes red with pain. It was a reflection of my own grief and somehow I felt I already understood. He lifted me off my feet as we embraced for the last time and thereafter I took my leave. Our meeting was short, so very short.

I felt the full force of my emotions welling up as I walked down the corridor and away from this man who was so much a part of my life. The waterway was beneath my feet to collect the tears that were now beginning to flow freely and I was crying hard with abandon. I avoided the mates as I coursed the waterway and descended the plank. I looked back one last time across the dock to see Mr. O'Kurk waving and blowing me kisses from high in the shrouds. I waved back and then turning my back on him, I stepped out of his world and into the coach that would take me forever away. I never expected to lay eyes upon him or set foot upon the good ship REBECCA ever again.

I saw my image slip across the vermilion finish as the driver opened the door and Lady Rebecca's name swung out of view. I sat down upon the cushioned seat. The door was closed, sealing me into the silence of luxury that was crafted to pamper me. I gazed at the waxed woodwork of the cabin, the burled walnut, the leather upholstery, and finally the blanket draped upon the seat.

It was my ship's blanket. I remembered the hours I sat alongside Lady Rebecca at the hearth as she knitted it for me. I remembered the nights we sat huddled in the coach wrapped in it to stave off a winter chill. I studied it as sunlight flashed off the edges of the polished reading lamps and grazed the tears in my eyes. I reached for the blanket and pulled it about me. I rubbed my face in it to soak up my tears and inhaled deeply the scent of lavender that lingered to remind me of whom this coach belonged.

I closed my eyes. I so desperately wanted to see her, to feel her comforting touch, for everything in this silent cabin was perfect. This had been our place and everything was here except for Lady Rebecca. I had never felt so alone. I cried out to her, begged her to come back. I wanted her. I wanted Mr. Claussen and Mary. I wanted it to be once again the way it was when I first rode in the Claussen coach.

I wept until I found myself completely empty, drained of feeling, a ghost from the past given no choice but to wander. When I left my mother, I believed myself to be going on a holiday and was excited to be off. Now, I felt abandoned. No ties, no family, no history. It was just me…left behind in the New World with nothing but a day to face tomorrow, and the day after, and forever forth. I lay down upon the seat and closed my eyes to a land and future I had no desire to face. I prayed I might disappear—*like everything else that had meant anything in my life.*

REBECCA'S SONG

WORDS AND MUSIC BY:
C. JOHN COOMBES

TRANSCRIPTION BY:
MATTHEW KENNEY

VERSE II

AYEEE, TH' BOYS DEY BE A WAITIN'
BUT FOOR 'ER T' TAKE A MAN.
SHE CARES FOOR NAUGHT AN' PATIENTLY
AWAITS UPOON TH' LAND
FOOR ONE T' COME B'FORE 'ER
AN' SWEAR UPOON 'IS KNEES
T' SWALLOW TH' ANCHOR IN 'ER NAME
IF THAT BE WHAT SHE PLEASE.

OH REBECCA, REBECCA, REBECCA DARLIN' DEAR
THINK ON ME FOREVER AN' FOREVER I'LL BE NEAR

OH REBECCA, REBECCA, REBECCA DARLIN' DEAR
SAVE YOOR 'EART AN' I'LL BE BACK
ME PROMISE BE SINCERE.

VERSE III

AYEEE, TH' TALL SHIPS SAIL FOOR ENGLAND
AN' WHEN TH' ISLAND'S FOUND
FROOM EV'RY MOORING IN TH' PORT
TH' SAILORS COOM AROUND
BUT NAUGHT T' SEE TH' ABBEY
OF WESTMIN'STER OR TH' CROWN
ONLY TH' LOOVLY LADY
OF TH' THAMES OF LONNDON TOWN

OH REBECCA, REBECCA, REBECCA DARLIN' DEAR
THINK ON ME FOREVER AN' FOREVER I'LL BE NEAR

OH REBECCA, REBECCA, REBECCA DARLIN' DEAR
PROMISE ME YOU'LL SAVE YOUR 'EART
AN' I'LL BE BACK I SWEAR

Where Credit is due...

I dedicate this novel to all my friends,
who assured me that anti-social behavior was normal.

To my wife, Nancy, who nourished me during the years I spent
daydreaming obsessively in dark corners as our house crumbled.

To Maria E. denBoer, my editor, who gave my ego the boost
that only a mother could duplicate.

To my family, and these friends and advisors, Cynthia Guy,
Dawn Lynes, Steven L. Gerbers, Nancy Jesko, Debbie Martinez,
Cathie Leonard, Marcia Marshall, Amy West, Kelly Mc Gee,
and James R. Ward, many who suffered through the early
manuscripts of this volume and trashed me with joy.

To Matthew Kenny, who brought the sound of music to my eyes.

To my lifelong and fairweatherly friend, Jon Hunter,
whose nautical expertise and 'knowledge of the ropes' helped
keep me afloat.

To Martha Hart, whose generosity, advice, and encouragement
made this 'MH' edition possible.

Finally, to my daughters, Britany Michelle and Tawnie Allison, who
taught me how make-believe is properly presented with
conviction.

I thank you all.
C. John Coombes

www.ingramcontent.com/pod-product-compliance
Lightning Source LLC
Chambersburg PA
CBHW032248020726
47495CB00001B/23